BYZANTIUM

YZANTIUM

MICHAEL ENNIS

A MORGAN ENTREKIN BOOK
THE ATLANTIC MONTHLY PRESS
NEW YORK

Published simultaneously in Canada
Printed in the United States of America

Library of Congress Cataloging-in-Publication Data
Ennis, Michael.
  Byzantium.
  "A Morgan Entrekin book."
  1. Varangians—Byzantine Empire—Fiction.
  2. Byzantine Empire—History—1025–1081—Fiction.
  I. Title.
PS3555.N63B98   1989   813'.54   89-6892
ISBN 0-87113-275-3

Design by Laura Hough

The Atlantic Monthly Press
19 Union Square West
New York, NY 10003

FIRST PRINTING

FOR MY MOTHER AND FATHER

The gods make mighty him who bows to their yoke.
　　　　　　　　　　　—Homer, *The Iliad*

FOREWORD

n the first half of the eleventh century, while Europe lumbered fitfully toward the end of the Dark Ages, the Byzantine Empire stood at the apex of its power. Direct heir to the might and glory of ancient Rome, the Empire of Byzantium already could look back on seven uninterrupted centuries of world dominion. The hub of this enduring and seemingly invincible power was Constantinople, the magnificent fortress capital founded in A.D. 330 by Constantine I, the first Christian Emperor of Rome. Invulnerable behind miles of towering walls, the Queen of Cities was a luxurious metropolis of a million inhabitants at a time when London and Paris were squalid, overgrown villages of ten or twenty thousand.

Presiding over the splendor of Byzantium was the most powerful man on earth. Lord of the Entire World, the Byzantine Emperor was thought to rule literally side by side with the Lord of the Universe, Christ the Pantocrator. But the Emperor's divine prerogative was coveted by many, and this all-too-fallible mortal often feared for his life even in the staggeringly opulent sanctuaries of his vast palace complex. For this reason the Byzantine emperors surrounded themselves with an Imperial bodyguard of Viking mercenaries, men of unquestioning loyalty and unyielding ferocity. Known and feared throughout the world as Varangians, these few hundred Viking warriors became essential to the stability and survival of the world's mightiest empire.

The most famed of all Varangians was a young Norwegian prince named Haraldr Sigurdarson, who would play one of the most fateful roles any man has ever undertaken on the stage of history. This is his true story.

While this is a work of fiction, it has been based very carefully on historical fact, a truth more extraordinary than any fiction. All except the most incidental characters actually lived and died almost a thousand years ago, and all of the major events actually took place.

In the interest of authenticity, various measurements and terms actually used in the eleventh century have been retained here. The units of measurement most commonly used by the Norse were the thumb, about an inch; the ell, a span of eighteen inches (based on the measurement between the elbow and forefinger); the bowshot, a distance of roughly two hundred yards; and the rowing-spell, a distance of about seven miles. The Byzantines used the fathom—six feet—as well as the Roman foot. The stade, a measurement based on the length of the hippodrome track, was about two hundred yards.

The Vikings of the eleventh century never referred to themselves by the sobriquet they earned in later centuries; they called themselves simply Norsemen, while the word *viking* described an activity roughly translatable as "adventuring in search of wealth." The word *Varangian*, which was widely used in Scandinavia as well as Byzantium, literally meant "pledgemen," as the Norse warriors obeyed an inviolable pledge to defend one another, and their sworn leader, to the death. The Norsemen called the Byzantines Griks and their Empire Grikkland or Grikia; the city of Constantinople was often called Miklagardr, the Great City. But the Byzantines, who in fact spoke the Greek language and incorporated all of Greece in their Empire, emphatically considered themselves and their Empire "Roman"; Constantinople was often referred to as New Rome. The Byzantines frequently referred to Norsemen in general as Rus, because the Norse usually reached Byzantium by a route that took them through Rus Land, which later became Russia. In elegant court circles, Norsemen were also known as Tauro-Scythians, a condescending and affected anachronism that meant Scythians (i.e., savages) from beyond the Taurus Mountains. Of course, in the eyes of the Byzantines all foreigners, regardless of status or place of origin, belonged in one basic category: *barbaroi,* or barbarians.

PROLOGUE

STIKLESTAD, NORWAY
31 AUGUST, 1030

educed to predawn embers, the hundreds of campfires speckled the still-darkened meadow like a constellation of dying stars. Each was the site of an anxious communion, as a thousand men whispered a question only one man could answer: Will we fight today? The cumulative sound of this hushed speculation was an eerie, detached sibilance, as if giant wings slowly fanned the darkness above.

The King of Norway stared into the faintly pulsing coals at his feet and repeated the name he had murmured a moment before. "Ingigerd."

Jarl Rognvald brushed the shag of frost-white hair from his forehead. The Jarl was well into his sixth decade, his walrus-tough skin slit with deep creases. Like the King sitting beside him, he was dressed for battle, in a knee-length coat of chain mail called a byrnnie. "My King?" he asked absently.

King Olaf sat erect; the links of his byrnnie chinged in a tiny, sad note, the instrument and its music suited to the man. Olaf was thirty-five, huge, with the face of a scowling, oversize boy who had shed his baby fat and become a tough, overbearing bully. And yet his painfully blue eyes were gentle and haunted; not a sensitive boy's eyes but those of a man long pursued by an unkind fate. "The last time I saw Ingigerd," said the King, "I promised her that before I died, I would hold her in my arms again." He stirred the coals with his boot, and sparks flew up as if sucked by the vast whisper in the air. "I held her in my arms last night. A dream so real that I could taste her flesh and feel her heart beneath mine."

Jarl Rognvald knew then that the King had made his decision. Ingigerd, the King of Sweden's daughter, had been the love of Olaf's youth; though Olaf had never admitted it, Jarl Rognvald was certain that they had slept together. Perhaps for that reason the King of Sweden had always despised Olaf, and had married Ingigerd to Yaroslav, Great Prince of the Rus. Olaf and Ingigerd had not seen each other for almost twenty years.

"Where will we fight them?" asked Jarl Rognvald.

"Here. When they see how few we are, they will come down from the high ground."

The two men stood and looked to the east. The forest began on a small

3

slope at the edge of the meadow where Olaf had encamped his army; it seemed filled with an unnatural, incandescent orange mist that illuminated the bases of the pine trees. All night long Olaf's scouts had gone out into that forest and returned with a grim accounting of their enemy's strength, so evident in the massed light of their campfires. They were seven times as many men as Olaf had mustered, a mercenary mob hired by an unlikely coalition: the owners of Norway's largest estates, who envisioned a Norway fractured into their own sovereign principalities, and Knut, King of Denmark and England, who envisioned a Norway shackled to his empire. And once Norway's King was out of the way, Knut could easily impose his vision on his erstwhile allies.

"We could still pack our gear bags and leave this field before dawn," Olaf said, "and live to meet them at a time of our choosing. But as word spread that King Olaf had run, their ranks would increase. We would simply die on another day, but in retreat, rather than with honor. No king could ever follow me, except a foreign king." Olaf turned to face the Jarl. "My choice is simple. If I live to fight again, Norway will die. If I die today, Norway lives."

Jarl Rognvald removed the conical steel helm from his leather gear bag and cradled it in his hands, his rough fingers tracing over the intricately scrolled dragons engraved around the rim. The Dragon of Nidafell, the Jarl silently noted, the giant-taloned serpent that would fly in the last black night of the world. The creature with the jaws of infinity, the beast that would draw all creation, the works of men and gods alike, into its endless maw. Jarl Rognvald still believed in this pagan apocalypse, despite Olaf's relentless campaign to establish Kristr as Norway's God.

Olaf watched the Jarl deal with doom in the fashion of his youth. "I know you still believe in the old gods," he told him softly. "I wish I could have placed your feet on the ladder to Paradise. But when you drink at the ale benches in the Valhol this evening, tell Norway's Kings that I tried to honor them with my death, and that no man honored me more with his life than Jarl Rognvald."

The Jarl's thick neck pumped with emotion. "What of Norway's next King?"

Olaf strapped his sword belt around his waist. "Yes. Where is Haraldr?" Haraldr Sigurdarson was Olaf's fifteen-year-old half brother and next in line for the throne; Haraldr's father, Sygurd Syr, had been King before Olaf. But Olaf had been much more than half a brother to Haraldr; Sygurd Syr had died when Haraldr was only a small child, and Olaf had become by any measure Haraldr's father.

"Haraldr is with the skalds," said Jarl Rognvald. The skalds were the court poets. "He will want to fight."

"All boys who have never fought want to fight. It is time for Haraldr to learn that sometimes it requires more valor to live than to die."

"Where will you send him? His life will be worthless in Norway."

"Kiev, in Rus. Ingigerd will look after him there."

"They will hunt him down in Rus, even. Every hired thug, sand wanderer, and Dane's slave will want to earn the price on the head of the Prince who did not die at Stiklestad."

"He will take a new name. Within a year he will probably grow so much, he will look entirely different. I am not worried that other men will take him for the Prince of Norway, if he can keep quiet about who he is." Olaf glowered, the light of the dying fire on his troubled eyes making him seem more haunted than haunting. "I am worried that Haraldr himself will forget he is the King of Norway."

† † †

"Steadfast will we feed the gulls-of-blood." The skald pulled anxiously at his whiskers, contemplating his newly minted verse. If he had to recite it this morning, he realized, it would probably be his last.

"Gulls-of-blood," repeated Haraldr Sigurdarson in his piping, occasionally cracking adolescent voice; he stood next to the pensive skald, no such doubt reflected in his swaggering version of a court poet's elegant oratorical pose. He was immature for his age, his lean, fine-featured face all pale down, his long golden hair almost as beautiful as a woman's. His blue eyes were said to be the image of his brother's. His metal-studded canvas byrnnie swallowed skeletal limbs; only his man-sized hands and feet hinted at the stature he might acquire. "That is the kenning for raven," Haraldr said authoritatively; kennings were the elaborate metaphors favored by Norse poets. "The gull is a bird, and the bird that drinks blood is the raven. We will feed the ravens the Danemen's blood."

The skald ignored Haraldr and squinted at the men approaching in the dim light. He dipped to his knee when he recognized King Olaf. The King was attended by Jarl Rognvald and two of his house-karls, members of his personal guard.

"Olaf! Jarl Rognvald! Listen! 'Dark nigh the dread of arrow-storm—' " Haraldr broke off when he saw the grim set of Olaf's face.

"Haraldr." Olaf's beefy hands engulfed his brother's frail shoulders.

"This morning I am going to ask you to serve your King and our Norway with a hard task. It is the most difficult I will ask of any man this entire day."

Haraldr had already imagined so many acts of his own heroism that he hardly knew which image to supply, now that his years of daydreaming had culminated in reality. What feat did his brother and king require?

"You cannot enter the shield-wall today."

Haraldr's head snapped back as if he had been struck. He was too shocked to say anything.

"Guaka and Asti"—Olaf indicated the house-karls—"are going to take you to Rus. You have heard me talk of the Rus Queen, Ingigerd. I want you to stay at the Rus court in Kiev until you are told it is safe to return home. Your name will be known only to Guaka and Asti, and to Ingigerd and her husband." Olaf squeezed Haraldr's shoulders so hard that the boy's eyes glazed with pain. "You must swear to me on your father's soul that you will tell no one else your name until you are able to return home to Norway. No one. If anyone discovers who you are, you will never come home. I can promise you that."

Haraldr sniffled and tried to force his shoulders up and his chest out. "I won't go to Rus. My wand-of-wounds will feed the raven-wine to those Dane-sucking dung haulers!"

Olaf squeezed Haraldr's shoulders again. "Haraldr, you have not passed fifteen summers. I never intended to let you fight. No boy your age will ever die for me."

"You went a-viking in your twelfth summer."

"I carried water skins to men who had gone a-viking."

"The skald Thorfinn Munnr says you killed a man that same year."

Olaf shook his ponderous head wearily. "When a man becomes King, he magically grows two ells taller and suddenly he has plowed the belly-barley of a different woman for each night since he was a swaddled infant. The truth is that I became strong because I was not asked to pull an oar until my back was ready for it. That is how I intend it for you."

"My back is ready. If you are going to fight here, I am staying with you."

"I do not have the time to convince you that I am not jesting, little brother. We are not playing games at Nidaros."

"I am aware of that."

Olaf's hands gripped so hard that Haraldr thought his bones would be ground to meal. "You are about to shame yourself. If I have to have you tied up, I will."

"And if I have to tie my sword to my hand, I am going to fight today!" Haraldr was momentarily startled by his own shrill shouting. His face was suddenly brilliant with outrage.

Olaf reached swiftly for Haraldr's sword and whipped the blade out of his brother's scabbard. Haraldr leapt like a springing cat, his eyes wild. He clamped both hands on Olaf's wrist, which was as thick as a small tree, and wrestled it with mad fury, as if it were indeed a tree he was trying to uproot. With his free hand Olaf tried to prise Haraldr's astonishingly powerful grip but after a moment gave up. He drew back his immense fist and clobbered Haraldr just behind the ear.

Haraldr dizzied and fell to his knees, sparks popping in his head. "You don't have to truss me up," he said meekly. This isn't finished, he told himself.

Olaf gave Haraldr's sword to Guaka. "You must go before it gets too light." He brought his bristling, burly face close to Haraldr's and his eyes were dark, endlessly deep, as if fate had somehow chased the entire star-flecked universe into their void. This can't be happening, Haraldr told himself. But Olaf's eyes said it was. "Do you swear on your father's soul not to reveal your name to anyone?"

Haraldr swallowed thickly; a cold stone seemed to be stuck in his throat. "I swear it."

Olaf's eyes filled again, not with life but with the swirling mists of memory. "Haraldr, when you get to Rus, you must remember me to Queen Ingigerd. Tell her she was with me." He snatched his brother into his arms and held him against his massive metaled chest. "I will always be beside you," Olaf said. "No matter where you are, no matter where I am. I love you, little brother."

The next thing Haraldr knew, he was walking into the pall of the new day, Guaka and Asti flanking him, and the tears on his cheeks were cold.

† † †

"I'll carry it." Guaka shrugged and handed Haraldr his sword. The dense forest was dappled with mid-morning light; the patches of sky visible through the trees were like glazed cerulean tiles. The ether of the pine resin was intoxicating. To the right, only fifty ells away the woods parted and a field of large jumbled black rocks descended to a nearly dry creek.

"Guaka, I have to piss."

Guaka turned to Asti. The towering, armored house-karl shook his head as if to ask, "We have to go all the way to Rus with him?"

Haraldr pointed to a dark, almost mysterious clump of pines to his left. "I need to go in there."

Guaka grinned knowingly at Asti and again shook his head. "You can go right here. We don't mind."

Haraldr hiked up his byrnnie and tunic. His urine splashed over the pine needles for a moment and then he turned quickly and directed the stream over Guaka's bare knees.

"Kristr, damn!" shouted Guaka, and he danced backward several steps. Haraldr immediately dashed to his right, through the woods and onto the field of boulders. In spite of his gawky frame, he moved across the big rocks with the grace of a panther. The house-karls followed, bellowing obscenities, but they had nowhere near Haraldr's agility or speed on such crude terrain. Haraldr crossed the trickling creek, loped over the rocks on the opposite side, and disappeared into the forest.

† † †

Haraldr crouched behind a parapet of smooth black boulders on a small hill overlooking his brother's encampment. The meadow was like an emerald platter before him; at one end a half dozen huge, fractured black boulders lay on the grass as if tossed there by a giant's hand. Olaf's men had already set themselves in the classic shield-wall defense, a circle three men thick and five hundred men around, shoulder to shoulder, an enormous ring plated with steel and bristling with spears. Inside this human fort were the King, his skalds, and his house-karls. Haraldr could easily distinguish the tiny, jewellike figure of Olaf; he wore a blue silk tunic over his lacquered steel byrnnie, and his white enameled shield was embossed with a large gold cross. Three bowshots beyond this formation, almost directly opposite Haraldr, the forested, slightly elevated rim of the meadow teemed with the vanguard of the opposing horde. In their predominantly brown canvas byrnnies they looked like a muddy wave, silted with silvery steel blades and armor, about to burst from the forest and crash down the slope.

The battle oath of Olaf's army was clearly discernible: "Forward, forward, Kristr-men, cross-men!" The shield-wall advanced toward the line of trees, virtually without distortion of its immaculate geometry. From the forest came a vast exhalation: "Thor crushes all!" The metal-flecked, turbid wave of the Dane's men came out of the trees, multihued battle standards carried along like the masts of a vast, miniature fleet. Dense clouds of arrows rose up from both armies, flying as swiftly as passing shadows. Spears and javelins darted in quick, glittering volleys. The wave surged against the the shield-wall and halted.

Haraldr watched the miniaturized conflict in utter fascination, forcing himself to adhere to his plan: Wait until the crucial moment and then rush to his brother's rescue. He had a vision of himself in the setting sun, acclaimed on the field-of-fray, amid the corpses of his foes, the youngest marshal in the history of Norway. As he dreamed, he vaguely wondered why the sky was darkening.

A small portion of the shield-wall buckled in and Haraldr's heart thudded as his brother's gold-embroidered standard, ringed by his housekarls, moved to buttress the defense. But it was not yet time; the breach was quickly repaired. Haraldr noticed that the cloud had still not moved from the sun and that it was a very dark cloud. Yet why was the rest of the sky a flawless, deep cobalt blue? He finally gave up a moment of his battle for a look over his head. He gasped and stood, gaping, no longer concerned about revealing his hiding place.

It was another wonder, a celestial parallel to the marvel at his feet. In the still-brilliant, unmarred sky, the sun was dying. It was as if a crescent chunk had been taken by some great jaws. He distantly remembered a man at court talking about a day when the sun had vanished and the midday became midnight. Much more distinct in his mind were the pagan tales he had raptly listened to; Jarl Rognvald had often talked of Ragnarok, the doom of the gods, when the wolf Fenrir would swallow the sun, only to be devoured in turn by the black Dragon of Nidafell in the last night of creation. Haraldr weighed the two theories and concluded that this portent was too coincidental with the affairs of men to be merely an accident of nature. It was the work of the old gods.

He squinted at the sky until his face hurt. Fenrir only slowly ingested the sun, but the day darkened more quickly than a sunset in a deep fjord. The din of battle fell in concert to the fading light. Thousands of heads tilted upward to watch an even more epochal confrontation. The unearthly wails of the wounded, no longer masked by the screams of combat, carried across the meadow.

The landscape became coppery, almost fiery, as the mythic jaws swallowed all but a final, desperately glimmering fragment of the sun. Haraldr looked at his sword, his arms. Blood. Blood sun, blood sky, blood on the land. His mind went blank, perfectly suspended between wonder and fear. The wind gusted from the meadow, carrying with it the ferric scent of opened flesh. The dying voices rose in a harrowing dirge. Haraldr plunged into fear. He scrambled from his redoubt, tumbled part of the way down the slope, and then he was conscious only of the blood-tinted grass racing beneath him.

No one stopped Haraldr from entering the shield-wall. He looked about, bewildered, at the craning warriors. A wounded man moaned, only a few ells from him. Shouting began, from the front of the shield-wall, but Haraldr could not see what was happening because the huge armored backs of the house-karls blocked his view. Men pushed back toward him in large groups, their faces drenched with sweat. The shouts were louder still, and they were joined by the shriek of metal on metal; it seemed to Haraldr that he could actually feel the noise, like needles in his bones. A house-karl staggered toward him like a careening metal beast, coughing up blood, his lips and chin glazed crimson.

And then they were all running. He followed them to his right, not really knowing why, until they stopped abruptly. He did not know where he was until he realized that the huge black boulders he had seen from his perch were now at his back; he could reach out and feel the cold stone. He saw Olaf's standard only a half dozen ells in front of him, the gold dragon embroidered on it bloodied by the moribund sun. The grip on his arm was like a sword stroke.

"By all the gods, where did you come from!" shouted Jarl Rognvald. His byrnnie was smeared with blood and two deep, open cuts intersected the seams on his cheeks. The Jarl bellowed almost frantically for Olaf. Olaf finally shouldered through the crush of house-karls. His demon-chased eyes did not change expression when he saw Haraldr. He shouted in Jarl Rognvald's ear. Without looking at Haraldr again, he turned and immediately went forward. Jarl Rognvald let Haraldr's arm go but stayed by him.

It was too much for Haraldr to acknowledge that this was all that was left, that the shield-wall had been shattered and most of Olaf's men engulfed by the brown wave, that the house-karls had set this last line of defense against the boulders. Instead a heedless bravado seemed to pump up his gangling limbs and he wriggled between the metal torsos of the house-karls, pushing to the front. The enemy, seperated from the house-karls by a no-man's-land no broader than two arms spans, were a sword-waving, spear-thrusting, barking, howling wall, teeming like an immense pack of monstrous deadly vermin. He was close enough to see their gnashing teeth. Their eyes were thousands of fiery coals.

An eerie hush fell as five huge men stepped into the no-man's-land.

Four of them wore steel byrnnies, but the man in the center, the tallest and stoutest of them, wore an armor of layered hides with the fur still attached. Berserk, thought Haraldr with horrified rapture. Another pagan tale come true; the Berserks, or bear-shirts, were said to wear such hide armor, and when Odin gave them the Battle-Rage, no man could stand before them.

The Berserk took another step forward. His black beard had white streaks; his eyebrows, hacked away in countless frays, were bestial, whiskered tufts above tiny red eyes. The end of his nose had been sliced off in one of his previous combats; his truncated nostrils were huge and upturned like a pig's snout. "I am Thorir, called the Hound," he said, his voice strangely tranquil. "You are lost. Give up your King and your Prince, and our accounts will be settled."

The house-karls answered with a gale of obscenities. "Sow fucker!" "Corpse lover!"

The Hound calmly waited, eyes flickering, until the outburst had ended. "Then you will all die," he said. "I know the King." He pointed at Olaf. "When we begin again, I will kill him first." The tiny red eyes began to roam among the house-karls, as piercing as hot, sharp irons, and Haraldr knew what they were searching for. He was too mesmerized to look away and the moment of contact was like a knife slitting him from his groin to his windpipe, ripping out his fool's courage and replacing it with a cold, leaden, mortal dread. "I think the boy is the Prince," said the Hound; he turned to the silent army behind him for confirmation, and several men nodded. "I will kill him as well."

Olaf's vast bulk hurtled from within his cordon of house-karls. Someone grabbed Haraldr and pulled him back and he fell hard on his seat, but before he went down he glimpsed his brother's sword pound into the Hound's furry hide armor. Men stepped over and on him and he thought he would be trampled. He heard a moment later the explosive collision of the two armies, the screech of clashing steel and the desperate, thundering oaths of doomed men. Then he could see Olaf and Thorir the Hound again. They seemed to move so slowly, like figures in a nightmare. Olaf's blade flashed in long, ruby-tinted strokes, again and again, and yet the Hound still stood. Then a third man entered the dreamlike vignette, one of the huge men who had come forward with the Hound. This intruder crouched low, and when his sword scythed parallel to the ground, Haraldr perceived it moving much more swiftly, everything was speeding up, and the blade struck Olaf's massive leg and recoiled and Olaf's knee seemed to disintegrate and he was falling. Another man stepped into Haraldr's suddenly rushing nightmare and his spear caught Olaf under his byrnnie, jerking him up and sideways before it was pulled from his belly. Olaf's hand clutched but he could not grasp, and his slick, coiled bowels began to ooze down his thighs. A sword struck his neck and his head tilted freakishly to the side and blood pumped onto his shoulder.

The blow knocked Haraldr on his back and something flew swiftly into his eye like an angry bird, and his vision flooded with warm serum. *Stand to fight!* shrieked a voice so loud, it could only have come from inside his skull. But his limbs were locked in an icy dread and a terrible truth quarreled with the other voice: *I am a coward,* it said, as his fright gushed out of him and soiled his breeches with a repulsive warmth. A boot crunched with stunning force into his chest; his heart, painfully bruised by his ribs, seemed to beg for death; if only he would not have to stand and face it.

The Hound was above him. The huge nostrils, the horrible sucking. Haraldr lay there, frozen with terror, his head screaming with the dark poetry of the last instant in time. The Hound's sword rose high, lost in blood-tinted night; it was no sword, it was a creature, a raven's beak descending, falling from night into night. Then there was a terrific concussion, as if the sun had exploded in its final dying fury, and Haraldr fell away from its heat and light, falling, falling endlessly into the vast, airless, utterly black craw of the last dragon.

† † †

The man from Denmark grasped the jaw and turned the corpse's puffy claret face toward him; the head flopped as if no longer attached to the neck. He fanned away the flies and slipped open the livid eyelids for a moment; the blue eyes glared in a ghostly fury. He stood and faced the Hound. "This is King Olaf. Now show me the Prince. Haraldr Sigurdarson."

The Hound's chest heaved and the air wheezed through his gaping nostrils. "I struck him on the helm. There was blood all over his face. Then two men attacked me. When I finished with them, I saw him still lying there. I don't see how he could have gotten away."

"But some men were able to flee?"

"No more than two or three. Cowards."

"Or men intent on saving their Prince." The man from Denmark removed a bulging leather wallet from his expensive Frisian wool cloak and shook out four gold bezants. "My King said he would pay you the bounty for the King of Norway and his heir. I give you partial payment as the task has yet to be completed. But consider how much easier your errand has become." The man from Denmark hefted the wallet. "Before today, you had to kill a King and a Prince to earn this. Now you only have to kill a fugitive boy."

The Hound held the gold coins in his flat palm and gently prodded them with his scarred, blood-smeared fingers, almost as if they were small, delicate creatures of a species he had never imagined existed. "Haraldr Sigurdarson," he said quietly, and then he closed his huge fist.

ISLE OF PROTE,
SEA OF MARMORA
SEPTEMBER 1030

earning is but foliage compared to the fruits of a holy life, and the tree that bears nothing but foliage must be cut down and burned. But the finest result is when the fruit is set amongst its foliage.' " Father Katalakon permitted himself the vanity of a slight smile as he finished his impromptu recitation. He was a tall man, his long but neatly combed hair and beard the color of the gray sea mist that on this bright day was, blessedly, still only a dreary memory of winters past and a foreboding of the cold months ahead. Indeed, all of the fruits the Pantocrator had delivered to his Holy Brethren on the Isle of Prote were on this day brightly lit by the brilliant candle of Our Lord's glorious vault. The September sun gleamed off the floor of rose-veined Proconesian marble and burnished the gold acanthus-leaf pattern that bordered the lacquered, coffered ceiling of the library. Father Katalakon turned to the man next to him. "Of course I do not intend to convey that your intimacy with the words of Theodore the Studite requires a restorative from my lips, Brother Symeon."

"Wisdom is never disgraced by repetition, Father Abbot, as holiness is only cultured by our efforts to emulate it." Brother Symeon, the new Chartophylax, or archivist, of the Monastary at Prote, was content to allow the Father Abbott to meander toward their objective. After all, Brother Symeon reminded himself, he would not have been summoned here to Prote had he not long ago achieved the state of *apathia* that bridled impetuous, worldly desires. He looked about the library with admiration; the sumptuous marble revetments and gilded scriptoria attested to the material abundance of Prote, while the shelves stacked with books—some bound in oak, many sheathed in carved ivory, cloisonné, or gems—revealed spiritual wealth. Brother Symeon peered through the clear glass panes of the gracefully arched windows; beneath him, sunwashed rocks fell away to the gem-blue Sea of Marmora. So what I have been told of Prote was no exaggeration, reflected Brother Symeon. The island scarcely has enough arable soil to support a herb garden, and yet the splendors of the establishment rival those of the monasteries at Bithynia and Chios. Ah, well, Christ the Pantocrator will no doubt soon

14

reveal the identity of Prote's benefactor. All things according to His immutable plan.

Father Katalakon appraised his new archivist; like the Father Abbot, Brother Symeon wore the long black wool frock and high round cap common to all the monastic orders of the One True Oecumenical, Orthodox, and Catholic Faith. Yes, Father Katalakon was satisfied that his careful inquiries had indeed been rewarded. The aged Brother Symeon had manifested no impatience on this deliberately circumlocutional tour of the facilities, nor had he evidenced any curiosity as to the source of this magnificence. Of course, Brother Symeon had become noticeably weary of the walking, his thin shoulders slumping and his lips purpling against his snowy beard. Hopefully the new Chartophylax would live long enough to finish his archival research here on Prote; most certainly he would not live long enough to speak of those labors elsewhere even if his worldly passions were somehow revived by what he might find amid the late Father Abbot Giorgios's voluminous archives.

Well, it was time. "One could linger here in contemplation of these glories until the Trumpet of Judgment sounded." Father Katalakon graciously extended his hand to Brother Symeon. "But I am sure you are curious to see the documents of which I have written to you."

The carved wooden door slid noiselessly to reveal a chamber lit by an ornate glass-and-gold candelabra and a single window looking onto an enclosed, private court. Brother Symeon virtually gasped in astonishment. The floor, paved with moss-colored Thessalian marble, was almost entirely obscured by dozens of stacks of unbound parchments; some of the bundles, wrapped in silk cords, rose almost to Father Katalakon's lofty chin. Surrounded by these thousands upon thousands of documents was a marvelous little writing cabinet with an ivory and niello top and gold fittings on the lacquered wooden drawers.

"Yes, you see that I did not embellish fact when I wrote you that Father Abbot Giorgios, may Christ the Pantocrator bless and sanctify his soul, was an extraordinarily prodigious correspondent. And certainly you can see why a Chartophylax of your eminent repute was required." Father Katalakon slid the door closed. His hazel eyes took on a flinty texture in the light from the window; his voice lowered and lost its unctuous buoyancy. "Father Abbot Giorgios was a man of unusual energies and occupations. Not only did he correspond copiously with other Holy Men from places as distant as Cappadocia and Rome, but he also exchanged letters with many eminent persons in the world our Lord has inveighed us to turn our backs upon. No doubt he diverted many souls from the foul paths of perdition to less errant if more arduously inclined avenues of righteousness."

Father Katalakon looked out on the courtyard. A blue-and-gold-tiled fountain lofted pearly spray. "Father Abbot Giorgios gave these weary souls the accumulation of his own holy wisdom, and they in turn gave to his holy establishment at Prote from their worldly accumulations." Father Katalakon looked directly into Brother Symeon's eyes. If he saw any retreat there, he would send the man away.

"The foremost patron of Prote was the purple-born Eudocia," resumed Father Katalakon after his searching pause. "Niece of the late Emperor and Autocrator Basil called the Bulgar-Slayer, daughter of the late Emperor and Autocrator Constantine, sister of the Empress and Basilissa Zoe the purple-born, and sister of the Augusta Theodora. Under the blessed Eudocia's generous auspices, the *typicon* granting our establishment its current rights and privileges was signed by the Emperor and Autocrator Basil the Bulgar-Slayer. Father Abbot Giorgios was Eudocia's friend and counselor; it was he who persuaded her to renounce her temporal ambitions and their concomitant woes and join the Sisters of the Convent of the Theotokos in Protovestiary." Father Katalakon paused again and lowered his steel-colored eyebrows. "Father Abbot Giorgios was also the purple-born Eudocia's confessor."

The fountain in the little courtyard faintly gurgled over the long pause. "I am not a *hesychaste,* a silent monk," Brother Symeon finally offered in a soft yet implacable voice. "But in the matter of the archives that Christ the Pantocrator has placed in my keeping, my silence has been vowed for many, many years."

"Yes," said Father Katalakon as he slid the door open and prepared to leave his new Chartophylax to his Holy duties. "I knew that when I asked the Pantocrator to send you to us."

Father Katalakon quickly left the library and walked past the towering domed apse of Prote's splendid Church of the Holy Apostles, through the colonnaded arcade that fronted the barrel-vaulted cells of the monks, and entered the lovely cypress grove that carried the procession of the arcade out along the wooded green spine of the little island. He walked swiftly, savoring the rich sea air, his step lifted by the conviction that he had acted both decisively and prudently. If the Sisters of Theotokos in Protovestiary were not overly apprehensive—and he had never known them to be so—then the purple-born Eudocia would soon escape the miseries and blandishments of the flesh and take her place at the feet of Christ the Pantocrator. And then who would prevent Prote's generous *typicon* from being redrafted by the new Emperor? Unless, of course, there was an heir to whom the rights to the Holy Establishment at Prote might be transferred.

The tiny convent at Prote lay just beneath the point where the verdant spine of the island again dipped a rocky flank into the sea. The chapel had three small domes, and the cells, refectory, and larder were wrapped around the landward pointing apse like a bent elbow. The moldy stone complex was deserted, having been occupied only once, for less than a year, and that seventeen years ago. Father Katalakon had been on Prote then, though he had only been cellarer at that time. As such, he had not been privileged to visit the little convent. Still, he had heard the play of promiscuous lips among some of the Brethren.

Father Katalakon descended to the flagstone path in front of the stark, empty cells. The plaster had begun to chip from the walls, and here and there weeds prised apart the underlying courses of bricks. The wind came from the north; in the woods behind the empty convent, leaves rattled. The wooden doors to the cells were rotting and the Father Abbot decided not to open one.

I am certain it was the purple-born Eudocia who resided here, thought Father Katalakon. *As to the rumors of the child born here, I am certain of that as well, and I expect Brother Symeon to provide me proof. But that will not be enough to save our establishment. What Brother Symeon must uncover are the names. Who was the father? And yet more important—vastly so—where is the child?*

The wind gusted and eddied, swirling leaves against the doors of the cells. Father Katalakon looked north, toward the unseen but profoundly felt presence of mighty Constantinople. He shuddered despite the dazzling silver light on the heaving sea. Having taken this step, he now had to admit to himself that it was not simply the fate of their Holy Enterprise on Prote that was at stake. If Father Katalakon succeeded in finding this child, the fate of the Empire was in his hands.

I

KIEV, RUS LAND, A.D. 1034

am condemned to spend my life looking out windows."
Elisevett sighed, trying to sound as weary of life as possible for a fifteen-year-old virgin. She settled into the embroidered cushion she had placed in the deeply recessed
window seat; her scarlet silk robe was varnished with the
candlelight diffusing from the adjacent clerestory. She pressed the tip of
her long-bridged nose to the glass and looked out into the night, past the
dim outlines of the domed and peaked palace roofs and down the pine-
shrouded bluffs of the Citadel of Kiev. The Dnieper River looked like ink
striated with gold, the shimmering reflections of the hundreds of torches
that flared along the sandy beaches. The pounding of the shipwrights'
hammers and the shouted commands to the porters were a muffled,
distant din. If she were the merest fur-trader or *strug*-poler, Elisevett
reflected, or even a reeking Tork slave girl, she would be able to journey
down that river. But of course the Princess of Rus would not be permitted
to go. No. She would spend her life in *terems* and churches, first waiting
upon her father's bidding, then upon whomever he chose for her. Elisevett thought of her mother, so dry and wasted, like a tree with the sap
drained. That would be her fate as well, to look out windows while the
life ran out of her.

But on this night she would escape that fate. On this night she would
journey, go away forever, right here in the very cathedral where they had
so often paraded her, dressed like a jeweled, silk-wrapped little *rusalka*
doll, for every gaping *miuzhi* and *liudi* in the entire world to stare at in
slack-jawed wonder. No, tonight would not be at all like that. Tonight she
would kill the little doll.

"Come here," she said. "You can see the lights by the river." She
turned. "Come here."

Haraldr looked back through the low, arched entrance of the tiny
storage room on the third floor of the Church of the Tithe, praying that
the cathedral was indeed empty. He squeezed awkwardly into the window
seat. He had never been this close to her before. Her sandy hair, pulled
back and tightly coiled on either side of her head in the Greek fashion,
seemed streaked with gold. He could smell her rose-water scent and hear

her breathe. He tried to suck air into his constricting lungs. He could not imagine what the touch of her would do.

"Look at them."

Haraldr watched the points of light swirl like fireflies as the workers moved among the blunt prows of the beached river ships. The dark forests beyond the left bank of the Dnieper stretched off to an eerily orange-fringed horizon, the corona of thousands of campfires. Haraldr shuddered. The Pechenegs were on the land.

"Jarl Rognvald told my father you are not going down the river with him. My father was *not* pleased. Why are you staying?" Elisevett leaned away from Haraldr and ran her fingers over the luminous pearls that studded her high silk collar, taunting her earnest Nordic swain to answer the question she knew he would not. While she observed his torment she considered how extraordinary it was that Christ—she doubted that the Lord's sinless Mother would have interceded on her behalf in this mat-ter—had answered her prayers by providing the hapless *detskii,* Haraldr Nordbrikt. He was a suitable vision, of course, tall and silky golden and so broad in the chest and shoulders, with those dazzling blue eyes and that interesting scar that pulled his right eyebrow up slightly. But then rakish Nordic giants were a plague in Rus these days, due to her father's relentless ambitions. No, what was truly wonderful and extraordinary was the manner in which Haraldr Nordbrikt affected her mother and father. She saw the way her father glared and gasped; if this mere *detskii* in his Lesser Druzhina offended him so much, why didn't the Great Prince just send him off against the Pechenegs and be done with him, instead of keeping him around Kiev to collect tolls? And her mother. *She* all but reached out and caressed Haraldr with her eyes, not in a leering fashion as an older woman might but with this strange glimmering ember deep within. But if Haraldr were her mother's lover, then her father would also send him off against the Pechenegs. Or could he? How mysterious. And how wonderful it would be if Haraldr Nordbrikt were her mother's lover.

Elisevett lowered her thick, dark, resin-coated lashes, an utterly feigned expression of modesty. "I think you are staying because of me."

Haraldr wanted to clutch desperately at this great secret that had just been wrenched from his breast, and yet its leaving also filled him with immense joy and relief. *Nothing will ever take me from you!* his head sang triumphantly. But dry chalk seemed to fill his throat, and he had to strangle a pathetic, creaking whimper.

Elisevett silently acknowledged this initial milestone on her journey and forged ahead. She removed a tiny folded parchment from the sleeve of her tunic. When Haraldr recognized the scrap, he became vertiginous with panic, and for a moment he imagined himself pitching forward through the window and plunging to his death. Elisevett squinted over the awkward Slavic script. "What is 'gold-wreathed goddess'?" she asked.

Haraldr raised his hand in the feeble gesture of a dying man and finally forced a syllable out. "Your . . ." His palm fluttered near the ornate gold bracelets that twined her arm. "Arm rings. You are wreathed in gold."

"I did not say for you to point at me as if I were a serving maid," Elisevett snapped. "My father could have you flogged in the Podol Square if he knew you sent verses to me." She lowered her head for a long moment and wondered what she would see when she arrived at her destination. It did not matter, as long as it was not *this*. She wondered if he would be fearless—and foolish—enough to follow.

Elisevett looked up at Haraldr again, her smoky-blue eyes wide. "The embassies have come since I was four months old. Three weeks ago the Prince of Hungaria. Last fall a king of Langobardia. I am the third daughter of the Great Prince, to be auctioned off like some shackled *kholopy* in the Podol market in order to bear the swinish brood of some petty tyrant with filthy habits. The gifts they have sent my father already fill a chamber." Her voice lowered to a mysterious, wistful sigh. "You are the first to send me something forbidden." She hissed conspiratorially. "Your own verse."

Haraldr's heart rose in his chest like a desperate caged bird. The life that had ended four years ago at Stiklestad could begin again. *Gold-ringed, cherished, snowy vision, I am not worthy of you but you have accepted my verses.*

"Touch me." Like some wizard's conjuring, the scarlet robe slinked fluidly past her knees to reveal several inches of firm, pale thigh. Her whisper was like cat's fur. "Touch me."

Haraldr inhaled sharply; even the damp air seemed to stick in his throat. Not in this holy place, and with the ax her father, Yaroslav, held over his head.

"If you don't, I will tell my father that you did."

Haraldr was conscious only of a bead of sweat rolling down his back. He watched his trembling hand reach out with the sickening fascination of a boy watching his first execution. Elisevett's eyes were spikes. But his hand crept closer, more assured of its desire.

Her thigh was like a rose petal, summer-plush, smooth and warm. Her white hand pulled his higher. His insides were liquid and his skin was pelted with sleet. Higher, downier, softer. If he went farther, his heart would stop.

"Stop." Elisevett pressed her legs together and slowly pulled his hand from between them. She knew now that he would have to go with her. "You could die for what you just did," she told him. She brought her lips closer, and her eyes were fierce, manic. "You know what we must do now." She pressed Haraldr's face with her silky hands. Her heavy lashes folded down and her face turned up in bitter triumph. It would be over soon.

Haraldr watched her eyes pulse beneath her pale, almost translucent lids. Her wine-red lips twitched. He distantly remembered one of Olaf's skalds using the word *dangerous* to describe a woman.

Like an attacking beast, her arms were around his neck, overwhelming his senses: the smell of her, the petal-soft cheek, the hot breath. He spasmed at the first lancing touch of her lips against his, and then flesh melted and fused. They held, gasped, teeth grinding. Then she pushed him away, her high breasts heaving beneath her silk. This was the moment. Her eyes found his and made certain that he would obey. "You know I am as pure as the Mother of White Christ," she said. "You must teach me."

The rest was a dream. In a pile of white priests' vestments, silk sliding, hard lilac nipples, probing the hot, downy center, each contact excruciating. She was so slick, like curiously hot ice—one slip and he would be gone.

It ended suddenly, with consummation still in progress. Haraldr could not believe the paralyzing surge in his gristled loins. Before, with the whore Jarl Rognvald had purchased for him, all the ale he had consumed to prepare for his initiation had dulled him sufficiently to allow for what had then seemed a lifetime of wondrous exploration. But with love and without ale, lovemaking was clearly different.

Their hearts pounded in concert for a moment. Then Elisevett heaved with a single sobbing inhalation. She had rid herself of the detestable innocence that tied her childhood; the little doll had been smashed by his bludgeoning manhood. But there was this strange new sorrow. Where would she go now? The still wet new wings of womanhood began to wilt, and suddenly she had a maddening desire to undo all this, to go back to the *Him* she had renounced for this new *him*.

Haraldr clutched his new life in panic; why had she begun to cry like this? He tried to caress her but she wrenched away and furiously pulled her robe out from among the scattered, crumpled vestments. She stood, tears welling over her dark lashes, her scarlet silk draped in front of her. "I am going to have to tell my father what you did," she said, sobbing.

† † †

Two guards preceded him and two followed. The noise from the river was now an assault; the musicians had started a tinny rehearsal. The warmth of the day lingered in ponds of still air as Haraldr and his gaolers ascended the steps to the summit of the Citadel of Kiev. They turned beside a stack of freshly quarried granite blocks and entered a colonnaded walkway bordered with newly planted cypresses, finally pausing in front of a bronze door embossed with a trident, the family crest of the Great Prince Yaroslav of Rus.

Haraldr was ordered to wait in an antechamber. The guards locked the doors as they left. The candelabra were not lit and the only light came from two brass oil lamps hung on opposite walls. Along the far end of the chamber, scaffolding had been erected by visiting Greek artists, and the chalk outline of a mural traced a phantom image in the faint light.

He waited on his feet, too stunned with terror to begin an accounting of his misery. After what seemed like hours he heard footsteps and voices, then nothing. His legs ached and he slumped against the wall, then sat on the cold marble floor. His resurrection last night had ended so quickly, it might never have happened, a butterfly that had flickered across his vision one summer afternoon and was gone. Kristr was cruel, he gave pleasure and then punished for it. No, this was Odin; the prophet of fate had finally come to claim the ending that had been stolen from him four years ago. The thought provided a melancholy comfort; the terrible dark fall that had begun at Stiklestad was almost over.

"Nordbrikt! Get up, you hamster-eating moron! You'd sleep on the gibbet!" The lamp flared and Yaroslav's scar-faced bailiff kicked at his feet. "You kissed the Devil's ass this time." He gave Haraldr a shove toward the double doors.

The Great Prince Yaroslav's office was lit by a single flickering lamp set on a massive ivory table inlaid with silver tridents. Leather- and ivory-bound manuscripts were stacked at Yaroslav's left elbow and he pushed them away. The Great Prince's stubby, larvaelike fingers crept over the tabletop as if he were fumbling for something in the dark. Finally he looked up. His face had a greasy, slightly jaundiced pallor that closely matched the color of the tabletop. Purple folds almost like separate appendages hung beneath his wide, hen's-eggs eyes.

"Haraldr Nordbrikt, Haraldr Sigurdarson," said Yaroslav in a weary, rattling voice; it was as if he were deciding which of the two names offended him the most. "I spend too much time dealing with"—Yaroslav paused and gasped—"you." Yaroslav's right hand snatched a small jeweled replica of a cathedral and his busy fingers went to work on it. "Now, I understand that you have brought some sort of . . . suit to my third daughter."

The Great Prince's voice was so introspective that Haraldr was not certain he had heard properly. Did he dream this? He soared on a gust of bewilderment and hope.

The Great Prince rose, stepped around the table with his jerky lame gait, and stood with his stout belly aimed at Haraldr's belt. His glaring pop eyes offered no hope at all. "You are the opposite of me in every way. God in his ineffable wisdom made you tall and straight. I am short and crooked. Your father and then your brother worshiped you as if you were the sacred skull of St. Andrew. My father, the blasphemous fornicator, banished me to Rostov and then still tried to extort tribute from me, and I fought my brother, Syvataspolk, he of the foul-smelling grave, for ten years for the right to rule this city!" The Great Prince's voice was steadily rising; his face darkening. "And yet I am the one called the Great Prince, and all Europe comes to me, and even the Greek Emperor calls me friend, and you"—Yaroslav gulped for air like a fish out of water—"you are a prince without a name, much less any subject who would raise any sword for him or tithe a grivna to his cause. Your rank is *detskii* in my Lesser Druzhina. I believe you now have the lofty responsibility of collecting the toll at the Lybed Bridge. And I can tell you on good authority that you will never be promoted even to *pasynok.*"

Haraldr boiled in the acid of four years' humiliation. Another voice screamed at him, but it was not Yaroslav's.

"I know why you regard me with such contempt." Yaroslav paused like a man on the brink of a sheer promontory, then gulped and stepped forward. "You affront the Great Prince because you know, as indeed the scabrous tales are recited in every court in the north, because your brother"—Yaroslav stuttered with rage—"your brother knew my wife. Because your brother fouled my wife with his stinking lechery! Your brother put his hands all over my wife and spoiled her, and after all I did for him he rutted her like the drooling satyr he was. He ruined her with his filthy lusts!"

Haraldr had not known this. Yes, his brother had always spoken of Ingigerd with reverence, but Haraldr had never imagined that they had been lovers. His frigid, leaden stomach plunged toward the floor. Now he understood the sin for which he had been punished for four miserable years.

"Stop this, Husband." Haraldr peered with terrified wonder into the dark corner of the room. Gaunt, wraithlike, a cloak wrapped around her like a burial shroud, sat Ingigerd, Queen of Rus. Haraldr had not even noticed her when he had entered. The outline of her broad, angular shoulders became visible as she rose from her chair. "You knew that I was not pure before you ever held me. I have given *you* four sons and three daughters. It was my father, the same who forbade me to marry the man who touched me first, who sent as my dower the Swedish mercenaries who defeated your brother, Syvataspolk. It was my *lover"*—she spit out the word—"Olaf, who sent his friend Eymund to take Novgorod for you." Ingigerd stepped toward the light and clapped her hands to the breasts, now low and shriveled, that men had once called the great snowy joy-cliffs of Sweden. "Your dynasty is built on this corrupt flesh, Great Prince."

Yaroslav returned to his chair and sat with a cringing posture. He deeply regretted that the sight of Norway's royal excrement had caused him to vent his old jealousy in this unfortunate display. He considered again the counsel his wife had offered him earlier in the day, when his daughter Elisevett had come to him with another of her endless vexations. Haraldr, as Ingigerd had pointed out, was Norway's rightful heir; and *reliable* Norse military assistance, such as might be provided by a grateful son-in-law, was essential to the survival of Yaroslav's dynasty. And then Elisevett was no prize: she was a mere third daughter, an intractable child whose precipitate temperament might break an alliance as easily as her precocious loins might build one. But the problem with this marriage was—as were all problems of statecraft—pecuniary.

Currently Haraldr offered nothing but liabilities. The reclamation of his throne would require a considerable fortune, and at the moment Haraldr was worth more dead than alive: the purse now offered for the head of Haraldr Sigurdarson was a staggering one thousand gold bezants, and it seemed that virtually every Norseman in Rus was intent on winning that bounty, save the most ardent Norwegian patriots; Yaroslav, himself, had been tempted more than once to solve several of his problems by surrendering the fugitive Prince of Norway. Of course, his wife would have bitten his balls off, so it was just as well he had resisted. Haraldr, however, was not the kind of man who seemed likely to win men's loyalty, so it would be pointless to risk a single silver grivna on the chance he might reclaim his throne. But if Haraldr could finance his own re-conquest of Norway, he would be worth the risk of a third daughter. Of course, Haraldr would need the money quickly, while Elisevett was still young; without an heir to bind Norway to Rus, the exercise was pointless. And there was only one place in the world where a layabout like Haraldr could acquire a fortune virtually overnight. And if Haraldr never returned from that journey, what would have been lost? Even Elisevett had dozens of other suitors.

"Haraldr. My father married no less than the daughter of the Greek Emperor. Do you know what he gave the Emperor in exchange for his bride? Kherson. The entire city of Kherson."

Haraldr stared maniacally at Yaroslav. It was all he could do to keep from shouting, "I'll give you a nation! Denmark or Angle-Land or Bulgaria!"

"Haraldr. It would be enough for me to know that Norway was a grandson's birthright. But presently you are sovereign of nothing beyond your own boots. And I cannot worry about defending you against your legions of enemies when my own cities are beseiged by Pechenegs and I need the cooperation of all Norsemen in ridding Rus of the eternally menacing pagan horde." Yaroslav's throat rattled, and he sighed as if he could hardly go on. "You are aware, of course, how valuable your corpse is. I feel that if you stay here, it is only a matter of time before you are found out. Yesterday I received a correspondence from a Jarl of Denmark who has served me ably in my Druzhina in Novgorod—I won't reveal his name to you, as I will not reveal yours to him—a correspondence inquiring if I harbor the Prince of Norway at my court. A week ago my own *podiezdnoi* asked me if I had heard rumors that the lost Prince of Norway, the one who ran from Stiklestad, is a fugitive in Kiev." Yaroslav paused and looked at Haraldr searchingly. "Are you beginning to understand?"

Haraldr was too stunned to think. An alarming metallic buzzing echoed in his ears.

Yaroslav sucked in a weary, rattling breath. "Haraldr, my concerns are those of statecraft." He glanced surreptitiously at his Queen. "Had your brother paid more attention to that discipline and less to . . ." He hesitated. "Well, yes, had your brother been more careful, he would not have confronted King Knut when he did in the way he did, and perhaps I would not at this time be concerned with *your* enemies—" He stopped, distracted. "I forget myself. . . . Yes. Well, then, as you might know, the Pechenegs have blocked the Dnieper for eight years now. So now my primary concern is to open the river to commerce once again, employ our profits to summon additional military assistance, and exterminate the

Pechenegs as we have the Avars and Chuds and, most recently, the Poles. Your countryman Jarl Rognvald has gratefully accepted my commission to lead the trade flotilla to Constantinople. Perhaps you could in some small fashion contribute to the success of this enterprise."

The words were like an ax thudding into Haraldr's neck. The journey down the Dnieper was a game of chance that few would win; even Jarl Rognvald admitted that he, himself, would be unlikely to see the walls of Constantinople. The Jarl would risk the deadly voyage on the slimmest wager that Norway might profit, but he did not think Norway would gain if her Prince slept in the Dnieper. Haraldr had in turn hardly pushed to go, and not simply for *her.* Since Stiklestad he had known sorrow and loneliness until they were like faces before him. And even as his breast ached at the thought of leaving Elisevett, he knew that he could somehow endure this terrible extra measure of longing. But on the river he would have to look at a face he knew he could never confront again. He would have to look again at fear. And fear would humble him before the whole world, because fear had been with him that day at Stiklestad—even now the blood-dark nightmare flew before his eyes—and fear knew him for what he was. A coward.

Yaroslav's small ragged teeth appeared briefly. "Cheer, boy. Many rewards wait at the river's end. Surely even an idler like yourself has dreamed of service in the Emperor's Varangian Guard. Indeed, we have received an eminent representative of the Emperor's guard this very afternoon, a man of Greek subtlety and refinement. Hakon, called Fire-Eyes. You would do well to emulate his industry."

Haraldr turned from the nightmare past to the nightmares that waited ahead on the river. Hakon Fire-Eyes. Second in rank to Mar Hunrodarson, the wide-famed commander of the Great King's Varangian Guard, and next to Mar himself the most feared and brutal warrior in the world. For weeks now it had been rumored that Hakon would join the expedition to Miklagardr, and that he would bring with him five hundred handpicked candidates for the Varangian Guard. Now fear would have five hundred faces. And a demon to lead them.

"So there," said Yaroslav, rising and holding his stubby fingers out to Haraldr. "Lesser men then you have ventured to Constantinople and returned with a king's endowment. So might you. So. Good-bye to Haraldr Nordbrikt. Let us hope that if we see you again, you will be someone else."

Ingigerd followed Haraldr into the antechamber. She caught his arms and turned him, the long, wilted stems of her fingers about his wrists.

"You know it is the only way now. Jarl Rognvald will care for you, and Elisevett and I will pray for you." She surprised Haraldr with a wiry, intense embrace; she had never even touched him before, always staying back, as if his flesh might rouse some banished specter. "I will miss you more than Elisevett shall. She is young. I am . . . finished." Her irises were like melting blue ice. She took his face in her hands and gazed into his eyes, as if this were the last time she would ever consume that life-giving draft. Her throat corded with a sob. "Your eyes . . . " said Ingigerd, Queen of Rus, as softly as a deathbed prayer. "In your eyes he lives."

he slap on the back of his head was playful, but Haraldr wrestled for his sword with hands clumsied by wine.

"Leave that in your scabbard. River-farers and woman-praisers need their fingers." Jarl Rognvald grinned. He had also been busy at the mead trenches. But the Jarl lost only his melancholy in the ale.

"Jarl . . ." Haraldr held up his sloshing wine bag in mute apology.

"I know. I talked with Yaroslav. But you're sailing with me! Tomorrow we'll be on the Dnieper! You leave nothing here, my boy, nothing. But think what you might return to!"

Haraldr tried to focus. "Jarl, do you think that Yaroslav will really consider my suit—"

"Haraldr, my boy! In the morning we put out for Miklagardr. Miklagardr! To seek the widest fame and goldest glory a man can seek. The Grik Emperor can bestow a princess's dower as easily as a Norse king might give his man an arm ring. Your dreams await you there!"

Yes, my dreams, thought Haraldr, for a chilling instant sobered.

Jarl Rognvald observed the shadow on his ward's face and grinned foolishly while the demons of his own mind soughed and shrieked. To-morrow morning he would lead almost five hundred ships and twenty thousand men down the Dnieper. If Odin were extraordinarily lavish with his favors, a third of those ships and men might return to Kiev. Jarl Rognvald had accepted Yaroslav's onerous charge through the same rigid sense of duty that had driven him throughout his life; he was the best man, Norse or Slav, to command the flotilla, and as far as he was concerned, that alone obligated him to lead, however ill advised the Great Prince's venture might be. But that was before Norway's fate had been cast upon the murderous Dnieper.

"Haraldr. We all fear the river." The Jarl wrapped a big rough hand around Haraldr's neck. "Why do you think that every man of us has tonight summoned the heron of forgetfulness?" He grabbed Haraldr's arm. "Let's walk. I must find the Grik trade ambassador. And the entire world is here to see!"

The flat, sandy plain just north of the bluff-walled Citadel of Kiev was strewn with acres of cargo lit by moving torches: corded stacks of furs; endless buckets of beeswax and honey; and groups of predominantly dark-hued, resigned slaves, enough for an army, roped together at the feet. Farmers dragged their sledges full of cabbages, turnips, and onions. Barrels of ale and salted meat were rolled along the maze of timber paths to the Dnieper. Screeching from their canvas booths, merchants did a lucrative last-minute business in tools, armor, and burlap for tents and awnings. Strange foreign tongues clashed like flocks of exotic birds. Yaroslav's military band filled the air with the whirling, tinny melodies of pipes, tambourines, and horns. The fat-bodied river ships lined the ghostly gray sand-shore like an enormous herd of beached leviathans.

The Jarl pointed out two silk-sheathed figures. He straightened his own tunic and fastened the top two buttons of Haraldr's jacket. His voice returned to its usual gravity. "Haraldr, the Grik trade ambassador will have an interpreter with him, a Grik likewise, but this man speaks our tongue as well as you or I. Like many Grik court-men, this interpreter has been gelded so that he may serve the Emperor without aspiring to his throne. He will have a face as smooth as a woman's. Please do not stare at him. He still has his dignity."

The Byzantine trade ambassador wore an ankle-length tunic of red silk; dark, tightly-ringed hair and a curling beard framed his high, feminine cheekbones. He seemed to peer through the Norseman as if he were looking through a pane of glass. The little hairless man beside the ambassador, robed in plainer silk, smiled broadly. The ambassador still evidenced no awareness of the two Norsemen. After an awkward moment the eunuch spoke in a high, humming voice. "Greetings, Jarl Rognvald." Haraldr was astonished at the flawless pronunciation and undetectable accent. The eunuch cleared his throat for ironic emphasis and his eyes sparkled conspiratorially. "We both greet you. At least I am certain that the august ambassador would greet you if he were not so busily engaged in ignoring you."

"Gregory," offered Jarl Rognvald, "I want you to meet Haraldr Nordbrikt. I ask you to treat him as you would my son. You'll find him different than most young men of our race. He has a special passion"—Jarl Rognvald pounded his breast—"strong but gentle. He writes verse." The Jarl rustled Haraldr's long silky hair. "Sometimes we say that our skalds 'drink the ale of Odin.' Well, tonight Haraldr has drunk only ale."

"A poet," said Gregory appreciatively. "Then he must learn of Homer."

The ambassador wiped his mouth, as if trying to remove some contami-

nation, and spoke sharply to Gregory in the flowing, interminably circuitous rhythm of the Greek tongue. His comments went on for several
minutes. Gregory nodded respectfully from time to time.

"Jarl Rognvald, it is sometimes argued that in our government a man
rises on the accumulation of his words," said Gregory when the ambassador had finished. The little eunuch struggled to combat a smile. "Of
course, that is not true. If it were, our august ambassador already would
have ascended to the Imperial throne. What he has said is this. First, I
am not to exchange inessential pleasantries with you 'northern *barbaroi.*'
Forgive me, but I am afraid you will have to become accustomed to that
term. More pertinently, the documents for the entire fleet of four hundred and eighty-six ships are now in order. There is nothing to prevent
our departure. Unless, of course, the august ambassador decides to deliver an address to inaugurate our voyage."

Jarl Rognvald forced himself not to laugh; he presumed that the ambassador would be only too eager to take offense. "Have you seen Hakon?
I don't want to wait until the morning to speak with him."

Gregory lifted a wry eyebrow. "I am afraid I have seen more of the
Manglavite than I had hoped."

"Manglavite?" asked Haraldr.

"Hakon Fire-Eyes holds the official title of Manglavite. He symbolically
clears the path for the Emperor in official processions," said Gregory. "It
is an extraordinary honor." He did not add that it was a particularly
extraordinary honor for a *barbaroi,* and a frightening testament to the
enormous, malignant power of Hakon's patron, Mar Hunrodarson.

Gregory led the Jarl and Haraldr to the Varangian encampment. It
seemed as if all of the five hundred swaggering young warriors had
assembled in a rollicking mob around some central attraction. Haraldr
reluctantly followed the Jarl into their midst; though he was taller and
broader than all but a few, he felt as if his cowardice were a physical defect
they would immediately recognize and ridicule.

At the center of the crowd was a naked woman, a coarsely ruddy farm
girl with short-cropped slave's hair, firm heavy buttocks, and small
breasts with boyish nipples. She stared numbly at a man sitting on an ale
barrel; he was huge even by Norse standards. He wore a short lacquered
gold byrnnie but was naked below the waist; his legs were so thickly
muscled, they seemed like the pillars of some colossal temple. His head
slumped toward his chest, and his long golden hair concealed his face.
He held a hand to his crotch, as if he had been injured. It was a moment
before Haraldr realized that the giant was actually stroking his own geni-

tals, apparently trying to coax an erection so that he could publicly pene-
trate the unfortunate slave girl. Then Haraldr noticed the other naked
slave, a slender girl who sat forlornly in the sand; blood smeared her
inner thighs. She was no doubt the reason for the giant's temporary
impotence. Several more slave girls, roped together and wearing coarse
wool tunics, stood behind her, dreadfully waiting their turn.

The giant looked up. His long golden beard was plaited into dozens
of tiny braids and spangled with shimmering bits of gold. The eponymous
orange flecks in his blue irises were clearly visible. Hakon's fire-eyes
swept about crazily, as dangerous as weapons, and finally targeted Jarl
Rognvald. Hakon's thick, brutish lips parted, offering a huge ivory grin.
"Jarl Rognvald," he said casually. "It seems my quiver is temporarily
empty." His head slumped again, and he returned his attention to his
limp penis.

Jarl Rognvald was rigid with disgust. To capture, own, and trade in
slaves was accepted in the north, but to abuse them, particularly in this
fashion, was an outrage. But there was trouble enough waiting for him
on the Dnieper, and he could not afford a row with the leader of the five
hundred most able warriors under his overall command. "I'll speak with
Hakon in the morning," he told Haraldr wearily.

A young man with wispy chin whiskers bounded from the crowd and
began a recitation in the strident tones of the skald. "Sater-of-ravens!
Full-strong arm of the Great King! He whose forehead-moons glow with
the stars-of-hearth!" He raised his arm and flourished his hand as if
scattering gold dust into the sky.

Hakon looked up at the young skald. "Grettir!" He chortled. "Have
you found me fresh meat? Something to temper my Frey-spike?"

"Yes, heretic-hewer." Grettir moved his hands in suggestion of a
woman's curves. "*Itrvaxinn!*" Good lines, like a well-crafted Norse dragon-ship.

The naked farm girl was pushed aside. Two Varangians dragged the
next victim through the crowd. At the sight of her Haraldr knew he could
not leave.

Though she was cloaked in a dirty burlap tunic and bound at her wrists
and ankles, this young woman obviously had not been born to accept
slavery. Her skin was as lustrously white as her uncropped hair was black.
She snapped like a badger at Grettir's hand, and he had to wrestle her
chin up for Hakon's inspection. Her agate eyes were brightly polished
with anger; her nose was long and fine with a delicate, sharp tip. Even in
the face of the humiliation that awaited her, she had an unmistakable

nobility. Haraldr's breast ached with her loveliness and her terrible fate. A voice whispered at him, then faded. He did not know what it said. A torrent of obscene speculation followed from the crowd.

"Imagine the dark foliage that garlands her thigh-gorge, heretic-hewer." Grettir grimaced as he struggled to steady the girl's writhing head. "You had better expect a fight if you try to sail up this fjord."

Hakon grinned. "The blood from the wound Freyja hews will bless our journey!" His disproportionately small penis now stood with plum-hued stiffness. He reached out with an enormous apelike arm, seized the girl's long black mane, and forced her to stumble between his massive, spread thighs; she became curiously acquiescent, and merely glared as he brought her mouth to his. There was a moment of contact, and then her head jerked violently. Hakon bellowed and almost pitched backward off his perch. Blood streamed from his lacerated nose.

Hakon dabbed at his nose with one hand. The other wrapped almost entirely around the girl's neck. Jarl Rognvald decided that he would intercede if Hakon tried to kill the girl. The lewd chorusing of the Varangians quieted. Hakon's eyes wandered, as if he were looking for a signal. The clearly voiced verses lilted over the crowd.

> *Sable-haired*
> *Plundered from the strand that is sea*
> *Dauntless to spill the wine of ravens*
> *Swan-white stands she.*

A fair snippet of verse, thought Haraldr as he savored the skald's words. The poet has imagined her coming from the desert, which is said to be a sea of beaches, and because she has spilled the brute's blood she can yet wear her hair uncovered, like a maiden, and so is still white and pure. . . . *Why are they all looking at me?* Haraldr wondered. Then he realized what had happened, and his veins iced. He was the poet. He had spoken aloud, perhaps not in his own voice, but the words had certainly come out of his mouth.

"Hvat?" bellowed Hakon, as astounded as he was furious. Grettir took two slow paces toward Haraldr and looked at him as if he had just seen a serpent talk. Jarl Rognvald's heart soared in the instant before he furiously began to reason how to get Haraldr out of there alive.

Haraldr felt the pressure of Hakon's dagger against his windpipe almost before he saw the gleam of steel. "I'm sorry, Jarl Rognvald, but your bodyguard has mocked me," Hakon growled; there was no sorrow in his voice. "I'm going to have to ask him if his sword is as sharp as his tongue."

"He's carved from a tall tree," jibed Grettir, "but it looks as if the wood is still green."

"Hakon!" Jarl Rognvald's hand gripped the pommel of his sword. "Hold back. This boy is my ward. He is not paid to defend me. But I am bound by honor and love to defend him."

Hakon weighed his own decision, the satisfaction of butchering a meddlesome old Jarl against the huge bonus he would receive when he delivered his recruits in Constantinople. And he needed the Jarl's Rus pilots to insure that delivery. But when they reached the Rus sea and no longer needed the river men's expertise, he vowed that the lobsters would taste old Norse meat. And as for the Jarl's turd-chewing ward, he would never see the river's end.

Hakon dropped his sword and he shrugged and sniffed contemptuously. "Yes, Grettir, this wood is too green to whittle. Perhaps," he added ominously, "a few weeks on the river will season it."

The Varangians hooted with derision. "Too green to whittle!" echoed through the crowd.

Grettir turned back to Haraldr. "It would have been an honor to die at the hand of Hakon. But listen to the praise they're singing you now. You've a hard tongue but a soft back." The laughter rose like the thunder of a coming storm. A wind screamed inside Haraldr's skull, whipping humiliation into a suicidal frenzy.

Haraldr's wet palm slipped against the bone handle of his sword, but almost at the same moment Hakon flung his arm toward the sand and something thudded against Haraldr's foot; he felt a minute searing, as if he had stepped on a spark. He looked stupidly at his feet and saw a gold pommel staring up at him. Hakon's dagger had sliced through the sole of his heavy boots and had just nicked his big toe. Haraldr reflexively tried to pull his foot away, but his boot was pinned to the firm, damp sand and he stumbled. He lost his balance and fell to his knees.

The laughter shrieked like a tempest. "Hakon has toppled the tallest tree with a nick of his dagger!" Grettir chortled.

"Green-wood!" bellowed Hakon.

"That's his name, Green-wood!" echoed voices from the crowd.

"Green-wood, next time I see you with your hand on your sword, I'll aim two ells higher. I'll make you the tallest geld in the East." Hakon paused, hocked, and spat a great yellow wad on Haraldr's hand. "And then I'll make you shorter by a head."

The howling north wind blew away the drunken haze. Haraldr recognized a voice that he knew but had not heeded since that terrible day four years ago, when he had shut his ears to it. It was strange, so thunderous and yet so intimate, as if it not only knew him but also was of him, as if another soul, separated from him at Stiklestad, stood partially inside him and partially outside, sharing some of him and rejecting the rest. There had been times when Haraldr had sensed that he could completely enter this twin soul and share his power, which he knew to be considerable, for he had on occasion felt the other's fist, as hard as an iron ingot yet as light to lift as down. Still, he could not simply take a slight step and embrace his fugitive twin; he knew that he had to cross through the spirit world, cold and ancient, filled with the furies of the old gods and the beasts of the deepest abyss. So he had long feared the other and had struggled against him, fettering the part of him that wanted to begin that journey.

Now, for the first time in four years, he pulled against those bonds, somehow feeling that the fetters might at last be broken if only his will to do so was great enough. His vision darkened with a ferocious mind storm, and his hand flexed and trembled and strained for the handle of his sword. If only he could reach it!

Jarl Rognvald's hands clutched Haraldr's arm like a vise, but it was not that which was able to restrain him. "Wait," whispered the strange inner voice, which for an instant was his own. "Wait."

is Imperial Majesty, the Emperor, Basileus, and Autocrator of the Romans."

The Empress Zoe sat up. The head of her chamberlain, Symeon, framed by the leaden silk curtains of her canopy and illuminated by the single oil lamp he had brought into her bedchamber, seemed to float in the darkness, an ancient, hairless mask of white parchment. She nodded quickly and the curtains swished vaporously aside. Zoe stepped onto the thick carpet beside her bed. She was entirely naked, and for an instant her generous bosom and satiny flank gleamed like honey-tinted white marble. A second eunuch wrapped her in a gauzy robe. Her already erect nipples, dark and thick, pressed against the sheer fabric. The two eunuchs left a lamp on a small table and swept silently out of the room, their slippers whispering on *opus sectile*.

She met the Emperor in the more intimate vestibule of her cavernous, domed bedchamber. The miniature eagles embroidered all over his robe flickered dully, like gold insects flitting in the moonlight. She could see at once the hint of weariness in the otherwise impeccable carriage of his broad shoulders and muscular chest. She pressed her lush bosom against him and kissed him fiercely. She had become accustomed to his slight, almost palsied recoil.

"I . . . I came to say I will be unable to stay with you," he said when she took his hand and urged him in the direction of her canopied bed. His voice, deep and resonant, had a natural command, but this was offered without inflection. He was apologizing, though he did not wish to.

"You are still working?"

"I could work for the next ten years and not repair the damage done by my . . . predecessor. I had no idea what he had done. No one did. Not even my brother. The substance of it, yes. Not the extent of it." The Emperor's lustrous, dark eyes contracted for a moment, hardening. "Even if the Rus trade resumes, we must institute another surcharge to the window tax. The Dhynatoi will do everything they can to oppose us." The Dhynatoi were the empire's enormously powerful landed aristocracy; among the myriad Imperial exactions, the window tax—based on

38

the number of windows in a dwelling—was one of the few levies that fell more heavily on the owners of large estates than it did upon peasant freeholders.

The Empress Zoe brushed the dark curls from her husband's forehead and again drew him toward her bed. The Emperor did not resist. He sat on the edge of the enormous sleeping couch, his back perfectly erect. He relaxed his shoulders and exhaled, audibly, through his nose. Zoe began to unlace his robe at the back. She unlaced the fine linen undershirt as well, and peeled away both layers to expose her husband's muscle-dimpled back. She slipped out of her wrapper and pressed her breasts to his flesh. His back tensed.

"Stay with me," Zoe whispered into his ear.

He turned, his face fixed with a kind of horror, as if her breasts were diseased. "He was murdered." The Emperor's tone was now vaguely frantic. "Your husband. The Emperor. I am certain of it."

"You are my husband. You are now the Emperor."

"Romanus was your husband when you—when you and I—" The Emperor seemed to strangle on the words. "When he asked me about us, I lied to him in the sight of the Pantocrator. I perjured myself on the holy relics. And then I turned away while he was murdered. Does mere acquiescence make the mark of Cain upon me any less indelible?"

Zoe pulled her robe over her breasts. Her recitation was ritualistic, an oft-repeated exorcism. "He was near death. The last of his innumerable follies was his final ablution. His doctors warned him not to bathe. He simply drowned. You saw the corpse. Perhaps the servants were . . . *inattentive.* But they were not assassins."

"They say someone held his head under. A Varangian. The Hetairarch, they say."

"*They* say? The hirelings of the Dhynatoi, who will repeat anything for a price? There are many powerful men who would have preferred a far less . . . *vigorous* successor to Romanus. This is how they attack you, and the men who stand between you and their obscene ambitions. If any hand held my . . . your predecessor's head beneath those waters, it was the hand of the Pantocrator Himself. Romanus was a plague. Your hands cured me of him. Now they will cure my people."

"And who will be physician to my affliction?" The Emperor stood up, pulled his robe over his shoulders, and stepped away from his wife's bed. "For even if I wash seven times in the River Jordan, I cannot heal the infection of my soul."

on't touch it!" The arrow had drifted lazily out of the sky like a wounded bird and clattered harmlessly on the deck. "It might be poisoned." Jarl Rognvald walked to the foredeck, crossing the planks that covered the main cargo hold. He carefully picked up the metal-tipped, neatly feathered shaft and held it up for all to see. "What a bowshot." He looked across the still, yellow river toward the startlingly green, thickly wooded bank. "I'd measure it over five hundred ells."

"Gleb!" shouted Jarl Rognvald to his Slav pilot. "Call for a tight file."

Haraldr squinted at the mysterious, dense wall of foliage. Ten days already on the river, the placid monotony of the waters like the sultry, unsettling stillness before a lightning storm. Each day with its whispered, drifting warning of the hidden enemy. The eerie tranquillity of the star-flecked nights, and the creeping, subtle terror that one might awaken to find that one's boat has drifted from anchor and thudded into the bank, into the hands of the unseen demons. (It had happened to one crew last night; the watch had gotten drunk, and in the moonless night no one knew until they heard the screams.) Jarl Rognvald was increasingly withdrawn when he was not preoccupied with command, staring down the river like a seeress struggling to spy the future. And for Haraldr, dreams. So many dreams here. Not only of a dying sun and blood on the land but also of a place of wind and cold and endless blackness. The voice, always that voice now, whispering, cajoling, drawing him into that deepening dark void where his fears stalked on nightmare feet. On the river, the beasts of those inner depths had become more fierce, and his fugitive soul seemed ever more distant.

Haraldr was certain he saw a glint of metal in the distance. Another. Yet another! Far ahead, the left bank lowered and the verdant screen was interrupted by a dun patch filled with colors and flashes of steel and bustling movement. "Larboard bank! Larboard!" he yelled. "Pechenegs!"

Gleb the pilot limped along the gangplanks, coming forward to stand in the prow with Haraldr and Jarl Rognvald. He was a short, gray-eyed man who shaved his head save for a long gray lock above each ear. Gleb had obtained his limp on his first Dnieper trip, when his boat had been tossed on the rocks. After that he had lived to "vanquish the river," and that was why he had taken three more trips. But it was said that Yaroslav had had to make Gleb's sons and grandsons rich men before he could persuade Gleb to become lead pilot for this expedition. "A man needs the luck of the whole world to go four times down the Dnieper," Gleb had told Jarl Rognvald. "By the time he starts his fifth trip, he will have used up all the luck there is."

"They'll be giving us a show now," muttered Gleb.

Jarl Rognvald looked at him quizzically.

"That crew they captured," groused the pilot, "be sure that they haven't yet killed all of them."

A distant shout boomed across the water. "The famished eagle feeds at last!"

Haraldr's stomach roiled. Several ships, oars churning, had moved up fast on the larboard. From the prow of the lead boat, gold returned the sunlight: byrnnie, helmet, and gold-tinseled braided beard. Hakon.

Little had been heard from Hakon since they had left Kiev. He had communicated with Jarl Rognvald through a messenger, and his men were quietly disciplined on the water. Now, just when Haraldr was beginning to think that Hakon was simply another of his deviling dreams, here he was.

"Jarl Rognvald, we must moor our ships up ahead!" Hakon was commanding, not requesting. "The skeleton-copulators are sure to entertain us. I want them to know that we also have art-skills!"

Jarl Rognvald cocked a frosty eyebrow at Gleb.

The pilot nodded. "Fear is the Pecheneg's sharpest blade. We need to show them that our steel is just as good."

The Pechenegs had trampled a path to the river like a vast herd of giant lemmings; only a dozen or so trees at the water's edge, stripped to mastlike shafts and curiously paired, rose above a river of human and horse heads thousands of ells wide and long enough to disappear over a hill far in the distance. The warriors had dismounted and stood in their own rough clothes as well as the plunder of a dozen other races: homespun robes with leather caps and jerkins, skin and fur tunics, spiked and conical helmets over glossy black hair, tattered Frisian cloth, byrnnies of chain mail and iron discs, even a cluster of Pecheneg potentates in silk robes and gleaming armlets. The makeshift horde erupted into a cataclysmic, shrilling, droning welcome.

Hakon's ship drifted closer to shore. "Bring me the instruments on which I'll play my ditty!" hollered the gilded giant. Five dark little men, roped at hands and feet, were brought to the prow of the ship; the Varangians had captured some Pechenegs just outside Kiev and intended to sell them as slaves in Constantinople, if they did not find more expedient uses for them.

Hakon began to speak again, but his words were lost against the screeching gale from the shore. There was a flurry of movement around one of the pairs of tree trunks. The two towering shafts were bowed toward each other until their tips crossed, forming a crude arch.

The Rus boats buzzed with speculation. Gleb spat angrily and his jaws clenched. A struggling, flailing man, his naked white skin clearly visible, was hoisted up and tied between the tree trunks, his arms and legs spread wide so that he looked like a huge white spider amid a rope web. The Pechenegs howls ascended and then abruptly drifted away until only a single sound floated across the water: the sound of one man screaming.

A Pecheneg sword flashed like a silver spark at the base of the nearest tree trunk. The crossed tops of the trees twitched almost imperceptibly. Then, with a terrifying suddenness, the shafts snapped apart and the white spider exploded in a burst of crimson. A torso seemed to spin slowly through the air. The trees snapped upright, each dangling one arm and one leg.

Hakon's face was sunset-purple amid the ashen complexions of his Varangians. Without speaking, he selected his instrument; the dark little man let out an unworldly shriek until Hakon clamped one huge hand around his windpipe. In his other hand Hakon held a broadax polished to an antimony gleam. He turned the Pecheneg's back toward the riverbank and laid it open with two lightning-quick strokes along either side of the spine. Before the blood could really flow, Hakon had dropped his ax and cracked open the ribs and peeled them back. With both hands he scooped into the body cavity and drew out the foaming pink lungs. He held the Pecheneg by the hair and spread the lungs like wings over writhing shoulders. The little man's mouth spewed pink froth, and Hakon let him slump to his knees, then tore away his loincloth. He grabbed a spear and carefully probed the Pecheneg's rectum. After several deft shoves the gory tip sprouted between the spread lungs.

Hakon seized the spear shaft with both hands and held his creation aloft like a winged battle standard. "The blood eagle, marmot-fuckers!" he screamed. "The blood eagle, wives of dogs!" He shook his macabre standard in fury. "The blood eagle! We'll strangle you with the cunts of your women!"

The Pechenegs on the shore had prepared another victim. The trees snapped and limbs dangled again. Hakon raised another gory standard in response. The ritual exchange continued until five Varangians held the purpling blood eagles aloft and the Pechenegs had run out of trees.

An almost palpable silence descended, as if the air had become thick with some sound-absorbing ether. One of the blood eagles twitched like a fish on a pike. Finally a group of silk-robed Pechenegs moved to the water's edge. The vividly colored chieftains held pinkish, hemispherical bowls in their hands. They raised the vessels and chanted a salute to the wallowing Rus ships before emptying greedy drafts into their upturned mouths.

"They're wassailing us?" asked Haraldr numbly.

Gleb spat. "No. They are showing us their new drinking vessels. Cut from the skulls of our men."

Hakon shifted his grim, fire-flecked gaze to the remaining Pecheneg. He yanked the wide-eyed little man in front of the first of the blood eagles. His dagger flashed and severed the impaled Pecheneg's testicles. "We'll fatten him with belly-oysters!" crowed Hakon as he popped the surviving Pecheneg's mouth open with one hand and shoved the bloody morsel down his throat with the other.

Hakon went down the row of blood eagles, harvesting each man until his dinner guest, stuffed mouth clamped shut by Hakon's massive hand, writhed and gagged, his throat gurgling obscenely. Finally the Pecheneg's bulging eyes mercifully closed, and he slumped, black-faced with asphyxiation, to the deck.

† † †

"No one speaks!" Gleb raised his hand to command silence. The ships had strung out down the river again, and the crew lolled in the late-afternoon heat. "Listen."

Drugged by the torpor, Haraldr at first allowed himself the thought that they had already reached the sea. The barely audible noise, like the muffled crashing of distant waves, entranced him, and for a sharp moment his breast longed for Norway.

"Do not sleep!" barked Gleb.

Haraldr started, along with most of the crew.

"That's the name of the first of the river's seven cataracts," explained Gleb. " 'Do not sleep.' Now we begin to game with the Dnieper." He eyed the descending but still white-hot sun. "No use starting now. The last ships wouldn't make it through the first cataract before dark. If we set out at dawn tomorrow, we can all pass the first four cataracts before the sun sets." Then Gleb spat and rasped so softly that he must have been addressing only himself. "Of course we will be a much shorter file by then."

† † †

The river was ice-smooth and raven-dark. Haraldr held the night watch. Occasionally a scream lifted from Hakon's boat and pealed into the night; apparently the day's blood had whetted Hakon's appetites. The boat rocked in the current, a reminder of the relentless force that Haraldr knew carried him toward an inevitable reckoning.

"Haraldr."

Haraldr started and turned. He was relieved to see Jarl Rognvald.

The Jarl looked out over the black-onyx surface of the Dnieper for several minutes. He knew that there was little time to say what he must. "Haraldr, you know I have never lost my faith in the old gods." Haraldr nodded. "That does not mean that I do not believe in Kristr. I think that all the gods exist, and the only difference between them is the gifts they present to the men they favor. Now this Kristr, grant you, is probably the greater god. He is a builder. In Norway He has built roads and bridges for his priests, and a *kirke* in every town. You can also see what Kristr has enabled Yaroslav, no very great man, to do in Kiev. And of course Kristr has helped the Griks build Miklagardr. By that measure alone Kristr's power is superior to any other. But sometimes I think that Kristr loves buildings more than He does men."

Jarl Rognvald theatrically spread his hands out over the water. "Odin," he said expansively, "is the more generous god. The tale is told that Kristr hung from a cross for one day, in order to show men the way to Paradise. But Odin hung himself upside down from the rootless tree for nine days, waiting to snatch the mead of poetry from the depths of the Underworld. He has shared that drink with men, with those who dare to accept his gift." Jarl Rognvald looked intently at Haraldr, his eyes glaring in the blackness like winter ice. "That verse you recited on our last night in Kiev . . . so sharp and true, and it came as quick as a thunderbolt. It is a madness, a madness given by Odin. Just like the Battle-Rage."

Haraldr said nothing, his thoughts smothered in fear. He had witnessed the Battle-Rage of the Berserks at Stiklestad: the Hound, the sucking nose, the red eyes. He had even worn the skin armor told of in all the tales. Yes, Haraldr reminded himself, the Rage is more than a pagan fable. It exists. And it is indeed a madness.

"The other night in Kiev I watched you. Something held you back from striking Hakon, which took a greater valor than foolishly spilling the wine-bag courage in your veins. Perhaps even Odin himself held your arm. Well, I know it was not my hand. I think the wounds of Stiklestad have finally healed. I think that you are ready to accept a second gift from Odin, the gift of the Battle-Rage."

"You were with me in my last battle, Jarl." Haraldr's tone was self-accusatory. "Would you want me beside you in your next?"

"I could wish for no better comrade. Haven't I taught you all I know?"

Indeed, the Jarl had. Endless hours of drills with sword, ax, and spear, and swimming and wrestling and riding as well. If kingdoms were won in mock combats, Haraldr would own more subjects than the Greek Emperor. But Jarl Rognvald could not teach him the inner defenses a man needed in real fights. "Green-wood." A strong arm but a weak breast.

"The fault isn't with your teaching, Jarl. You know that that has meant more than anything to me. But I have a battle-fetter that no skill of yours or mine has been able to remove. If I thought Odin could release me, then I would ask his help. But I know that the strength to break that bond has to come from within. The gods cannot answer every question in a man's mind."

Jarl Rognvald looked over the river for a long time. A feathery insect flew against his face and he brushed it away. Finally he spoke. "Haraldr, I have been a warrior all my life, and that is most of what I know of life. I am not a poet like you, and I can only tell you what I know." The Jarl paused and examined his hands. "I have been to the spirit world. Believe me. It is an inner landscape inhabited by anything the imagination can provide, and yet it is no less real for that. Each man conjures his own inner beauty, his own hidden demons, and the gods only guide him to them. Men think that when possessed by the Rage, a man becomes a beast. That is wrong. The Berserk, in fact, is a beast-slayer. He enters the spirit world and confronts the demon-beast that has held his soul captive. That beast is his fear, and when he has faced it or even slain it, when he has put his faith in his own force, his own will, then all things are possible—even miracles of the sort that are ascribed to the gods."

Haraldr knew then that he and the Jarl had looked out on the same desolate landscape of mind and memory, and that his own spirit-journey over that strange and terrible terrain could no longer be postponed. "Yes. I know that a beast waits for me there, a fear as terrible as the world-devouring dragon itself. And when I awaken in the middle of the night, I am certain that if I ever face it, I will die."

"You are ready to face it. Even the last dragon itself. You are a poet and a warrior. You showed that the other night in the Podol. And you have learned, far earlier than most men, how bitter is the outer world when a man seals off his inner world, thinking that the demons he never confronted will no longer trouble him. You know that that is no life to be clung to, not at the cost of a pure and honest soul."

The Jarl turned away from Haraldr and faced north, thinking of the cool emerald and azure summer in a land he would never see again. "Haraldr, even when you were a boy, I knew you had a mind that someday no man, perhaps even no god, could ever command. I choose to believe that Odin will guide you to your beast and help you confront it, but your own will is equally capable of leading you through the spirit world. Chosen by Odin, chosen by your own will, what does it matter? I only know that you are ready to stand before the dragon."

Jarl Rognvald said nothing more. He left Haraldr to his thoughts and the death-dark, murmuring Dnieper.

aria, Mistress of the Robes, fanned the eunuch away; her milky hand moved like a ghost through the thick steam. Despite her utilitarian-sounding title, she was the second ranking lady at court; only the Empress Zoe and the Augusta Theodora, who no longer resided in the palace precincts, were accorded more prestige. Maria studied a rivulet of perspiration as it descended from her cleavage to her navel. She pressed her finger into her navel and drew a liquid line to her glossy black pubic triangle. She pulled her legs up and thrust her arms between them, a curiously simian posture for a disturbingly beautiful woman. Her blue eyes were like tiny, miraculously illuminated grottoes in the heated mist. "Your husband's brother has sent Irene away," she said languidly. Her voice chimed against the marble walls of the bath.

The Empress Zoe toweled her moisture-beaded breasts. "We are already surrounded by his spies." She sounded drowsy. "And our companions are no doubt happier elsewhere. But I will miss Irene. Remind me to have Symeon send her something."

Maria turned to the Empress, who sat next to her on the marble bench; their shoulders touched lightly. She decided not to ask the question she had considered; Zoe would speak of it when she wished. But it had been two weeks now since the Emperor had spent the night in his wife's bedchamber. "Ata came to see me yesterday," said Maria. "He advises that I have neglected the amorous component of my nature."

Zoe's eyes opened; they had a lovely amethyst cast. "Ata? Oh, yes, the palmist who came to us out of the Orient, in the company of that rather charming yet woefully disenfranchised emir." She paused to recall the name. "Salah. We haven't seen much of Emir Salah since my husband's brother extended the generosity of our treasury. I believe he has taken his pension and has bought some estates near Nicaea. I presume this Ata still finds our court rewarding. Darling, wasn't the Emir one of your . . . *amusements?*"

"I will never allow a dark-skinned creature to crawl into my bed again. He wanted to impale me from behind like one of his goats, and when I insisted otherwise, he was finished before I could draw three breaths. He then remarked that his wives were more submissive. I told him that if he was at all representative of his race, the appropriate custom would be to have one wife for twenty emirs, instead of the other way around. I could not understand what he said next. I arranged to have him ejected from my chambers as quickly as he had spewed his dubious manhood into me. The next time I saw him, I spit in his face and told him I now presumed to have given him as much pleasure as he had given me."

"Little daughter! You know I worry when you are so . . . *vehement.*" The Empress spoke gaily, but her eyes winced, showing fine wrinkles at the corners.

"My next lover will be entirely Western in concept. Golden skin and hair. There are some Athenian types in the Scholae who so closely resemble the ancient statutes that one wonders if they were hewn from stone." The Scholae was the elite Imperial household cavalry.

Zoe's eyes had forgotten the moment of melancholy; her vividly red lips curled salaciously. "Darling, I can only assume that you have already been . . . *reconnoitering.* Can I also assume that my use of military terminology is rather apt? I have heard that you were a spectator at the pentathlon last week. I was intrigued at your sudden interest in athletic contests, until I learned that this was an intramural event for officers of the Scholae. All those oiled young gallants, and all of them lodged here in the palace precincts."

"I have found the perfect pair. Hermes and Apollo, I call them. They are beautiful, as vain as Narcissus, and insufferably arrogant. They are also inseparable, though whether it is a friendship in the style of the ancient Greeks whom they so closely resemble, I am as yet uncertain. Of course, I intend to separate them. I am dining with them both tonight."

"Little daughter! You are scandalous. But so deliciously . . . *inventive.* How I envy your freedom. Not from convention; may the Holy Theotokos forgive me, I have never been constrained by that. But to be able to make love and yet be untrammeled by love. How I envy you that."

eifor!" yelled Gleb. "The pelican roost. The fourth cataract. The most deadly." But the noise of Aeifor was not that of any water. It was that of a living thing, a monstrous, baleful groan, as if some titanic beast had been stirred from sleep. As the sound rose, the Rus oarsmen looked anxiously at one another. In one morning they had already passed through a lifetime of terror. The walls of giant-set stones across the river; the sucking, dizzying, mortally cold eddies; ships disappearing behind the foaming veils; and timbers showering up over the great rocks as ships exploded. The hideous flotsam, shattered strakes, cargo pods, and the limp, seemingly boneless pulp that even now chased them down the death-strewn Dnieper like shrieking ghosts. Perhaps a hundred ships and their crews had been lost already. What lay ahead?

Aeifor first appeared as a white haze over the river. A few herons and pelicans emerged like snowflakes from this mist and flew overhead in greeting. Within minutes the current began a rapid acceleration, and then huge, jagged rocks loomed toward the starboard. The pelicans swarmed. Clouds of spray boiled into the air. Between two massive, cathedrallike rock upthrusts was a vast, swirling maw.

The ship seemed to hit something solid. The steering oar at the stern jerked like a giant arm and swatted the steersman into the river; the hapless Rus shot past with both arms raised, almost as if he were waving good-bye, then surrendered to the Dnieper. Haraldr dashed for the wildly swiping steering oar as the ship spun and then heeled, almost capsizing. With Gleb virtually clinging to his back, he put all his weight against the bucking shaft. The oar settled and the ship fought the current, heading hard larboard.

Over his shoulder Haraldr saw a ship disappear into Aeifor's white shroud. The deadly mist parted for an instant, and a prow, then the entire ship, shot high above the lip of the great whirlpool, men leaping overboard, the abandoned oars flailing like the legs of a desperate centipede. Then the prow lurched down and the ship simply vanished, swallowed whole by the beast Aeifor.

The beach that ran along the larboard bank was sandy with periodic eruptions of jutting rocks. The oarsmen rowed for their lives; the iron grip of Aeifor never slackened, as it had near the banks skirting the other cataracts. They would have to come fast against the suction to firmly ground the ship on the beach.

Fifty ells to the shore. Haraldr braced for the shock. An oarsman lost his grip and slumped from his sea-chest. The shaft of an arrow sprouted from his neck; crimson rivulets oozed from the wound. Seconds later the ship jolted, timbers swayed, and the prow lifted. Haraldr swung his shield around from his back and jumped to firm, welcoming sand. To his right, Hakon's ship slid onto the strand.

The arrow blurred past Haraldr's ear, for an instant buzzing against the terrifying groan of Aeifor. The Rus set their wall of shields in the Norse fashion, crouching and anchoring their long spears against the sand.

A very long time seemed to pass. Haraldr feared that Aeifor only masked the shrieks of the Pechenegs; certainly they were a few dozen ells away in the thick brush, readying a massive charge. But the wall of foliage beyond the wall of shields was quiet. The leaves hung motionless; the sun glinted off them like a reflection in a stagnant pond. Jarl Rognvald knelt beside Haraldr. "I think we have surprised them," he yelled. "They haven't been able to assemble for an attack." The Jarl located the lone Pecheneg sniper and signaled for an archer. After the Rus bowman had fired two arrows, the Jarl stood up, lifted his helm, and stroked his sweat-matted white hair. Haraldr felt as if he had miraculously escaped another humiliation, and yet he also had a strange, haunting sense of disappointment, as if he had taken the wrong road and would now miss some extraordinary marvel.

The ships were lifted over log rollers and moved along the old portage trail with surprising speed. Hot dust clogged windpipes, and the sun glowered through a metallic haze. The afternoon wore on, an orchestration of endless, groaning motion. The portage followed a relatively cleared path through a generally wooded area; porters cut away the brush and small trees that had grown up in eight years. Occasionally runners trotted up to the Jarl with reports of men lost to Pecheneg archers, but there was no word of any concerted attacks along a line of ships that now extended down the riverfront for half a rowing-spell. Varangians detailed to various potential trouble spots along the line came and went in groups of fifty or one hundred, marching in smart order in their gleaming byrn-nies.

Haraldr was surprised to hear Gleb announce that the portage was almost three-quarters complete. Defenses relaxed; a few men at a time could now slump for a rest on a pile of furs or a barrel of pickled meat. Hakon, trailed by his dogs, wandered the beach, dragging the gilded spear point of his enormous, gold-inlaid broadax in the sand. He saw Jarl Rognvald, Gleb, and Haraldr and walked over, grinning like a beaver. "Jarl Rognvald," he called out as he approached, "you see what has happened, don't you? The turd-suckers know Mar Hunrodarson well, and it seems that they have also heard of his man, Hakon Fire-Eyes." He raised his ax to his chest. "They won't come against us." With comic emphasis Hakon warily rubbed a finger over his immaculate ax blade. "Folk-Mower, here, is angry with the corpse-eating savages. He is thirsty for the wine of ravens." Then Hakon swiveled his sparking eyes toward Haraldr with feral menace. "Why, Green-wood! I hardly recognized you in your battle toys. And on your feet instead of your knees!" He rapped Haraldr's breastplate. "You must have bashed up some old woman's kettle to make this." Haraldr was annoyed at his own passive, silent response; it was as if his body and mind were suddenly drained of will, even thought.

Bored with this game, Hakon wandered back to his ship, detailed some more of his Varangians upriver, then talked with his two concubines and some slave girls before returning with his hawk on his arm. "Pelican harrier!" he announced to everyone within earshot, his grin boyish and proud. He removed the plumed golden hood from the sturdy, chevron-breasted bird.

Gleb wrinkled his red, swollen nose. "I don't like that smell."

"My hawk smells better than you, louse-eating Slav!" snapped Hakon.

Gleb ignored Hakon and looked at Jarl Rognvald. He had not been referring to the bird. The hawk spiraled into the air, and Gleb continued to sniff. Haraldr noticed that Hakon's dogs had picked up their ears. He retrieved his spear.

A puff of feathers in the coppery haze. Hakon's hawk fell toward the river like a stone. "Shield-wall!" shouted Gleb.

The wailing shriek that came from the woods pierced even the monstrous plaint of Aeifor. The first wave of Pechenegs seemed, almost deliberately, to fall on the upraised spears of the hastily constructed shield-wall, though in fact they were pushed by the crush from behind. Within moments the shield-wall staggered back from the sheer weight of the Pechenegs, then fractured. The horde poured through, and this time, unlike in Stiklestad, Haraldr watched death stalk in the searing light of day. He was pushed back inexorably toward the river, a witless participant in a mortal dance. He watched with idiotic clarity as the polychrome

Pecheneg horde surged to the river's edge on his left and Hakon's daz-zlingly metallic Varangian force retreated with shocking alacrity even farther to the left, falling back upriver, disappearing through a clump of trees. He could see the figure of Hakon in his golden byrnnie, as distinctly as a magically animated little statue, running.

The hostile Dnieper was the only refuge for those who had not fled or already fallen to the swarming Pechenegs: Haraldr, Jarl Rognvald, Gleb, and maybe a half dozen Varangians who either had had the misfortune to miss Hakon's precipitous retreat or had the good sense to protect the expedition's pilot. Before his boots were even half submerged, Haraldr could feel the icy current swiping at his legs. When the rushing snow-melt seized his testicles, Haraldr heard the dark voice from the pit of his soul: You are going to die.

The vanguard of the Pecheneg horde stood at the water's edge, a jeering riot of antic brown limbs and flashing blades. They were less than thirty ells away. An archer wearing only a loincloth came out to test the water and made it halfway to the tight cluster of Norsemen before he shot down the river as if yanked on a string. A hundred ells downriver, his head went under, not to be seen again.

But the Dnieper offered a precarious sanctuary even for the huge Norsemen. One of the Varangians lost his footing, and the entire group staggered before they could make common cause against the rushing river. When they had steadied somewhat, the tallest Varangian spoke. He was about Haraldr's age and size, and impressively handsome. His voice was as calm as if he were sitting on a stump whittling a stick. "Hakon will be here within a quarter hour," he assured his comrades. "He was wise to fall back and summon the rest of the Varangians from upriver. Soon the corpses of these shitheads will be colder than we are."

Jarl Rognvald turned to the Varangians. "Yes. All we need do is stay on our feet until then." But inwardly the Jarl suspected not. What he had seen looked more like a treacherous desertion than a strategic retreat.

Aeifor roared on. The Pechenegs jittered and waited, occasionally launching a few spears or arrows; the Varangians fielded the missiles on their shields as though playing a game. The game became less amusing as the current continued its numbing assault; Haraldr's legs were turning to dead stumps. Finally there was a commotion, and the teeming mass of Pechenegs was parted by a silk-clad chieftain accompanied by three or four byrnnie-clad subalterns and dozens of variegated retainers, includ-ing some women in expensive Frisian cloth robes apparently just looted from the Rus ships. "The turd on top of the dung heap," said the handsome Varangian in a remarkably laconic voice.

The Pecheneg chief had wide, thick shoulders; a scowling, beetlish face peered out beneath a finely embossed Norse-style helm. He stood with his hands at his hips and shouted furiously at the Norsemen, then at his own men. He stomped up and down the beach for a few minutes, every now and then pausing to exhort the heavens or kick at the sand. This exhibition concluded, he simply sat on his haunches and waved his retainers away.

The Varangians began to discuss a breakout, but the handsome young Varangian was adamant in his faith in Hakon. "We're pledge-men," he reminded his comrades. "That's what *Varangian* means. Men who pledge their lives in defense of one another. It is an inviolable troth." It was as if this Varangian believed the invocation of this pledge would almost magically transport Hakon and the rest of the Varangians to their side.

"Maybe they are pinned down upriver," offered a shorter, thick-necked Varangian with boyish, rock-crystal eyes.

Haraldr admired the loyalty of the Varangians. They're good men, he decided. They deserve a better leader.

The Pecheneg chief suddenly leapt to his feet, screaming and gesturing as if he had been seated over a fire. Almost immediately the Pechenegs swarmed the nearest ship upriver from the Norsemen. The blood that chilled in Haraldr's aching limbs seemed to crystallize, cold water turning instantly to ice.

"We've got to move now!" shouted Haraldr; he did not bother to explain why, and only distantly wondered why he was giving commands. "If we clasp arms and form a ring, we can drift together until we get to the rocks!"

The handsome Varangian quickly appraised the situation. Like industrious ants, the Pechenegs had already lifted the massive hull from the log rollers and were creeping toward the water. "That's the best plan now," he calmly agreed. He eyes had a wounded look, not of fear but of betrayal. Hakon has lost something more valuable than all the gold in Grikia, thought Haraldr.

The ship was almost floated, due less to organization than to the numbers and the verminous frenzy of the Pechenegs. Thirteen ells at beam, fifty ells long, and careening down the river, the big river craft would crush the Norsemen like snails. The desperate human raft floated away just as the looming hull began to bob toward them.

The Dnieper's suction drew them on at a fantastic speed, but the ship, a more seaworthy craft, came on faster. The white water was just ahead. Haraldr's foot smashed into a rock but his feet were so numb that he hardly noticed. His head went under, and water surged up his nostrils like solid plugs of ice. The ring broke up. Insensible feet scrambled to gain a foothold on the treacherous bottom. The ship whoosed past; seconds later a series of muffled cracks announced its destruction on the rocks.

"Make the boar!" yelled Jarl Rognvald. The boar-array was a wedge of men driven into the heart of the enemy. The Varangians quickly found their places. Jarl Rognvald took the snout, grabbed Haraldr's arm, and placed him at his right flank; the handsome Varangian took the same position on the Jarl's left. The essential Gleb was tucked safely in the middle of the wedge.

The boar moved warily through the spiky, foaming shallows. The Pechenegs crowded the bank, spears thrusting and sabers waving. "Follow my cadence!" growled Jarl Rognvald. The Pechenegs were only a few ells away. Voices were screaming deafeningly both inside and outside Haraldr's skull.

"Fast!" Jarl Rognvald lurched forward at a near run. His ax rose and fell like a woodcutter's. Haraldr pushed against the mass of Pechenegs with his shield, but it was as if the beast of his fear had seized his sword; he still could not lift it. He struggled to keep moving forward against the weight on his shield. He could see a rock-strewn rise ahead and promised himself that if they made it, they would live. Then sun-flared metal showered over the rise. Not Norse steel but Pecheneg mail jerkins and captured Hunland swords. The Pechenegs had brought up their best footmen.

The Pecheneg footmen pushed forward, crushing their less heavily armored comrades against the Norse boar. The wedge quickly became a circle, a desperate shield-fort. The crystal-eyed Varangian took a spear in his thick neck, drew a final, desperate arc with his ax, and fell. Another Varangian raised a forearm lashed to a limp red rag by the Pecheneg sabers. Jarl Rognvald smashed two Pechenegs with his ax and sent them reeling in a mist of blood, but three more leapt forward and clutched at his shield and the Jarl could not throw them off. Thin sabers whirled around him like furious, shrilling birds, and long red streaks appeared on his face. A spear drove into his byrnnie, and he fell.

Something struck Haraldr's chest so hard that his lungs emptied and he thought he had lost his sword in the darkness. The noise of the battle was like a great wind that kept him from regaining his breath. His upper arm touched something white-hot, and his forehead tickled. He shoved hard with his shield to keep it from crushing his chest, but a greater force pressed back. All he could see was blood, not before him but in memory. Black-red blood. Stiklestad. His body began to freeze. He saw Elisevett, very clearly for a second, and then his mother. He fell, not to the earth but in a great spiraling plunge to the abyss of his own being, a spirit world haunted by mythic beasts given substance by the real horrors of Stiklestad. Here, not in the realm of flesh, would be Haraldr's last battle, here his tormented soul would finally be forced to confront its own demons.

Haraldr knew he had been here before. It was a dark, featureless plain scoured by a bitter-cold wind that wet and stung his eyes. Someone told him that if he stopped to rest, he would be warm forever but another voice thundered and ordered him on against the ravening gale. The fire exploded before him but it was colder than the wind and blacker than burned coal. Within the lightless magma he could see the great gaping black jaws. The Dragon. *You can run, now, forever,* he told himself, but the voice commanded him to stand, and the creature blasted him with its cold obsidian-hued flame. He stood and faced it. . . . The journey ended, as suddenly as a fitful dream.

He awoke to ice crystals in the sun. Steel-ice. The Pecheneg wore a conical Norse-style helm, a steel jerkin sheathing his stocky chest. Haraldr's body was liquid and iron at once, flowing, changing between the two at some unthinking but complex suggestion. His sword at last lifted, blown by the cyclone from the spirit world. And then it fell.

The Pecheneg's sword arm and half his torso were gone, and the gaping slash spewed blood as if his heart had exploded. It is not a rage, Haraldr thought very clearly, but a will, a cataclysmic necessity that must discharge itself as a storm cloud spits fire. His sword lifted again, no longer a thing of steel but a force of nature that beat like the raven's wing, ripped like the eagle's talon. The Pechenegs fell inexorably back from the horrifying circle that it described.

Three Varangians were still beside him, and Gleb was huddled at his back. Haraldr reached down and grabbed the collar of Jarl Rognvald's byrnnie, and as he did, he saw a force of armored Rus battling over the rise, only sixty ells away.

Dragging Jarl Rognvald and carving his terrible crimson path through the Pechenegs, Haraldr led the rest to safety.

o we have ascertained that Alexandros is no enthusiast of romantic verse." Maria's eerily enchanting blue eyes roamed from Alexandros, the young man seated at her right, to Giorgios, on her left. Her velvety tongue flicked at the gilded rim of her murrey-tinted agate goblet. "And what do you think of the *Digenes Akrites,* Giorgios?"

Giorgios extended his tautly muscled neck slightly, as if he found the high, pearled collar of his ceremonial robe too tight. He had curly, sand-colored hair; an elegant, Grecian nose; and strangely innocent brown eyes. His sweat-glazed forehead glowed in the light of the huge pewter candelabra that floated high above the table. He glanced nervously at his friend, as if seeking direction. The evening had not been what they had expected. They had heard the tales about the Mistress of the Robes, of course, and they had envisioned an evening of sexual abandon that could otherwise be provided only by the pox-eaten whores of the Studion, Constantinople's notorious slum. Instead the Mistress of the Robes had confounded them with rigid decorum and a trying discussion: Ancient Hellenist philosophers, the several religious heresies with which the city was currently rife, and the economic possibilities presented by renewed trade with the northern *barbaroi;* it had been rumored that a trade fleet might arrive from Rus within the next few weeks. Now the subject was literature. The *Digenes Akrites* was a popular epic of heroism and romance on the far-flung borders where the Empire abutted the Saracen caliphates and emirates.

"I would not think that the *Digenes Akrites* is an accurate depiction of life on the Eastern frontier," offered Giorgios hesitantly. Maria had quickly concluded she preferred Giorgios to Alexandros, though the latter had a piercingly blue-eyed, scarcely restrained lasciviousness that she found appealing. But Giorgios, despite his studied Scholae swagger, had the gift of self-doubt.

"But truth and romance are two very different qualities," said Maria. In a choreographed burst, five silk-robed eunuchs swept away the large golden tureens containing the dessert fruits, poured unwatered wine into the agate goblets, and promptly vanished. The heavy bronze doors slid silently shut behind them. "If we perceived only truth, we would be incapable of love."

"Do you mean physical love or spiritual love?" asked Alexandros. "Perhaps a spiritual love could fool the senses. But a physical love?" Emboldened by the wine, he allowed his eyes to rake his hostess. She lifted her dark eyebrows slightly and focused on him; he felt as if a current had swept from her eyes into his testicles.

"You are asking in what fashion naked bodies can withhold the truth?" Maria wryly pursed her livid, glistening lips. "But if a lover could see the truth of his partner's flesh, its conception in the bowels of a woman, and its decomposition into putrescent sludge, and the trail of mastications and excretions and discharges that flesh will deposit in its transit between those two states, then I fear we would all become eremites, happy with the solitude of a barren cell."

Giorgios leaned forward. "But isn't truth what is, not what has been or what will be?"

"That is merely the state of a thing. What cannot conquer time has no truth."

"Then beauty has no truth? Only decay and death?" Giorgios frowned.

Maria tilted her head slightly. Her sable-black hair was parted in the middle and coiled at either side of her head; the coils were laced with pearls. "Plato believed that beauty resides outside of a thing, in an eternal state. Or so Psellus informs us."

"Psellus?"

"He is one of the Hellenists at court. The most gifted, I think. He is quite taken with this Plato."

"The Hellenists are heretics," Alexandros said petulantly.

Maria's lips hovered over the rim of her goblet. Like a snake striking, her hand flashed out toward Alexandros. The full measure of wine struck him directly in the face and he jerked with surprise, flung his head, and rubbed his eyes. Giorgios stared in astonishment. Maria rose without a word and went to Alexandros. She wiped at his eyes with her linen napkin. After a moment she began to laugh, an elegant, musical sound. "Your robe is soaked," she said. Her teeth were like perfect pearls. She unlaced Alexandros's robe and yanked it to his ankles. Giorgios stood up as if frightened. Maria pulled Alexandros's linen breeches down and took his penis in her hand. He was almost immediately erect. With her other hand she swept Alexandros's goblet and chased silver platter to the floor; the clatter echoed harshly, as if malevolent spirits were mocking her laugh. Then she pulled her scaramangium, a tight robe of scarlet silk, up to her waist. She sat on the edge of the table, spread her legs, and guided Alexandros inside her. She gasped and wrapped her legs around his back.

"Unlace me!" she shouted to Giorgios, twice. When her scaramangium was unfastened, she threw it over her head; she wore nothing beneath. She had rounded woman's breasts and delicate white skin, but there was an athletic, almost adolescent sinuousness to her arms and legs. With the fingernails of one hand she raked Alexandros's pumping buttocks. Her other hand found Giorgios's, and she placed his trembling fingers to her searing breast.

is vitals have been pierced." Gleb shook his head almost in rhythm with the gentle rocking of the ship in the Dnieper.

Haraldr leaned over Jarl Rognvald and lifted the linen bandage they had applied to the gaping wound in the Jarl's abdomen. They had given the Jarl a drink of leek-mash, and now the escaping odor told them that the organs had indeed been punctured. No man survived such injuries.

Jarl Rognvald opened his eyes. His irises were dark, as if already clouded with a vision of the waiting spirit world. He parted his mist-blue lips in a painful effort to smile. "The death-fragrance," he said. "But I knew I would die before the spear struck me. Odin's third gift is prophecy."

Haraldr clutched the Jarl's cold, rough hand. He felt that if he spoke, he would release the terrible sob clawing at his throat.

"You took the gift today. Didn't you?" The Jarl's voice was weak but still commanding. His business in the middle realm was not done.

Haraldr fought for control. Had he really entered the spirit world? Where had the dream ended—for surely his encounter with the beast had been a dream, a dream in an incredible instant of sleep—and the reality resumed? And he had just as surely led them out of that ring of death; other men had seen it. Yet those last moments on the beach had also been part of his dream. Where had the dream ended? And what had reddened the wolf's jaws in that time of indescribable terror, beauty, and rage? His mind or his arm?

He did not know. But, yes, it had happened.

Haraldr leaned next to Jarl Rognvald's ear. This was their secret, the bond that would tie them between worlds and beyond time. "I met the beast. I stood. But I think there is still a test ahead of me."

The Jarl turned to him, his lips barely moving. "There is always another beast to slay. When the last beast is slain, time will end. I will be there then, to raise my sword against the last dragon. Now I know that you will be there as well. So I die happy."

The sob struggled out of Haraldr's throat.

Jarl Rognvald mustered a final, robust grip. "Don't mourn this old pagan," he said. "Odin has already set my place at the benches in the Valhol. I will drink with your brother tonight. Honor me by listening to me now." The Jarl paused to marshal his strength. "I'm turning my command over to you. The entire flotilla. I've already talked to Gleb, and he agrees."

Haraldr was shocked. What did he know of command? Wasn't it enough that he now commanded his own courage? "Jarl, I'm not—"

The Jarl cut off Haraldr's protest. "Yours is the blood of kings and the gods. King Haraldr Fairhair was your great-great-grandfather, and he was descended from the god Frey. That's what gives you the power to command. It was there today, just like the Rage."

Is it? considered Haraldr, wondering at the person he had discovered on this bloody day, unable now to discount any possibility. *Perhaps it is. Your father was a king from kings. You sat in many times on your brother's counsel. You did not always fear to lead.*

"Anyway, I am not asking. My last command is that you assume my duties. I'll have you roped with the slaves if you disobey. Now bring me my sea-chest."

Haraldr set the weathered wooden box by Jarl Rognvald. The interior gleamed with the treasures and utilities of a lifetime. Tools, knives, gold and silver coins, a walrus tusk, a silver Hammer of Thor, glass beads, a robe of Frisian cloth and another of silk, a bear carved in wood. And a superb byrnnie with tight, heavy links, polished and lacquered like new. Haraldr hadn't known that Jarl Rognvald had two byrnnies. He never wore this one.

"I've talked with Gleb. He says there is a place at Kherson where Kristr's wizards will clean the flesh off my bones and put them in another chest. Then I've arranged to have both chests shipped back to Norway. I won't lie in the Rus Sea or this cursed river or Yaroslav's dirt. I'll go home at last."

Haraldr started to close the chest.

"Wait. There is something in there that I won't need in the Valhol. It belongs to you. That shirt."

Haraldr started to stir through the clothing in the chest. What did the Jarl mean?

"The shirt the hammer sews."

Haraldr was speechless. He reached out tentatively and touched the cold, almost silky smooth links of the byrnnie.

"Well, put it on. It's Grik steel and construction, built to fit a Norseman's size."

Haraldr slipped into the byrnnie; it fit as well as a fine wool tunic, so snugly and evenly that its great weight was hardly noticeable. The shirt the hammer sews, the invulnerable second skin of the mightiest warriors.

"Emma is her name," said Jarl Rognvald. "I bought her for you in Kiev, when I learned that you would come with me. I was going to give her to you when I knew she would fit. Now she does."

Haraldr realized that if Jarl Rognvald had worn Emma today instead of his own byrnnie, the spear never would have pierced his side. He knelt and put his head on the old man's shoulder. He could not control the sobs.

"It's cold where I'm going," said the Jarl. He shuddered, and dark blood spilled from his wound. "The wings of the Valkyrja are blocking the sun."

Haraldr clutched the Jarl's hand again and felt the last surge of life.

"There is a saying," whispered the Jarl. " 'Wealth dies, kinsmen die, and a man himself must likewise die. But word-fame never dies for him who wins it well.' " The Jarl coughed and shivered. "I am an old pagan who served the Kings of Norway, the sons of the gods. But I want to be remembered as the man who served King Haraldr Sigurdarson, Norway's greatest king. Promise me you will go back and claim Norway."

"I swear it on my soul." The enormity of the pledge swallowed Haraldr, and he felt himself plunge toward a distant, unseen fate.

The Jarl paused, his grip slackened, and Haraldr thought he was gone. But his ghost-lips parted slightly and he continued. "Yes, I know you will keep your pledge; Odin is telling me that right now. But you'll need wealth. You can get that from the Griks. And allies. Probably Yaroslav. With money he can be bought."

The Jarl started to go off again, but his grip was suddenly fierce, as if all his life were now transferred to Haraldr's touch. "Remember what you promised your brother on the last day of his life," he said raspily. "It is more important now than ever. You know about the bounty on your head, and how many Norsemen hope to win it. But you must also protect yourself against discovery by the Griks. They have a prophecy that a fair-haired race will destroy them, and they have good reason to fear that a Norse leader might assemble a great force against them. It has happened before. They will never allow a Norse king to come among them, much less serve their Emperor. And now you have men under your keeping. If you are careless with your name, you may condemn them as well. I die knowing that you are Haraldr Sigurdarson again, which is why you must be all the more vigilant in denying him."

The Jarl seemed to collapse inwardly with the huge effort of his admonition. "I promise you, as I promised Olaf," murmured Haraldr.

Jarl Rognvald coughed blood. His last words were like leaves rattled by the barest summer breeze. "Good-bye, my . . . son. . . . I'll see you next at the benches—" Then his pale lips froze and the spirit visibly fled from his face.

When all human warmth had vanished from the Jarl's body, Haraldr released him from his embrace and gently folded the lids shut over the old man's empty eyes.

† † †

"Hakon. Pah." Gleb spat angrily into the black water.

Haraldr stomped over to the pile of gear he had left on the deck. His sword was beside his old Slav breastplate. He strapped his sword belt on over Emma. "Get the dinghy ready," he snapped to a Rus oarsman.

"No!" Gleb shook his head. "We've still got three cataracts and the ford at Krarion ahead of us before we reach St. Gregory's Island. You might kill Hakon, but what about the five hundred with him? We all need to work together for now." Gleb spat and looked off into the night. "Then when we get to St. Gregory's Island we'll think of some way to feed Hakon to the pelicans."

After Gleb retired, Haraldr said he would take the early watch and he stood for a long time at the stern of the ship, looking down the faintly stirring, deceptively tranquil Dnieper, trying to make sense of a day in which he had freed his own lost soul and had lost the dearest soul left to him on earth. He sobbed quietly for a long while, but eventually his agony lightened with the thought of the Jarl already seated at the benches with Odin's chosen champions, hoisting his mead horn with Olaf and Sigurd Syr. Now Haraldr would have to earn his seat alongside them in the Valhol. He had stood before the beast of his own spirit but he had not slain it. And now he would also have to slay the demon who stood before him in the flesh. Hakon.

Haraldr started. What was out there? Pechenegs? They would not go out on the water. He searched for the point where he had heard the faint inconsistency in the rippling of the river. Merely a fish?

A dinghy. Haraldr tightened his hand on the pommel of his sword.

The shape took on contrast against the black Dnieper. Two men, from the size of them Varangians. Haraldr slowly and soundlessly slipped his sword out of his greased scabbard. With his left hand he removed his dagger from his belt.

The dinghy impacted the river ship with a light thud.

"Watch. You!" came the urgent whisper from the water. "We want to see Jarl Rognvald and Haraldr Nordbrikt."

"What do you want with them?" Better to let them guess about the Jarl's fate. Bastards. Their treachery had been the deadly blade today, not the Pecheneg spear. Haraldr's grip tightened on the steel that would mete his vengeance. He was not afraid. He would enjoy this.

There was a long pause. Haraldr heard whispering below. "With whom do we speak?"

"A man trusted by Jarl Rognvald and Haraldr Nordbrikt as themselves."

Another pause and a brief whispering. "You pledge it, Norseman?"

"I pledge it on the soul of the Jarl." What ruse were they about?

The two Varangians engaged in a lengthy, hissing discussion. Finally Haraldr snapped, "Tell me your business. Except for the handful who fought with them today, Jarl Rognvald and Haraldr Nordbrikt have only cold breasts and colder steel for you Varangians."

"I'm one of the men who fought with them today. Ask them to come look."

Haraldr peered warily over the railing. A man was standing in the dinghy, face up. Kristr's Mother! It was the fine-looking, laconic Varangian who had been with them in the river.

Haraldr was still uncertain. Hakon could easily be this clever, and a Varangian this treacherous. "I'm Haraldr Nordbrikt. If I'm wrong, excuse the indignity. Strip!"

The handsome man grumbled, but both men complied. There were no byrnnies hidden under their tunics. "Put them back on and climb aboard."

With his sword Haraldr motioned the two to sit on the deck.

"My name is Halldor Snorrason," began the handsome one. In his tunic he seemed even more powerful than he had in his byrnnie, but his features would have made a woman happy; he had a thin, graceful nose and the finest silken hair. "This is Ulfr Uspaksson." The smaller man nodded. He had a strong, blocky face with big, sensitive eyes. "We're comrades from Iceland. From the same village."

Haraldr nodded silently. Let them announce their intentions.

"Where is Jarl Rognvald?" asked Halldor.

Haraldr quickly decided that he needed a reaction, a gauge of Halldor's sincerity. He watched his face carefully. "Jarl Rognvald is at the ale benches. In the Valhol."

Halldor's face registered nothing. Then he said, "That shames us. I, and the men with me who survived, owe our lives to the Jarl. And you." But Halldor's voice was a dry drone, as if he were idly passing off some clever, ironic remark.

Haraldr stared coldly, and his grip welded his hand to his sword. Hakon could at least have sent an able performer.

Ulfr looked nervously at Haraldr and then at Halldor. "Halldor," he said, "I think you had better let me empty our breasts." Ulfr's voice had the low-key resonance of the careful-tongued, sincere sort of skald. Haraldr guessed that he might be a fellow poet.

Ulfr turned anxiously to Haraldr. "Excuse my friend. His voice is like a road in Rus Land. Never up, never down, just straight on forever. But as I'm sure you know, the melody of a man's voice has little to do with the music in his breast."

Halldor just shrugged at the comments. In spite of himself, Haraldr was charmed by the relationship between the two men. They weren't lying when they said they were friends. He went off his guard a bit and wished that he had been able to enjoy companions his age these past years. But his only friend was an old man now lying under a canvas shroud.

"What we would like to say," Ulfr went on, "is that we are all ashamed. Hakon easily could have saved your Jarl. And our own men. The Pecheneg helmet-hail did not pursue Hakon. He spent the afternoon executing prisoners, and with the exception of Halldor and those few who were with you, we Varangians spent the day kicking sand. Hakon never told us that there was any trouble up the beach. He deliberately let those men die. And we are ashamed to be pledged to such a man."

"Most of you seemed to enjoy your employment in Kiev," snapped Haraldr angrily. "But now that a few of you have been offered up to the gulls-of-fray, you come whining to me." His tone implied the obvious question. Why?

"We're not all loudmouths and strand-wanderers," answered Ulfr. "Why, you won't find better men. Certainly they scorned you that night in Kiev, but I can assure you they laughed the way the rooster laughs when the ax is over its neck—"

"Well, you did look foolish that night," interrupted Halldor. Ulfr shot him an uncomfortable glance. "But then"—he shrugged—"the mead horn has cut down more men than the sword."

Haraldr cocked his eyebrow. He liked this Halldor's tart candor. If Hakon had been interested in concealing a treachery behind flattery, he wouldn't have sent this one.

"What we're saying—" began Ulfr.

"What we're saying is this," droned Haldor. "There's not a man among us who enjoys the leadership of Hakon. He disgraced us all today, and believe me, none of us admire his oafish behavior. We're not simple bumpkins. But we are pledge-men and we made our oath to him, and that pledge is the single honor we must preserve. Otherwise we are not Varangians."

Haraldr deliberately made no response. Halldor searched Haraldr's face for a moment and then smiled. "Besides," he said, "Hakon is an important man in Miklagardr. We don't want to be known as the unit that mutinied against an officer of the court. The only honorable and acceptable way for us to eliminate Hakon would be for one of us to challenge him to an island-going." Halldor looked over at Ulfr. "But there isn't a man among our five hundred who would return from such an excursion with his head still attached to his neck."

"So I shovel the Varangians' dung heap," said Haraldr evenly. "A spade carved from green-wood."

Halldor looked Haraldr right in the eyes. "Yes." Then he smiled at Haraldr's barbed jest.

"I would think the main requirement for fighting your Hakon would be feet swift in pursuit," said Haraldr.

Halldor fixed Haraldr with eyes as implacable as slate. "Hakon did not run with fear dribbling from his breeches. You know that. Ulfr says that after he deserted you today he deliberately let himself be surrounded, and then killed a dozen Pechenegs by ripping their windpipes out with his bare hands. I will be honest with you. I think you alone have a chance against him. But a very slender chance. Still, our honor commands us to risk a wager on your chance."

Haraldr returned Halldor's obdurate stare. "It seems as if *my* life is a small enough risk for you. What do *you* risk?"

Halldor paused, making sure of his next words. "If you challenge Hakon to single combat, Ulfr and I will stand as your seconds. If you lose, so will we, but in that way our deaths will insure that the honor of our unit will remain unstained."

Haraldr nodded. A few minutes ago he would have suspected that these men would second him with a dagger in his back. Now, almost instinctively, he believed he could trust them. They had just placed their lives in his hands.

"And if I win?"

Halldor and Ulfr both grinned broadly. "If you win," said Halldor, "you take everything that is Hakon's. His tunics, weapons, coins, treasures, slaves." Halldor's laconic tone took on a droll hint. "His women too." Then he paused and his voice became grimly earnest. "And also the command of his five hundred Varangians."

hen Maria awoke, she smelled the sea. She had left the arcade of her summer bedchamber unshuttered, and the breeze, warmed by the morning sun, was already sultry. The light flooded the open balcony overlooking the silver-spangled water and blurred the white columns of the arcade into molten shafts. She turned away. Giorgios was looking at her, his fawnish eyes intent and adoring. Alexandros was still asleep.

She kissed Giorgios and pressed her body fully along his, reveling in his tension, his heat, and the steely erection against her thigh. When he tried to enter her, she pushed him away. "Don't." Giorgios's eyes were wounded; she had not allowed him to make love to her the previous night, though she had let his hands explore wherever he had wished.

Maria turned back into the morning's flaring apocalypse, wrapped her hand around Alexandros's priapic, dream-swollen shaft, and squeezed tightly. Alexandros's eyes shot open. She mounted him swiftly and began a slow, churning ride, her breasts swaying to the rhythm of her pleasure. She looked down at Giorgios and smiled.

Her paroxysm came even before Alexandros's, and she quickly dismounted and walked naked out onto her balcony. Giorgios squinted and could no longer see her; it was as if she had been consumed by the white fire of the new day.

es, *silki*. I could well pay that toll. I could afford a hundred of you, in fact. Hakon is no mean diminisher of ice-of-arm." Hakon's skald, Grettir, pointed to the silver arm bracelets that coiled up his left arm. The girl smiled. She was young, and her healthy white teeth sparkled against her thin flushed lips. "Of course," continued Grettir, resuming his caress of her fine blond hair, "I would first have to see if Freyja's pleasure hut is as well thatched as this, and make sure that a good fire awaits me within." With oily stealth Grettir lowered his hand and stroked her linen-cloaked flank. "Well, there will be time for that after our Hakon finishes his woodcutting."

He turned and gestured at the arena that had been prepared for the morning's combat. A burlap cloth ten ells on a side had been spread over flat ground, surrounded on three sides by trenches and then a rope fence. Outside the rope, the enormous throng was already assembling; despite the carnage on the river, seven, perhaps even eight, thousand Rus had reached St. Gregory's Island. As Hakon had requested, Grettir had seen to it that the prettiest slaves were brought up closest to the rope. Hakon had mentioned something about wanting to see "their white skins speckled with raven's-wine."

No trench or rope ringed in the fourth side of the cloth. At the suggestion of Hakon—and strangely enough, the condition had been acceded to by that eagle-meat, Green-wood—the fourth border of the arena was a drop of one hundred ells off the sheer rock cliffs that thrust the island up from the Dnieper.

† † †

Haraldr had ordered everyone out of his tent. If his hands shook, he'd just as soon keep that to himself. A high-pitched, steadily whining ring filled his head. He had not slept all night; over the past few days he had confirmed too many grisly tales of Hakon's prowess to think he could still defeat the demon who waited for him at the black center of being. He remembered an old saying: "No man lives to evening who the fates condemn at morning."

Haraldr had already honed his sword, and now he took a piece of pumice and roughened the bone handle. The sun slipped behind a cloud, darkening his tent like dusk. For a moment he had an ineffable vision of some vast catastrophe, perhaps the vanishing of an entire age, that he would join with his death. He recalled another verse. An ax age, a sword age, shields are ripped asunder. A storm age, a wolf age, before the world-orb shatters. Man will offer man no mercy or forgiveness.

And then the last dragon will fly in the darkness.

Haraldr tested the sword handle. Ready. The dragon waited for them all, man or God. Even all-conquering Kristr would one day be swallowed. There was no shame in that. The important thing was to spit in the beast's eye. Haraldr stood up, pulled his sword girdle around Emma, collected his spear and shields, and walked out of his tent. The sun suddenly emerged from the clouds, and the brilliance of his polished byrnnie dazzled him. He thought how happy he would be to see his father, Olaf, and Jarl Rognvald again.

† † †

"Not here, marmot-mind, I can't see!"

"I'm wagering fifteen grivnas."

"That's him! He's big enough—"

"Hakon pulled the hearts out of the Pechenegs with his bare hands and fed them to his women!"

"Your tongue is drunk."

"They say a giant snake fell from the sky this morning. . . ."

Gleb led Haraldr through the confused chatter of the traders and slaves. Rumors had buzzed in the night like mosquitoes. Most who knew anything at all were incredulous. Jarl Rognvald dead, and a member of the junior Druzhina, Haraldr Something-or-other, challenging Hakon for command of the fleet. And what was Gleb the pilot doing, championing the upstart?

Haraldr felt as light as down in the wind, dizzied by the warmth, dazzled by the multihued finery that the crowd had donned in celebration of their passage of the cataracts. Silk and Frisian cloth bloomed like bright flowers; pendants and arm rings sparkled like dewdrops on a bright spring morning. The slave girl, the raven-haired one he'd praised in Kiev, waited for him by the rope, her lips as red as blood. She was his Valkyrja.

The blow on his chest almost knocked him over.

"You're not here to nap!" Gleb spat at his feet, doughy mouth working pugnaciously. He looked as if he'd like to shove Haraldr again. "And that's no down mattress with a Roman-cloth pillow." He pointed to the dull brown burlap square and the ominous opening to Haraldr's right.

Ice frosted Haraldr's bones. He felt the anxiety, not the gaiety, in the crowd. Their fates hinged on this. Then he saw Halldor and Ulfr only a few steps away, waiting to come forward and second him. It was not so easy to die when other lives were at stake.

"Diminisher of the wolf's hunger! Hawk-hill of the Great King!" Grettir strode onto the burlap square with arms raised. Hakon's brutish head and oxen shoulders thrust above the crowd. Crushed herbs and dried petals flew in the air before him. Pipes skirled. Hakon's byrnnie iridesced like golden glass; his tallowed yellow hair gleamed. His two concubines, surprisingly lovely young women with ornate embossed silver belts cinched around their narrow waists, massaged his huge shoulders.

Grettir stood in the square and explained the traditional rules of the island-going contest. Battle to the death. Three shields only. One spear, one sword, one ax. A man can step into the ditch—though of course he would be put at quite a disadvantage by doing so—but if he goes beyond the rope, voluntarily or not, he must forfeit all of the stakes. Oh, and one final point, though it was rather obvious: A man who goes into the river has also lost.

Stanislav—an assistant to the Bishop of Kiev, who had come with the fleet as its spiritual leader—stepped into the square and motioned the combatants forward. Hakon's grin was mocking, and a pungent oil glistened on the the fine, tight braids of his beard; the gold spangles winked. The thin, sallow priest raised an ornate gold censer and swung it hesitantly. A few droplets sprayed in the air. "God the Father said, 'Inasmuch as I destroyed mankind with water because of their sins, I will now wash away the sins of man once more through. . . .' "

"I met a man who knew your mother, Green-wood," Hakon barked over the priest's invocation. "He says your father was a hound, not a man. Though your mother rutted with a shipload of Estlanders, she couldn't whelp until your flea-crawling father vomited in her cunt. It's no seed of man you were born of, Green-wood."

The priest would have swooned, but Gleb rushed up and snatched him back into the crowd. Grettir came forward. "Announce the seconds! Then let the Valkyrja weave their crimson cloth!"

Hakon's paint-rimmed, ember-flecked eyes probed through the thickening din of the crowd and clutched at Haraldr's soul. His brutish nostrils flared and he turned to his entourage. "My seconds. Alfhild and Inger." Hakon grinned and snorted. The silver-girt, silk-skirted concubines stepped forward, burdened under shields and weapons. The crowd tittered nervously and some of the Varangians guffawed stiffly.

Haraldr calmed himself with the observation that the Varangians had not enjoyed the joke at his expense nearly as much as they had the other night. He turned and waved his arm to his side of the square. "My seconds. Halldor Snorrason and Ulfr Uspaksson."

The veins at the corners of Hakon's eyes twitched wildly. "You're pelican meat!" he shouted to his erstwhile followers. "I'll fly your skins from my mast!" But the buzzing among the Varangians and the crowd did not offer a chorus to Hakon's outrage.

"Ravens flock and eagles gather! Folk-Mower prepares to sip the raven-wine with his thin lips!"

Grettir finished his overture with a bow. Out of the corner of his eye Haraldr saw a metallic flash and a blurring shaft; Hakon had already begun his attack. The spear struck his conical helm with a dull clatter and caromed off into the crowd. Haraldr's head whirled, and brilliant little sparks scattered in the descending night. Some reflex urged him to launch his own spear before his knees weakened and his vision darkened. Through a watery blur he saw Hakon bat the flying spear away, spin, and raise Folk-Mower flaring into the sky. Hakon's ax thundered against Haraldr's shield, almost immediately shattering most of the wooden boards. Drop it! Haraldr screamed to himself. It's useless! Where's Hakon!

Folk-Mower drew back to strike again. Haraldr leapt forward to defend himself with an attack, his head woozy and his mouth coppery with fear. His sword hammered against Hakon's shield three times in rapid succession, and sharp linden splinters sprayed. The gold giant stepped back, mildly shocked at the impact of Green-wood's fusillade. He withdrew dangerously close to the open side of the square as Haraldr continued his frenzied, booming attack. The crowd cheered wildly. Another step and the Varangian bully would be on a fast trip down the Dnieper.

Hakon halted his retreat at the lip of the drop and crouched beneath Haraldr's blows. The giant's shield was little more than an iron rim. Then, incredibly, his ax slipped from his hand. He dropped Folk-Mower! Haraldr exulted. It's over!

Hakon swiped with a preternatural arm, and Haraldr's feet jerked out from under him as smoothly as if he had decided to leap on his own. He saw a glimpse of cobalt sky, and then, below him, sparkling white foam over blade-sharp rocks. Some calm center, still functioning, told him that he had just been flipped over Hakon's back, and that only the rock-strewn

Dnieper would break his fall. Time was suspended for a fateful instant in which he might still save his life, and his desperately flailing hand caught the collar of Hakon's byrnnie. He clutched the metal hem with a death-cheating grip as his momentum sent him flying out over the roaring, silver Dnieper.

Hakon's crushing paws wrapped Haraldr's wrist in an effort to pry him loose. Haraldr held on; Hakon's counterweight arrested his fall, and his knees smashed into the sheer rock face just below the lip of the cliff. Hakon looked down, eyes afire, and grimaced fiendishly as he attempted to snap Haraldr's wrist. Haraldr could feel the bone scream with stress, and he knew his respite would be brief and would end painfully. There was no decision to be made. He glared back at Hakon and with all his force pulled down toward death, trying to bring Hakon over the edge of the cliff. The embers fanned in Hakon's eyes but he could not combat Haraldr's desperate weight. Unable to free himself and unwilling to share Green-wood's mad fall, Hakon planted his huge legs, pulled with a bestial grunt, and, with Haraldr's scrambling assistance, dragged his opponent back onto the burlap square.

Haraldr sprinted for his seconds. His knees were bloodied and he had lost his sword in the river. He grabbed his second shield from Halldor and his ax from Ulfr. His heart, throbbing with delayed fear, was strangling him. He turned to face Hakon again. He felt as if his limbs were trapped in cold black pitch, like a fly stuck in pine resin. He could hear the carrion-devouring ravens shrieking in his ears as Folk-Mower destroyed his shield in two lightning-quick flurries. Ulfr pressed a new shield on him. "Your last shield!" Ulfr screamed.

King from kings. Haraldr forced his body on. His sword lifted, but before he could get off a good stroke, Folk-Mower lashed out and Haraldr had to parry with his shield. Hakon's blade thudded deeply and stuck fast in the boards, and the light of hope flared again in Haraldr's eyes. *I've got it! I've trapped Folk-Mower!* Haraldr twisted the shield with all his force in an effort to wrench the shaft of the deeply embedded ax from Hakon's hands. An alarming resistance shocked back through his forearm. *Kristr! No!* The iron handle of his shield was ripped from his grip. He watched with morbid detachment as Hakon stood admiring the trophy Folk-Mower had gaffed, then blithely discarded the ax, Haraldr's last shield still attached.

Hakon removed the gold-pommeled sword from his scabbard. He stood with his tree-trunk legs spread wide, grinning like the head of death. "I've yet one more surprise for you, Green-wood," he slowly drawled. "Folk-Mower was but my toy. My sword is my *weapon.*"

Haraldr gripped the handle of his ax with both hands. Good hard oak, it might shield him from at best a dozen strokes before it was hacked to splinters. After that Hakon would need scarcely more than an executioner's skill.

Hakon delicately stroked the luridly blue-tinted, almost phosphorescent blade. "Come kiss these lips, sweet Green-wood," he said mockingly, pursing his thick lips and making contemptuous kissing sounds. "My wand-of-wounds will take your nose first. Then your ears. Then your hands . . ."

"Then take my nose, sow-lover!" Haraldr came forward screaming, determined not to beg for mercy in the jaws of the beast, determined to die with a courage worthy of the kings who had come before him and the good men who would soon have to join him in this death. The blue light of Hakon's blade flashed before eyes. His cheek itched. He struck Hakon's shield a glancing blow. Hakon's retort skidded off the ax shaft and ripped into Haraldr's forearm. Deep, too deep. Haraldr could already feel the blood streaming down the sleeve of his byrnnie.

"I'm whittling you away, Green-wood! Bit by bit, Green-wood! I'll cut you down until all that's left is your asshole! Then I'll make an arm ring out of it and give it to your mother!"

Now the blows came at Haraldr's shoulders, sapping his arms, softening him up so that he could indeed be sliced bit by bit, slowly, without dignity. A metallic ringing rose to a quick, clamorous crescendo. Hakon's blows were battering his steel helm. Resolve draining with every pulse of his ebbing lifeblood, Haraldr ducked his head and the strokes fell on his back and shoulders like ripping dogs. The sun faded, and he followed the echoes of memory into the night.

Haraldr slowly began to walk across the dark tundra of death. This time he went on farther than he ever had before. His destination was announced by the roar of the beast, the sound of all creation shattering into oblivion. The blast struck Haraldr and flattened him into the stinging slush. His face was unfeeling, solid ice, and he could hear nothing.

Except the voice. Whispering, very faintly: *Kill it. Kill the beast.*

Haraldr's arms were frozen in the ice, but he strained and shattered them free and struggled to his feet. His hands were numb and the ax handle burned like hot iron, but he forced himself to grip it. He peered into the endless blackness, and there, within the howling maw, saw the dark heart of the dragon. He hunched his shoulders and went in after it. . . .

When Haraldr returned to the light, the pain in his arms was gone and for an instant he wondered why he was being slapped on the head. Then he knew. He pushed forward with his arms and the weight that was on them flew away.

Nearly flattened by Haraldr's explosive shove, Hakon wheeled his feet as he struggled to stay upright. He staggered back, veering to avoid the drop to the river below. His fire-irises were rimmed with white wonder. For an instant, only an instant, Green-wood had been a beast! But Green-wood couldn't have the Rage. Only Mar has it! Only Mar! Hakon steeled himself. He was still Hakon, whose forehead-moons glowed with the stars-of-hearth, raven-sater, din-hastener, arm of the Great King, second only to Mar Hunrodarson. He advanced behind his shield and drew his sword back, preparing to draw a final, fatal arc through Haraldr's neck.

In the spirit world the dragon let forth its monstrous death scream. The earth-shattering bellow came out of Haraldr's throat. Hakon's sword arm froze, petrified by his opponent's inhuman oath, a sound known to any seasoned warrior, the terrifying peal of Odin's favor. Haraldr's ax lifted high, then struck like a thunderbolt.

Hakon's shield was air, a mirage that had formed in the sun. It blew apart like chaff. His byrnnie was the barest sheet of glass, twinkling as it broke. His skin was a petal, bruising and then ripping. His bones were twigs. Haraldr's blade did not slow until the earth that would soon claim those bones finally resisted its descent.

There was no sound except the rushing of the Dnieper over the rocks below. Hakon's vivid arterial blood bubbled around the ax shaft that sprouted from the huge gash in his chest. His legs jerked spasmodically.

Haraldr bent over the fallen Titan. Indigo lips parted and the ivory teeth chattered. "Mar . . ." Hakon said, his voice rattling. Blood gushed from his lips and the teeth were no longer white. "Mar, avenge me. . . ."

hat's the last of them," said Halldor as he lowered the flap of Hakon's silk pavilion, blocking out the inky blue wedge of sky. Even Halldor's imperturbable voice was edged with weariness and irritation.

Haraldr turned to Ulfr, seated on the simple camp stool next to him. "What do you think, Counselor?"

"I'm satisfied," said Ulfr. "I'd say the loyalty of two dozen of the Varangians will be suspect, and perhaps one or two of those will have to be watched. But I think your ears will tell you the feeling of most."

Haraldr smiled. The Varangians were already rowdy with tales of the combat and with extraordinary inventions about the origins and background of their mysterious new champion and leader. There were at least a dozen pagans, young men from small rural communities in Sweden, who were steadfastly certain that Haraldr was Thor in the guise of a mortal.

"And the Rus?"

"Well, to my thinking, as good as can be. They'll all follow Gleb, at least until we reach the Rus Sea. We have assurances from the leading traders. And surely you filled their breasts with joy this morning."

Yes. What a moment. There had been a hushed silence as Haraldr knelt over Hakon. After the blood had pooled and Hakon's feet had stopped twitching, no one had moved. Then Gleb had walked forward, sagging cheeks working, stood over the corpse, and ceremoniously spit on it. With that the crowd had erupted in a delirium of joy and praise. Then the Varangians had carried their new leader to the late Hakon's grandiose pavilion and had entered one at a time to pledge homage and loyalty. And after that came the Rus merchants and traders, begging concessions and asking Haraldr to settle disputes.

"Now we only need worry about the response of the Griks," said Halldor. He was carefully cleaning his nails with his short eating knife. "And the commander of the Imperial Guard."

Haraldr nodded wearily. The Byzantine trade ambassador had been noticeably absent among the day's endless procession of congratulants and supplicants. Gregory, however, had come by. "An unofficial visit, Haraldr Nordbrikt," the little eunuch had whispered hastily. "I want to express my singular delight in your victory over that gangster, a joy that is only surpassed by the august ambassador's acute discomfort at the news of your triumph. He hated the Manglavite as he hates all *barbaroi*, but he views with great trepidation the reaction that Hakon's death will evoke from Mar Hunrodarson, a man far more powerful than even the august ambassador." Then Gregory had looked about nervously. "I am not certain that I will have an opportunity to speak informally with you again. I would like to be able to tell you what you may expect when we reach the Empress City, but I fear that fortune still spins that wheel. I am certain that the fact that the Manglavite joyfully acceded to your challenge, in front of many witnesses, is an element in your favor. But much is changing in our Empire. The planets are reeling, and what their final configuration will be, even an astrologer could not say."

Haraldr had been less concerned about the fate of the Byzantine Empire than the vastly more chilling certainty that he would soon have to come face-to-face with Mar Hunrodarson. He remembered what Jarl Rognvald had said: "There is always another dragon."

"And you should have killed Grettir." Halldor continued to clean his nails as he delivered his admonition.

"Halldor, you don't understand the bond among poets," said Ulfr. "And Grettir's just a boy. The bitter taste on his praise-tongue today will make him a better man."

Haraldr nodded his agreement. Grettir had come literally on his knees to Haraldr, begging forgiveness and a chance to serve. Haraldr had demoted him to a menial stewardship but had promised him consideration as a skald if he showed a more worthy attitude.

"Well," said Halldor dryly, "it's as useless to argue with poets as it is to butt heads with an elk. That's my advice, and I leave it at that." He slipped his knife back in its sheath and stood up. "It's not an urgent matter, anyway. Sleep is." He examined the blood-encrusted linen bandage around Haraldr's deeply gashed forearm; other than that and a quick rinsing of the blood from his face, Haraldr's wounds had yet to be treated. "I've found a healer for your wounds. This healer is from someplace to the east. They say she's very skilled. She speaks some Norse." Haraldr thought he detected some signal in Halldor's implacable eyes. "I've told her to be available for as long as you need her." Halldor turned and left without further ado; Ulfr embraced Haraldr and followed.

Sable-haired and swan-white, thought Haraldr as the healer entered the pavilion. She was the slave he had praised in Kiev. Her chin was cocked haughtily and her agate eyes confronted his. Her linen petticoat whisked over glimpses of white ankle. Her bare arms cradled a small carved wooden chest, folded linen, and a silver bowl.

She set the chest and linen and bowl on the camp stool next to Haraldr. Standing while he was seated, her eyes were slightly higher than his. She was more beautiful than Elisevett, Haraldr thought. The closeness of her made his breath come with difficulty.

"Take off." Her voice was high and melodic, with a thick accent Haraldr had never heard before. She gestured with elegant movements of her slender fingers.

Haraldr blushed. The healer seemed amused and politely looked at her feet while Haraldr removed his sweat-soiled wool tunic; he was wearing only breeches beneath.

She began with the lesser wounds. He closed his eyes when she washed his forehead, and he could smell her sweet skin, faintly scented with myrrh. She tended a shallow gash on his thigh, and he was embarrassed by the stirring in his groin.

Her eyes searched his with a seemingly innocent curiosity. "I call you Jarl?"

Haraldr shook his head. "I'm not a Jarl. And you no longer have a master."

Her eyes narrowed suspiciously. "You . . . not master?"

"I gave all of Hakon's slaves their freedom." Haraldr spoke very deliberately so she would understand. "You are free."

"Yes," she said proudly, as if he had merely expressed the natural state of things. She pressed her lovely fingers to her breast. "Khazar."

So, thought Haraldr, she *is* from the desert. The Khazars were a proud and noble people who had once owned a great empire around a vast inland sea to the east. Lately their power had been usurped by a race of horsemen said to be as dark and savage as the Pechenegs but far more intelligent.

"You don't belong here, do you," said Haraldr, almost to himself.

"Caught," she said angrily. Apparently she understood Norse better than she could speak it. "Brothers . . ." She vehemently brushed the air with her hand. They had been wiped out. She probably had been sold to Norse traders in Khoresm.

She touched her breast delicately again. "Princess."

The word seemed to strike Haraldr's heart. Yes. She had the air. She probably had learned to heal by binding her brothers' wounds. She'd certainly not been raised as a servant. His breast pained for her as it had that night in Kiev. *I already love you,* he silently confessed. *But I can see that you have another love, and because of it, you could never be happy with mine.*

With one trembling finger he touched her chin. She did not flinch. "When we get to the Rus Sea, twenty of our ships will leave to dock at Kherson. I'll send you with them and see that from there a ship takes you east. Home to your people."

She understood. "Home," she said. Her eyes shifted focus, as if she could see some glorious vista far beyond the silk walls of the pavilion.

When she had finished with the small wounds, she began to rummage through the gear scattered about the pavilion; she finally located a half-full wine bag. As she moved about, the lamplight shone through her linen petticoat and Haraldr could see the outline of her slender flanks and the contour of her breasts. She took a small silver goblet from the chest and mixed an ocher powder with the wine. She drank some first to show Haraldr that it was not poison.

"Not hurt," she said as she began to pull the blood-caked linen from Haraldr's forearm. The wound was deep but clean. She daubed ointment from a jar into it. Haraldr began to feel drowsy and very comfortable. His head nodded.

"Lie." She gestured at Hakon's bed. It was an enormous, intricately carved wooden frame covered with thick, down-padded silk covers. Disgusting, Haraldr had thought when he had first seen it that morning. Just another reason why Hakon's Varangians, who would sleep tonight on hard ground beneath coarse blankets, had so willingly endorsed the usurpation of their leader.

Haraldr shook his head and looked for his own gear bag. He couldn't find it amid Hakon's splendid clutter. He did want to lie down.

The healer guessed at Haraldr's reservations and dragged the down covers off the bed and spread them on the floor beside him. Haraldr wondered briefly if she had been forced to sleep beneath them. He felt very good. He slid off the camp stool and lay down on the covers.

The healer knelt beside Haraldr and began to wrap clean linen around his forearm. The light behind her gave her raven hair a golden aura. He reached up and grazed her arm with the very tip of his fingers. He did not feel her soft skin so much as a curious shock, like the sparking when one touched a kettle or a knife on a cold, dry day.

She shuddered at some similar sensation. She studied the cup of medicine for a moment, and then drank the rest of the narcotic draft. The wine slicked her lips with a brilliant sheen.

"Swaa . . . swaan?" she asked.

Haraldr's groin tingled. She remembered his words in Kiev. "A swan is a white bird," he answered, drawing the curve of the neck in the air. "Noble and white. And soft." He touched her again.

Her erect torso swayed slightly. "Serah," she said, touching her breast.

Her name was unlike any Norse sound, and it made a beautiful and mysterious music. He thought momentarily of Elisevett, but she was a distant thing of cold beauty, a glacier diminishing into a sliver of icy light beyond the horizon. Serah.

Serah's hand burned and chilled his chest. His body lost weight, as when he had flown above the river today. But now there was no fear.

Wizard-quick, Serah rustled, white revealing white. She threw the linen petticoat aside. Dark hair fell around Haraldr's face. Serah tugged at his breeches. The still air felt like a summer sea-wind over his nakedness. He was as hard as an ax staff. Serah's body settled over him like a silk drape.

This was different from the two times before. The first, a whore, had been a meaningless lesson in the art-skills a king must know. Elisevett had been a passion that had rushed along like a torrent before exploding in a moment of aching, ungraspable ecstasy. Tonight was a deep pool, dark and warm, and in it Serah slid against his tingling flesh, drawing him deeper into the iridescent blackness. There is another place, Haraldr whispered to himself. Not the cold, dark place where the dragon lurks. A place he had never sensed before, a place where only a woman could take him. He plunged deeper into these depths, his pleasure more liquid and languid, only a single steel core left to his body. For an instant he wondered if there was danger in this place as well, but Serah gripped him and whispered, and the thought drifted away on the warm current.

Long after they had finished, they held each other and listened to the sigh and hiss of the Dnieper. Finally Serah tilted her head to look into his eyes and said, "Serah. Princess. Khazar." Her finger gently pressed against his chest. "Har— Har-aldr . . . ?"

Haraldr held her close again. "Haraldr. Prince," he whispered distinctly, realizing she was no threat, wanting her to share with him the secret that he held as dearly as life. "Like you, I am far from my people."

She understood, and this new bond brought desire to another pitch. Her hands began to brand his chest. Her lips devoured his face and neck.

"Haraldr, Prince," she said next to his ear, her voice urgent with passion. Her lips moved down his chest.

Neither of them heard the slight stirring of the silk curtain, or the lithe footsteps in the night.

will see him, Nicetas."

The eunuch bowed and the doors slid shut behind him. Maria turned to Ata, her palmist. "This is Giorgios. The one I like." Ata grinned; his teeth were very bad, though he could not have been much older than thirty. He stood up, smoothed the wrinkles out of his robe, touched his hand to his forehead, bowed, and also left the room. Giorgios was shown in a moment later. He wore the uniform of the Imperial Scholae: an embossed gold breastplate over a short-sleeved crimson tunic, and a short leather kilt. His tanned face was flushed with exertion; he probably had been riding.

Maria kissed him on the forehead and brushed his blond curls back. "Why did you come? Is Alexandros with you?"

Giorgios eyes were wild, like a pursued stag's. He stammered. "I . . . I love you. My every thought is of you. You consume me. I can't bear to watch you." His neck corded. "I can't eat anymore. Do you . . . love Alex?"

"Alexandros disgusts me. He is a boor." There was no expression on Maria's face. She was as serene as a marble Aphrodite but more beautiful.

Giorgios blinked rapidly, as if he had been slapped. "Then why . . . why . . . ?"

"I want to inflict upon you the pain you will cause me to suffer."

Giorgios blinked again.

"Ata says that for me fate and love have crossed once before. Though he could not know it, he is right. Now he says that my next crossing will bring together fate, love, and death. He says that a man will destroy me with his love. A fair-hair. Perhaps you are that man." She paused. "I am almost certain that I love you."

Giorgios wavered as if he would topple. It was a moment before he could speak. "I would never . . . I adore you, I worship you, I would die before—"

Maria put her fingers to lips. Her eyes were like blue flames. "I know," she whispered. "Now go. I won't see you for several days. But know that when you are thinking of me, I am thinking of you. Now go."

Giorgios made his way to the vestibule with intoxicated steps. As the eunuchs slid the ivory-inlaid doors open, he turned and looked at Maria pleadingly. "I am sleeping with Alexandros tonight," she told him.

hat hole is no deeper than a man's member," said Halldor. His words were whipped by the stinging, salted gust. "But many a man has fallen to his death within it." He nodded at Haraldr, staring morosely out over the deep blue swells of the Rus Sea. "Its a good thing that Khazar girl went off for Kherson. She only had him for five days, but by the end of that time I feared for him more than I did when he was in the death-square with Hakon."

Ulfr smiled fondly. Three weeks ago they had sailed out of the broad estuary of the Dnieper into the Rus Sea, and they had dispatched the contingent of twenty boats bound for Kherson. Haraldr had arranged transport for the Khazar girl, and when he had bid her farewell, he had kissed her all over her face and hair, and then tears had visibly streaked his face as he watched her ship disappear into the eastern horizon. Many of the men present had been shocked by this weakness in their new hero; a warrior was supposed to bid his woman farewell with a smile and a wise remark. Let her do the pining. But Ulfr himself knew how a poet's heart was, and he had gone among the men to explain that the same passion that had crushed Hakon's chest like a bird's made Haraldr's own breast tender to a woman's touch. Within a few days it became the fashion among the Varangians to lament lost loves they had hardly thought about for months.

Haraldr remained statue-still in the prow. Gleb looked at him, then at Ulfr and Halldor, and spat. "Well," he growled, "he is about to meet a woman who will make him forget all the rest." He paused for effect. "The Empress City." He gestured south, where the coastline was just a dark, greenish line on the horizon. To the west the ascending sun punched a brilliant hole in a seamless sheet of smoked blue. "By mid-morning we'll reach an opening on that coast. It's a strait the Greeks call Bosporus. At the end of it, a half-day's sail south, is the Empress City. I'll never forget my first sight of her."

"Look. Another one," said Halldor. He faced the stern and pointed into the steel-hued sky. A messenger pigeon made one last spiraling turn before heading off to the southwest. "That's the fifth bird the Grik ambassador has sent out since yesterday morning."

"He's telling them to prepare our welcome," said Gleb.

"What nature of welcome?" asked Haraldr. He had left his lonely perch while Ulfr, Halldor, and Gleb had been distracted by the pigeon. "That's what troubles me."

"Well, I'm glad something besides that girl troubles you," said Gleb. He spat and smiled like a father forgiving a foolish son. Then his malleable face puckered with concern. "I'd say we're in danger. If only because there's no knowing the mind of these Greeks. They're a nervous people, they've never trusted the Rus, and this business with their Manglavite, which they surely know of by now, has got to alarm them. It's obvious from the way their ambassador has acted."

Indeed, thought Haraldr. For the past three and a half weeks the Byzantine trade ambassador had rebuffed every attempt at communication with the curt message "maintain course." In fact, they had seen neither the ambassador nor the interpreter, Gregory, since leaving St. Gregory's Island.

"Can we fight them?" asked Ulfr.

Gleb tugged at his doughy jowls. "Long before I made my first trip down the Dnieper, a Rus fleet attacked the Greek navy right in front of the Empress City. But these were swift warships manned by thousands of Varangians; Swedes, I believe they were. Even then the Greeks were able to call on their lightning from heaven and set the water on fire. They say you could walk across the shores of the Bosporus for a rowing-spell and your feet would never touch anything but the bodies of sailors, both Greek and Rus. Ten ships returned to Kiev. That's when the Emperor and the Great Prince decided a treaty was preferable to such slaughter."

"Then that treaty will protect us," said Ulfr hopefully.

"Unless they view the death of their Manglavite as a breach of that treaty; indeed, an act of aggression against the very Emperor whom Hakon served," added Haraldr.

"We don't even know who the Emperor is now," said Halldor. "It's fairly certain that Basil Bulgar-Slayer is dead." The Bulgar-Slayer had ruled Byzantium for so long that he had become a legend, even in the far north, long before Haraldr had been born. "All we know beyond that are reports of mutterings made by Hakon when he was drunk, of a second and even third Emperor after Basil Bulgar-Slayer, and something about a 'bitch-whore' who has had a very great hand in this succession of

Emperors." Halldor looked around at the group and gave his usual insouciant shrug. "There are times when a man finds himself far from shelter on a moonless night, with his tinder wet. There's nothing he can do but wait for the sun."

Haraldr envied Halldor his innate calm as much as he hated his own gut-churning helplessness. He was no Halldor, but he knew that Halldor was right. They could only wait. And watch. "Who's got the sharpest eyes?" he asked Gleb. "Send him up the mast."

Gleb snapped an order, and Blud, a young Slav oarsman, clambered up the mast like a monkey and stood atop the single cross-spar from which the billowing square sail was suspended. Blud waved happily at his comrades below and then intently began to study the empty Rus Sea.

† † †

"Bosporus." Gleb pointed to the now clearly visible fissure in the green band of headland. He called out for the following ships—at last count there were one hundred and fifty-four vessels remaining of the close to five hundred that had left Kiev—to make a broad starboard turn and close up formation.

The sun was rising to its zenith and the water glittered. The sky was an immaculate cerulean. Soon it became apparent that the Bosporus was a good fourth or even third of a rowing-spell in width. Dozens of small boats with square and triangular white sails cruised along the coastline. Scattered clusters of white buildings gleamed on the high, grassy, tree-spotted escarpments of the nearest shore; some of these apparent suburbs of the Great City were more extensive than any town Haraldr had ever seen, save Kiev. After an hour or so the Bosporus narrowed to several thousand ells. The immense buildings scattered on the headlands became clearly visible; domes like those of Yaroslav's cathedral, though much larger, rose from yew-colored woods.

"A-heaaad! A-heaaad! Off the prow!" Blud looked like a mad seabird leaping up and down on the cross-spar, flapping his free arm and screaming himself purple. Haraldr dashed to the mast, grabbed a rope, and pulled himself up the timber spire.

At first it seemed like a necklace on the water, flashing in the sun. Within a few minutes the jewels could be distinguished as gilded, swoop-necked prows. Dragons, like the ships of Norse kings. But there had been only a handful of such ships in the entire north. Now there were hundreds out there, spread across the entire width of the Bosporus.

Gleb came scrambling spryly up the mast, his limp no handicap in the rigging. He frowned as he appraised the dancing gold on the water.

The fleet was approaching rapidly. Haraldr counted perhaps a hundred large ships, surrounded by several hundred smaller supporting vessels. Though still too distant for an accurate gauge of length, the biggest ships were clearly of enormous size, with double banks of oars, twin masts, and what looked like huge gold beasts—perhaps panthers or bears—looming at both bow and stern.

"*Dhromons* of the Imperial Fleet." Gleb spoke as if he were describing a huge wave rolling toward them, a natural phenomenon that a man could only curse helplessly in his last instant of life. "Fire-ships."

"In what formation?"

Gleb cleared his throat with an angry growl. "Battle formation."

If we are to die, Haraldr told himself, *we will not make it easy for them.* He shouted down to Halldor: "We must give no provocation! Reef sails but don't furl them. Oars and weapons ready but out of sight. Keep men in place to quickly furl sails at my command. We'll wait for them, but if they come closer than two thousand ells, we'll furl sails and row for the shore. Those big ships may have trouble maneuvering up against the headlands!"

"So will these Rus washtubs!" answered Halldor. Then he shouted the orders down the line. Within minutes the entire Rus trade flotilla had stopped and sat bobbing like a great flock of waterfowl resting on the water. The Imperial ships continued to advance, their formation perfect, oars slitting the water in precise rhythm. Haraldr could see metal scintillating on the decks, and distinct figures clambering about. The range was down to three thousand ells. A fearsome, oxlike bellowing echoed across the water.

Two thousand five hundred ells. Haraldr looked at Gleb. Gleb just shook his head and worked his jaws. Perun be praised that he had exacted enough gold from Yaroslav to ensure that his grandchildren would never have to look down the angry snout of an Imperial *dhromon.* If his death could buy that, then death take him.

Two thousand two hundred. The *dhromons* bellowed again, louder, as if the leering golden spouts had been transformed into the creatures they resembled. Two thousand one hundred. At two thousand ells Haraldr hesitated and decided to wait a moment longer. He was no exact judge of distance. A few hundred more ells would still give them time to break for shore.

Eighteen hundred. Haraldr could see that the men on the decks of the giant Byzantine ships wore armor. *Kristr, my fate is in your hands. Odin's gift is of no use here.*

Seventeen hundred. The command could no longer be delayed. "Hal—no, wait!" Signal flags wriggled up the barren first mast of the lead *dhromon.* The double rows of oars lifted glistening from the water, bristled in the air like the spines of strange sea monsters, and vanished almost simultaneously into the hulls of the *dhromons.* The Byzantine ships slowed and then stopped. They were about fifteen hundred ells away.

Gleb looked at Haraldr. "Don't assume anything when you deal with the Greeks. They love a ruse."

The motion at the periphery of Haraldr's vision sent his pulse hammering. What fool had broken rank? Then he saw the crimson sail puffed out like a fat silk cushion: the trade ambassador's ship furiously rejoining its own. The ambassador stood in the prow like a victorious admiral. A few paces behind him a little bald figure turned, looked up to the mast of Haraldr's ship, and waved. Gregory. He looked lonely and wistful, as if he were bidding his Norse friends a permanent farewell.

A single small warship slipped out from between the monstrous *dhromons* and came very rapidly toward the ambassador's vessel. The two ships drew even, halted, and bobbed in unison. Haraldr could see the flash of armor as several men leapt from the warship onto the deck of the ambassador's stubby vessel. An animated discussion seemed to commence. On and on it went, arms raised on one side and then the other in a distant, mimed debate. The wind flapped the reefed sail of Haraldr's ship and he imagined that it was the sound of the Griks quarreling among themselves. Good, he told himself, clearly there is a lack of resolution here. But remember what Gleb said about Grik ruses.

The armored figures leapt back to the warship. Oars dipped into the water and the ambassador's ship went on toward the line of *dhromons* while the small warship moved forward. The question thundered in Haraldr's head: Will the *dhromons* follow? If the the seagoing monsters now moved even an ell, he could not hesitate to give the last order of his short-lived command.

But the *dhromons* remained motionless except for the slightest swaying; it was as if the colossal warships were great buildings anchored in the earth rather than vessels floating on water. The small Byzantine warship came on with startling speed. It seemed no larger than the Rus ships, with just a single row of oars. The pitch-slathered hull was solid black, but the railing, prow, and swooping stern were brilliant arabesques of gold and red enamel. The planked deck, painted a gleaming white, supported enormous crossbows on wheeled carriages. Most of the men on deck wore steel jerkins or bright blue steel byrnnies and conical helmets.

The Byzantine ship closed, oars almost brushing the hull of Haraldr's ship. An armored figure, apparently an officer, and a single civilian came to the railing amidships. The officer's head was uncovered, and his short, curly hair was raked by the breeze; his beard was neatly trimmed. He wore a mail jerkin and a short scarlet tunic. The man beside him was swathed from head to toe in a solid black robe. Only a stubble covered his head and squinched, distorted face.

The wind slackened. Haraldr could hear snatches of the two men conversing. He scampered down the mast. Gleb followed.

"Haraldr Norb— Nord-briv!" shouted the man in black. His Norse accent was not nearly as good as Gregory's. "You are now under the authority of Michael, Lord of the Entire World, the Emperor, Autocrator, and Basileus of the Romans. His Imperial Majesty has sent as his representative the Droungarios of his Imperial Fleet, Nicephorus Taronites, who has sent as his representative the *komes* Bardas Lascaris." The officer narrowed his dark eyes menacingly and barely nodded. "I, John Stethatus," continued the man in black, "temporary secretary in the Office of the Barbaroi under the Logothete of the Dromus, speak for the *komes!*"

"I am Haraldr Nordbrikt! This fleet is under my authority. And I speak for myself and those under my command!"

The two Byzantines spoke rapidly in Greek. The question was settled quickly. The man in black shouted in Norse again.

"Then the command you will give your fleet is this: Wait for our signal." He pointed to the single mast of the warship. "One red flag and one white! Then follow us, under sail, in single file. We will escort you to the Queen of Cities!"

The warship moved quickly to a post fifty ells ahead of the Rus vessel. A single yellow flag went up its mast. An answering yellow flag went up one of the masts of the nearest *dhromon,* and the beasts bellowed again. The spiny oars of the *dhromons* emerged and slapped the blue-slate surface of the Bosporus. The great ships began to fan off their formation and head south along either bank of the strait. It was as if the Byzantine warships were forming a huge funnel to draw the Rus flotilla down the Bosporus. Or to surround and annihilate it.

Haraldr turned to Gleb, but the old Slav just chewed and ground his boot against the rough planking. "I've never seen an 'escort' in such force. But remember that the Greeks rarely do the obvious."

Haraldr had already made his decision. "We're sailing Rus washtubs, not Norse dragons," he said, forcing a jaunty smile at Halldor. "If we run, if we fight, a dozen ships might survive to reach the Dnieper, and how many of those would survive the Pechenegs? No, that way death is certain. We don't know how the Griks think, but we know that this trade must be of value to them or it would not have continued for so many years. This way we have one gaming piece on the table."

Ulfr swallowed thickly and nodded. Gleb chewed and spit. Halldor shouted the order back. The red flag went up on the mast of the small warship just ahead. The white flag followed. Oars dipped and the Byzantine warship began to move forward. Gleb ordered the sail set, the gust caught, and the ship lurched forward. The rest of the Rus fleet followed.

Soon the giant *dhromons* flanked the Rus River ships on both sides, at distances of only a hundred or so ells. They were floating islands: three, perhaps four times as long as Olaf's dragon-ship, a vessel that had been the marvel of the north. The massive black hulls were as high as the walls of Yaroslav's palace, and a gilt-and-red building as big as the average Norse farmer's dwelling sat on each foredeck. The spout-snouted beasts at the bow and stern of each ship were more than twice as tall as a man, and there was a third such spout on the deck between the two masts. Some of the spouts had been turned at angles to face the Rus ships; apparently these man-made dragons could swivel their necks just like living creatures.

The *dhromons*, oars methodically plodding at the sluggish pace of the merchant ships, continued to flank the entire Rus fleet as it moved south. The buildings on either shore, but particularly to the starboard, became more closely spaced and yet more complex in structure. We have already passed the dwellings of a dozen Yaroslavs, thought Haraldr. But if this is Miklagardr, where are the Great City's fabled walls?

An apparition appeared on the horizon, a wavering ivory line flecked with bits of coral and silver. Haraldr shouted at Ulfr and Halldor and pointed. Gleb watched the three huge Norsemen standing there jabbering like excited boys and smiled knowingly. Haraldr scrambled for the mast, followed by Ulfr and Halldor.

"Kristr the Pure!" Haraldr gasped. From the top spar he could see the immense sprawl of miniature palaces on the starboard shoreline. Though still diminished by distance, the buildings would have to be as large as those they were passing now, but the sparkling little domes and cubes now densely blanketed an area that stretched as far as the eye could see. Haraldr's knees weakened. Men could not build this! Gods, perhaps, but not men.

Ulfr shouted and pointed to larboard. No! It was simply not possible, even for the gods. Another Great City on the opposite shore of the Bosporus! Had the Griks built a twin of Miklagardr? Impossible. Kristr's Mother! This Miklagardr was no less sprawling and lavish and brightly twinkling than the other. *We have left the middle realm,* thought Haraldr. *We sail on the clouds, toward the city, the twin cities, that Kristr built in Paradise. He is truly the conqueror.*

The ship pitched on a wave and metal glinted on the water directly between the twin cities of Miklagardr. Haraldr's bowels knotted with alarm: another fleet, even greater than that which already surrounded them. And the purpose of this second armada was obvious; there was already sufficient escort. Haraldr whipped his head around to observe the *dhromons,* expecting them to initiate the slaughter. Ulfr continued to elaborate on his discovery of the second Miklagardr, struggling to come up with some clumsy verses.

"Look." Halldor spoke with his insistent reserve. He pointed toward the deadly scintillae of the second great fleet.

A heavy, cresting swell tossed the bow high again. Haraldr's feet slipped and his fingers clawed the mast. He looked at the frothing wake below and his heart raced. When he looked up again, Halldor was still pointing. Only his eyes spoke. Haraldr sighted down Halldor's trembling finger.

All the gods. All of them conspired to create this vision, Haraldr told himself, *this dream that mocks mortal existence until it seems nothing. The twin cities that we thought were Miklagardr are merely court men, skalds who announce the entrance of the glorious Sovereign of the Entire World. All the gods. I have seen what I will see when I close my eyes for the last time.*

Gold and silver bubbled up from the sea, shimmered and froze, a froth of enormous bubbles that rose and fell over hills of solid ivory. It was an enormous island of gold and silver and ivory. No, it was perhaps a huge finger of land jutting into the sea; one could not see where it ended.

Wind rattled the rigging and the ship sped toward the vision. The shimmering bubbles were domes, like the ones they had seen earlier, but hundreds and hundreds and hundreds, climbing up and down gleaming hills, domes built upon domes to rise like globular mountains. Forests of enormous pillars stood in polychrome rows, and window glass, almost unknown in the north, sparkled like diamond dewdrops. Constantinople, the Queen of Cities, rose from the sea like a huge gem-encrusted reliquary.

On they sped, the vision steadily rising from the water, becoming more intricate in its fantastic, multicolored details; awnings winked into view and tiny figures appeared on scrolled balconies. The vast seawall, a towering, elaborately crenellated structure of brilliant ocher brick, girdled the entire visible stretch of waterfront like a huge golden belt.

"Asgard," said Ulfr numbly. The city of the gods. On the deck below, the Rus traders and oarsmen crowded the railing, exclaiming in wonder. "A miracle wrought by the angelic host . . ."

"Father Almighty . . ."

"Christ the Pure has brought us to his heavenly mansions. . . ."

The Byzantine warships slowed and veered hard starboard, toward an arm of the sea that embraced the city on the north. The entrance to this prodigious harbor was marked by a soaring turret of mournful, ashen stone set at the edge of the water. The grim tower was a sinister contrast to the vivid color of the buildings behind it; for some reason Haraldr shuddered as if he had seen a vision of his own grave. Gleb had already shouted the order to stop when Haraldr saw what the old Slav pilot was pointing at. The mouth of the harbor was blocked by a colossal boom of skiff-size metal chain links alternating with wooden floats the size of tree trunks. The daunting waterborne barrier extended from the brooding gray tower to the teeming docks on the opposite shore, a span of about fifteen hundred ells.

A tender towed the boom toward the tower, and the two fleets resumed their procession. In the distance, perhaps half a rowing-spell off, checkered dun-and-green hills sprinkled with chalk-white dwellings rose above what Haraldr assumed to be the western terminus of the harbor. The harbor was crowded with perhaps a thousand ships: *dhromons,* smaller galleys, exotic merchant vessels, many of types Haraldr had never seen before. Along the shoreline, as far as one could see, enormous warehouses supported on pilings extended from the towering seawall out over the water; from the landward side of the city's girding wall, palatial stone edifices, some of them extravagant concoctions of clustered cupolas and meandering arcades, ascended the hills to the shallow summit of the city's long, languorous spine. Broad white avenues, teeming with laden porters, mules, carts, and four-wheeled wagons as big as Norse cottages, disappeared into the architectural maze of the city.

As the Rus fleet sailed on into the harbor Haraldr turned and again studied the harbor chain. No hull could challenge the cyclopean links and floats. When the boom was drawn back behind them, they would leave here only with the permission of the Griks.

† † †

"Emmanuel counted them. He says there are only one hundred and fifty or so. The Prefect had anticipated four or five hundred ships. Now he will start gouging the butchers and the silk merchants to make up the shortfall. I wouldn't be surprised if we find he has set the prices higher tomorrow." The Augusta Theodora stood on the third-story balcony of her ancient country palace; her home was sufficiently far from the city to be considered a place of exile. She had a view across the olive-green hills, occasionally speckled with white-marble porticoes and red-tile roofs, that sloped to the distant, slablike surface of the Golden Horn, the enormous natural harbor flanking Constantinople on the north. The sails of the usual merchant traffic surrounded the wharves like swarms of white-and-beige butterflies. In the middle of the harbor the Rus ships, lashed together in a long single file, looked like a wooden causeway set between two rows of giant, metal-beaked *dhromons.* Constantinople seemed cool, silent, almost misty in the early-evening light. The last rays of the sun caught the ornate palaces high on the city's spine; from this distance the long expanse of enormous buildings appeared to be a single intricate carving in gleaming ivory.

"I am told they have brought some very fine sable skins," said Maria. "I intend to get enough to line three coats, even if I have to auction a vineyard to pay for them. Of course, the price will go down next year when the Rus return in greater numbers, but whatever I might save on next year's sables won't keep me warm this winter."

"The Rus may never return, at least to trade. Emmanuel says"—Emmanuel was Theodora's chamberlain; although he had accompanied her into exile, he still maintained a priceless network of informants among the eunuchs of the Imperial Palace—"that both the Grand Domestic and the Droungarios of the Imperial Fleet favored attacking the Rus fleet in the Bosporus this morning. Apparently the Manglavite was murdered by one of the Varangians he had recruited, and now the murderer commands the entire Rus fleet. It is claimed that this Varangian is a dangerous privateer and an 'enemy of Christendom.' "

Maria snorted with disgust. "I would consider the murderer of the Manglavite a friend of Rome."

"Perhaps so. But the military clique and their Dhynatoi sponsors are still looking for an incident to spark a confrontation."

"What does Joannes say?"

"He is holding them back for the time being. As usual, his real interest is obscure. I think he might use the Rus to bargain with the Dhynatoi, then give them up. If Joannes and the Dhynatoi ever came to an accommodation, I would fear for my sister's life." Theodora pursed her thin, spinsterish lips. She was tall, with an angular frame and a disproportionately small face; her immature, pinched features gave her the aspect of a small child grown into middle age without ever ripening into womanhood. Though she was younger than her sister, the Empress Zoe, Theodora often seemed old enough to be Zoe's mother. "How is my sister?" she asked.

"Unhappy. Her husband has not spent the night with her for almost a month."

"I had hoped she would find . . . peace with him. After Romanus . . ." Theodora paused and scraped at the coarse stone with her silk slipper. "Are you happy, darling?"

"I think I am in love." There was a curious melancholy to this pronouncement.

Theodora smiled, though her face seemed capable only of irony, never genuine mirth. "Is it one of them, or both?" She peered down into the unkempt yard directly beneath the balcony. Alexandros and Giorgios looked like little boys foraging; they were peeling the thick layer of ivy from the weather-worn statue of an ancient Roman deity. "I could tell immediately that the brown-eyed boy is in love with you."

"He is the one," Maria said numbly.

"Darling, you know I have always tried to refrain from judging you. But will you be careful? I think of my sister and how different everything might have been. . . ." Maria knew that Theodora was referring to her older sister, Eudocia, who had conceived a child out of wedlock, given birth in a convent, and had died shortly thereafter. The baby was always said to have been stillborn, though Maria sometimes wondered if it had been adopted by a simple family, and now, oblivious of its Imperial destiny, lived a far happier life than its mother ever could have enjoyed.

"I know all the precautions," Maria said. "There is even a physician from Alexandria who specializes in the field."

"I don't mean those precautions, darling, or even the measures one must take to guard the heart. I mean the precautions of the soul."

Maria nodded vaguely and studied the line of Rus ships in the harbor.

t shames heaven. Kristr forgive me, but it shames heaven." Ulfr shook his head and stared.

The Great City blazed away in the night. How many lights? Enough to make it like day down by the wharves where porters still struggled with sacks and barrels and bales, enough to turn the enchanted crown of the city into a dazzling universe. Drapes and garlands of winking lights spread over the hills as far as one could see. The stars in the glassy black night were barely visible in comparison.

Haraldr let the boy stand for him before this vision; the man, the commander of a fleet, had given his orders and slipped off to await the day. The boy stood in the inky night and saw a dream—every Norse boy's dream of distant, magic Miklagardr—become real.

"Haraldr!" Gleb hobbled frantically across the hold, his face lobster-red. His breathing was virtually apoplectic, and he had to clear his throat several times before he could speak. "It's Lyashko. He's a merchant from Novgorod and a fool. . . ."

Haraldr quickly remembered who Lyashko was; he was as big around as he was tall, with a blunt nose and a greasy bald head. He'd made trouble ever since St. Gregory's Island, lagging behind and then sailing out of sight ahead of the file until Haraldr had threatened to chain both him and his equally foolish pilot. After that he had simply sailed up every day to grumble about "incorrect headings."

"Yes, the very one," Gleb said, seeing the recognition in Haraldr's eyes. "He's gotten himself and his men drunk. Says he's going into the city to find Greek whores. Perun strike me if he didn't threaten my life when I tried to stop him!"

Haraldr left Gleb far behind as he sprinted along the bridge of lashed-together Rus ships, hurdling railing after railing. Damn fool Lyashko. After they had entered the harbor that afternoon Haraldr had been called upon by an official announced as the "Legatharios to the Prefect of the City," a pale, emaciated man dressed in the most intricately embroidered silk robe Haraldr had ever seen; though the Legatharios had merely gazed into some metaphysical distance throughout the interview, his interpreter (the first Norse-speaking Byzantine they had met who was not a eunuch) had issued a long set of directives Haraldr and his men were expected to observe under the Byzantine–Rus treaty. The Byzantine officials had expressly instructed them to lash their ships together and remain anchored in the middle of the harbor until a complete inventory of their cargoes and crews could be taken; any vessel leaving the rank was to be considered, in the interpreter's words, "a brigand, and will be dealt with as such by elements of the Imperial Fleet." Haraldr had spent the rest of the day making certain that every shipowner and pilot understood the Byzantine orders. A single ship out of formation and the lurking *dhromons* might be provoked into attacking the entire Rus fleet.

Haraldr must have leapt over a hundred railings before he saw the crews that had crowded the ships next to Lyashko's. He moved through the jabbering, excited throng, and the exclamations of "It's him, It's him" and "Hakon-Slayer" and "Mighty-Arm" began to circulate. He reached the gap in the line of lashed-together ships and looked across the murky water. Nothing.

"He left like that, Jarl!" said a gnarled old pilot with an eye patch, slapping his hands briskly. "Nobody could stop them! Elovit, there"—he pointed to a boy with linen wrapped around his arm—"took a good cut. They'da killed us!"

Kristr damn Lyashko. Haraldr continued to search the black water between the line of Rus ships and the harbor, but he could discern nothing; the lights from the harbor didn't illuminate the entire stretch of water, and even Lyashko wasn't enough of a fool to go in with a lantern shining from his mast.

"Close this gap!" shouted Haraldr. "Get a torch or a lantern up on every cross spar and keep them burning. We've got to convince the Griks there's only one renegade!"

Halldor and Ulfr arrived, both out of breath. Halldor made sure that Haraldr's order started down the line. "Find a healer for this boy," Haraldr told Ulfr. He looked out over the water again and thought he saw the silhouette of a Rus river ship against the fringe of light spilling from the docks. But the fleeing shape slipped back into the night.

Lights began to appear from the mastheads of the Rus ships. As if in response, rows of lanterns appeared before and behind the Rus ships at a distance of several hundred ells. Haraldr watched the flaring lamps with utter horror. The lights were paired, one from each mast of the mighty *dhromons.* The beasts were stirring in the night.

The *dhromons* bellowed as they had during the day, but their lights remained motionless, a still, precise constellation against the dark water. Haraldr searched the brilliant formation for movement. The beasts bellowed again. Again Haraldr saw the darting gray silhouette of Lyashko's ship.

Two lights began to move, passing the motionless row of similar pairs. They were tracking in the direction of the evanescent silhouette. The twin lights moved swiftly, heading east almost a thousand ells away.

In an instant the night became day. With a whooshing, roaring sound, a liquid comet, a searing, exploding rainbow of fire, arced over the water. The huge flame-spitting snout of the *dhromon* glared like molten gold. At the other end of the terrible arc, Lyashko's ship exploded in a volcanic pillar of flame.

The storm of fire almost immediately wilted the rigging of the Rus ship and the human forms that for an appalling instant could be seen staggering within the inferno. Daylight burst again, and the water itself began to burn around the red-veiled shape of the boat. Before the brilliance of the second fiery rainbow had faded, a third spout of flame arced from the *dhromon* in a monstrous exhalation.

Lyashko's ship, laden with wax, simply exploded. A ball of fire thundered back into the sky and rolled toward the vault of heaven. Only splintered timbers were left to be consumed by the flaming waters.

The rows of twin lights, their work done, winked out, leaving the blazing slick to light the pall like a solitary, eerie eruption from the darkest depths of the sea.

Haraldr spent the rest of the awful night staring out at the incandescent city from the prow of his ship. *The dragon I have slain,* he told himself, *was merely a toy of the mind, a creature of my thoughts. Tonight I have seen real dragons, the creatures wrought by men, and they are infinitely more terrifying. And how, if I must, will I ever slay them?*

† † †

The backs of the porters glistened, doused with the heat of the high afternoon sun. Haraldr stood uneasily on the dock, trying to regain his sense of the earth beneath him. He imagined he would never become used to the din of this city. It was a human cataract that roared, shrieked, and buzzed unceasingly.

"Five more barrels and we're done!" sang out Gleb in his happiest growl. "Then we'll drink Greek wine and all have aching skulls in the morning!"

Haraldr was about to turn to Halldor and ask him to check on the progress of the off-loading of the other Varangian ships. They all needed to gather and discuss—

"Haraldr Nor-briv."

Haraldr stared in astonishment. The dark little man tugging at his sleeve looked like a marmot, dark and hairy-faced and no larger than a five-year-old Norse boy. He wore a dirty, pale yellow cap, tied around his head with a ribbon, and a faded, yellow silk robe with several tears and holes in it. He might have just crawled out from a burrow, but he spoke Norse!

"Quickly, quickly, Haraldr Norbriv. You have five hundred Varangians conscripted with you. Nicephorus Argyrus knows; indeed he does." The marmot-man pointed to the crest of the city where the great palaces ran on endlessly. "Nicephorus Argyrus. Yes, indeed he does know." The marmot-man chuckled conspiratorially. "Well, he wants all five hundred. Yes, yes, you heard me correctly—all five hundred." Marmot-Man tugged frantically at Haraldr's sleeve and tried to pull him closer. His breath smelled like fish. His voice dropped to a harsh whisper. "Nicephorus Argyrus offers you five bezants to enroll each man, and wages to consist—" Marmot-Man broke off and his dark pupils dilated with fright. He maneuvered himself behind Haraldr.

Haraldr turned at the sound of hooves clamoring on the paved street that ran by the wharf. Mounted on dazzlingly white horses, a contingent of perhaps two dozen men in short red tunics, bronze breastplates, and kilts made of leather strips swept aside the dockside traffic; they were armed with short, thrusting swords and long-shafted spears from which flew scarlet-and-gold banners.

The horsemen stopped in formation a few paces from Haraldr. A single rider moved forward, reined his immaculately groomed horse, and looked down at Haraldr. The rider had clipped-short dark hair and beard and taut, leather-tough, tanned skin. His hard, unflinching eyes were colored like the Rus Sea at dawn.

The horseman peered around Haraldr and saw the cringing little Marmot-Man. He exploded in a fury of apparent obscenities, lowered his spear, and teasingly prodded Marmot-Man and sent him scurrying off. Then he turned to a handsome, barrel-chested blond man in the first rank behind him and spoke rapidly. Haraldr heard the words *Nicephorus Argyrus*, *Varangian*, and *Basileus* mentioned. The dark-haired horseman didn't seem faintly amused, but the blond-haired man smiled, showing perfect white teeth, and shook his head.

"Aral-tes . . . Ork-vit. So-ree. No . . . talk Tauro-Scyth."

The dark-haired man held up his hand. "Wait."

Haraldr understood the crude stab at his name and the message. But Tauro-Scyth? Was that the Greek name for Norse? As Haraldr considered this two more figures emerged from the dockside traffic and walked toward him; the two men daintily pulled up the hems of their street-length blue silk tunics and gingerly picked their way over the paving stones as if they were walking in cow dung. Haraldr immediately recognized the arrogantly contemplative Legatharios who had so studiously ignored him the previous day, and the short, blond-haired interpreter who had instructed him in the treaty provisions.

As he had the day before, the interpreter carried a stack of documents written on a curious, very thin, and supple membrane unlike any parchment Haraldr had ever seen; the neatly inked characters seemed to dart across the page like busy insects. The interpreter spoke for a moment with the dark-haired horseman. Haraldr sensed a controlled but still quite evident antagonism between the two; he also noticed with great interest that the Legatharios was ignoring the Byzantine horsemen as magisterially as he had the Rus *barbaroi*.

The dark-haired horseman reached into a leather pouch attached to his saddle and produced a folded, curiously purple-tinted document tied with a cord secured by two coin-shaped seals, one of red wax and the other seemingly pressed in lead, or perhaps even pewter. He handed it to the interpreter.

The interpreter placed the sealed document beneath a single sheet on top of his stack. Then he turned to Haraldr and read from the sheet. "First, Haraldr Nordbrikt, I wish to convey the concern of the Imperial administration over the impudent and unprovoked violation of harbor protocol on the previous evening. Any further contradictions of Imperial authority can result in the abridgement of privileges extended under the terms of our mutual agreement." He paused and removed the message from the top of the sheaf. "We are almost finished checking off your cargoes. When the process is completed, the Prefect will require your entire contingent to reembark for your final berthing place near St. Mama's Quarter. As principal authority over the Rus fleet, Haraldr Nordbrikt bears overall responsibility for the orderly execution of this procedure."

"St. Mama's Quarter?" asked Haraldr.

"The traditional lodging place for you Rus. Outside the walls." The interpreter pointed to the western terminus of the harbor.

"Then we are not to be permitted into the City?"

The interpreter sniffed with contempt. "Once approved by the Prefect, the Rus will be admitted to the city. With escort, and in groups not to exceed fifty men." The interpreter cut off the discussion with a curt nod. He handed the sealed document to the Legatharios, who pressed it to his forehead and then kissed it. Then the Legatharios broke the seals, made no attempt to even unfold the sheet much less read it, and handed it back. Kristr, these Griks are curious, thought Haraldr. Does anyone here do anything for himself?

The interpreter unfolded the document and read it carefully. When he had finished, he spoke to the Legatharios, who snapped back at him irritably. Then the interpreter spoke to the dark-haired horseman, who responded in a steely tone. The only words that Haraldr recognized in the entire exchange were *Varangian* and *Basileus*. But there was also another name that was repeated—Joannes—always preceded by some sort of lengthy, tongue-tangling title. And the name Joannes seemed to settle the matter.

The interpreter glanced at the document and then looked at Haraldr and gestured with his hand as he spoke, as if paraphrasing. "This Topoteretes of the Imperial Scholae requests that in your capacity as commandant of five hundred Varangians you assemble your men when you reach St. Mama's Quarter. You are to be lodged separately from the rest of the Rus. When you arrive, present this order to the Imperial official in charge of final disembarkation. Then you will be escorted to your quarters."

The interpreter handed the document to Haraldr. The writing was in Greek, and in a reddish ink. The broken seals seemed to be impressed with the likeness of a bearded man with long hair; he held a staff with a large ornamental knob. The back of Haraldr's neck tingled. Was this the Emperor?

By the time Haraldr looked up again, the Legatharios and his interpreter were gone, and the horsemen had wheeled their mounts and cantered off in stately procession.

† † †

"This is certainly no prison," Haraldr told Ulfr and Halldor. As he paced, his footfall resounded off the green marble floor and echoed through the vast hall. "Could it be one of their barracks?" He bent over and examined one of the cots that ran in long rows, separated by an aisle, the hundred-ell length of the room. The simple wood frame of the cot, though dented and nicked in places, had been smoothed and finished. The linen-covered mattresses were yellowed and covered with the rings of old stains, but they seemed to have been washed. And they were stuffed with cotton, not straw.

Halldor sat down on one of the mattresses. "There's no inn in Iceland this good. Perhaps they aim to soften us up with comfort. Then . . ." Halldor drew his hand across his neck and grinned.

Haraldr couldn't share Halldor's amusement. He strode to the row of elegantly arched windows that lined the inner wall of the hall. Through the clear panes of glass—some were cracked and a few were missing—he could see the Varangians milling and arguing in groups on the broad lawn that covered the large interior court of the building. Beyond this court was a parallel wing of the huge villa, also filled with beds. At the left end of the court was a complex of empty stables and locked rooms, and at the right end were more rooms and a gate flanked by two large marble pillars. The wooden gate was open, and a wagon loaded with numerous sacks of grain and barrels of ale or wine had just rolled through. Haraldr had no doubt that the gate would again be locked behind them once the stores had been unloaded.

But other than his suspicion that they were under a polite form of arrest, Haraldr had no signal of what the Griks intended to do with him or his pledge-men, and he was wondering if the Griks themselves knew. And what about Marmot-Man? He was no official, but he knew about the Varangians and was trying to hire them, apparently for someone named Nicephorus Argyrus. One thing was certain, however. Haraldr couldn't let the Griks' confusion or subterfuge infect his relationship with his new followers; he had already heard one of the malcontents grumble to the effect that Hakon would already have had them feasting in the Imperial Palace. It wasn't a moment too soon to organize the men into companies and begin to fashion them into a disciplined fighting unit. There, at least, he was on secure ground; as a boy he had seen Olaf turn ragged raiding parties into well-schooled armies a dozen times. And the thought occurred to him that if he was to one day be a king, then he would have to begin his own training. Now.

"Halldor! Ulfr!" barked Haraldr. They looked up, surprised at the unexpected sternness of his tone. "Get the men in here and assigned to beds. In one half hour have them dressed in full armor for drills in the courtyard."

here would you like to be?" asked Maria. She stood before her bedchamber's arcade, and the color of her eyes was so closely keyed to the hot, flat cerulean sky and sea behind her that it appeared they had been painted with the same precious pigment.

"I am at your discretion, mistress," said the eunuch. His name was Isaac. Despite his beardless skin, his jaw was tense and muscular. In his elegant, perfectly fitted silk robe, his frame seemed lithe and supple but with broad, masculine proportions. His blond hair was long and lightly curled.

Maria laughed delightfully. "No, I intend to leave this entirely up to you. Surprise me."

Isaac did not have to deliberate. He was a *vestiopratai,* an Imperially licensed dealer in the finest finished silk goods, and while he numbered many of the Dhynatoi and high-ranking ladies of the court among his customers, this was his first summons to the Gynaeceum, the Imperial women's apartments. He had prepared thoroughly; he could describe the plan and furnishings of the Mistress of the Robes's apartments as accurately as if he been there a dozen times previously. "You are not troubled by the heat?" he asked.

"No. I hate to be cold."

Isaac led Maria to an observation cupola on the roof; he sent her eunuchs for cushions and cold wine. The breeze that whispered through the delicate columns was like silk tissue teased over the skin. He had long ago learned to be expedient, and as soon as the cushions and goblets had been properly placed, he unlaced Maria's scaramangium. She stepped out of the robe and stood on the marble bench so that her body was exposed to the breeze. Isaac hardened her nipples with butter-smooth fingers, then took the chilled wine in his mouth. When he touched his cold tongue to her nipple, she convulsed and whimpered. His tongue slid toward her navel but she pushed him away. She unlaced him and stripped off his robe. He was as solid and as smooth as a statue. She fell to her knees and ran her tongue along the tawny mass of scar tissue at the base of his erection, then toward the engorged tip. "It is so beautiful," she said. "When you are almost ready, come inside me."

Isaac was in fact both a eunuch and a silk dealer. But his principal vocation was making this sort of call on wealthy, highly placed women, a vocation for which he was uniquely suited. While the operation to create a eunuch was usually performed in childhood, some boys like Isaac had their testicles surgically removed in mid-adolescence. Although their bodies might never develop fully masculine characteristics, their ability to function sexually, and their desire to do so, could sometimes remain intact. Such a eunuch offered a highly placed woman two invaluable attributes. He usually would not arouse suspicion, and he could not impregnate them.

When they had finished, Isaac reclined on the tasseled cushions; he always provided his customers an opportunity to talk. Maria sat and shaded her eyes against the sun as she looked out toward Chrysopolis, the huge city across the Bosporus. "You are better than I had hoped," she said.

Isaac smiled. "Most eunuchs can function physically, I have found. Unless, of course, they have had the entire male apparatus removed." But this catastrophic surgery was rare; because the operation was so dangerous and the wound caused recurring problems even when healed, it was usually only performed on Pechenegs or other *barbaroi* races. "That they do not is usually a matter of inadequate desire. Or technique."

Maria laughed. "What technique was required for me?"

"That was desire. Is there any man who hasn't desired you?"

"I want something beyond desire. Still, I enjoyed this. You are like a boy, and yet also a man. I will want you again. I have a lover, and another boy with whom I am in love. But my specialist advises me that on certain days I must abstain if I do not want unintended consequences. Still, the more regularly one enjoys passion, the more one becomes addicted. If I did not have a lover now, I would not need you so badly."

"I am at your discretion, Mistress."

"Do you work with men?"

"Only if a lady asks for another man to join us."

"Have you ever had a Tauro-Scythian?"

"No. I would try to find one if you are interested."

"No." Maria looked down and stroked her flat, velvet-soft belly. "Do you know what they are going to do with those Tauro-Scythians they are calling pirates?" Maria understood the efficiency with which information passed among the city's highly placed eunuchs; it was as if they had all joined in some secret pact to punish the society that had deprived them of their manhood by exposing its secrets.

"They are still arguing. The military are quite set on simply massacring the entire lot now that their ships are unloaded. They say there is still a threat of invasion."

Maria snorted. "The military are the stooges of the Dhynatoi. The Dhynatoi have never forgotten how Basil the Bulgar-Slayer used the Varangians against them." Almost a half century earlier, Basil the Bulgar-Slayer had recruited a large force of Norse mercenaries to put down a revolt of the Dhynatoi. The Varangians had been so effective in crushing internal opposition that Basil had created the Varangian Guard to permanently institutionalize their role as the sentinels of Imperial power; over the succeeding decades the Varangians had come to be seen as the champions of the middle and lower classes, who relied on the protection of a strong Emperor, and the sworn enemies of the selfishly ambitious landed aristocracy.

"Somehow the rumor has gotten started that there is a Tauro-Scythian Prince among the traders," Isaac said. "The Grand Domestic"—the Grand Domestic was the Empire's highest-ranking military commander— "has elaborated this gossip into a theory that this prince intends to enter the city with his Varangians, then summon a huge invasion force lurking somewhere in the Rus Sea, and open the gates for them when they arrive. The Grand Domestic is determined to find this man, even if it means resorting to the kind of crude measures with which Herod hoped to indemnify himself against the Christ child. He has already had the Rus traders interrogated."

"How fascinating!" Maria's eyes sparkled like a child's. "I wonder if the fair-hairs will eat our flesh and drink our blood, as the prophets have foretold." For centuries the "fair-haired nations" had been cast as the agents of doom in so many Byzantine tales of the apocalypse that their role was as well-known as that of the Antichrist.

"I think it is all nonsense," said Isaac. "Of course, there is no such prince, and all the talk of action on the part of the Grand Domestic is bluster. It always is. What everyone will probably end up agreeing to do is to execute this bandit who killed the Manglavite, though they should rightly give him a palace near the Forum Bovis—send the rest of the Tauro-Scythians off to garrison Ancyra, and be done with it."

"Yes," said Maria distractedly. She put her hand on Isaac's thigh. "I suppose that compromise would make everyone except the Tauro-Scythian bandit happy."

he bronze breastplates and the brilliant white horses flickered in the sun. The same mounted contingent that had greeted Haraldr three days ago at the docks rode stiffly into the courtyard. The tough-looking Topoteretes dismounted and looked around. Haraldr discerned that the Byzantine officer was more than a bit impressed by the sight of almost five hundred armored Norse giants slashing, shoving, and grunting in martial cacophony.

A black-frocked civilian mounted on a mule rode in among the horses: John, the interpreter with the squinched, hairless face. Interesting, Haraldr thought, that the same interpreter was assigned to the navy and now this group of horsemen. Perhaps there were fewer Norse interpreters than it seemed at first. That meant they might run into Gregory again. And then they might be able to get some information about the bewilderingly formal, circuitous Griks.

John the interpreter looked about, spotted Haraldr, and nudged his mule toward the *barbaroi* chieftain. "Haraldr Nordbrikt, come with us," he said as if he were a gaoler addressing a prisoner.

"Where?" shot back Haraldr. His blood was spiced from three days of hard martial drills, and he decided to get some answers from these Griks for a change.

The interpreter stared sullenly. Haraldr noticed that his head and face were freshly shaven; with this smooth skin John looked like a pink frog.

"Where?" Haraldr repeated.

"City," said John, as if answering an insistent, squalling child.

Inside the walls! Haraldr's breast drummed. He snapped for one of the Byzantine servants—or were they spies—who were always loitering around. With hand motions he indicated he wanted a washbasin and a clean tunic.

"That won't be necessary," snapped John.

Haraldr's stomach plunged like cold lead. In his sweaty, torn tunic the only place he would be fit to be received would be in a slave-gang. Or a dungeon. Well, he would not let this black-frocked frog march him off. He continued to motion to the servants and sent them twittering on their errands. John stared angrily but said nothing. The Topoteretes walked over and spoke to the interpreter, who rattled on irritably and pointed at Haraldr. Many *barbarois* peppered the recitation. The Topoteretes shrugged and went back to studying the drilling Norsemen.

Halldor walked up. "I'm going into the city," Haraldr told him. "You've got command until I return; Ulfr is your marshal and counselor. You know the drill schedule, so keep to it. I'll be back." The servants brought up the washbasin and one of Hakon's silk tunics, and Haraldr splashed water on his face and toweled dry. When he looked up, Halldor was still observing him earnestly. "Yes. If I don't come back," Haraldr concluded, "you have the command permanently."

† † †

The mounted escort wound through the narrow streets of St. Mama's Quarter, looping around the back of a domed church, huge by Norse standards but relatively small in relation to the surrounding buildings. As the stone-paved avenue straightened out, Haraldr could see an expanse of mowed grass ahead. He looked up and gasped.

The great land wall, which traversed the width of the peninsula on which Constantinople had been built, had been only partially visible as they had sailed into St. Mama's Quarter. Now, from an unobstructed head-on view, it seemed like a vast, tiered, many-towered city unto itself. The first line of defense, a moat as broad as a small river—it was partitioned by a series of dikes that enabled it to climb up and down the gently rolling hills—would alone have been the engineering miracle of the north. Just beyond the moat was a brick parapet about as high as the walls of a Rus city; then a broad, graded path; and finally a second wall of unimaginable dimensions; the alternating courses of stone and brick rose a good twenty ells and were studded with massive stone turrets at regular intervals. Beyond this colossal defense was the main wall.

This third wall was at least as tall as a Norse dragon-ship stood on end, and yet the towering rectangular fortresses set against the sheer brick-and-stone surface at intervals of sixty ells (they looked like the teeth of some world-devouring beast as they ran off into the distance as far as one could see) were twice again as tall; each of these Titan-made towers was a soaring castle capable of defending an entire city the size of Kiev. Perhaps the gods had built these defenses, but not even the gods would dare come against them.

A small, open gate framed by carved stone beams punctured the great wall. Several officials in long silk tunics—one of the silk-clads seemed to be a eunuch—examined the documents presented by the Topoteretes, then began to question him insistently. The eunuch looked at Haraldr and shook his head. The Topoteretes pointed to something in the document and began a heated discourse. Haraldr observed that Basileus and Joannes and Manglavite figured in his argument. The eunuch protested again but the documents were returned to the Topoteretes, and he signaled his men to ride on. The escort tunneled through the wall and emerged on a brilliant white landscape.

A stone-paved avenue more than a hundred ells wide extended beyond the wall toward the distant heart of the city. On either side of the street the three- and four-story buildings rose like sheer cliffs, though these palaces often had marble-columned arcades at street level and elaborate balconies and rows of arched windows on the upper floors. Pack mules, wagons, slave-borne canopied litters, and ordinary pedestrians jammed the street; they passed one four-wheeled carriage with an elaborately gilded, curtained, boxlike enclosure for its invisible occupants. Haraldr struggled to capture details as his escort led him down the avenue at a brisk canter: an arcade rollicking with roughly dressed men who hoisted wineskins as they disputed over board games and tossed dice; a statue of an unclothed man set into a niche above a brass-fitted oak door, so astonishingly lifelike that one could see the veins beneath his pale marble skin; a shorn black-frock, like John the interpreter, offering bread to three ragged beggars who sat on a scrolled stone bench. There were far fewer women than men about, and most of them had wrapped bright cloth veils about their faces and moved in protective clusters. But one young woman with a brightly painted face strutted alluringly alone.

The escort paused at a major intersection less than a dozen blocks into the city. Looking south, down the paved street perpendicular to the main avenue, Haraldr saw enormous, featureless, russet-brick edifices, looming some six, even seven, stories high. People milled about on the street and stuck their heads out of the innumerable windows. For the first time Haraldr noticed that the sky over the Great City was strangely dingy. He quickly established the source of the pollution; maybe another dozen blocks due east from these buildings was a huge, gritty pillar of smoke, fouling the entire horizon. Not far away, another shaft of soot rose above visible tongues of flame; glowing cinders shot up into the roiling black column. Was the Great City on fire?

Neither the Topoteretes nor his men took notice of this catastrophe; they had been distracted by the approach of another contingent of a dozen mounted men quite similar in arms and attire to their own. The leader of these horsemen had a sweat-beaded, squarish face and red, irritated eyes, as if he had just ridden right through the smoke. The Topoteretes tipped his head deferentially, and the red-eyed man spoke with animated gestures. Then the red-rimmed eyes turned to Haraldr, widened in surprise, and he immediately gave the Topoteretes what seemed to be a brusque order. The Topoteretes produced the magical documents again and the red-eyed horseman looked at them, handed them back, and thought for a moment. He snapped to one of his men, there was some probing of saddle packs, and a length of dark cloth was finally handed to the Topoteretes. The Topoteretes then spoke to John the interpreter.

"You have to be blindfolded."

Haraldr iced with terror. There was no reason, unless they intended to put a blade to his neck. Two horsemen were already at his side. He reflexively pushed them away. His horse reared, and more horsemen closed around him. He threw one right out of the saddle, but a blow cracked his head. Sparks showered as he sent another Byzantine flying off his horse. Hands clutched all over him, he heard a sound like a glacier fracturing and smashing into his head, and a brilliant light exploded into darkness.

ce. He was in a huge ice cave. His head throbbed and his neck ached. How had he gotten back to Norway? Had he ever left? Yes. The pounding in his head had a pattern; he could think between the metallic throbs. Yes. He had left. River. City. Haraldr jerked erect. His eyes focused. Ice. Somehow the Griks had carved a room from ice. The pure white light, more diffuse than day but almost as bright, momentarily defeated Haraldr's quest for reason. Then he shaded his eyes and concentrated, bringing his mind back. The ice was stone. Incredible stone. A dazzling white marble with sinuous blue veins. His head lolled and he strained to study the complex pattern on the floor, knowing that if he understood it, his mind would come back. The floor was paved with polished marble, a woven pattern of bands and circles of emerald and ruby-colored marble. The light that glazed the marble seemed to come from high above. He looked up. Light flooded in from a ring of windows set at an impossible height.

"You shouldn't have fought." The frog face of John the interpreter leered at him, but he was speaking the words of the Topoteretes, who crouched over Haraldr with apparent concern. "The blindfold was just a precaution."

Against what? thought Haraldr, painfully reorienting. *To keep me from seeing what? So I won't know my way to . . . what? Where exactly am I?* Haraldr rubbed his head and looked around the vast hall. Dozens of finely dressed eunuchs circulated, buzzing in discussion with one another as well as some soldiers, four or five dark-skinned Saracens, and several big, shaved-headed men in poor brown wool tunics little better than those worn by Norse slaves.

Just a few paces from Haraldr an excruciatingly thin eunuch with a curiously flabby, pale face abruptly terminated his conversation and minced delicately, on slippered feet, toward Haraldr's group. With one sweep of his narrowly spaced hazel eyes the eunuch managed to look right through the Topoteretes, give the merest hint of contempt at the sight of the black-frocked interpreter, and completely ignore Haraldr. One hand propped on his bony hip, the eunuch extended the spidery fingers of the other. The Topoteretes placed the documents in the eunuch's outstretched hand. The eunuch unfolded the packet with the very tips of his fingers, as if the pages had been dipped in fresh dung. He was clearly less impressed than the previous inspectors; he brusquely flipped through even the purple-tinted document. But the eunuch did pause over a plain-colored sheet, and something he read caused one of his thin, seemingly painted-on eyebrows to quiver slightly. That was the only reaction he betrayed. Without a word he folded the packet, turned, and walked off.

"You follow him," commanded John the interpreter in his sourest tone. "And don't try any more stupid *barbaroi* tricks."

The eunuch never once looked back to see if Haraldr was following. He exited the great hall and, after a long, winding transit over marble-paved corridors, stopped in front of heavy wooden double doors laced with gilt trim. He pulled a yellow silken cord that dangled near the door frame; to Haraldr's astonishment the doors slid silently open, as if they ran on greased tracks. Without even looking at Haraldr, the eunuch rolled his eyes toward the aperture.

The room was bright and strangely warm and humid; marble benches and compartments lined the walls. Two young boys dressed in short white tunics waited by the doors. "Clothes," said one of the boys in a heavily accented attempt at Norse. With motions he indicated that Haraldr should take his clothes off. They don't bathe a man before they toss him in a dungeon, thought Haraldr with constrained relief. Still, he could not escape the sensation that death, however perfumed and silk-frocked, stalked this place. He remembered what Gleb had said. The Griks were never straightforward about anything.

Haraldr stripped and was shown through a door at the end of the room. He was greeted by a blast of hot, steamy air. His eyes watered and for an instant he thought he would be attacked. Then the wonder of the place hit him. The large domed chamber was almostly completely filled with a brilliantly blue pool; at the bottom of the pool was a shimmering illusion, a twining green garden depicted with multicolored bits of tile.

Haraldr luxuriated in the cleansing heat and the cold water; how long had it been since he had enjoyed a sauna? The pain at the back of his head subsided to a dull ache and he began to reassemble his scattered wits. *Put aside your fear,* he told himself. *Presume that you come as the leader of five hundred Varangians, not a condemned criminal; they had you at their mercy on the street, and yet look where you are now. You have the instrument to serve the Griks, and they clearly have the wealth to serve your ends. But why with every question that*

*is answered are there two new ones? Who is Nicephorus Argyrus? And what was it
the Griks didn't want you to see?*

When he had finished bathing, Haraldr was toweled and combed and
rubbed with scented oil, then dressed in a long tunic of very fine white
silk; the high collar was crusted with heavy embroidery. Back in the
marble hall, two eunuchs, both of them surprisingly stout, waited for him
along with the birch-thin eunuch who had led him here originally. His
head cocked in annoyance, the spindly eunuch cast his eyes over Haraldr
as if he had been forced to look at a mutilated corpse. He turned to the
other two and compressed his thin lips in an attitude of bored, barest
approval; then his wretchedly bony shoulders shuddered slightly and he
minced off.

The two big eunuchs flanked Haraldr and each firmly but decorously
took an elbow. The hallway eventually turned into a large, sun-flooded
arcade. Haraldr squinted out over a blazing expanse of white marble. He
could see patches of peacock-blue sea framing a massive templelike structure several hundred ells away. Then he turned to his left. He gasped and
knew for certain where he was.

Spread out over a gentle slope was a glittering jewel box that was an
entire city. Fantastic, multicolored buildings stood on verdant terraces
laced with neat rows of flowering trees, shimmering azure ponds and
pools, and beds of vermilion blossoms. Scores of domes, held aloft by
columns of brilliant jade-green marble or deep plum-colored porphyry,
formed swirling patterns so deft and intricate that they seemed to have
been painted against the backdrop of sea and sky. Here in a magical city
within the Great City was the home of the Emperor.

The eunuchs tightened their grip and led Haraldr toward the prodigious building straight ahead; six white columns, so huge in girth that
were they hollow a man could build a comfortable cottage within them,
thrust up to a marble roof at a dizzying height. Beneath the portico,
two-story silver double doors, embossed with fierce-visaged, armored
eagles, were surrounded by a perfect, motionless semicircle of powerful,
dark-eyed men in burnished steel breastplates and steel helms. Haraldr
observed the guards' dusky, foreign features with a sharpness in his
breast; these men were Khazars, from Serah's homeland. The armored
arc split momentarily to allow Haraldr and his escort to pass. The enormous doors slid open as silently as those in the bath.

Paradise. It was not simply the vastness of the hall; a bowman could not
have shot the length of the jeweled cavern and the ceiling, coffered with
elaborate gold beams flecked with silver medallions, soaring like a fantas-

tic sky. It was the supernatural sumptuousness: pearl-white marble columns topped with plum-colored capitals wreathed with carved vines and flower buds, candelabra that looked like lacy silver clouds dotted with glinting ice crystals, drapes of braided ivy, garlands of pink roses, hanging tapestries stitched with lustrous flowers.

The entire back of the hall was cloaked with a vast purple drape, damasked with hundreds of huge eagles embroidered in gold. Forming a sort of funnel beneath the hangings were two ranks of soldiers in golden armor, bearing standards topped with golden eagles and dragons. A single figure stood at the very end of the funnel, in front of a now-visible seam where the two halves of the curtain met. Haraldr's heart leapt to his throat.

This man was as tall and broad as Hakon. He wore a golden breastplate and a plumed golden helmet with metal cheek pieces folded over his entire face, concealing all save glints of blue behind the eye slits. A Varangian Guard, certainly, and very likely Mar Hunrodarson himself. *I would not have expected this Paradise to end at the executioner's block,* thought Haraldr with a groin-stabbing renewal of his fear. *But I am told that the Griks rarely do the expected.*

The Varangian stood perfectly motionless, an immense silver-bladed broadax inlaid with elaborate gold niello pressed to his chest. Like a rodent mesmerized by a snake, Haraldr was drawn to the eerie glimmer of life visible within the eye slits, expecting some evidence of malice or recognition. But the guarded irisies were so still, they might have been bits of glass.

The curtain drew aside slightly and the eunuchs led Haraldr past the rigid Varangian. The rest came like a frantic episode in a fantastic dream. He was in a vast, rose-scented, many-domed hall echoing with an unsettling, powerfully sonorous music that pulsed within his very bones. The hall was filled with a living rainbow, hundreds of utterly motionless, silk-sheathed, bejeweled figures arrayed in perfectly concentric semicircles, each ring a different dazzling hue. The rainbow was broken in the middle by a great massing of incandescent gold: a throne the size of a small building flanked by two large trees with leaves of delicate gold; gem-bright birds perched in the gilt branches. As Haraldr approached, the birds tittered and called in a supernatural melody, cocking their brilliant heads and flapping their wings. Haraldr came to the terrifying realization that the birds were in fact jewels, creatures of enameled gold to which somehow the Griks had given the power of both movement and voice. Then the beasts came to life from behind the trees and the blood drained from Haraldr's face and his knees buckled. Lions! Creatures of the gods! The great beasts rushed forward to devour him, tails pounding the ground and huge jaws gaping. They roared like the trumpets of doom, and Haraldr reflexively felt for the pommel of the sword that he had been forced to leave back in the barracks.

The lions halted as if the gods themselves had turned them to stone. Reason tried to command Haraldr's whirling senses. Not stone but metal. The lions were incredible metal creatures, just like the birds. But this deduction did nothing to assuage fear. What wizardry, or, more frighteningly, what knowledge did this Emperor possess?

The huge throne was covered with a purple satin canopy and encrusted with gemstones and iridescent white pearls. The giant god who might have occupied this grandiose furnishing was not present. Instead, a mechanical man sat to one side of the vast cushion. His body was metal. No, he was swathed in a full-length tunic of stiff purple brocade covered with mazelike courses of gems and precious spangles and flocking eagles of flickering gold thread. He wore a jeweled, helmetlike cap, and no winter sky was as thick with stars as this cap was with gemstones; they spilled from the crown in sparkling runnels that streamed down the mechanical man's eerily human cheeks. The device's eyes were agates polished to a watery sheen. Kristr! Not agates. These eyes moved! They were wet with life. This was a living man! No, not a man. A god. Perhaps all-conquering Kristr himself.

The two eunuchs threw Haraldr to the floor and prostrated themselves alongside him; this ritual of obeisance was repeated three times. Then the eunuchs raised Haraldr to his feet. He looked for the throne and moaned with awe. The entire gold edifice floated high overhead, the purple canopy seemingly grazing the gold-flecked dome. Kristr—He could be no other—looked down on him from his rightful position above all mortals.

His head craned back, dully gaping, Haraldr tried to focus his entire will on reason's moribund whispers, and for a moment he found a certain mental equilibrium. Metal dragons and lions and birds and fire that burns on water and now this. The rest are the creations of men, and so this must be as well. He clung to that thought even as his terrified awe rushed him off, as savagely as the currents of the Dnieper, on the dark river of ignorance and superstition. No, no, reason struggled, all the works of men. But if this is the Emperor, does it matter that he is not immortal Kristr? He is a man made a god, with the power of the gods.

An elderly eunuch in a gold-hemmed robe approached slowly and deliberately; age spots covered his bald head. He looked directly at Haraldr, his steady gaze a startling contrast to the condescending evasion practiced by the lesser officials. The eunuch's pale gray eyes were sad, weary, and ancient, as if he had seen the cares of a dozen lives. He motioned for Haraldr to bring his head down.

"Your father, the Lord of the Entire World, Emperor, Basileus, and Autocrator of the Romans, greets you, his son," the eunuch whispered next to Haraldr's ear; his Norse was fluent. "His Imperial Majesty has taken a personal interest in the matter of the death of the Manglavite." Haraldr's entire body quaked as if he were bewitched. "After ordering officers of the court to take depositions in the matter, and advised of their findings, he has instructed the Logothete of the Praetorium to release his files concerning the incident of the third of June, fifth year of the indiction, year of the Creation six thousand five hundred and thirty-three. Your father the Emperor offers you probationary conditions, subject to summary revocation. You may remain past the winter, but you are not to be readmitted to the palace, nor will you or your men be offered service under the Imperial standards until your files have been readmitted to the Logothete of the Praetorium." The eunuch paused and furrowed the thin, veined skin of his brow. "That will be in approximately eight months, before the spring campaigns. You may reenter the city during this period only under conditions of private employ approved by the Logothete of the Symponus."

Reason quickly revived under the comforting aegis of relief. *I have been partially exonerated,* thought Haraldr, his newly unburdened mind more supple than it had been all day. *But for obvious reasons the Emperor still questions the loyalty of myself and my men. Private employ? Could that be what this mysterious Nicephorus Argyrus is about?*

The aged eunuch tugged at Haraldr's sleeve and brought him even closer. "That is his Imperial Majesty's position of record." The eunuch's pale eyes roamed for a moment, and then his voice dropped to the barest audible level. "Privately, his Imperial Majesty asks that you be advised to leave the Queen of Cities, and the Roman Empire for that matter, altogether." The old eunuch paused and looked up at Haraldr. "Immediately."

The eunuch released Haraldr's silken sleeve and the two stout eunuchs spun him about and led him from the throne of the Emperor, Basileus, and Autocrator of the Romans out into the lesser light of day.

hrow him out?" asked Halldor. "No, you don't have to worry that I did that. I've been trying to get information from him for an hour. He chatters like a rodent, but not much gets said. These Griks just aren't very forthcoming with foreigners. He claims that his master, this Nicephorus Argyrus, knows quite a bit, however. He even says that you've seen the Emperor and been granted what he calls a 'conditional amnesty.' He says that we are free to accept private employment. And that's why he's here. He says that Nicephorus Argyrus invites you to dine with him tonight and discuss his proposal."

Haraldr looked at Ulfr—his relief at Haraldr's return was as obvious as Halldor's was deceptively concealed—then at Halldor and nodded. Nicephorus Argyrus did indeed know. Haraldr had left the presence of the Emperor only several hours ago; he had been detained for a while in several parchment-piled offices full of fluttering eunuchs and pale clerks and scribes. Apparently Nicephorus Argyrus had somehow received word of the ruling and had dispatched his emissary almost immediately.

"Well, let's hope the rest of his information is as good," said Halldor. He grabbed Haraldr's arm and led him and Ulfr into what must once have been a supply room—the wooden shelves were now barren—and shut the door.

Halldor lowered his voice cautiously. "When we were recruited by Hakon, he led us to believe that after a short training period those of us who qualified would be initiated into the Emperor's Varangian Guard. According to Marmot-Man, that would have been impossible. Not only do members of the guard have to complete a period of service outside the Great City, but also to enter the guard they have to pay an entrance fee. Well, I asked how much that might be, and since I don't know how Grik money works, I opened up Hakon's chest and took out one of his gold coins and held it up. Marmot-Man just laughed. Then he reached in the chest and pulled out Hakon's belt, the one entirely covered with hundreds of gold coins, and said, 'About this much.' I said, 'You mean for all five hundred?' He just laughed again and said no, that all the gold in Hakon's belt was probably enough to pay the entrance fee for *one* man."

Haraldr blinked incredulously. There was enough money in Hakon's belt to purchase several counties in Norway. And this was what one man paid to *serve* the Emperor?

"According to Marmot-Man," continued Halldor, "Hakon never intended for us to enter the Guard. His plan was to contract our services for the Emperor's campaigns, pay us a few pieces of silver, and keep the rest for himself. And this on top of a substantial bonus for recruiting us in the first place. If we had started to grumble about our wages, he would have seen to it that we were sent on an expedition far into Serkland or some such place, from which few if any of us would return. Marmot-Man says that he's already done this with two smaller groups of recruits in previous years."

"The Emperor permits this?" asked Haraldr. "I'd hardly pay a cheat to guard my back."

"Perhaps the Emperor does not know," offered Ulfr.

Perhaps, thought Haraldr. *And what else might be beyond the Emperor's knowledge, and perhaps also beyond his control? I could not tell whether the "advice" the Emperor presented me with today was a threat or a warning. And if it is a warning, is it possible that the Emperor and I share the same enemy?*

"Could you discover what role Mar Hunrodarson plays in all this?" asked Haraldr.

Halldor shook his head. "I just mentioned the name Mar Hunrodarson to Marmot-Man and I thought he was going to scurry out of the room. You might have thought I had offered to conjure a demon."

"My feeling," said Ulfr, "is that by Grik standards Hakon was just a sand-kicker. Mar Hunrodarson, on the other hand, is playing a game with the gods."

"You may be right about that, Ulfr." Haraldr went on to describe the message he had received in the presence of the Emperor. "If the Griks love a ruse, what ruse could be more fitting than for this man-god that I saw today to have a personal guard he cannot trust? Consider that the Emperor had the power to swat me like a bug today, and who would have protested, or for that matter even have known? Instead he pardoned me for the slaying of a high Imperial official, yet in the next breath he made it quite clear that my life was in jeopardy here. And who more than Mar would want me dead?"

"But what you are saying is that the Norseman is playing the ruse on the Griks," said Ulfr.

"No," said Haraldr. "What I mean is that there may be a hidden power that Mar and his Varangians really serve, and that the Imperial Throne itself is a ruse, or at least a sort of illusion." The thought, even as speculative as it was, made Haraldr shudder. What power could be greater than the man-god Emperor, except the power of the gods themselves?

Haraldr looked at Ulfr and Halldor. "It's time I greet our visitor. And get one of Hakon's best robes ready for me. Tonight I'm meeting Nicephorus Argyrus."

† † †

Maria placed her palms flat on Alexandros's powerful chest and waited until he had stilled. She did not look at his face. She raised herself slightly, and his slick, now flaccid penis fell out of her. She swung her leg over his body and padded to the floor. She walked naked into her antechamber; her breast was still rouged with passion, her hair tousled. Giorgios sat at the small ivory-topped table, staring morosely at his long, artistic fingers. Maria sat beside him and took his hand; it was lifeless, unable to respond to her caress. "I love you," she whispered.

Alexandros came in, also naked, his ample manhood flapping like a banner of his virility. Maria stood and flexed her back; Alexandros came around behind her and kissed her neck and raised her nipples with his fingers. After a moment Maria pulled loose. "We are going to have the most extraordinary evening," she said. "We are going to Nicephorus Argyrus's." Everyone in Constantinople knew the name; Argyrus was a former provincial army commander who had become the most successful merchant in all Byzantium; some said he was even wealthier than the Emperor, although that was also said of several of the Dhynatoi. But Argyrus was the only merchant who could persuade the august Dhynatoi to dine at his town palace—at least those Dhynatoi who had been forced, because of overenthusiastic land speculation or simple mismanagement of their estates, to borrow money from Argyrus. The very integration of the classes—and sexes—at Argyrus's dinners was considered a scandal of itself; the tales told of his entertainments were a catalogue of vices, though most of the gossip was patently false or, at best, wildly exaggerated.

"Argyrus has brought us a famous eremite from Cappadocia, I am told. They say he last left his cave when the Bulgar-Slayer was a boy. I don't believe that for a moment. But he will bring us luck. Also, Argyrus is going to display for us the Tauro-Scythian who murdered the Manglavite. I have been told that this is the last opportunity we will have to see him." Alexandros seemed very keen at the mention of this attraction; even

Giorgios cocked his head with interest. "I am taking all my little ladies-in-waiting so that they can see him, and the Hetairarch has agreed to come and translate for me, though I think Argyrus also has a man." Alexandros did not seemed pleased that the Hetairarch would be along; he had heard that Maria had once kept company with him. "Then, when we leave Argyrus's, I can send my ladies home with the Hetairarch." Alexandros's scowl fled. "And we three can visit that inn in the Venetian Quarter."

Alexandros and Giorgios looked at each other with naked alarm. The Venetian Quarter, home to the considerable contingent of traders from Venice, was almost as notoriously lawless as the vast Studion slum, though it was a much smaller enclave. The Venetian sailors were considered virtual savages, and the only women who ever entered their environs were the most used-up and disease-ravaged whores, who could find employment nowhere else. Maria had several times expressed an almost morbid interest in a Venetian Quarter inn where these women were said to service their customers on the tabletops.

"I don't think you would be safe there," said Giorgios, his eyes mournful and frightened.

Maria opened her knees slightly and stroked her fingers once along the tops of her inner thighs, just beneath her vulva; the gesture was as mechanical and distracted as an animal cleaning itself yet almost breathtakingly erotic. She looked up at Giorgios. "If you don't think you can protect me, then don't go."

he black waters wrapped around the brilliant galaxy of Constantinople at night. Haraldr knew the source of many of the lights now: behind him, the flares along the great wall; to each side, sloping away from the spine of the city, the still-bustling wharves and factories; and just ahead, viewed as if from the mast of a ship, the lights of the Imperial Palace. It was as if he stood at the very center of this wondrous constellation, and all around him the Empress City glowed and winked with the splendor of her nocturnal life. And tonight, robed in silk and perfumed with myrrh, Haraldr felt part of her. His fears only seemed to inflame his ardor for this new woman in his breast, to encourage the strange feeling that no matter how perilous this seduction, he did not want to stop it.

"Nicephorus Argyrus has a palace larger than this on the Asian shore of the Bosporus, indeed he does," Marmot-Man interjected into Haraldr's reverie. "Larger still is his palace near Ancyra. Yes, Yes, Nicephorus Argyrus owns a third of the Bucellarion *theme.* But he got out of his Macedonian estates when Basil the Bulgar-Slayer died. Didn't think this new lot could hold the Bulgars back—no, indeed he did not. Still, he likes his town palace best. He hates provincial life, and this terrace is his favorite place."

"This new lot" apparently is not as powerful or competent as the old Bulgar-Slayer, thought Haraldr. Despite the narcotic luxury of the evening, he was endeavoring to note any snippet of information that might be useful.

Haraldr looked around the terrace atop the fourth floor of Nicephorus Argyrus's palace. He could well imagine that a man with this treasure would long for no other place. The rooftop Eden had been planted with small flowering trees, neatly clipped shrubs, and beds of flowers; shallow pools with spouting fountains were surrounded by mossy lawns. Delicate marble pavilions, lit with softly glowing, glass-sheathed oil lamps, were sprinkled among the gardens, and marble pathways meandered from pavilion to pavilion.

"Well, let us return to the main hall, Haraldr Nordbrikt. Nicephorus

Argyrus prefers to conclude his business before he dines, indeed he does." They descended a spiraling marble staircase and emerged into a miniature palace hall, much smaller than the Emperor's but even more splendid; it was paved with pale green marble inlaid with whorls of pure gold and silver and lit by candelabra that looked like silver pine trees bearing scores of light-filled glass cones.

The gathering crowd was equally ornamental. Men and women alike wore elaborate, gold-embroidered silk tunics with high collars and long, gold-laced hems and sleeves; on many of the younger women the fabric seemed little more than a coating of iridescent paint. While virtually every guest was dressed as lavishly as a Rus prince or princess, none of them was accorded the respect shown a miserable beggar literally dressed in rags. His white hair and beard were crudely cropped; his wizened, ghostly pale skin pocked with crusty sores; and his stench was detectable from a dozen ells away. Yet the most corpulent, jewel-laden princes and their ladies crowded around the foul-smelling wretch, kissing his gnarled hands or filthy chest and pressing gold coins to him even though the old beggar simply let the offerings clatter to the floor.

Haraldr was clearly the secondary attraction. Nicephorus Argyrus, a short, well-weathered man with a deeply recessed gray widow's peak and a stout belly that swelled against his carnation-and-gold silk tunic, periodically flicked his hand discreetly in Haraldr's direction, apparently briefly explaining to various guests the identity of the giant curiosity.

Argyrus started toward Haraldr. *Good,* Haraldr thought, *let me do what I came to do, before my wits are seduced by this luxury.* But a eunuch whispered in Argyrus's ear and he stalked off to the entrance vestibule at the far end of the room. The doors opened and a flock of shimmering eunuchs bustled into the hall, followed by a group of very young, very pretty women; almost all of them had their hair coiled on both sides of their heads, and the tightly wrapped tresses were traced with spirals of sparkling pearls and gems. The resplendent young women tried to appear grave and dignified as they entered, but they began to talk animately and even to giggle as they were greeted by the other guests and absorbed into the crowd. Then everyone turned expectantly toward the doors.

She is not real, was Haraldr's first thought of the woman who now entered the hall. *She is the product of the Grik artists who can surpass nature.* Her hair was raven-black, and the pearls set into the twin coils glittered like the lights of the city. Even viewed from across the room, her cobalt-blue eyes were luminous. She wore a tunic of the sheerest alabaster silk veiled with gold floral patterns, yet both her front and back were more modestly concealed by a long, rectangular, scarflike garment of gem-studded carmine brocade.

"Maria," said Marmot-Man worshipfully, as if the name itself were a confession of love. For some reason Haraldr repeated the name softly to himself. He remembered that Maria had been the name of Kristr's mother, the Queen of Paradise.

"She is Her Imperial Majesty's cousin," volunteered Marmot-Man. "The Mistress of the Robes." Marmot-Man wandered toward the vision, drawing Haraldr with him. Two young, arrogant-looking men attired like officers of the Scholae followed Maria into the hall; the longing in the soft brown eyes of the thinner of the two was obvious, and it made Haraldr wonder what his own face now betrayed. Another man entered after the two officers. Haraldr felt as if a sword had whirred through his legs at the knees, leaving the severed halves stacked like segments of a column; if he so much as leaned forward a thumb's width, he would collapse.

The Norseman who walked into the hall was a giant, as tall as and even broader than Haraldr, and yet he bore his enormous strength casually and gracefully. He had a sensitive, slightly feminine mouth and a high, intelligent forehead; the silk-fine hair that swept straight back to his jeweled collar seemed dusted with gold. Haraldr had expected Mar Hunrodarson merely to be a more detestable thug than Hakon; this man had the noble stature of a king. How could he be Mar? And yet if he was not Mar, who was he?

"Who is that man?" asked Haraldr urgently, his blood icing at the frozen look on Marmot-Man's dark little face.

"The Hetairarch," he answered with a tremulous voice.

"His name!" demanded Haraldr, irritated by his own rising panic.

"The Hetairarch . . ." repeated Marmot-Man weakly. He waved his arm like a drowning man, apparently trying to draw the attention of his master.

Nicephorus Argyrus had already moved to greet the Norseman with an effusion that he had shown toward none of the other guests; he chattered nervously and flicked his hands about. The Hetairarch glanced over at Haraldr, but the look was idle, disinterested. Maria turned to the Hetairarch and in a familiar, faintly erotic fashion touched the Norseman's sleeve with her beautiful white hand; Haraldr could see the statue-firm contour of her arm through the gauzy sleeve of her tunic. The two officers who had accompanied Maria made no attempt to mask their glaring disapproval of this contact. Haraldr understood their ire; for a moment he, too, was a jealous boy, raging as he watched his secret love make love to another.

Nicephorus Argyrus flicked his hand toward Marmot-Man and without a word the Marmot-Man scurried away from Haraldr and joined his master and the Hetairarch. The three men and Maria studied him more than casually; their discussion was fairly animated. Unarmed, tongueless without his interpreter, Haraldr felt naked and chained. Had Nicephorus Argyrus been the ruse all along? Would Mar—if this was Mar—kill him here, a mere entertainment for the Empress City's decadent elite?

The three men and woman walked toward Haraldr, bringing along the other guests. The beauty of Maria numbed his fear; if this was his Valkyrja, then Odin favored him even in death. Maria moved like a dancer, her hips swaying gently, exposing a heart-stopping curve as her flank swished against the sheer tunic. Her laughter was like music, her delicate white fingers languorously stroking the air as she talked.

She was close enough that he could smell her, an indescribable fragrance, like a rain-drenched, exotic flower but with the merest hint of musk. Her bow-shaped lips relaxed whimsically, almost teasingly. Her eyebrows were thick, almost gold-tipped near her nose, then thinned and darkened as they rose and fell in gull's-wing curves.

Maria spoke to Marmot-Man, then looked up at Haraldr. Her eyes seemed to have lights behind them.

"She wonders," translated Marmot-Man, "if you know that we Romans have a legend that a fair-haired race will destroy us."

Haraldr was taken aback; her delivery had been trifling, yet the question was taunting, ominous, and melancholy all at once. Let Odin reply, he told himself. An ancient voice whispered back. "Yet among us," Haraldr said with an evenness that surprised him, "it is the dark-plumed raven who heralds doom."

Marmot-Man translated. The gull-wing eyebrows rose slightly, and Maria looked at Haraldr with mixed surprise and amusement.

Maria spoke again and Marmot-Man turned to Haraldr. "She wonders if you know this Tauro-Scythian prince everyone is looking for."

Again the sword went through Haraldr's knees. Could they have tortured Gleb? How many knew? His forehead seared. Even Odin could not offer him a response.

The Hetairarch saved Haraldr with a half dozen sentences in mellifluous, perfectly accented Greek. He ended his discourse with a wry smile but did not seem amused; it was as if he were scolding the rest of the guests. Haraldr was certain that his heart could be heard thudding in the chastened silence that followed the Hetairarch's discourse. The Byzantines began to whisper self-consciously among themselves. The Hetairarch turned to Haraldr.

"I told them to stop badgering you with that fable," he said in Norse; the accent was Icelandic. "I told them that a single Norseman could come sailing down the Bosporus in a hollowed-out log, and half the people in the Great City would proclaim him this mythical Norse prince leading the force that will finally sack Constantinople. It is incredible. They are surrounded on every side by very real enemies, but they have decided that we fair-hairs, who have loyally served them for three score years, are going to pull their walls down, all because of one incident lost in the mists of time, and a few prophecies. When you get to know these people as I do, you will realize that for all their knowledge, they are sometimes like credulous children. I suspect you might be worried about false accusations being directed against you or one of your men. But don't be concerned. No one has come up with even a single hair of this supposed Norse prince, and the authorities have closed the matter. It was all rumors to begin with, and now it is nothing but dinner-party gossip."

Haraldr's lingering guilt was overwhelmed by relief. This man was hardly his enemy. Perhaps he was even a rival to Mar Hunrodarson. "Thank you," he said stiffly, offering the Hetairarch a polite nod. "I can see there is much I need to learn."

"We'll speak again, comrade," said the Hetairarch genially; he raised his eyebrows conspiratorially. Haraldr could scarcely wait to tell Ulfr and Halldor that he had discovered an ally, a Norseman with considerable knowledge of the Griks and their curious ways. Already he had been given priceless intelligence.

Maria apparently had become bored by the exchange in the guttural *barbaroi* tongue, and her lips grazed the ear of the stouter of the two officers of the Scholae who attended her. The fashion in which she smiled as she whispered was almost like a hand on Haraldr's genitals; it was as if his previous conversation, with all its terror and relief, had been blown from his mind by a gale of lust. He was certain that Maria and this blue-eyed officer were lovers, and with a curious sensation, both sickening and thrilling, he imagined her naked and writhing with passion.

Nicephorus Argyrus stepped forward and placed his hand on Haraldr's arm. He spoke to everyone and they laughed politely as he swept Haraldr out of the circle of guests. "My master told them," translated Marmot-Man, "that they can examine the fair-haired agent of our destruction during supper, but for now we must discuss the demise of the enemies of Nicephorus Argyrus."

† † †

Marmot-Man and Haraldr sat behind a large ivory table; Nicephorus Argyrus stood in front of a wall covered with a truly extraordinary mosaic. It was a map of a world that Haraldr had previously only vaguely assembled in his mind. Though the names were in Greek, he thought he could make some sense of the places. The gilt eagle certainly marked the Empress City; there was the thin blue slit of the Bosporus, the oval of the Rus Sea, Rus, Estland, Sweden, Norway, Anglia, even Iceland. But where were Greenland and, far to the west, Markland and Vinland? Clearly these Griks are not all-knowing, he surmised. Still, it was daunting to see the vast expanses of Blaland and Serkland that they had mapped; the extent of Serkland, which extended so far to the east that it seemed to wrap up half of the world orb, was particularly astonishing.

Nicephorus Argyrus's gold signet ring rapped against the mosaic at a point just below the boot shape of what appeared to be Langobard-land. He barked a single word; Marmot-Man quickly translated.

"Pirates!"

Nicephorus Argyrus ejaculated a few more words, almost as if he were angry at Haraldr.

"Saracens, yes, uh, Afrikka, that is, Blaland . . . uh, Maumet's men, heretics," Marmot-Man said, fumbling.

Haraldr nodded. Saracen pirates who sailed the waters off Blaland. He had heard tales of them since he was a boy. They were said to be vicious, tricky, and their ships were as quick as narwhals. But surely the Griks, with their fire-spitting *dhromons,* feared no pirates.

Nicephorus Argyrus went into a long discourse that sounded like a recitation of dates, names, numbers. None of it made much sense.

"He's recounting the cargoes that have been lost to the Saracens in just the last year. He says that he alone had to sell three good estates in the Bucellarion *theme,* as well as his monastery near Chrysopolis, simply to cover his losses."

"Monastery?" asked Haraldr.

Marmot-Man looked at him incredulously. "A community of monks." He rolled his eyes at Haraldr's continued lack of comprehension. "Blackfrocks," he said as if to a slow child. "Men who devote their lives to Christ."

Is there no end to the strangeness of these Griks? wondered Haraldr. So these black-frocks are Kristr's wizards. And wealthy men can buy and sell them like trains of Pecheneg slaves!

Nicephorus Argyrus rapped the mosaic map impatiently.

"He offers you ten fast ships with tackle and provisions, one solidus per man guaranteed, and thirty percent of any booty above twenty solidus of gold per man."

"How much is a solidus?" asked Haraldr coolly. He was determined to deal hard, as he had seen his brother Olaf do so many times.

Nicephorus Argyrus unlocked a small cabinet set into the wall next to the map. He removed a bulging chamois sack, thudded it onto the table, removed a small embossed gold coin, held up one finger, and said, "Solidus."

Haraldr pondered. Twenty solidi was considerable gold, though only a fraction of the entrance fee for the Imperial Guard. But catch the pirates when they were laden with plunder—that would be essential to vanquishing them, anyway—and yes, they could well exceed such sums.

"Your ships," asked Haraldr. "Describe their construction, number of benches, armaments, and condition."

Nicephorus Argyrus rattled off the specifications. The ships were light galleys of the type that had initially greeted the Rus fleet in the Bosporus: thirty benches, about the size of a Norse dragon. They had heavy arrow launchers, but of course Haraldr must understand that only Imperial vessels were permitted to carry "liquid fire."

"Ten solidi per man guaranteed," shot back Haraldr. "Fifty percent of all booty, period."

Nicephorus Argyrus frowned at Marmot-Man and barked something in Greek that was not translated, but the general thrust was clear: "I thought you told me this boy was a bumpkin who would trade a dozen gold arm rings for an iron kettle." Then he turned his comments to Haraldr.

"He doesn't think you understand your position here," translated Marmot-Man with a slithering menace in his voice. "You have entered the city under his escort, with the assurance to the authorities that you were in his employ. And you have enemies here, perhaps even in this house, against whom only Nicephorus Argyrus can protect you. His terms are fair. Still, his generosity is legend. He will offer you three solidi per man, and forty percent above fifteen solidi. He's taking enough of a risk as it is. What if these pirates add you to their plunder? He's lost ten good ships."

Haraldr's stomach churned at the bald reference to his enemies. And in this house? Was the Hetairarch in fact Mar? No, Norsemen did not smile at their mortal foes. Then it occurred to him that it was in the nature of the Griks to hide the problem at hand behind an imaginary concern. *Yes,* he told himself, *you've struck this Nicephorus Argyrus a good blow. Follow it up.*

"And my men are risking their lives," said Haraldr with a hard edge on his voice. "What good are your ten ships sitting in the harbor? Does Nicephorus Argyrus think that five hundred more Varangians will come down the Dnieper tomorrow? If he doesn't like my terms, let him find some camel drivers to sail his ships. We Norsemen know what our skills are worth."

Nicephorus Argyrus clapped his hands sharply. The doors to the little room slid open immediately, and in popped two stocky, dark-faced men in steel jerkins. They aimed the steel points of their spears at Haraldr. He leapt forward and grabbed a shaft with each hand and jerked the spears back so violently that the guards crashed against the wall. He kneed one guard in the gut and left him doubled up on the floor, then dropped the other with a mighty hand slap to his ear. He picked up one of the spears and turned on Nicephorus Argyrus.

"You just raised our fee by ten solidi a man and twenty percent," growled Haraldr. The terrified Marmot-Man meekly repeated the figures.

Nicephorus Argyrus's eyes revealed more surprise than terror; he had clearly seen death before. After a moment the coal-colored irises brightened, and he grinned slyly before beginning his response.

"He asks you to put away your weapon. He says a man with your special skills is certainly worth the extra pay, though it will probably cost him his profit and then some. He's doing this as a service to the Empire."

Of course, thought Haraldr. He's probably already extorted the entire cost of the expedition—as well as a good profit—from the other merchants who ship in those waters.

"He says that now that our business is concluded, he wants you to eat well. You'll need your strength out there." Nicephorus Argyrus reached up and put his arm around Haraldr and began walking him out of the room. Marmot-Man followed with a running translation. "Yes, the risks are great but I have every expectation of a successful venture. After all, you Varangians grow up fighting on the sea. Why, I might even gain some profit in the end. Why not? Of course you'll be a rich man. And when you return, we'll talk about making you wealthier still, and by that I don't mean chasing more Saracens around Italia. There are still some superlative properties for the taking out there, particularly in Thrace and Thessalonica, where the Bulgars will never touch them; they're undervalued simply because the Dhynatoi have this prejudice about setting foot west of the land wall. Of course, if you really want to ruin the value of even an eastern estate, send the son of a Magister out there to manage it. Yes, my friend, I'm the one to talk to if land is your business. It's not enough to know what to buy, it's the 'when' that makes the difference between profit and penury. I always buy after a raid, and sell when everyone says the frontier has never been quieter. . . ."

† † †

Nicephorus Argyrus's guests dined on silver plates embossed with scenes of legendary heroes and sipped wine from carved agate goblets rimmed with silver and pearls. It was an excruciating experience for Haraldr; he did not know which foods should be eaten with the hands— such as the tiny berries and fish roe and other curious morsels that were served before the meal—or which should be picked to bits with the curious little silver ladles and prongs each guest had been provided. And even when Haraldr cued himself by watching the other guests, the effort in managing the delicate implements was maddening.

When not struggling with the dining protocol, Haraldr was surreptitiously studying Maria. Her nose alone was a fascinating work of art; it was narrow, with an erotic, slight flare of the nostrils, and somewhat long, very subtly curving inward along the bridge and then rising to a sharp, chiseled tip. She was a goddess to whom Elisevett and Serah were only handmaidens, and yet she sat between her Scholae companions as if she were their whore, touching their hands and nuzzling their shoulders.

Eventually Maria caught Haraldr staring at her. Impelled by a force that seemed to gather him up like a huge surf, he did not turn from her blazing cobalt-blue eyes. She made no expression or gesture whatever, and yet her unwavering gaze drew him within the ice-tinted fires. Haraldr felt the same sort of convulsive shudder that he had when he'd touched Serah, yet this sensation penetrated to his soul. The voice in his head spoke so clearly that he wondered if the others had heard. Thoroughly spooked, he closed his eyes for an instant and a fantastic vision composed of images so fleeting that he could not discern them flashed before him. He felt something strike his neck quite perceptibly, and he could not breathe. His eyes shot open and his hand jerked up to his neck and he was surprised to find nothing there. Maria was still looking at him. Her lips softened into the barest hint of satisfaction, as if she acknowledged the vision to which her powers had drawn him. The voice spoke again, this time as softly as a woman's silken touch.

The shouts broke the frighteningly irresistible connection. Disappointed and relieved, Haraldr turned toward the commotion at the entrance to the dining hall. A giant figure in a black-frock and high black hat—a "monk," Haraldr reminded himself—lurched forward as if he would topple, yet slapped his gangly, curiously shaped arms at the distraught, silk-clad eunuchs who were trying to prop him up. The black-frock took several unsteady steps toward the table, and then, his shoulders wavering in an almost constant rotation, leered over the guests.

Like the other monks Haraldr had seen, this man had cropped his beard and hair, apparently just recently; his skin was as smooth as a woman's. But his features were huge, distorted, almost monstrous: a nose like a great, swollen eagle's beak; an upper lip as thin as an engraved line; a thick, almost purple lower lip; and a grotesquely heavy, bestial jaw. His tangled dark eyebrows seemed to merge with his small dark irises, and his eyes rolled about with a manic, piercing fury. After a moment Haraldr realized that this baleful monster-monk was not freshly shaven. He was a eunuch.

The monk's strident voice rumbled over the table, the slurring of the words only adding to the inherent menace in his discourse. A swarthy, sumptuously dressed man seated across the table from Haraldr inclined his head toward the painted cheek of his lady and mumbled some commentary on the monk's discourse. Haraldr strained for some recognizable words or names and was startled to hear "Joannes." The same Joannes whose name he had heard invoked so often?

The monk heard his name as well, and his already angry features shadowed with rage. His explosive response was entirely verbal, but the resounding sentences seemed to assault the swarthy man physically; the man's head snapped back and his dusky complexion ashened. He rose, his entire body trembling, bowed to Nicephorus Argyrus, and hurriedly led his obviously terrified wife from the room.

The monk went back to his wavering vigil. Someone tipped over a goblet of wine and a few guests tittered nervously. Maria tilted up her exquisite nose and dabbed her lips with a linen napkin. She spoke very slowly to the monk, using the name Joannes quite clearly, and there was no mistaking the timbre of annoyed sarcasm in her musical tones.

Joannes replied precisely and gravely, almost as if had suddenly been released by the herons of the ale-benches. His tongue was a thick reptilian pad that slid over his lower teeth as he talked.

Maria followed his words with a quick glaring retort. When it seemed that the goddess and the monk would remain locked in this exchange of hard looks and words, Nicephorus Argyrus rose, said something to the guests, and clapped his hands. In a flash of brilliant hues and dazzling flesh, several acrobats in colorful jackets and brief loincloths flipped over the table. The guests laughed and clapped. His audience lost, Joannes stalked from the room. Haraldr noticed with considerable curiosity that the monk moved much more steadily than he had when he entered. Had he only been feigning drunkenness? And why? And who was he? Kristr's chief wizard?

The acrobats bounded into the main hall and the guests rose and followed. Dancers and more acrobats on stilts gamboled about to the whirling rhythms of cymbals, pipes, and stringed instruments. Eunuchs brought fresh goblets of wine, but many of the guests were already making their farewells to Nicephorus Argyrus. Maria's entourage of pretty young women had returned to her side, and the two officers of the Scholae and the Hetairarch were strapping on their swords.

Maria turned, and the stunning blue eyes glanced in Haraldr's direction. His heart hammered at the thought that she might be thinking of him, as he was of her. She reached out to the Hetairarch, again placing that infuriating, familiar hand on his arm, and spoke to him for a moment. Then she turned amid her train of lovely young ladies and vanished like an achingly beautiful dream.

The Hetairarch walked straight for Haraldr, his step graceful, the heavy, jeweled sword and scabbard riding his brocaded hip.

"The lady has a message for you," the Hetairarch said pleasantly, with a touch of genial man-to-man ribaldry. Haraldr thought his heart would thunder out of his chest.

The Hetairarch slapped Haraldr's shoulder and said, "Follow me, I'll give it to you away from prying ears." He led Haraldr to a small clerk's room with cases for files and a few parchments piled on a plain wooden table; it was lit by a single ram-shaped iron oil lamp. The Hetairarch turned and faced Haraldr, his features flickering in the light.

"She says she hopes your fair-hair will not bring about your own doom before she has a chance to see it again."

Haraldr was confused. Was she warning him as well, or just teasing? And was this the extent of her message? Why this secrecy? His skin began to crawl.

The Hetairarch seemed to sense Haraldr's unease. "Well," he said affably, "I wanted to give you advice as well." He smiled and stepped closer. His eyes were rimmed with a touch of black paint. Haraldr's instincts warred; he desperately needed this alliance, yet he was becoming acutely uncomfortable.

The Hetairarch came a half step closer, still smiling. "You don't know what the Hetairarch does, do you?" His inflection was curiously lilting. He reached out and lightly touched the ends of Haraldr's silky blond hair.

Haraldr cringed, rocked by revulsion. Kristr damn all! A crooked! Pervert! Boy lover!

"You still don't know who I am," the Hetairarch said, still smiling, but there was a strange metal-edge to his lilting voice that made the hair at Haraldr's neck rise. No . . . *no!*

It all happened at once. The handsome, slightly feminine features darkened as if a great storm cloud had passed over them, and in an instant the Hetairarch had the face of the beast: nostrils flared murderously, mouth blackened and snarling, eyes veined and bulging with rage. Odin's Rage. Haraldr already felt cold steel at his throat. The Hetairarch slammed him against the table as if he were a puny child.

The voice roared and howled like the last dragon. "The Hetairarch," the demon spat in terrifying, barking convulsions, "commands the Imperial Guard!" The syllables, each a separate explosion of rage followed by a thundering gasp, jolted Haraldr like the blows of a broadax. *"I! Am! Mar! Hun! Ro! Dar! Son!"*

The sword slid against Haraldr's neck and he could immediately feel the tickling flow of blood. He could do nothing; it was as if a crate loaded with anvils had rolled upon his chest. *Odin!*

The beast fled from the face of Mar Hunrodarson. Haraldr now merely faced the most terrible, intimidating human visage he had ever imagined. The great force relaxed slightly but the sword stayed at his neck.

"Just so you know that the Rage is no weapon against me," Mar said, his voice still metallic and his teeth clenched. With a lightning-quick movement he thrust the bloodied sword back in his scabbard. Most of the deep crimson hue of the Rage receded from his face. He pulled Haraldr up by his bloody collar.

Haraldr's head spun and he sat meekly on the edge of the table. He was the new boy at court who had taken a profound thrashing from the reigning tough. And that was all he was; no son of the gods, no king from kings, not even leader of five hundred Varangians.

"I hope this proves to you that I am not the one who wants you dead," said Mar, his voice even if not genial. "It was I who made certain that no one meddled with the investigation into Hakon's death. A fair ruling was all I sought, and I helped to see that you got it."

Mar confidently turned his back on Haraldr. "Hakon was a buffoon. I had reason for encouraging his rise at court. But he had become a liability, even an affront to the Imperial dignity. And I was appalled when I learned that he was going to sacrifice five hundred good men in another of his foolish cheats. If you hadn't killed him, I would have."

Mar turned and placed both hands firmly on Haraldr's shoulders. There was nothing remotely suggestive in the gesture.

"Yes, your life is in danger here, but not by my hand. It would hardly be in my interest to kill you." Mar grinned tightly. "I have use for you."

Mar threw back his head. The grin spread over his entire darkly flickering countenance before he lowered his gaze and fixed his glacial eyes on Haraldr again. "Yes, Haraldr Sigurdarson, Prince of Norway. I have use for you."

he building had been an old Roman inn, and it stood between crumbling, centuries-old brick tenements. The street in front had stone curbs, but the ancient pavestones were invisible beneath a thick layer of silt and garbage. A sailor in a ragged fustian tunic sat against the building's soiled marble facade, his head ducked between his knees. A prostitute paced before him, her face painted as garishly as a wooden puppet; she seemed at least fifty years old. The music of some kind of stringed instrument came from inside.

Alexandros and Giorgios had consumed enough courage at Argyrus's to boldly cast aside the filthy sheet that served as the inn's front door; Maria followed. There was but a single large table, and no one was having sex on it; a half dozen Venetians howled as they gathered around a furiously attentive young man rapidly and deftly pounding a huge knife blade between his spread fingers. Less interested in the game were four or five prostitutes and another dozen sailors who milled beside the row of marble basins that had, in better days, dispensed food to the establishment's patrons. The current habitués scarcely acknowledged the new arrivals; they discreetly gestured to one another while taking furtive glances. One man plucked tentatively at a lute.

Maria watched a sailor slip his hand inside the coarse linen tunic of one of the whores and knead a sagging breast. "I am so disappointed," Maria said. "Perhaps we have come on one of their Saint's days."

"We have seen enough," said Giorgios, slurring slightly. At that moment the sheet over the door swept aside and at least two dozen people and assorted creatures burst through the arched doorway so convulsively, it seemed that the little inn had somehow ingested them in a single gulp: Sailors in coarse tunics; more affluent traders in relatively cheap export-grade silks; some young, not unattractive prostitutes; several musicians with lutes and pipes; yapping dogs, screaming monkeys, and a small spotted panther on a leash. The music shrilled in frantic circular rhythms, and almost immediately a woman whirled on the table; after a very short performance one of the silk-clad Venetians wrestled her to the floor and began removing her robe.

Maria's eyes ignited. Several of the newly arrived traders noticed her, shouted curiously among themselves for a moment, then gestured for her to dance. Alexandros took her arm and urged her toward the door but she pulled away. She unwrapped the long, scarflike, jeweled pallium that covered her sheer tunic at both front and back, and threw it at Giorgios. She leapt onto the table.

The Venetians backed away slightly, thunderstruck by this vision faintly cloaked in almost transparent white silk. Maria began to dance slowly, with the sinuous control of a professional. The tunic restricted the movement of her legs, so she pulled it high on her hips and knotted it. As she spun more rapidly the truncated garment hiked up farther, and her black pubic triangle teased her audience. Two traders began to close in on the table. Alexandros swept his cloak aside and slowly drew his short sword. A hand reached out and Maria kicked at it. A dozen hands grasped for her.

Alexandros and Giorgios savagely hacked the Venetians with their swords. Somehow Maria kicked herself free and leapt from the table onto Giorgios's back. They were able to retreat behind Alexandros's whirring blade, but only because Maria's gem-studded pallium had been dropped in the melee, and most of the Venetians considered it an equally valuable and far less fiercely contested prize. Three of them lay bleeding on the floor while the rest ripped the garment to shreds and scrambled after the loose baubles.

Alexandros and Giorgios—with Maria still on his back—raced uphill, in the direction of the still-glimmering spine of the city. After a half dozen blocks they stopped and ascertained that no one was following. Giorgios wrapped Maria in his cloak; her tunic was in tatters. Her face betrayed nothing, but her eyes were startling, their hue visible even in the dark. "There is a lovely park just a little farther up the hill," she said. It was as if nothing at all had happened back at the inn.

The park was a small, nicely maintained refuge in the midst of a cluster of upper-middle-class town houses; a ring of cypresses shielded a little pool and an adjacent marble pavilion. Maria spread Giorgios's cloak on the neatly mowed lawn. "Alex," she said, "go to the corner and watch for the cursores." The cursores were the city's nocturnally vigilant police force. Alex looked quizzically between his friend and his lover, then shrugged and walked away.

Maria feverishly removed Giorgios's clothing. For a moment she reverently caressed his painfully erect shaft. When he penetrated her, she gasped as if stabbed, and her fingernails brought blood from his back.

They rolled ferociously in the grass, and her moment came quickly. She screamed, a short, sharp note, then clung desperately to Giorgios. "Holy Mother, how I love you," she gasped. She fell silent and licked his neck and wondered to herself, *I do love Giorgios. But why did I just feel the Tauro-Scythian deep inside me, like a knife in my womb?*

II

hey are the offal of the Empire, the horseman observed to himself, the effluence of the stinking sewers in which they spend their days hiding from the sun and the police. Armenian peasants, Selucid mongrels, mutilated criminals, all of the outcasts who have come to the Empress City to exist as human cockroaches, two-legged insects who scurry from the dark alleys at night to cut purses and throats. The horseman counted five of these nocturnal predators; they had set a barrier of refuse across the narrow, unlit side street, a trap for any citizen foolish enough to stray near the putrescent arteries of one of Constantinople's largest slums. But the horseman, who was in his own way a denizen of the night and the less decorous recesses of the city, had seen them even before they discerned his giant silhouette against the distant backlighting of the Magnana Arsenal. He made no attempt to alter his course.

Hooves clamored on ancient paving stones, then quieted as they slowed on the silt and trash that had begun to bury this forgotten, reeking little lane. The five waited, listening for the hoofbeats of an escort, and satisfied themselves that their victim was alone. But when they distinguished the black-frocked figure and the huge head, they postponed their assault, wondering if this was the man who rode in the night. They whispered their confusion, and the horseman, who had learned to make out murmured confidences across a room full of tittering dignitaries, smiled and listened.

"It's the demon-monk. I'll swear to it on the hair of a saint's ballpouch."

"No. We'll see demons 'nough when we're called to Hell."

"Won't be Christ the King nor Devil's disciples you'll have to fear if he catches you first. He's an unholy black whirlwind, set down by a conjurer, then he's somewhere across this cursed city a wink later."

"Listen to that while you still got ears, brother. Let's beat out of here and lay ourselves upon some sotted whore so to thank the demons who saved our balls from Joannes."

Before the five could vanish into the shadows, the horseman had charged into their midst. The cutthroats looked up in terrified rapture, then shrank from the monstrous leering head as if it were a lighted torch thrust into their faces. *Mark me well,* the horseman thought as the five stumbled into the dark crevices between the towering hovels. *Spread the word like poison into your fetid warrens, let every miserable, damned soul in these pestilent warehouses of human refuse know who I am. I am more than power, that all-too-recognizable face of uniformed authority that clubs you into your stinking lairs by day and gives you short leash by night. I am something more formidable, that ultimate alloy of power welded to the implacable resolution to wield it without hesitation or pity. I am fear.*

The horseman, whose name was indeed Joannes, now returned to his intended route; he spurred his horse up the good stone road to a hill crowned with a large, plain-fronted town house. He circled around the back of the building, then turned off the street into a colonnaded arcade screened with vines. A boy in a short silk tunic recognized him and slid open a gate that led into a large interior court. As he gave up the reins to another stable boy, Joannes looked at the outlines of the elaborate topiaries in the court: a boar; an incredible crouching lion. He traversed the long interior arcade to the large brass double doors, where he was greeted by two armored, stubble-faced Alemmanians, taller even than the black-frock himself, and quickly ushered inside.

"Orphanotrophus," said his host, using Joannes's official title in the Imperial Administration of the Roman Empire. The candelabra were not lit, and the single row of candles in sconces on the walls cast a wavering, hallucinatory light over the mosaics above them; here and there golden tesserae glimmered like little stars.

"Logothete of the Dromus," answered Joannes; this was the official title of the man responsible for all intelligence gathering, both foreign and domestic, in the Roman Empire. Joannes pointedly ignored the Logothete's honorary rank of Magister, the highest for any administrative officer in the Roman government, though such an address would not be neglected by any other courtier who hoped to keep his manhood. The hollow-eyed, glowering monk had no use for the complex apparatus of court ceremony, just as he gave little thought to his own meaningless title: Orphanotrophus, or Guardian of Orphans, head of the Empire's vast network of charity hospitals and orphanages, and not, incidentally, sole authority over hundreds of thousands of solidi in charitable "donations"—usually extorted by various threats—for which he was accountable to no one, and which rarely redressed any of the Empire's social ills. Titles might have currency to the posturing milksops at court. But tonight a simple monk had the real business of the Empire to conduct.

Joannes knew his way and silently followed the mute-eyed servant to the corner of the room. The servant, a pale, blond-haired Thracian in an oversize silk tunic, pressed against the wall. With a slight exhalation the smooth marble panel swung aside. Joannes and the Logothete entered a small, cool chamber; the servant followed with a single brass lantern in the shape of a ram. The servant bent over and pulled a thin stone slab from the floor. A chill gust swept into the chamber, and the Logothete shielded the lantern. The servant descended into the dark hole.

After feeling his way down the familiar wooden steps, Joannes let the servant guide his legs into the small boat. He swung to the side and sat. The lantern, to his acute eyesight, lit the entire cistern. As the servant paddled the boat through the inky subterranean lake, Joannes counted the rows of algae-striped columns and studied the patterns of the bricks in the rounded vaults overhead; numbers and order were the two fundamentals for which his mind instinctively quested. When they had passed beneath twenty vaults, they reached the far end and climbed to a small wooden dock. They ascended a short flight of stone stairs that led to a stained oaken door. The servant unlocked the door; the room they entered smelled of incense, good wine, and a woman's perfume.

"I have something special tonight," said the Logothete as he and his guest lowered themselves to tasseled brocade couches. The Logothete had dark, piercing Asiatic eyes that sparked ferally as the servant began lighting the sconced oil lamps. Like Joannes, he had been born to a low-level bureaucrat and had suffered a family disgrace; his father had been paymaster to a provincial regiment and had been cashiered for skimming funds, while Joannes's father had been a minor legal clerk in the Black Sea port of Amastris and had been caught forging deeds of sale. This was the bond between Joannes and the Logothete, worth more than any momentary political allegiances or utterly fictional declarations of loyalty.

"You'll find this quite remarkable," said the Logothete. His servant poured wine from a glazed clay jug into silver goblets. "A Sicilian vintage. It will be past its time in two or three weeks, so drink copiously." The Logothete smiled. Joannes would drink liberally whether or not the wine was good, and certainly regardless of any invitation. The Logothete waited until Joannes had downed a full goblet and half of a second; he knew from long experience that Joannes never exceeded his considerable capacity but often drank enough to convince others that he had gone beyond his limits.

"The information comes from my usual correspondents at the court of

Yaroslav, as well as interviews with Rus traders who have journeyed from what are commonly referred to as the Islands of Thule, though we are certain that Thule is actually a collection of separate nations, some of them islands, some of them large peninsulas, linked by a common language. My offices have also had conversations with Frankish traders and diplomats who know and deal with these northern *barbaroi,* whom they call, with their characteristic simplicity of expression, Northmen." The Logothete paused to sip, then placed his goblet on a small ivory-surfaced cabinet. "The facts are thus. The level of military organization among the northern *barbaroi* is much higher than the Strategus of Kherson, our putative expert in these matters, has led us to believe. Land battles involving tens of thousands of men have been reported, and fleets of hundreds of fast craft manned by heavily armed Marines regularly launch lightning attacks on their neighbors. Because these northern nations are not dominated by a single great power, there is considerable political flux among them, and the northern *barbaroi* kings regularly depose one another. Bands of warriors—often considerable in number—disenfranchised by these conflicts are almost always available for hire, or simply for the promise of booty, to the next usurper."

Joannes thought for a moment before speaking in his sepulchral baritone. "So. The military resources for an invasion by the northern *barbaroi* certainly exist. This is one of those rare instances in which popular hysteria has a basis in fact. It is quite coincidental, of course. If a blind man spends enough time groveling in the street, eventually he might chance across a gold coin someone has dropped."

Joannes signaled the servant to fill his cup, settled back, and looked. steadily upward, as if he had just located some hovering phantom he wished to address. "Of course, the military capability of these northern *barbaroi* is in itself hardly alarming, merely another name added to the litany of antagonists who ceaselessly harass our borders. But alone among our multitudinous adversaries, the northern *barbaroi* have the seafaring abilities to threaten the Queen of Cities herself. If they did mount such a naval belligerency, and had the good fortune to find their assault coincident with, let us say, an incursion by the Bulgars across the Danube estuaries, then we would find the northern *barbaroi* a serious menace." Joannes snapped his gaze back to the Logothete. "However, you mention this political flux in the northern nations. As long as thieves quarrel among themselves, the gatekeeper has little to worry about. Without strong leadership any northern *barbaroi* incursions would be little more than ill-fated acts of piracy, even with half the Imperial Navy dispatched elsewhere."

"You discount the notion that a *barbaroi* prince arrived incognito with the last Rus trade flotilla?"

"You found nothing. It smacked of the usual Dhynatoi rumormongering."

"I am not entirely satisfied with what I found. The rumor may have started among the Rus."

"Continue to work on it, then. As much as I would like to build the Rus trade, if this Prince is produced, I would have no choice but to make cause with the Dhynatoi in urging the extermination of all the northern *barbaroi* who arrived with that fleet."

"Would that be enough? Suppose one of the these *barbaroi* thieves, to follow your metaphor, was already the gatekeeper?"

Joannes's dark, oily eyebrows descended toward his stormy irises, and for an awful moment the Logothete wondered how he could have so miscalculated his ally's loyalties. But Joannes then nodded appreciatively at the extrapolation of his metaphor. The Hetairarch, the northern *barbaroi* Mar Hunrodarson, opened the gates to the Imperial Palace each morning. And the Hetairarch was perhaps a servant who had begun to imagine himself a master. "Develop your theory," rumbled Joannes.

"The Hetairarch Mar Hunrodarson has long openly petitioned for greatly increased recruiting of Varangian mercenaries. Lately he has focused on my office, almost daily providing me with intelligence—some legitimate, some highly exaggerated—regarding suspected civil uprisings in the City, and suggesting that a new, lesser Varangian guard be created and posted in the city, though outside the palace, for riot control. Interesting, isn't it? The champions of the common folk petitioning to become their oppressors."

Joannes nodded and gulped another draft of wine. "Mar Hunrodarson is clearly an exceptional *barbaroi*. He has learned to thrust and cut with Roman paper almost as well as he can with Frankish steel." Joannes drank again and reflected silently. If things were going well in the Imperial Palace, this would be the time to eliminate the *barbaroi* upstart Hunrodarson. But things were not going well at all, and the wily Hetairarch would have his role in the drama that surely would be enacted over the next few years.

"Yes," said the Logothete, his eyes keen and fiery as he responded to his guest's twitching brow. "The Hetairarch Mar Hunrodarson is extraordinarily patient for a man capable of such ill-tempered eruptions. I believe he will wait, strengthen his hand with the increasing insinuation of his fellow *barbaroi* in the military affairs of the Roman Empire, and when the time comes"—here the Logothete tread warily, knowing the relationship between the Emperor and Joannes—"position himself to broker the succession. With a sufficient force of Varangians in or even near the City, it would be possible."

"Then we must either make Mar Hunrodarson our broker, or find someone who will break his sword when that time comes," said Joannes, as much to himself as to his host. He covered his deeply set eyes with his long, misshapen fingers, pressed in, then moved the spatulate fingertips to cradle his chin. "Perhaps we can do both."

The Logothete showed decay-rimmed, ragged teeth. Most officials of the Imperial Administration exerted their power like porters hefting heavy crates. Joannes was a juggler, capable of keeping several contradictory goals in the air at once. "I suppose you have this Janus already in mind? The information you wanted from Italia?"

Now Joannes raised his thin upper lip in what appeared to be a snarl, though the Logothete knew it as a rare expression of genuine, if sinister, mirth. "Yes. I believe this man, Haraldr Nordbrikt—I presume that is the correct pronunciation of yet another ludicrous barbaroi name—that this Haraldr Nordbrikt and Mar Hunrodarson have a relationship that is rather, one would say, pregnant. As you know, when the Grand Domestic wanted this Haraldr Nordbrikt and his men butchered in Neorion, Hunrodarson interceded and provided information that justified the murder of the Manglavite."

"Yet consider their only meeting," said the Logothete, contributing the presumed antithesis. "My man in the house told me that they closeted, argued, and perhaps struggled. And Hunrodarson made no attempt to get Haraldr Nordbrikt a posting anywhere near the city; it was he who insisted that the Imperial pardon banish Nordbrikt and his men for a period of months."

"A deception? Perhaps Hunrodarson wishes to allay any suspicion of his barbaroi accomplice."

"Or he thinks that Haraldr Nordbrikt will fail in his mission for the merchant Argyrus, leaving a powerful force of Varangians looking for a more effective leader. Better than martyring their hero, is it not?"

"A possibility that certainly would have occurred to me, were I standing in Hunrodarson's boots. Well, right now all we have are possibilities, but possibilities that we can quite likely turn to our advantage. What word do you have of Haraldr Nordbrikt?"

"The last landfall was Brindisi, almost two months ago. They had been at sea for several months without sighting the Saracen fleet. They provisioned very quickly, and there was a detail you might find interesting.

Unlike most *barbaroi* wine bags, who prefer to drink barrels of that piss they call ale, Nordbrikt loaded his ships, almost until the rails were awash, with barrels of plain spring water. I would suspect he was heading south toward Libya and intended to remain at sea for some time. He may be a resourceful man."

Joannes grunted. Monkeys in the Hippodrome could also perform tricks. Still, something about this Haraldr Nordbrikt interested him. He had possibilities, but better yet, he was entirely expendable. There was absolutely nothing to lose in using him, and possibly the Roman Empire to be gained.

Joannes gulped a full cup, belched deeply, rose, and motioned the servant to let him out without even gesturing to the Logothete. At the door, however, he turned. "If this Haraldr Nordbrikt makes a return landfall, see that I know at once."

† † †

"Giorgios?" Her voice was visible in fine silver bubbles, and she knew that it was not Giorgios who was there. The sea around her was a vast azure platter with a pure gilded rim. She was cold and he was like the sun, his hair a golden halo high above her. "Mar?" Again the silver bubbles. He was not Mar. The other one. The silk, the wicked scar. He was like a sun. But the sun was gone, and the sea, fiery as opal, lit them from below.

The ships flew over the dimming horizon, and the blue glow from the sea candled the faces, hundreds of them, hollow and ghostly, their dead teeth chattering obscenities. But the fair-haired sun made them shrivel and they floated away like dry leaves in the soft breeze. The fair-hair climbed aboard and he was gone, and her heart tore with a pain so real. Then he stood before her again, and in the wooden chest he held the sun. With his hands he scattered light, and she could feel the hot incandescence when his arms took her up.

e tells you to behold the Pillars of Heracles, Haraldr Nordbrikt. The ends of the Earth." Marmot-Man, Haraldr, and the Byzantine pilot stood in the prow of Nicephorus Argyrus's galley. The deck pitched in a south wind with the same harsh, steamy rasp as a harlot's love cries. Marmot-Man had been forced to join this mortifying pirate-hunting expedition as interpreter for the pilot, who otherwise could not have warned these reckless *barbaroi* that they were rapidly approaching uncharted waters.

"There is a sea beyond these Pillars," said Haraldr. He pointed to the west. A molten sun hovered above a watery horizon the color of steel. Haraldr shielded his eyes to discern the slight shift of hue that marked a spit of headland jutting into the sea.

"A sea indeed, but it would not be wise to venture into it for any great distance, Haraldr Nordbrikt. It is the moat that separates the world of men from the walls that thrust up the vault of the firmament." With his hands Marmot-Man drew the shape of a box. "So that living men cannot attain these walls and climb into paradise, Lord God has furnished this sea with every imaginable ferocious creature of enormous size, and some so frightening to behold that their gaze alone will shatter a ship to timbers."

Haraldr continued to study the sun-hammered horizon. "As a boy, I spoke with a man who sailed this great western sea with Bjarni Herjolfsson. They ventured as far as Vinland and saw no walls. Another man sailed with Leif the Lucky and went ashore on Vinland. There was no paradise, only miserable *skraelings*—savages." Haraldr rotated his palms to sculpt a sphere in the air. "The world-orb has no walls."

Marmot-Man sighed. "Well, Haraldr Nordbrikt, that is also the opinion of certain overly learned heretics at court who read the words of ancient Greek pagans." Marmot-Man rose on his toes to approach Haraldr's ear more closely. "Haraldr Nordbrikt, believe me, you do not want these heretics as your friend or their enemies as yours," hissed Marmot-Man. "Haraldr Nordbrikt, say no more of this earth shaped like a Persian melon."

Haraldr looked away, weary of Marmot-Man's pointless, often conflicting confidences. Almost four months at sea, and Marmot-Man had furnished nothing more than incidental glimpses of the vast structure of Grik—no, Roman, he reminded himself—power. It was as if, even at the limits of the Roman world, Marmot-Man were reminded of a sword over his neck.

The ravens took wing in Haraldr's gut as he remembered the blade that threatened his own head. Each day for the last four months he had ached with the shame that he could not reveal to Halldor, Ulfr, and the rest of his pledge-men all that had transpired in his meeting with Mar Hunrodarson. Yet how could he admit to his physical fear of Mar, and, far worse, tell them that Mar held knowledge that could prevent all of them from ever seeing their homes again? What fate was Mar, even at this moment, divining? Haraldr had heard nothing from the terrifying Hetairarch during the week they had remained in St. Mama's Quarter, preparing to sail; but now, alone at night on this distant sea, it was as if Mar's mighty grip was an ever-tightening noose about his neck. Lately he would awaken, hardly able to breathe. And what of these other enemies Mar had alluded to, perhaps even more deadly than the Rage-filled Hetairarch?

Yet when Haraldr thought of sailing right through the Pillars of Heracles to the sanctuary of the cold green sea that Norsemen alone commanded, he was pulled irresistibly back. The Empress City. He wanted her embrace, her scent, her heat, her . . . Maria. With some strange clarity undiminished by time and distance he could still see the brilliance of her lips and eyes, hear her speak, watch her hips sway. In his endless rocking fantasies each night upon these fevered southern seas, Maria and the city had become the same imaginary lover, and when he finally held Maria against his breast, loving her so deeply and limitlessly that he would melt within her, he would know then that the Empress City had trothed herself in return. They had already loved a hundred nights in as many different places within the Empress City, the night before on a marbled terrace, lying upon silk, naked to the whispering breeze, her swan-white skin iridescent like the lights of Halogoland writhing against an arctic horizon. He had been away from her, both of her, so long.

Haraldr struggled against the torpid seduction. It was this unearthly heat. The heat attacked reason. The heat was death, and death waited out on this flaming sapphire brine. He could consider what awaited him in the Empress City, when, or if, he returned to her. "Count no day until the sun has set," he reminded himself as he squinted into the boiling copper disc looming over the western horizon. This day was far from ended. He called for Ulfr and Halldor to join him forward.

"We come in with the sun at our backs."

Ulfr nodded. *"Ja,* my friend, if the men don't fight these Saracens soon, I think they'll begin to set their sword upon the wind. They've given you a name now. Hardraada. Hard-ruler."

"If they are still full-strong enough to praise me with such curses, then I have served them well." At least about this Haraldr could be pleased. At their last landfall, now almost two months ago along the coast of Langobard-land, Haraldr had provisioned his ships with water rather than the local wine, to which the men had greatly taken. The men had complained bitterly then, and the hard-mouthing had continued for the next month while they had searched for the Saracen pirate fleet at open sea. Then they had sighted the Saracen masts rising against the bleached horizon like a seagoing forest and for another month had dogged the huge Saracen fleet along the endless coast of Blaland, the vast landmass sometimes called Afrikka. Haraldr had enforced strict water rationing among his own men while staying at sea to block the Saracens from turning into the Afrikkan ports. Yes, his men were as testy as penned stallions scenting a mare in heat. But consider what entreaties the crews aboard the Saracen ships now would be issuing to their Devil-God, Maumet. If indeed they had the spit to speak.

Haraldr studied the Saracen mast-forest, sails unfurled on the eastern horizon like enormous white leaves. He squinted to discern the formation of the bobbing dark hulls, wondering if he had found his answer. He could not be sure. *Odin,* he prayed, as much to himself as to the god, *I lay it all in your hands.* Then he turned to Ulfr and Halldor and sucked in a parching breath. "There will be no battle cry," he said. "We're going in by ourselves, just this ship. I alone will board."

Halldor's blackened, sun-split lips slackened in shock. Ulfr's jaw dropped.

"Yes. I have invited the ravens to join me." Haraldr looked hard at Ulfr and Halldor. "But the men are nearly mutinous. In this hot blue sea they have long ago forgotten that day beside the white waters of the Dnieper. Yet if my strategy has been successful, I will have both saved a good half of my force and given them as their leader a true favorite of Odin. When we return to Constantinople, they will cleave to me as if I were their Emperor. And when we return to the city, surely I will need nothing less than fanatics to guard my back."

Ulfr conveyed the order down the line of ten fully rigged galleys; soon Haraldr could see arms, swords, and spears gesturing with confusion atop the decks. He ordered his own crew to furl sails and take their places at the oars. As his ship moved swiftly out of line, the crews left behind stilled and hushed. Soon the only sounds on all nine ships were creaking tackle and flapping canvas, the splash of waves on hulls, and the invisible abrasion of the wind. A man was about to show them that he was a god.

Haraldr caught the spray at the foredeck as the fast galley charged; the droplets stung his sun-tormented face like flung sand. Here the sun rises so high that it does not offer a shadow for much of the day, he thought, vaguely considering what mechanism of Kristr's doing had created this phenomenon, so different from the long shadows of the northern lands. He focused on the mast forest, trying to discern if he would win this wager or lose everything.

It was confusing, so many masts—three to a ship—so many sails, all crowded together. Then the formation began to make sense, and he whispered his thanks to Odin. It was as he had expected; the Saracen vessels were clustered in groups of from three to a dozen, and they bobbed and yawed curiously; the hulls often bumped together.

"You are indeed as clever as Odin," said Ulfr as he and Halldor came forward and observed the curious progress of the Saracen fleet. "I hope you are as lucky."

Halldor waved his arm as if anointing the careening lines of Saracen ships. His byrnnie glistened with sweat and his teeth were as white as bleached bone against his cooked face. "A ghost fleet," he said, "intended to function like an army of false campfires. As their men perished of thirst they abandoned ship after ship, towing the dead vessels along in files to deceive us that their strength was intact."

"That must be their flagship," said Ulfr, pointing to a deep-hulled vessel with a kind of house on the stern, three seperate masts, and perhaps a dozen empty oar ports to a side. "It leads the line." Despite the growing chaos within the ranks of the ghost fleet, most of the ships had been rigged to run with the wind, and the flagship cruised smartly ahead of the long, swell-tossed files. Haraldr observed the lead ship carefully. Odin enjoyed tricks. He squinted for resolution, and as they approached the flagship his hopes plunged in sickening concert with the pitching deck. He had indeed offered the one-eyed god a premature thanksgiving. A full crew manned the top frame of the Saracen flagship, as well as the half dozen ships to her stern. Steel jerkins glinted over white robes, and flashing spearheads and curved, silvery steel swords pointed to attention in immaculate rows.

"We change the orders?" asked Halldor.

"No," said Haraldr raptly, as if he suffered from some narcosis of fear. "Odin has led me here. If Odin intends to offer me to the ravens this day, not ten thousand men could save me." Is it the heat? he wondered as he distantly contemplated his deadly folly. Or was fate so thick around him that it had charged the air with the heat of its vast cauldron?

"Boarding ropes!" shouted Ulfr. The galley swung parallel to the hull of the flagship and prepared to drift into position for a fast boarding. Ulfr and Halldor worked frantically with the boarding ropes, too mesmerized with Haraldr's god-driven fury to try to stop him. But why was he laughing? The heat. The heat and the fear had driven him mad; the line between the madness that saved a man and that which doomed him was finer than the finest silk filament. Odin had finally forsaken their hero, and they would joyfully share his fate.

"Look!" shouted Haraldr. He was still laughing. "My foes will have to dismiss their unbidden supper guests before they can fight!" Haldor and Ulfr raised their heads, at first bewildered by Haraldr's babble, then incredulous at what they saw at the railing of the Saracen ship. Ulfr coughed, revulsion gagging his throat. Dozens of sea gulls had descended upon the Saracen warriors; they perched on unmoving shoulders and pecked the eyes from unprotesting heads. The ghost fleet had also been provided a ghost crew.

Haraldr leapt to the deck of the Saracen ship. The stench was appalling; he had never imagined such decay, but then he had never known such a sun. The Saracens had their backs strapped straight against their spears and were lashed to the railing. As he walked the deck, slimy with the the foul droppings of the carrion birds, Haraldr felt the spirits of the dead hovering about their unburied corpses; their sighing plaints were a hot miasma in his nostrils. He looked straight ahead as he went aft, but he could not ignore the awful cooing and clucking of the birds, an obscene satiation worse even than the cawing of hungry ravens. He saw the door to the cabin at the stern of the ship; he now only wished to escape the sun and the spirits that were sucking away the air around him. He wondered at the strange, partially peeling blue script that bordered the rose-enameled wood. The door rattled as the ship pitched, then suddenly swung open.

The scimitar raked Emma with a dry screech; the sound was far more alarming than the impact. Haraldr lashed out with his shield and felt as if he had crushed a bird's chest. He stepped back and with his sword probed the blue-black pall inside. A spear jutted past him and he snapped it like a twig. He placed his shield beneath his chin and tried to adjust his eyes to the darkness. Then he saw the nimbus of light around the curtains and ripped the fabric away with his sword.

The Saracen sat at a large table of carved wood inlaid with rosettes of pearl and ivory. He was coal-bearded, still almost as juicily plump as a fat partridge; a clean white cloth covered his head. Beside him stood a single wraithlike guard in a filthy, stained smock, a curving dagger swaying in his withered grip. The Saracen pushed the guard back and immediately opened a black lacquered box set before him on the table. The light from the portals glossed a small, flat, gold ingot, then another, then another, until the Saracen had placed twenty ingots on the table. Haraldr extended his sword and pricked the man's windpipe. He held up his other hand and flashed his fingers to signal "five" four times. Then he shook his head no, and began to flash five again and again and again, until it seemed he had done it a hundred times. When he was finished, he cut a small nick on the Saracen's well-fleshed throat.

The Saracen shrugged, turned up sausage-thick fingers almost immobilized with gem-encrusted rings, and waved Haraldr to a latticed hatch at mid-deck. He opened it and climbed into the hold at the point of Haraldr's sword.

Light from the oar ports sliced the hold with hot white blades that flickered as the ship gently rocked. The Saracen very slowly pulled aside a dingy canvas, revealing seven large wooden chests bound with bright brass fittings. The Saracen hiked up his billowing cotton robe, shrugged at Haraldr, and assumed a ridiculous posture as he probed his bowels. He winced as he withdrew the key.

The Saracen unlocked all the chests before opening any of them. When he began to lift the lids, he went about it so quickly and dramatically that Haraldr expected a ruse, Saracen warriors springing from their last hiding place. But it was not ice-of-battle that glimmered in the thrusting light, it was Roman gold. Enough shimmering solidi and golden ingots to buy all of Europe. For a moment Haraldr saw Olaf's last moments at Stiklestad, heard the dying words from Jarl Rognvald's sky-blue lips, and saw the ice-white swords of retribution bloody the northern horizon. And then, in a blinding epiphany, all he could see was the Empress City, luminous in her aureate mantle, receiving him into her scented arms.

aria asked her guard to have the carriage stopped; brakes whined and the enclosed compartment pitched and canted slightly back. She slid across the cushioned satin upholstery and nudged aside the shell-pink brocade shade. She could see over the queued-up crowd at the news bulletins posted by the great bronze gate to the Imperial Palace complex.

"What is it, Maria?" asked Anna Dalassena, daughter of the Grand Domestic, in her chiming voice.

"Look. Remember the Tauro-Scythian we saw last summer—where was it?—the nervous one with the clumsy hands and the agile tongue?"

"No," demurred Anna with a leisurely folding of her thick dark lashes. She indeed remembered the towering *barbaroi;* hadn't she in fact lain in her silk sheets later that night, her head whirling from wine, and for a dreadfully fascinating instant imagined those huge arms enfolding her? But as the flower of Anna's maidenhood had yet to be pruned, she was obliged to coyness. Maria, on the other hand, in the months that Anna had waited on her, had alluded to the most delectable, most extraordinary intimacies between men and women. Anna supressed a giggle; Maria had no chastity to protect. How exquisite that would be.

"Oh," said Maria, the elegant line of her lips scrolling with amusement, "I had rather a fantasy of the Tauro-Scythian that night. As I recall, I saw to it that he was rough with his hands."

Anna blushed profoundly. "Please, Lady, tell me what this man has done for his name to be posted by the Chalke gate. They haven't cut off his hands, I beseech the Holy Mother."

Maria smiled, thinking that it was time that bright, spirited little Anna learn a woman's pleasures. She needed to think of someone suitable, someone gentle yet vigorous. Perhaps Isaac would know.

Anna's face pressed next to Maria's, and the braided loops at the sides of their heads touched. "Holy Mother!"

The bulletin was framed and set in the usual marble niche. Maria read the florid script with mock gravity. "Varangian champions defend Christendom at edge of the world; restore Roman riches to furtherance of

Glory of Christ the King. Varangian Nordbrikt, his arm strenghtened by the Mother of God, single-handedly vanquished the infidel."

"They say he's now rich enough to buy Nicephorus Argyrus's palace!" blurted Anna.

"Anna," said Maria musically, "you suddenly recall the man?"

Anna smirked. "Yes." Then her face dropped. "My father isn't happy about this Tauro-Scythian's success. I heard him." She sighed, trying to imitate the mysterious note of melancholy that so often crept into Maria's discourse. "I don't suppose we'll ever have him to banquet in our chambers."

"No," answered Maria. She pulled the shade back and motioned the carriage on. "I fear the Tauro-Scythian's enemies have multiplied as rapidly as his riches."

Maria settled back against the cushions and closed her eyes as the carriage rumbled up the Mese, the city's main artery. Extraordinary. The dream had been months ago. And how vivid it had been. Perhaps more than a dream. Perhaps a vision like those of the prophet Daniel: the fair-hair, the fleet of ships manned by specters, a chest of gold as brilliant as the sun. But there were other dreams. No. She could not recall them. Would not. Fair-hair haloed by horrible black flocking creatures, frozen waters dark as onyx, awakening with fear on her tongue. Had she some gift of prophecy? There were many in the city who claimed it, but, as with virtue, that gift was much more often claimed than possessed.

Maria opened her eyes and clutched her hands tightly together. Yes. The fair-haired *barbaroi* was a harbinger of death, but she had not seen if the death that haloed his golden head was his own or that of another. Maria started; it was as if an icy finger had suddenly brushed her cheek. She whipped her head, expecting Anna's cheerful confession of the prank, but Anna had slid across the seat to peer intently through her own window. Maria touched her faintly rouged cheek as if daubing a wound, and shuddered that she found nothing but her own silken warmth. Tonight in the Hagia Sophia she would pray to the Mother of God that the fair-hair not visit her dreams again. And pray for his soul, because in her silent heart she would pray that it was his own death she had foreseen.

† † †

"Who is he?" asked Thorvald Ostenson, centurion of the Grand Hetairia, fourth in command of the Emperor's Varangian Guard. The leather fittings of Ostenson's new gold breastplate creaked as he came around the chair on which the man sat, hunched over, his back trembling in soft heaves like the belly of a small, wounded animal.

"This pitiful head upon whom the ravens have chosen to defecate belongs to John Choniates, a petty tax officer from the Anatolian theme." Mar Hunrodarson folded his arms atop his writing table and studied the wretch who sat before him. The man's eyes were pools of vitreous red surrounded by enormous purple bruises, and his chin was as raw as fresh meat where his beard had been plucked. His short, stiff fingers were swollen and caked with blood.

"So why are they feeding these little mice to Varangian lions?" asked Ostenson. "Don't the ball-less paper stuffers know that we are already overburdened with felons above the rank of patrician, and our strength is short as it is? Besides, a Varangian takes little pride in playing a broken reed like this. The men are malingering when they're asked to perform these inconsequential interrogations."

Mar looked up at Ostenson; he had just promoted the lanky, straw-headed farm boy from Iceland to centurion. Mar had learned his lesson with Hakon. When he had seen to it that Hakon was elevated to the honor of Manglavite, he had thought that it was more important to find a man who was suitably vicious—something Mar knew couldn't be taught—than to look for intelligence in his key subordinates; Mar had reasoned that he had enough wits for all five hundred members of the Grand Hetairia and then some. Well, Mar also had the wits to know when he had been wrong. Ostenson was part of Mar's new strategy to surround himself with men who did not run out of words after *ax*, *ale*, and *cunt*. This new centurion had the keenness to understand the intricacies of Roman power, if he were taught well. And it was clearly time for the education of Thorvald Ostenson to begin.

"Ordinarily I would have flatly refused the use of my offices to execute sentence on such a menial bureaucrat," explained Mar to his coarse-featured but sharp-eyed subordinate. "But here my own objectives are served." Mar paused like a rune-mentor. "You understand the significance of Anatolia and the rest of the Eastern themes, do you not?"

Ostenson nodded. He knew that the Anatolian theme was the richest of the eighteen Asian themes, or provinces, that comprised the breadbasket of the Empire.

"The wealth of the Eastern themes," continued Mar in a pedagogical rhythm he had learned from listening to the endless discourses in the Emperor's chambers, "is not simply the endless sacks of grain they provide the Imperial granaries, or the yet more extraordinary harvest of taxes they provide the Imperial Treasury. It is military manpower. By this I mean the thematic armies."

Again Ostenson signaled his understanding. Each theme was able to mobilize a highly competent citizen army, both to protect its own borders against minor incursions as well as to supplement the Imperial Taghmata, the Constantinople-based standing professional army, in times of major conflict. Fully mobilized, all of the thematic armies could quintuple the size of the Imperial Taghmata.

"And you understand the system of inalienable military freeholds, then?" asked Mar, certain that his new centurion had not troubled himself with such arcane details; Ostenson's bewildered eyes quickly confirmed his doubts. "Well," Mar continued, "understand that these citizen soldiers cannot magically transform their hoes into spears and their burlap tunics into armor. If you travel through Asia Minor, as I have, you are struck by the prosperity of the small farms, strip after endless strip of shimmering grain and dewy pasture. For centuries Roman law has required each of these prosperous small farms, which are the freeholds of the peasants who work them, to provide and equip one soldier to remain in readiness for service in the thematic army. The Emperors have long understood that Roman power is dependent on the survival of these military freeholds, so for centuries they have enforced laws strictly banning purchase of the freeholds by the Dhynatoi."

Ostenson's eyes narrowed. The Dhynatoi not only wallowed in the centuries-old fortunes provided by their vast landholdings but also dominated the Roman Senate and had placed their stooges in many of the most important Imperial military commands. The Dhynatoi were vain, ostentatious, and insufferably arrogant; when one of them occasionally ran afoul of his own kind and ended up in Numera Prison, the Varangian centurions would cast lots for the privilege of attending to him.

"Unfortunately," Mar went on in the wry tone he used when he criticized official policy, "recently these laws have proven difficult to enforce. The peasant freeholders, who are called upon all too frequently by the Imperial tax collectors, as well as by their local military commanders, wish to elude these obligations by illegally selling their farms to the Dhynatoi. The Dhynatoi, for their part, are only too willing to illegally purchase these properties, which they acquire by the hundreds, even thousands, and consolidate into vast estates."

"So a peasant feels his lot is bettered by becoming a serf on the estate of a Dhynatoi rather than owning his own farm." Ostenson shook his head. "Then this tax gatherer is one of the bloodsuckers who are turning these soldier-farmers into slaves. No wonder the Emperor wishes to make an example of him."

Mar grinned. In the matter of thinking like a Roman, Ostenson was a newborn. "The obvious deduction, which you must never make if you wish to fathom the Roman mind. It is not the Emperor but the Dhynatoi who have sent this wretch to us, bundled up with a dozen more tax officers from other districts and themes. The Dhynatoi wish to make the example of them."

"Why?" Ostenson looked like a boy playing his first game of checkers with a man.

Mar's lips contorted with sarcasm. "This pathetic fool officially protested that the two largest estates in his district were harboring former peasant freeholders, now serfs on these estates, who had illegally surrendered their farms to the Dhynatoi. The local judge quickly convicted this troublemaker of fraud and extortion, and then the Dhynatoi sent him along to the Great City for punishment, so that the message might be spread to overzealous tax officers throughout the Empire."

Ostenson was astute enough not to have to ask why the Emperor permitted the Dhynatoi to cheat him of taxes and soldiers. Instead he raised the less obvious question. "I'm not certain what our interest is in serving the Dhynatoi."

Mar nodded soberly. "As the thematic armies are inevitably weakened by the disappearance of the military freeholds, the Imperial Taghmata will increasingly require the support of foreign mercenaries in times of great need. And with my devotion to our Father the Emperor, and indeed to the ideals of Rome itself, I would like to see that the Roman army is served by nothing less than the finest warriors on the world-orb." Mar paused and flashed his perfect teeth. "Norsemen."

Ostenson looked down on the quaking back of John Choniates. "Then there is great worth in the punishment of this doubly cursed villain. What is the disposition of his sentence, Hetairarch?"

Mar forked two fingers and pointed them to his eyes. "Take him to the basement of Numera Prison and blind him with irons. Then transport him to the Augusteion, chain him upside down between the pillars, and let the simple folk of the Great City show him their charity."

Ostenson jerked the whimpering tax collector to his feet and dragged him off. This departure was immediately followed by the appearance of a decurion of the Grand Hetairia who handed Mar a rolled and sealed document. Mar looked carefully at the lead seal dangling from the cord. When he identified the author of the missive, he flipped the seal contemptuously.

Mar considered the Grand Domestic Bardas Dalassena, Commander of the Imperial Taghmata, to be, as Mar had once said, "a puffed-up, strutting cock who holds his position only because of the position he holds—bent over with his hands on his ankles—whenever the Dhynatoi request protection for their estates." The Grand Domestic had vehemently resisted Mar's initiatives to recruit more Norsemen into the Roman army; his opposition not only reflected the traditional interests of his Dhynatoi sponsors but also his own conservative, defensively oriented approach to battle tactics. As Mar had put it, "Dalassena's idea of an aggressive campaign is to bribe the opposing commander not to transgress Roman borders for a period of six months."

Mar ripped the seal off with irritation, expecting another protest about his petitions to expand the Varangian Guard. But his face settled into intense concentration as he unrolled the document and began to read. *What* was *this?* The Grand Domestic was proposing that he and Mar put aside their animosities and join forces to counter the precipitous ascent of Mar's fellow Tauro-Scythian, Haraldr Nordbrikt. *What?* Mar had been nothing less than delighted by Haraldr Sigurdarson's success; now the fugitive princeling could not only contribute his title to Mar's ambitions but also his fortune. And why deprive the lad of any incentive to fatten his already considerable purse? Whatever the slave earns, the master keeps. Mar shook his head. *Dalassena,* he told himself, *is a bigger fool than I had thought.*

No. No man rises to the rank of Magister without a modicum of cunning, even if he has only acquired his guile by aping the patrons whom he serves. No, Dalassena was not a complete buffoon; was he privileged to information Mar was not? Or was the intent here simply to burden Mar with suspicion? No, Dalassena was not *that* clever. The Grand Domestic's concern probably could be taken on the face of it. But then who would be sponsoring Mar's pet princeling behind his back? Not Nicephorus Argyrus; he was merely a grotesquely inflated merchant masquerading as a Dhynatoi.

Well, such speculation was at this moment pointless. Mar did not want to be like one of these so-called Hellenists at court who read the ancient Greek philosophers and postulated endlessly on ultimate causes; a Hellenist would stay rooted in the path of a runaway horse, debating over the great forces that set the event in motion, rather than just simply getting out of the way. Or better still, taking a horse staff and goading the beast back into its stable. Indeed. If the fugitive princeling was perhaps soaring too high, this would be the time to remind him of the chains that held him to earth.

Mar remained fixed in thought for some time, then took up his quill pen and dipped into the gold ink pot given to him by Romanus on the occasion of the late and emphatically unlamented Emperor's last Easter among them. He wrote at length, checking the details carefully. Then he removed his ring, lit the red candle he had taken from his writing cabinet, and applied his personal seal to the paper. He clapped his hands with pleasure; in the Imperial Palace a bowshot was not well-aimed unless it brought down two birds at once. And this single arrow might just skewer three fat, unwary fowl.

"These are instructions for our friend on the Street of St. Polyeuktos." Mar handed the sealed document to the waiting decurion. "Double his usual fee. Make certain that he understands *everything*. And tell him that his brother, who unfortunately has come to lodge in Numera Prison, is well cared for. We have petitioned for his release, and he may be free before he has to spend the winter there."

The decurion bowed, turned briskly, and headed toward the palace gate. Mar Hunrodarson looked through the large, vaguely green-tinted, arched windows that illuminated his third-story office; he had set his writing table so that he faced north. There was a uniform grayness to the view; even the great silver dome of the Church of Hagia Sophia was dulled by leaden skies that here and there dipped to earth in wispy, ashen shafts of rain. The waters of the Bosporus, sprinkled with white, resembled gouged pewter. How gentle those waves lulled next to the memories of the vast, furious northern ocean that had tested Mar as a boy and had brought him to manhood.

Mar opened the doors to his colonnaded balcony and walked outside. A north wind carrying the first intimations of winter funneled through the marble portico. Mar savored the refreshing gust; the air seemed cleansed of the appalling fetor of the long, sweltering southern summer. What these Romans have built is magnificent, Mar told himself as he surveyed the Great City. But think how much more magnificent all this will be when it has been scoured by the tempest that rages out of the north.

† † †

"He assures this price is below the cost to him, Haraldr Nordbrikt. He only begs you accept because of the prestige your patronage will bring to him." Marmot-Man paused and reflected that this hand-wringing rug merchant, with his oiled brow and desperate eyes, had neglected to add a tip to the minimum fee that Nicephorus Argyrus, via his representative,

Marmot-Man, was collecting for arranging audiences with the fabulously wealthy *barbaroi* pirate-slayer. Besides, the perplexingly tight-fisted *barbaroi* had already refused a number of tempting propositions from agents representing Nicephorus Argyrus's own business concerns, and some of the proposals even offered legitimate profits! There wasn't time to waste with this greasy carpet peddler. Marmot-Man waved aside the scrofulous boy and crooked-backed old man who had carried in the merchant's wares. "No, Haraldr Nordbrikt, slayer of Saracens, this merchandise is inferior, indeed to such a degree that this purveyor might well be reported to the Prefect."

"No more merchants!" growled Haraldr in the passable Greek Marmot-Man had taught him during their long voyage.

"Yes, I've asked him to go, Haraldr Nordbrikt."

"Not him only! All! All merchants!" This time Haraldr drew his finger across his neck.

Marmot-Man nervously stroked his new robe of Syrian silk as he surveyed the mob of dealers in precious gems, icons, glass vases, carved ivories, Egyptian carpets, chased silver and gold serving vessels, furniture, polo mounts, and even concrete-and-steel strongboxes. The merchants waited impatiently in the courtyard of the Norse compound, bobbing up and down to practice their shrillest solicitations or jostling as they fought for position; there had already been several bloody noses and one attempted stabbing. And these were supposedly proprietors of the most respectable shops on the Mese, men who wore embroidered Hellas silk to work! Marmot-Man shook his head and calculated that there were thirty-five, forty tips still to be collected. And four—no, five—that would have to be refunded. And here was Haraldr Nordbrikt making like Christ the King expurgating the moneylenders from the temple! Still, had not Haraldr Nordbrikt given Marmot-Man a full Varangian's share of his booty, which was ten times what Nicephorus Argyrus had paid him? Marmot-Man quickly decided where his true allegiance lay. He raised his hands and flew at the merchants like a peasant woman shooing a herd of lumbering oxen out of her herb garden. "Out! Out! Be gone quickly! Quickly! The Slayer of Saracens casts you out! He casts you out! You have angered him with tawdry wares and meretricious claims! Be gone quickly, before you bring his magical sword from his scabbard! Out! Save yourselves!"

Haraldr put his hands over his ears to block the unearthly wails of protest and withdrew into the barracks.

"Marmot-Man described these for me." Halldor was sitting on his cot leafing through a sheaf of parchments. "A shipyard in Langobard-land, or as the Romans say, Italia. An estate, in a place called Melitene, which is somewhere off in Serkland. This estate encompasses ten entire villages. There are at least three score opportunities right here in Constantinople. A candle factory. A palace not one street from Nicephorus Argyrus's. A home for black-frocks, or 'monastery,' that includes a newly constructed 'mortuary,' which is a building where corpses can be prepared for burial." Halldor looked up. "I think we could make some money on this."

Haraldr simply groaned and sat on his cot. How many agents for such properties had already assailed them in the two days since they had docked and returned to their St. Mama's Quarter barracks? One hundred, perhaps, another hundred right now howling outside the compound gate like a starving wolf pack with a caribou in sight. And then there were the merely curious, conducting some sort of strange vigil outside. Thorir from Upsala had gone through the gate to fetch a ball he had kicked over the wall, and so many of the men, women, and children of a half dozen nationalities had crowded forward to touch his cloak that he had nearly died of fright; apparently they had thought that the towering, moon-faced Swede was the famous Haraldr, Slayer of Saracens.

"We are invited to purchase other properties as well," said Ulfr, who had just descended the stairs that led to the second-story gallery. "The Romans call them 'ladies of the roof,' though I hardly know why, since they are always on the streets. At least they are all on our street. Right now there are three painted whores outside for every man inside. You would not believe it. The traffic is entirely blocked." Ulfr did not need to add that the noise from the street made the din of battle seem like the music of a mountain rivulet.

"Well, let the whores in," said Halldor matter-of-factly.

"Halldor may be right, Haraldr." Ulfr looked out into the courtyard where the Varangians were squabbling over the trinkets they had purchased, playing dice, wrestling, and throwing knives and axes. "Besides, breaking up all the fights over the belly plunder would give us something to do."

Haraldr looked down at the cracked marble paving stones. If Odin and Kristr had not favored him with his successful stunt in the oceans of Blaland, he already would have lost the confidence of his pledge-men. He shook his head at his two friends. "I don't understand. Nothing. No word from the Imperial authorities, other than that eunuch tax gatherer who came to count our gold. Nicephorus Argyrus sends only this plague of merchants, most of them probably representing his own businesses, as if it is now our duty to serve ourselves up to these gold devourers like trussed pigs. Not even any word from rivals of Nicephorus Argyrus hoping to hire our services away from him."

"Believe me," said Ulfr, "you still have the absolute allegiance of your pledge-men."

Haraldr smiled, grateful for his friends but unable to share their belief in him. He had thought that his newly won wealth would open the gates to the Imperial Palace immediately, and it was his secret, desperate hope that even Mar would be so impressed by his coup that he would accept him as a valued and respected ally. Mar. No word from him, either. The knifing guilt that he had not, could not, tell everything to his pledge-men. And each passing hour tightened the fetters of anxiety. Haraldr could almost sense his destiny being determined by forces beyond his reach, perhaps even beyond his knowing. Was Mar himself devising his use for Haraldr, or were others now taking up the threads of his fate, and those of the five hundred he had pledged to lead? Two days ago he had been a triumphant god. Now, waiting outside the walls of the Empress City like the mendicants outside his own gate, he was but an infant desperate for his mother's breast.

"Haraldr Nordbrikt! Haraldr Nordbrikt!" Marmot-Man tugged on Haraldr's sleeve. "You must talk to Euthymius!"

Haraldr took his sword from his scabbard and checked its polish and edge against the light from the freshly lit oil light. Night was falling quickly, and the sky smelled almost like damp earth. "Is a Euthymius a merchant?" he snapped. "An agent for some property owner? A tax collector? A whore? If it is any of those, I'd like to test my blade on this Euthymius."

"No, no, Haraldr Nordbrikt, indeed he is not, indeed. He is Euthymius. *The* Euthymius. You can't imagine what his coming here means. Quickly, Haraldr Nordbrikt, quickly!"

The man who strode jauntily through the doorway was tall, perceptibly bony even in his stiff robe of damson silk, and he moved so strangely that Haraldr wondered for a moment if a Euthymius was another of the Emperor's magical metal beings. This note of artificiality was heightened by the man's face, which lay beneath more paint than Haraldr had ever seen on man or woman; it was as if Euthymius had been lacquered and dipped in wax. His long, sweeping golden hair scarcely seemed more real—had it been hammered from brass?—and his equally golden, pointed beard might have been beveled with a chisel. He spoke, in Greek, without prompting, and sounded as if he were projecting his words through a large tin funnel.

"Haraldr Nordbrikt, Slayer of Saracens, to whom brilliant Achilleus and resourceful Odysseus and indeed the entire host of strong-greaved Achaians are but phantom mists seared to oblivion in the withering sunburst of your fame! Rise up, O former denizens of Olympus, a man lives among us who would be our successor to your Heracles! Rise up, O Christendom, embrace your new champion! Rise up, O ye firmament that doth illuminate our flickering lives. A new beacon is set among you!"

Euthymius advanced, fell to the floor, and threw his arms around Haraldr's new leather boots. "Haraldr Nordbrikt, I greet you with as much felicity as can surmount the towering edifice of reverence already constructed to your immortal memory!"

Haraldr understood only a fragment of this; he had been told of Odysseus and Achilleus and Heracles, heroes of the ancient Greeks, and he knew the terms for *ghosts* and *sun*. But he hardly needed a complete translation to understand what a Euthymius was; he had finally met a Roman skald.

"Tell him I thank him for his verses," Haraldr told Marmot-Man. "Unfortunately I have both Ulfr and Thorfinn the Otter to serve me in the role of skald, and possibly Grettir before too long. Besides, from the look of him, even now I could not afford his upkeep. But tell him his verses would surely please Odin, our patron of poets."

"No, no, Haraldr Nordbrikt, this is *the* Euthymius, as he urges me to tell you, 'impresario of entertainments, husbander of amusements, commander of an army of mirth.' He offers you one of his amusements, celebrated in the Hippodrome and throughout the Empire. Theater. Dance. Song. Comedy. Drama. All specially created for the entertainment of you and your men. Believe me, Haraldr Nordbrikt, this is an honor you will enjoy beyond all others!"

† † †

"I will be all right, Nicetas." Maria whisked her hands gracefully at the concerned-looking eunuch. He bowed and retreated into the villa.

Maria turned to Giorgios. "How did you find me?"

Giorgios's face was flushed from his run up the flight of marble steps, and contorted with pain. "I followed the Imperial galley. I thought you might be on it." He did not need to remind her that he had been trying to see her for weeks, and that her servants and guards had rebuffed every attempt.

"This is my villa," Maria said. She stood on the portico with her arms folded beneath her breasts, as if defending it. Behind her, the great cities on either shore of the Bosporus were framed by scudding rain clouds and metal-hued water; her villa was on the Asian side, to the north of Chrysopolis. "I don't want you here."

Giorgios's brown eyes were wet with confusion and sincerity. "I can't play this game any longer. I am useless without you. You must . . . please."

Maria stepped toward him, her jaw tensed. "I know more amusing games. This is not love play, little boy. I have refused to see you because I do not want to see you."

Giorgios swallowed as if preparing to attempt some athletic feat. "You said you loved me. The things we have done . . ."

"Do you think you are the only man I have done those things with? You saw me do some of them with Alex. I despised him. It would make you sick if you knew some of the men I have been a whore to, and what I have asked them to do to me. And what I have done to them."

Giorgios sprang forward, seized her arms, and shook her like a doll for a moment. When he stopped, his lower lip quivered. "Why did you ever say you loved me? You must despise me too."

"I did love you."

"Then why . . .?"

"Why do I no longer love you?" she asked rhetorically. "You were only beautiful when I hurt you. You only had life when I caused you pain. I could no longer go on creating you anew each time." Maria's eyes were cast down, and her tone was inexpressibly melancholy. "I realized I can only love a man whose pain I do not have to provide. A man bereaved in a way I cannot understand, so that I must enter him when he enters me and find the thorn that has impaled his soul. In you I could only find myself." Her pearllike teeth nibbled at her wine-dark lower lip. "And I am empty. I am as cold and dark as the deepest abyss."

"There is another man?" Giorgios sounded curiously hopeful, as if he could deal with that eventuality. It was the utter frigidity of her demeanor that baffled and frightened him.

"There is no one. You were the last man in my bed. If I could both love you and be kind to you, I would love you still."

Giorgios's mouth trembled with anguish. He squeezed her shoulders gently, and when he closed his eyes, tears spilled to his cheeks. Clutching his forearms, she removed his hands from her shoulders. "Farewell, Giorgios."

An awful, muffled keening came from Giorgios's throat and he fell to his knees. The tip of his bronze scabbard clattered on the marble paving stones. He wrenched his sword free and with trembling arms held it to his own throat. "I want you to see the wound in my heart," he sobbed. "I want you to see the proof of my pain!" His neck corded against the sheer, polished steel.

Maria's eyes were disinterested, seemingly dulled by the baleful pigmentation of the Bosporus. "I am cold, Giorgios. I am going inside. Please go before I call for my guards."

She walked swiftly past Giorgios and disappeared into the pillared entrance. After a moment Giorgios lowered his sword and sobbed quietly, still on his knees. He finally left an hour after dark.

† † †

Euthymius's little army of mirth put the finishing touches on their courtyard theater; the stage they had erected, with its gilded proscenium and brocaded drapes, was as splendid as the palace of a Norse king. Neither Haraldr nor any of his men could divine the use of the rest of the apparatus this "impresario" had assembled, but the Varangians, who had already littered the courtyard with empty kegs, jars, and wineskins, were loudly speculating on the possibilities offered by the dozens of variously costumed, lithe young women—all painted nearly as brightly as Euthymius himself—who scurried about, trilled brief notes, or performed agile exercises. Haraldr had nearly choked when Marmot-Man had first proposed Euthymius's "expenses and honorarium—the rest of his costs are an offering, a veritable human sacrifice, to the Herculean demigod, the Slayer of Saracens, and his dauntless band of incorruptible Christian heroes." But now, even before this "amusement" had begun, Haraldr knew that the gold spent would be more than recaptured in the heightened spirit of his men.

The performance opened with an explosion of two dozen male and female athletes, clad only in loincloths spangled with shiny, rainbow-colored metal bits, who could spin like tops, roll like hoops, and whirl through the air like throwing axes; eventually they built a human tower crowned with the bare-breasted women. Then came dogs that dressed and walked as men; monkeys that raced into the audience and plucked coins from men's purses, then danced in celebration; a lion whose roar seemed to shake the walls, then a lion with stripes; a striped horse with a neck so long, it seemed certain he would topple over; and finally an incredible beast with a back that reached to the second-story balcony, legs shaped exactly like tree trunks, and most wondrous of all, a snout as long as a man was tall that could also pluck coins from the audience (leading Halldor to ask if there was any living creature in Constantinople that could *not* find a man's purse).

Then came the truly extraordinary portion of the amusement, if indeed this was an amusement at all. It was well past midnight, the Varangians roaring with wine and lust, when a chorus trilled and the stage was momentarily screened. The brocade curtains parted, and the music, provided by a portable pipe organ, droned dramatically.

"I'll draw the curtain! You find Euthymius!" Haraldr shouted to Halldor. Wearing purple brocade, a dark, full beard, and an elaborate sparkling diadem, the first actor was clearly a representation of the Emperor. Haraldr's heart screamed with alarm as he rushed to the stage. Was this a plot to involve them in a treason? Clever, indeed!

"Haraldr Nordbrikt! Haraldr Nordbrikt!" shrieked Marmot-Man as he clung desperately to Haraldr's thigh. "Haraldr Nordbrikt, you must stop! Please! If only for a moment!"

Haraldr finally gave up. He was not making much progress through the crowd—the Varangians kept clasping him gratefully—and the enactment was rapidly proceeding. The mock Emperor had already been followed onto the stage by a second, thinner actor, also dressed in mock Imperial raiment, and then three younger, purple-robed women: one beautiful, one less attractive, and one wearing a mask representing some sort of pox or skin disfigurement. These five characters burst into simultaneous action. The first Emperor mimed the defeat of numerous men in rough brown tunics who streamed endlessly onto the stage; the thinner, purple-clad man drank from a wineskin and rolled dice; the beautiful woman primped and dabbed paint on her face; the plainer woman looked on enviously; and the ugly one retired to a corner and knelt in prayer.

"Haraldr Nordbrikt!" gasped the shaken Marmot-Man. "You must know that this is customary among the Romans. It is permitted to lampoon the Emperor even should he himself be seated among us. In fact, there has never been an Autocrator who did not himself witness at least one such performance at his expense. Believe me, Haraldr Nordbrikt. Euthymius says he has prepared this mime particularly for you!"

Haraldr understood. A Norse king would also permit a skald to jest with him. Of course, the skald who dared such jibes was like the man who hunted walrus alone in a small boat; if he was not extremely skilled, he was dead. Haraldr waved Halldor back, and they stood together to watch the show.

"Basil the Bulgar-Slayer?" asked Halldor as the first stage Emperor continued to bash various mock enemies.

"I think so," said Haraldr. "Bulgars wear those brown tunics." Suddenly the Bulgar-Slayer slumped motionless to the floor, and the other actors indulged in great floor pounding and wailing. The Bulgar-Slayer's crown was handed to the thinner man, who after placing the diadem on his head paused and appraised the beautiful woman and the not-as-beautiful woman; the disfigured woman apparently had disappeared, though Haraldr had not noticed her departure from the stage. Another actor, a rather elderly man in a green robe, entered, and with elaborate comic motions the Emperor urged the not-so-beautiful woman to embrace this new character, but she merely turned her head and turned up her nose. Then the Emperor cajoled the beautiful woman, and after considerable reluctance she finally took the green-robed old man in her arms; the not-so-beautiful woman erupted into hysterical, mocking laughter. The Emperor threw up his arms in glee, promptly fell in a heap, and the beautiful woman picked up his crown and purple robe and gave them to her aged companion. Once crowned, this new Emperor piled bricks into little walls and sprinkled them with coins, to the accompaniment of long-haired men who threw pages torn from books in the air and shouted in a nonsense language.

Then something quite remarkable happened. The pace of the actors' movements slowed, the music became funereal, and a towering black-frocked monk entered, mounted on a real horse, and pranced about the stage.

"Not the black-frock you saw at Nicephorus Argyrus's?" asked Halldor.

"I don't know. Perhaps we have reached the present Emperor. This one is certainly portrayed as a buffoon."

The black-frock paused for a moment to study the new Emperor and the beautiful woman, who had turned their backs to each other. The monk cantered offstage for a moment, and when he returned, another man, much younger than the Emperor and clad in a very plain yellow wool robe, rode behind him on the horse. Both men dismounted, and the monk took the yellow-robed man by the hand, pointed out to him the apparently feuding Imperial couple, gave him a pat and a kiss as one might to a young child, and shooed him over to the woman. The beautiful woman took the yellow-robed man's hand, held it shyly for a moment, then devoured him with kisses, knocking him to the floor.

"Fuck her! Fuck her!" The first few Varangians to shout were quickly joined by a rhythmic chant.

The couple kissed prone for a moment—the not-so-beautiful woman just observed all this with elegant amusement—then rose, turned to the Emperor, and stood and watched while he grabbed his throat like a man choking or poisoned. Neither they nor the monk attempted to help, and the Emperor collapsed in a heap.

"They're saying someone murdered an Emperor!" hissed Haldor. "His wife and her lover."

The monk plucked the Imperial diadem from the fallen Emperor's head and removed the purple robe. The monk then placed the crown on the yellow-robed man's head and wrapped him in the purple robe. The beautiful woman turned to the not-so-beautiful woman, erupted with arm-flailing anger, and drove her off the stage. Then the beautiful woman went to one side of the stage to paint her face while the newest Emperor sat contemplatively on his gilded throne, the monk hovering over him in a somewhat sinister tableau.

"Kristr!" Haraldr released the strangled oath as a tall blond man wearing huge padding and the uniform of the Varangian Guard entered the stage. The make-believe Varangian stood on the side of the throne opposite the monk, his great ax extended over the Emperor; it was unclear as to whether he was protecting the Emperor or preparing to behead him.

"Mar Hunrodarson?" asked Halldor.

Haraldr nodded, his veins iced. He had suspected that the Imperial Throne might be an illusion masking a greater and more sinister power, but to finally see his speculation confirmed by a Roman source, and to know that Mar himself was that power . . . But it wasn't that clear. What of the black-frock? Was he the mysterious Joannes, and if so, did he and Mar share power?

Before Haraldr could begin to sort through these alarming new questions, the organ raced to a triumphant flourish and a second tall, blond, padded, and armored actor entered the stage, followed by a band of makeshift Varangians. This second mock Norseman was quickly swarmed by a band of actors wearing white robes; he held his Varangians back, then stepped forward and one by one knocked the white-robed actors to the floor.

"Haraldr! Haraldr! Hardraada! Hardraada!" chanted the audience.

Haraldr uncomfortably watched his stage persona finish bashing the mock Saracens, then reach into the stage floor and pull out a chest filled with brilliant gold coins. The mock Haraldr proudly displayed the chest to the Emperor, and as he presented the offering, both Mar and the black-frock bent simultaneously and mimed speaking garrulously to the Emperor, each taking an Imperial ear. With that the curtain was drawn.

Haraldr leapt for the stage, intent on asking Euthymius just what message this cryptic, unfinished drama had been intended to convey, even if it meant posing his question with the blade of his sword. But he was quickly intercepted by his pledge-men.

"Haraldr! Haraldr!" yelled the Varangians as they swarmed around him.

"Find Euthymius!" Haraldr frantically shouted to Halldor.

The Varangians boosted Haraldr to their shoulders, then ebulliently tossed him high into the night sky; they caught him and continued to throw him into the air again and again.

After several minutes Halldor returned and shouted to his still soaring leader. "I can't find Euthymius!"

Someone opened the gates and the whores came in.

† † †

Silence. The Grand Domestic Bardas Dalassena turned the brass cock at the base of his water clock and emptied the fluid into a washbasin he kept beside the machine's ponderous, brass-pillared base for precisely that purpose. Even though the hourly whistle did not sound at night, he hated the insidious racheting of the mechanism that caused a small statue of a beast—a different one for each hour—to appear in a miniature arcade. Visible now was a bear, indicating the ninth hour of the night. Dalassena looked at the erect gold creature (its finely modeled little paws clawed the air) with his usual vague dread, a psychic burden he carried so habitually that it seemed to press on his shoulders physically, bowing him forward like an aged porter. Three hours until the first hour of the morning, five hours until he would once again be at his office in the Palace. He hated this reminder of the routine that had chained him, but the clock had been a gift from the Senator and Magister, Nicon Attalietes. So he was obliged to display it prominently in the office he kept in his home, the hilltop palace that he had acquired through the generosity of Senator Attalietes and his circle.

But for a moment at least, Dalassena was free from time and its irksome herald, sound. His wife Eudocia had long since succumbed to the oppressive gaiety of their evening at the Palace of the Zonaras; the price of being among the Dhynatoi but not of them was that one had to pretend to enjoy the social rituals that the Dhynatoi themselves disdained with weary sarcasm. His daughter, Anna, also had come home, though only an hour ago; he ached to think of the corruption of her doe-eyed innocence, but since Anna now often dined only a chair removed from the Empress, he endured the pain of her despoliation like a soldier in a field hospital stiffening against the amputation of his leg. The only sound from this quiet precinct of the sleeping city was the occasional rattle as armed guards checked locked gates, and the ghostly sough of the wind through columned arcades.

Dalassena went to his lacquered wooden writing table and removed the sheaf of dispatches that he regularly brought home and studied, as if in taking these profound drafts of his predicament he could somehow find expiation. The dispatches reported raids near Hadath and Raban; some large estates had been torched and a distant nephew of a senator had been slain. Bulgars had come across the Danube near Nicopolis and had penetrated almost to Trnovo in Paristron theme. The continuing fester of Sicily, where Abdallah-ibn-Muizz was taking Christians captive by the thousands. Libyan pirates had sacked three coastal villages in southern Crete. The successes were almost as nettling: The siege of Berki would soon be concluded now that a force of Varangians had arrived; and, most appalling of all, the victory by this new Tauro-Scythian menace over almost two hundred pirate vessels, at the very ends of the earth. Just the kind of thing that would kindle the dangerous imagination of the mob.

Dalassena clenched his still powerful fists. Madness. His generous appeal to the self-interest of the swellheaded Hetairarch Mar Hunrodarson had not brought a breath of reply; apparently Hunrodarson was unaware of the directive from the Emperor's own offices to explore expansion of the Middle Hetairia, the less prestigious Imperial Guard that been virtually defunct for decades and was now manned by only a few well-born fugitives from Saracen courts, ceremonially invested to reward them for converting to Christianity and swearing allegiance to the Emperor. This directive proposed to revive the Middle Hetairia to accommodate a second force of Varangians, a force that would be equal in numbers to Mar Hunrodarson's Grand Hetairia. And this initiative had not been sponsored by Mar Hunrodarson; Dalassena was certain of that. No, he reflected, Hunrodarson has taken to making his appeals to the Logothete of the Dromus, with all these not entirely unfounded claims of massive civil discontent in the city and his continued lobbying for another Varangian unit to be posted outside the palace; even Hunrodarson is reluctant to invite any more of his *barbaroi* band of cutthroats within the Chalke Gate. So it is clear that the extravagantly lucky thug, Haraldr Nordbrikt, is the beneficiary of some other highly placed patron, perhaps someone promoting a rival to Mar Hunrodarson. Why can't Hunrodarson, who is as clever as he is mendacious, see that he is being asked to share his bone with another equally vicious dog?

Dalassena shuffled through his writing cabinet, took out his pen and ink and a sheet of Alexandrian paper, and laboriously scripted a note to the Domestic of the Hyknatoi—one of his key subordinates in the Imperial Taghmata—instructing him in the course of action they should now take. He decided he had better use his personal seal on the document, rather than the official stamp of his office. As he fingered the small, cone-shaped stone implement, he noticed that traces of wax had been left on the the face, and he picked the engraved surface meticulously clean. Had his wife Eudocia been using his seal again, perhaps to place orders with the Vestiopratai, the imperially licensed dealers in silk garments; wasn't it enough that she had one eunuch silk merchant who called weekly? That was simply not acceptable; the woman was determined to make a travesty of his marital dominion.

Bardas Dalassena pressed the stone seal into the glimmering hot wax, then put his writing instruments away and savored silence. Within seconds he had completely forgotten the diatribe he had intended for his wife.

he sound of steel striking brass echoed through a cavern. Haraldr felt the pain and wondered how he had come to sleep with seals, slippery seals, soft, down-covered seals, their bodies beneath and atop and beside him. But seals did not have furless arms or legs or great hanks of wet hair. Still, seals could smell like this.

Again the noise in the cavern, but this time it was someone screaming. Haraldr struggled to raise his torso, and bodies slithered away from him. He saw the whore, her face paint smeared into a blurry mask, and then the dancer. Around they went, pulling hair, grunting, and squealing. Haraldr dragged his legs from under a bedding of flesh punctuated with bulging breasts, jutting buttocks, and staring, wheat-thatched belly furrows. He shook the whore; she had to stop screaming. But she wasn't screaming. Haraldr struggled to his feet. The brass was shattering inside his head.

The courtyard looked like the aftermath of a terrible battle; the wreckage of Euthymius's stage was scattered amid a vast carpet of naked men and women, their clothes, and empty containers of various intoxicating beverages. Odin, the herons of forgetfulness must have plucked every mind last night, thought Haraldr, his stomach retching and his head bursting with hot metal and the horrible shrieking. Then he saw the actual source of the screaming, an olive-skinned dancer rising above the prone but obviously not totally incapacitated form of a wild-haired Varangian. At first Haraldr assumed that only an excess of pleasure filled the dancer's throat, but then he saw it too.

It had been a Varangian, when it had forearms and calves and bowels and genitals and a head. It now hung naked, six feet off the ground, from its own small intestine, which had been wrapped around its waist and then tied to the balcony above, so that the truncated body spun slowly within one of the broad, soiled, white plaster arches of the courtyard arcade. Haraldr bent over and let the bitter alcoholic bile surge over his tongue and onto the pavement. The vomit filled his nostrils and he retched some more, choking and sputtering like a child. Another woman screamed, and a Varangian began to shout.

Haraldr held his hands to his screeching head. The screaming and shouting became a chorus. Ulfr came running; he had remained sober to guard the gold, along with a few of the most devoted disciples of Kristr among the Varangians, who would neither drink for pleasure nor fornicate. They had been at their posts in the strong room all night.

"A message has been left," said Ulfr as he stood over a disembodied arm lying on the stone pavement a few ells from the corpse. The stiff, purple forefinger had been carefully arranged to point directly at a large, algae-tinted terra-cotta jar resting a few ells away against the inner wall of the arcade.

Haraldr looked inside the jar and gagged. Steeling himself, he reached in. His trembling fingers found a single, grotesquely slippery lock of hair; the bowel-knifing touch told him that the rest of the scalp had been flayed to the bare skull. He forced back the bile and commanded himself to bring the head up. He stood and looked with uncomprehending terror into the face: no lips or ears, a shriveled, bruise-colored penis in place of the nose, and a rosy testicle in each eye socket. A piece of parchment was clenched between bloody, grimacing teeth. Shaking from head to toe, nauseated beyond anything he had ever imagined, Haraldr prised the teeth open, removed the parchment, and clawed with bloody fingers at the crimson wax seal. He read the message, crushed it in his hand, fell back against the wall, and slumped to the ground, holding the bloody skull against his chest like a boy cradling the dead body of a beloved pet.

† † †

One by one they entered, their robes of glossy white silk stiff with gold thread, to stand at their places around the polished ivory table. But the black-frocked Orphanotrophus Joannes did not acknowledge or even see them. He had gone home to Amastris. He smelled the dust of Asia Minor in the hot summer wind and heard the buzz of the locusts.

"But I did the sums."

"You can't have finished all of them," his mother had said. She held the lump of cheese in her hands, squeezed, and the thin, milky liquid oozed between her thick, mannish fingers. He remembered that distinctly.

"But I did. If Stephan and Constantine are going, I must be able to go too." The sea was where he had wanted to go, the coarse wet sand of the beach near the docks and the big cool pebbles around which he could curl his toes.

"I need you to look after Michael. He's everywhere at once and into everything now. Look." His mother swept up the naked infant, who had almost disappeared into a half-empty grain sack.

Joannes could tell that his mother was concealing something from him. He knew then that this day would not be good. He said good-bye to Constantine and Stephan and waited, quietly doing sums in his head. After what seemed a very long time he heard his father's voice, that beaten, whining voice that alone of all sounds terrified him, for he knew the defeat in it. His father, tall yet paunchy, with his reek of fish sauce and cheap wine, was in the company of a second man, and Joannes shrunk from this man immediately. He had the ugly, hairless chin of a eunuch; jaundiced, squinty eyes that made him look like a snake; and a tunic stained like a butcher's smock.

"This is the one," Joannes's father told the snake-eyed eunuch. "He reads better than boys twice his age and there is no function of arithmetic he cannot already perform."

The eunuch slipped Joannes's tunic over his head and looked at him through his reptilian slits, then felt his arms and poked at his chest and belly. He turned to Joannes's father and said, "He's strong enough for the operation. I can proceed right away. He'll have some pain but little bleeding." The rest had been an unimaginable nightmare. No blade, only a silk ligature wrapped tightly about the top of his tiny pink scrotum, the searing pain that had come within minutes, then the numbness and the horror of the next two weeks as he had watched a part of him die. Every day the eunuch came to smear the purpling, yellowing, blackening flesh with ointment, and every day Joannes smelled the rot of the life he might have had, the games with other boys, and that vague future of manhood that he could sense only well enough to know he was now denied it.

Joannes's father had not explained it all until the the shriveled vestige of Joannes's scrotum and testicles had sloughed away. "This is so you can stand next to Emperor, as I will never do." The next day Joannes had been sent to a school in Constantinople.

And so he had come to stand next to the Emperor. The Orphanotrophus Joannes looked down upon the living heir of Christ the King, seated on his golden throne as he attended to this meeting of the Sacrum Consistorum, the group of fifteen men who constituted the Emperor's cabinet. The Emperor turned and looked up at Joannes, his dark, tired eyes questing for assurance, and Joannes nodded and replied with a look that communicated the almost suffocating love he felt for this Sacred Person. He had never loved a woman, but was not such feeling, even at its purest, a hollow profanity next to the love he held for the Lord's anointed representative on earth? For in loving this Emperor, Joannes could restore the life—no, not simply the life, but the *immortality*—that had been shorn from him so long ago. Joannes looked again at the Emperor Michael and, for a searing instant, filled his heart with the dream that burned in his soul.

Joannes studied the assembled cabinet. They were pieces on the board at which Joannes daily played the ages-old, endless game of Roman power, a game where a man might wager his life and win eternal life, his name forever inscribed in the halls of memory. There isn't a real player in this lot, thought Joannes. The Grand Domestic Bardas Dalassena, clutching the golden wand of a Magister as if he were showing off his erect manhood, his arrogant chin and barrel chest thrust forward. Dalassena was a career military officer, his family just wealthy enough that he had been able to start out in the Imperial Scholae, but not wealthy enough to make him a member of the Dhynatoi, to which he so desperately aspired. Will you be so proud, Dalassena, when you ride through the city backward on an ass? And the Logothete of the Dromus, a thorough, potentially formidable man who had become so timorous of his own spies that he could hardly speak without locking himself in that absurd "secret" chamber of his. Joannes's eyes flickered; what would the Logothete say if he knew that his trusted servant was in the pay of the Orphanotrophus? The Prefect of the City, white-haired and frail, was a harmless criminal, a competent administrator content to ploddingly enforce his exacting regulations and enrich himself with a steady flow of petty graft. The Quaestor, his fat, round head bobbing with palsy, was the highest judicial officer in the Empire and reputed to hear his cases in such a state of inebriation that he had once sentenced his own secretary to hanging; fortunately the lawyers had been able to turn him to the accused before he had had the horrified functionary dragged off in irons. The Sacellarius, a stooped, almost vacant-looking eunuch, was Joannes's personal property; as supervisor of all Imperial finances from the Emperor's estates to the Empire's staggering tax revenues, he was a relentless cipher who provided Joannes with the real key to his power: a knowledge of the origins and ultimate disposition of virtually every solidus that entered the Imperial Treasury. Then several august senators of Magister rank, the obligatory representatives of the mindless Dhynatoi and their reclusive swineherd, the Senator and Magister Nicon Attalietes. The Dhynatoi, Joannes thought scoffingly, were willful children who produced nothing and were intent on consuming everything, and in the Eastern themes they were shaping the noose with which they would hang themselves. Then the Imperial Government would come in and restore the timeless order of the Roman system.

The meeting droned on. The principal concern was the quivering-jowled Quaestor's continuing dispute with Alexius, the Patriarch of the One True Oecumenical, Orthodox, and Catholic Faith. The Patriarch Alexius was attempting to appropriate into the Patriarchal Courts some types of cases previously relegated to the civil courts. In this Joannes would oppose the Quaestor, though he personally despised the unctuous, excrement-tongued Patriarch perhaps more than any other man, because when Joannes had deposed the Patriarch, he would wish to expand the authority of the ecclesiastical courts beyond even Patriarch Alexius's insanely grasping ambitions. The Grand Domestic reported on the siege of the Saracen fortress at Berki in eastern Asia Minor, which was finally showing signs of a successful conclusion. Yes, Dalassena, Joannes observed silently, because you were finally able to blockade the fortress when a force of several hundred Varangians was brought in by your subordinate, Nicholas Pegonites, over your objections; hadn't you, Dalassena, at first threatened to make a eunuch of Pegonites? The Sacellarius gave the usual summary of the declining tax revenues from the Eastern themes, though as usual his figures, at Joannes's behest, did not reflect the true immensity of the problem; wait until the patient is gravely ill, Joannes reasoned, and he will accept even the most drastic treatment.

Then came the matter Joannes had prompted the Logothete to raise. "The new Caliph of Egypt, Moustanir Billah," the Logothete humbly intoned, his stubby fingers clasped almost penitently to his chest, "is proving himself the very manifestation of peaceful coexistence between Rome and the Arab world. He has released tens of thousands of Christian captives from the caliphate's dungeons. He has entered into a thirty-year treaty of peace with the Roman Empire. He has kept passage to Jerusalem open to Christians who wish to journey to the Holy Shrines. And to crown his achievements, he has authorized rebuilding of the Church of the Holy Sepulcher in Jerusalem. Is it not time to honor this Saracen avatar of Christian virtues with a gesture of regard for his estimable conduct?"

The Emperor nodded.

"What is your suggestion, Logothete?" asked Joannes.

"What better way to express our respect and trust for the Caliph, and indeed convey to the ordinary Roman taxpayer the peace that Roman hegemony has brought to the entire civilized world, than for eminent and honored Roman dignitaries to lead a pilgrimage to the Holy Sepulcher of Christ Pantocrator in Jerusalem?"

"And what dignitaries would the Logothete suggest as appropriate to the significance of this new accord in the lands where Our Lord was sinlessly made incarnate in flesh?" asked Joannes. "We must not offend the Caliph by sending him any less than his equal in rank and diplomacy."

"It would, of course, be inconceivable to ask our Emperor Father to make such a time-consuming journey at a time when his children are in desperate need of his Holy Presence. But perhaps the Empress Mother, who has spared no effort on previous occasions to vouchsafe her exemplary piety, would lead the Roman standards on a pilgrimage of such profound implication that it may well be thought to augur the millennium of the Pantocrator's Holy Kingdom. I pray that our Emperor Father will bless us with the loan of his living treasure, though it is certain that for him, and indeed for those of us who will remain in the Empress City, each moment without our Blessed Mother will be a torment to echo the diabolical distresses Christ Pantocrator Himself endured in the wilderness."

Joannes looked around the room. The Dhynatoi would concur in this initiative, since such a profound expression of Saracen–Christian accord would almost immediately escalate the value of their estates in the Eastern themes, which had long suffered from Arab raids. And their dung hauler, the Grand Domestic Dalassena, would certainly have to join their accord, even though he knew that he could not even guarantee the Empress safe passage from Cesare Mazacha to Adana in the heart of Roman Asia Minor!

Joannes turned his lowered palm forward, signaling the Emperor that he should reply. Of course the Lord of the Entire World would accede to this request; the idea of a pilgrimage would appeal to his ardent piety, but less so than the opportunity to remove himself from the scheming harlot who plagued him to distraction with her unyielding demands for the most lascivious affections. The woman was a menace, and Joannes longed for the day when she would prove unnecessary.

When the Emperor had given his approval, Joannes thought of the small matter that had troubled him earlier. He was fatigued from the meeting but reminded himself that the enormity of his responsibility required unremitting attention to detail.

"Your Imperial Majesty," said Joannes, "let me presume to acknowledge the angelic quality of your affections for our Mother the Empress, a model of devotion such that even those of us who love the Holy Theotokos as we do cannot hope to exceed the adoration you have vested in our earthly Mother's precious vessel. And so to protect this wondrously adorned yet fragile vessel, I would suggest her guard be augmented with a special gift to her Holy Presence, a force of Tauro-Scythians of proven ferocity and dauntless ability in dealing with foes of Christendom. The Tauro-Scythians who vanquished the despicable Saracen miscreants off the coast of Africa are languishing in disuse, and I fear that their services will soon be lost to the Roman Empire if they are not given employment suitable to their evident worth as champions of Christ. Name these men as the Empress's special guard, and the Mother of God herself will take our Mother's hand as she ventures forth to pray for us at the shrines of Christ the King."

The Emperor quickly agreed, and Joannes watched the Grand Domestic Dalassena's eyes, looking for a sign. As he had suspected, he saw nothing.

† † †

"Purple." Even Halldor's voice was edged with fatigue, shock, and rage. Asbjorn Ingvarson's funeral pyre, which had burned in the courtyard all afternoon, still sent a raven-sooted plume into the indigo sky. The authorities had barred the gates and prevented the Varangians from burying the young Swede at sea, and it had taken all of Haraldr's force as a leader to keep his men from breaking out and assaulting the city walls.

"Purple?" asked Ulfr numbly. He jerked his head up. His chair scraped against the stone paving of the little storeroom.

Halldor spoke like a man in a trance, determined to make his point to listeners he could scarcely see. "When the first two Emperors died, the woman passed the crown to their successors, neither of whom wore purple when they first appeared. Purple implies royal lineage."

Haraldr tried to focus on Halldor's words through his own scarcely controllable fury. Although he had not known Asbjorn Ingvarson well, the agreeable young pagan had been one of his most devoted pledgemen, and his death screamed for Odin's vengeance; Asbjorn's soul could not begin the long journey through the spirit world while his murderer remained in the middle realm. But Haraldr realized that his sword was sheathed by his own ignorance; as yet he could only guess at the identity of the murderer of Asbjorn Ingvarson. He was convinced, however, that

Euthymius's curious mime provided them important clues. He struggled to make sense of Halldor's reasoning.

"So you see," Halldor droned on, "the man the monk brought in on his horse, who was surely intended to represent the Emperor who received you, Haraldr, is not of royal blood."

Haraldr nodded, his intellect finally stirring. "So this 'bitch-whore' is the last of the Bulgar-Slayer's lineage, and the kiss of her loins can legitimize any would-be Emperor skilled in aiming the lance he carries between his legs."

"The monk gave the last Emperor his crown," rebutted Ulfr.

"But the Emperor still had to embrace the 'bitch-whore' in order to receive the crown and purple robe," countered Halldor.

"Why would the monk pick this particular man?" mused Haraldr, almost to himself.

"You're certain this monk is the same one you saw that night at Nicephorus Argyrus's?" asked Ulfr.

"No. There are so many black-frocks among these Romans, I could never be certain. But this Joannes—I am certain that was his name—inspired fear, as if he could indeed topple an Emperor and raise up another in his stead. And his name is whispered, here and there, again and again."

"I believe that this Joannes was the monk portrayed here last night," ventured Halldor. "And clearly the Emperor, a usurper with no blood claim to the throne, is but a puppet of both Joannes and Mar. The question left is: What were they telling their puppet to do with you?"

Haraldr massaged his aching temples. "I'm not certain any of it is that simple. Yes, Mar and Joannes are very powerful, but the very fact that they might need a puppet to represent them indicates the limits of their power; after all, one is a eunuch, the other a *barbaroi.* I have also seen the array of court-men who surround this Emperor, and among those hundreds there must be other factions as well." Haraldr placed his hands together and looked searchingly at Ulfr and Halldor, his scarred eyebrow twitching slightly. "Consider this. What if, in the play, Mar and Joannes were actually disputing for the Emperor's ear? If Mar is my enemy, then Joannes might be my friend."

"Or the other way around," said Halldor.

Again Haraldr felt the awful stirring deep in his entrails. Even now, especially now, he could not tell everything to Halldor or Ulfr or any of his men. It was not only the oaths he had sworn to Olaf and Jarl Rognvald, but he now realized that the Jarl had been agonizingly prescient when he had warned him that his deadly secret could also condemn the men pledged to his keeping. Haraldr would have to deal with Mar as he had dealt with Hakon, in the arena from which the only exit was victory or death.

Haraldr pressed out the piece of parchment prised from Asbjorn's frozen teeth. The message had been written in runic symbols, obviously drafted by an interpreter who had made several mistakes. Still, the message was clear enough. Haraldr read it aloud again, as if the words were some sort of chant that would induce a state in which a greater truth would be revealed. "Haraldr Nordbrikt. The next head is yours. Think well with it while you yet own it. Leave Miklagardr."

"Mar would not have needed an interpreter to write the runes," offered Halldor.

"Perhaps the interpreter's hand is a clever ruse," suggested Ulfr.

Haraldr followed his own silent line of reasoning. Why would Mar want Haraldr to leave if he had, as he had said, use for him? But perhaps Mar had butchered Asbjorn Ingvarson simply to unnerve Haraldr, to remind him of the blade he held at Haraldr's back. If Haraldr could prove that, he would not wait. He would ask Odin to choose between his two Rage-gifted champions. But what proof? A mistaken judgment now would almost certainly doom five hundred men.

Haraldr examined the remains of the red wax seal, again cursing himself for destroying most of it that morning; by the time he realized what he had done, the remaining bits had been flattened on the stone walkway by dozens of feet. Still, the fragment that remained had a recognizable detail, an arm holding a sword. That could easily be Mar, but then many men carried swords—though it was unlikely that monks did. Haraldr fixed every detail of that fragment in his memory. If he saw it again, his sword would be swift.

"Could it be Mar's seal?" asked Ulfr.

"Why would Mar use his own seal but try to disguise his hand?" countered Halldor.

"Or perhaps Joannes is trying to make us think that Mar opposes us."

Haraldr just shook his head. Each thought was like a box within a box within a box. Were Mar and Joannes themselves merely ruses? Was the whole intent of the play and its grisly aftermath to confuse? Yes, a man could be beaten by ruses alone. To march on the city that day would have been suicidal, but soon Haraldr would have to take some action; they could not fester here indefinitely, eventually to turn on themselves. He considered the bitter irony: By defeating an army of phantoms he had won enough gold to buy a kingdom, but now all the gold in the East could not help him against the phantoms the Romans had set upon him. And the names of these phantoms were fear, confusion, and indecision.

ow could a garden so beautiful be so empty? she had wondered, but she knew that only the iridescent peacocks watched. The huge leaves, so green that they seemed flaked from giant emeralds, bowed deeply with the moist heat. Her robe was hot, so she had slipped it up to her hips as she sat on the cool marble bench and dangled her legs in the little pool. The peacocks rustled and spread their silky fans. She touched herself, and she was already wet. Then his hand came over hers and held it there. He stroked her gently with her own finger, her spine became fluid, and she rocked her head back and saw the sun, distant and filtered through the emerald canopy. His other hand pulled her robe up and the silk seemed to dissolve over her arms, and she shivered when he touched her hard nipple. She floated on the pool, the water warm.

He tossed her like a doll and she faced him, he standing, she poised, weightless, legs wrapped around him, sensing the searing gristle just beneath her. She lowered herself and he was like a shaft of rock covered with hot unguent, sliding deep. She pressed her milky breasts to his chest, pulled his silky hair, and kissed his soft golden eyebrows, her tongue darting over the hard ridge of the pale pink scar. She rocked and rose, and the birds made a single noise like the note of a golden hymn.

Her scream shattered the glassy leaves and brought the night like a black hammer. The obsidian head of her lover leered, his horrible beak tittering and the nacreous beads of his eyes reaching for her soul. She screamed and screamed again, and her lover's wings rose up like storm clouds. She awakened.

"Mistress," lilted the eunuch Nicetas. He stood at Maria's bedside, a silver tray and golden goblet balanced on his slender fingertips. "Mistress, would you care for your draft?" The Mistress of the Robes usually requested this narcotic when she awakened in the night, if she did not have a companion to ease her nocturnal anxieties.

Maria looked around the bedchamber. "No, Nicetas, light a lamp." Nicetas found the brass lantern on the dresser and lit it with his own oil lamp. "Is our Mother awake?"

"Yes, Mistress." The blessed Mother was often awake, since she was so rarely rendered pacific by the attentions of her husband.

Maria put on her beryl-green robe and padded down the marble hall-ways in her silk slippers. She paused before the eunuchs who guarded the Empress's antechamber and was nodded past. The antechamber was brightly lit by the silver candelabra; the floor of opus sectile resembled a meadow of crocus and hyacinth. Two more eunuchs in lacquer-stiff silk greeted her and went softly to the huge ivory doors, incised with the Imperial eagles, and slid them slightly apart. After a moment one eunuch turned and nodded, and Maria crossed the room.

Columns of white-veined Carian marble supported the soaring golden dome of the Empress's vast bedchamber; the walls were reveted with alternating panels of deep red porphyry and moss-green Thesallian marble. Maria observed that the Empress had expanded her cosmetics factory. Three servants attended tables covered with vials, jars, mortars and pestles, and rows of braziers simmering dozens of pungent-smelling potions.

"Little daughter!" cried the Empress Zoe as she swept across the room to greet Maria, her flawless white arms extended, her sheer gauze gown clinging to her full yet youthful form like a windblown cloud. She drew the small clay jar in her hand beneath Maria's nose—it smelled vaguely of whale oil—and then dabbed with her fingers, gently massaging a cool cream into Maria's forehead. "This is new. It will erase a frown as if an angel had passed his hand over your face."

Maria acquiesced; was not Zoe's own unsurpassed pulchritude proof that her endless cosmetic inventions had merit? Still, the Empress's obsession was desperate, as if she believed her beauty might flee in the night if she did not remain awake concocting ways to preserve it. Of course, Maria acknowledged that she, too, would be as vigilant when she reached the Empress's age. She hated to think of herself as prune-faced and desiccated, no longer able to contort her lithe spine against the supple body of a young athlete. But perhaps she would not live that long.

Zoe stood back and admired Maria. "Already the care has been absorbed from your skin." She handed the jar of ointment to a servant. "I guess you have heard?"

"That the Senator and Patrician Andronicus Cametus has been murdered by one of his conquests? It's not entirely true; the boy's father was the assailant. He hid in the Senator's bath."

Zoe waved her hand as if the entire scandal were a wisp of stagnant air to be fanned away. "No. I can see that you don't know." She parted her bow-shaped, blood-red lips in a curiously triumphant pout, inhaled as if to speak, and then paused, savoring her coup. "We're going to Jerusalem," she finally said. She fluttered her hand frivolously. "My devoted husband commands it, so I must obey. Should I have occasion also to submit myself to the sinful pleasures of Antioch and the appalling decadence of the Levant on this holiest of ventures, it would simply be as the dutiful wife of our Holy Emperor Father."

"Then I am bid to suffer these scourges at your side, my blessed Mother," said Maria, her eyes cast down in mock humility. Then she looked up earnestly. "But isn't it in truth dangerous?"

"I think not, at least once we leave Roman soil. The Caliph is reputed to be most gracious. And"—Zoe drew the word out with a delicately salacious flourish—"we are to have a special guard attached to our regular military escort. Those Tauro-Scythians who have made themselves so rich, and the monstrously acquisitive Nicephorus Argyrus so much richer."

Maria felt as if the blood in her face had been sucked away by a shrieking dry winter wind. She could only stammer. "I—I—Mother . . ." Her teeth began to chatter slightly.

"Little daughter! The Tauro-Scythians are such . . . *luxuries!* They amuse us." Zoe placed her arms around Maria. "You have never been afraid of northern *barbaroi* before, and you have even met the commander of these men. Why, you said he was partially civilized, in a grim sort of way. I do remember."

"I fear he is too grim for me. I have had dreams."

"Ohhh . . ." Zoe let the exclamation breeze through her lips. "I am so . . . *stimulated* by your dreams, Maria. Had I had your . . . *imagination* when I was your age, perhaps I would have been more . . . *deliberate* in my choice of companions."

"Mother, these dreams bring me no pleasure." But Maria realized that there was even now a residue of the ecstasy she had known in the dream garden, and that her memory of that passion was all the more vivid because of the horror that had followed. "No, that is not entirely so. There is pleasure and there is terror. My dreams offer love and death, twined so tightly that you could not get a knife between them. Perhaps death is the ultimate desire."

Zoe's icy amethyst eyes seemed to darken, like crystal pools shadowed by a cloud, as she thought of her own troubles. "Yes, little daughter, love and death are but the different sides of one coin. How well your Empress Mother knows the truth of that."

ou may not." John the frog-faced interpreter held the document against his chest as if he were a woman shielding her bare breasts. "I have translated each word exactly as written." He fixed his eyes defiantly on the ceiling.

"Let me read!" snapped Haraldr in Greek so that the Topoteretes would hear.

The tough-eyed, leather-skinned Topoteretes, who had been absorbed in studying Halldor's sword, looked up in surprise. After a moment he barked at the surly, black-frocked interpreter, who sulkingly handed the paper to Haraldr.

Haraldr studied the claret script. He made out the term for the Emperor, and also another Greek word that troubled him. "It says something about my going by ship," he told Halldor and Ulfr. "My previous journey to the Emperor's Palace did not require a sea voyage."

"I smell the raven-slime," said Ulfr. "They could plan to take you to a place of imprisonment. I've heard they frequently exile their own to islands from which there is no escape."

"Or just feed you to the lobsters," offered Halldor.

Haraldr decided he would balk on this issue. He tapped John on the arm; the interpreter jerked it away indignantly.

The dam Haraldr had built against his rage and frustration could hold no longer. He leapt to his feet, grabbed John's gown at the chest, and with one hand jerked the astounded interpreter over his head; his other hand quivered over the pommel of his sword, waiting, if necessary, for the Topoteretes. "Ask the Topoteretes why they are transporting me by sea! Ask him!"

To Haraldr's surprise the Topoteretes laughed, his head back, showing big white, horsey teeth. He even poked Halldor and gestured, showing how much he appreciated this treatment of the interpreter. "Ask him!" shouted Haraldr to his red-faced, flailing captive. The interpreter translated frantically, and Haraldr, recovering his control, dropped him hard on his feet.

The Topoteretes shrugged and explained. The interpreter stepped back and made the sign of the cross; he spoke in unsteady Norse. "He says they want to receive you in the palace harbor. It's more appropriate."

Haraldr looked at Haldor and Ulfr. He raised his eyebrows quizzically.

"I think we can trust our friend the Topoteretes," said Ulfr.

Yes, thought Haraldr, *I can assume I am going to the palace. But has Mar sent for me, or is it Joannes? Do Mar and Joannes work in concert?* Then all of the pieces shifted and he felt a sudden tranquillity, almost as it had been when he was a boy struggling to learn the runes and suddenly he had made sense of it all. Fate alone would greet him at the end of this day's voyage, and the masks destiny wore were not important. If he died, it would be a better end than remaining the wealthiest prisoner in St. Mama's Quarter. If he returned, it would be with the answers to these deviling questions.

A small warship waited at one of the commercial wharfs in St. Mama's Quarter. Haraldr was actually greeted by the kentarchos, the captain of the ship, a wiry man of about thirty who wore a bright brass breastplate embossed with a lion. The kentarchos told Haraldr he could roam the deck freely; Haraldr studied the great throwing engines with their bewildering complexes of gears, ropes, pulleys, and windlasses, then went to the bow and examined the ornate bronze spout, shaped like a bellowing lion, that could belch forth the terrifying flames he would not have believed in had he not already seen their devastating effect.

The warship passed the enormous harbor boom and the foreboding gray tower and skirted the tip of the finger of land that thrust the Great City into the sea; in ancient times, Haraldr had learned, this entire peninsula had been called Byzantium. The sun parted the slate-colored base of the roiling cotton clouds, projecting a broad shaft over the eastern prow of the city, and Haraldr once again gaped at the thrilling panoply of glistening domes.

The ship docked at a wharf next to a large, blocky gate house projecting from the towering seawall. Soldiers armored like the Topoteretes and clearly under his command joined Haraldr's escort and led him up wide marble steps to a series of grass- and ivy-covered terraces lined with stone statues, some of them as startlingly lifelike as the ones Haraldr had seen in the city, but others standing stiffly at attention, arms at their sides. As he walked among the stone figures Haraldr noticed that their eyes had a strange life force, as if they were filled with visions of distant realms and other times, times before there were men and only gods inhabited the earth. For how many aeons had men preceded him up these steps, beneath this stony scrutiny?

The terraces climbed to the Imperial City within the Empress City.

Haraldr had seen the palaces from a distance, and yet then they had seemed a miniature world too fantastic to be real, like looking into a knothole and finding a splendid city inhabited by elves. Now this world surrounded him in its dazzling actuality, the rows of carnation and sulfur-colored marble pillars towering above him like gleaming stone forests, the spray from the fountains turning into crystal fragments that melted against his face. He wondered at an enormous golden building made of domes fanning out like the petals of a flower, cyan-blue ponds teeming with darting orange fish, marble cypresses carved into foliate traceries so delicate that it seemed they would crumble in the breeze; in the distance shimmered a vast silver dome, huge enough to swallow a *dhromon.* Chalk-white avenues fanned out in the sun, swarming with eunuchs in silk, soldiers in armor, and occasional groups of ladies who seemed to float along in the coral-tinted shade of endless porticoes.

The escort steered Haraldr sharply right in front of a massive, shell-colored building; Khazar bowmen stood at attention within a towering portico. Haraldr and the Topoteretes were admitted through the massive silver doors. They crossed a marble hall busy with scurrying, sumptuously dressed eunuchs, then wound through a jade-columned portico, a courtyard with gurgling fountains, and halls decorated with endless ocher and gold mosaics depicting scenes of battle; a half dozen times they had their passes inspected by guards posted at each entrance to a new room or passageway. Finally they halted in front of a cottage-sized, vaultlike structure made of porphyry marble as deeply purple as a ripe plum.

Two Varangians in their golden armor stepped from a door at the side of the vault and looked at the passes. The Topoteretes nodded and stepped aside while the Varangians came around Haraldr's back. Haraldr hated the fear that crawled up his spine; had he not resolved to remove all speculation from his mind and leave his questions to Odin and Kristr? And yet how else could he feel at this moment?

"Sir, please accompany us," said the one of the Varangians in Swedish-accented Norse. The menace thawed slightly, and Haraldr stepped into a lurid purple chamber. A half dozen armored Varangians stood rigidly at attention; a single Varangian faced them, his huge back to Haraldr. The golden broadax crossed over his chest glimmered as he turned.

Haraldr resisted the swoon. Yes, he had been prepared for this encounter. But now, face-to-face with Mar Hunrodarson, he wanted to fall to his knees and toss the fear from his surging stomach.

Mar stepped forward, the ax moving in his hands, and Haraldr heard the rustle of the raven's wings. But Mar merely passed the ax to the Varangian flanking Haraldr on his left. He extended his hands in greeting. "Haraldr Nordbrikt," he said, without even the ominous emphasis on the last name that Haraldr would have expected. Then Mar grabbed Haraldr's arm and drew him close. Haraldr could not mask the terror in his eyes.

"Before you go in, listen," Mar whispered. "I have heard of a plot against you. If you have been threatened, I must know of it." Mar paused and drew Haraldr into his insane, glacial eyes; the rest of the Hetairarch's face was utterly void of meaning or inflection, as if he were a walking corpse that had lost its spirit but not the heat that still flushed its cheeks. Haraldr remembered that he had been fooled once by that face.

"You wear doubt like a battle standard," Mar continued. "But you have nothing to fear unless you challenge me. I would use your secret as a shield for myself, not a sword against you. Look, my plan will benefit us both. We are both Norsemen . . ."

Mar stepped away as two eunuchs entered the chamber through a rear door. The taller and elder of the two was a pale-browed but firm-fleshed man who wore cream-hued silk so heavy, yet so finely woven, that it seemed like a metal foil. The other man, similarly splendid, held an ivory baton with a golden dragon atop it. This eunuch was short, with a receding jaw marked with a large dimpled scar just below the corner of his mouth.

The white-haired eunuch reached out and fingered the heavy blue fabric of Haraldr's new tunic of the finest Hellas silk. He nodded and the eunuch with the scarred jaw spoke in Norse.

"Haraldr Nordbrikt, I am the Grand Interpreter of the Varangians. The honored dignitary assisting me in preparing you for your audience is the Imperial High Chamberlain. Listen carefully to your instructions. You will enter and prostrate yourself three times. At the command *Keleusate,* you will be invited to stand. Your Father may wish to examine you. Should you be questioned, the High Chamberlain will nod if you are permitted to answer. You may look upon the face of the Autocrator, but be certain that your expression is one of reverence, humility, and gratefulness. When the interview is concluded, your Father will bless you with the sign of the cross. You will immediately withdraw, arms crossed over your breast, from the presence of the Pantocrator's Hand on Earth."

Haraldr's blood, drained by fear, almost audibly roared back into his veins. He had expected he might be displayed to the Emperor again, and perhaps receive yet another warning from this curiously godlike puppet of a Norseman and a monk. Yet to speak with him! Haraldr could look this man in the eyes, weigh the timbre of his voice, and in every way discern if he was a man to command all men or a mere illusion. Perhaps Haraldr had seen nothing in the inscrutable face of Mar Hunrodarson, but now the veils of Roman power would be stripped aside. He would see into the heart of the Roman dragon.

The two eunuchs preceded Haraldr through an antechamber with a gold-coffered roof; Mar, his ax upon his chest, followed at Haraldr's back. Four Varangians stepped aside while two white-robed eunuchs parted the silver doors.

After the ritual prostrations were completed, Haraldr stood and steadied himself. Above him soared a vast, celestial blue dome speckled with golden stars, but the area in which he stood was a small one, cordoned off with heavy scarlet brocade curtains. The Emperor, seated in a jeweled gold throne, was flanked by several standing, white-robed eunuchs. He was aflame in scarlet silk medallioned with gold eagles, but he wore no crown upon his head. Haraldr noticed out of the corner of his eye a man in monk's garb; for some reason this figure was the only person of the eight or so in the room who was seated in the presence of the Emperor.

Haraldr reminded himself that he was of royal lineage and that this Emperor was not. He breathed deeply and forced his eyes to search the face of the man who sat no more than three ells from him. His hands trembled, but he locked his gaze upon the sable-hued irises. Within seconds he knew that everything he had assumed about this Emperor was wrong.

He was no god, certainly, but a handsome man of perhaps two score years with a bold, sharp nose; noble, high forehead; and long, gray-flecked dark curls. But he was also just as clearly a man above all men. His entire carriage as he sat bespoke stature and confidence, his red-booted feet flat upon the floor, his shoulders square and chest erect, his hands set in his lap with the fingertips lightly touching. Haraldr had grown up in royal courts, and he knew the importance of a king's sheer physical presence in maintaining the respect and fealty of his subjects. But he knew just as well that this mysterious aura of command was not as simple as donning silk robes or projecting a fine masculine swagger. It was something in the eyes, an intangible yet undeniable quality that left no question of a man's mastery of both himself and those around him. Haraldr had seen this look before, and he had learned to discern men who pretended to have it and did not. And what he saw in this Emperor's black, chasm-deep eyes was all he needed to know; they were somehow infinitely sorrowful yet terrifyingly obdurate, the shafts to some unshakable resolve. This Emperor was no puppet; even a man like Mar would be but a toy to him.

The Emperor spoke several sentences in an even, deep, yet natural voice that did not turgidly solicit respect, as did the exhortations of so many weak leaders but simply projected keenness and innate authority. The Grand Interpreter translated, maintaining much of the Emperor's original inflection.

"Your father greets you, Haraldr Nordbrikt, and applauds your resourcefulness in dealing with the plague of Saracen pirates who have disrupted our maritime commerce. There were some who did not welcome you when you first came to our environs, but his Imperial Majesty has seen to it that your enemies now respect you as a true soldier of Christ. Your Father asks if you are now willing to perform a task that will more directly serve his Holy Person."

Haraldr was almost euphoric in his desire to serve this magnificent man, and yet another region of his mind screamed with confusion. He had burned the body of Asbjorn Ingvarson only yesterday. Had these enemies been chained in hours? And even so, the young Swede's soul pleaded for revenge. He again saw the monk at the corner of his vision and thought of Mar at his back; it was likely that Asbjorn's murderer was no more than two steps away.

Haraldr noticed that the High Chamberlain was nodding at him. He broomed his mind by drawing in his breath, then gave his tongue to Odin. "Your Imperial Majesty and chosen hand of Kristr, though it is my most passionate desire to serve you in any way I can, your invitation assumes more honor than I am now worthy of. Two nights ago one of the men pledged to my keeping and guidance was slain in a cowardly and villainous manner. Until I avenge this murder I am soiled by a disgrace that renders me unfit to serve a sovereign as glorious as the Emperor of the Romans."

After the translation the Emperor stared intently at Haraldr; it was everything Haraldr could do to keep from flinching before that lancing gaze. Then the Emperor looked up at the eunuch nearest to him—Haraldr recognized this man as the aged, sad-eyed eunuch who had spoken to him at his first audience—who bent to the Emperor's ear and began a whispered discussion that lasted perhaps a minute.

The elderly eunuch disappeared through the red curtains behind him while the Emperor studied Haraldr in almost total silence; the seated monk seemed to have difficulty breathing and wheezed slightly. Haraldr also noticed that the seated monk's robe was rough brown burlap; hadn't Joannes worn fine black wool?

The eunuch reemerged and whispered to the Emperor, who nodded and immediately addressed Haraldr.

"His Imperial Majesty is pleased to tell you that even now the assassin is being interrogated. He has confessed to everything. You will be able to see the perpetrator when you leave His Majesty's presence. Will this satisfy the admirable requisites of your honor?"

Haraldr could scarcely believe his ears. He cast his eyes quickly in the direction of the monk. Kristr! He was almost certain that the seated monk was *not* the Joannes he had seen; this monk was much smaller, with a crown of short hair. Could Joannes possibly be this "perpetrator" now in custody? That was too unlikely, given the monk's evident power; not even this Emperor's justice would be so implacable. But clearly Haraldr's enemy had been identified and dealt with, and he would soon know him.

The Imperial Chamberlain nodded again, and Haraldr gushed praise. "Your Imperial Majesty's pursuit of justice, as swift as the flight of an arrow, makes me all the more eager in my desire to dedicate to you my arm, my allegiance, and my life, and the lives and allegiances of the five hundred men I have pledged to lead to glory in the service of the Emperor of the Romans." Haraldr's skin tingled with conviction; he meant these words with all his suddenly unburdened heart.

Haraldr raptly watched the Emperor reply. He thrilled at the eloquence of His Majesty's speech and imagined himself walking beside him in stately procession. And yet some tiny parcel of Haraldr's intellect saw something else, even as the rest of his consciousness floated on this dream. What was it? Something about the Emperor, the shape of his cheeks, his lips; where had he seen these features before? But the memory was too fleeting.

"His Majesty delights to command an arm so strong and yet so obedient. His faith in you is boundless, so he offers you a task that might have exhausted Heracles, and yet he is assured you can perform it." The Grand Interpreter went on to describe the pilgrimage to Jerusalem; an entire regiment of the Imperial Army would accompany the Empress and her ladies, but Haraldr and his men would comprise the Empress's personal bodyguard. It was a honor second only to guarding the person of the Emperor himself.

Haraldr quickly and ardently accepted, and the Emperor rewarded him with an intoxicating, perfect smile. The Emperor began another address, and Haraldr was again transported with devotion. But the Emperor blinked in mid-sentence, stopped, and tipped his head slightly toward the seated monk.

The commotion was immediate. The High Chamberlain glared at Haraldr and made an entirely indecorous whisking motion. Haraldr sensed Mar, still at his back, spring forward. The crushing grip stung his arm, and then Haraldr spun; his heart, now cold lead, slammed against his ribs. No! The ultimate ruse!

Mar's grip vanished and Haraldr stood outside drawn curtains that seemed to shrink around the Emperor and his party like a crimson silk cocoon. The Grand Interpreter was beside him; he yanked Haraldr's arm and frantically urged him into the guardhouse. Behind him, Haraldr heard a rustle of brocade, calm whispers, and painful gagging, as if someone had gotten a bone lodged in his throat. Haraldr's mind raced. Had someone become ill? Had someone, perhaps even Joannes, sent an assassin to avenge himself on the Emperor? Just when he had thought he knew the heart of the Roman dragon, this. What was happening?

Mar, still inside the curtains, watched with disgust the twitching figure on the floor before him; he reflected that this spectacle was becoming enticingly common. But the Emperor's disclosure had caught Mar by surprise. Had they really caught the Norseman's assassin, he wondered, or was this "perpetrator" merely the usual scapegoat to be sacrificed to the absurd notion of Roman justice?

† † †

Haraldr scarcely noticed the clicking feet around him. The Topoteretes, one of the eunuchs who had attended the Emperor, and the black-frock interpreter had taken him completely across the palace grounds, past even the huge silver-domed cathedral. Now he looked up at the sheer, round tower that brooded over the entrance to the harbor, a doleful stone shadow against the shimmering harbor beyond. His mind was a tempest of suspicions and fears.

The entrance to the sinister turret was a steel door set into grim, cinereous granite. The Topoteretes spoke to Haraldr; for once John the frog-faced interpreter seemed eager to translate.

"Do you know this place?"

Haraldr shook his head. The tower was a giant crypt; it even smelled of death.

"It is called Neorion Tower. Pray to your god that you are never invited to stay the night here."

Unseen machinery seemed to crank the steel door open. Gloom, wet, and decay seeped into the sunlight. As the shadows engulfed him Haraldr felt that he was entering the dark world of spirits.

Two dozen Khazar guards armed with swords stood watch in a perfectly barren room that seemed even darker because of the flickering lamps that could only establish dirty brown penumbrae in the foul pall. A Roman officer approached and inspected passes. Machinery clanked again. Stairs fell from the ceiling.

The Topoteretes led Haraldr and John up the wooden steps and into a narrow, sooty shaft encasing stone stairs that spiraled endlessly up. Oil lamps in the form of wolves sputtered greasily. At intervals dark steel doors waited next to narrow stone landings. Haraldr could only observe all of this with nightmare acuity; like a man in a dream, his fate was no longer subject to reason or even speculation. It was as if the ascent were actually a journey deep into the Underworld. What demons awaited?

The Topoteretes rapped on steel, and an almost obscured grate slid aside. The entire door wrenched open. At once Haraldr smelled the carrion the ravens would take from this place, and his weary stomach heaved. He coughed to disguise his retching.

They followed a guard down a long corridor; the dingy walls seemed to radiate cold, as if they were not blocks of stone but dirty ice. The darkness and the smell of death and spoil and new blood were suffocating. The walls closed like black jaws.

A grimy steel door groaned like the dead and took them in. Lights flickered. Enormous steel double doors faced Haraldr across what seemed to be the antechamber to a fair-sized hall. A man was seated at a small table to Haraldr's right, his massive, dark shoulders hunched over as he studied papers by the light of a table lamp.

Haraldr knew the man, and his own fate, as soon as the monk's huge head lifted to confront him. Joannes.

Joannes's eyes were hot charcoal bits with a faint nimbus of red. What seemed a flat statement rumbled from the tomb of his breast.

"You know him," said the interpreter.

Haraldr looked directly at Joannes and nodded. The monk's voice pounded again.

"Do you know this seal?"

Haraldr was startled. The monk's curiously flattened fingertip pushed a small folded document, addressed with a few lines of Greek, across the tabletop; the attached lead seal was intact. Haraldr leaned forward, feeling as if he were coming too close to a dangerous wild beast. He recognized the tiny sword arm at once; it was identical to the wax fragment he had studied a thousand times. The complete figure was a man armored like the typical Roman military officer. "Yes," Haraldr answered grimly. "I think it belongs to a murderer." And then he asked Joannes silently: *Are you the murderer? If you are, before I die—and take you with me to the spirit world—I must barter for the lives of my pledge-men.*

Joannes glanced once at a paper before him; the document was covered with dozens of lengthy Roman numbers and haphazard lines of Greek writing. He settled back in his chair and looked at Haraldr carefully. Haraldr was aware of a faint sound, almost like a spirit moaning from the depths. His nerves were shards. The monk spoke.

"You were the victim of a plot. The late Manglavite had a criminal associate, a middle-ranking Roman military officer, in the palace. This associate, deprived of his nefarious income by the death of the Manglavite, sought revenge against you and carried out his plot with professional stealth."

Haraldr nodded, and relief began to fill him like a warm draft. This was more than plausible. He and Halldor and Ulfr had perhaps been overly impressed with their importance among these Romans; they had not considered that Hakon would have had friends, coconspirators at court, lesser men who might have acted entirely without the knowledge of Mar or Joannes. But the monk now telling him this had a face no man could trust.

"The murderer has already reaped the whirlwind of your Father's implacable justice. Do you wish to see the vengeance God grants the Emperor of the Romans?"

The huge steel doors at the back of the antechamber slid open, and two men brought out a canvas-shrouded parcel on a pallet. The intestinal stench engulfed Haraldr like the breath of a howling carnivore. The pallet was set down and the shroud pulled away.

The lump of gristle, bowels, glistening organs, and stacked appendages was surmounted by a helmet of flayed, featureless viscera; incredibly, the teeth still chattered.

"Yes. This lives, for a moment still. You may finish him, or leave him to further contemplate the immutable virtue and implacable will of Roman justice."

Haraldr turned away from the horrifying bundle. If this was the murderer, then the soul of Asbjorn Ingvarson had been avenged in kind.

Joannes spoke at length, then watched Haraldr keenly during the translation.

"I understand you saw our Father this very hour. Let me explain to you what occurred, to put your mind at ease. His Imperial Majesty enjoys the company of holy men like myself, some of whom are given, unlike myself, to convulsive visions that yield extraordinary prophecies. It was discerned by His Imperial Majesty that the monk you saw during your interview was about to experience one of these transports, and he did not want to trouble you with the monk's outburst, for many things are said that would summon demons if they were heard by ears innocent of the knowledge to resist them."

The interpreter paused and conversed with Joannes, apparently to straighten out something the monk had said, and then continued the translation. "Nordbrikt, I am aware that you have recently been exposed to the fantasies of naked chorines and sotted actors, and perhaps you have mistaken these shameless libels as some accurate representation of my humble role in the vast scheme of Roman power. You must understand now that you and I merely serve the same master. I am friend of all who truly love the Emperor, unrelenting foe of those who would try to deceive or harm him."

After this translation Joannes began again, and Haraldr focused on the face of the giant monk. True, the monk seemed to be the living face of evil. And yet when Joannes had spoken of the Emperor, the passion in his countenance had transformed it; the love that had radiated from that monstrous visage was too fierce—as fierce, in its way, as the Rage—to have been feigned. Haraldr could trust nothing about this monk, except that Joannes truly loved the Emperor whom he served. And perhaps that was a common turf on which they could meet.

The translation began again. "You have been successful here, Nordbrikt, and yet you have held your arms out to death more times than is prudent even for a man who apparently sits in fortune's lap. You are of no use to anyone if you continue to use your life as the vane to detect the direction of the winds of Roman power. You are a seafaring man, of some renown now, and you would not go into strange waters without a pilot. Just so, you need a guide to plot your course through the shoals of our Roman system. You need a patron who can see that opportunities, not deadly obstacles, are placed in your path."

Again the interpreter paused for clarification, then quickly resumed the translation. "I would like to sponsor you. Not formally; certainly neither of us will have occasion to recall this conversation to others. But when your course needs proper steering, I will be there."

Haraldr soberly considered the monk's words. Olaf had once told him that the best tutor in games of power was the man other men feared and avoided, not the man who nightly drew the skalds to flatter him and heap him with praise. But a powerful instinct warned him that this monk's lessons might well be fatal. Still, the faith they shared in one man was enough to tip the scales. And what would he gain by refusing?

"I share your devotion to our Father," said Haraldr, searching for the correct tone; with the Romans, it was obvious one always had to speak as artificially and obsequiously as a skald. "I believe your offer to be the most generous gift I have received here, even more generous than the gift given me by the Saracen pirates I recently met. I am grateful, and in need of any assistance your offices might provide." As his response was translated and Joannes replied in Greek, Haraldr studied the monk's distorted features and remembered his fleeting perceptions in the presence of the Emperor. Strange, he thought, and unlikely, but it would explain much. He abandoned the notion when the Norse translation began.

"Good. I have a letter for you bearing my seal. It contains no threats or warnings. It is rather an introduction to my brother, the Strategus— that means the military governor—of Antioch, a city you will pass through on your Holy mission to Jerusalem. I want you to be known to my brother, and he to you. I also have a nephew there, about your age, though he sadly lacks your ambition. Perhaps he could learn from you."

Joannes reviewed his own concerns during the translation. The assassin had died before he had revealed the truth; Joannes was certain of that. He looked again at the seal he had shown the hapless Nordbrikt. The Grand Domestic Bardas Dalassena was just arrogant and stupid enough to have put his personal seal on such a crude enterprise. Yes, this would have been his fashion, but the indisputable fact was that the by now demon-racing assassin had named the Grand Domestic far too early in the interrogation and had lingered far too painfully while insisting that he was telling the truth. Someone else was using the Grand Domestic to screen his own intentions. But who? Surely the Hetairarch Mar Hunrodarson did not know that Joannes had already moved to preempt the Hetairarch's proposed expansion of the Varangian Guard.

Joannes refused to consider further the myriad possibilities. He tried to look composed as the obviously befuddled Varangian Nordbrikt was led away. He chided himself for the time wasted on this inconsequential project. Varangians, even the Hetairarch, were hardly worth the effort. Not now. Not when so much else was at stake.

Joannes lowered his head to the paper-strewn table and went home to Amastris, to the time when his being had split into the two persons who now so desperately struggled to achieve a single voice. He felt the hot dust on his lips and lay again on his back, the pain still in his testicles, his arms strapped to his sagging cot so that he would not loosen the ligature. Michael, dear little Michael, crawled, stumbled, shakily stood, and gurgled beside him. The infant grabbed for his brother's finger, caught hold, and held, cooing with delight. And the love entered Joannes, and the pain vanished.

Back in the Neorion Tower, watched only by a corpse without eyes, the huge black-cloaked shoulders of the monk trembled with sobs. "Michael, Michael, dear little Michael," he murmured, choking with grief. "Now you are afflicted and is there nothing I can do to succor you?"

o you are not keeping company with either of those boys?" As she waited for Maria's answer the Augusta Theodora sipped from a goblet fashioned of embossed gold leaf pressed between clear glass. She was fond of elaborate table settings, but otherwise the apartments in her country palace were almost barren; the only decoration on the dull terre-verte marble walls of her dining chamber was a small enameled icon of the Virgin, framed in gold.

"No." Maria paused for a silver forkful of fish. "It was a mistake. They say that love is a flower that can only bloom once. If it withers without bearing fruit, there will never be another blossom. My first man was a mistake, and so all of the rest have been."

"I wish you could forget about that, darling. No one blames you." Maria took several silent bites while Theodora watched her expectantly. "I think you might be happier if you tried to remain chaste," Theodora finally said. "And as much as I am concerned about your journey, darling, I feel that this pilgrimage will be a salve to your soul. Allow the Christ to fill your heart. The Patriarch has helped me to see that when we love the Christ, we are never without love." Alexius, Patriarch of the One True Oecumenical, Orthodox, and Catholic Faith had become Theodora's spiritual adviser and personal friend during her exile.

Maria ran her tongue over her teeth. "Alexius is as determined as Joannes to keep you and your sister apart."

"My sister is determined to keep us apart. She will always blame me for Romanus. That I refused him and she was forced to marry him. I thought that it would all be buried in the same crypt as Romanus. But it will always be there."

"Joannes is responsible for this breach. He never could stand up to the the two of you together. He told the Emperor lies about you, and the Emperor repeated them to Zoe. You believe anything from the mouth that drinks your soul."

"Emmanuel says that the Emperor has not taken that draft for some time. Perhaps on this pilgrimage she will have an opportunity to consider who truly loves her and who is merely using her." Theodora frowned like a troubled child.

"I know how much she loves you. That is really the reason it was so easy to turn her against you." Maria tapped her goblet with her fingernail, a staccato pecking that went on for almost half a minute. "It is strange how thin the membrane of love is," she finally said, "and how precariously it withstands the pollutants of the soul. Sometimes when I am with a man I love, I feel that I can reach inside him and find only decay."

"Darling. Someday you will find the proper kind of love with a man. Give yourself time to find the Christ's love, and then you will find a man's true love."

Maria chattered her front teeth in minute, nervous little clicks. "I feel that on this journey I will find a resolution. I will either fill my soul, or my being will completely evaporate, like a dead lake. But I will not be this empty, cold thing anymore, a shell with no light inside. My palmist, Ata, told me that soon love, fate, and death would collide in my life. I am not afraid to die, because I am already dead. But once before I die I would like to love a man and not feel the rot in his soul." Maria looked at Theodora almost belligerently for a moment, and then her face slowly began to contort. She burst into tears.

III

he world was a reflection in a copper sheet. The dust stirred by the horses' hooves swirled up into the dust already suspended in the air like a dry, chalk-fine fog. The approaching horses of the scouts merely added to the choking ocher cloud.

The scouts, dark, wild-eyed men called akrites, wore jerkins of quilted cotton over short linen tunics. There were four of them, silver helmets dulled to brass in the dusty pall. They rode directly to the Domestic of the Imperial Excubitores, bowed in their saddles, and began talking with animated gestures. Haraldr had difficulty with the dialect—the akrites were from Armenikoi, a theme halfway to Khoresm—but he understood. A Saracen raiding party, fair-sized, was just ahead.

"It appears that the Saracens have positioned themselves to block the Cilician Gates," came the quick, effortless translation.

Haraldr pushed his helmet back, wiped the grit from his forehead, and smiled at Gregory Zigabenus, the interpreter who had accompanied the Rus trade fleet. "I understood some of that already, Gregory." Then he said in Greek, "Because you . . . teach well." He added his own silent thanks to Odin and Kristr for this gift of the little eunuch. The assignment apparently had been by chance, but the adventuresome, unfailingly cheerful Gregory was as welcome as a third hand in a single combat. Like every Roman, Gregory was mute on the subject of the Emperor and his immediate circle, but otherwise he had been a continuing education in what Joannes had called "the shoals of the Roman system." And strange waters—not to mention dangerous—they were indeed.

Haraldr looked down the road up which he had just ridden, along with two dozen horsemen of the Imperial Excubitores. The graded path, here only wide enough to draw a wagon through, wound down through the russet haze toward a dull, brownish-gray plateau ringed by the slightly darker convolutions of the Taurus Mountains as they rose to their snow-crested heights. He had never imagined so much land, or so little beauty. And yet the mute austerity of the terrain bespoke the power of the Romans. For almost six weeks, at a clip that surely measured at least two and sometimes three rowing-spells a day, the Imperial entourage had traversed territory not unlike this. Not as dusty, certainly; farther to the north the peaks were less precipitous and the pastures still held some of summer's verdure. But the distances, the isolation on many stretches, surpassed anything imaginable even on Norway's barren central plateau. Yet, most remarkably, just when one thought that the Romans had finally run out of folk with which to populate this prodigious domain of theirs, the endless road (paved as neatly and much more sturdily than the floor of a Jarl's hall) would enter the tree-rimmed perimeter of yet another pasture; pass through the rich, dark, relentlessly cultivated communal fields and orchards speckled with ripe fruit; and lead them to the clustered mud-brick, thatch-roofed huts of yet another Roman village. The industry of these provincial Romans, lost in this frightening vastness, was something to behold; hoeing their fall harvest of vegetables, chopping wood for winter, sacking grain, bundling fodder, driving their massive oxen to and fro, they had coaxed a bounty from a wasteland that a Norse farmer wouldn't give a piece of silver the size of his fingernail for. And yet, as Gregory had explained, many of these proud, busy people preferred to become rich men's slaves because of the burden of Imperial taxes on free peasants.

"The Domestic wonders if you wish to go forward with them. He says if you do, you will see a Roman ambush."

Haraldr turned to Nicon Blymmedes, Domestic of the Imperial Excubitores: thick-chested, wiry-limbed, about two score years old. Blymmedes was accompanied by two dozen mounted soldiers wearing waist-length mail shirts and conical helms, with their bows and tooled-leather arrow quivers slung over their backs. The rest of their vanda, a company of about two hundred strong, were footmen who had disappeared up ahead, seemingly swallowed by tortured rock and swirling dust clouds.

"Yes, thank you, I will," said Haraldr directly to the Domestic. He had come to like the hawk-nosed, constantly frowning Blymmedes. The Domestic, unlike so many of these endlessly scheming Romans, seemed solely concerned with doing his own job properly—no, perfectly—and seeing that his subordinates performed with similar punctiliousness. Yet he was eager to teach, and he had accepted Haraldr as a fellow warrior with perhaps a different philosophy of warfare but of considerable aptitude in martial affairs.

The small contingent started up the steeply climbing roadway. Blymmedes fell back between Haraldr and Gregory and began another of his tactical discourses, vigorously illustrated with his leather-tough hands.

"You see, I have sent my infantry up ahead"—Blymmedes thrust both his hands forward as Gregory translated—"and positioned them in the heights on either side of the road." He pushed his hands apart to show the dispersal. "Now we will come forward past the position of our hidden infantry. We will appear to be a mere scouting party, but one that offers the prize of a foolish officer of the Roman Imperial Taghmata. The Saracens will see us and advance quickly to profit from my impudence. Prudently we will retreat the way we have come. They will follow us, lusty with the promise of my ransom. When our pell-mell retreat has lured the Saracens beneath the positions held by my infantry . . ." Blymmedes brought his hands together with a loud clap.

"Deal with the enemy on your terms," said Haraldr directly, repeating one of Blymmedes's axioms.

"Yes," said the Domestic, hazel eyes flashing eagerly. Then he shook his finger. "But meet the enemy. The ambush does not work if you simply run away. Retreat alone cannot win victory."

Gregory pretended to translate. "You understood? I thought so. The Domestic, I think, feels that Roman strategy has become too cautious under the man who commands him. This is as far as he can go in criticizing the Grand Domestic Bardas Dalassena, however."

Blymmedes was now occupied ahead, having taken the point of the column. He signaled to his unseen forces in the hills. The road continued to climb and narrow, the crumbling, shard-strewn rock walls rising ever more steeply. They rounded a blind turn and looked up to a narrow defile backed by nothing but thin coppery sky. Blymmedes fell back for a moment and whispered to Gregory, then went boldly up ahead.

"These are the Cilician Gates," whispered Gregory. "The Domestic wanted you to know that Alexander brought his army through this pass."

Haraldr nodded. Alexander of Macedon, or the Great Alexander, had been a Greek King who had conquered the world to the Gates of Dionysus in the days before the Roman Empire even existed. Alexander sounded more like a god than a man, but the Domestic often referred to his tactics and courage and seemed very proud to speak the same language as this great demigod.

The horsemen wandered slowly into the massive jaws of the Cilician Gates. Haraldr caught a breathtaking glimpse of rugged terrain falling away to a dull green plain.

The Saracens seemed to come out of the rocks. They led their horses by the reins, then saddled up deliberately, as if they had enough time to pause and straighten the quills of their arrows. A few bright curved blades began to flash, and bows rose in disjointed arabesques against the met-aled sky. The Domestic, conspicuously displaying himself four ells in front of the rest of his horsemen, held his reins deftly, almost as if he were preparing to touch a woman's face. Horses snorted, but no one on either side made a sound. Then the nearest Saracen, a beetle-brown face with a coal-black beard and eyes rimmed with glaring whites, raised his arms and legs like a four-winged bird preparing to fly. Arrows hissed from quivers.

It was as if the mountains behind them had found huge metal voices. Even the Domestic whipped his head around with astonishment. Then his face almost instantly purpled. In that same instant the Saracen leader let his limbs relax and fall. He neatly wheeled his horse about, and the rest of his band just as suddenly turned their rearing mounts and began to vanish into dust and rock.

Haraldr had no idea of the specific meanings of the raging oaths the Domestic began to bellow with bulging-eyed fury, but a translation was hardly necessary. Blymmedes spurred his horse and charged back down the road. The *komes* in charge of the vanda ordered the rest to follow. The Domestic's curses were quickly swallowed up by the unearthly, blaring, pounding, whistling din of the lifeless crags.

A short way down, Haraldr reined his horse around a switchback and saw the source of the sound. The road was jammed with armored horse-men and footmen as far as anyone could see; the files of soldiers in mail coats and breastplates glinted through the dust like strands of silver thread as the road zigged and zagged thousands of ells down the moun-tain. Jammed in among the vanguard of this army were two dozen musi-cians equipped with every manner of drum, horn, bell, and whistle one could imagine. Haraldr knew immediately what he beheld; ever since they had crossed the Bosporus into Asia, the citizen-army of each provincial theme had, as soon as the Imperial caravan had entered their territory, joined the Imperial Taghmata to guard their Empress and her Holy pilgrims. But the meeting places had always been carefully appointed. This was a curious breach of protocol and military discipline.

The Domestic's livid face was inches from the rather puffy, even some-what indolent features of a man mounted on a huge white horse. The horses trotted in quarter-circles as Blymmedes bellowed furiously. The other man simply sat higher in the saddle, like a traveler trying to ignore a troublesome dog. Finally Blymmedes abruptly ended his diatribe, shook his head like a tutor puzzled by a witless student, and motioned with his hands, as if he were attempting to push the entire thematic army down the mountain. The other man ignored this signal and rode past the Domestic, stopping just in front of the Excubitores; Haraldr was close enough to detect the perfumed fragrance that surrounded both rider and horse. The man was groomed like a courtier, his brown beard immaculately trimmed, the beautifully chased dragons on his gold breastplate still bright beneath a thin layer of dust; even his horse's bridle was brightly enameled. His indigo eyes, which despite the slackness of his face had a command to them, swept over the Excubitores, Gregory, and Haraldr with no acknowledgment whatsoever that they were separate individuals but as if collectively they represented a single large deposit of donkey excrement to be avoided on his upward journey. Then he turned, spurred back to his waiting army, and shouted a command in a brisk, imperious voice. With the same musical cacophony that had heralded its arrival, the thematic army turned and began to lumber back down the mountain.

Blymmedes rode back to his men, shaking his head. "Next lesson," he shouted to Haraldr, "I teach you how to keep the thematic army from scaring off your quarry when you've already got their heads in your game bag!"

"Who was that man?" asked Haraldr.

The Domestic's eyes flared again. "That eminent tactician was Meletius Attalietes, Strategus of the Cilician Theme and the first son of the Senator and Magister Nicon Attalietes."

† † †

"You see, Mistress, interruption of the effluent phlegms that produce these desires is the reverse of the procedures that stimulate the sexual inclination. One must simply manipulate the organs with careful consideration of vortices that regulate the discharge of the vital humors. Mother of God willing, we have every reason to assume that you will be relieved of your grievous and insolent inflammation before the hour of Compline."

The Empress of the Romans, Zoe the Purple-Born, ordered her face toweled by white-robed Leo, her eunuch vestitore, and considered for a moment the advice of this new specialist in the treatment of sexual disorders. The deathly pale, long-faced eunuch physician, who always seemed to perspire above his upper lip, was in countenance alone dour enough to dissipate the carnal appetite. But as for his procedures, Zoe seriously had to consider that perhaps she had exhausted the knowledge of these learned charlatans. What good had the specialists done to facilitate marital relations with her late husband, Romanus? The endless applications of aphrodisiac ointments prescribed by these experts had done nothing to restore virility to the senescent manhood of a white-haired windbag. And now that she herself required the reverse procedure, due to her present husband's persistent neglect of his marital obligations, their success seemed equally unlikely. Michael. No, she would not think of him any longer. The disappointment was too acid.

"Maria," asked Zoe, "what do you think of this physician's ambitious promulgations? In your experience is desire physical, something that can be manipulated by pressure on the offending internal organs? Or is it rather spiritual and therefore beyond the probing fingers of our learned specialists?"

Maria puckered her brow, cracking the dried cosmetic paste the Empress had applied all over her face. She sat on a gilt camp stool set in front of the Empress's portable Magyar steam bath; only Zoe's flushed face was visible at the top of the round leather cabinet that enclosed the Imperial body. "I am certain that it is both. Of the two components of desire, the physical is easier to assuage. The spiritual element of desire, however, can lead one to overcome even a physical repulsion and enjoy the love of a man who is fair neither in limb nor in countenance." She idly dipped her finger in the silver bowl of rose water set on the cabinet beside her chair. "I have never loved both the spiritual and physical aspects of the same man, at least not at the the same time. Who knows? Perhaps that is an explosive combination of elements, like the ingredients of liquid fire. It would incinerate the soul. But I have never met a man who, having aroused my body, was sad enough to arouse my spirit."

"How interesting, little daughter." Zoe reclined her head toward the crimson silk canopy of the bathing pavilion. The lamps had already been lit; the sun had just vanished behind the peaks of the Taurus. "Do you realize that you have lately come to speak of your amorous pastimes with the most curious melancholy? I advised—no, implored—you to bring some sort of . . . *diversion* with you to prevent just this sort of malaise. And this ceaseless wandering in the wilderness would have taxed the virtuous patience of Moses, the chosen of God. It is the vastness of Asia that afflicts the mind with such lassitude and apprehension."

"I felt this emptiness before we even departed the Empress City."

"Oh, well, little daughter, you certainly must know that the brighter the flame of passion, the more rapidly the fuel of desire is consumed. Your problem is that you stoke the flames too quickly and awaken in the middle of the night to find that your bed is cold." Zoe relaxed as the steam dissipated the road weariness in her back. Michael. She could not elude him. He was the heat that still fevered her nights. If only Joannes had not quenched Michael with lies about Romanus (not lies . . . you watched as they held his head under . . . he came up once, gasping, eyes bright). Zoe felt an internal cold, the jeopardy of her immortal soul, as the memory flew by her like a dark comet. But they *were* lies in the context of her love for Michael and her people. Even Joannes had known that. Joannes. To have had the man who seared her soul wrenched from her scorching grasp by the malignancy she found repellent beyond all else: Joannes. *He is the one who has banished me to this life of saintly contemplation. So contemplate I will, though of matters saintly it will not be.*

"Mistress?" asked Maria. "Is my own melancholy infectious?"

"I was thinking," said Zoe with a frown that indicated she was still thinking. "The Tauro-Scythian. The *komes* of my own personal Varangian Guard. Haraldr something—I think they all have the same family name, all probably having had the same father. Anyway, he of pirate-slaying fame." Zoe's voice was almost chilling in its deliberation. "We have so rudely neglected him, shut up in here with our tittering little birds like Anna and that dreadful Hellenist bent on ransacking the library at Antioch."

Maria looked down at the thick blue carpet. She had not dreamed of the Tauro-Scythian harbinger of death since they had left the Empress City. And peering out at him several times a day through the curtains of the Imperial carriage, she had come to see him as simply another oversize *barbaroi* curiosity. But to look in his death-filled eyes again? She realized that she had seen the doom in his icy irises even that night at Nicephorus Argyrus's; for a fleeting moment she wanted that tragedy deep inside her, and her womb stirred. But this man would not be a harmless pet like Giorgios. He was a murdering savage from Thule. She had lied to her Aunt Theodora. Out here, in this barren post-apocalyptic vastness, she realized she was afraid of death, and always had been. Her entire life had been driven by her fear of death's ineluctable darkness. "Is it wise?" she asked. "Are we not convinced that he is an informer for Joannes?"

"Symeon assures me that he is," said Zoe with bland indifference. She needed no further proof; her Chamberlain Symeon, a vestitore to her uncle, Basil the Bulgar-Slayer, for decades, had so many ears in the palace precincts that he would know if a mouse squeaked in the Triclinium (a largely unused ceremonial pavilion) late at night. "He says that Joannes himself sponsored the Tauro-Scythians under this Haraldr in the Sacrum

Consistorum. And later this Haraldr met alone with Joannes at Neorion."

Maria crossed herself quickly at the mention of the gruesome tower. "Then we have been laudably prudent in excluding him from your presence so far. Why would we now wish to invite this snake into our gilt cage?"

Zoe arched her perspiration-slickened eyebrows. "Except for Symeon and Theodore and Leo and you, darling, I am surrounded by Joannes's spies as a fishmonger in his booth is by his stinking fish. Besides, I am not suggesting that we uncover our metaphoric bosoms to this Cyclopean menace Haraldr whatever, or even our physical breasts. It's simply that there is a primitivism, a . . . *vigor* to his race that I find . . . *enchanting*. We will converse with him, beckon him to share drink with us perhaps, and encourage him to speak to us of his perpetually frozen homeland"—here Zoe smiled maliciously—"and any other matters we may find to our interest."

Maria offered her own bewitching smile for the first time since the morning sun had glared over the snowcaps of the Taurus. Zoe, she reminded herself, had been Basil the Bulgar-Slayer's favorite niece, and while Zoe's father had been a blathering sophist with the sole ambition of totally depleting, within the providentially brief three years of his reign, the bulging treasuries his older brother had won in a glorious half century of relentless conquest, Zoe had been the heiress to the Bulgar-Slayer's strength and wiles. Yes, this evening would be amusing, after all. She and her beloved Empress would give Joannes's Tauro-Scythian busybody all the information he could stuff within his thick skull.

† † †

"You're certain it is the Empress herself you are to see and not Symeon, that—" Halldor was about to make some satirical reference to the Empress's prize geld. He caught himself out of deference to Gregory, who had just entered Haraldr's tent.

"Symeon brought me the message himself. Signed in purple ink just like the Emperor's missives." Haraldr looked over at Gregory, who had put on a white silk robe that swallowed him up as if he were a boy in a man's tunic. "You appear more nervous now than when we faced four times our number in Saracen brigands this afternoon, my friend. Don't tell me your fearless breast is quavering."

Gregory was indeed nervous; he hardly smiled at Haraldr's attempt to lighten his burden. Blessed though the Holy Mother and Father of the Romans indisputably were, it simply was not safe to come too close to them. As he began his career in the Imperial Administration Gregory had never imagined he would have reason for that concern, and was more than happy to think that his viewings of their Imperial Majesties would be from no greater proximity than those permitted the rabble of the Empress City. Now to think of entering an Imperial pavilion and—may Christ grant him absolution for thinking so—especially that of Her Imperial Majesty, who could quite clearly eliminate anyone who gave her offense, even an Emperor and Autocrator! No, he cautioned himself, it was too irreverent, as well as profoundly unsettling, even to think such things. "There is an ancient Greek story I have not told you of, Haraldr Nordbrikt," Gregory said weakly. "About a man named Daedalus, who built wings of wax for himself and his son. The boy flew too close to the sun and perished."

"Well," said Haraldr, "I don't think my problem on this journey has been one of overexposure to the Imperial sun." Haraldr shook his head in bewilderment. He had quickly learned that an assignment to guard the person of the Empress actually meant guarding the swarm of eunuchs who in fact guarded the person of the Empress. These pale drones, who on this journey had probably not tread with their silk slippers more than two ells of their Empire's vast expanse of naked earth, became angry hornets defending their nest when even the *komes* of Her Majesty's special Imperial Guard approached the Imperial Carriage and Pavilions. Gregory had insisted to Haraldr that these imperious functionaries were versed in a combat at which he was ill-equipped to best them, so Haraldr had observed the curious protocols and had been rewarded with an occasional sighting of blurred crimson silk as Her Imperial Majesty was escorted from her brightly gilt carriage into the scarlet pavilion that the advance party had waiting for her every evening.

And Maria. He was certain she was among the ladies who occupied the four curtained carriages; perhaps she even rode in Her Imperial Majesty's carriage. A eunuch had whispered her name in one of the endless, flustered, hand-wringing deliberations over protocol. Maria. Haraldr could not describe the agitation that had seized him just to hear the name. Was she waiting with her mistress now? How could he keep his face from coloring like a maiden's when he finally saw her? No. He must not think of her. He was here to serve the Emperor.

"I am certain this will be a brief interview," said Haraldr as he gave his hair a final combing; a servant held a mirror above his silver washbasin. "Just as one is not permitted in the presence of the Emperor and Autocrator for any length of time."

The eunuchs met Haraldr and Gregory just inside the encirclement of one hundred and fifty Varangians that secured the complex of Her Imperial Majesty's domed brocade pavilions; anyone who came within an ax shaft of this human barricade without plainly declaring a password that was changed each evening would have his skull instantly split. The ritual the eunuchs explained to Haraldr was identical to that for his audience with the Emperor, but with a surprising exception: "Her Imperial Majesty," the wizened Symeon had unctuously droned, "expects you to reply without prompting from her Chamberlain."

The entrance to the main Imperial Pavilion was curtained with brocade so thick, it seemed to be made of lead. The sound of some sort of stringed instrument, much more elegant and melodious than anything Haraldr had heard at the court of Yaroslav, sweetened an atmosphere already rich with the scent of fresh roses. Walls of heavy brocade divided the pavilion into separate spacious rooms with gauzy canopies overhead. Haraldr and Gregory were led through two fabric antechambers before they were finally thrust to their faces in the thick nap of a carpet that smelled of myrrh.

A eunuch guided Haraldr to a couch covered in glass-smooth silk. Cushions thick with down seem to swallow him up, producing a disorienting, weightless feeling. The lamps flickered. He dared not look directly at either woman, but he already knew. His heart pounded his ribs with huge, hollow thumps and he was certain his voice would quaver. This was worse than any battle. Helpless, sinking, he gave himself up to the god who had suffered unspeakable torment to give men the beauty of verse. Let this torture make him as eloquent in the face of her beauty. Maria.

The voice was throaty, almost mesmerizing, flowing forth like a thick fragrant syrup. Haraldr could only distantly observe that it was not Maria who spoke. "Your Mother the Empress greets you and thanks you for the assurance your offices have given her on this most arduous yet joyous pilgrimage." Gregory, seated to Haraldr's left, translated with considerable fortitude. Haraldr forced himself to concentrate.

When the translation was finished, Haraldr knew he should look upon the Empress. Kristr! Which of the two was lovelier? The Empress was like a living statue, a beauty so ideal that it could exist only in the imagination. Or upon the face next to her. In fact, they looked almost as alike as sisters. The same pearl-laced coils framing the same exquisitely contoured, slightly rouged cheeks; the glistening, deftly sculpted lips. But the eyes of the Empress were ash-tinted with a sorrow that showed even in the surrounding flesh, in minute creases that shadowed the corners of her eyes. Maria's eyes, almost amethyst in this light, challenged him; they were as hard as the gem they resembled. It was as if she knew of the liberties he had taken with her in his fantasies. He was shamed, a boy confronted by his secret love.

The Empress said something to Maria about "gold" or "golden," and "hair," and Haraldr's wealth; it was an aside that Gregory was not invited to translate. Maria's gemstone eyes remained obdurate, fixed on a point somewhere to Haraldr's left and considerably behind him. The Empress laughed, showing perfect, small teeth; for the first time Haraldr registered that her coiled tresses were as stunningly golden as Maria's were raven-black. An uneasy silence followed. The Empress looked at Haraldr steadily, forcing him to lower his eyes. His head buzzed with tension. Was this acute coyness his fantasy lover's fashion? Hadn't Maria haunted him with her eyes on their previous meeting? Hadn't she hoped to see his fair hair again? Oh, no. What a fool, he suddenly realized in the pit of his stomach. That declaration had only been manufactured by Mar to his purpose.

Maria spoke an aside to the Empress, her tone like a knife's blade. "Tongue" and "oxen"; something to the effect that one should not expect a beast set to the plow to regale one with wit. Haraldr felt as if hot irons had been placed to the backs of his ears. He knew his forehead visibly flamed. Why would not Odin release his tongue? The weight on his chest was crushing.

The Empress spoke again and Gregory translated. "The lady Maria says she has dined with you on a previous occasion and that your tongue was, shall we say, charmingly . . . *audacious.* It would distress your Mother so to think that the honors and wealth you have won since then have made you reticent among us."

Maria's lips flickered with the barest discernible taunt. Haraldr wondered if his chest would explode with excitement. She remembered him! Her demeanor now was the ruse. Haraldr closed his eyes as an ancient wind swept his mind. Odin was ready to speak.

"Forgive my insolent silence, my Blessed Mother. I can only say that since coming among the Romans I have seen many wonders that have brought comment spontaneously to my tongue. Your Imperial Majesty is the first such wonder to deprive me entirely of the faculty for speech."

The Empress's wine-red lips parted and her pearl teeth sparkled in a display of glee. She sat up and pulled her arms about her knees; her long, elegant white fingers stroked the raised golden-eagle medallions on her silk robe. Maria shifted to place her elbow on a thick maroon cushion. She cast her eyes down.

Zoe signaled with the merest nod, and a white-robed eunuch passed among the couches with silver goblets on a silver tray. The wine was strong and aromatic and seemed to change flavors in Haraldr's mouth, ending its passage with a faint sweetness that dissolved on his tongue. A drink for the gods, he thought. He was seduced by the heady vapors and the down and silk that wrapped him up.

"What place in Thule do you come from . . . Har-aldr?" Zoe successfully feigned interest in her own question.

"Norway."

Zoe nodded. "Nor-way. And before you earned honor among the Romans, what were you?"

Haraldr was instantly cold, but almost as quickly he realized that the Empress was asking one question only to get to another. "I was a land man at the court of the Great Prince Yaroslav."

Maria's laugh was as harsh as breaking glass. She spoke several sentences to Zoe; Haraldr made out the word *servant* three times. He was thought a servant's servant; apparently the Romans were not impressed with the Great Prince, and certainly not with his former toll collector. The blood pounded in Haraldr's ears.

More wine was served. Zoe spoke between sips. "I have heard such tales of you Tauro-Scythians. Is it true that one man may have many wives?"

Haraldr flushed with wine and embarrassment. He tried to shift his body but the downy cushioning gave way, trapping him as if he were struggling in a spiderweb. "Not for those who believe in Kris— Christ. Pagans, perhaps."

Zoe's eyes bored away with insistent insincerity. "Yes. I have seen some of you who wear amulets dedicated to a heathen god. He is a bull?"

Haraldr was confused for a moment. Then he understood. Many Norse pagans wore the hammer of Thor, while the Greek word for *bull* was the similar-sounding *tauros*. He explained to the Empress.

Zoe tired of these preliminaries. She lowered her voice to a gentle growl. "So. I have heard that followers of this Thor-god will take a woman and have intercourse with her before an entire multitude. A man will spread his harlot's haunches atop him even as he sits playing dice with his friends."

Haraldr's face was singed with embarrassment. Was the Empress testing his modesty? Then he remembered the scene in the play, how she had rolled on the floor with her lover. And Hakon had called her a "bitch-whore."

Maria again directed an aside to Zoe. Haraldr could tell she made an obscene jibe; he did not know many of the words except *donkey.* He looked sharply at Maria. Who was she but a presumptuous lady-in-waiting, while he was rightful King of Norway. Odin filled his throat with a fate-tempting voice; hadn't the Empress asked for audacity? "I am certain, your Imperial Majesty, that were a Roman to observe our lovemaking, he would not find it different from the habits he is accustomed to. Unless, of course, his own practices were as curious as those you have described."

Zoe looked slyly at Maria, whose cheeks became slightly tinted. The *barbaroi* had a certain deftness, Zoe observed to herself; by making his hypothetical Roman a man, he had avoided a direct aspersion to the Imperial Dignity. In the manner one should treat a lover found more skilled than one had expected, it was time to lead this Haraldr on to more . . . *intriguing* postures. "Maria says you are a harbinger of our destruction. I have often wondered why so many of my children have an inordinate fear of you fair-hairs. Of course, your role in casting us into the abyss has long been chronicled in The Life of St. Andrew the Fool, and in our time this sagacious oracle seems to be present at every meeting of the Sacrum Consistorum—though God accepted the saint's worthy soul half a millennium ago. However, since you are of the fair-haired race and St. Andrew was not, might we know if you are an agent of such sabotage?"

Haraldr's heart seemed to constrict involuntarily at this line of questioning, but he was certain that his identity was not what the Empress wanted to know. What was she getting at? He cautioned himself that this Imperial beauty was a thorn-girt rose; her question had ridiculed both him and Maria and apparently also disparaged the policies of Imperial officials, all to an end that was no more discernible than a headland lost in a fog.

Answer soberly, Haraldr instructed himself; you have permitted yourself enough recklessness for the evening. "It is true. If the Empire of the Romans turned against my Father the Emperor and my Empress Mother, I would be the agent of the Romans' destruction."

Maria spoke to Zoe, waving her hand dismissively; Haraldr recognized the words *serpent,* and *flatterer.* Haraldr felt as if she had physically slapped him; his bed and his heart would be empty tonight. It saddened him to think that his fantasy love had been inspired by such an astringent reality.

Zoe sipped with both hands on her goblet, as if she were a priest consuming the blood of Christ. "I understand that you have made yourself most favorably known to my husband's brother." Zoe's voice was devoid of inflection, neither innocent nor accusing.

Haraldr made no attempt to conceal the shock of realization. Of course! The mouth, the eyes. One face a grotesque inflation of the other, and yet . . . Brothers! That was why the Emperor had appeared to be a mere puppet of Joannes; more likely his Imperial Majesty, who lacked none of the aptitudes for leadership, simply valued the advice of his older brother. It explained so much.

"The Orphanotrophus Joannes," prompted Zoe, dismayed by the *barbaroi*'s crude disingenuousness in attempting to conceal the liaison. Surely he was more skilled than this.

"Yes . . . Joannes," said Haraldr, recovering. "He had suggested I not boast of the honor he has paid me. Yes, he indeed offers me the inestimable gift of his guidance."

"But of course. Our Orphanotrophus guides all of our earthly fortunes much as Christ the Pantocrator guides our immortal souls. He has the hands to mold whatever he will with the clay of our beings."

Maria spoke sharply. Something about hands too big and statues lacking in grace; Haraldr would remember to ask Gregory later. Then he was chilled to the core despite the swaddling warmth of the down cushions. Kristr! Maria hated Joannes. There had been no doubt of her enmity that night at Nicephorus Argyrus's. Could the Empress share this animosity? Had there not been a strange timbre to her voice when she had spoken of him? Cold, stormy, mortally dangerous, these Roman waters were indeed.

Zoe looked keenly at Haraldr. She was certain that this interpreter was good, and that the *barbaroi* was really almost a semi-*barbaroi* with a fair command of Greek already. And yet he had betrayed nothing when she had mentioned sabotage, and had stumbled with witless guile over her mention of the grotesque monk. He was either an innocent or a dissimulator worthy of Odysseus, an actor to make the entire Hippodrome weep. Either way he would be useful. But before she took this . . . *seduction* further, she would need to know which. She signaled Symeon to escort her guests out, and spoke in parting.

"Your Mother has enjoyed this interview," translated a gratefully exhausted Gregory as Zoe finished. "When we arrive in Antioch and begin our official entertainments there, I will ask that you be seated at my dining couch."

† † †

"Brother," muttered Constantine, mocking the imperious tone of the letter's perfunctory salutation. He continued to read.

> My instructions will arrive in two seperate missives. This is the first. As is your duty as Strategus of Antioch, you will send the escort you are obligated to provide her Imperial Majesty to the scheduled rendezvous at Mopsuestia. At Mopsuestia your Turmarch (I of course presume that you will not accompany your army into the field, given the ever-present threat to Antioch itself) will not accept the transfer of command from the Strategus of Cilicia. Instead, due to the temporary depletion of your own ranks and the necessity of defending your own city, the Strategus of Cilicia will be humbly beseeched to continue his escort of the Imperial Party as far south as Tripoli. You are to pay for the accommodation of the Cilician troops within your theme with the surcharge to the land tax I ordered earlier this year. I trust you will show the Strategus Meletius Attalietes every hospitality your splendid city has to offer.
>
> Your second set of instructions will be delivered to you in the form of a letter introducing the *komes* of Her Majesty's special Varangian Guard. This Tauro-Scythian, named Haraldr Nordbrikt, is a tool I plan to use for one surgical procedure, after which he will be blunted to uselessness. Until then, see that he is particularly well cared for.
>
> With affection and in the service of our Holy Brother,
> Joannes Orphanotrophus

Constantine took a small key from an unlocked drawer beneath his writing table, then opened the lock of another drawer. He removed a box with an ivory lid, unlocked the padlock that secured the sliding top, and deposited the letter in the box, then locked everything back up again. He sat for a moment with his hands clasped across his chest, his beardless, slightly sagging chin slumped forward.

Brother. Never consulting, never asking, always the command: Brother. Yes, his brother, Joannes, had pulled him along as he rose in the Imperial Administration; and yes, Joannes had engineered the stunning deification of their precious little Michael, over whom Joannes doted as if his youngest brother had sprung from his own mutilated loins. But had anyone ever wondered how Constantine might have performed on his own, had he been the firstborn? Or had he been the last-born, permitted to go through life with the undamaged reproductive equipment that had placed Michael on the Imperial Throne? Yes, Joannes had given up his manhood, but so had Constantine, and yet everyone revered Joannes as if he alone had made this ultimate sacrifice for the family. And Michael, now unbelievably the Emperor and Autocrator of the Romans, had given up nothing for the family! Yet now, from beneath the Imperial Diadem, he looked down upon his "second brother," Constantine, as if the Strategus of Antioch were merely a court fool dressed for the part, incapable of performing the simplest Easter distribution without the personal intervention of the all-knowing Orphanotrophus Joannes!

The fountains gently tinkled in the courtyard, balming Constantine's anger. A man does not say when or who will bring him into the world; only the Pantocrator determines that fate. Joannes's schemes had worked in the past, and this current exercise, however nebulous it might seem at the moment, would no doubt bring them all further success. And someday Constantine would be brought back to the Empress City, and there he would prove to both his eldest and youngest brothers the true measure of his abilities. Until then, Antioch was the fairest exile a man could know.

He rang for his chamberlain. "Basil," he told the bowing eunuch, "order the Turmarch to my office right away."

† † †

"You would prefer we discuss this flatulent Plato our Hellenist is always ranting about? The man is an Aeolus, so prodigious is the hot wind he makes." Zoe was irritable after the jolting, pitching descent from the Cilician Gates.

"I simply do not think that this single Tauro-Scythian offers anything other than his own considerable wind. While we toy with this savage the repulsive Orphanotrophus Joannes continues to strengthen his stranglehold on your people. I would not be surprised to hear that in your absence he has snatched up the Imperial Diadem and placed it on his own head."

"Joannes could not keep the brother I have crowned on the throne for a day without my Purple-Born connivance. The people would put the palaces of the Dhynatoi to the torch and then smash down the palace gates to evict the usurper." Zoe's voice was as fierce as her pride in the devotion the common folk—the merchants and laborers and fishers and butchers and porters—reserved solely for the authority derived from birth in the porphyry Purple Chamber of the Imperial Palace. She and her sister, Theodora, were the last Purple-Born survivors of the Macedonian dynasty established by their uncle, Basil the Bulgar-Slayer, and woe betide the upstart who would attempt to take from the folk of Constantinople the living legacy of the Emperor who for half a century had lifted them up and protected them against the Dhynatoi.

"No," Zoe said, "Joannes is as presumptuous and arrogant as Babel rising from the Plain of Shinar. But we must not forget that he is also thorough and patient. Which returns me to our Tauro-Scythian. Why would Joannes sponsor a *barbaroi* upstart if the *barbaroi* did not figure in some important equation? If this Haraldr is innocent of Joannes's wiles— and despite your protests, I believe that this is possible—if he is innocent, we can turn him to our purpose. And if he is a willing accomplice of the grotesque Joannes, then we can send him back laden with poisoned treats to offer his patron. And what could *we* possibly betray of our own objectives? Between the sexless brute Joannes and myself is that absolutely transparent intimacy that can exist only between the most implacable foes."

"I do not assail your logic, Mother."

Zoe pushed the curtain slightly aside to see why her carriage, and presumably the rest of the Imperial caravan, had stopped. "Well, you know I value your intuition, little daughter. What is it?"

"For a moment I got the sense that this Haraldr fancies himself . . . I don't know. He looked at me as if he considered himself a king."

"Well, he certainly cannot think he will conquer the Roman Empire with his five hundred Varangian malfeasants. But do you think he has ambitions for himself?"

"Ambitions? I am not sure that is the correct term. Fate rules all, and yet fate has no ambition. This man . . . he chills me. It is not as if he is an agent of some worldly power but an emissary of destiny itself. There is this current of raw fate that seems to surround him, almost as if you could touch him and . . ." Maria clasped her hands, as if to stop them from quivering. "I do not make sense, I know. But I have told you what Ata said about the three lines crossing. He never said that the man might be a *barbaroi* fair-hair. I don't know."

Zoe placed her hands over Maria's. "I think this Tauro-Scythian is a chorus player in this drama of ours. But perhaps . . . don't take offense, daughter, but you said once he brought you pleasure, if only in the evanescence of sleep." Zoe smiled wryly. "Perhaps he is an instrument of a simple fate. I know you find the Tauro-Scythians pleasurable to countenance, and you never did conclude your . . . investigation of the Hetairarch's . . . abilities. Perhaps you make too much of a basic desire, the one, as you so astutely pointed out the other day, that is easiest to assuage." Zoe laughed delicately. "You would hardly be the first lady of my court to take a Tauro-Scythian *barbaroi* to your bed."

"Perhaps. I confess that he was in my bed last night after your conversation with him." Maria's eyes widened as she recalled the vision. "May I tell you?"

"Oh, yes, little daughter," said Zoe, all weariness forgotten.

"He came to me, quite naked, his chest covered with hair like golden threads, his arms as hard and smooth as sculpted stone. He ripped my gown away. I submitted totally, willing it. Mother, it embarrasses even our confidence to mention my shamelessness—I begged him to enter every orifice with the most savage thrusts. I screamed at him to break my flesh with his teeth, to bite my lips and nipples, and blood and sweat mixed to a hot oil spread between our merciless breasts. And then I rose above him, now pulling his hair, then clawing his eyes, and he knew my pleasure. We rose, conjoined in ecstasy, toward a golden dome, and in my hand I discovered a knife, a cold, icy blade, and at the moment of supreme passion I plunged it with all my force into his neck and he faded, he died as I was transported, raised by the last warmth of his burning member as his body froze, and the arms of the sun held me. When I awakened from the dream, I was drenched in my own effluxions."

"Maria! You exceed yourself! Your nocturnal musings would make our esteemed specialist in sexual disorders faint away like a maiden at the sight of her first unsheathed column! So you see, you can have your pleasure of him. But I think we ultimately can dispose of our overweening Tauro-Scythian in a fashion that might be less . . . provocative, but more useful to our cause."

Maria nodded, her jaw still tense. Yes, she could finally admit that the desire existed; after all, it was of the type easiest to assuage. What she could not confess, even to her beloved Empress mother, was that her dream had demonstrated to her a frightening but essential truth. Her desire could only be quenched in the moment that its object was destroyed.

† † †

If Constantinople was the Queen of Cities, stately and elegant, then Antioch was a ravishing courtesan. The walls, golden in the late-afternoon sun, were almost as vast and proud as those of the Empress City; studded at intervals of a bowshot with huge round towers, they rose from a glowing emerald-and-ocher valley to the pine-dotted heights of a mountain ridge thousands of ells above. The city tumbled down the slopes; beneath rocky heights were terraced fields, rowed vineyards, and gardens dotted with lemon and orange and ivy, interspersed with the white domes of vast palaces. The buildings thickened as the incline graduated to the flat plain before the river, crowding together in fantastic arrays of domes and spires and colonnades that faded into the southern horizon.

For almost a rowing-spell the people of the surrounding villages had come out to stand by the road; they were simple farmers in brown tunics brightened by vivid shawls and sashes. They threw flowers and aromatic herbs beneath the wheels of the Imperial carriages and chanted in Greek mixed with a tongue Haraldr did not know. The women held their children and pointed, saying, "Theotokos"; apparently many of the peasants could not distinguish between the Mother of the Romans and the Mother of God.

The city became more distinct as the Imperial party advanced parallel to the looping, sluggish yellow river that flowed toward the city's eastern flank. The buildings seemed more open than those of Constantinople, with rows of wide arches and canopied balconies to draw the breeze that wandered idly through the valley. Banners fluttered and glazed domes sparkled.

"It does not have the aspect of a virtuous city," said Halldor lightly.

"She is a whore," offered Ulfr admiringly. "Goddess of neck-ice, golden-haired shaker of the limb of Frey's orchard."

"Please repeat that," asked Gregory. "That was a very difficult kenning."

"He means that this whore is both very beautiful and very skilled," said Halldor. He gave his horse a little spur and came up beside Haraldr. "You haven't had a woman in some time. I think abstinence has made you despondent. Your comrades have decided to plunder this wanton city until we find a woman who will put the fire back in your eyes."

Haraldr struggled to smile. "I can always count on you to be blunt." He thought for a moment. Halldor had bedded a woman in Nicomedia, one in Nicaea, one in Ancyra, one in Adana. None of them whores, either, but seemingly well-born women prominent in provincial courts. The one in Nicaea, with dark hair and dark eyes and a waist like a wasp, had rivaled even Maria in Haraldr's fancy for several restless nights. Why had he not considered this before? If a man's arrows consistently missed their target, should he not ask the advice of an archer who inerrantly struck that at which he aimed? Haraldr asked Halldor to join him in riding up ahead of the Varangian ranks.

"I knew you were lovesick," said Halldor when Haraldr had finished his tale, "but I thought it was still that Khazar girl." Halldor rubbed his fine nose with his forefinger as he thought for a moment. "Haraldr, do you know why I drink a full cup of love for every drop that dampens your lips?" he asked rhetorically. "Because you approach love like a poet, your breast bared for all to see, while I approach love like a trader with his hacksilver hidden in the lining of his girdle."

"But you have never had to pay for a woman's favors."

"Exactly. Look. The wise trader sees an object he must acquire. He does not run pell-mell to the merchant's booth, swoop the desired merchandise into his arms, with heaving chest declare that his life will end if he cannot have this exquisite item, and then offer to hack off a limb to place on top of the merchant's price so that he may have it. No. The wise trader in fact strolls idly by this merchant's booth, then looks for hours, perhaps days, into the booths of the neighboring merchants. He examines their wares and sets his praise-tongue wagging over the quality of *their* merchandise. Then, his bag already full of items he has purchased at the other booths, he walks by, almost walks on, thinks better of it, and pauses to poke here and there among the wares that surround his treasure. He asks the price of this and that, and then, well, since he is here, what about this? And then of course he haggles, as if this treasure is nothing more than dried dung to be burned, and how could he possibly pay such a price and so on. Soon the merchant is so convinced he will never be relieved of this worthless item that he virtually gives it away. So as I see it, this Maria is a wise trader playing games with you. Now all you need to do is turn the tables on her."

"That is remarkable, Halldor," said Haraldr with genuine respect. It had never occurred to him that one needed to deal as hard with a woman he hoped to clutch gently to his breast as he did with a man with whom he was doing business. The wise trader indeed. The next time he saw Maria, he would not offer so much as a sideways glance at the wares in her booth.

✝ ✝ ✝

"Haraldr Nordbrikt! Of course! Haraldr Nordbrikt!"

Constantine, the Strategus of Antioch, virtually leapt from behind his ivory-surfaced writing table. Haraldr observed that Constantine was a beardless eunuch like his brother, Joannes, though he had been spared the grotesque giantism of his brother's features. In fact, there was more of the Emperor himself in Constantine's look. As he came closer, though, Haraldr noticed the glaze of nervous perspiration on the Strategus's forehead and upper lip, and he wondered if this man was so daunted by his brother that he grew anxious in the presence of someone merely bearing a letter from him.

"Welcome, welcome, welcome. My brother, Joannes, has not only told me to expect you, but word of your fame has already begun to buzz about my city. We are verily beneath the blade of the Saracens here, so your proficiency in exterminating heretics is particularly well valued in fair Antioch." Constantine fluttered his hands and hated himself for it. *Mother of God, what a monstrous thug,* he thought, *albeit splendidly formed. The scar over his eye gives him the sinister aspect. Certainly the type of delinquent my brother would enlist in his employ.*

"Thank you, Strategus," said Haraldr in Greek; he had specially prepared this address. "I wish . . . I hope I may serve you well . . . as well as I am devoted . . . to serve your brother, Orphanotrophus Joannes, and . . . our father. And may I . . . present this." Haraldr handed the rolled and sealed letter to Constantine.

Constantine thanked Haraldr and returned to his seat behind his writing table before unsealing the document. *I wonder if my omniscient brother knows that his pet brute is acquiring the power of speech,* he thought as he nervously peeled the embossed lead from the string. *Is Joannes's ambition making him careless? And if he plots an errant course, to what end will the rest of us be led?* Constantine unrolled the letter, apprehension already lurking in his stomach.

Haraldr watched carefully as Constantine read. Kristr! For a moment Haraldr wondered if someone hiding beneath the table had just knifed Constantine in the groin; he was suddenly virtually chalk-faced. Haraldr's own skin crawled. Had his patron, Joannes, been entirely sincere? This could not be simply a friendly letter of introduction. And wasn't it considerably longer than it would need to be for that purpose? On the other hand, perhaps Joannes sensibly appended other news to the letter, and perhaps not all of it was good. But the reaction was most curious, and Constantine did not seem to be recovering well. This was doing nothing to allay Haraldr's doubts about Joannes's credibility.

Constantine put the letter down with trembling hands; he had not needed to finish it to be virtually numb with shock, and he certainly could not read on in front of this brute. He grinned forcibly, sweat beading his brow. "Well, Haraldr Nordbrikt, I am afraid official duties beckon me to return to them. But I understand that I will see you this evening. We are both seated at the Imperial Table."

When Haraldr had left, Constantine picked up the letter again and studied it for almost an hour, forcing himself to consider carefully all of the details. The plan was astonishing in concept and would be exceedingly taxing to execute; it was certainly more than just another of Joannes's elaborate schemes. And yet Joannes promised far more reward than he had ever offered before for the complicity he now desired. It was incredible, but yes, it could be done. And, of course, now there was no question. It would have to be done.

† † †

"Get your face away, swine-breath!" shouted Grettir, though he knew these beetle-faces could not understand Norse. At every street they swarmed around him, touching his tunic and the white skin of his arms with their filth-blackened fingers, then abandoning him to the rabble that assumed the chase at the next block. This is a mistake, Grettir told himself, in every way. Haraldr Nordbrikt was no longer his enemy. After months of a woman's scullery work, Grettir now rode with the skalds again; few other masters would have been as generous, particularly not Grettir's former patron, Hakon. Grettir cursed the impulse that had led him, those long months ago, to contact the Heta-mark, or whatever they called that Icelandic devil. Well, the ogre had him by the belly purse now, and he would have to ransom his own soul to shake him loose. If these nut-faced demons did not take him first.

The beggars crawled from their rag nests, set against the scum-coated walls. Empty eyes, legless torsos, lipless mouths, jabbing stumps. The sores, the stench, the pall of fat, lazy flies. Grettir swatted the attacking human miasma around him and looked for the landmark, as he had been instructed. There. Odin be praised. The blue tiles, the tower rising. How he had found the place through this rat's warren in this vast, strange city, he did not know. Perhaps fortune was still with him.

It was the place indeed; as he turned the corner Grettir saw the golden-tipped spires rising above the blue dome. The street in front was blocked with every damned soul Kristr had cast into Hel. They wailed and beseeched like screeching birds and chattering rodents, rags hanging off their scabrous, desiccated limbs. Men with cloud-white eyes, a woman with ragged black hair pulled out in angry red patches, children with pox-eaten faces. They saw him, and they came after him.

Instinct took over, and Grettir struggled for his knife against the probing of skeletal, slimy fingers. He waved the blade, and the man in front of him pressed his hands to his bleeding chest. The rest hesitated, a wolf pack deciding if hunger or fear would command their guts. Grettir wheeled, crouched, let them all see the blade. They stood dull-eyed and sightless, moaning and jabbering.

Grettir took one step. No one moved. He thrust ahead with the knife. A man with a huge, swollen, oozing leg stepped back. Another step. The pack responded. Slowly, step by thrusting step, Grettir passed beneath the blue-tiled dome. Suddenly they were gone, vanished like malignant *fylgya* returning to the spirit world. Grettir looked down the dark, narrow alley ahead with tears in his eyes.

The absence of traffic was as disconcerting as the mob. The crumbling mud walls almost met overhead, and a dank smell pervaded the chilly air. A rat scurried across the narrow dirt path. He listened to the faint cries of the mob; the once hideous wails were seemingly sponged from the air by the ancient earthen walls. He squinted into the darkness.

A man. Bent over a sort of crude stone table. He worked at something; edging closer, Grettir saw a boot, a few scraps of hide. He gasped; the man was huge! But the enormous figure did not turn from his table. He was filing something, slowly, wearily, as if for the rest of his life he would file away in this strange dungeon.

Grettir fought the gorge in his throat and nostrils as the man looked up. No nose, only gaping, wheezing slits. Yet the eyes were light blue, and the filth-encrusted hair had once been golden. Odin, what caprice of yours condemned this Norseman to this Hel? The giant's tunic hung in greasy tatters.

The man spoke. "You have business here?" The language was Norse, the accent Icelandic.

"Wh-what?" mumbled Grettir.

The eyes burned in the darkness, ice beneath a haunted moon. "You have business here?" The voice was strangely passive, yet Grettir's tuned ear detected the strong current of menace beneath the calm surface. Quickly reveal your errand, he told himself. "I am told to give you this." Grettir dug the ring from the lining of his belt and cautiously placed it on the stone table. The next thing he knew, he was on his back, the dankness suffocating, the pale luminescence of the eyes above him, the sharp point at his throat. "What does Mar Hunrodarson want?" The voice was the wolf's.

Grettir whimpered but fought to find words; his tongue had always been his livelihood but now it was his life. "He said you would not need to ask that."

- The knife vanished and Grettir was jerked to his feet. "You live, then," growled the beast, "as Mar once let me live." The noseless giant said nothing else, only stared at Grettir for a long, horrifying minute, as if he could pull from Grettir's terrified gaze the memories of a homeland so far away. Finally he spoke again, with calm finality. "The name of the man?"

"He is called Haraldr Nordbrikt." Grettir gulped the dry rock in his throat. "His real name is Haraldr Sigurdarson, Prince of Norway."

cannot bear to look," said Gregory. He shut his eyes and would have buried his head in his hands if he had not thought he would be immediately flogged—or worse—for such a violation of protocol. "You don't know how many of them fall. I've seen it before in the Hippodrome."

"I can't take my eyes from her," said Haraldr as he raptly watched the acrobat. The rope had been strung taut between the the the far ends of the two half domes that thrust up the gilded central dome of the Strategus's palace. The acrobat stood on one pointed toe, just beneath the balustraded rim of the central dome. Her arms stretched wide like a bird's, and her breasts, covered only by tiny golden leaves placed over the nipples, were pulled firm against her sculpted rib cage. Her bare buttocks were tensed; a third leaf between her legs was all that concealed what little modesty she had left. She pirouetted and waved, then leapt almost weightlessly to the safety of the stone-railed balcony. The Strategus's guests, several hundred of them at more than a dozen large tables covered with white brocade cloths and silver settings, roared in acclamation.

"He wonders if you would like to speak to the acrobat." Gregory translated for Constantine. "Her name is Citron. A very private conversation, he assures you."

Haraldr looked at Constantine, who reclined across from him, next to the head of the T-shaped table. "Yes," he answered in Greek. Then turned to Gregory, who stood in attendance directly behind him. "Tell him I do not intend for the shroud of night to conceal from me the beauties of Antioch."

Constantine smiled obsequiously. Haraldr noticed that the Strategus of Antioch was in an active sweat; a bead dripped from his eyelash and darkened the carnelian silk upholstery of the dining couch on which he reclined. Haraldr settled comfortably on his left elbow; Constantine had called this dining "in the Roman fashion," and Gregory had reported that this was considered the height of elegance. One of Constantine's eunuchs scurried over to arrange the silken pillows to support Haraldr's back. He studied the gleaming silver knives and forks set before him; after practicing for months with the absurd instruments, he could use them as well as ax and sword. And after all, he reminded himself, these are in a sense the weapons of the Romans.

The young man who came to stand beside Constantine at first seemed to be the Emperor. Another moment's scrutiny revealed a less robust torso and more delicate features, but he was a very handsome young man. Constantine gestured between the new arrival and Haraldr. "This is my nephew, Michael Kalaphates. Michael, you are privileged to meet the renowned slayer of Saracens, Haraldr Nordbrikt."

Haraldr stood and bowed. Michael seemed genuinely enthusiastic, his dark eyes lively. "Sir, I am your servant," he said in an elegant but slightly quavering voice. "The smallest thing you wish, or if you wish the greatest thing of your admirers here in Antioch, I would find any request an honor to fulfill. And even if there is nothing I can do for a man as resourceful as your feats prove you to be, I hope I will have the good fortune to converse with you before you leave our city." He bowed and took his seat. Haraldr remembered that Joannes had remarked on his nephew's lack of ambition. But Haraldr also observed that same had been said of him not too long ago, and he felt an instinctive affinity for this lesser Michael.

Meanwhile Constantine had begun to dither with the eunuch he called Basil; something about his anxiety as to when the Empress and her ladies would appear. Haraldr counted the empty places; the Empress would clearly take the purple-upholstered couch at the head of the table; two guests would be seated between him and the Empress, another directly across from him. Haraldr worried that Maria would take the seat one removed from him; then he would not be able to conspicuously pass her booth without so much as a single glance at her wares.

Constantine frowned involuntarily and then brightened into a clearly extorted greeting. He stood, grinning and perspiring. "Strategus Meletius Attalietes, you do us honor!"

Attalietes waved as if he were fanning a slow, stupid fly. He settled languidly onto the couch opposite Constantine's. Haraldr was astounded to observe that Attalietes's gold-hemmed tunic was almost as berry-purple as an Imperial robe; everyone else was in white. This could not be an Imperial blood relationship; was it effrontery? Attalietes made the merest inclination of his head in Haraldr's direction; the small nostrils that pierced Attalietes's snub nose flared slightly and then compressed, as if expunging a disagreeable odor. He turned back to Constantine and spoke in a scrolling tongue more imperious, more florid, than even

Symeon's. Haraldr heard *barbaroi* clearly, of course, and something about vulgarity, bad taste. Constantine seemed flustered; his forehead was covered with huge beads and his bare cheeks flushed.

"The Dhynatoi wants to know why you are seated at his table," whispered Gregory. "He also says it is vulgar to entertain before dinner. He says that out of deference to Her Imperial Majesty he will suffer these affronts to propriety and remain at the table."

The music of the organ was the signal for all to rise; like a huge flock of white birds, the snowy-robed guests stood and waited. The large bronze doors at the end of the room slid aside, signaling the prescribed chants. "Come forth, Empress of the Romans!" The dome echoed with the reverent words and Haraldr calmed himself with the reminder that he had dined at a king's table for most of his life. "Come forth, God-protected splendor of the crown! Come forth purple-born glory! Shed light on your slaves!" The white-robed chamberlains, led by the frail Symeon, preceded the glittering ladies-in-waiting through the door; Haraldr saw Maria, sheathed in tight white silk, just before the Empress appeared in a burst of brilliant purple. Every head in the enormous hall bowed deeply.

Eunuchs fluttered about the couches. More white-robed figures took up positions behind the head of the table. Silk rustled, and Haraldr, head still bowed, saw a gold-threaded white hem a few ells from his feet; the erotically tiny white slippers were studded with little pearls. He thought of Halldor's lesson and relaxed. The wise trader. The white-robed figures at the head of the table began to chant, one after the other, in a tongue Haraldr could not understand. When the chants were done, it was permissible to look up.

Zoe reclined at the head of the table; a young woman bearing a golden wand stood motionless directly behind her. The Empress turned to her right and said, "Constantine, Strategus of Antioch." Constantine removed the long white sash he wore over his shoulder, then reclined on his couch. Zoe turned to her left. "Meletius Attalietes, Strategus of Cilicia." Attalietes removed his sash as floridly as a dancer discarding her robe and reclined in a single effortless motion, as if he dined in this position each night. Still facing left, Zoe addressed the woman next to Haraldr. "Maria, Mistress of the Robes," said Zoe in her voluptuous, slightly sibilant voice. Maria settled on her couch; Haraldr could not restrain a glance at her white slippers and a flash of bare ankle. "Anna Dalassena, Silentarias." The girl who removed her sash and reclined just opposite Haraldr was like a gorgeous bird; her lips bright red, her black hair coiled and set with pearls, her cheeks blazing. She was smaller than the Empress and Maria, with a delicate silk-sheathed neck, and probably not any older than Elisevett.

"Haraldr Nordbrikt, Slayer of Saracens and Komes of Her Imperial Majesty's Varangian Guard." Haraldr could not suppress his excitement and vanity as he removed his sash and settled back on his couch. As the rest of the guests at the Imperial table were announced and seated, he noticed that the Empress gave Michael Kalaphates a wry, meaningful look.

The five white-robed chanters, or *voukaloi*, began their sonorous, rhythmic exchanges again; the eunuchs fluttered forward and began to mix the wine with water. Haraldr looked across at Anna. He nodded and her brilliant cheeks grew deeper. Her dark eyelashes dipped, but her lips quivered with a faint smile. Haraldr decided he would praise these wares with a tongue that would make Odin blush.

"She wants to address you," said Gregory in a panic that almost tied his tongue. Haraldr put his goblet down and looked at the Empress.

"Have you ever dined in the Roman fashion before?" asked Zoe. Haraldr could hear Attalietes snort.

"The position is familiar to me, as we do not have seats on our longships. The comfort, of course, is quite superior, and this I attribute to the glory of the Roman Empire and the divine offices of your Imperial Majesty." Haraldr thanked Odin for his words.

The *voukaloi* again droned their chants and the servants brought the first course: miniature olives in silver bowls; boiled artichokes; eggs, cooked and shelled, and cradled in shells of blue enamel set on individual silver trays and served with a long silver spoon. Haraldr thought better of tackling the egg and instead scooped fish roe from a silver bowl onto a biscuit.

"Anna Dalassena." Haraldr was surprised at the civility of Attalietes's address; somewhat condescending but spoken as if the girl were human. "Your father is well?"

Anna blushed. "Oh, yes, very well, thank you, Strategus."

"Yes," said Zoe, pausing to press one of the miniature olives to her erotically puckered lips, as if kissing the tiny morsel. Gregory quickly poised himself to translate, as Haraldr had asked him to do whenever she spoke. "The Grand Domestic has to be magnificently . . . robust. He has so many masters to serve that his errands are endless, and it is a pity that those for whom he so diligently labors are never satisfied. I pray for him often, don't I, Anna dear?"

Attalietes dabbed his mouth with his lace linen napkin. "I am certain that is a comfort to the girl. I know how devoutly you prayed for the health of your late husband. May Christ the King—"

"Strategus, your tongue is not so glib that I could not have it removed." Zoe's voice was a dagger in each heart within hearing. Haraldr could scarcely believe her screaming eyes; *this* was an Empress who could daunt any king he had ever known. He almost flinched as she gestured toward him. "You have met the *komes* of my guard, have you not, Strategus? He has hewn stiffer stuff than your neck." Zoe fixed Attalietes for a moment, then turned and with absolutely deft fingers selected another tiny olive. Her eyes wandered again, to Attalietes. "Strategus, I suddenly realize that naughty Symeon must have failed to communicate to you the proper attire for our dining. Symeon, you must make amends. Take our Strategus to the kitchen and find him a garment in a more . . . harmonious hue."

Symeon came up behind Attalietes; the Strategus colored like a maiden but his haughty eyes were unrepentant. The wrinkles at the corners of Zoe's eyes twitched slightly.

Haraldr quickly rose and stepped over his couch. One of the eunuchs handed him his single-bladed ax. Haraldr slammed the blade flat against his chest with a resonant thud.

Attalietes's jaw quivered with astonishment and anger. He rose reluctantly and Haraldr stepped closer. Attalietes turned to the urging of Symeon's withered hand on his arm. Haraldr wheeled to follow.

"No, Komes Haraldr," said the Empress. "I assure you Symeon has the strength to provide a suitable escort for our Strategus. Besides, you would leave my darlings bereft of company. Resume your place."

Haraldr returned his ax to the eunuch and settled back onto his couch. He knew he had made an enemy but he had realized an inescapable truth. He was at the Empress's beck and call, and like her husband, no matter what rumors one heard of her, she was more than capable of that command. Whoever was her enemy was his. A truth, he reflected, that brought him little comfort.

The second course was a large poached fish smothered in the oily, tart sauce called *garos* and topped with more tiny fish eggs. Haraldr was pleased with how he had handled the thin, two-pronged silver fork, particularly since he was still rattled by the incident with Attalietes.

Zoe spoke with Anna for a while; the girl seemed to have taken the outburst with aplomb. Haraldr found this attractive; she seemed so young and blushing, yet she had a woman's grace. When he had finished his fish, he kept glancing at her until he caught her eye. She looked at him and cocked her head slightly. "Komes?"

Odin. No, Homer. Gregory had set him upon the study of the famous ancient Greek skald, saying that it reflected well on one to recite his verse. Haraldr frantically reviewed some remembered passages. " 'Laodike, loveliest . . . of all . . . the daughters . . .' "

Constantine's fork clattered on his silver plate. He stared as if he had heard a dog speak. Even Zoe's jaw sagged slightly. Anna blushed furiously and fluttered her lashes. Then her eyes widened and her teeth flashed as she spoke. " 'Tall Hektor of the shining helm . . .' " Haraldr understood immediately; Hektor was the hero of Homer's seemingly endless lay called *The Iliad.* But wasn't Hektor killed at the end of this lay?

Zoe leaned forward, her eyes sweeping from Haraldr to Anna. "I have certainly heard many far more subtly . . . allusive citations of the Bard," she said, "but none quite as . . . extraordinary." Zoe looked at Maria— Haraldr would not turn to see Maria's reaction—and then back at him. "I had no notion that your . . . inclinations extended to verse."

"I hope that your Imperial Majesty and this estimable lady do not consider it an indignity. In my own tongue, which has not the grace of the Greek but is not without its own beauties, I have composed verses of my own. And I have three men in my company who record in verse the valor of the Varangians as we serve your Majesty. It is customary for a Norse king never to be far from his poets. We call them skalds."

"But you are not a king."

Haraldr concentrated on not lowering his eyes. "No," he answered firmly. "But then no Norse King has had the privilege to stand next to your throne. Perhaps I imagine myself above them, though I am just the servant at your feet."

"Anna," said Zoe, turning to the rapt girl, "I believe you have found a gallant. If he can celebrate your beauty in our tongue, think what glories he might ascribe to you in his own."

Haraldr only wished Halldor could hear this. He turned and glanced quickly past Maria, as if he were checking on the eunuch who held his ax. Hah! She was looking at him.

The second course was a whole goat stuffed with delicate miniature onions and other tiny vegetables. Haraldr was grateful for the distraction, as he realized that Halldor's first lesson had not included all he needed to know. If he lingered by Anna's booth too long, pointing and jabbering, then certainly Anna would demand a price he could not meet, or else shoo him away. It was endless.

Fortunately a dance with men and women in sheer gauzy costumes gyrating madly to wild, ringing, circular music followed the dinner. Haraldr watched the Empress for a moment; her eyes seemed to fill with the music and sinuous movements as if they gulped the pleasure of love. She devoured, with those eyes, the dancers, Kalaphates. The Strategus Meletius Attalietes, now wearing white, was readmitted to the table. Maria began to converse animatedly with him.

When the dancers were finished, Haraldr drank deeply and met Anna across the table. He desired her now; he felt she desired him, and there seemed to be no caveats against a woman of the court freely enjoying a man, even a *barbaroi*. She raised her goblet to him, he to her. They remained locked, sipping, their eyes like stroking fingers, their tongues darting over silver. Haraldr's head dizzied; they no longer mixed the wine with water. He signaled the eunuch and told him that Ulfr should assume command of the Varangians for the rest of the night.

Zoe rose and drank toasts, and the *voukaloi* chanted. First to Constantine, then to Kalaphates. Shockingly Kalaphates came beside her. He sat on the couch next to her. "Nephew," she said, and she pressed her wine-dark lips to his forehead and touched his hair. Haraldr felt the seduction around him like a great, hot, yet fragrant wind, sweeping, sucking. It was their perfumed scent, the vague outline of nipples beneath silk, perhaps the air of this place. He desired.

The *voukaloi* celebrated the pastries and fruits. Haraldr took a fig. Someone was on the rope high above again. Anna nodded, eyes heavy with desire. She bared her teeth, she . . . Kristr! Anna's head bobbed and then plunged to the table, nearly crushing a silver-wreathed pastry. She raised her head again, but the eunuchs were around her like white spume and whisked her away like a white cloud riding the wind. The Empress had not even noticed. Haraldr steadied himself. Halldor, he lamented dizzily, now there is only one booth open.

Citron was at his side like an answered prayer. Her gauzy robe hid little more than her working costume had; the nipples were dark. Citron sat, bringing a mist of rose and pine with her. Her arm was smooth and cool around his neck, her breath hot on his ear. Another white arm drew her back.

So. Haraldr turned and met Maria's eyes; it was she who had taken Citron away from him. Even with the herons fluttering in his head she was as detailed as one of the Empress's jewellike icons. The scroll of her lips, seemingly painted with blood; the slight flare of the delicate nostrils and the chiseled tip of her nose; the gull-wing brows. She did not flinch from

his rapture, nor did her blue silk irises flare with jealousy. She stared at
him for a moment and then her glistening lips descended on Citron's ear,
almost as if she, too, desired the lithe acrobat. But Maria only whispered
something, then drew away. A eunuch bent to Maria, listened for a moment, and nodded to Citron.

Citron almost imperceptibly tilted her head. Then she wrapped Haraldr like a hot breeze, like cool marble, her fevered lips on his.

† † †

John Chimachus, Turmarch of the first Brigade of the Imperial Thematic Army of Antioch, waited alone in the darkness. He watched as the
pearl-faced moon settled just above the eerily luminous crest of Mount
Silpius. He did not like it on this side of the mountain, with Antioch
hidden to the west. Silpius was the city's great natural shield, and on this
eastern slope of the peak he felt about as safe as he would were he
advancing into battle with his shield behind his back.

Something rattled, and Chimachus gripped the pommel of his sword.
He looked back at the skewing arms of the thick-trunked old tree, isolated
in a rock-strewn pasture. The peasants had tied talismans in the branches,
bits of cloth, bells, entire weather-shredded garments hanging like moss.
To appease the djinn of the place, thought Chimachus. He wished there
was some djinn he could appeal to; things had been so much easier when
he was a mere *komes* in command of a vanda. Then he simply had to worry
about fighting Saracens. Not about making deliveries to them in the
djinn-haunted night.

Chimachus looked at the leather bags at his feet. His Strategus, Constantine, ran an army in a queer sort of way, all his letters and dispatches
and sealed missives. And for the past two days, Theotokos! Four of the
dispatch unit's fastest horses were lame and a good messenger was even
now being treated with St. Gregory's salt in the Brigade hospital. Of
course, something was up; why else would a Turmarch be standing alone
in a Christ-forsaken pasture? But the Strategus who had ordered these
strange things was very close to the Imperial Dignity. What he bid was
done, and questions were a waste of time.

Good. He heard the hoofbeats. If they had wanted to come with stealth,
he would have seen them first, and by then it would have been too late
to outrun the Saracen horses. Then he saw the silhouettes as the horsemen rode over a slight ridge to east, just four of them. Four black horses.

They do not like this night, thought Chimachus, *and perhaps this errand, any more than I.*

The horses wheezed, sweat lustrous on their necks and flanks. The black robes of their riders concealed all but black faces. White teeth, lit by the moon, appeared with frightening brilliance. "Yes?" asked the black face from atop the largest horse.

"Yes." The Turmarch grunted as he handed up the first bag. The other horsemen came forward in turn. After the fourth bag had been laboriously hoisted, the horseman who had spoken nodded, spurred his horse, and led the others galloping into the night.

The Turmarch returned to his own horse and gently soothed the beast's sweat-crusted neck. A pack mule would have been better suited to this mission, he thought; fortunately the stallion hadn't been lamed by the load. The Turmarch looked over his shoulder; he could no longer hear the riders, but he again saw their silhouettes on the ridge; in an instant they were gone. As considerable as that weight had been, it did not warrant the apprehension he still felt. The Turmarch decided he would walk his horse at first. Yes, that had been a great deal of gold. But the Turmarch was certain that it had not been the final payment.

n the darkness he felt silk on one cheek; something lighter, almost as fine, on the other. "Ar-eld?" she whispered, her hair over him like a shroud. She burrowed beneath him like a silken otter, turning him on his side. It wasn't dark, he realized as the shroud fell away. His Frey-spike was tempered as hard as Hunland steel, and her hand tightened around it. "Citron," he mumbled.

Her dark tresses receded down his gold-flecked, huge torso, her course as direct as it had been all last night. Kristr! Odin! And that had been only the prelude. Citron's tongue had been insatiable, as if she were a hummingbird who could only take sustenance through that medium. Odin! Kristr! The things she had done with that tongue, he had never imagined. She was doing some of them again. Haraldr moaned and writhed, as if she were sucking the life from him. When she was done, he slept again.

He awoke. Light filtered around the brocade curtains. He vaguely recalled the room in the palace Citron had taken him to. She was standing by the window, wrapped in a green silk robe. She opened the curtains slightly and returned to him. She bent over and the dark hair fell and she brought her lips to his again. She reached within the sleeve of her robe and took out a white slip of Alexandrian paper and laid it on his chest. Then, springing as lightly as if she were once again cavorting high above the Great Hall, she danced to the door, slid it open, and vanished.

"Citron . . ." Haraldr lay back on the pillow and looked at the red wax seal. Who would be summoning him here? He decided not to prolong his anxiety and broke the seal.

The message was written in runes, in Gregory's hand:

> Sir,
> We game with one another. Such pastimes are for girls like Anna. I hope Citron has reminded you that there are other games. Today we go to Daphne. You will be with me.
>
> Maria

† † †

"Daphne?" Nicon Blymmedes could in no way believe what he was hearing. "You received none of my intelligence? Do you think I employ akrites and a kambidhouter and a mandator because they amuse me with their inventions?" Blymmedes's face was ripening rapidly. "The indications are unmistakable. We have evidence of very large movements to the west of Aleppo. And one of the brothers at St. Symeon was blessed to elude a reconnaissance party."

Constantine toyed with the large clamp used to stamp his seal in lead, absently snapping the iron jaws shut several times. Delightful, he thought, the way the birds had added their early-morning chorus to the melody of his fountains. "Domestic," he said insouciantly, "I am most impressed with the fashion in which your barbaric akrites can examine a pile of camel dung and from it deduce the size of the Caliph of Egypt's army. However"—Constantine rattled a sheaf of documents—"I have here my own intelligence, and it is considerably more eloquent than the carefully studied excrement your akrites offer us." He threw the papers down. "Assurances of safe passage from the Caliph of Egypt, as well as his vassal, the Emir of Tripoli."

"It is never safe to be careless!" thundered Blymmedes. "All I am requesting is another day or two to send two light cavalry vanda west as far as Harim."

"Our Mother does not wish to wait a day or two. She wishes to leave for Daphne immediately. She does not wish to await the winter inclemencies while your cavalry collect more droppings to display to you."

"Fine," said Blymmedes, calming and searching for compromise. "We will leave today, but we will move quickly and set a proper camp for the night. Daphne is not defensible."

"The Empress wishes to stay the night there. I am certain that with two thematic armies in her cordon she will not need the worries of the Domestic of the Imperial Excubitores to safeguard her Blessed Person."

Blymmedes saw that there was no hope; even one Strategus outranked him, and apparently the two he now had to contend with agreed on this foolish course. The only other recourse was dangerous insubordination. And these two Strategi, whatever their woeful shortcomings at military command, had the abilities to see that he would be punished promptly and mercilessly for any usurpation of their commands. Well, defending Daphne would at least be a challenging exercise in tactical deployment.

Blymmedes bowed crisply. "We will be ready to leave Antioch within the hour."

† † †

"These, Mistress." Symeon's scarcely living, parchmentlike fingers decorously placed the documents, broken seals dangling, next to Zoe. The Empress was stretched out under iridescent purple covers; her ponderous gilt and white-lacquer Imperial sleeping couch required an entire wagon for transport.

"These are the original documents?" asked Zoe as she read; her varnished fingernails picked at the dried emollient that masked her face.

"Oh, yes, Mistress. After we have opened them we always feel it is better to make an exact copy with a fresh seal and send on the duplicate. A keen eye can detect a seal that has been restored."

Zoe continued to read and pick for several minutes. She leaned back against her pillows and closed her eyes. Symeon stood patiently, a single bluish vein throbbing just beneath the membranelike skin of his ancient temple. "How interesting," said Zoe finally. "Do you really think it is Attalietes?"

"No, Mistress," said Symeon without hesitation. "These came to us too providentially for even Providence to account for reasonably."

"How interesting. Then it is someone else who wishes to make a fool of a fool. And only our Mother in Heaven knows what they plan for us. How very interesting." Zoe's eyes were still closed and she seemed to drift off for a moment.

"Mistress?" asked Symeon. "Is there something you wish done about this?"

Zoe seemed not to hear at first. "Oh, Symeon . . . No, if you please. Nothing. We will do nothing."

† † †

"Blymmedes seemed quite convinced," said Ulfr. "Of course, we have not surveyed the terrain at this Daphne, but what he told me made sense."

"I have no doubt we will find the situation as Blymmedes described it," mused Haraldr. He looked at the lifelike, almost crocus-golden statue of a woman that stood beside the broad, paved, gently rising avenue. Set well back from the road, a large villa glimmered like ivory behind a screen of cypress trees. Haraldr turned to Ulfr and Halldor. "I smell something rank and foul here. I smell a plot." He went on to describe the vitriolic exchange between Attalietes and the Empress the previous night.

"Perhaps," considered Ulfr. "But Blymmedes said the Empress herself had commanded this, and that both the Strategus of Antioch and the Strategus of Cilicia were in agreement."

Haraldr thought for a moment. He knew that Attalietes was the Empress's enemy. If Joannes was also the Empress's enemy, then Constantine could well be allied with Attalietes, despite the disdain of the Dhynatoi for the eunuch. "I think I will find out what the Empress commands with my own ears," Haraldr said, motioning to Gregory to join him. He spurred his horse and turned back toward the Imperial carriages.

The Imperial Chamberlain Symeon rode in his own carriage with his own eunuchs riding in attendance. He pulled back the crimson curtain and peered out; his slightly jaundiced, watery blue eyes looked as if they would slide off his face. Deceptive eyes, thought Haraldr; he had seen the authority in them the night before. "Chamberlain, I hope you will not think it impertinent if I discuss with you my anxiety about the safety of Our Mother." Symeon nodded. Haraldr recited Blymmedes's concerns while Symeon fixed him with a curious look; not indifferent, but perhaps regarding Haraldr as only one of an entire multitude of things he witnessed at once. Then Haraldr added, "You will see that we are dependent on the thematic armies to guarantee the security of such a diffuse perimeter. Tonight will we sleep with the assurance that these bricks have been set with the proper mortar?"

"Komes," Symeon intoned with ancient resonance, "the Empress herself is the architect of her fate. She has set these bricks you speak of in the pattern she finds most pleasing." Symeon closed the curtain and his carriage rumbled on.

† † †

"Daphne." Zoe pulled aside the curtain and inhaled deeply. "You can smell the roses." She watched as her carriage passed a long marble pergola smothered with ivy. She inhaled again. "The air is as fragrant and pure as the water. You know how they say, 'Antioch, near Daphne,' don't you, dear? You have to be here to realize how true that is." Zoe again imbibed the fresh, floral-scented air. "Cypress, pine, roses . . . paradise!

Fair Daphne, your virtue is our reward!" She turned to Maria. "You are not troubled, are you, little daughter? Symeon simply thought we should know. I can hardly see that it changes anything."

Maria's nostrils flared. "It means that this Haraldr is almost certainly a principle in this conspiracy. If it is to happen near St. Symeon, and this Haraldr says it is to happen here, is he not saying watch out for the dog at our feet when he knows that the lion approaches from behind?"

"But Komes Haraldr implies that Constantine and Attalietes are allied in this enterprise. There is no sense to that accusation, unless—"

"Yes! Yes! The best actor is both a liar and a madman! Euthymius would pay a thousand solidi for this Haraldr's talents!" Maria's cheeks glowed, stoked with outrage.

Zoe settled Maria's hands. "I believe he is innocent simply because there is no method, no plan to his contrivances. Why would he have so visibly challenged Attalietes last night if he was in league with whomever wishes Attalietes to play the ass? In doing that, he has already made Attalietes the fool, thus relieving the scene that will follow of its necessary drama. And why would he warn us of a conspiracy we have already been far more subtly, and misleadingly, alerted to?"

"So you believe it will happen here?"

"Oh, dear, I have no concern where it happens." Zoe settled back and admired the sad elegance of a crumbling arcade. "You must enjoy your day here, my darling. Simply remember that I now regard my Tauro-Scythian, Komes Haraldr, as wedded to me by a loyalty that would embrace death with greedy arms. You must only think to weld him to our cause with a yet more implacable bond."

Maria looked out on the dead splendor of Daphne and said nothing.

† † †

"Who are these men?" White wisps of hair clung to the parchment scalp behind Symeon's ears, and several errant strands floated in the breeze like gossamer. The Varangians stood at rigid attention, breast-plates gleaming.

"I have detailed these men to follow the Empress at a discreet distance wherever it is her pleasure to go." Haraldr stood with his single-bladed ax pressed against Emma's polished links.

"These men are not necessary." Symeon studied the Varangians with his watery stare. "They are relieved from their martial duties so that they may imbue themselves with the culture of the ancients. It will heighten their appreciation for the glories of the Roman Empire. Certainly that will make them better servants of Her Majesty." Symeon returned to Haraldr. "The Empress believes you alone are sufficient escort for her Sacred Person and her ladies." Symeon's bony fingers moved through the air like the passage of an apparition. "And, Komes, do not go to her in your war costume. She does not want to be reminded of military matters in any fashion."

† † †

The Empress was accompanied by the eunuchs Leo and Theodore, two serving ladies, and Maria and Anna. She waited for Haraldr and Gregory beneath a single large laurel tree; her own fragrance and that of her ladies blended with the scent of the leaves. "Komes!" she offered enthusiastically. Haraldr mastered his urge to look at Maria's face. He knelt before Zoe and she gave him her hand to kiss. When Haraldr and Gregory stood again, Zoe regally scrutinized Gregory. Then she spoke sharply to him.

"She asks if you can trust me. . . ."

"I understood, Gregory." Haraldr looked at Zoe. "With my life," he said in Greek.

Zoe nodded slowly and graciously, then lifted her crimson hem and whirled. "Daphne!" She plucked a leaf from the tree and pressed it to her cheek. "Dear little Daphne. Do you know her story, Komes Haraldr?" Haraldr shook his head. "Daphne was the fairest nymph who lived in this, the fairest place on earth. Apollo, son of Zeus, devotee of beauty, looked down upon her as he rode in the chariot of the sun. Struck by mad longing, he leapt to earth and pursued her! She fled in terror to save the lovely flower of her chastity!" The ladies seemed highly amused by this passage. "But Apollo was swift and relentless! He was upon her, his golden shaft poised to pierce her with the wound from which there is no recovery! Was there no pity among the gods! Daphne pleaded and sobbed, and good Gaea, Mother of the Earth, was stirred to mercy. 'Poof!' Gaea decreed. Even as Apollo held her in his arms, Daphne bloomed into the very tree we see here!" Zoe pressed the leaf to Haraldr's lips. "You see, she still has the freshness of a virgin." Zoe turned to her ladies. "And she will be fresh and pure forever, for that is the reward for woman who has never known man." Haraldr was startled; the Empress had been so gay a moment before. Zoe whirled again. "Ah," she said, the lust returned to her voice, "but to have loved Apollo even once, to have felt the heat of his golden arms!"

Despite the frivolity of the tone in which the Empress had told her tale, Haraldr sensed that the Romans still had a reverence for their old gods. He looked about at the wonders of Daphne. Behind the laurel tree stood a row of columns, half toppled, with fragments of architraves forming zigzag patterns; the crocus-veined marble was chipped and weathered and spotted with lichen. Beyond these ruins was a perfect grove of ancient cypresses set as formally as the row of columns, and above these cool, dark spires unfolded a tumbled-down city of enormous crumbled columns and jagged walls and ruptured towers and curious rows of small stone terraces, all of it set as if by giant hands into the garland-scattered limestone cliffs. The old gods, the gods of the ancient Greeks and Romans, had lived here once.

"Nephew!"

Michael Kalaphates strode among the Imperial party, his sparkling robe of white Hellas silk far superior to the tunic of Syrian silk he had worn the previous night. Kalaphates knelt and kissed the Empress's hand. She clasped his shoulders and raised him up, then turned and whispered to the youthful, full-jowled eunuch, Leo. Although the Empress gave no signal that Haraldr could discern, the ladies stepped away from her. Haraldr was confused; he wondered if he should stay and guard his mother, or offer her his own discretion.

The hand on his arm was as light as if a butterfly had settled there. Maria smiled up at him without guile, her coiled hair almost touching his upper arm. The crimson lips, the pearl teeth; he shuddered perceptibly at the thrill of her presence. *You will be with me.*

"May I use your name?" she asked. Did the multihued, ethereal lights of Halogoland have a sound? If so, her voice was it.

Haraldr nodded. "May I call you by your name?"

"Certainly, Har-aldr." The weight of her hand increased minutely. "And perhaps you will think of another name for me before we leave Daphne." Her tone was an invitation.

Yes, thought Haraldr, your name is already snow-breasted goddess.

"May I show you Daphne?" White silk dazzled as she waved her ivory fingers toward the ruins on the heights. With Gregory, the unseen voice, following behind them, they crossed to a paved path that rose in a series of worn stone stairs flanked by small, disarrayed columns. Birds sang and a green lizard scampered from atop a chunk of white stone carved with a floral pattern. Soon the rows of cypresses draped them in cool misting shadows.

"Did you enjoy our mother's tale of how Daphne gave her name to this place?"

"I found it quite beautiful. A skald will often use a tree kenning to describe a lovely woman."

"Ken-ning. I'm afraid that word does not translate into the language of Homer." Gregory elaborated in Greek. "Oh, yes, when a poet likens one thing to another. 'He went on his way like a snowy mountain.' So the Bard spoke of fair-helmed Hektor, because his size and ferocity and, some would say, his arrogance put him above other men."

There was no dominant tone here that could guide Haraldr. Was she teasing him, or was there a threat in her bewitching melody? Had Hektor been too arrogant, too bold, and if so, was Hektor/Haraldr considered to share the same faults? "Yes, a kenning is much like that, though not entirely so. Take this example: Raven-flocked laurel tree of the golden sea cliffs."

Maria stopped for a moment and looked up at him. Her silk-sheathed breast brushed momentarily against his sleeve. "Whatever might that be?"

"You. The lovely laurel tree, with hair as dark as the raven's breast, who comes from the Great City where the mountainous walls that face the sea are golden in the sun."

Maria simply looked at him for a very long moment. It was as if her eyes were mysterious chasms with blue lights in their depths. She turned and guided him up the steps and out of the cypress grove.

Incredible, thought Haraldr. How could such things be built and then discarded? Men would not abandon such a place, only gods. The huge marble structures clung to the cliffs, dappled all over with flowering vines and lacy ivy. Haraldr and Maria and Gregory walked toward two broken towers surrounded by the glacierlike rubble of their former magnificence.

"Rome built this," said Maria. "The old Rome that rose by the river Tiber in Italia."

"But you are the Romans."

"We are the new Romans."

The ruins of the towers lay in huge ashlar blocks among which berries and flowers had begun to grow. Here and there were fragments of carved human forms, a muscular leg, an arm and shoulder, a partial head covered with short curly hair; it was as if here the old gods had waged their last battle, their bodies now frozen amid the titanic wreckage of that ultimate struggle. "The old Romans," asked Haraldr, "what happened to them?"

Maria stooped to caress the ancient stone face of a beautiful young man, a fragment so curiously lifelike that it seemed as if the delicately parted marble lips might take in air and restore a blush to the weathered cheeks. "Travelers who have visited the old Rome make the cross of Christ the King when they talk of it, so vast is that tomb, as vast as the Queen of Cities, yet peopled only by spirits and demons and slinking dogs. All like this. Stade after endless stade, all like this. A vast sepulcher. So sad. To think of them . . ." Maria touched the stone youth's lips. "They were flesh as we are, soft lips . . . dust. All to dust." She drew back as if the lips had burned her fingers, or, perhaps, as if they had stirred to life.

She took his arm now, curling her elegant, statue-smooth fingers just above his elbow and pulling him next to her so that her silk flank swished against his. Haraldr was stirred and yet the awe, the holiness of the place, overwhelmed him. He looked up at a wall covered with carvings of young men; naked athletes, not armored warriors. Maria led him beneath an arch that pierced the wall and descended a dozen steps into a brilliant field of light. Haraldr gasped; what was this place? It was a vast, long field of unkempt grass and shrubs surrounded by row upon row of steps. No, seats, as if for a thing-meeting. But there was room enough here for every man in Norway, it seemed.

"The stadium," said Maria. "For the games."

Haraldr shielded his eyes from the glare off the bleached stone seats. "What sort of contests?"

"The ancients called them Olympics, for the mountain on which Zeus dwelt. The man who won here became a god. As one, every citizen of Antioch stood to sing the victor's name." Maria paused. A flight of small black birds descended on a shrub at the end of the field nearest them and chorused noisily. "Can you hear the name they are singing?" she asked wryly, though her scrolled lips had a bitter set.

Maria guided Haraldr around the pathway at the top of the stadium to a row of almost intact, neatly fluted columns. The columns were the entrance to a large, cottage-sized niche carved into the very rock that seemed to embrace the long southern flank of the stadium. Haraldr peered into the gloom behind the sun-warmed columns. In the shadows a huge figure loomed. Haraldr bent for the dagger he had hidden in his boot.

"You think he lives." Maria laughed. Haraldr's eyes adjusted to the light. He saw a stone man taller than himself, even if the statue were to be taken off the stone pedestal upon which it stood. The figure's marble arms were coursed with living veins, and every other detail was equally lifelike, even the curl of hair that crowned his manhood. Haraldr was embarrassed.

"Heracles." Maria sighed, as if she were a rapt maiden. "He was half man, half god. They say that Apollo and Hermes were fairer. Perhaps. Yet one does not reflect on their beauty in his presence." She stepped around an empty basin that stood before the statue and wrapped her fingers about Heracles's veined marble ankle and softly ran her fingers up to his bulging stone calf. She pressed her cheek to the leg and nuzzled it for a moment, then leaned her head back and looked directly at the demigod's flaccid, strikingly human organs. Haraldr could not believe her immodesty, but her boldness stirred him far more than downcast eyes and fluttering lashes.

Maria slowly released the demigod and stepped toward Haraldr. Her hips inclined slightly forward, only a thumb's width from his thighs. She held her hands just above his chest and spread her fingers. For a moment she looked directly at him, her eyes reflections of the brilliant azure sky outside, her lips slightly parted. Her fingers touched his chest like the barest breeze. That was all. She closed her eyes for a moment and stepped away. She looked once again at the towering Heracles and then went into the sun by herself.

"It is so dark in there," she said, taking Haraldr's arm again. "Sometimes in the dark I feel I cannot breathe." They entered a shaded arcade roofed with thick ivy. She was quiet for a while. They left the stadium and wandered in a small poplar grove, poking at statuary fragments with their feet. Between the rows of trees, the limestone cliffs fell away to the green-and-gold plain below. The trees that ringed Daphne shimmered in the late-afternoon breeze. Maria's fingers moved softly against Haraldr's sleeve. She spoke as if mesmerized. "Do you fair-hairs believe in the Apocalypse?"

Haraldr asked Gregory to clarify, but Maria interrupted. "The End of Creation." She looked out over Daphne, now a mosaic of golden spires and long, misty, smoke-purple shadows. "We shall subdue the sons of Hagar, the Emperor shall regain Illyricum, and Egypt shall bring her tribute once more. And he shall set his hand upon the sea and subdue the fair-hair nations." Her recitation was dreamlike. "Then a base woman will rise up and rule the Romans and there will be conspiracies and slaughter in every house and this impure queen will anger God and He will stretch out His hand and seize His strong scythe and cut the earth from under the city and order the waters to swallow it up. And the waters will crash forth and raise the city spinning to great height, and then cast it down into the abyss."

Haraldr knew that Maria had sensed his tremor of anxiety. Was she testing him with this reference to an "impure queen"?

"I see I have frightened you," Maria said, her voice light. "It is such a wicked tale. Do you have one like it?"

Haraldr assumed she had only been playing "Yes. Ragnarok. The Doom of the Gods." Haraldr watched Daphne glitter in the lowering sun and felt Odin stir to life. "The sun turns black, earth sinks in the waves, the blazing stars are quenched from the sky. Flames leap fierce to scorch the clouds, until Heaven itself is seared to ashes." Haraldr lost the skaldic rhythm with the words that followed. "And then the wolf, Fenrir, will devour all, even one-eyed Odin the All-Father."

"Odin? Is he your fair-hair demon?"

"He is the god of war, verse, and vision. He hung from the tree of infinite roots to seize the mead of verse from the Underworld, and in his palace, called the Valhol, slain warriors raise their swords again, to wait for Ragnorak."

"So you do not believe in Christ the King."

"I was baptized with the water of all-conquering Christ."

Now Maria seemed perplexed. "So you believe that Christ will rule in the end, after Odin perishes?"

"Yes."

"Do you believe you will be spared to enter the New Jerusalem?" She gathered that he did not understand. "You see, when the Empress City has been cast into the abyss, God will allow the fair-hairs to rage forth upon the earth and they will consume blood and flesh and the sun will turn to blood and the moon darken. And then the Antichrist, a serpent in the guise of a man, will arise to battle Christ. After terrible tribulations Christ will cast the Devil and all of the unjust into a lake of fire. And the just shall be brought into a great city of crystal and gold, the new Jerusalem that will descend from heaven." Maria seemed to recite from some text. "And there shall they dwell in the sight of God, and there shall no longer be night, nor need of lamp or sun, for the Lord God will give them light, and the just shall reign for eternity."

Haraldr pondered this tale in which the Norsemen played such a menacing role. Was this why the Romans feared the northern nations, even with their God-granted gift of liquid fire? He looked down and saw Maria's flickering blue challenge. "So you believe that we fair-hairs will hasten the rise of Christ's great foe the Devil Antichrist?"

"Those are the visions of the prophets." Maria paused and reflected, as if she gave partial credence to these visions. "What do you think?"

Haraldr remembered the words of the Christian skalds at Olaf's court. "We believe that . . . that after Ragnarok, Christ will raise up a hall more fair than the sun, thatched with gold, at a place called Gimle. Perhaps that is this New Jerusalem you speak of. It is said that the gods shall dwell there in innocence and bliss."

"How extraordinary! That you fair-hairs would also know of the Holy City of God."

"That is not the end of the tale." Haraldr felt as if he could see beyond sun-flecked Daphne to the dark border of creation. Maria clutched his arm tightly. Odin spoke, death dark on his own tongue. "Now comes the last black dragon flying, the glittering serpent from Nidafell. He is a blackness that will consume all flesh, all life, all light, even his own being. When he soars in the darkness, all creation will cease to be."

"Then no one will judge you in the end, and bring the just to everlasting life?"

"No one, man or god, will be left to judge. A man will judge himself, by the courage with which he stands before the last dragon."

Maria looked down for a long while. Finally she blinked, and a tiny tear hung on a painted lash. "Your tale is better than mine," she whispered. "It is so brave, and so sad."

The wind fluttered the leaves in the grove behind. Gregory spoke in Greek; someone was approaching. Maria turned and waved. She let go of Haraldr's arm and advanced a few paces to wait for Leo, who attacked a flight of stone steps with red-faced vigor. Leo whispered breathlessly into Maria's ear, then held out his arm to her. She placed her white fingers on Leo's silk sleeeve and turned to Haraldr. "Thank you for your lovely tale. Anna is coming for you." Then, with dancing white slippers, Maria descended the golden steps of Daphne.

hat ass has more sense than the man who beats him," muttered the Keeper of the Imperial Beacon at Toulon; he plucked at his short black beard with consternation. "You be careful with those!" The Keeper quickly steadied the stumbling pack mule and made certain that the load—two large terra-cotta canisters—was secure. "Fool!" he shouted to the batman, a small Cilician whose weathered dark skin was the same color as his sweat-stained brown burlap tunic. "You break one of these and your own piss could set it off so quickly that you would wish for Hell-fires to save you from the flames."

The batman grabbed the mule's harness to steady himself and looked back at the narrow, rocky path he had just ascended; it led from the main road which threaded through the Cilician gates. "Well, your Sirship, accustomed I am to the loads of faggots we bring up here, and that is no worry to me, for my children would not go fatherless. But you want the Devil's spittle, and for good reason I do not know, and you pay only what the load of faggots is, to boot." The batman pulled the long-suffering mule over the last steep step-up. A small stone-walled fort stood at the flat top of the crest. The batman slapped the mule's rump; the beast trudged toward the fort's heavy wooden gate. "It's me that should be protest, Sirship."

"It's you that should protest," mumbled the exasperated Keeper as he followed the delivery through the gate. They stepped into a deserted court; a rectangular, three-story stone tower rose at the northwest corner of the walls. Atop the tower was a flat bronze ellipse twice as tall as a man, surrounded by four workers who busily polished the shimmering surface. *I should protest,* thought the Keeper; *I am asked to maintain Toulon with one assistant and five lice-eaten guards. When the sainted Bulgar-Slayer was alive, the frontiers were important and we would sometimes have an entire vanda posted up here. Now the corvée that would provide us with even temporary reserves from the thematic army has been eliminated by the offices of the Strategus Attalietes. Fine, he will one day learn his lesson when the sons of Hagar pour through the Cilician gates and darken his own fields and there is no thematic army to resist them, and the*

Imperial Taghmata cannot be summoned because the Imperial Beacon at Toulon has been destroyed by the heretics! The Keeper hitched up his belt and strode to the tower.

He ascended the gray stone steps and stopped in the clock room. His young assistant, the Superintendent of the Imperial Dial, maintained the room spotlessly; the afternoon sun through the grilled glass windows lit scoured stone. The brass tank of the water clock gleamed, the gears and pulleys beneath it clicked like busy beetles. With a habitual reflex the Keeper checked the time on the large engraved bronze disc. He looked for the coin-size gold pin that signified the sun and then plotted it against the overlying grid of arcing wires that indicated the hours. Tenth hour of the day; four hours past the red-enameled vertical wire that marked the meridian, two hours above the red arc that indicated sunset. It was the hours after sunset that mattered to the Keeper. "Let's check the beacon," he said to the Superintendent, a studious young graduate of the Quadrivium in Dorylaeum, whose once-sallow cheeks had taken on a healthier brightness from his mountain posting.

The pair climbed through the small circular stone stairwell to the roof of the tower. A charred stone tub three arm spans wide took up most of the roof space. Towering above the tub was the elliptical copper mirror; the guards had just finished their meticulous polishing and the slight concavity captured a compressed, distorted image of the mountain landscape. The Keeper looked north, imagining that he could see the summit of Mount Arghaios a dozen leagues across the dull, olive-gray expanse of the Taurus plateau. May the clouds stay away and your watchmen stay awake, he thought, silently invoking the beacon keepers' prayer for his counterpart atop the distant mountain. And for you also at Mount Samos and Kastron Aiylon and Mount Mamas and Kyrizos and Mokilos and St. Afxendios and of course the Grand Superintendent of the Imperial Dial in the great Magnara in the Empress City. The Keeper sighed, thinking of the distance that separated him and his ambitions from the Queen of Cities; he attempted to assuage his melancholy with the thought that he was the most important of the Keepers, for he started it all. And he would at least not have to worry about his watchmen sneaking wine to their posts and drifting off; his message would come by swift courier from Antioch by way of Adana.

The Keeper inspected the improvised crane that would lift the terra-cotta canisters to the roof of the tower. "Yes!" he shouted down, signaling the guard to attach the clay jars to the hoist.

"I'm not comfortable with the idea of using liquid fire," said the Super-intendent. "I really think it might melt the mirror and burn through the roof."

"I guess when you studied the Quadrivium they didn't teach you that a wood fire can actually burn hotter than that stuff," said the Keeper good-naturedly. "The advantage to liquid fire is that it ignites instantly and the flames leap more vigorously. When Basil the Bulgar-Slayer—may Christ the King preserve and keep his immortal soul—was alive, we used it all the time. Look, you can figure it before I can say it. Even when the flame is up to maximum visibility in four minutes . . ."

"True. Four minutes for each beacon, times eight beacons in all, totals more than half an hour. And given the usual delays, it is quite possible that a message sent from here in one hour could be received at the Imperial Palace in the next. Hasn't it happened before?"

"Indeed it did, the year before you came here. We were told of the capture of Edessa by the Saracens. At that time the schedule called for the beacon to be lit at the fifth hour of the night to signal that particular event. But the light finally arrived at the Magnara in the sixth hour of the night, signaling that Edessa had resisted the siege. By the time it was all straightened out, the relief force was two weeks late. The problem was traced to Mokilos, where the Keeper had allowed two women of a nearby village to inspect his 'facilities' that night. Needless to say, that particular Keeper no longer has that particular equipment to display. Nor does he have eyes with which to miss beacons shining brightly in the night."

"So why do they give us liquid fire but cut a watchman from our roster every month, it seems?"

"Well, something big is afoot down there in Antioch." He pointed south. "They want to make sure this message is not delayed. And you and I are going to have to share in the watch duty." The Superintendent groaned. "Let's look at the new schedule," said the Keeper; he genially slapped the bony shoulders of his assistant.

They descended to the clock room and the Keeper went to the polished wood cabinet in the corner opposite the water tank. He unlocked a shiny brass padlock, removed the sealed document, and displayed it to the Superintendent. The Superintendent examined the seal. "The Orphano-trophus Joannes," he said with youthful awe. "Usually it is the Grand Domestic who sends us the schedule."

"Yes," said the Keeper, "I wouldn't be entirely surprised if someday the Orphanotrophus Joannes appeared at our gate to set your clock. They say his seal is on everything these days. Perhaps I should petition *him* to find me a posting in the Empress City. Well, let us see what the new schedule is." The Keeper peeled apart the seal; the Superintendent crowded in so that he could read the paper as soon as it had been unfolded.

After a moment the Keeper and the Superintendent looked at each other in shock. The most important messages were always scheduled for the second and third hours of the night, while the evening winds still whipped clouds and fogs from the peaks. For years now the message reserved for the second hour had been "Antioch besieged," and for the third hour it had been "Antioch has fallen." Now there was a change. The message for the second hour was "The Empress has been attacked." And for the third hour, "The Empress is dead."

† † †

"So this Plutarch was a Greek ruled by the old Romans and he wrote of both the Greeks and the Romans. But before Plutarch, in the time of Alexander, the Greeks ruled the world."

"Yes, Har-aldr," said Anna happily.

Haraldr leaned against the stone seat and watched a shaft of sun project a vivid aquamarine stripe over the darkening waters of the semicircular, stone-lined pool. A column, toppled from the row behind him, lay across the seats nearby like a huge recumbent figure. The temple to Jupiter, the old god the Greeks called Zeus, stood ravaged at the far end of the pool; only four delicately fluted columns remained to glow in the dying day. Behind the temple a much larger reservoir sat deep and still; water from the limestone springs beneath Daphne was collected here and sent to Antioch via the soaring-arched aqueducts that sloped away from the far end of the reservoir and disappeared into the distance. All this had been built by the old Romans, yet much of it, according to Anna, in imitation of the style of the ancient Greeks. Haraldr marveled at these dense, intricate layers of time. The world he had grown up in was so new; in Norway wooden shrines to Thor that could not have been more than two hundred years old were all that could inspire memories of the ancients. Here, amid these giant stone relics, he could reach across time and touch the world of the old gods.

"It is said that Hadrian, the Emperor of Rome who built this place, also built a wall somewhere near your home in Thule. Is that possible?"

"Perhaps so. I remember once when my brother returned from Angle-Land, someone talked of a wall." Haraldr shook is head in wonder. In

Norse the terms for *fool* and *stay-at-home* were the same. Yet as far as he had now come from home, he felt like the fool next to this bright, beautiful girl. He studied Anna's vivid, almost unreal color; her face was like a painted statue, her skin so white and her lips so intensely red. And yet, Haraldr reflected, her enchantment was not simply beauty. If the Empress was beauty enhanced by power, and Maria was beauty enhanced by carnal invitation, then Anna was beauty enhanced by knowledge. She had said it was her mother who had insisted she learn of ancient texts that revealed the thoughts and breasts of men who had lived long ago, when the old gods walked the earth and Daphne was new. Incredible. The more he observed them, the more bewildering and beguiling these Roman women became.

"We must go." Anna sighed. The shadows had dissolved into a lustrous twilight and the pillars of Daphne were transforming into towering ghosts. "Maria says that every sunset is a tragedy. She does not like the night. And yet . . ." Anna trailed off with an enigmatic smile.

Maria. A witch who shunned the darkness that Haraldr had seen deep in her own eyes. In spite of Anna, he could not rid her from his mind. He would have to talk to Halldor; what did the wise trader do when the merchant gave him gifts from his competitor's booths? If he and Maria no longer gamed, what was this?

"There is one thing I must show you," said Anna as they descended from the reservoir. A moment later she turned off the path and entered a small grove thick with vines; here night had already settled. She took his hand and he marveled at the impossible smoothness and delicacy of her flesh. The vines arched over them. Haraldr peered into the miasma ahead. "Wait for your eyes to become more adept," said Anna confidently. "There."

The stone architrave, supported by two columns, materialized from deep shadow. Soon Haraldr could even distinguish the Greek letters chiseled onto the crumbling architrave. H-E-C-A-T-E.

"The Temple of Hecate," whispered Anna. "The Greeks worshiped her as the goddess of diabolic magic. She could raise the dead and make them appear to the living."

"*Fylgya,*" said Haraldr with genuine respect. "Spirits that wander among men."

"You know them," whispered Anna. "Come. I want to tell Maria we went down there. She will be terrified that we even speak of it."

"Down?" Haraldr's neck and shoulders tingled.

"Yes." Anna's whisper had become a mysteriously urgent hiss. "Hecate lives in the Underworld. Look. You can see the steps."

Barely. The narrow stone steps faded into the murk after a few ells.

Gregory crossed himself. "Haraldr Nordbrikt, I do not see well in the dark."

"Stay here," said Haraldr mercifully, "in case we become lost." Anna clutched Haraldr's hand tightly and led him down step by step. Behind him, Haraldr could hear Gregory reciting one of the poems, called psalms, that the warrior David had long ago composed for Christ's Father.

Soon there was an utter stillness, broken only in the instants that foot touched stone. The dampness made Haraldr think of Neorion, the Hell that rose in the sky. Ever down, the smell of ancient stone more and more suffocating. Haraldr counted over a hundred steps, and still they descended. Anna bumped against him and gave a little cry. Haraldr fought the reflex to grip his dagger; he had been the fool once already today. "O sky!" whined Anna. Haraldr heard her hand slap stone. She said something to the effect that they could go no farther.

Haraldr reached out and felt the cold, grainy stone. "No farther," he said hopefully, in Greek.

"No farther," whispered Anna. "Can you see me?"

"Not well. No."

Anna lifted Haraldr's hand and slowly took it to her warm, marble-smooth face. Then she took his fingers away from her cheek and brought them down until he felt the lightest touch of silk. She pressed his hand toward her, and he could feel her hard nipple and small soft breast. She exhaled once, took his hand away, and pulled him behind her as she scampered back up the steps.

Anna smiled impishly in the relative light at the surface and said to Gregory with a sigh, "We did not get to see the shrine."

"We did not go all the way?" asked Haraldr in Greek.

Anna smirked. "No. The shrine has a step for every day of the year. We only took one hundred and seventy-two steps. The stairs have been blocked. But we will still tell Maria we saw the shrine." Anna wrapped both hands around Haraldr's arm and led him away from the Temple of Hecate.

† † †

"Certainly you may have your leave, Brother." Zoe sat in her gilded, portable throne, the rounded back piled high with cushions of scarlet and sky-blue silk. She curled her gold-flecked slippers beneath her. "You have provided us with all splendid Daphne has to offer." Zoe raised her hand to indicate the marble-reveted hall her throne had been set in; beyond the melon-colored columns that ringed the courtyard, lanterns played off the waters of a chiming fountain. "And our nephew has graciously consented to . . . attend to myself and my ladies until we are safe in Tripoli. So go, Brother, defend the trust my husband and your brother has given you. And be assured that the convivial and benign reception accorded by your Antioch will remain a cherished memento in my grateful heart."

"Your words are my solace," answered Constantine, his brow gushing. "For tomorrow I will awake in a city that has lost its sun. Farewell, sister, Mother, Light of the Roman world, chosen of God." Constantine crossed his arms over his chest and backed out of the room like a dog sneaking a stolen morsel.

Haraldr stood rigid beside his Mother, wondering if he was able to conceal his shock and dismay. Now it was as plain as the nose on a face. Joannes, through his surrogate, Constantine, was behind a plot against the Empress, one that would surely take place before sun dappled Daphne again, and one that played Haraldr as a dull-witted accomplice in the usurpation of his Empress. But why did his Mother do nothing? She had just permitted Constantine to withdraw his thematic army to Antioch, citing some clearly contrived Saracen threat to the city. And Blymmedes's Taghmatic forces and Haraldr's Varangians could not, as the Domestic had warned, defend the entire perimeter of Daphne. They had had to rely on Attalietes's utterly incompetent, and most likely disloyal, thematic army to complete the cordon. On the road from Antioch that morning Haraldr had had the opportunity to inspect Attalietes's troops, and he had been astonished to find that most of them were baggage handlers and batmen for the pack mules, and that many of those who were armed did not have proper weapons or healthy mounts. It was a disgrace. How could they all be so blind?

Haraldr looked at Maria and Anna, rolling dice at a table in the corner of the room opposite their mother's throne. Their laughter fused with the music of the fountains. He was suddenly in the cold embrace of a theory he had never considered. This was all a ruse. There was a plot indeed, but one of Romans devilishly conspiring to rid their Empire of the fair-hair menace. But then why had all these Romans constructed such an elaborate ruse simply to eliminate him? They had already had him in Neorion. Had they since then discovered his identity—there had been so many cryptic allusions—and considered such extravagant measures justified by their morbid prophecies of a fair-hair apocalypse? Did they intend to slaughter his pledge-men as well, once they had eliminated him? Such reasoning was self-inflicted torture. Only one thing was certain: He would not sleep tonight.

† † †

A dog barked in the ruins and a cock crowed prematurely. It was still four hours until dawn. The fountain in the courtyard of the Empress's villa masked the Norsemen's words.

"We wager on both stallions," said Ulfr. "If it is the Empress who is to be a victim of this plot, I will embrace the Valkyrja at her side."

"And if it is you, Haraldr," said Halldor, "together we will summon every carrion bird in Serkland."

"No," said Haraldr. "That honor is too great for me if I have led you into this. If it is me who is to be attacked, you must live to lead my pledge-men to safety. I know that the Romans have enemies nearby. If you can fight your way out of here, you could parlay with them. My pledge-men may yet see their homes again, with little thanks to their foolish leader. Besides, I have learned an interesting tactic from the Romans: how to bait a snare. And perhaps tonight by offering myself as the bait I may win something more valuable than all the Roman gold we have acquired." He paused and looked at his two stern-faced comrades. "I may win some answers."

The white-robed figure emerged like a ghost from the dark hall. Symeon was indeed as indefatigable as a spirit. It seemed as if he could not take the next step, and yet day and night he was there, attending to the smallest detail. The wraithlike eunuch swished to Haraldr's side. "Mother wish to know guard relieved," he croaked in a condescending bastardization of good Greek.

"You may tell my mother yes," replied Haraldr as fluently as he could. He nodded to Ulfr, and the grim-faced Norseman followed Symeon into the Hall.

Halldor fixed Haraldr with his implacable stare. "Well," he said with a faint smile, "I have no lady. I guess I will have to spend this night with my sword in my arms." He turned to walk away. "Oh. In the morning I think I need to tell you some more things the wise trader must know." As casually as ever, Halldor vanished through the gate.

Haraldr shook his head in amazement. When the Valkyrja came for him, Halldor would ask them to spread their legs. His bravado bolstered by his friend's insouciance, Haraldr began to reason where he could best place his snare. His listened to the gurgling fountains. A two-week-old moon silvered the dancing droplets. Here. Of course. Symeon already knew where he was; no doubt others did as well. Wait here and they would come to him. He sat on the damp tile enclosure of the fount. To come behind him, they would have to splash through the water, a variation in the night's music that he could easily detect.

The dog barked again, more distantly. Lost in this ancient world, Haraldr wondered if the gods had a purpose. Had they spared him at Stiklestad, along the Dnieper, among the Saracen corpses, only that he should die here tonight? That could not be. He was part of their plan. Haraldr felt a strange power surround him in the night, wrapping him like the layers of fur that had armored the terrible Hound. He was destiny's instrument. And when fate called him to the last battle, he would come with his sword in hand.

He did not wait for long. Heels clicked on marble and the white robe came into the light. Leo. He reached down and handed Haraldr a tiny slip of paper. The eunuch turned quickly and vanished with his bounding step, heedless to Haraldr's plaintive "Leo!"

The message was in Greek. Apparently the conspirators could not risk asking Gregory to write the runes; he might have warned Haraldr. That was obviously why the Empress had wished to know of the bond between the interpreter and Haraldr. Haraldr studied the brief message. The translation was quite simple, especially since he had seen the name written before. "Come to Hecate. Now."

Haraldr had to compliment the Romans on the elaborate construction of their trap. The girl as the lure, the perfect place for an assassination. He removed his sword and set it by the fountain, then raised his robe and snugged his dagger into his boot. What could be more disarming than a man walking unarmed to his own execution?

Daphne's shattered face was pearllike in the moonlight. It was bright enough for Haraldr to find the path that turned into the grove easily. Then the ivy bowers closed overhead and the light faded. He walked slowly ahead and almost collided with one of the columns. The inscription was unreadable now, but the impenetrable void just beneath Haraldr's feet was proof that this was Hecate.

Haraldr descended into the earth, carefully counting each step, his fingers darting against the damp, increasingly slimy wall to maintain his orientation; it seemed to him that if he lost contact with the wall, he would not know up from down—much less right from left—in this inky oblivion. After an eternity he reached the hundredth step. At one hundred and sixty, he would pause and listen for his murderer.

One hundred and forty-eight. A noise! Something brushed past his leg and scurried up. It was not relief that caused Haraldr to shudder. The *fylgya* would often take the form of small beasts.

One hundred and fifty-eight, fifty-nine, sixty. Haraldr waited for his heart to cease echoing off the coffinlike walls. He listened. Nothing, even to ears strengthened by blindness. Nothing. Hecate was as still as death.

Another five steps and Haraldr listened again. Four more. Haraldr's skin crawled and yet he could sense nothing, even this close to fate's answer. Then the light of realization dawned. *The Empress! It is her they have plotted against, after all! As I voluntarily bury myself in this dungeon, my mother and my pledge-men are probably struggling for their lives!* Haraldr pivoted frantically, lost his balance, and stumbled.

Haraldr pulled himself up, his veins ice. He had fallen three, four steps. He reached ahead. Nothing. No stone. The barrier he had felt that very afternoon was gone. Very slowly he descended another step. Gone. Haraldr paused on a threshold of fate. Up or down? Then something told him that the beast he could not run from waited below.

At two hundred and fifty steps the walls closed in. Haraldr had to turn sideways to squeeze through. Then there were no walls, no steps. He walked forward and smacked into a wall. He ran his hand over the slimy surface. He looked down at his feet, and he could see them, vague shadows against other shadows. And the stairs were to his right. Down he went, the light coming up to meet him like a winter dawn; he was almost able to see each step before he set his foot on it. At three hundred and twenty-five steps he squeezed through an even narrower passage than the one before and turned again in a grim vestibule lit by a flickering from below.

The last forty steps were straight down. Carved pilasters marked the entrance to the shrine. The single lamp within the dark-walled chamber was set just above the doorway. The sputtering flame flicked light over a tile basin filled with water. The water was covered with a pale mist. No, steam; the air was warm, almost as sultry as a sauna.

The statue of Hecate stood on a low platform behind the basin. It seemed as if she had been draped with a real robe of fine black fabric, for only her delicate alabaster ankles and feet showed. Her head was bowed, her hair painted so lifelike that it might have been as real as her cloak.

The statue moved. Haraldr stooped to pull his dagger from his boot, never taking his eyes from the startling motion. He backed away, seeking the corner to protect his back and flanks, if there were others.

The robe slid from the shoulders and the statue stood revealed in flawless alabaster, except for the dark nipples and sable pelt between the legs. The face turned up. The lips were red and the eyes blue, even in this light. Haraldr reeled from the blow he had never expected. Maria was his Valkyrja, her white skin drawing him on into the last black night of his mortality.

She stood still, hair shimmering, piercing azure eyes unblinking, almost armored in her nakedness. Haraldr took a tentative step forward, and then his boots were wet, and he was stumbling through the warm water. She still beckoned, her blood-red lips faintly parted. He stood, dumb, disbelieving the perfection of her body. The full woman's breasts, the erect areolae, the unflawed curve of her hip, the glistening pelt. He stepped closer, rapt at the flaring of her chiseled nose. He did not see the knife until she had already raised it from her thigh.

He was powerless, now refusing to believe that such beauty could be wedded to death. He watched the heaving of her breast as her arm shot out; there was a faint blue vein beneath the mercurous ivory surface of her skin. The blade flickered against his throat. She held him with her eyes. He remembered the last time he had seen Olaf's eyes, the sense that all time had fallen into that void. It was as if his fate were within that abyss, waiting for him to find it.

The knife moved swiftly. When she cut his collar open, she nicked his neck and the warm blood trickled. Never blinking, she ripped downward, slicing the front of his robe open. Her arm fell wearily, as if she had freed herself of a great burden, and the knife clattered on stone. Her breasts rose with a violent inhalation and she attacked the incisions in his garments, ripping at silk and linen. When she had exposed his almost immediate erection, she knelt and pulled off his boots. Then her face was above his, her hands searing velvet claws on his shoulders as she lifted herself. Like an adder, she brought the point of her nose toward his. He could no longer look at the blue fire in her eyes. Her smell seemed to drown him and his steel member reached for her. She settled, and he felt the fiery point of wetness. She held there, tantalizing, pulling his hair hard, pulling his head forward.

She came down slowly, a consummate torturer. If he arched upward, she drew back, now raking his neck with her nails. He placed his hands beneath her tensing thighs and could feel her wetness spilling onto the soft down beneath the sable patch. She let her body slump against his and they both convulsed.

Haraldr knew that the stars in the heavens reeled and pitched from their orbits. There had never been a Rage like the fury of this pleasure. Her spine was willow-supple and he pressed her to him, her breasts kneading his chest. Then she would stiffen and tease him with the merest touch of her hard nipples. She would writhe until he thought his brittle member would snap, and then rise, tightening, rippling, soothing him with her lips, those delicate crimson lips, gentle on his forehead. And then she was mad, sucking at his eyes, his nose, his lips, sucking the blood at his neck, biting and ripping until he felt fresh blood flow. And in all this there was pleasure, rising like the molten spume of a huge burning mountain.

Maria rocked, wrapped in coruscating clouds of sensation. The scent of his blood, the giant arms pressing her breathless, the power that she could so willfully control. He was like the sun inside her, his golden hair glowing with that sun, the hardness of him, all over, yet the softness of his brilliant skin, like gold leaf hammered to the suppleness of velvet. And the death in his eyes. What gods does he dance with now? she wondered, swaying and pumping, listening for the music she knew he heard. She pressed his chest, clawing the curling gold threads, her wide eyes reaching his and forcing him down to the cool marble slab. She was close now. Close to the knife.

She felt the sun exploding inside her and knew she would be gone, and it was now! She strained for the knife and felt its silver handle hard and, in an insane instant, wondered if he would stay hard afterward, and could she keep him in until he cooled, letting the night enter her again? She had the knife now, but she did not have his eyes. There.

And then she went beyond. The eyes before her floated with their white-ice blueness and she was beyond. Beyond him, his one death, to the thousand thousand souls he held in his eyes, and she knew it would not end here. There was more. She dropped her knife, the sun in her novaed, and she fell away from her body, her soul drifting with the glassy stars.

Haraldr strained with every fiber to contain her violent spasms, and then he burst inside her, his whole being drained in an instant. For a moment it was black before him and he wondered if he had been taken into her eyes, into the whirling black vortex of fate.

Haraldr saw the dagger before he saw his attacker's huge shadowed form looming above him. The knife fell like a comet toward Maria's still spasming back, and he rolled, flinging Maria away like a doll. He was on his feet before he could think.

The Hound! his mind screamed for a moment. But the metal-swathed giant in front of him was not the same; the Hound still had a piece of his nose, but this man had only two inhuman gills. The giant's dagger swayed in front of him, its movement hypnotic. Haraldr looked at the awful face, ringed with helm and byrnnie like some demon warrior, and knew that the Rage was on it. Without armor and or even a weapon, Haraldr's fate was indeed here in Hecate.

Haraldr waited for the monster to commit himself; the knife continued its lulling serpent dance. Maria thrashed in the water near him, momentarily distracting him from his attacker's menace. Was Maria the assassin's helper as well as his bait?

Maria lurched toward him. The pommel of a knife touched his outstretched hand. He could not look, and for a moment would not believe. A dagger, and not his; he could tell from the feel of silver rather than bone. She pressed it into his grip.

Haraldr did not wait for Odin, and his arm was as swift as Thor. The monster's dagger swiped against Haraldr's shoulder, but by then the point of Haraldr's blade had crunched effortlessly through the gaping, artifical orifice in the center of the monster's face; his eyes rolled back, and when Haraldr pulled the dagger from his brain, he dropped like a dead walrus into the pool.

Maria came to Haraldr sobbing, her hair plastered to her skull. She nuzzled into his arms, her heart pulsing like a bird's, and pressed her cheek against his chest. Her tears were warm.

Haraldr turned her head with one hand and with his foot tilted up the lolling head of the floating corpse. "Who was he?" he demanded.

"I have seen him before," Maria said with a horror innocent beyond any conceivable guile, and in that moment he was certain he could trust her. "In the Grand Hetairia."

She turned again to his chest, her cheek smeared crimson from the wound on his shoulder. She sniffled and stopped her sobs. Then she placed her lips against Haraldr's chest and touched her velvet tongue to his trickling blood.

† † †

"Remember. Shoot the horses. At close quarters, spear the horses. With your swords, gut the horses. Keep your shields up and don't even concern yourselves with the riders until you have gotten them off their horses." Blymmedes looked at the incredulous faces of his Norse colleagues. "Believe me, the Saracen values his horse above the life of his closest comrade. Without his mount he is literally a legless man on an endless plain without food or water. The value of his horse exceeds anything he could win in spoils or ransom. Kill enough horses and you don't need to kill Saracens."

"That's sensible enough." Haraldr nodded. From what he had already seen, the Saracens' huge, swift horses were more formidable foes than the men who rode them. "But perhaps the ransom available to them here will incite them even to fighting on their own legs."

Blymmedes turned in his saddle and checked again on the progress of the distended baggage train. The Imperial caravan had just left the cross-roads where the road from Antioch met the coast road, an ancient high-way that ran a few miles north to the seaport of St. Symeon, and south past the port of Laodecia all the way to Tripoli, Beirut, Caesarea, finally turning inland at Arsuf to their destination of Jerusalem. "I am certain they will consider the Imperial baggage train a more convenient target than the Sacred Person of our Mother. An abduction of the Empress would provoke massive punitive action. As I'm certain you have seen, the value of the baggage train is an Empress's ransom, without the attendant risk of retaliation."

"So you think that is why the astute Strategus Nicon Attalietes has ordered the Imperial Excubitores to guard the Imperial baggage train?" asked Haraldr with wry emphasis. "What if the Saracens are to receive a ransom for *not* sparing the life of our Mother?"

Blymmedes pushed back his golden helm and massaged his temples. The Varangian, Haraldr Nordbrikt, was a clever boy, thought the Domestic, but perhaps his intellect was a bit too active; he saw conspiracy in the rising of the sun each morning. Only one man in the entire Roman Empire was both devious and able enough to carry out such a plot, and the Orphanotrophus Joannes knew that his brother—*Lord God, forgive me for thinking such a thought*—would not go shod in the Imperial buskins for a single day without the Divine sanction of the purple-born niece of the great Bulgar-Slayer. But what about a plot engineered by the Orphano-trophus Joannes to embarrass the Senator and Magister Nicon Attalietes through the agency of the Strategus Meletius Attalietes? After all, the Orphanotrophus Joannes was a dedicated enemy of the Dhynatoi, and blessedly so, for if Joannes and Nicon Attalietes ever joined forces, the result would be too disagreeable to contemplate. But if this conspiracy only aspired to slitting the throat of the scapegoat, Meletius Attalietes, let the Orphanotrophus Joannes conspire. The purple-born surely was safe.

The Domestic looked at Haraldr. "My friend, I'm certain I would see demons scampering about by light of day if I had seen what you saw last night." Blymmedes thought of that obscene giant, his brains oozing from the hole in his face, and wished he could have seen Haraldr dispatch him. "But I know the man who tried to kill you served in the Hetairia and I'm almost certain that he was punished and expelled by the Hetairarch for some illegal confiscation. He had a grudge, and you were the most convenient Varangian. I'm certain he is not an agent of some plot against our Mother."

Perhaps. Haraldr, mind aching from sleeplessness and worry, tried again to make sense of it. What if the giant had not acted on his own? Who had sent him? Haraldr was too fatigued to think of the possibilities. And his mind was too full of Maria. She appeared in a flash of alabaster; he could feel her smooth, wet skin. The previous night he had taken her back to the villa before he had alerted his own men to the attempt on his life. At the gate she had given him a kiss more erotic, certainly more emotionally powerful, than their embrace in the Temple of Hecate. She had saved his life, and he hers. But that kiss had told him that they had yet to plumb the depths of their shared fate.

"There!" Blymmedes stood in his stirrups and pointed to the rugged crags that pushed the coast road against the azure band of the sea. Haraldr saw nothing, but Blymmedes assured him that a large Saracen force was stirring dust in the heights. "We're vulnerable now that we have turned south to Laodecia. They're waiting."

"I'm going to the Empress," said Haraldr. Signaling Gregory to follow, he spurred ahead, passing the huge baggage train of Attalietes's thematic army. Incredible, he thought as he observed the rugs and pillows and wine jars these so-called soldiers had brought along. Before he had transited half of the thematic army's line of creaking wagons and groaning pack mules, he was passed by two akrites heading in the opposite direction, their dust and sweat-stained mantles flying and their horses whipped to a furious, foaming gallop. Only minutes later Blymmedes came by, heading toward the Imperial carriages like a whirlwind. "This is it!" yelled the elbows-akimbo Domestic.

Haraldr whipped his horse in pursuit of Blymmedes, but by the time he reached the Imperial carriages, the Domestic had already dismounted, stopped the caravan, and engaged himself in discussion with Symeon and the resplendently armored Meletius Attalietes; Halldor, who had remained with the Empress's carriage, looked on helplessly. Haraldr was grateful when the dogged Gregory arrived less than a minute later, though even without his interpreter he had already discerned that the argument was over the disposition of forces to defend against an imminent attack.

"I gather that Domestic Blymmedes wants to disengage half his force," said Gregory breathlessly, "in order to protect the Empress if the Saracens move for the Imperial carriages, or, should the Saracens capture part of the baggage train, to pursue them while they are laden with spoils. The Strategus Attalietes forbids this. He commands the Domestic Blymmedes to use all his forces to guard the Imperial baggage train. As far as the Strategus Attalietes is concerned, the matter is settled."

Blymmedes continued his livid, arm-thrusting presentation of his strategy, but Attalietes merely stood with his arms folded and his snub nose lifted. Blymmedes finally stopped, stomped the dust layered over the paving stones, and turned away. Then Attalietes spoke to Symeon.

"You will not like this, Haraldr Nordbrikt. The Strategus suggests that the Empress, in the person of her Chamberlain Symeon, command the Varangians to guard . . . to guard the thematic army." Gregory cleared his throat anxiously. "Excuse me, I am embarrassed to have to clarify that. To guard the baggage train of the thematic army."

Haraldr's aching skull could not even momentarily contain his fury. "Symeon," he shouted, "I am ordered by the Emperor himself to offer my life and that of all my men in defense of our Mother! I will not guard donkeys while she goes undefended!" Haraldr stepped toward Attalietes and narrowed his eyes at the arrogant Strategus, with satisfaction detecting the spark of fear. "Symeon, you tell this strutting peacock that we will die before we withdraw from the person of the Empress, and if the Strategus Attalietes wishes otherwise, he will first have to convince my own sword!" Haraldr did not add that there was now another life in the Imperial carriage for which he would sacrifice his own a thousand times.

Gregory translated with admirable emphasis. Attalietes's pale forehead colored, Blymmedes made no attempt to conceal his smile, and Symeon stared as if Haraldr had worn red silk to an Imperial banquet. His lifeless fingers suddenly clasped in relative agitation, Symeon walked a few paces to Her Imperial Majesty's carriage and tapped the window. The door opened slightly and Symeon stuck his head in. After a moment he walked back to the still speechless group of military men, his corpselike composure restored. He said nothing.

The door to the Imperial carriage opened wide. Gilded wooden steps were placed in the dust, Leo dropped out in sparkling white silk, Theodore following with a gold-tasseled silk parasol he quickly opened. Michael Kalaphates leapt out, cinching the leather straps of a bright new bronze breastplate embossed with a rearing lion. Leo extended a hand into the carriage, and the pearl- and gold-studded red silk slipper of Zoe the purple-born reached for the great Roman road upon which she had traveled, for perhaps a hundred rowing-spells, without ever setting down her foot.

Supported by Leo, her face discreetly veiled in crimson gauze, Zoe watched as her commanders fell to their faces before her. When they stood again, she spoke to Gregory in a husky, fearless tone.

"The Strategus Attalietes is the ranking military commander, and as such he represents the will of my husband, our Father, in the matter of my defense. Komes Haraldr, if you do not carry out his order, I will command your centurion here to administer summarily the punishment for treason." She turned and fixed Halldor with a stare that blanched even his face. "If your centurion will not perform this duty, I will order the Domestic Blymmedes to carry out the execution of both traitors."

Haraldr looked at Blymmedes and saw no indication that his friend would not do as his Empress had commanded. He mastered his rage at his own impotence, but his breast was leaden with the thought that Maria would share her Empress's fate. But perhaps Blymmedes was right; the baggage train would be the objective. What could he achieve, anyway, now forced to place Halldor's head on the block and challenge his friend, Blymmedes. And it seemed the Empress was determined to perform her own execution. Almost unable to breathe, Haraldr bowed deeply, gave the order for the Varangians to re-deploy, and backed up to his horse with his arms crossed over his breast. At least he had another answer. It was the Strategus Meletius Attalietes who wanted his Empress dead.

Shielded by her parasol from the glancing late-afternoon sun, Zoe kissed Michael Kalaphates on the forehead and wished him the Beneficence of the Theotokos. Then, assisted by her eunuchs, she returned to her carriage and settled beside Maria.

"We will wait here," Zoe said calmly. Her lips mused sensuously. "When we are finally put away and at our privacy, you must tell me about your . . . interview last night with the Komes. You have put such a fire in his eyes, and, my darling . . . well, I have never seen your countenance quite so . . . avid. We will talk of it during the long days ahead. You know your Mother is fascinated by . . . details."

Maria said nothing, lost in her labyrinth of fear and desire. Could this be the death his eyes had promised her the night before? Was this where the three lines crossed?

"Little Daughter!" the Empress said soothingly. "Surely you are not worried about . . . *this.* " Zoe waved her hand languidly. "Symeon assures us that the Emir of Aleppo is most hospitable."

† † †

Blymmedes pointed to the dust cyclones that had appeared at the head and tail of the long, motionless Imperial columns. His infantry were raising their own reddish clouds as they returned to formation after spreading thousands of spiked iron balls, called caltrops, on the plain between the road and the sea. "There, Komes Haraldr. You see how they are flanking the column at both ends. Now they will circle back to come in with the sun behind them. That's why I spread my caltrops to the seaward side. If I were giving the orders, I would send my light cavalry there"—he pointed north to a distant point along the coast—"and there"—now Blymmedes pointed south—"and crush them in my pincers when they fell on the baggage train." Blymmedes slapped his hands together and looked with admiration at the line of Varangians in gleaming byrnnies. "Fortunately your men are adept at static defense. Well, good luck, Komes Haraldr." Blymmedes waved dashingly as he galloped back to the Imperial baggage train.

Haraldr turned to his men, dismounted, and lined up facing the sea as Blymmedes had suggested; Haraldr had placed archers behind the first spear-wielding, shield-raised rank. The overloaded mules behind the archers wheezed and brayed, and the batmen chattered with nervous excitement. Haraldr rode out in front the Varangians, stood in his stirrups, and tried to strike a balance between his own utter despair and the kind of valiant exhortation that would merely humiliate his men further; they knew they guarded mules and rugs.

"This time the Maumet's men will not be ghosts," he shouted evenly, as if giving routine instructions. "Remember, we must first shoot horses, then spear horses. Then, if men still come against us, we will let them feel the bite of Hunland steel!" Haraldr had expected the halfhearted acknowledgment he received, but the muttering only fueled his anxiety. The men had every right to be dispirited, he thought, stallions asked to pull the plow alongside the ox and the mule.

After perhaps a quarter hour the sound came from the sea. At first the noise was almost like wind whistling through a narrow opening, but it quickly rose and fragmented into the trillings of an enormous and angry flock. A rusty pall soon shrouded the sea, and then the glittering cloud of dust boiled out of the sun. The noise seemed to advance and retreat in a horrible, shrill wailing. The Saracen host rode forward at a pace that seemed unreal, as if nature had somehow compressed time. They were dressed much like the Romans' own akrites, spectacularly in silver and white, helms and curved blades glimmering before the dust cloud that they seemed to outrace. Their unearthly shrieking, rising and falling in violent rhythm, scraped the nerves. Haraldr stood at the center of his Varangian wall, his shield set, and gave his bowmen the order to fire. Almost instantly the huge white and black and gray dappled horses in the vanguard toppled, legs buckling and skewing. But the rest leapt over the writhing beasts and their hapless riders, making little attempt to avoid crushing their own men. Haraldr took a step forward and set his spear. Arrows clattered against the Varangian shields—Haraldr wondered how men on horses were attaining such prodigious bowshots—but the return salvo brought down another rank of horsemen. Still the rest came on, now only a hundred ells away.

The horsemen abruptly veered, whipping light throwing-spears against the Varangian shields as they turned off toward the north. Another salvo from the Varangian archers and the horses and riders began to pile up; the following ranks were refusing to advance beyond the flailing parapet of fallen mounts. Saracen arrows still rained with surprising force against the Norse wall of shields, but Haraldr could not see a single Varangian down. Haraldr yelled for Halldor and Ulfr to come to the center.

"Have we slain enough of their horses?" asked Halldor dryly.

Haraldr shook his head. "They seemed bold enough even within our bowshot. Perhaps they are tempting us to begin our own offensive. . . . Kristr!" Haraldr's sudden epiphany clutched at his belly. "This is only the feint! The Empress!" Haraldr brought his head back and bellowed so that he was heard over even the cataclysmic shrilling of the Saracens. "Boar!"

The line of Varangians almost instantly re-formed into the impenetrable wedge of the swine-array. Haraldr took the snout, flanked by Halldor and Ulfr. The Saracens quieted for a moment as Varangian axes pounded on shields. As the boar moved to the south, the mounted fury of the Saracens raced to blunt its snout.

Haraldr did not know how long the Rage seized him. So immense was the relief of feeling Odin's favor again, he thought he could slash and hack until his blade wore to a nub. The Saracens were indeed brave; they came forward in endless files with their howling black faces and agate eyes, their silver arcs swishing. And they fell relentlessly to the Norse blades. Haraldr's boots were soaked with blood when the Saracen horde finally disappeared, almost vaporously, like a sea mist rolling back from a morning sun.

The road ahead was littered with corpses. Like terrible blossoms, white robes and quilted cotton jerkins were spotted with brilliant crimson. Roman and Saracen corpses at first, then a growing preponderance of Romans, quilted armor soaked, sleeveless byrnnies glazed red, conical helms cast everywhere. Horses bleated in agony, joined by the screams of men. The vultures made obscene circles above. The thematic army of Cilicia had been virtually annihilated.

The Imperial carriages were surrounded by a low ridge of corpses. Several white-robed eunuchs sat wailing, beating their chests and tearing at their silken hems; Symeon stood like a corpse that had neglected to fall. A dark-haired, silk-clad woman wandered dazed, and Haraldr, breast exploding, began to run to Maria. But no, it was Anna. Then Haraldr saw the Empress's purple-paneled carriage. The lumbering four-wheeled wagon had been tipped over. The gold-scrolled, white-lacquered door on the upturned side was open. Numb with horror, Haraldr peered inside. The scent that lingered, her scent, choked him with anguish. The carriage was empty.

Blymmedes charged up and leapt off his horse, his face pale and scowling beneath his golden helm. Clearly shocked, he stumbled over the corpses and looked inside the carriage. He turned to Haraldr with pain in his eyes and whispered, "You are the better tactician, my friend." Then he turned over one of the Saracen corpses. The man had a neat black beard and decayed teeth that showed between slightly parted, claret lips. One of his eyes had become a livid bruise, but the other was open, and the staring iris was as black as a raven's plume. "Not Saracens," said the Domestic hoarsely, tears welling in his eyes. "Seljuks."

Haraldr looked across the plain to the sea; the sun skimmed rays over distant golden ripples. He turned and the snowy crests to the east flared with the glow of the plunging orange globe. Where was his Mother? And where was his love? Distractedly, the pain too great for thought, he began to check the fallen for signs of life. He nudged a shoulder and turned a limp body on its back. He knew the now-battered bronze breastplate before he saw the face. Michael Kalaphates. Haraldr ripped away the breastplate and hollered for water for the bloodied lips. Kalaphates was alive.

"Komes!" Haraldr left Kalaphates with the water bearer and ran to Blymmedes, who knelt beside a corpse he had uncovered from beneath several slain Seljuks. His arrogant features almost serene, the Strategus

Meletius Attalietes's body reposed in eternal sleep, his golden breastplate punctured by a broken spear and his golden helm crushed into his skull just above his ear. Blymmedes sealed Attalietes's partially open eyes with respect, closed his own, and whispered an epitaph for the Strategus. "He fought bravely."

he Magnara Palace was dark and empty, the tapestries shrouds on the wall, the golden throne a looming silhouette. The carpets had been rolled up and the black-frocked figure paced the the bare marble; despite the size of his enormous spade-shaped boots, the Orphanotrophus Joannes made no sound to mask the whisper of his fine wool frock. As he walked, he calculated the time as he calculated everything—in his head, with unerring precision. He did not need to rely on the endlessly clicking water clocks that coerced lesser men, because he could rely on the sound—no, not the sound, but something more subtle, more intuitive—of the city. His city. He could sense its rhythms, the rising in the morning and the settling at night, with ineffable, primal instinct, in the way a bee might locate its hive. It was a vibration only he could feel, and it told him the time with far more precision than the grandiose machines the Dhynatoi amused themselves with. And from the movements of his city he could also discern much that those clocks would never tell their owners high on their hilltop palaces. But at this moment only time concerned him.

It goes well; this much he permitted himself. The message received in the second hour, exactly according to plan. The third hour had passed with no signal; that was an enormous relief, particularly given the unpredictability of the agents they were dealing with. But the excruciating effort would be for naught if the the fourth hour passed without a message. And his city told the Orphanotrophus that the fourth hour of the night was three quarters gone. The message was already a few minutes overdue.

Hating his own lack of control, the Orphanotrophus walked behind the throne; left the audience chamber through the silent, hidden entrance used by the Emperor; climbed the large spiral staircase to the cabinet chamber, and took the smaller staircase up into the clock room and observation deck. The attendants went about their duties, accustomed to if not comfortable with the lurking presence of the giant monk. Joannes stepped out onto his own private balcony adjacent to the observation deck. Lamps flared along the towering seawall beneath him, and the bright points of ship lanterns drifted on the Bosporus. Here and there the Asian palaces of the Dhynatoi formed little constellations off into the east. He knew the exact position of Mt. Afxendios and stared without blinking. Only ten minutes left in the hour.

Eight. The beacon glimmered for a tantalizing instant. Then, more brilliant than the evening star, the light that had begun in faraway Toulon exploded and flared across the last expanse of Asia Minor. A pity, thought Joannes as he quickly turned and headed back into the palace. The Senator and Magister Nicon Attalietes has lost his favorite son.

Joannes opened the door to the small ground-floor antechamber, a disused room once employed for storage of the censers and icons that cluttered the Magnara on ceremonial occasions; Joannes had had many of these superfluous treasures melted into more utilitarian assets. His guest waited in darkness and Joannes lit a single oil lamp; he had learned years ago that men found flickering light on his face far more frightening than simply his voice emerging from the shadows. "Thank you for waiting," Joannes told his guest.

The man shifted his clumsy, sandaled feet and bowed deeply. His rough burlap tunic exposed thick burly calves. His face was round but had long seamlike scars from which his jowls seemed to hang as if wired to his face; his richly veined nose was studded with two warts. He smelled of cheap resiny wine.

"I wanted you and your friends to know the truth before the Dhynatoi begin to shovel their lies about the city," said Joannes. "A terrible tragedy has occurred due to the negligence of the powerful who have so much while you have so little. The powerful who impede every effort your Imperial Administration makes to ease your suffering."

"No one has done more for us than yourself, who we worship as the blessed hand of Christ the King, Orphanotrophus," said the man in a brutishly obsequious voice, the growl of a bear paying sincere homage to a lion. He clutched his broad, scabbed fists to his tunic as he spoke in a gesture of humility and anxiety. "You know how much we folk are beholden to what you have done."

Joannes studied the clutching, ham-hock fists with satisfaction. The Butcher—he did not know the man's real name, nor did he care to know—had in fact been a real pork butcher once. He had run afoul of the Prefect for buying his swine outside the city at prices below the officially mandated wholesale rates, then charging an exorbitant markup at his shop in the city. Of course it was not that crime that had condemned him;

his fate had been sealed by his refusal to share the requisite portion of the illicit profit with the Prefect. Joannes had found the Butcher in the Neorion Tower, where he often browsed for suitable instruments of his myriad policies. And now the Butcher was still a butcher of sorts.

Joannes stepped forward and enveloped the Butcher's powerful shoulders in his grotesque fingers. "I prayed all afternoon to the Holy Veil, begging the Holy Mother for the strength to convey my sorrow to my friends in the city, who should know first of this calamitous event." Joannes stroked the Butcher's shoulder paternally and lowered his voice to an awkward, rasping whisper. "Our purple-born Mother has been raped by the Saracens."

The Butcher's bleary eyes froze with shock and then thawed with flowing tears. "Theotokos, Theotokos, Theotokos," he wailed frantically, "oh, beseech we, Holy Mother, spare our Mother, spare our Mother. . . . Oh, Theotokos, Theotokos . . . my Mother, my Mother." The Butcher thundered his chest with his rock-hard fists, slumped to his knees, and began to rip the front of his tunic to shreds. Joannes watched, incredulous as always at the devotion of the rabble to the painted harlot they called their Mother. In Zoe's case it was not simply the centuries-old association of the Empress of the Romans and the Mother of her people with the Empress of Heaven and the Mother of God; Zoe also had the legacy of the Bulgar-Slayer dyed into the weft of her purple-born being, the Bulgar-Slayer who had diligently and, when necessary, ruthlessly protected the people of his city and his empire from the merciless depredations of the Dhynatoi. Seeing the wailing Butcher before him, Joannes again reminded himself that the Macedonian Dynasty would have to be excised from the hearts of the clamoring mob with the greatest of surgical precision.

Joannes knelt beside the slobbering Butcher and cradled the greasy, rough-fleshed head. "Brother, Brother," he said in a low rumble, like a distant shaking of the earth. "Fear not for our Mother. I have already dispatched the Grand Domestic and our Imperial Taghmata to effect the rescue of her sacred person." The brutish eyes turned to Joannes gratefully. "Yes, Brother. Let us now think to transform our tears into a righteous vengeance. There has been fault here." The Butcher stiffened. "Yes. It was the Dhynatoi Meletius Attalietes who cravenly abandoned our Blessed Mother to the unclean heretics. That vile recreant is beyond our reach now, but the father, the demon-sire who engineered this plot against our Mother, is well within your grasp."

The Butcher bolted to his feet, his fingers strangling the air. His chest heaved with rage.

"There!" boomed Joannes. "Do you see him!" Joannes extended his vast arm span to a dark corner of the antechamber. "The Archangel Michael! He appears to lead you in vengeance against those who, having deprived you of everything save the love of your Mother, now wish to deprive you of your Empress! Go to your friends in the City and tell them what the Archangel has commanded you to do!"

"Archangel Michael, messenger of God!" roared the Butcher, his rapt eyes fixed on the empty corner.

† † †

The Augusta Theodora wrapped her long arms around her slender torso, her limbs tense and her expression pained, as if she were trying to crush her own ribs. Her eyes welled with tears; for some reason grief made her look much younger, almost boyish. "Thank you for telling me yourself, Father. You know your guidance is the balm for all my disquietudes."

Alexius, Patriarch of the One True Oecumenical, Orthodox, and Catholic Faith, smiled gently. He had come to Theodora's country palace as soon as his informants in the Magnara had brought him the news of her sister's abduction. The Patriarch showed no sign of fatigue from his long night on the road. He had a powerful yet elegant face; his nose was long and jutting, with a craglike tip poised above thin, almost feminine lips. His heavy, somewhat brutish eyebrows were streaked with black, and they ended at his temples in wiry tufts; his beard was like an extrusion of fine, pure silver wires. His small black eyes were fierce but controlled, like leashed hunting cats.

"I was frightened for her," said Theodora. "May the Pantocrator forgive me for not setting my pride aside and going to her with my fears. I will never forgive myself."

"There was no reason to be apprehensive about this pilgrimage, at least within the Saracen territories. I myself made inquiries." Alexius's voice was a heavy tenor; like his eyes, seemingly capable of vastly more powerful effects than the Patriarch cared to display at this moment. "I will probably be unable to confirm my suspicions. But I believe this abduction to be the work of heretics who call themselves Christians, and not the Sons of Hagar."

Theodora immediately understood to whom Alexius was referring.

"Father, I cannot believe that even Joannes could consider this. Father, he could not keep his brother on the throne without my sister. Why?"

"If it is he, he would not be acting against your sister, and indeed I believe she will not be harmed. I suspect some fashion of maneuver against the Dhynatoi. Your sister is merely in a jeopardy we all share. In his demonic pursuit of his personal ambitions, in his persistent and diabolical attacks upon my person and the One True Faith under my stewardship, Joannes threatens every soul born into the world from now until the trumpet of judgment sounds. It is not Joannes the murderer of men I fear. It is Joannes the murderer of souls. Do you understand the true seriousness of his crimes, my child?"

Theodora stared thoughtfully at the floor. "I know that he is trying to redraft the *typica* of hundreds of monastic establishments to withdraw them from your jurisdiction." Alexius ruled a virtual empire within the Empire, consisting of thousands of churches, vast landholdings, an entire system of patriarchal courts, and a huge bureaucracy to manage it. One of the principal sources of revenues was the income from monasteries granted their *typica,* or charters, by the Patriarch; by issuing *typica* under Imperial sanction, Joannes could divert those revenues from Alexius's empire to his own.

Alexius placed his long, elegant fingers together just beneath his chin; his golden rings caught the light from the single brass candelabrum. He wore a thickly embroidered white robe and a white shawl emblazoned with gold crosses. His eyes were unleashed now, stalking a prey. "Joannes weakens the One True Faith at the moment that it requires every resource to combat a far more malignant infection. The Bishop of Old Rome is a wily servant of the fallen Archangel, and what Satan himself could not accomplish, these so-called Roman pontiffs may succeed in achieving with this *filioque* they are demon-bent on inserting into the Holy Creed. Their insistence that the Holy Spirit proceeds from the Father *and* the Son, rather than from the Father *through* the Son, denies the operation of that Spirit in our souls. Indeed, it denies the Pantocrator Himself His divine patrimony from God the Father. If the Latin creed is allowed to become standardized throughout the Christian sees, then every soul receiving the sacraments under that doctrine is in jeopardy. With that single unholy word the infidel will have defeated us, and the Gates of Hell will receive all the descendants of Adam. But I cannot combat this infection until I have extirpated Joannes."

Theodora crossed herself. "I have always despised Joannes. But before tonight I had not fully understood the urgency of opposing him. I will help you in any way I can, Father."

Alexius looked away and his eyes finally pounced on some invisible quarry. "Yes, my child. I am certain you will."

order a halt," said the Strategus Constantine.

The Domestic Nicon Blymmedes turned to him; Blymmedes seemed to have aged a decade in a single night.

"This pursuit is useless self-excoriation," continued Constantine. "We will be too exhausted to fight when we get there. And that presumes that we are even taking the proper route. After all, your so-called intelligence is responsible for this catastrophe, that and the foolishness of Attalietes, may the Pantocrator have mercy on his soul. Had I known we were dealing with Seljuks, I certainly would have stayed with the Empress and taken command myself. This never would have happened."

Haraldr listened, already hating that name. Seljuks. They were believers in Maumet, or Mohammed as he was known to the Romans, who was either the son of, or wizard to, a god named Allah. The Seljuks had many of the characteristics of the Pechenegs: they migrated in great hordes on veritable herds of fast horses, which they rode expertly; they were heedless of their lives in combat; and they even had the same beetle faces. But the Seljuks were wealthier and more organized than the Pechenegs, because they already had begun to conquer less warlike Saracens in a rich place far to the northeast called Persia. Blymmedes said that the Seljuks had never been this far west before, and that this was probably a renegade tribe hired out to the Emir of Aleppo. However, the Domestic had also told Haraldr that he considered the Seljuks a "plague" that would someday spread west and make the Romans forget all other foes.

But right now these Seljuks were retreating east at an astonishing pace, and despite the gut-jarring evening and night in the saddle, the swift, light cavalry units of the Imperial Excubitores and the thematic army of Antioch—there were virtually no surviving horses or men from the thematic army of Cilicia—could not bring them in sight. The pursuit through the plains of the Orontes River Valley had been especially brutal for the Varangians, who simply couldn't ride with the Romans but had maintained the pace through sheer endurance and tenacity. And now they were going up again, back into the rocky foothills that would soon rise to even more torturous heights.

Blymmedes heard approaching hoofbeats and hailed the rider, one of an endless relay of akrites who had ridden ahead of and behind the column all night long. He turned to Constantine. "If we do not intercept them before they make Aleppo, I am certain we will not see our Empress for some time. And the ransom could be insuperable."

"I assure you our Father will bear any demands to obtain the safety of his wife," said Constantine indignantly. He did not add that the price had already been fixed and in any event would come from a contingency fund that Joannes had amassed with a triple surcharge to the window tax, levied a year ago in all eighteen Asian themes.

"The Emir of Aleppo has made an alliance he will soon regret," said Blymmedes. "He may not be able to control his Seljuk servants. And I assure you they are nowhere near as cognizant of Imperial protocol as the good Emir is."

Constantine straightened in his saddle, the alarms clanging in his road-assaulted skull. That would be the end of them all. Why hadn't Joannes thought of this? Then the alarms were replaced by a sweeter music. Well, perhaps the august Orphanotrophus Joannes simply could not dictate everything to "Brother" out here in far-flung Antioch. Perhaps "Brother" would have to rescue this perhaps not-so-thoroughly planned enterprise with his own astute initiative. Ah, but "Brother" must be careful; he was reaching high, and he should provide a bed of straw to cushion his fall if he did not attain his objective. "What is your plan, Domestic?" growled Constantine with feigned disinterest.

"I believe they will stop, water and fodder their horses, and rest for a few hours. Then they will send half their force in one direction to mislead or even harass us, while the rest will proceed directly to Aleppo. I believe they will make this stop at a fortified place."

"Between here and Aleppo?" asked Constantine irritably; Blymmedes was falling to pieces. He was a typical career military man, Constantine reflected, crowing lustily atop his own dung heap but at an utter loss in true adversity. "The closest fortification is only eight leagues from Aleppo. Why would they pause there?"

"Have you ever sent a reconnaissance as far as Harim?" Blymmedes was astonished. The Saracens exerted control of the countryside only several leagues east of Antioch; wasn't Constantine concerned as to what the infidels might be up to right on his own threshold?

"Our tax collectors don't go out that way anymore," answered Constantine. "We don't need those revenues, and not many peasants are willing to farm out there, what with nothing to protect them save the ruins of the kastron near Harim." A kastron was a fortified town. "I suppose you would suggest I rebuild the kastron? The cost would hardly be offset by the increase in tax revenues. You should focus on military matters, Domestic, with which you seem to have ample difficulty as it is. Leave civil administration to those with the requisite expertise."

"You would not need to rebuild the kastron, Strategus. My akrites have seen it recently. The Saracens have rebuilt it for you."

For a moment Constantine refused to believe Blymmedes. Very well, he then conceded to himself, perhaps one did become contemptuous of Saracen threats within the walls of Antioch. "So you think they will pause at the kastron. If it is such a threatening fortification, how do you expect to besiege it with several exhausted droungos of light cavalry?"

"I think if we appear, we will bottle them up. Then we can bring up siege machinery and go to work on the walls."

Constantine frowned, trying to make sense of this new music. It was becoming increasingly titillating to his ear. Yes, most pleasant. With the siege engines in place, the leader of the Seljuks might be compelled to negotiate independently of his agreement with the Emir of Aleppo. He might be convinced to surrender his prize at a significant discount. And the Emir could hardly grumble, because he had already received partial payment and would be relieved of having to compensate his Seljuk hirelings. And the enormous sum left in difference, well of course that would be returned to Joannes's special treasury—minus a suitably ample reward for the extraordinarily illustrious engineer of this successful conclusion. Ah, very sweet music indeed. But what if the Seljuk beasts are not so reasonable? Well, that was the risk one had to take, or else remain in Antioch forever. Besides, there was an easy way to indemnify himself.

Constantine pulled himself erect. "I concur with your judgment, Domestic. But since your intent for the moment is merely to frighten the infidels into remaining at the kastron, I reason that it would make sense for me to withdraw my forces to Antioch and begin requisitioning the appropriate siege equipment." Constantine tugged his horse's reins and rode off without waiting for a reply.

† † †

"What a filthy man." Zoe pulled her veil more tightly around her face. Her blue eyes shone like gems in the dismal room. The eunuch, who spoke only the local Arabic dialect, set the silver tray down, then bowed and retreated as if he had been addressed with appropriate decorum.

Maria sat cross-legged on a stained linen cushion, balefully studying the four Saracen women who sat against the wall opposite her; the plaster was new, but the tapestry that covered much of it was moth-eaten and faded.

"Can you imagine?" said Zoe airily. "I had heard that their women were veritable chattels, but the emirs and ambassadors we have dealt with were always so civilized. Apparently, here they are rather less gracious. I'm certain that their stables are cleaner than their women's quarters. Of course, given the choice, the brutes who have absconded with us might prefer the enchantments of their steeds to these greased piglets they call their wives."

The Saracen women—three chubby, barely pubescent children and one darkly pretty young woman—tittered shyly at the Empress's dismissive gesture and then resumed their entranced study of the silk-draped woman they understood to be the mother of the prophet Christ. Maria caressed the back of her hand with the fingers of the other and avoided Zoe's inquiring look.

"Little daughter," admonished Zoe, "you are making far too much of this. Tomorrow we shall be in Aleppo, we shall have our Leo back, and no doubt the Emir will immediately regale us with tales of his exotic land. You know that their literature is so much more . . . forthright than ours, don't you, dear? I suppose that explains why all the sons of Hagar are so frightened of women that they must keep them locked away. After all, they have heard so many epics of these . . . temptations. Pity that the reality is so artless. Have you noticed the coarseness of their complexions?"

"We will never see Aleppo." Maria's voice was so deep and soughing that it scarcely seemed to be her own.

"Little daughter! Don't tell me the Prophet who haunts the Orient has taken you as his deputy. You are as gloomy as a Bogomil. From wherever have you received this . . . *intimation?*"

"He told me." Suddenly Maria whipped her head, her eyes fired, and she spat the words out. "He told me while he loved me!"

Zoe pursed her lips in deliberation. "My darling," she said with paired concern and anticipation, "would you like to elaborate on that?"

Maria's eyes were almost phosphorescent. "I had intended to kill him. As I had in my dream. I even had the knife."

Zoe shut her eyes and leaned against the wall. "Oh, darling, I had hoped that was all done with. That was so long ago. You mustn't go on reliving that . . . accident with every other man. Everyone knows you were not at fault."

"There has never been a man like this man. This Haraldr." Maria clutched her arms and cocked her head; her voice was hypnotic. "All the rest have simply drawn the poison out of me, sucking away the putrescence of my soul with the proboscis between their legs, feeding on that obscene gruel because it is the only sustenance their own corruption can digest. They leave me empty, yet cleansed of my own toxins. This man filled me with the brilliance of the stars. The sun. A thousand suns. A light pure and searing. An incandescence in which every fate is revealed. A light in which I saw love and death as lovers, joined in the mad ecstasy I shared with them. At the moment that light flared to infinite brilliance he offered me an exchange. He offered me that light in exchange for my life. He offers that trade to everyone he touches. I saw it in his eyes. There are souls trapped in his eyes, a thousand thousand souls for a thousand years. I know. I am with them now. He lives, and I will die."

Zoe slid next to Maria and took her limp, almost lifeless hand. "Little daughter," she said with a sigh, "now you have entered a realm I perhaps know better than you." She wrapped her arms around Maria's vision-stiffened shoulders. "Our Komes Haraldr has beguiled you. Fear is the most powerful aphrodisiac; it not only arouses passion but also bonds souls. You were there when he killed that man, weren't you?"

Maria nodded numbly. "Blood excites me. I wanted him to make love to me again."

Zoe raised her eyebrows for a moment. "Well," she said conclusively, "we are each plagued with our passions. I am a slave to simple caresses and the merest devotions, while you, being rather more . . . cosmopolitan, have developed more . . . complex desires. We can never fully exhaust these passions, and yet we can acquire the wisdom to endure them. You are wise, my child, you will endure long after this Komes Haraldr has gone back to the frost-breasted maidens of distant Thule." Zoe kissed Maria's forehead. "I rather think your unwarranted inquietude at our predicament has inflamed your memory of the golden giant. When we see him again, you will find him just another Tauro-Scythian curiosity."

"You are not afraid, Mother?" Maria's eyes were wide and incandescent.

"Of course not. I am the most valuable being beneath our Lord's sight. The ransom I can bring is worth far more than any goal that might be obtained by placing my soul before the judgment of God. No one clever enough to steal me would be fool enough to kill me."

Zoe stroked Maria's downy temple with her fingers. No, little daughter, I do not fear the hands I have fallen into, however rough and unwashed they may be. I do not fear a confinement that will probably be long, longer than I can permit your precious heart to suffer before it must. But now I know what must be done when we finally return to my city and my people. And when I think of that, I know fear.

† † †

The Mandator, chief intelligence-gathering officer of the Imperial Excubitores, spoke in Arabic to the squat, scruffy-bearded man, a petty merchant from the look of his uncallused hands and his dirty linen robe. The merchant showed several blackened teeth as he jabbered in a sing-song voice; as he spoke, he seemed to clutch frantically at the vague, ground-clinging, early-morning mist. The Mandator gestured to the man's cup and ordered a batman to fill it with more wine. He bowed to the merchant and stepped back to talk with Blymmedes and Haraldr.

"He's an Arab from this place, not a Seljuk," said the Mandator, a wiry, spooky-eyed man who usually dressed just like the akrites he supervised. "He says they rebuilt the kastron for defense and they have no wish to invite quarrel with the Romans. According to him, the Seljuks have murdered the governor of the kastron and have sent out couriers to the east." The Mandator lowered his bristling, sun-bleached brows, for a moment fixing his usually wandering eyes. "He is telling the truth. I have no need to intensify his interrogation."

Blymmedes nodded agreement. "See that the paymaster attends to him." He turned to Haraldr. "It appears the hireling has initiated his own scheme. Are you prepared to interrogate the Seljuk?"

Haraldr pulled his knife from his belt and nodded. Blymmedes's akrites had chased down a contingent of the Seljuk rear guard and had succeeded in capturing a Seljuk warrior.

"Good," said Blymmedes. "It is important that you do it. They think you fair-hairs are demons, Christ's avengers."

The Seljuk waited on his knees, his arms bound behind him. Haraldr forced his hands to steady. This was not his kind of business, and it required a kind of courage that he had not considered before. But Blymmedes had convinced him how important this was. And he needed no convincing of the importance of the lives this wretch might save when his tongue was persuaded to glibness.

The Seljuk's bright, feral eyes widened when he saw the golden giant approach. Then he remembered his own fierce father, and his big brothers who had swatted him, and he spat at the demon's boots. Allah would soon embrace him.

Haraldr held the Seljuk's eyes. He reached around and slit the rope that held the Seljuk's hands, then raised him up. He signaled the batman to give him a bowl of steamed grain with bits of sliced lamb. The Seljuk looked at the bowl, sniffed, and barked something in his staccato tongue. An akrites who knew the Seljuk dialect—many of them did—spoke in Greek to Gregory, who then translated for Haraldr.

"He says why should he poison himself? He—excuse me, Haraldr Nordbrikt—calls you a huge pig."

Haraldr looked into the furious, curiously smug face. The man was not much older than Haraldr, with a dense black beard and a sharp handsome nose. He clearly prided himself as an indomitable warrior and was probably one of their officers. Haraldr took the bowl from the Seljuk's hands, shoveled several handfuls of the food into his own mouth, chewed at length, and swallowed before handing the bowl back. The Seljuk snatched the bowl from Haraldr and devoured the rest of the dish like a ravenous dog.

"Does he wish more?" asked Haraldr. The Seljuk nodded and another bowl was brought, tested by Haraldr and served. And then another. Did their guest wish to drink? Watered wine was brought, tested, and poured for him. Was their guest at last satiated? The Seljuk nodded, eyes gleaming, certain that Allah had bewitched his foes.

Haraldr gestured that he would relieve the Seljuk of the burden of his empty goblet. When he had given the cup to the batman, he turned suddenly, clamped his hand to the Seljuk's forehead like a vise, and neatly sliced his right ear off.

The Seljuk was rigid with shock; blood streamed down his neck and dripped off his shoulder. Haraldr seized the Seljuk's jaw, popped it open, and stuffed the ear in. "Tell him to eat his ear!"

The Seljuk fell to his knees, retching and coughing. Haraldr knelt with him, his hands over the Seljuk's mouth and nose. "Eat!" The Seljuk's eyes seemed to grasp for the air denied his lungs. Haraldr held his knife to the desperate face again. "Tell him to eat his ear or I will feed him his other ear and then his nose"—Haraldr waited for the translation and sliced skin from the tip of the nose—"and then I will make him eat the nose that droops between his legs." He lowered the knife to the man's belly, slit the coarse linen robe, and made a shallow cut across the abdomen. "And if he does not eat, I will find another way of filling his belly." Haraldr then placed the bloody point of the dagger against the tear gland of the Seljuk's right eye. "When he has seen all this, we will provide him a dessert. He will have no trouble swallowing his eyes." Haraldr pushed against the Seljuk's face and toppled him backward. "Then our physicians will make certain that he lives."

Haraldr stood over the Seljuk like an ancient Titan. "The first question saves his eyes."

After a few minutes of verbal interrogation the Seljuk had gratefully saved everything except his previously forfeit right ear. It was an ominous tale. The Seljuks had been in the pay of the Emir of Aleppo but now planned to keep the Empress as their own property. They intended to rendezvous with a larger Seljuk force riding from the east, then retreat with their prize to a series of mountain redoubts in northern Persia, beyond the reach of any power, even the Romans. The ransom they extorted would finance their westward ambitions. For this reason they saw no need to deliver the Empress once their demands had been met; for if their demands were met, they would soon enough be at war with the Romans.

Blymmedes asked Haraldr and Gregory to accompany him. They climbed a rocky path that snaked to the summit of a sheer outcropping. The kastron, now four or five bowshots away, was a sinister apparition in the moonlight, a dungeon rather than a town. The dark walls were only about two bowshots on a side, but they were a good twenty-five ells high and were rooted in a roughly faceted summit that scarcely allowed purchase to a few scrubby trees. Toothlike merloned battlements ran along the top of the wall; in the crenellated openings the robes of the Seljuk sentries were visible as a pale luminescence.

"I don't like sieges," said Blymmedes. "It is work for engineers, not soldiers. Towers, tortoises, fire blowers, mangonels. Of course it would take weeks to bring the equipment up here, dig the tunnels and entrenchments, and erect the engines. And there are too many Seljuks inside such a small place, so they would first slaughter the inhabitants to preserve food. A disagreeable business altogether." Blymmedes paused and frowned even more deeply; the lines were like slits in his leathery forehead. "Of course that is the simple problem, and now its solution offers us nothing. My akrites have already encountered the reconnaissance elements of the Seljuk force and have interrogated—though not as eloquently as you, Komes Haraldr—one of their scouts. The relief is quite a large force and only a day away. Even if my infantry arrives tomorrow evening to help us initiate the siege, we would not be able to withstand both the relief force and the force inside. And of course we do not know when Constantine will return with his thematic forces, though with such assistance as he will offer we might hope he is delayed indefinitely. I do not see any way we can prevent the Empress's abductors from escaping into the Plain of Aleppo, and from there to wherever they may wish to go." Blymmedes folded his arms, looked up at the brooding kastron, and shook his head.

Haraldr studied the walls. At the back of the kastron the crenellations were almost crested by a twenty-ell-wide lip of tortured rock that fell away to a sheer drop of almost two hundred ells. "How wide are those walls on top?" asked Haraldr.

"Three men abreast," answered Blymmedes, his brow slightly unfurrowing.

"So despite the considerable number of these Seljuks inside, were I to gain access to those walls I would only have to worry about three men. At a time, that is."

"True," said Blymmedes. "But how would you get on the walls, and what objective could you accomplish on the walls alone, for you could never survive a descent into the town."

"My comrade," said Haraldr with renewed vigor, "the Seljuk who leads this army impresses me as a bold, ambitious leader who can count on the fanatical loyalty of his men; why else would they have joined him in this daring escapade? Up on those walls, my objective will be to meet face-to-face with this noble warrior. But before I can achieve this intercourse, I will need you to help me with a diversion."

† † †

The drums broke the dawn. The kastron was a blocky silhouette against a radiant sunrise still hidden by the summit. Five light cavalry vanda of the Imperial Excubitores and four hundred Varangians advanced in stately formation to within a bowshot of the walls. The Mandator of the Imperial Excubitores, Domestic Nicon Blymmedes at his side, formally called upon the walled town to surrender to his Majesty Michael, Emperor, Basileus, and Autocrator of the Romans. For several minutes the only sounds were the snorting of horses in the Roman ranks and the faint crowing of roosters from inside the Citadel.

The scream began inside the walls. For a very long minute the sound left the kastron and was amplified among the surrounding crags, finally assaulting the Roman forces like a dry, biting, nerve-scraping wind. Then the scream lifted into the sky and became pure and clear: sheer human terror. The body flew against the lightening sky, arms and legs milling madly. For a moment it seemed to succeed in gaining desperate flight.

Then it plunged sickeningly, the scream lowering in pitch and ending with the sound of a bag of wet sand smashing into a wooden wall. Naked, arms akimbo like a huge, pitiful, plucked bird, the body lay on the rocks in front of the Roman formation. The head was cocked perpendicular to the spine; Blymmedes walked forward and gently lifted it. Haraldr did not know the man at first because the facial skin had been slit at the forehead and peeled off like a rabbit's pelt. Then he saw the eyes, terror still intact. Leo, the Empress's eunuch.

Blymmedes faced the Citadel. A figure stood framed in a crenellation just above the thick wooden main gate. The Seljuk's white silk seemed to have a phosphorescent corona. He called down in a powerful voice that bounded stridently off the rocks. The mandator translated.

"His name is Kilij. He is the leader of these Seljuks. He says withdraw or he will see if the woman can fly any better than the eunuch." Cold hands knotted Haraldr's intestines. He struggled with a maddening urge to run forward and settle with Kilij. But no. The plan. He must meet this Kilij.

Blymmedes and Haraldr discussed Kilij's ultimatum with animated gestures, just the type of argument among commanders one might expect before a cowardly retreat. After a few minutes Haraldr stomped angrily to the rear. Blymmedes gave the order to withdraw. Within minutes the cavalry and the Varangians were winding down the narrow, dusty road to Harim. Haraldr could hear the Seljuks jeering from the walls, and the cold hands made the knots ever tighter.

† † †

Grettir squinted. The sun was now a golden globe just resting on the kastron's east wall, preparing to break loose and float into the sky. The mist had contracted into purplish streaks in the shadowed ravines. Grettir stepped forward proudly and gratefully. Odin had favored him by sparing his leader, Haraldr Si—no, Nordbrikt, if he so wished, and by giving his tongue Grettir this chance to atone for his stupid treachery. The eagle-feeding Saracen-Slayer had asked for the most amusing man among them, and Grettir had been a virtually unanimous choice. Well, it was true; a skald who skinned onions for half a year had to become a prankster or he would drown in his own tears. Besides, as Odin's din hastener had told him, today his humor would be worth a thousand swords. Judging that he was just outside bowshot, Grettir cocked his big knife-edged hat and stepped onto his stage, a patch of fairly even ground illuminated by a sun that had now been freed to the pond-blue sky. *This morning I'll teach even mischief-making Loki a thing or two,* Grettir told himself, hoping to calm his quaking hands.

Haraldr waited at the base of the sheer drop beneath the east walls of the kastron. When he heard the dim but clearly perceptible sound of a human imitating, with comic hyperbole, the crow of a cock, he turned to Halldor. "Good. Grettir has begun." Haraldr looked two hundred ells up the crusty face of the cliff. Wafting slightly in the breeze, the rope ladders hung like glorious braids in the dazzling sun. Haraldr clapped Joli Stefnir-son and his brother, Hord, on the back and winked at Ulfr. "I told you that any man from Geiranger can climb like a goat. But Joli and Hord can fly. They are Norway's eagles, and today they will bring us Seljuk meat." Next Haraldr checked on the preparations of a single Roman infantry-man, who carried an apparatus the Domestic had called a "fire blower." This was a long brass tube attached to a leather bladder worn on the back. The infantryman carried the hollow tube in his hands and had a wood-and-leather bellows strapped under his left arm; tapers tipped with some incendiary substance used to ignite the liquid fire were stuck in his belt. "Let's give Grettir enough time to win his audience," Haraldr told the clustered, eager-eyed Varangians.

Grettir skipped drunkenly; dozens of arrows bristled the ground a few steps in front of him. Doffing his hat with exaggerated gestures of defer-ence, Grettir veered toward the arrows with freakish bounding steps, stopped suddenly as he encountered the feathered shafts, teetered for-ward while waving his arms as if he were about to pitch into an abyss, then staggered backward before tripping over his flapping legs, tumbling into a heap, and starting all over again. The Seljuks, at first incredulous at the assault of this single addle-brained infidel, had begun to join in the game, sending down their arrows every time Grettir lurched close. Grettir saluted the salvos with increasingly elaborate flourishes of his silly hat. The jeering Seljuks soon crowded the walls.

Suddenly Grettir dropped his hat and jerked his head up as if a rope were pulling against his neck. Swiveling his head on his distended neck, he reached down and clutched at his crotch, then began increasingly vigorous scratching motions. The Seljuks howled with laughter. Grettir turned his back to the walls, pulled from beneath his tunic the specially shaped pig bladder he had contrived and pumped his hips and jerked his free hand up and down as he blew into the bladder. When he had the device inflated and in place, he turned with his arms wide. The Seljuks shrieked with delight and began an immediate chorus of trilling observations. Grettir surged wildly with his hips, showing off a pig-bladder phallus as long as a man's arm, complete with a melon-size scrotum.

Grettir continued to stalk with his absurd giant steps, his hips pumping in enormous circular motions. Within minutes the Seljuks had several of their concubines up on the walls, stripped naked and gyrating their pelvises in reply to Grettir's prodigious thrusts. The walls swarmed with Seljuks now; they jammed the crenellated openings and balanced on top of the merlons. One warrior fell from his perch and lay in a cream-colored heap at the base of the wall; no one even noticed. "Loki," Grettir said aloud, as happy as he had ever been, "I have shamed you."

At the base of the cliff Haraldr could clearly hear the rising din of mirth. He started up the rope ladder first, followed by Halldor, Ulfr, the fire blower, and then a gradual procession that ultimately would total a hundred picked men. Haraldr climbed quickly, repeating the phrases the Mandator had taught him and reflecting on the strange hilarity that accompanied their grim ascent. He soon reached the jagged rock lip at the summit; he gripped the stone and easily pulled himself over the natural obstacle.

The lance blurred by him and he heard Halldor grunt. Haraldr swung his shield to his front and looked back. Halldor hung by one hand, his face gushing blood. Haraldr's shield took a blow and he had to turn. His sword lifted the Seljuk into the air and sent him flailing into the gorge. Haraldr crouched atop the rock lip. He could see right through the crenellation into the walled town. As if the kastron were a box tipped to one side, every man in the city seemed to have spilled onto the west wall or stood below it, waiting for an opportunity to view Grettir's performance; apparently only a single guard had remained posted along the entire east wall. Haraldr surveyed the route he intended to take as the others began to gather beside him. Halldor's face was severely gashed. "Can you go on?" asked Haraldr.

"They didn't cut my legs off," snapped Halldor.

Haraldr dropped to the gray-brick pathway atop the wall. They already had twenty-five men on top now; enough. The rest should be able to join them quickly. Flanked by Halldor and Ulfr, Haraldr took his ax with one hand, set his shield, and positioned the Roman with the fire blower almost against his back.

The first Seljuks to notice the Varangian invaders were lost in the clamor near the center of the west wall. Haraldr could see them distinctly, pounding and tugging at their fellows like miniature actors in a raucous comedy. Then a few more Seljuks began to turn, but most were held rapt by Grettir and the naked mime of their whores. When the Varangian phalanx reached the southwest corner of the kastron, they met the unwary Seljuk spectators like a whirring, relentless steel engine.

The carnage was apalling; hastily produced scimitars did almost nothing to deter the Varangian advance. The first Seljuks to fall screamed their oaths to Allah or simply ululated with surprise, but their distress was blanketed by the blaring revelry of their fellows. Only after dozens had pitched off the battlements did the change in tenor begin to spread orchestrally north, to the center of the wall, but the crowding made a concerted defense impossible. Only the sheer weight of frantic bodies began to stop the Varangian push. Haraldr shouted to the infantryman armed with the fire blower.

The long brass tube, a glowing taper now fastened to the tip, jutted past Haraldr's shield, a phallus far more obscene than the pig bladder Grettir still played with below. Haraldr grimaced against the intense heat as the fire streamed out. The molten lance virtually seemed to blow a hole in the first Seljuk, then splattered; Haraldr quickly stomped his boots to shake off the singeing droplets. The spout of flame swept in a slow arc across the breadth of the battlements, quickly extending its reach as flaming Seljuks plunged from the wall. Within seconds the Seljuks began to leap well in advance of the fiery tongue. When the liquid was exhausted, Haraldr looked ahead, just past the blackened bricks that defined the fire blower's deadly range. Waiting for him was an armored guard cordoning the white-silk-clad figure of Kilij. With Ulfr and Halldor at his side, and now almost a hundred Varangians on the walls behind him, Haraldr pushed forward across the scorched bricks. The Seljuk guards died quickly, their elegant scimitars and oaths to Allah no match for Hunland steel and Odin's fury.

"Kilij," said Haraldr. He handed his shield to Ulfr and gripped his ax with both hands. He had already calculated that the next arc of his blade would be perhaps more fateful than the blow that had killed Hakon, and yet he did not need Odin to strengthen his arm, only to assuage his fears. Before he had climbed to these walls, he had been certain that when Kilij's head rolled into the streets, his Seljuk followers would immediately give up their cause and their captives. But now that wager seemed far less certain.

The Seljuk leader was viciously handsome, his dark, sharp features framed with a dense beard and a beautiful engraved silver helm. Holding Haraldr's blade with his eyes, Kilij slowly knelt, removed his helm, and began a recitation punctuated with many Allahs. Haraldr ignored the appeal and stepped forward, conscious that if he had erred in his judgment, he would never escape these walls alive. He caught the Seljuk's night-filled eyes and in Odin's ancient voice recited the phrase that the Mandator had taught him. The words were said to mean, "I am the Avenging Angel."

Kilij lowered his forehead to bricks speckled with the blood of his guards. Atop the walls, the silence was now complete. From the city below came the wails of badly burned men. Haraldr told Halldor to hold Kilij's head up. Halldor yanked on the glossy black hair, bringing the dark face to that of the golden angel. Kilij's pupils became antic flying insects seeking escape from a doomed head. Haraldr lifted his ax high, his own fate as tentative as his victim's.

To the left, down in the town below, Kilij's desperate eyes found their sanctuary. He lifted his head defiantly and his left arm shot out, a gold-ringed finger pointing. He smiled wickedly.

Down below, on the street just inside the gate, another Seljuk ululated insanely. Kneeling at his feet was a woman in a white silk robe, her raven hair long and undone. The Seljuk who had cried out jerked the flowing tresses and forced the face of the kneeling figure to look up. Instantly numb, his upraised ax suddenly freighted with the huge burden of this revelation, Haraldr could only murmur the name once, somewhere in the last redoubt of his reason. Maria.

A second Seljuk stepped forward, touched a heavy-bladed scimitar to Maria's neck, then raised the blade to the sky. The swordsman looked up to the walls, and Kilij grinned like death. The exchange was now stated in terms so graphic that no language would be needed. The life of Kilij for the life of the Roman woman.

Maria did not lower her head, nor did Haraldr lower his ax. Their eyes met, her blue fires perhaps pleading, perhaps challenging, clearly questioning him. A simple instinct bound his arms for a heartbeat, and then he listened to some vastly more profound intuition. He found the answer he would give her beyond love, beyond death, somewhere amid the black ice of eternity.

The only sensation Haraldr felt as his ax descended in a whooshing arc was the slight vibration of Kilij's skull splitting and the virtually simultaneous cracking of his coccyx. The ax clanged on brick.

Halldor held the two halves of Kilij together at the shoulders, but feces and bowels still gushed onto the bricks, and the neat seam along his chest spurted blood. In the courtyard the Seljuk executioner wearily lowered and then dropped his scimitar, stunned by his leader's demise and utterly astonished at the huge golden demon's ferocious disregard for the life of the woman second only to the prophet Christ's mother. It was so quiet that the sound of the Seljuk's blade clattering to the street seemed like a small rock slide. The Seljuk who held Maria's hair let it slip from his fingers like a bewitched man watching the gold in his hands turn to sand. Her face radiant, her cheeks and neck flushed as if with lovemaking, Maria stood and stared at the vision on the walls above her.

Haraldr pulled his ax free. With each hand he grabbed a lock of Kilij's hair but saw that the scalp would simply pull away from the skull. He found a grip on each side of Kilij's neck. He lifted, oblivious to the horrifying scent of the spilling organs. His arms swooping wide like the giant-taloned wings from Nidafell, Haraldr raised the butchered halves of Kilij, turned to face the courtyard, and stood with arms out and elbows locked, like a hunter displaying a brace of rabbits. "I am the Avenging Angel," he told the Seljuks in their language. "I have come for my Mother."

The Seljuks' billowing robes seemed to collapse like felled tents as every man among them threw himself to the ground and pressed his lips to the dust. A frightening silence followed this huge rustling homage to the terrible golden avenger. Only one person remained standing within the Citadel, her brilliant face still lifted to Haraldr, her gem-blue eyes telling him that she was the fate to whom he had just given his reply.

o one present could remember having seen the Senator and Magister Nicon Attalietes walk for at least ten years. But the old man, his spine grotesquely conformed to the shape of the chairs in which he spent his days and nights, hobbled to the window. He placed his thick, gouty fingers against the marble-reveted recess and pushed his deformed nose toward the glass. He hacked wetly as he always did before he spoke. Everyone quieted. Despite his massive chest and the leonine growl with which he habitually cleared his throat, the Senator and Magister Nicon Attalietes had a voice like a whisper beside a grave. "Dogs, whores, lepers. Look how they lick their adulterous mother's pustulant afterbirth."

Attalietes shuffled around to face his retinue. His thin white hair curled slightly at the nape of his neck, and his gray beard fell in sagacious disorder to his chest. A large purple blotch spread over his broad, nut-colored forehead; his nose and cheek below his left eye were scarred by surgeries to remove similar skin malignancies. Several years ago Attalietes had sent for a specialist in facial restorations from Alexandria but had dismissed the man for reasons he would never discuss. The Senator and Magister Nicon Attalietes was not accustomed to giving reasons.

"You get over here." He jerked his swollen hand at his son, Ignatius, as if he were strangling a chicken.

Ignatius Attalietes had the same indolent features as his late brother, Meletius, but as he preferred to avoid altogether the salutary effects of outdoor exercise—having hit his head badly while taking instruction at polo as a very young boy—he had a particularly spectral pallor. Boils spotted his forehead and nose, as if some mysterious demonic force had directed his skin to emulate his father's afflictions. He lowered his head and minced toward his father.

"Get over here, you spineless milksop." Attalietes batted his son's ear. "Mele's dead and you wring your wrists like the capons at court. Mele would have sent that holy turd a pile of their whoreson noses. But you. You tell me what you see."

Ignatius inclined slightly toward the window with the vertiginous sense of a man looking into an abyss. He could see all he needed to see. Three stories below, the street was solid rabble, and for that matter every street as far as he could see down to the distant pale square of the Forum Bovis was jammed with the clamoring beasts. They were disgusting, the terrible anonymity of their ragged, brown-tunicked poverty. It was as if the sewers beside their tenements had flooded, and now the feculent sludge had filled the streets. They had set fires at many of the intersections, and the smudgy pillars were choking off the sun, deepening the vile coloration of the scene. Ignatius didn't care anymore. He was frightened. He began to sob softly beside his father's wheezing face.

Attalietes decided not to humiliate his son further. What was the use? As much as Ignatius was a coward, Mele—he still could not believe it—Meletius had been a fool. What was he doing south of Antioch in the vanguard of the slut's escort? No doubt the holy turd, Joannes, and his sexless brother, Constantine, were laughing richly over Mele's corpse. And now this. Oh, the black-frocked excrement's slimy hands are all over this, certainly. *Damn fool,* Attalietes thought, admonishing himself. *I should have withdrawn to Arcadiopolis or Nicomedia when I heard of the whore's abduction.* But there was so much to do here, what with the plunging value of land in Cilicia and Teluch and Lycandus. My God, even Armenikoi has shown some downward trends. Too much to do, too much possible still. God is so cruel. When Nicon Attalietes had been young and vigorous, Basil the Bulgar-Slayer had limited the universe of the Dhynatoi to polo and banquets and hunts. Those luxuries had cost the Dhynatoi more of their vitality than if they had rebelled and had been cast into the Numera or Neorion. But now, when there was so much to be taken, so much simply waiting to be plucked, there were only feeble old men without the strength to grasp it, and callow youths without the courage to reach for it. Perhaps Mele would have been the one to extend the Dhynatoi's grasp again, Attalietes silently lamented. But Mele is dead and the mob is at the door.

"Manganes." Isaac Manganes, a short, Asiatic-featured man who glowed like an icon in his robe of Hellas silk, came to the window. A former middle-level military commander from Armenikoi who had been denied promotion by less competent superiors, Manganes had begun working for Attalietes as manager of several estates in Armenikoi. He had proved himself so much more able than the network of cousins, nephews, and—yes, sons—who supervised most of Attalietes's properties that he had soon risen to overseer of all the Asiatic estates. When the position of Strategus of Cilicia had been purchased for Meletius, Manganes had been summoned to the Empress City to become the elder Attalietes's next-in-command, with responsibility for the enormous body of day-to-day details the old man didn't like to bother with. That is the plight of the Dhynatoi now, thought Attalietes as Manganes came to his side. To have to depend on the lowborn for our survival. Well, at least Manganes appreciated the luxuries to which he had become accustomed.

"I have to tell you, the situation is hopeless." Manganes knew his patron preferred blunt talk to the florid dissimulations one heard at court. That, less than health concerns, was why the old warrior had not entered the Chalke Gate to the Imperial Palace for perhaps five years. Besides, as Attalietes always said, "Why should I go to his palace and endure his strutting capons and branded felons when I have a dozen of my own palaces?" Unfortunately, considered Manganes as he watched the mob surge against the gates of Attalietes's vast hilltop residence, this palace is about to sacked and burned by the unclean horde. Unless . . . Well, the old man will have to suggest it first. There are some things a hireling from Armenikoi can never say.

"You've considered . . . everything?" Attalietes's black-streaked white eyebrows quivered as he faced Manganes.

"Senator, it has been well conceived. The . . . duping of Meletius, the abduction of the Empress, the dispatch of the Grand Domestic and the rest of the Imperial Taghmata to recover the purple-born. You'll recall that I cautioned against the reduction in your personal guard even though we were all convinced that under the Grand Domestic Bardas Dalassena the Imperial Taghmata had become our personal guard. This is just the sort of eventuality I was concerned about. As long as the Taghmata is under the authority of the Emperor, our assurances of its protection cannot be absolute."

"All right, Manganes, you've made enough noise shutting the gate I left open." Attalietes wheezed irritably. "Why can't we buy off the mob's leaders? Surely the walking dung heap has not paid this stinking herd so well?"

"Senator, the Orphanotrophus Joannes has a unique system of inducements. In his one hand he offers the carrot: his orphanages and charity hospitals. Entirely inadequate for the demands on them but sufficient to offer hope. In the other hand Joannes carries his whip. Neorion. And of course, in this matter an even more powerful force is at work."

Attalietes nodded slightly. The purple-born harlot. *His* legacy. Attalietes could still see the Bulgar-Slayer strutting before the Sacrum Consistorum, hands thrust against his hips, pausing to twirl his black beard as he pondered the next advance of Rome's borders. The arrogance of his simplicity! Throwing away his purple robes and rings and diadems to receive his supplicants bareheaded in a tunic the color of ashes. Always surrounded by his *barbaroi* goons, as if he could not trust his own courtiers; it was he who had invited the fair-hair menace to the very bedchamber of Roman power. His lifelong hatred for the Dhynatoi was evident in every rough, clipped utterance, in every brutal, larcenous action. His vicious Novel No. 29, forcibly returning estates of the Dhynatoi to the dull-witted slovens who had not maintained them in the first place! Why hadn't the Bulgar-Slayer seen the true glory the highborn would have afforded him if only he had included them in his vision of Rome. Instead the glowering, ruthlessly simple despot had raised his throne on the offal of peasants and laborers.

"No one can buy their devotion from the purple-born," emphasized Manganes. He coughed deliberately and dared to prompt the inevitable. "Still, even the purple-born has her enemies. We have ample proof of that in this conspiracy in which we have become pawns."

Attalietes turned slowly from the window and with laborious motions and rasping breath returned to his gilt-and-velvet chair. His brilliantly robed retinue faced him from a respectful distance: two elderly senators; his useless nephew, Manuel; four glorified accountants with what seemed to the old man almost uniformly pinched, narrow faces and squinting, myopic eyes; his eunuch chamberlain; and the obligatory staff of three additional fluttering capons. If any sight could compel the unprecedented step he was about to take, they were such an epiphany. Yes, their faces told him what he had long suspected but until now would not admit. The Dhynatoi could no longer stand alone. They would have to make an alliance. An alliance with the Devil. But which Devil?

Attalietes rattled the phlegm in his throat. "Well," he said, exhaling, "you have all read the proposals from the two extortionists who have offered to save us from the mob. What do you think, if that is not asking the impossible?"

Manganes surveyed the numb faces and coughed again. "Senator, we know the Hetairarch has the lesser ambition."

"I know the Hetairarch," offered Ignatius with a sudden brightening. "We have spoken about horses three or four times. He is very civilized."

"Yes." Fools, thought Attalietes. Manganes is too young to have seen the Varangian victories at Scutari and Abydos, the victories that had saved the throne of the Bulgar-Slayer. What dung! He had been no Bulgar-Slayer, just a Varangian payer. And now this *barbaroi* Hetairarch who was far too civilized for anyone's good. Fools.

The white-haired, immaculately groomed Senator and Magister Romanus Scylitzes spoke up. Owner of huge chunks of the themes Thessalonica and Dyrrachium, his speech reeked with presumed Hellenistic elegance. "My esteemed colleague, virtuous mentor, and indefatigable paramount. Might I offer a deduction of my own? I declare the Orphanotrophus the inferior source of jeopardy, offering these substantiations. The Orphanotrophus and his egregiously purple-clad sibling suffer from the dilute blood of the plebian classes. Because they are not conditioned to the obligations required by their station, they will rapidly weary of their lofty occupations. Suffering from languishment and irresolutions due to these exhaustions, the midnight-cloaked will be forced to gesture forth with his own hand, not in augur of our own despoliation, but suppliantly, in reciprocation of the gesture he would have us perform today, though vastly exacerbated against restraint."

Insufferable, turd-spewing windbag. Joannes hardly needs an hour's sleep each night and his brother has the endurance of a pack mule. As usual, it was pointless to counsel with these parasites. An old man would decide the way an old man best decides. With his ancient, ulcerous, churning gut. And that decision had already been made. "Chamberlain. Send my secretary." Attalietes raised and shook his bloated fist. "The rest of you, get out."

† † †

Children hid behind their mothers' rough wool tunics. Men stared with wooden fright and then lowered their gaze to the littered paving stones as the man on the black horse came close enough for his swollen, immense face to reach out and mark them. Joannes was on the streets.

The clamoring died in inevitable sequence as the black-cloaked monk ascended the rise to the palace of the Senator and Magister Nicon Attalietes. The great, hollow stillness that preceded the Orphanotrophus Joannes like some force of nature was neither sullen nor reverent but profoundly respectful. Who did not have a friend or neighbor or relative who had received free treatment in one of the Orphanotrophus's hospitals? And who did not know of someone who had vanished in the night?

As was his custom, Joannes rode alone. He dismounted in front of the brass-ornamented oak gate of the Attalietes palace. Rough hands came tremulously forward to gently hold the halter of the Joannes's horse and stroke the animal's quivering obsidian flanks, as if in assuaging this great beast they could somehow gain favor with the other.

"Orphanotrophus." Attalietes's chamberlain bowed deeply. The arcade led through a courtyard in the style of a Moorish palace from Iberia, a glittering fantasy of gold and lapis lazuli and checkered ceramic tiles and azure pools flecked with crimson fish. Joannes enjoyed the irony of his monochrome intrusion in this brilliant setting. He was a moving shroud, his black breast a sepulcher for an old man's dreams. He would enjoy crushing Nicon Attalietes. There were only two people on earth whose destruction would give him more pleasure.

The silver doors emblazoned with virtually life-size embossed lions slid open. Joannes almost gasped. Unbelievable. Attalietes did not style himself a mere emperor, the chosen hand of God. No, his ambition exceeded even that blasphemy.

Attalietes sat enthroned in the middle of a vast hall; the golden tesserae that covered the dome high above him glittered like the sun. Flanking the gilded throne, which resembled a small chapel in its ornate architecture, were long, gold-tiled pools lined with a carved stone menagerie spouting dazzling sprays of water. As he came forward Joannes marveled at the mathematical intricacy of the floor, the way the scrolls of rose and white marble created fantastic three-dimensional patterns against a background of gold-serpentined green marble and black onyx.

"Orphanotrophus." Attalietes's eyes were like stone. The tombs of hope, thought Joannes.

"Brother." Joannes used the greeting that would most offend Attalietes, the salute he would offer any of the rabble outside.

"At what price do we purchase our lives?"

Joannes slapped his leg with his riding crop. "With what would you pay, Brother Attalietes? You borrowed from Nicephorus Argyrus's arguoprates to buy most of Cilicia and Armenikoi. I understand that the merchant Argyrus instructed his agents to charge you the usurious rate of twelve percent."

Attalietes thought he would choke on his welling phlegm. It had been humiliating enough to have to shake hands with a man like Argyrus, a man whose hands were stained so deeply with the filth of commerce that they would never be clean no matter how many silk robes he donned or palaces he built.

"I have instructed the merchant Argyrus that I will remit the penalty for his usurious exaction if he will immediately bring his promissories due." Joannes gleefully watched as the old man's face colored to the extent that his skin lesions were hardly noticeable.

Attalietes didn't know the exact figures and he didn't need to. He had rushed to acquire the vast holdings in Teluch and Cilicia when he had learned of the imminent accord with Caliph Moustanir Billah, and then on top of that the office of Strategus of Cilicia had opened and had brought a damnable price—at first in solidi, then in the incalculable loss of his son—and then the untimely demise of the Senator Andronicus Cametus, leaving the old pederast's estates in Armenikoi available at an enticing discount. Yes, each acquisition had made good sense at the time. But now, with the plunging value of land all along the Saracen frontier, the arithmetic of disaster led to an inevitable solution. He could not meet the damnable merchant's notes even if he sold everything.

Attalietes lifted his thick fingers from the skulls of the golden lions that snarled at the arms of his throne. "Since I cannot pay this debt in solidi, what currency do you ask?"

"Complicity." Joannes lowered his black, wiry brows. "You and the entire Attalietes clique in the Senate."

Attalietes felt cool, soothing air surge into his burning, gasping lungs. Was there a way to work with the Orphanotrophus Joannes? The fact that the huge black capon did not simply let the mob do its work was evidence that he did not consider his own power secure. Might the monk be willing to compromise? Might they eventually arrive at shared goals? "How could an old man reduced to penury share your lofty visions, Orphanotrophus?"

"Obliquity does not suit your delivery, Brother Attalietes," admonished Joannes in his menacing rumble; he was pleased, however, that the beast he was about to yoke still had enough spirit to be useful. "I offer you this, in brief form. You will donate to the offices of the Orphanotrophus two thirds of your entire holdings in Europe and Asia. Nicephorus Argyrus will forgive the debt on your remaining properties in exchange for the monopoly he is about to be granted on trade with Venice, Amalfi, and the Rus. And in gratitude for your generous donation to the indigent of our city, taxes on the estates still held in your name will be excused by beneficium for a period of ten years. I believe that when these transactions are completed, I will find myself with an ally who is more fiscally powerful than ever. And wealthier in wisdom as well."

Attalietes wheezed with relief. Life was still sweet. Tonight he would ask the Khazar girl to take him in her soft lips and let him feel the bursting ecstasy of his youth. He blinked away the tears and saw the monstrous face through a golden haze of hope. "I am in your debt, Orphanotrophus."

"I will make certain that you remember, Brother." Joannes turned and found his way out without escort. The mob hushed again as the gate swung open and the Orphanotrophus reappeared. Joannes quickly mounted and wheeled to face the expectant throng.

"God has granted me the privilege of announcing to the blessed children of our Sacred Empress news of the most extraordinary miracle. Yesterday, Christian warriors led by the Archangel himself and that dauntless foe of heresy, the Strategus of Antioch, challenged the devil-worshiping hordes and effected the rescue of our Mother! Our Mother returns to us!"

The din of the joyous response made Joannes's head ache, and he struggled to maintain his concentration as he headed through the wildly cheering, praying, and sobbing crowd. Almost by some divine intercession petals began to drift like snow to the pavement before him, strewn by hands that only seconds before had clutched stones and staves.

Remarkable, reflected Joannes, no longer giving thought to the celebration swirling around him like a cyclone. Two very remarkable things. The astonishing rescue of the slut; Joannes had been prepared for a much lengthier period of negotiation. The result was certainly not undesirable, though it had proven quite prudent to have moved quickly to incite the rabble against Attalietes; the scum hardly would have been so vehement if they had known their precious slattern was safe. But who had executed this miraculous deliverance? Of course, not Constantine, though it was reassuring to know that apparently he had not sabotaged the endeavor. Blymmedes? That might be a problem, since Blymmedes was known to disapprove of the Grand Domestic Bardas Dalassena, and now Attalietes's soldier-stooge belonged to Joannes. Was it possible? Well, the Tauro-Scythian Haraldr Nordbrikt was already celebrated for his martial escapades, and indeed he might be the most likely hero out of all this, though of course Constantine would have to receive official precedence. How incredible that would be. It would be as if fortune had blessed Joannes again, considering the other remarkable discovery of the previous night.

Quite extraordinary. The Logothete of the Dromus had brought him a transcript of the letter the Hetairarch Mar Hunrodarson had dispatched to the unfortunate Senator Attalietes; the Senator's son, Ignatius, often surrendered such information in exchange for the Logothete's collusion in the matter of young Attalietes's appetite for well-formed officers of the Scholae. Hunrodarson's letter had offered his Varangians to relieve the siege of Attalietes's palace. A simple mercenary transaction? No, Hunrodarson would have known of Attalietes's acute shortage of solidi—the *barbaroi* was friends with Argyrus—and so he had sought the same medium of exchange that Joannes had just secured. Simply remarkable. The Hetairarch Mar Hunrodarson was announcing his ambitions, apparently for all to see. Hunrodarson was not a foolish man, either; what could possibly have prompted this impudent assurance on his part? Well, no matter. Let Mar Hunrodarson dream. The hero, Haraldr Nordbrikt—and he would be a hero even if he had tried to defect to the Saracens—would now be a formidable rival to the Hetairarch. Yes, Joannes's instrument would return from Asia more finely honed than ever. And how pleasurable it will be, thought Joannes as the petals flew around him like a blizzard, to see the two overinflated Tauro-Scythian *barbaroi* impale themselves on each other's blades.

araldr Nordbrikt, you must know that I am hardly expert in these matters." Gregory blushed, almost restoring the sun-flamed color that had begun to fade in the last few weeks. "That is, I have no practical experience. Of course, one hears many things if one is curious about the subtleties of language. And, well . . . I confess that I have read some of the romances in the corrupt vernacular. Only to relieve the stress of studying serious literature, of course."

Haraldr looked over the misty plain of the River Sangarius, his amber-tinted face a vivid contrast to fields now dulled with winter. He wrapped his woolen cloak about his shoulders and enjoyed an internal warmth. By tonight he would have memorized every endearment, every anatomically explicit term the Greek language had incorporated in the eons since Alexander had marched east to the land of the Brahmans.

Ahead, the Imperial carriages were gilt and scarlet lamps in the midday gloom. Farther beyond, the bright standards of Constantine's thematic army were already lost in the leaden pall. Until today the retreat from Antioch had been strangely foreboding, in spite of every reason for celebration. Of course, the pilgrimage had been terminated after the Empress's harrowing ordeal; clearly the Saracen guarantees of safe passage were worthless. Haraldr had held his guard in constant battle readiness until five days ago, when the Imperial party had come as far west as Ancyra, where Saracens had not penetrated for centuries. And Blymmedes still sent out two reconnaissance vanda well before each dreary dawn. Even Constantine, who had been so dilatory before the abduction, had insisted on contributing his thematic army to Her Imperial Majesty's safekeeping and now quite obviously intended to personally command the escort all the way to the Empress City. Certainly his principal motive was to reap an undeserved share of the credit for Her Majesty's deliverance, but nevertheless he had taken his command seriously on the return journey.

Apparently the Empress had suffered greatly from her captivity. She had seemed well enough and at ease when she had received her champions after her rescue; Constantine, Blymmedes, Haraldr, and Kalaphates had all been honored with gifts of robes and solidi and profusely grateful benedictions from the lovely Imperial lips. But then the Empress had plunged into deepest seclusion. Each day she ordered the carriages to begin their creaking advance before dawn and would not command halt until the tinted twilight had begun to char into the smothering blackness of the Anatolian night. Then she would disembark directly into her tent. Symeon had turned into a fierce, ancient reptile, hissing at the merest suggestion of an intrusion on her Majesty's privacy. Even Kala-phates, who had recovered sufficiently from his mostly superficial wounds to join his uncle's retinue, had not been permitted to see his Blessed Mother.

And Maria. Since their eyes had met that terrible and beautiful morn-ing, nothing. For six weeks now, no word—not even a glimpse of her silk slippers. Just the memory of what had passed between them in that moment when love and death had embraced over the great abyss of time. They were still together, plunging into a blackness lit only by the torch of their joined souls. That was the truth she could not confront.

Until now. Haraldr put his hand to the message he had placed against his heart. "Tonight," she had written, "I will send for you."

† † †

"Komes." Haraldr was doubly shocked. He had not expected the Em-press, and not in this setting.

Glowing braziers offered the only light, and a dry, clean, aromatic heat. Everything was tinted red; the Empress's lips were like fresh blood. Zoe curled on the cushions like a panther; there was a sense of power, even viciousness, latent in her lithe limbs. And there was much of her limbs to see. The sheerest lilac silk, hardly more opaque than the drizzling mist outside, clung to her breasts and hips. Haraldr helplessly noticed that his Blessed Mother's nipples were large, flat areolae.

"Komes Haraldr." The voice was like liquid desire. "Can you speak without your little tongue?"

Haraldr had been asked to come without the ubiquitous Gregory; now he was grateful for the concentration Greek required. "Yes. I have learned a great deal on this long road."

"Yes, you have," Zoe said, enunciating carefully. "I am impressed by your fluency."

Haraldr thanked Christ's Father, Lord God, for the many tongues he had created in his tower at Babel. The barrier of language seemed to take the seduction out of Her Imperial Majesty's voice. "It is my intention to become, as you Romans say, 'civilized.'"

Zoe's eyebrows quivered and set with a slightly elevated arch. "Yes. But you must retain the . . . impetuousness of your race. I believe I owe my present comfort, if not my very life, to your . . . instincts. I want to thank you more properly and more privately." A serving eunuch brought wine in response to some signal Haraldr had missed.

Haraldr took his goblet. Perspiration began to bead on his back but he felt a certain stimulation. Maria had proven herself fond of such preludes. Then he almost choked. Christ! Citron! Surely he was not intended to use the Empress as he had Citron?

"So, Komes Haraldr." Zoe raised her goblet, her smooth white arm compressing her ample breast. The nipple had now become slightly erect. "Let us raise a cup to your future as a civilized man. And let us hope that you do not become too civilized."

Suddenly Zoe stood, and Haraldr scrambled out of the couch and onto his knees, his head bowed as prescribed by protocol. He could hear the Empress swish toward him. He closed his eyes in terror like a man expecting the blade to kiss his neck. The Imperial fingers tousled his hair like a breeze. "Golden silk," she said, her voice frightening, but only in its sorrow. Then the touch of the purple-born fingers was gone. Eyes shut tight, Haraldr again heard silk rustle.

"You may rise, Komes Haraldr," said Theodore in his droning tenor. Haraldr stood and crossed his arms over his breast. Zoe waited by the curtained brocade partition, apparently to take leave of her guest. She was now wrapped in a glistening black sable cape faced with purple satin.

"Komes, am I a fool to be certain of your loyalty?"

"We would both be fools if you could not be certain of that loyalty." Haraldr's unhesitating pledge brought him not even an inkling of anxiety; in the long, monotonous weeks since the rescue he had allayed many of his suspicions. The Romans, he had concluded, were more incompetent than treacherous; when the arrows had begun to fly, they had defended their Empress with absolute unanimity. The sorely misjudged Attalietes certainly had been a colossal blunderer, but ultimately he had given his life to defend the Empress. Constantine was equally inept, but had he truly conspired against the Empress, he would have obstructed or opposed Blymmedes's rescue mission, rather than approving it and in fact facilitating it with his temporary withdrawal. And Joannes's nephew, Michael Kalaphates, had come very close to his own mortality fighting at the door of the Empress's carriage. Certainly the Romans had their internecine feuds—every court did—but in this case it was obvious that the "conspiracy" he had imagined was actually a Seljuk adventure. And as for the attempt on his own life, he still did not discount Mar's involvement, but he was certain that no Roman had sent his would-be assassin.

Zoe fixed Haraldr with the certitude of centuries-old power. Her seductive lips became muscular, shaping her words as if they were to be carved in stone. "Komes, Maria is coming for you. She has much of which to speak with you. But she will also ask a question in my name." Head erect, Zoe vanished in a whisper of sable and silk.

Theodore ushered Haraldr back to the lavishly cushioned couch. He waited, smothered in down and plied with wine, for what seemed an hour. Then the brocade was lifted away and Maria appeared with heart-stopping suddenness. She wore a coat of pale blue silk trimmed with white ermine; the collar of snowy fur came up to her chin, and her skin seemed like the whitest marble against it. Her raven hair was loosely pulled back and set in a single braid.

"I am sorry. Our Mother wished to speak with me." She looked at her slippers, the same white silk with pearl beads that she had worn to the banquet at Antioch. There was no intimacy in her voice. It was as if Hecate—Haraldr sucked in a breath almost audibly at the memory of what lay beneath that coat—had never happened. "We are only two days from Nicaea. In a week we will be in the Queen of Cities. I long for my home. Do you miss your home?"

"Yes." For the first time in weeks Haraldr thought of the debt he must pay to the kings in whose footsteps he followed. And yet how could he leave her now?

"Do you remember the stadium in Daphne?"

"Yes. I remember everything at Daphne."

Perhaps her cheeks became more deeply tinted, perhaps it was the play of the braziers on her usual glow. "Together we heard the echoes, the acclamations to the heroes of ancient Hellas and old Rome. When we return to the Empress City, you will be the hero of new Rome. In the streets they will sing your name." She looked up at him for the first time. The intense blue of her eyes was always a fresh marvel. "Who will one day walk in those ruins, to listen for your name? Will they be as we were, lovers in search of their own fate?"

Haraldr felt the surging in his breast and the stirring in his loins. She acknowledged . . . them. Or was it no longer them but a single being, a new soul born in that terrible instant? "I know my fate," he told her softly.

"Yes. So do I." She stood suddenly. "Come to my bed."

Haraldr struggled to his feet and reached out with a trembling hand.

Maria stepped away. "No. You must promise not to touch me except where I touch you. You cannot ask me except what I ask you." Then she touched his hand with the hot brands of her fingers.

The partitioned chamber in the Imperial Pavilion had room for little more than a large wooden bed frame covered with thick down quilts. There was no light from lamps or braziers but the room was quite warm. Maria stood and held Haraldr's hand in the darkness for several minutes. He could hear her breathe occasionally, but the silence was otherwise absolute. It was as if they were alone in the vastness of Asia Minor. Her touch seemed to fill him with a warm liquor that quickly dissolved his bones.

She dropped his hand, and he could see the motion and hear the sigh of silk as she removed her coat. He could sense that she was naked. Her vague form vanished and the quilts were ruffled by a breeze. From the bed she said, "Come to me like Heracles."

Haraldr stripped as naked as the statue and found his way to the bed. He lay down carefully, unwilling to break the strange spell she was casting. After a few minutes she took his hand again. She sighed, or perhaps it was a muffled, tiny sob. Then she began to explore his arm.

Time became suspended. She traced every vein, every indentation, the outline of every muscle, and he in turn claimed the same territory from her. How long did they float through black oblivion before she stroked his nipple and pressed her satin palm against his huge pectoral? How long before her fingers crept to his belly and his to her wet fur? And then the ritual repeated, this time with lips instead of fingers. They had long ago passed the stars; there was no heat except their own. Finally she held over him, just as she had in Hecate, but this time she lowered her nose to his, the fine-tipped nose he now knew like his own flesh. Perhaps it was a freak of the shadows, perhaps not, but her eyes seemed to light from within and he could see the lapis gleam. "You are my angel," she whispered. "My avenger and my destroyer. I love you." Then she settled and brought him inside her.

How long they rocked on that warm, impossibly brilliant sea, he also did not know. This time it was slow, endless, a complete dissolution of the flesh. At the end they shuddered only slightly but in perfect concert, and ceased to be. They were utterly exhausted.

"Who are you?"

Haraldr started; he must have dozed off. Had it been a dream?

"Who are you? You are no land man from Rus."

Haraldr felt her eyes on him, and reality reconstituting his body, if only because for a moment he had actually considered telling her everything, not merely the cryptic affinity he had offered Serah. But the oaths he had taken to that secret were too strong, the risk too great even for love. And then he realized a stunning new truth, that this new love, Maria, also commanded his silence: In Maria's arms he wanted to remain Haraldr Nordbrikt. In her arms he wanted to end the flight that he had begun at Stiklestad, to stay here among the Romans, to become civilized, to serve his Mother and Father. And to love her, here, forever. He knew that he could not indefinitely share both these loves, Norway and Maria, yet he would lose them both if he told her now. So for now he would offer her the only truth he could. "I cannot tell you who I am."

She wrapped her arms tightly around his back and pressed her lips softly to his neck. He nuzzled her lustrous hair and whispered in her ear. "Who are you?"

Maria kissed Haraldr on the lips and then released him and rolled away from his body. "I do not know," she said.

Her voice was so plaintive that Haraldr reached out for her with pain in his heart. What sorrow was hidden so deeply? But Maria sat on the edge of her bed and draped her coat over her shoulders. "It is almost time to prepare for our day's journey," she said wearily. "You must leave." She turned to face him. "My last question is for our Mother. To it you can reply only yes or no."

Haraldr sat up and stroked the raven's plumage. She threw her arms around him and kissed him fiercely, as if it were her last. And then she pushed him away and stood up, her arms wrapped against some inner cold. "Our Mother asks if you will, when she commands, sever the head of the Imperial Eagle."

eleusate." The eunuch's voice clattered like broken porcelain on the bare marble floor. Mar Hunrodarson lifted himself to his knees in response to the invitation but did not rise to his feet. This was a calculated act of protracted obeisance; the purple-born Augusta Theodora could still look down on him as they spoke. Theodora's thin lips, drawn like a string across her small face, flattened into a wry suggestion of a smile. The pale blue eyes sparkled like ice in the cold room, as if the giant Hetairarch were merely a callow suitor whose attentions Theodora found too fervent and clumsy.

"Hetairarch." Theodora held her arms out and extended her long pale fingers toward the Hetairarch's shoulders, as if she were a conjurer commanding him to rise. Again the eyes flashed, droll and challenging. Theodora turned swiftly and reclined on her couch. *"Keleusate,"* offered the eunuch again; he gestured for Mar to sit on the blue silk couch opposite the Augusta.

"You are accompanying our Father to Thessalonica?" Theodora's question was rhetorical. "How unseemly that he did not greet my sister or her rescuers on their return, leaving their reception to the offices of his brother, Joannes. I understand that he has not even sent her a message of welcome. And now it seems that my sister embarrasses his piety to such a degree that that he must flee to the arms of his saint before he can even look upon her again."

"St. Demetrius has issued our Father an urgent summons," said Mar. He tried to imagine the pain and frustration cloaked behind Theodora's chalky, impassive features. With her reddish-blond hair drawn back into a single tight braid, the Augusta not only looked older than her sister but also, curiously, more innocent; the rumor, widely bandied about by the satirists and street gossips, was that Theodora was still a virgin.

"And while he obeys the summons of his patron he permits his Hetairarch to make his own pilgrimages." Her inflection was acid. "Perhaps customs have changed since I . . . left the palace. I had always assumed that the Hetairarch kept a relentless vigil at His Majesty's side."

"I will rejoin the Imperial procession this evening," said Mar without a hint of apology. "It is often my habit to depute the care of his Imperial Majesty to my lieutenants."

"I see." Theodora's grim lips pursed as they resisted a mocking grin. "You are so often occupied with more important errands." The Augusta looked straight at Mar and then laughed, the throaty, masculine laugh of a woman too clever to really care about her sexuality. "Such an ambitious man. Indeed, haven't I heard of your ambitions . . . somewhere . . . wherever? You know I do not go out much." She fluttered her hand in a gesture of mock femininity. The voice that followed cut like a newly honed blade. "Why do you think I would wish to further your desires?"

Mar composed himself, determined to meet this notoriously direct woman with his own candor. "Because I believe your Majesty and I share a common enemy."

Theodora smiled at Mar as if she were indulging a small child in some elaborate masquerade. "But of course you must know that out here I have no enemies. Only water bugs. And servants who prefer gossip to work."

Mar leaned forward slightly. "Have your tongue-wagging servants told you of the Orphanotrophus Joannes's most recent success?"

Theodora snapped back: "What do you mean, Hetairarch?"

"I know that Joannes engineered the abduction of your sister."

"There are many of us who suspect that."

"I can offer proof."

Theodora considered what use such proof might be to her sister or her mentor, Alexius. Very little, without command of the Imperial Taghmata. But any knowledge of Joannes was a potentially deadly weapon. "Can you produce this evidence?"

"Shall I have Ignatius Attalietes sent to you? He and I had a brief . . . misunderstanding, but I assure you that now his greatest delight is to do what I bid him."

"It will be sufficient for you to speak in his stead, Hetairach. I am well aware of your reputation for thorough interrogation."

Mar went on to describe the plot as revealed in an antechamber of the Numera by the virtually hysterical Ignatius; a few seconds of listening to the screams of some of the other guests had turned the Attalietes scion into a pop-eyed, desperately rambling geyser of information. Enough information to expose the handprints of Joannes all over the entire scheme.

Theodora absorbed Mar's account impassively. When he had finished, she rose quickly and lithely. She walked a half circuit of her apartment's bare, dull marble walls, then stopped to look out an arched window toward the distant city; Constantinople was invisible in the mist. When she turned back to Mar, her face seemed pinched, even smaller than usual. "How would you check Joannes, Hetairarch? You acknowledge his freshly wrought alliance with the Attaliates clique, but you did not mention that Joannes, now equipped with the resources of the Dhynatoi, is sponsoring a rival to you, the Tauro-Scythian who effected the rescue of my sister. This Haraldr whose name is on everyone lips. He has been named Manglavite, and the Middle Hetairia has been expanded to receive his band of cutthroats. Joannes has given him a palace near the Forum of Constantine." She looked at Mar piercingly. "As I told you, my servants have time for nothing but idle chatter." Theodora wondered again if the rumors she had received about Maria's liaison with this Haraldr were true. Of course, it was only one of Maria's caprices, but this one seemed more reckless than usual.

"This Haraldr will soon turn on his patron, Majesty. At my command." Mar reflected on the good fortune that had thwarted his own efforts to have Haraldr Sigurdarson eliminated. When he had learned that Joannes was Haraldr's sponsor—the meeting in Neorion had left no doubt—he had considered the princeling to be far more of a liability than an asset. But in that impetuous decision, Mar now realized, he had behaved like a Norseman, which was not the way to deal with these Romans. Now he could see that Haraldr Sigurdarson was more useful than ever. Vastly so.

"Indeed," said Theodora. "You have persuaded this Haraldr as you did Ignatius Attalietes? I would think one your kind far more resistant to such blandishments than a pathetic Dhynatoi sodomite."

"Even the gods could not save Achilleus once his peculiar vulnerability became known."

"Well. Between your abilities and those of this new Tauro-Scythian Achilleus, whom you alone command, it would seem that we Romans are already as helpless as Isaac upon Abraham's altar. Why offer an alliance to a scorned, indeed discarded, Augusta, when you fair-hairs have merely to let the sword fall? Do you pity me so much? Strange that I never suspected you of charity, Hetairarch." Theodora's mouth worked in minute contractions, and her eyes glistened.

Mar ignored the taunts, as well aware as the purple-born Theodora of the power a Norseman could never acquire no matter how keen his blade or intellect; he would not insult either of them by mentioning it. Instead he would propose a more subtle form of patronage. "Would I be too bold to admit that I envy the friendship you share with the Patriarch of the One True Oecumenical, Orthodox, and Catholic Faith?"

Theodora showed small, uneven teeth. "You have become so much more interesting than when I was previously acquainted with you, Hetairarch. You have become so much more . . . Roman." The corners of her eyes crinkled as she mused on the proposition. Fortunately the Hetairarch had been clever enough not to propose making an Empress of her; Theodora had no intention of challenging her sister, even if Joannes's carefully seeded lies had convinced Zoe otherwise. But consider how profoundly the defense of the One True Faith might be enhanced if the Patriarch Alexius's mighty spiritual sword were joined by the Hetairarch's mighty secular sword.

Theodora signaled her eunuch, Emmanuel. *"Keleusate,"* intoned the tall, important-looking chamberlain. Mar rose and Theodora walked directly up to him, her face vivid, almost girlish. "I shall ask our Patriarch to instruct you in the One True Oecumenical, Orthodox, and Catholic Faith, Hetairarch. Strange that I had always thought you an irretrievable pagan."

† † †

"He is present," whispered the monk, Cosmas Tzintzuluces. "He is waiting for you in the ciborium."

Michael, Lord of the Entire World, Emperor, Autocrator, and Basileus of the Romans, stepped into the nave of the Church of St. Demetrius in Thessalonica. From the aisle vaults the brilliant, frescoed presences of the saints, the Holy Virgin, and the Pantocrator glimmered like welcoming friends. The Emperor was profoundly grateful for the familiar splendor of what was becoming if not his home, then his sanctuary. He did not come here for renewal—he never could expect that much—but for relief. It was a place of temporary sustenance, where he could arrest but not reverse the inexorable starvation of his immortal soul.

To the Emperor's left, midway down the nave, stood the ciborium, a miniature hexagonal temple, sheathed entirely in beautifully chased silver, the canopy topped with a large silver sphere and cross. The Emperor proceeded toward the ciborium, the thickly bearded monk Cosmas Tzintzuluces gently at his arm; both men seemed to glide over the marble floor as if drawn by some supernatural force. The monk paused and opened the silver door to the little chamber.

The Emperor entered and fell to his knees before the small silver couch. He did not need to see the physical presence of St. Demetrius to know that the holiest of martyrs and most potent of saints was spiritually present. St. Demetrius's *parreshia*, access to the Heavenly Father, was proven beyond all doubt. How many times had he saved Thessalonica from the Bulgars? How many torments of the flesh had he eased with his healing oil, how many carnal sins had he absolved with his cleansing waters? *Heal me, absolve me*, begged the Lord of the Entire World in silent, desperate prayer. *I know you have approached the Throne of Heaven so many times on my behalf, beloved Martyr. You have presented my case to the Divine Trinity with such graciousness and conviction that my heart bursts with gratitude for your Holy offices. And yet I still suffer. And yet I am not forgiven.*

Tzintzuluces knelt beside the Emperor, crossed himself, and bowed deeply in prayer. He took the Emperor's powerful hands in his own spindly fingers. He gently urged the Emperor's hands toward the empty silver couch. "Let him touch you," whispered the monk. "His one hand has now taken that of Our Father Almighty. His other seeks your mortal grasp. Reach out to him."

The Emperor's hands trembled slightly as he reached out. He sighed; it was as if his fingers had vanished into a warm ether, and the pain—the terrible strangling torment—flowed from his entire body, through his fingers, into this all-accepting void. It flowed joyously, cathartically, for a moment, and then the pain was suddenly excruciating, as if his skull had turned to hot iron and crushed in upon his brain. The effluence of pain trickled and ceased, obstructed by a sin too great to pass through any medium.

The monk looked anxiously at this suffering human being next to him. Yes, Tzintzuluces reflected, he could, without blasphemy—indeed it redounded to the glory of God—consider the Autocrator a far more humble man, indeed a mere novitiate in a universal monastic order. For when Christ the King summoned him, the King of the World would have to appear before the Heavenly Tribunal as naked as any man. And like any man, even the Pantocrator's Vice Regent on earth had to prepare for that time. For men, Tzintzuluces reminded himself, are like oxen whose life cannot last; they are like cattle whose time is short. "Let him guide you," whispered the monk.

The Emperor choked back the searing, vision-blackening pain. The Holy Martyr spoke, soothed, guided. His voice, transmitted through the spiritual ether within which he resided, seeped through the hard shell of pain that crushed upon the Emperor's brain. "Confess," whispered St.

Demetrius in a wonderful melody that was more music than voice. "Confess."

Dazed, the Emperor allowed Tzintzuluces to raise him to his feet and lead him to the vaulted crypt beside the altar, the very spot where St. Demetrius had accepted Holy Martyrdom. They stopped before the sunken marble font; the saint's holy oil shimmered, a fragrant, faintly golden pool. The Emperor fell to his knees again. When he looked up, two holy men stood before him. Both of these living saints were maned with voluminous beards and unshorn, lice-crawling hair but otherwise were as withered and desiccated as desert lizards; the taller of the pair wore a soiled loincloth, the other stood in a coarse, tattered tunic. If the Emperor noticed their unwashed stench, he gave no indication. Instead he turned to Tzintzuluces, hands clenched before his breasts, the tears welling in his eyes. "These are new treasures," the Emperor whispered hoarsely, and began to weep.

"Yes, yes," whispered Tzintzuluces, his own dark eyes glazed with adoration and rapture. "David and Symeon. The former a dendrite; the latter, as you have certainly heard, the stylite from Adrianopolis, the very Symeon whose fame has begun to spread throughout Christendom. They have left their perches to succor the holiest of all their brethren." Tzintzuluces looked aside briefly as a priest in silk vestments set a silver bucket, a sponge, and a towel beside the Emperor.

The Emperor spread his arms wide and his eyes swept from one Holy Man to the other like a drunken reveler forced to choose between two equally desirable courtesans. Finally he settled on the shorter, cloaked man. David the dendrite's tunic, hair, and bare legs were soiled with the droppings of the birds that had shared his home of the last four years, a solitary tree on the outskirts of a small Anatolian village; already the dendrite's virtuous self-denial had been credited with bringing widespread prosperity to the entire Charsianon theme. The Emperor reached almost reflexively for the pail and began to sponge the filth and bird excrement from the feet and legs of David the dendrite. He caressed the man's rough brown ankles and worked the sponge in between gnarled toes. The Emperor's eyes were stricken, tender, above all grateful.

After he had carefully toweled David's feet the Emperor turned to Symeon. The stylite had lived atop a single stone column for thirteen years now—the Emperor reflected on the holiness of this number, that of the twelve apostles plus their Lord. That Symeon the stylite had blessed the world with healing grace was beyond any doubt; hundreds of miraculous cures had already been attributed to his touch. In exchange

Symeon had surrendered his own flesh; his toes, eaten away by the maggots that lived in the filth—his own filth—at his feet, were raw nubs. Delirious with joy at beholding the evidence of this sacred act of mortification, racked with guilt over the crimes his own flesh had lured him to—yea, even to the very fires of perdition—the Emperor fell upon Symeon's grotesque, filth-encrusted feet; he kissed these feet, he bathed them with his tears, he salved them with the golden oil of St. Demetrius.

Finally the Emperor turned his tear-stained face to Tzintzuluces. He fought to control his sobs. "You know why the Pantocrator has struck me down with the lightning bolts of this madness that visits me, ever more frequently, do you not?"

"Why, Brother?" asked Tzintzuluces softly.

"I engaged in adulterous intercourse with her, even as I served her husband Romanus, the same Romanus who preceded me beneath the Imperial Diadem, even as I served him in the capacity of servant and friend." The Emperor snorted and struggled for air. "Suspicious of the rumors that attended our flagrant and unlawful—yea, unholy—dalliance, her husband and my Emperor questioned me of these matters and"— here the Emperor began to wail—"upon the Holy Relics I denied my crimes! If not damned before, there I threw my immortal soul into the fiery lake!"

Tzintzuluces crossed himself with a quick, frantic gesture.

"There is more," said the Emperor, his eyes now fixed with an expression of utter horror, as if he saw before him the demons who attended the gates of Hell. "They murdered him. It was not my hands that forced his head beneath the waters of his bath, but those hands acted in my interest. I know now the foul crime upon which my throne was raised. I will never escape the torment of that knowing!" The crypt echoed with the Emperor's shattered voice, as if the gates of Hell had now opened and the damned shouted forth, begging for release.

Tzintzuluces's face mirrored the terrible fear that racked his Imperial disciple. His lips parted with a curious slurping sound but he could say nothing. The Emperor stared at him, a drowning man who had just realized that his savior on the shore had no rope, no bit of flotsam to throw to him. And then Symeon spoke. His voice was shockingly elegant, as if he were an actor rather than a self-mutilated hermit. "Because you have listened to your wife and eaten from the tree which I forbade you, accursed shall be the ground on your account."

The Emperor, still on his knees, looked with shadowy, pleading eyes at Symeon. Symeon answered with barking syllables that echoed against the gleaming plaster vaults of the crypt. "And Cain sayeth to the Lord, 'Thy punishment is heavier than I can bear; thou hast driven me today from the ground and banished me from thy presence. I shall be a vagrant and wanderer on the earth and anyone who meets me can kill me.' And the Lord answered: 'No.'" Here Symeon's voice boomed mightily. " 'If anyone kills Cain, Cain shall be avenged sevenfold.' So the Lord put a mark on Cain."

The Emperor pressed his hands into his eyes. "I bear the mark," he whispered, his horror barely audible.

Symeon torturously bent his withered, arthritic legs and dropped to his knees beside his Emperor. "Though your sins are scarlet, they may become white as snow; though they are dyed crimson, they may yet be like new wool." He finished in a low, wondrous tone.

Tzintzuluces gave silent praise to the Pantocrator for the wisdom of the stylite. "The sight of a woman is like the venom affixed to a poison arrow," he whispered to the Emperor. "The longer the venomed barb remains in the flesh, the greater the infection of the corruption it carries."

Symeon's voice rose again, a booming concert to Tzintzuluces's note of caution. "And the angel of retribution sayeth this of the whore of Babylon, with whom the kings of the earth have committed fornication. 'Come out of her, my people, lest you share in her plagues. For her sins are piled high as Heaven, and God has not forgotten her deeds. Pay her back in her own coin, repay her twice over for her deeds!'"

Tzintzuluces realized that with the help of the thrice-blessed Symeon he had now found a voice of his own, a wonderful palliative for his Imperial novitiate's terrible distress. "If your right eye is your undoing," he intoned richly, "tear it out and fling it away; it is better for you to lose one part of your body than for the whole of it to be thrown into Hell. If your right hand is your undoing, cut it off and fling it away. It is better for you to lose one part of your body than for the whole of it to be cast into perdition!"

"You have fornicated with the harlot clothed in purple and scarlet!" boomed Symeon. "Now heed the warning of Jehovah's messenger and come out of her!"

"Cast the woman out!" thundered Tzintzuluces in a voice he had scarcely known he commanded. "Let not even the sight of her poison your immortal soul."

"Cast the woman out!" David the dendrite added his chorus to his colleagues' ringing admonitions.

To the Lord of the Entire World, the Emperor, Autocrator, and Basileus of the Romans, even the massive brick walls of the holy crypt seemed to tremble with the echoes of the righteous yet ultimately merciful wrath of the Pantocrator. "Cast the woman out," the Emperor said weakly, his agreement lost amid the clamoring oaths of the Holy Men.

icetas Gabras lifted the lid of the exquisitely granulated gold box and studied the seal on the rolled parchment tucked inside. "No," he said. He opened the second box, this of silver chased with what appeared to be, from Haraldr's vantage (seated behind his writing table) a hunt scene. "No," Gabras pronounced even more emphatically. The last box was blue enamel with red floral patterns. "No!" Eustratius, Haraldr's newly appointed chamberlain, turned to his master. He almost imperceptibly raised the silver tray that held the three boxes and bowed slightly. Haraldr looked at Gabras and raised his unscarred right eyebrow. Gabras ran the tip of his tongue very quickly between his lips and pulled reflexively at each long, silver-hemmed, silken sleeve of his tunic, as if he weren't certain that the garment fit properly. "The eidikos, rank disputor," said Gabras briskly. "Actuarius, rank protostator. A vestitore. None of them men of immediate consequence. I will indefinitely defer their urgent requests for interviews with the Manglavite Haraldr Nordbrikt."

Haraldr nodded at Gregory to indicate that he understood the Greek. Then he nodded at Gabras, who tipped his bulbous head, draped with long thin blond hair, at the chamberlain Eustratius; the willowy eunuch turned and walked out the door with curious, toe-bouncing strides. Haraldr dully praised Odin and Christ for the endless distractions of his new office, household, and fame, an opiate of details that were meaningful only because they momentarily contained the pain and the fear. He focused on the words, the bewildering "Roman system of titles and dignities." *Eidikos, disputor, actuarias, vestitore, eidikos, disputor, actuarias. . . .* The words rattled over and over in his head like an absurd ditty, briefly confusing the only thought he really had had for ten days now.

She had used him, of course, to an end so hideous that the memory of the words still froze his flesh to his bones: Sever the head of the Imperial Eagle. He had fled from her bed like a man fleeing a demon in a dream, hoping that as much as his night with her had been an incorporeal vision, so, too, would its nightmare conclusion. He had not seen either Maria or the Empress in the week and half since they had tried to make him the agent of their treason; mercifully protocol had shielded him on the road, and since the arrival of the Empress's huge caravan in Constantinople, neither woman had left the Imperial Gynaeceum. But what madness had kept him from going to Joannes as soon as he had returned? The intent of the two Valkyrja had been clear enough: the head of the Imperial Eagle was the Emperor, and how many times had Haraldr heard it implied that this Empress had already murdered one husband, as well as the rumors that she had been neglected by her new spouse? And yet he had been unable to accuse the Empress of such a conspiracy, much less sentence Maria to the inevitable "interrogation" in Neorion. Now it was quite likely that the plot had been uncovered—why else would the Emperor have been absent on his wife's return, and why were the two women virtual prisoners in their own apartments? And how soon would it be before the two silk-sheathed Valkyrja implicated him with the length of time he had concealed their terrible intentions? He had been mad to spare Maria, even for a moment, even after an eternity of her seduction. When the Emperor returned, Haraldr could only throw himself before the mercy of his Father and beg that his pledge-men be spared. But she had doomed him. And she had known that when she had led his soul into the depths. The pain of her betrayal was almost suffocating. Every word, every thought, was a struggle.

"Manglavite," said Gabras; he looked anxiously at the large bronze water clock near Haraldr's writing table. "Might I suggest that Eustratius inform your groom that one of your horses be saddled? You have a meeting at the third hour, in the palace, with the Grand Eunuch. Do you have a preference as to the horse, or perhaps merely the color? And would you—"

A shout came from downstairs. Gabras turned toward the door and pursed his lips in alarm. Surely the servants aren't quarreling, thought Haraldr distantly; Gabras has already got them working together as smoothly as the gears of this water clock. The shouts ascended the stairs and became an angry chorus, then a moment later crescendoed. In a blur of colors and cacophony of rattling armor, a lean, ruddy-faced blond in the full gold-and-red cermonial regalia of the Grand Hetairia lurched into Haraldr's office; he shook off Eustratius and two of his eunuch assistants like a wrathful bear shedding hunt dogs. Gabras's scarcely whiskered little chin dropped. Haraldr rose to his feet, stunned, uncertain whether to defend himself or to submit meekly to this emissary of the Emperor's justice.

"Manglavite Haraldr," said the Norseman apologetically. He made no effort to advance; instead he threw back his red satin cape and smoothed it behind his leather-kilted hips. His next words were in Norse with a slightly rustic Icelandic inflection, but with the perfect diction of a man who could read and write the runes as well as a skald. "I am Thorvald Ostenson, Centurion of the Grand Hetairia. I beg you not to regard the manner of my coming before you as an insult. I petitioned to see you in the accepted fashion, and your servant"—he gestured at Eustratius, who still glared at the Norseman with small black eyes—"simply placed my request with all the rest, even though I assured him that life and death were at stake in this matter." Ostenson held out a small rolled and sealed document. "The Hetairarch Mar Hunrodarson asked me to make certain that you have read and destroyed this message."

Haraldr broke the seal and unrolled the paper. The message was in runic symbols, a hand he had not seen before. "Sir," it read, "heed the warning of one Norseman to another. You are in grave danger in that house. You must meet me tonight at the Forum of Constantine at the seventh hour. I will wait for you beside the great statue. Make certain you are not followed. Your life depends on that."

"You understand?" asked Ostenson when Haraldr finally lifted his eyes from the message. Haraldr nodded, almost relieved at the simplicity of this ending. If Mar was in the city, then the Emperor had returned, and his mighty sword was now already poised above the necks of the traitors. The Forum of Constantine was to be the place of Haraldr's execution. Haraldr looked grimly into Ostenson's acute, cold blue eyes. Is it that simple? he asked himself. Is Mar acting as the Emperor's agent, or to his own ends?

Ostenson removed the paper from Haraldr's fingers and looked up at the ring-shaped candelabra that bathed the room in soft golden light; the gray and foreboding sky, visible through the three arched windows, offered little natural illumination. Ostenson placed the message against one of the flames, then turned the paper until it had been consumed to a brittle, curled leaf. He crushed the hot ashes in his hands and let the remains fall to the floor. The centurion bowed deeply to Haraldr and turned quickly. Before he left the room, he paused and caught Gabras's eye. Gabras turned away immediately, faced Haraldr, and pulled on his sleeves.

† † †

"I thought you would never come to me again," she told him, and he kissed the tears on her cheeks. "I love you," she said, his tenderness like a weight on her aching heart, forcing her to think. "I loved you for love of her," she explained very slowly, each word tearing out a fiber of her heart, "but our love was greater." The grief came over her like a wave, and she cried until it seemed she were actually screaming under water, unable to make herself heard, choking. But he held her and touched her hair, his fingers stroking her as if they were made of light. When he entered her, the light flowed through her veins and she arched her neck and cried. It was difficult to tell how long they made love. When he had finished, he rose above her and the light from the window made a halo around his golden hair. He smiled at her and then turned slightly, and his neck gushed blood. Once, twice, then spurting with every pulse, spilling down his shoulders and chest, she watched dumbly as tiny droplets bounced crazily against the silk sheets, and when she looked at his face again, the flesh had fallen away from it, rotting before her eyes, and his bare white teeth parted and he laughed. "I'm dead" he said matter-of-factly, laughing after the terrible words. "You killed me."

"Away, away, oh, wicked thing," murmured Zoe, cradling Maria's head and brushing at the tears that coursed down her cheeks. Maria's eyes shot open, startled, sapphire blue against her flushed face. "You have gone through an entire life on that couch, little daughter. Remorse, a most . . . profound ecstasy, and then a horror that chilled me as if death—" Zoe broke off, having conjured an image she did not want to see.

Maria suddenly remembered the nightmare she was awakening to and she sat straight up. She quickly emptied the silver goblet she had left on a small ivory table beside her couch; she hoped that the wine would wash the taste from her mouth, a bitter bouquet of fear and death. She looked at Zoe. "Is there news?"

Zoe nodded, her blue eyes as hot and unrelenting as a midsummer sky. *I don't understand her anymore,* thought Maria for an instant before the observation was engulfed by general anxiety. "He is back," said the Empress.

"It is over, then," said Maria, clutching at her silk-sheathed shoulders.

"It has begun!" snapped Zoe, her blood-red lips cruel and scowling. "Because you did not persuade your Komes Haraldr to kill for you does not mean that he has betrayed our intent!"

"We have been made captives." Maria pressed her hands to her thighs. The tips of her fingers trembled.

"A relative condition," said Zoe; her eyes shot about her apartment as if she were a general surveying a battlefield. "We are not allowed to go out. Otherwise we are at our liberty. We may summon whoever we please and send them out again with whatever we please. My husband is loath to see me because of his own guilt, which has clearly become a chronic disorder in our absence. He has no need to aggrandize that guilt, or contribute to the already unsteady tilt of the Imperial Diadem upon his head, by punishing me further." Zoe sliced the air with her delicate hand. "I believe the Komes Haraldr, or rather the Manglavite Haraldr, as he has now been so generously designated, is still considering our request."

Maria pressed her chin toward her snowy neck like a frightened swan. "I will not ask him to dance that closely with death again, Mother," she said in a small girlish voice. "You did not see the look of horror in his eyes, the betrayal, the wound, the outrage."

Zoe stared at Maria for a moment. "Oh, I am quite cognizant of your feelings," she said bitingly. "Our peril has somehow made this giant from Thule as precious to you as a little pet. I only hope you will not besiege me with your tears when I endeavor to slip my collar about his neck." Zoe narrowed her pitiless eyes. "I think your little pet can yet be goaded into devouring some of the palace vermin."

"But, Mother," pleaded Maria, "you have heard of the honors Joannes has showered on him. The wealth, the palace, the servants. Even if he was not Joannes's property before, surely his price has now been met."

"It only means that he is in a position to consider wagers of vastly greater currency."

Zoe's menacing tone silenced Maria. The air seemed to become heavy and stifling, as if filled with a deadly miasma. The double doors at the far end of the room slid open and Symeon floated toward the Empress and Maria. "Away!" Zoe snarled.

"Mistress," said Symeon softly, his ethereal progress undeterred, his words seeming to draw him forward into the room. "I thought you should know." Zoe nodded viciously. "Your husband has ordered that no one be admitted to your Imperial apartments without the approval of the offices of the Orphanotrophus Joannes. I have just spoken to the commander of the Khazar guard commissioned to enforce this directive." Symeon bowed apologetically.

The heavy silence resumed. Maria pressed her palms together tightly and her nails scored the milky back of her hand. "Very good, Symeon," said Zoe evenly, and the eunuch drifted away as he had come. Zoe pulled her legs up on the couch and began inspecting her pearl-studded red silk slippers. "Then I must be certain," she finally said in a curiously buoyant voice, "only to entertain guests who enjoy the favor of the Orphanotrophus Joannes."

† † †

The snow fell fitfully in dry, coarse flakes. The wind blew the sparse accumulation into thin, vaporous tendrils that swirled briefly above the darkened pavement and vanished into the night. Haraldr pulled his sable-lined cloak more tightly around his shoulders; perhaps his time in the hot southern realms had thinned his blood. The buildings to either side of him rose like shadowed cliffs; halfway down the block and three stories above him a single undraped window, lit by an oil lamp, seemed glazed with gold glass. He resumed his eastward progress up the side street. After another block he reached an intersection with a fairly large avenue. He looked around the corner of the last building on the block. Two blocks to the south was the Mese, Constantinople's broad, colonnaded central thoroughfare. This intersection was marked by the torches of the cursores, the city's ever-vigilant police. There were two of them, pitch-smeared tapers stuck in their crossed arms like scepters. One of the men coughed. The other stamped his feet and looked around briefly; Haraldr waited until the cursore's attention had returned to his boots before he darted quickly across the intersection.

Haraldr evaded two more cursores on a six-block, zigzagging journey down side streets and narrow alleys. His route ended in front of a long two-story building. Towering beyond the building, perhaps three bow-shots away, was an enormous dark column vaguely silhouetted against the snow-flecked night. On top of the column stood a solitary figure, a huge, heroic ghost gesturing into the darkness. Constantine the Great, the first Christian Emperor of old Rome, who long ago, in the twilight of Rome's old gods, had built the Great City that bore his name; thus had begun the glory of New Rome.

Haraldr decided not to risk further exposure to the cursores by looking for a more suitable route into the Forum, which seemed to be completely hemmed in by two- or three-story buildings; he crossed the street and quickly climbed the two-story facade, using the vines that had overgrown the featureless first-story wall and wreathed the rusticated stone windows on the second story. He pulled himself over the jutting cornice of the tile roof, scrambled to the peak, and crawled along the spine of the building.

He paused where the roof pitched down again. The Forum of Constantine was a large oval plaza defined by its darkness. For a moment Haraldr lingered over the view of the city, now softly sprinkled in light and surrounded by black water. He moved to the edge of the roof and looked down, startled for a moment by the figures waiting for him. The roof of the Forum's encircling arcade was a repository for dozens, perhaps hundreds, of statues, their gestures and poses so lifelike that they seemed to have arrested their motion only because they had sensed his intrusion. Haraldr lowered himself from the cornice, let go, and fell a few ells before his feet resounded against the arcade's wooden canopy.

Haraldr stopped to examine one of the marble figures, a woman almost as tall as himself; she was cloaked in a gauzy robe that swirled around her legs and clung to her full breasts; the sculptor had been so skilled that Haraldr could see her nipples pressed against the fabric. He reached out and touched the robe; it was smooth, almost without texture, as if it were made of real silk. He drew back. Her mouth was so delicate, so subtly nuanced at the corners that it seemed she might at a moment part her lips and breath life into her breast. He waited, poised on some great needle of fate. With terrifying sharpness he remembered Maria at Daphne, how she had touched a statue's lips and drawn her fingers back, as if she had come too close to the life locked in that ancient stone. Or had it been death she had touched?

Haraldr dropped quietly into the Forum and immediately ran toward the huge, pyramidal ashlar base of the column. He crouched beside the great marble plinth and looked up. The statue wore a strange crown, a fan of rays that projected about his head like shafts of frozen sunlight. He made his decision. If he opposed Mar, he would certainly die, no matter whom Mar was serving or what end he was pursuing. But if Haraldr dealt with him, he might at least save his pledge-men. He removed his cloak and placed it on the ground a few ells away from him, then took his knife from his boot and removed his short sword from his belt and placed both weapons on the cloak. He sat on his haunches and curled his arms around his knees, the posture of a defenseless captive. He waited.

The arm around his neck compressed his windpipe with paralyzing effectiveness, and his shout of alarm was strangled in his throat. He was jerked to his feet, and another arm wrapped his torso like a steel band. No man has such a grip, thought Haraldr with dull recognition. Only Odin.

"I swear our lives are worthless if you call out," whispered Mar Hunrodarson in a convincingly urgent cadence. Haraldr was released from the supernatural embrace and he rasped in cold air. Mar quickly scooped up Haraldr's weapons and cloak and shoved them back at him. "Not a sound," he hissed. For several moments Mar searched the emptiness of the Forum. His temple pulsed. "Follow me!" he barked as he dashed out into the darkness. Too stunned even to question his reprieve, Haraldr tried to maintain contact with Mar's fleeing back. The arcade loomed out of the darkness forty ells away, and Mar stopped. In a smooth motion he flung his briefly phosphorescing knife into the almost opaque passageway. A cry like a soughing wind drifted through the columns. Mar sprinted into the arcade.

When Haraldr arrived, Mar had already flipped the body over. The man had dropped his outer garment in his flight and wore only a good woolen tunic and long, dark woolen hose. His spiky, dark beard glistened with bloody sputum. "Do you know him?" asked Mar.

Haraldr shook his head. He had never seen this man before.

"He belongs to Joannes," said Mar. He stood up and fixed Haraldr with his fiercely intelligent blue eyes. "That house the Orphanotrophus Joannes so gratefully gave you is a nest of spies and informants."

Haraldr considered this twist with detached interest, as if he were now a spectator of his own life. "Perhaps Joannes merely assigned this man to protect me," he said, automatically reciting the questions of a mind too brutalized for guile.

Mar narrowed his eyes. "If you live long enough to become a king, they will call you Haraldr Ox-Wit. You saw how well this man protected you when it appeared that I had attacked you."

Mar's scorn was a reviving lash. The fates were giving him another toss, the Valkyrja hovered and waited. Deal with the demon. Had Joannes learned of the Empress's plot, and Haraldr's witless involvement, and for that reason had him followed? And if so, why would Mar have killed Joannes's informant, assuming they served the same master? Haraldr fought a retching shudder. Was Mar also part of the plot against the Emperor? Deal, fate told him. Deal as madly as you have ever gamed with me. "Perhaps Joannes suspects me of plotting against the Emperor."

Mar grabbed Haraldr's collar and jerked him forward. "Those are a dead man's words, little prince. If I had reason to believe you were capable of plotting against our Father the Emperor, I would leave you with this garbage tonight." He pushed Haraldr away. "Why would Joannes suspect you of such a plot?"

"He has reason." Haraldr's heart was a drum.

Mar's eyes were cold blue lights. "What plot do you know of?"

"I have information," said Haraldr. His chest ached from the effort of controlling his breathing. "It carries a price."

"What do you want?"

"We both share the gift from Odin," said Haraldr grimly. "I want you to swear to Odin the All-Father that my pledge-men will not be punished for anything I have done. Promise Odin this oath, that if you betray it he will draw back his favor." Haraldr knew that no man who had entered the spirit world and confronted his beast could ever break such an oath. The Christ might forgive those who broke his oaths, as He had Judas, but Odin's gifts carried the obligation to honor them.

Mar kicked over the corpse and pulled his knife out of the man's back. His glazed eyes reflected the seriousness with which he took this step. "Odin," he intoned with a voice unlike his own, "I offer you this foeman." Then he took the knife and slashed it across his forearm. "Odin, I offer you my blood if I forsake this oath." Mar lowered his arm and the blood trickled into his palm. His eyes now demanded as fiercely as his voice. "What do you know?"

"The Empress has asked me to murder her husband." The words came out like blood-vomit, the release cathartic, the taste as bitter as death.

Mar turned away from Haraldr and focused all his will so that he would not laugh out loud.

† † †

"You have exhausted me with pleasure."

"You are insatiable."

"It is true. Come up here where I can see you. No, no . . . I warn you, I can stand no more of . . ." Zoe reached behind her head and pulled her wet hair up and mopped it over her brow. She touched her fingers to her own engorged nipples and shuddered. "You . . . are . . . excessive . . . you . . . are . . ." Zoe ran her hands down her torso and then placed them under her surging buttocks, digging her nails into her own rich, smooth flesh. "Wicked . . . wicked . . . you . . . are!" She caressed her lover's cheeks and then pressed her hands to her loins, stroking her drenched pubic hair. "You are a sinner!" she suddenly shrieked, bucking madly and clenching her teeth. Her rigid body collapsed and she exhaled lyrically, explicitly, then lay with her head to the side for a moment before turning back to her lover. "Oh, delight, have I wounded you? Oh, no . . . is your nose broken? Come here and let me see it."

"To paraphrase a military maxim, it was not the force of the attack but the surprise."

Zoe laughed huskily. "Will you counter with a thrust of your own?" She rubbed her hand under his scrotum and along his erect shaft. "You are armed."

"I thought you found my attentions wearisome."

"So I do." Zoe closed her legs. "Do you worship me?"

"Yes."

"If I decreed that you should not?"

"I would disobey." He slipped his hand between her thighs.

"Beg me."

He licked her nipples; still erect, they tightened into hard knots.

"Beg me. Beg to worship me. Beg for my naked flesh."

"Lover, adoration, morning star . . ."

Zoe grabbed her lover's pulsing member and squeezed hard. "I will take your essence this time, little slave. But you must ask for permission. How will you ask for it?" She spread her legs suddenly. "Here, let me bring you in first."

Her lover moaned. "Oh, light, adoration . . . ohhh, take my soul's nectar . . . oh, perfection . . ."

Zoe ran her nails along his flank. "When it happens this time, will you swear to die for me?"

"I will," said Michael Kalaphates drunkenly. "My love, I will."

"Oh . . . you . . . wicked!"

† † †

"Here is my understanding of what is afoot," said Mar when Haraldr had finished his rambling, frantic exposition. They stood in what appeared to be a large park just south and west of the Forum of Constantine; cypresses towered in orderly rows and a pool shone dully a hundred ells away. "First of all, you must remember that the Empress herself did not importune you to murder anyone. I know the woman, Maria, though to my regret not as well as you do, and I believe I do no slander to the lady when I say that her beauty is matched by her volatility, her impetuousness, her wantonness. Forgive me, comrade, but she is reputed to be a woman of great passions and little discretion. I hope I am not wounding you, but when she was only a girl—this was eight years ago, when I was only a Decurion of the Guard—when she was only a bud, she took a lover, a distinguished Senator and military commander. I cannot say with certainty who murdered this man, but she was known to have visited him in his apartments shortly before he was found stabbed to death. Of course, the Empress protected the child and the scandal was suppressed, but I have always suspected that Maria killed the man. I suspect that now she thinks she is acting in Her Imperial Majesty's interests, as I do not question her love for our Mother the Empress. But I do not think she is acting at her Imperial Majesty's request.''

Haraldr's head ached from the metallic buzzing and his body seemed weightless. ''The Empress said that Maria would ask me a question in her name. And the rumors. You know how it is imputed that the Empress had a hand in . . . in the death of her husband.''

Mar's face hardened. ''How do you know that Maria asked you the question the Empress intended? And forget the libel of the streets and the theaters. I can tell you for certain that the Empress had no part in the death of Romanus, because I pulled his body from the bath in which he had drowned. May the Mother of Heaven forgive me, but the Emperor was under the care of his physicians, and besotted in spite of that. He must have fallen and hit his head. Perhaps he never should have been allowed to bathe alone, but that was no treason.''

Doubts still flocked like quarreling ravens. Was Mar performing his own drama? And yet what he said about Romanus could well be true.

''I think there is something else you don't understand. That was why I had to see you tonight.'' Mar held his hands up and examined his huge yet elegant fingers as if he were himself impressed by the marvel. ''If I had known what I do of you now, I would have behaved differently when we first met. Then I saw you as some sort of renegade, a man who did not understand our devotion to our Father and his Imperial dignity, a royal whelp who thought he could plunder the wealth of Rome merely to serve his own ends. I thought to teach you a lesson, intimidate you, use my knowledge of your background to frighten you into obedience. I didn't know then that you were a man of honor. Tonight I am certain that your devotion to our Father is as great as my own. I no longer mistrust you. But I hope, for your sake as well as mine, that you will begin to trust me.''

This was not a Norseman speaking; this was the oiled tongue of a eunuch. But why was Mar wagging a praise-tongue if he held the sword over Haraldr's neck? *He needs me,* Haraldr realized. *He needs my friendship more than he needs my fear. You have dealt once and won your pledge-men's lives. Deal with the demon again.* ''I trust that you will not break your oath to Odin. What would I gain by trusting you further? I have satisfied my honor. And you can only kill me once.''

Haraldr had expected at best the fury of Mar's anger; perhaps a final mortal struggle. But Mar surprised him with an intense yet even stare. "What you would gain, Manglavite Haraldr, is the honor of defending a worthy Emperor against a malignancy so foul that it threatens every life in the Roman Empire, our own included."

Haraldr could agree that the Emperor was worthy of defending. "I have told you of the plot I suspected," he invited.

"You say that Maria's words were 'Sever the head of the Imperial Eagle.' Perhaps she meant Joannes, not the Emperor. It is often said that the Orphanotrophus Joannes is the grotesque head atop the body of Rome. There are many who love our Father who would like to see his brother out of the way." Mar paused ominously. "The Orphanotrophus Joannes is evil. He does not serve our Father, despite his lavish protestations. He serves himself. Joannes has already designated you a plaything in his evil game."

Haraldr weighed his desperate hope that Maria's crime was lesser, perhaps excusable, against the fierce love he had seen on Joannes's face when the giant monk had spoken of his brother, the Emperor. "How would Joannes profit by opposing our Father's wishes? As I understand it, a eunuch would not be permitted to rule Rome."

"The eunuch Joannes will soon have enough power to have a porter from the wharves crowned Emperor to sit on the Imperial Throne as his surrogate. And when he acquires that power, no man or woman in Rome, including our Father, even including our purple-born Mother, will be safe. That is why we must work together to oppose him."

Haraldr looked down at the hard winter turf, listening to the appeals of two voices, neither one of which he could trust. Was it possible that Joannes's fierce love was for his own power, the power that only for the present he saw embodied in his brother? And if Mar were correct, then Maria's crime was only that of using him to defeat a monstrous evil. But could he trust Mar?

"I'm not asking you to accept my word on this," said Mar, addressing Haraldr's reticence. "You needn't believe that the man I killed tonight was Joannes's spy. I can offer you proof that Joannes has already moved against you with far more deadly intent."

"Why would he move against me, if, as you say, I am already his plaything?"

"He intends to make you a considerably more pliant instrument. As I say, I can offer you proof. You risked your life to parlay with me tonight.

If you meet me tomorrow night at the Chrysotriklinos, you will risk nothing further."

Haraldr nodded. His men would live to see their homes; he would live at least another day. That was vastly more than he had expected when he had ventured into this snowy night.

he stocky, dark-eyed little man had never known his real name, but as long as he could remember, his people—his people being his fellow denizens of the notorius Studion slums—had called him the Squirrel, and as far as he was concerned, Squirrel was his name, and his identity: quick, darting, able to climb anything. And perhaps he was a bit erratic, too, because in the Squirrel's business a man could not afford to develop recognizable patterns.

The Squirrel stood at the entrance to the vast, colonnaded, terraced square called the Augustaion. He looked without awe or interest past the enormous brick column that rose from the center of the square, thrusting up the huge bronze equestrian statue of some long-dead Emperor, now green with age, frozen in perpetual hubris, his great right arm pointing to the east, his left hand cradling a globe symbolizing the entire earth. The Squirrel did not care to know that this Emperor had been Justinian, who a half millennium ago had commanded an Empire even larger than that established by the great Bulgar-Slayer, an empire on three continents, stretching from Persia to the Pillars of Heracles, from the Alps to the far reaches of the River Nile. The Squirrel had no wish to know that Justinian's *Codex* had established the laws that would determine his fate should he ever stumble in the performance of his labors. He did not even care to know that Justinian had built the sole object of the Squirrel's attention, the great silver domes of the Hagia Sophia, the huge church to the northeast of the Augustaion. Today the glittering domes were as dull as the gray, mossy-textured sky. The Squirrel wrapped his dyed wool cloak around his torso, reflecting to himself that he probably would have been able to gain admittance to the palace grounds today without showing the guards his tunic of the cheapest, export-grade Syrian silk, the uniform of a low-grade secretary in the bureaus of the Sacellarius. Still, it was best to be prepared for any eventuality; if one was not prepared for the unexpected in this business, one would soon be most painfully deprived of the tools of one's trade.

The Squirrel proceeded at his leisure across the square, veering around a cluster of lawyers discussing a case in front of the massive marble columns of the Senate Building; some drivel about "the ecclesiastical canon asserting precedence in a case where customary, not secular statutes. . . ." The Squirrel suppressed his urge to spit at the feet of the barristers. They were windbags who blew nothing but ill to the people, that was certain. The Squirrel's demeanor brightened as he saw the Khazar guards moving into the northern exit of the Augustaion. So, the reports of the almighty Emperor's return were correct. Good information, the Squirrel told himself, shaking his head with satisfaction. There was no limit to the value of good information.

By the time the Squirrel reached the exit of the Augustaion, the Khazar guards had formed a cordon blocking the arcade that led from the square into the gardens and atrium at the west end of the Hagia Sophia. The public would be prevented from passing, but even minor Imperial officials might be admitted to watch the Emperor in his biweekly procession to the church. The Squirrel kept his cloak wrapped tightly about his tunic and produced a green sprig of myrtle, just as any boot-licking minor courtier would to celebrate the fleeting passage of his swollen-headed Father. The Squirrel clasped the myrtle reverently to his breast and was passed by the Khazars without a second glance.

The Squirrel's anticipation plunged like an overfed gull when he entered the cypress-walled courtyard in front of the Hagia Sophia. The fair-haired *barbaroi* thugs were already standing at attention alongside the route. But where was the mob of dignitaries and sycophants and functionaries who usually assembled with their sprigs and blossoms and wreaths, to cheer and chant their puffed-up Autocrator on his way to church? The Squirrel counted; maybe forty or fifty courtiers along the entire path, and each one of them with at least two of the fair-hair beasts to keep an eye on him. The Squirrel's instinct told him to take the rest of the day off, but a more powerful impulse drove him forward.

Choose your spot well, the Squirrel reminded himself, because with little or no crowd to hide your movements, you are only going to have one opportunity. There. About four paces to the right of a portly man in the green silk coat with the fur-trimmed collar. The Squirrel walked right up to the edge of the marble path and took his place. He bowed humbly to the portly man on his left, quickly noting to his amusement that the overfed Great Whatever couldn't even get the clasps of his coat fastened around his silk-sheathed belly; the man's ornate silver belt jutted out like the metal band around a bulging cask of fish sauce. Then the Squirrel bowed even more humbly to the towering fair-haired monster before him, not even daring to lift his eyes above the gilt leather kilt and polished gold breastplate of the Varangian Guard. Imagine *that* on your neck, he shuddered, eyeing the huge ax blade wrapped against the gilded breast by inhumanly thick forearms. It was a sight to make a man consider taking the tonsure and conducting his business only in the name of the Pantocrator. But if the Squirrel could practice his trade in plain sight of this brute, what a tale he'd have for his associates back at the Devil's Walking Stick.

What? The Squirrel watched the approaching horsemen in astonishment. Mounted Varangians, for certain, and behind them the Emperor on his white stallion with the gold-and-scarlet caparisons. But instead of a stately canter, they were all charging along as if fleeing the Last Trumpet. And where was the usual procession, the drums, the flutes, the massed courtiers in front, bearing their candles and chanting their gibberish? Something was very strange here; this clearly was not the time to try some fancy stunt. But to flee now would certainly arouse suspicion, and this unprecedentedly abrupt procession might in fact turn to the Squirrel's advantage.

The first ranks of Varangians clattered past, and then the demon of them all, the Hetairarch, with the devil's blue eyes glaring ahead; right behind the Hetairarch rode His Majesty. The Squirrel waved his sprig wildly and shouted, "Render homage! The sun's rays are upon us!" Still holding his myrtle high and dashing as if to follow the charging procession, the Squirrel headed straight for the portly official. It will take perfect timing, he hastily reminded himself.

Unnhhh! The portly official grunted as if the entire west wind had been disgorged from his belly. The Squirrel wrapped one arm over the official's shoulder to keep from falling, and with the other went about his day's work. "I have disgraced myself, oh, your plenipotentiary worship, sir!" the Squirrel pleaded, his labor already completed. "It was my unbridled love for our Holy Father, if I may beg the forgiveness of one who certainly stands second only to the sun that rises before us so that we may live each day! Oh, worship, pardon me, if only for my soul's sake and because your Christian charity doubtless exceeds your other uncountable virtues!"

"Go away, little . . . thing"—the official snarled viciously—"before I have these gentlemen here escort you to the Numera, where your witless life might pass without further hazard to those worthy to surround rightfully the Imperial Dignity! Away, refuse!"

The Squirrel bowed and began a slow, casual retreat, so as not to arouse suspicion; the official's purse was already safely snugged within the voluminous folds of his poorly fitting tunic. A fine grab! the Studion's most adroit cut-purse thought, exulting. And the fat goose had a purse as heavy as Judas's! But what now? The Imperial procession had halted, and the Varangians were leaping from their horses. Theotokos! Hadn't the Emperor himself fallen from his horse? Yes, indeed he was on the ground, and—the Squirrel could not believe what he was seeing—the sounds coming from His Majesty's throat! What! One of the *barbaroi* goons was rushing directly at him, and as the Squirrel looked about frantically he could see them thundering about like runaway bulls, rounding up all the other witnesses. A whore's spit they were; they could sew up these dignitaries in pork bellies and toss them in the Bosporus, but not the Squirrel!

The wind rattled in the Squirrel's ears as he took off across the garden. If he could reach the forest around St. Irene, the smaller church to the north of the Hagia Sophia, he could leap the wall and get lost among the warehouses behind the naval yards. Fear pumped his legs frantically as he dashed through a blur of winter-gray foliage; he did not look back until he saw the churchyard wall north of St. Irene. Damn his soul! The *barbaroi* was still after him, gaining with every freakish stride. The Squirrel bounded, body stretching, fingers clawing. His powerful, deft hands pulled and propelled his compact body over the wall.

The ground dropped away behind the wall and the Squirrel fell farther than he had imagined he would. No! Something snapped, and the pain made him shiver. He got to his feet and scrambled away from the rubble-strewn base of the wall toward the huge brick bulk of the nearest warehouse; it was only twenty paces away but each step was excruciating. If only he could find a door, a passageway. He looked back. The *barbaroi* came down from the wall like a great cat. *Oh, Theotokos, plead for me, for I never even knew the comfort of an orphanage, and I did what I had to do, only stealing enough to eat and perhaps to have some minor luxuries, and though I have fornicated, I have never, I beseech thee, never taken another life, oh, Theotokos!*

The Squirrel saw the small door, barely visible at the end of the building's east side. He forced himself to run, and ducked into the welcome darkness. The smell of mold added nausea to the knifing pain in his ankle. Sacks were stacked everywhere, musty burlap covered with dust. He crawled, quickly burrowing into a tumbled-down pile. Something kicked him in the face, and dust came into his eyes. Boots. Bags of campaign boots for some great army that had never been assembled. Then the Squirrel heard someone enter the warehouse and he winced, holding his breath. The footsteps meandered, pausing to kick at the sacks. He heard an entire stack topple, then another. Closer. Another stack tumbled down and the dust was suffocating. Theotokos! The dust! The Squirrel's ribs smashed against his guts and he saw brilliant sparks.

The Squirrel flew to his feet as if the hand of the Devil himself had jerked him up. The dust began to settle. The face of the *barbaroi* came out of the gloom. Fortune's scowl, the Squirrel told himself, finding irony in defeat. The devil's blue eyes. The Hetairarch himself had run him down. This could be a painful death, the Squirrel ruefully considered.

"What did you see?" barked the fair-haired beast in perfect Greek.

"See? Hetairarch, I am but a miserable thief who—"

The Hetairarch's knife blocked the vision of the Squirrel's left eye. "If your eyes are that useless, then I am certain you won't mind losing them," whispered the Norse giant.

"Well, worship, I . . . if I might presume in the presence of an eminence so overawing that I—"

"What did you see, rabbit turd?"

"I . . . ah . . . I believe someone has poisoned our Holy Father, has endeavored to snatch the very sun from our skies and leave us bereft in a darkness that—"

"Bite your tongue and listen, wharf rat."

"Certainly, worship."

"His Imperial Majesty is ill. More than ill. He is plagued by demons who drive the reason from him and will soon snatch away his life. Perhaps it is a punishment from the Pantocrator." The Hetairarch paused. "Do you know that our Emperor seduced your Mother?"

The Squirrel quickly crossed himself. There was only one woman in creation worthy of his respect, indeed his love. His purple-born Mother. "I have heard that, worship," whispered the Squirrel in a husky, truly humbled voice.

"Where do you live?"

"Studion."

"A long walk. Is your ankle broken?"

The Squirrel could scarcely believe his ears. Would a man who was about to slice his nose off and gouge his eyes out worry if he had far to walk? "I think it is broken, eminence."

"How much did you steal?"

The Squirrel pulled the purse out of his tunic and handed it to the Hetairarch. Mar hefted the purse and then pushed the man down on the pile of boots. "Wait here," he said. "Within ten minutes a man will come and bring you the donkey you are about to purchase." Mar reached in the purse and extracted a gold coin. "You will ride your new ass back to

Studion as triumphantly as your Christ entering Jerusalem." Mar tossed the purse, the remainder of the coins untouched, back to the Squirrel. "When you get there, go to your inn. Buy anyone who will listen a cup of wine. And tell them what you saw today, just as I explained it to you. Need I tell you that my own name is not to be mentioned?"

"Worship, you outdo fortune in the beneficence your unimaginably august and noble presence is capable of bestowing to those who are given life by the merest reflected ray of your shining being . . ." The Squirrel trailed off. The Hetairarch had disappeared through a doorway like the Archangel ascending back among the heavenly host. Theotokos. Theotokos.

The Squirrel clutched the stolen purse as if it contained his miraculously redeemed life. Good information, he happily told himself. There is no limit to the value of good information.

hat did you tell Gabras?" asked Mar.

"That you would be drilling me on the night postings around the Chrysotriklinos and Trichonchos," answered Haraldr.

"Good. You are starting to think like a Roman. Now, if he is told—and I am certain he will be—if he is told that we were seen together, he will think nothing of it."

Haraldr looked down from the terraced slopes that rose toward the massive, colonnaded flank of the Hippodrome. The lights of the vast palace complex glimmered below; the reflections off the variegated marble turned the intricate architectural tracery into a dazzling, multicolored blaze. It was impossibly lovely. And impossibly painful to think that Maria slept there; he could see distinctly the brightly illuminated porticoes of the Gynaeceum, the Imperial women's quarters. He could feel her breathing beside him like the faintest breeze, her slightly damp warmth. It hurt him more to think that she might have used him in a just cause; it was easier to imagine her as devoid of any redeeming virtue. With some perverse hope he wished that Mar's "proof" of Joannes's conspiracy would turn out to be as counterfeit as her love. Then he would give Mar a last battle that would awaken every old god who slumbered in this city, and die cursing her for her treachery.

"I could drink this view until the last dragon takes wing," said Mar, his eyes rapt at the shimmering nocturnal mosaic. "And yet here you must always be wary that you do not become intoxicated by this beauty." Mar shook his head. "Do you know the lays of Homer and the other tales of the Trojan War?" Haraldr nodded. "Helen. I think of her at these times. Too much beauty. When there is too much beauty, men will do anything to possess it, to feel that she writhes in their arms alone. Sometimes I think that is true of this city and the glory it can offer men." He looked over at Haraldr. "Were you thinking of Maria?"

"I . . . yes."

"You have loved the stars. I envy you. And I pity you." Mar clapped Haraldr on the back. "We must go."

The garden, with its neat rows of shrubs pruned back for the winter and its fountains stilled, ended beneath the Triclinium, a little-used ceremonial hall abutting the Hippodrome. Haraldr followed Mar through the main hall, a space so enormous that Mar's sputtering oil lamp could not illuminate the walls or ceiling. The two Norsemen's footsteps echoed eerily, as if they were giants overwhelmed by the dwelling of even greater Titans. Finally the embossed eagles on the bronze doors flickered and materialized; Mar took a key from his belt and unlocked them. They entered a gallery that abruptly narrowed into a passageway only large enough for three men abreast. Then another much smaller bronze door. The gallery turned this way and that. More doors, clanging like thunder in the dark, narrow passages. Up steps. Down. Finally they reached a large circular chamber. A marble-balustraded spiral staircase rose into the darkness. "The Emperor's box is above," said Mar, gesturing with the lamp. Mar turned toward the wall. The smooth plaster curve was frescoed with floral patterns; the squarish wooden panel hidden by twining painted vines was impossible to discern until Mar slid it aside and crawled through the opening.

Haraldr followed, sliding on his belly for a dozen ells. The crawlspace opened into another mazelike gallery. Eventually they halted at a banded iron door; after some difficulty with the lock Mar finally pushed the creaking door ajar. A large vaulted gallery led to a waist-high stone railing. Mar leaped over the barricade.

The night seemed almost lustrous; a whipping cold wind pushed the clouds toward the southeast and revealed a diamond-studded sky. The Hippodrome was completely darkened, but the towering obelisks and columns that ran the length of the central *spina* were sharply defined against the uncountable rows of seats; along the portico that crowned the enormous sweep of the stadium, hundreds of statues stood as silent witnesses.

Mar trotted across the firm sand to another arch barricaded by a stone railing. This gallery ended in a staircase that dropped two stories. Music and voices rose up as the Norsemen descended. An ancient crone waited on the landing at the bottom of the stairs. She turned quickly. "A divination," she crowed. "I'll divine the both of you for a single coin." She appraised the two giants with rheumy, sporadically focusing eyes, and smacked her toothless lips. "When I was a beauty, I took on two like you whenever I wanted." She tilted her head back and cawed. "You paid, and you came back the next night! Both of you did!" The crone crawled forward on her knees. "Don't I know you, gentlemen? Indeed! Indeed! Fair-hairs. The Bulgar-Slayer's boys. You've got gold, that I know. The

Bulgar-Slayer gave you each a coin for every nose you brought him. Butcher boys." She crawled closer, her eyes suddenly acute. "I'll divine you the time, my fair butcher boys. Then take her! The whore's yours; she'll spread her legs and take on every one." The crone punched her tiny, nutlike fist obscenely. "I know you boys." Her head slumped and she muttered something incomprehensible. Mar dropped a coin at her feet.

Beneath the southern end of the Hippodrome unfolded a tawdry, haphazard maze of stables, hovels, inns, brothels, and small tenements, all lit by so many flaring tapers that the smoke hung over the district like a local fog. Wherever a street was visible amid the densely packed buildings, people were visible coursing and clamoring along; little figures could also be seen perched in windows and balconies. "The Empress City has many faces," said Mar. "You will find this one interesting."

Mar followed a main street that zigged and zagged. Men in short tunics, some carrying sacks of feed on their backs, others driving donkey carts, zipped across at the intersections, heading down dusty side roads toward the Hippodrome stables. A cart with two huge, striped cats caged inside rolled past, followed by dozens of filthy, barefoot children who ran along singing a song. Beside an intersection a woman stood on her hands; her tunic had fallen away to leave her lower body completely exposed. A man threw a coin to the pavement beneath her head, and she spread her legs open. The various fortune-tellers were everywhere, sitting on carpets or sheltered beneath painted booths. A diviner, an old man with greasy silver hair, beckoned to them from one side of the street; a palmist, young, with beautiful black hair and a big scar that parted her chin, waved from the other. "Hetairarch!" she yelled; Mar nodded and walked on. A noseless man ran past them, a small costumed dog under his arm.

Mar turned left. A dwarf directed singing by three pretty, sad girls in clean white tunics; a large crowd joined in choruses and coins showered onto the filthy street before the poignant little songbirds. After a right turn the street ended against a cluster of wooden buildings wedged around a tenement with a crumbling, vine-laced facade. "Big man, big, big man . . ." The coarsely seductive woman's voice came from a shallow porch in front of one of the wooden buildings. Mar ignored the disembodied invitation and slipped into an alley next to the brick tenement. Finally they stopped at a thick wooden door at the rear of a large, newly plastered, three-story building. A viewing grate in the door slid aside at Mar's knock. The door opened. Inside was a storeroom that smelled of sharp fish sauce and flour. Another door and they were into the light.

"Hetairarch!" A short, bald man in a sparkling blue silk tunic clasped

Mar's arms. His crooked teeth flashed in an open smile. He had a clipped, dark, wiry beard. "Welcome! Welcome!"

Mar turned to Haraldr. "This is Anatellon the charioteer. He won seven races in the Hippodrome. The Emperor Constantine had a bronze bust made of him."

"Of course the Emperor also made a full-size bronze statue of my best horse!" said Anatellon. He threw his arms wide and emitted a curiously high-pitched giggle. He looked at Haraldr. "And you need no introduction, Har-eld, Slayer of Saracens and Seljuks, and now Manglavite of Rome." Anatellon extended his arms; his forearms were as thick as the forelegs of an elk and so hard that they seemed carved of marble. After clasping Haraldr's arms, Anatellon suddenly raised his hands over his head. "So you hacked him right in two!" he exclaimed, bringing his arms down in a huge motion. He giggled. "I like that!"

Haraldr looked around. They stood in a bright antechamber next to a heavy wooden spiral staircase. Whirling music and frivolous voices came from a larger room beyond; Haraldr could see only glimpses of bright silk through a wooden screen carved with intricate leafy patterns. Anatellon led the two Norsemen up the staircase to a dimly lit hallway punctuated with curtained openings every half dozen ells. A woman went past them like a wraith, her face as lovely and pale as a porcelain mask, her white limbs and large breasts seeming to fluoresce beneath a gauzy robe. Her glistening dark hair was coiled in the fashion of the court and sprinkled with gems. "She's an Alan," whispered Anatellon to his guests. "Too good for this place. I won't give her to just anyone, even if they can meet the price. I've already got a few highly placed gentlemen who want to take her into the palace and make a lady of her." He winked at Haraldr. "You could afford her."

The hallway ended at bronze double doors chased with images of four rearing horses. The doors slid open and a young eunuch with a sweet, cherubic face bowed. The principal furnishing of the room was a large canopied bed. Anatellon gestured to three silk-cushioned backless chairs with thick ivory armrests. The eunuch quickly brought wine; he served the glass goblets with overly elaborate gestures, an unintended parody of the polished elegance of the Imperial Chamberlains. Mar motioned with his head at the eunuch, and Anatellon nodded. The boy left the room and slid the doors shut behind him.

"I haven't told the Manglavite Haraldr any of the details because I wanted to hear the story myself," said Mar to Anatellon. "What, exactly, did you see?"

Anatellon bent forward and tensed his bulging forearms. "Three nights ago a man came to my establishment and sat downstairs. I recognized him immediately as Nicetas Gabras—"

"What?" blurted Haraldr. "Not my chamberlain, Nicetas Gabras?"

"Believe me, Manglavite, it would be most unhealthy for a man in my business not to know the faces of men owned by the Orphanotrophus Joannes." Mar nodded, apparently vouching for Anatellon's reliability. "Anyway, I made it my business to keep a sharp eye on Gabras. To no end, it seemed. He drank a few cups, then called for a girl. He wasn't with her more than a quarter of an hour. Then he left, but as he walked out he passed a man who had been sitting by himself all night, the kind who find melancholy at the bottom of a cup. Anyway, I was watching Gabras very closely, and as he passed this man he held his right arm by his side like this"—Anatellon let his arm fall straight to the floor—"and showed three fingers like this. A gesture you wouldn't notice unless you were looking for something. Anyway, Gabras leaves, and this fellow stays and drinks for another two hours, perhaps. Then he calls for the same girl Gabras was with and, well, you should hear it from her."

Anatellon got up and slid the doors open; he spoke briefly to the eunuch waiting in the hall. By the time he returned to his seat, a young woman had entered the room. She was not much taller than a girl but fully developed in the breasts and hips; she had heavy, sensual lips and a slight dusk to her skin.

"Tell these eminences what happened, Flower."

"Yes." Flower looked at the carpet; there was a soft green tint to her eyes. Her wavy hair, streaked with light and dark brown tufts, hung freely over her shoulders. "You see, I had intended to take this man to another booth, Daria's, because the previous guest had disturbed mine." Flower made a comical churning motion with her arms to indicate that the "guest" had apparently vomited. "This man insisted that I take him to my booth. The third booth on the right." Flower shrugged. "Why not? I decided. Men make strange requests. So. I removed the filthy bedding and he reclined himself on the bare mattress. I had begun to unveil myself in the manner most men find provocative when he told me to turn away. So. I uncovered myself and found him still fully clothed, with his arm reaching beneath the mattress. 'Turn away,' he said quickly, 'modesty commands me to ask you to turn away until I have become accustomed to my nakedness.'" Flower narrowed her eyes. "What? I have never heard this before. This is all becoming more curious than I can bear. So. I pretended to hide my eyes, but I looked at him through my hair like this, and as I spied, I saw him reach beneath the mattress again, and this time I discovered the cause of his modesty. From beneath the mattress he miraculously produced a great fat wallet. I could see it sag from the weight of the coins. He concealed it within his clothing, which he then removed. Then, of course, he asked me to join him and proceeded in the manner of men."

Haraldr shook his head. Gabras, the milk-mouthed little swine. "Do you have any idea who this excessively modest . . . guest was?"

"Yes, Manglavite," said Anatellon. "Having been advised by Flower of these further coincidences, I made inquiries among my clientele. The man is called the Physician. Not because he dispenses palliatives, purgatives, and healing drafts, but because he can so quickly alleviate all of the pain and suffering that this life brings upon us." Anatellon made a slashing motion across his throat.

"Where would two ailing Norsemen find this apothecary?" asked Mar.

"Studion," said Anatellon ominously.

"Studion." Mar's inflection was the opposite of Anatellon's. He said the word as if it were some sort of rare gem.

† † †

The oil lamps cast a yellowish light over the stacks of documents, making them seem ancient, archival. Joannes rubbed the deep sockets of his eyes, wishing that these papers did indeed reflect the great flow of history and not merely the fragile aspirations of a single man whose life span would be so evanescent, so insignificant against the great firmament of time. Unless. Yes. Here, surrounding him, in these figures, this legislation, these tax codifications, were the dimensions of his immortality. Yes. Just as the builders of the great Hagia Sophia had proceeded from mere wooden models to an edifice that would reign through the millennia until the Last Trumpet blew, then so these papers were the architect's vision of the great edifice to his memory. And yet like the ever-remembered architects of the Mother Church, he needed a builder, a back to hoist the bricks and place them within the exacting strictures of his schemata. Yes, he had thought he had selected his builder well, a back broad and noble. But now that back was bowed, afflicted; each day it carried fewer and fewer bricks to the Heaven-scraping vaults. Each day his builder fell behind the schedule that had to be kept.

Joannes looked at papers on his writing table. Brilliant. This series of novels—a novel was a new law mandated by the Emperor—would generate enough tax revenues to again fill even the great Bulgar-Slayer's vast underground treasuries, revenues enough to send armies and fleets to the Pillars of Heracles again, to regain Alexandria and Aleppo and bring Venice and Genoa to their knees, to again reap the wealth of the Tigris and the Euphrates, to humble the caliphates and the Bulgars and exterminate the Scyths from the face of the earth. The world as the Pantocrator had enjoined them it should be. And it was already here, in this beautiful paper construction! The numbers could not lie! Let the Sophists in their impotent bureaus invoke their mincing reservations about "an overburdened collection apparatus," let the hand-wringing Strategi protest about "the difficulties of enforcement." It would work! The numbers would become solidi, and the power those solidi could buy would reach out into the world; the numbers would increase and the power of Rome would be restored.

But it took the force of an Emperor to place such a sweeping reform before the people, for in truth wasn't the Emperor and Autocrator really the master builder who himself could not build without the hundreds of thousands of sweating backs who labored at his command. If the master builder was not there to lash and cajole and inspire his laborers to once again put their shoulders to the load even when they were slumped with weariness and exhaustion, then no edifice would rise. And for all the laborers of Joannes's new Rome now knew, the master builder was a phantom, a man who could no longer appear in public, even for the briefest ceremony. Theotokos. Today's incident in front of the Hagia Sophia could have been the end. Yes. That serious. Fortunately the *barbaroi* Varangians had been able to detain all of the witnesses and convince them of the inestimable value of discretion.

The *barbaroi.* Thugs who built nothing, only plundered what others had labored to construct. The Hetairarch Mar Hunrodarson was moving too quickly; even common gossip acknowledged that now. And Haraldr Nordbrikt. What a mistake. To see the witless brute serenaded in the Hippodrome, his head bowed meekly—as if there had ever been a humble thought in his vanity-engorged skull. Build Haraldr Nordbrikt up and he would be more dangerous than Mar Hunrodarson; the people of the city might actually come to like him. Haraldr Nordbrikt's ascendant power clearly required the pruning that had already been arranged for him. Was it to be tonight? He would have to check with Gabras.

Joannes shook his massive head as if awakening from a bad dream. That was what was insufferably offensive about these fair-hairs in the palace! The time one spent dealing with them added to nothing, and took away from matters of real importance! Look at him, sitting here fuming at pasty-faced pirates from Thule when history waited! Time, passing inexorably, demanded his answer.

Joannes brought his massive splayed arms down on his writing table, and the impact echoed through the empty corridors of the Magnara basement. Where was the answer? Where? And then like the voice of an angel, the answer came to him. Extraordinary. Was it possible? Perhaps it was. And yet to do it would be more difficult than passing the entire peninsula of Byzantium through the eye of a needle. Who could do that? Not even a conjurer. But perhaps . . . In the silence of the night the angels whispered again, and Joannes heard. Yes. Love. Love, which had created the entire world out of the formless abyss, had brought light to eternal darkness, and had vaulted the endless waters. Love had done it once. And might do it again. Love. And luck.

† † †

"What do you dream about?"

Halldor's eyes snapped open. He groggily pieced together the Greek sentence. Had he been asleep? How long? Odin! Well, it was no feather bed being Komes of the Middle Hetairia, particularly now that Haraldr was almost always occupied with his Manglavite duties, whatever they were. Ulfr, thankfully, handled the considerable burden of administration, but it was still Halldor who had to pound the excruciating ceremonial discipline of the court into five hundred swaddling-new guardsmen, most of whom still couldn't tell a lofty patrician from a lowly exarch or find their way from the Magnara to the Chrysotriklinos. It was sufficiently taxing to make a man fall asleep next to a woman as beautiful as this.

"You were dreaming. I can tell." The lady's blue eyes reflected the glowing candelabra far over her head.

Halldor pulled his legs up so the bulge in his robe wouldn't be so prominent.

"Don't be embarrassed," she said, laughing. "I am not a virgin."

No, you're worse, thought Halldor, you're the wife of some official whose title Halldor couldn't exactly pinpoint; the essential fact was that the husband had been exiled for several years as temporary special Strategus of some theme halfway to Vinland. The lady had issued Halldor an invitation to dine with her, and as some irascible old Magister had pointed out to him, it would have shamed the lovely woman had he refused; surely even a semi-pagan Tauro-Scyth understood that it was his

Christian obligation to console the lonely "semi-widow." So after a suit-ably proper five-day interval, during which the prospective liaison had become the titillation of half the ladies at court, here he was. Asleep, with nothing consummated.

"Did I bore you?" she asked, stroking his long blond hair with fingers like slender ivory flutes.

Halldor smiled at her. Her lips were as exquisite as a Greek Aphro-dite's, her hair almost pure gold in the lamplight. Her breasts swelled against her silk scaramangium. He touched his lips to her ear, inhaling the scent of roses and fresh meadow flowers. "When . . . did you . . . ever . . . bore a man?" Halldor surmised that his Greek had been fluent enough when she threw her arm around his neck and crushed her breast to his with an embrace as tight as a shipbuilder's vise. He finally prised his mouth away from the tender aggression of her lips to ask the salient question. "Where . . . would you like . . . to do this?"

"In my bath," she said, gulping, her eyes glittering.

† † †

The child looked up, his black eyes mesmerized by the sight of the giant fair-hairs and their woman. He hastily stripped the tattered rag from the torso of the fallen man and vanished. Squirming clusters of large rats continued to work on the face and toes of a fresh corpse only a few ells away. The fallen man groaned. Mar held Haraldr back. "A pox blotch," he said. "He will be dead soon, anyway." Haraldr look around, searching for an instrument of mercy. He saw a large piece of scorched masonry that had crumbled from the ruined, fire-gutted building to his right. He picked up the big stone and walked over to the now-naked, softly breath-ing man. Haraldr gasped; the man's face and most of his body were a mass of pustulant sores. Only the feverish eyes were human. They reached out and the man moaned. "Holy . . . cherubim . . . save me." Haraldr looked at the tittering, fearless rats, waiting only for him to step back before they began to nibble on living flesh. He brought the stone smashing down on welcoming eyes.

Mar held Flower in his arms. She had bravely agreed to come along and identify the Physician, if possible; she had not reckoned on this. "This is where they come to die, when even the streets turn them out," said Mar, as if anything could explain this. A man entered the intersection, his frock as black as the charred shells of the tenements that towered above him. The bearded monk bent over another corpse, one of a half dozen or so lying about in the muck, and silently arranged the stiff, chalk-hued arms. "They come here to die because they know the monks will find them," said Mar. "Over there"—he pointed north—"is the Studius Monastery. They have a fraternity of monks who do nothing but retrieve and bury the corpses that here are shunned by even the dirt." Mar walked over to the monk and bowed, then handed the serene-looking man some gold coins. The monk dipped his head perfunctorily and continued his work.

Mar took Flower's hand and looked at Haraldr. He spoke in Norse. "When you see the live creatures of the Studion, you will understand why I have taken us through the refuges of the dead."

They soon came among the living. A dark alley opened up onto a fairly broad avenue, which in spite of its breadth was almost completely canopied by jutting, enclosed wooden balconies and makeshift platforms that in many cases joined over the streets. The stench of human excrement was overpowering. The surface of the street was spongy, and to his horror Haraldr realized that it was paved with well-trodden mud, garbage, and sewage, perhaps to the depth of an ell. Beneath the precarious wooden canopies and reeking, slimy facades clustered hundreds of supine forms. The lucky ones were covered with straw; most of the rest, many of whom had bare skin showing through their rags, were huddled together in scores of human mounds, each several ells high. Haraldr was incredulous. "Won't the ones at the bottom suffocate?" he asked Mar.

"Look again. They are not piled on one another but on mounds of garbage. The heat of decay keeps them warm."

They began their stroll through Hell. The clumps of bodies stirred from endless wet coughs and moans. A man, his scalp covered with great black scabs, squatted in the street, groaning and clutching his knees. Two boys, perhaps ten, kicked at a solitary old man. A naked, filth-blackened child stood by a sleeping man and woman, wailing.

Block after block of this. A man, his greasy tunic thrown up, rutting like a dog with what appeared to be a very young girl, almost a child. In one tenement there was a party; two men stuck their heads out a window and tried to drop bits of their flaming tapers on the bodies huddled below. A naked woman squatted on a wooden balcony and urinated. A boy of fourteen, perhaps, handless, his mouth covered with sores, offered the Norsemen a sex act he could perform with the stump of his slender wrist.

Haraldr could scarcely believe his reeling senses. He had seen pockets of misery in Hedeby and Kiev, the offal-strewn, muddy streets crowded with cutpurses, charlatans, and crippled beggars. But the Studion was beyond his experience, beyond imagining. Now he understood why he had been blindfolded on his initial entry into the city, and why these wretches would attempt to burn their own dwellings. This offended the gods, and it should offend man. He had known the Empress City to be wanton, even cruel. But this was an infection of the body, a great corruption that would contaminate everything she touched. And yet the monk who came to bury the outcasts of the Empress City was a part of her, too; no Norseman would have had that kind of courage or devotion to the souls of strangers. The beauty and virtue of this ravishing city were beyond imagining, and so was her unspeakable evil. Perhaps that was also true of Maria.

† † †

Halldor draped the thick linen towel around his waist and waited. The steam glazed the green marble benches with a film of condensation and clouded the plastered vault overhead. Halldor enjoyed this Roman ritual, particularly when there was a woman waiting at the end of his sweat. When he had assessed that the foul humors—whatever they were—had been expunged from his body, he mopped his body with the towel and entered the next chamber. The large pool was almost obscured by steam, like one of Iceland's natural hot pools on a winter day. He heard a splash and saw a vague diffusion of pink.

Halldor rinsed himself in the tub adjacent to the pool and then walked carefully down the opus-sectile steps; he could see a mosaic pattern on the bottom of the pool but could not make out the motifs. The water was cool but not chilling.

"They say you are a great seafarer." Her voice was crystalline, delightful. Halldor began to suspect that he would want to dine here more than once. He wished the steam would clear so he could get a look at her. In his arms she had felt like one of those statues come to life, each curve perfect. "Can you cross the water that separates us?" she asked, her voice ringing delicately against a domed ceiling with a large glass oculus in the middle.

Halldor stroked easily; he had learned to swim at three summers. He touched the far end of the pool and wiped at the water in his eyes. "You didn't navigate properly." Halldor reached toward the teasing voice and made brief contact with slippery flesh. She thrashed away. Suddenly he could feel her against his back, her breasts and thighs sliding by. This time he got hold of an ankle and pulled her into his arms. "You have been netted," he said. She laughed and pressed her entire body against his and kissed him, letting the water drain from her lips like a thin, aphrodisiac oil. "Yes," she said, laughing, "but do you think you can spear me?" Then she ducked out of his arms and swam away.

† † †

The filth-paved road turned abruptly left, into the triangle created by the southward sweep of the Marmora coastline before it met the Great Wall of the city. "We have met all the honest folk of the Studion," Mar said in Norse, motioning back toward the long, dark boulevard of misery they had just traversed. "Let us now go among the liars, thieves, cheats, whores, and murderers."

The buildings here were better maintained, with plaster and wood patchwork frequently visible, though whole facades of crumbling brick and rotting wood also awaited repairs that might never be made. Signs, and even an occasional statue, appeared here and there above the arcades of dingy inns and food shops. Prostitutes, their faces virtually painted on, prowled like cats. "Pretty thing, Eminences," said one sourly as she passed, eyeing Flower enviously; beneath her caked-on powder, large boils raised pale welts.

Cutpurses ran beneath the arcades in shadowy packs, and they soon became bolder, swarming into the street to run about the Norsemen like crazy jackals trying to determine whether a lion was sufficiently wounded to permit an attack. At an intersection five or six whores held a man upside down by his quivering legs; another garishly painted woman sat by his head with a rock, bashing his teeth out. "Cheated her," explained one of the women to the gathering crowd.

The inns became larger, and crowds milled in the street; a man in silk passed, accompanied by more than a dozen retainers all wearing swords and cheap steel breastplates. "I get you best price for the girl," squeaked a voice that seemed to come from Haraldr's elbow; he never saw the source. An old man completely blinded by cataracts pounded on Haraldr's chest and vanished into the crowd. A woman smiled, her rotted teeth like old wood between her brilliantly painted lips.

Flower clutched at Haraldr. Mar had turned away and was bent over a young man who had fallen to his knees; he grasped the man's forearm in his huge fist. "The Squirrel," Mar hissed. "Your hand in my cloak told me you must know where I can find the Squirrel." The foiled cut-purse said nothing; his boyish face reddened and scowled. The crowd began to cluster. There was a snap, and the cut-purse howled and cradled his arm;

Mar immediately grasped the other arm. "When I finish with your arms, I'll start with your fingers. That might be a permanent disability in your profession." The thief whimpered and blurted, "The Devil's Walking Stick!" Mar let him stumble off through the crowd.

The Devil's Walking Stick was an inn situated in an ancient building several blocks closer to the seawall. The name derived from a trident carved in relief, apparently centuries ago, on the stone above the arcade. The street in front of the inn was almost solidly packed with boisterous, shoving young men and a few beleagured whores. "Cutthroats, the lot," said Mar, who had virtually hidden Flower inside his cloak. "If anyone makes a move toward you, kill them. You cannot expect to bluster past this kind simply because we are Varangians and might reduce the entire Studion to cinders if one of us is harmed here. These men don't care. They care about the next quarter hour and whether it will offer a strong draft and a tight cunt."

Haraldr and Mar walked side by side through the crowd, their huge shoulders forming a virtual arch over Flower. Hard eyes and scarred faces turned toward them, but the bodies moved aside. They walked beneath the arcade and through the arched doorway of the inn. The air was smoky and redolent of cheap wine and unwashed men. A dice game was under way at the nearer of two large tables; a great cheer accompanied each roll. At the farther table the center of attention was a small, dark-eyed man wearing an absurd-looking, brand-new brimless silk bonnet like those that were just coming into fashion with the Imperial courtiers. "I rescued a miserable cut-purse from the Numera the other day," said Mar. "He's over there. I'm sure he can tell me where to find the Physician. Stay with Flower. Remember what I said. They will try to insult you, and perhaps even our Father. Ignore the words. Watch the hands and the feet."

Mar shouldered through the crowd. The game came to a temporary halt. Flower trembled, her head hidden beneath Haraldr's arm like a frightened bird under its mother's wing. Dangerous, snakelike eyes began to examine the partially hidden female form beneath Haraldr's cloak. Mar reached the table and greeted the man in the red bonnet. A group of men at the near table, already turned to face Haraldr, stood up. They wore cheap silk and clearly fancied themselves successful rogues. The tallest was a giant among Romans; his dark beard stuck out like a shelf, and his eyes sparkled.

"Let us have a look, Eminence." The man's voice was deep, even, unthreatening. He nodded at his fellows. "We'll pay good for just a look at her." Haraldr gripped the pommel of his short sword; he wished he had worn Emma. But Mar had warned him that a byrnnie might inhibit the quickness he would need in these streets.

"He's dumb as a goat," said a smaller man with a sharp white streak in his dark hair. "You might as well pay to see a turd walk as see a Varangian talk."

"Well, there's one . . . no, two turds just walked in here!" a third said, chortling.

"Shut up!" barked the big man. "He knows what we're saying." The big man swayed as if he would take a step forward, and Haraldr prepared to take his head off. But the man's legs spread wide and he set himself, as if to declare his observance of a border between himself and the Norse giant. "Your Emperor will be dead soon," he said, his eyes grim. "He's abed now, dying. He's not shown himself to us or seen our Mother in all the new year. We'll put our own man up there before we let a corpse rule us while the unholy monk Joannes grinds us beneath his boot. Now you've seen Studion, Eminence. Do you think your Varangians can stop us if we get a will about us?"

Haraldr was taken aback. He had expected simple aggression, not the strange conviction of this criminal. The Emperor dying? It was true that he had not been in the city to welcome his wife, or the men who had saved her, and that there had been no procession on his return. But Haraldr had assumed that the Emperor was eluding his wife's treachery; after all, he could not simply throw the purple-born into Neorion. But this was certainly a new facet to the complex structure of Haraldr's doubts. If the Emperor was dying, then Joannes, no longer shielded by his Imperial relation, might indeed be driven to extreme measures in order to maintain his power. But why hadn't Mar told him this? That insight into Joannes's motives would have been much more convincing than this journey into Hell.

Haraldr watched while Mar, who had concluded his conversation with the red-bonneted man, made his way back through the crowd. He quickly responded to his impulse. "If a man wanted to . . . talk more of this, for whom would he ask?"

Now the big man did his own calculating. Finally he put his coarse, broad palm to his beard and compressed the springy mass. A large sapphire with a four-pointed star flashed from a thick finger. "The Blue Star," he said simply, then bowed curtly, turned, and sat down.

Out in the street, Mar pointed east. "Odin favors our enterprise. My friend had an associate who knew where the Physician currently reposes between cures. It is only two blocks away." Mar looked at Haraldr quizzically. "It is worthwhile to have friends in the Studion. Did you and that big man come to an agreement?"

"We exchanged greetings." Haraldr was acutely wary now. But if he had to fight Mar, he was more than prepared.

"You must water whatever they tell you here to arrive at the truth. These louts are spreading a rumor that the Emperor is dying. That, of course, is nothing like the truth. He has been ill but will soon recover. But they are worried that Joannes will rule in his stead regardless, and I think they will rise up if they imagine that tyranny to be imminent."

From what he had seen, Haraldr could believe the last part of Mar's explanation. But he was more convinced than ever that this "proof" of a plot against him was nothing more than a rambling ruse; was Mar hoping to exhaust him before he killed him?

The hostel where the Physician was reputed to live was perhaps the best-kept building in the Studion; it had been a great town palace once, and fit-looking horses were still stabled in the courtyard. The Physician lived on the third level, his room adjacent to a wooden staircase with rather delicately carved railings. Mar knocked on the door, waited a few seconds, then stepped back and shattered it with one kick.

A naked woman cowered on a small, linen-sheeted bed. Mar stomped around, throwing wide the curtains and rifling a large wooden cabinet set against the wall. He tossed some garish, cheaply dyed linen robes on the floor. He turned to the woman. She clutched the sheet up to her mouth, and her red-rimmed eyes shone with fright. "I want to know where the man they call the Physician has gone." The woman stared and pressed the sheet between long, pale legs blotched with several livid purple bruises. "You have three choices," said Mar, looking around the room casually. "Tell me now, and I leave you in peace, with a coin to buy you a room somewhere else. Tell me in the Numera, and depart with whatever I have not taken from you there. Third, do not tell me—"

The woman's trembling arm shot out. "I want to see the coin." Mar quickly produced a silver nomismata. "He went out. He said he was going to deliver a Varangian to the Neorion."

Mar and Haraldr stared at one another in surprise. "You still haven't told me," said Mar to the woman.

The woman stood up and wrapped the sheet around herself. "The name of the . . . patient was with the money." She pushed aside the cabinet, removed a chunk of plaster from the wall behind it, and thrust her hand in the hiding place. She cursed and turned. She held a flaccid leather wallet.

Mar snatched the wallet from the suddenly livid woman, probed with his fingers, and extracted a scrap of parchment. He showed the scrap to Haraldr. "Is this Gabras's hand?"

Haraldr nodded gravely as he read the name. "Who is it?" he asked, totally puzzled.

"The Strategus ex prosponon of Vaspurakan," said Mar, as bewildered as Haraldr. "He doesn't even reside in the City. He is in virtual exile. His wife stayed here. She is a vixen over whom many hounds have run themselves silly."

The cold realization reduced Haraldr's gut to an icy knot. "Halldor," he said weakly.

"Halldor Snorrason? The cockhound?" Mar's face registered the connection. "Theotokos! We'll get horses down below!"

† † †

"How many women do you have in Thule?" She fluttered her legs in the water and clutched Halldor's arms tightly around her breasts.

"Dozens."

She turned her head slightly and squeezed his arms tighter. "Do you keep them in a gynaeceum?"

"I let them . . . run . . . about . . . free. Naked. In a field. Like . . . deer."

"Extraordinary. How often do you make love to them?"

"Six . . . each night."

"How many times?"

"Once. Each . . . once."

She wriggled to face him. "Six times? One night?" She put her arms around his neck. "So we have three more times?"

† † †

Mar swung Flower off his wheezing, lathered horse and leapt to the ground. "Don't tether them," he yelled to Haraldr. He looked up at the sheer facade of the big town house. A light showed in a third-floor window. Mar pounded once on the great iron-studded wooden door and it immediately flew open. He turned back to Haraldr. "The lock has been broken."

A few candles in sconces lit the entrance hall. Mar motioned to the spiral staircase. They left Flower in the entrance hall and climbed silently to the third floor, short swords unsheathed. Haraldr put his hand down and felt the sticky, slippery texture of freshly pooled blood. In the dim light Mar pointed to the body lying at the top of the steps; the man was dressed like a typical servant in a wealthy household.

Mar signaled Haraldr to stay back and crept toward the light that filtered around a door, slightly ajar, at the end of the hall. Haraldr heard a noise at the second-floor landing. He looked down. Flower was crawling up the steps. Something crashed in the hall. Mar was on his feet whirling, his hands at his throat, a black shape like a giant hump clamped to his back. A horrible gagging came from Mar's throat, and Haraldr leapt for the deadly parasite on Mar's back, but before he could reach him, Mar turned and smashed his back against the wall, flying through the wood-and-stucco interior construction as if it were paper. Haraldr charged into the room through the hastily improvised opening, only to see Mar propel his unwanted passenger into the thick masonry exterior wall with a sickening crunch. The impact brought down great chunks of the ceiling and sent roof tiles clattering to the street below.

Mar staggered forward and the hump slid off his back like a half-empty sack. He pulled the attacker's silk cord from around his neck and rubbed his throat. "Bring Flower in here," he said raspily.

The attacker's face, unlike the back of his head, was intact. Haraldr took a candle from a wall sconce and held it above the inert form. Flower bent over, studied the face for a moment, and shook her head. "That is not the man," she said.

✝ ✝ ✝

Extraordinary, thought Halldor. Like a fist. In spite of his conviction that it was never wise to let a woman know she had given unusual pleasure, he groaned with enjoyment. He would indeed dine in this house again.

She sat up straight and let him take her breasts in his mouth. Her pelvis shuddered and contorted. "Do you want your Thule women now?" she teased, following with a hiccuplike laugh. "Thule is so cold. Here it is so hot. I will go around naked all day if you want."

Ohhhh, thought Halldor, *have I finally met an adversary equal to my skills? Freyja! Bitch! The woman can make the house shake. My teeth are rattling!*

Halldor was not at first certain what it was that plunged through the oculus high above the pool. It hit the water with a resounding impact, floundered, and then leapt for him. He knew when he saw the silver glint that it was a knife. He tried to throw his lover off him, but she held him with that particularly potent grip, and pain shot through his groin. He felt a searing in his left pectoral and plunged under the surface. The water immediately reddened. *Whether I live or die,* he thought with characteristic clarity, *no one will believe this.* She still had him, apparently thinking this was a game; then her eyes opened and she saw the blood and released him. Where was the knife! He saw the tunic billowing out in the water, away from him, and he realized that the assassin had come for his hostess, not for him. The knife shone with a terrible metallic brilliance through the steam, and it lifted over her bare white breast. Halldor could not reach it, but he splashed water at the assassin's face and the knife halted for an instant in midair. Halldor leapt like a dolphin. The man was strong but not nearly strong enough. For a moment the knife slashed like a silver fish just beneath the surface. Bubbles roiled the water above the man's head, and he went limp.

Halldor threw the body onto the tiles and took the lady in his arms. She cried for a moment and then kissed him, smiling through her tears. "Who wants . . . to kill you?" he asked. "Your husband?"

"No. He is happy for me to have lovers since it relieves him of a duty he finds—" She broke off in alarm.

Halldor looked toward the rinsing tub in sickening astonishment. Two more killers . . . where was that knife! Through the rapidly clearing steam he recognized Haraldr and Mar.

"Halldor!" yelled Haraldr; he jumped in the water and embraced his friend. Mar disappeared for a moment.

"What happened?" asked Haraldr.

Halldor casually pointed to the shattered oculus in the dome. "A spectacular leap. For some reason he wanted to kill this beautiful lady." The lady smiled at Haraldr, apparently concerned about neither her recent peril nor her present state of undress.

Mar reappeared with Flower and led her to the body. "It is the man I saw," she said immediately.

Haraldr shook his head and began to reconstruct the bizarre chain of events, theorizing aloud. "So Joannes learns that Halldor is going to visit this lady's house—the entire court has known for several days—and sends his man Gabras—my chamberlain, Nicetas Gabras—to arrange an assassination. But the assassin intends to kill the lady. Why?" He was posing the question to himself as well as to Mar.

Mar set his lips grimly. "Because that is the way the Roman mind works. And it is in particular the way our Orphanotrophus Joannes's works. This highly placed lady is murdered, and the accused, the obvious assailant, is the Komes Halldor Snorrason of the Middle Hetairia. Joannes coerces Haraldr with his comrade's scandal. Or perhaps he has a broader objective. I believe that in spite of his temporary buildup of your unit, his interest in the long run is eliminating the Varangian Guard entirely, so that no Emperor could enjoy the security we provide. As you well know, there are several factions at court, most notably the Dhynatoi, who share this objective. They would be only too happy to use this scandal to reduce numbers in both the Middle and Grand Hetairia. If Joannes goes directly after you or one of your men, he signals his intentions and invites your just retaliation. This way he forces you to defend yourself against the indignation of others. That the lady is dead is of no account. For Joannes, any treachery is conceivable, and any innocent life merely expedient."

Haraldr examined the face of the assassin again, then looked among the faces of the living, one by one. It was preposterous that Mar would have arranged such an elaborate drama—including an attack on himself—to make such an oblique point. And Gabras was a certain link to Joannes. This was not the kind of proof he had expected, which made it all the more convincing. Yes, Joannes was his enemy, an enemy far more devious and ruthless than he could have imagined just a few hours ago. And while that still did not make Mar his friend, he realized another essential truth. To fight this demon-monk Joannes, he would need Mar just as badly as Mar needed him.

The lady reached out and touched Haraldr on his arm, a look of concern on her face. "We are fine," she said. "We have not been hurt." She displayed a beautiful wet smile and looked over at Mar and Flower. "Since you are all here, why don't you stay?"

he komes of the Khazar guard looked at the list and frowned. "I am certain there must be some mistake, Manglavite. I don't have your name here." The komes looked up and shrugged sympathetically. "I could send a man to the Orphanotrophus's office and find out why. Most likely they are still working. As I say, I am certain there wouldn't be a problem for you."

"I appreciate your offer, Komes," said Haraldr, "but don't concern yourself with the matter. My business can wait." Haraldr nodded politely, turned, and walked back down the steps leading to the massive bronze doors of the Imperial Gynaeceum. He felt both relieved and ashamed: relieved that the Khazar guards at the entrance to the Gynaeceum had been unable to admit him—only the select few on Joannes's list were now allowed access to the Imperial women's quarters—and ashamed with himself for even trying to see Maria.

He wandered without direction among the terraced gardens beneath the Hippodrome. Lacquered with moonlight and beaded with lamps, the intricate architecture of the palace complex revealed a geometry concealed by the day's dazzling polychromes. Tonight he had given fate yet one more toss and had decided to confront Maria, to find out if she had meant Joannes or the Emperor, and in whose name she had asked her deadly question, and if *his* life had been of any consequence in the matter. But now fate had signaled agreement with what reason had told him all along: Forget her. It was of no consequence whether she had employed the ruse of love to kill a good man or an evil man. Not where love was concerned. He thought of what Mar had said the previous night about the "Roman mind." He had not until then fully understood the complexity—and cruelty—of that mind, and now he knew that if he was to leave here with his life and that of his pledge-men, he would need to anticipate and to an extent acquire that convoluted habit of thought. But one could not love with a Roman mind. The heart could not wear veils, could not embrace one thing as a means to acquire another. He had at least confessed to her that he concealed a secret in his breast. She had worn a mask from the beginning. And he hated her for that as much as he had once thought he loved her.

He stopped by one of the little pools, ringed by trees and bordered with stone benches. He sat and watched the fish slide silently through their pearled domain, their orange scales dull gold in the moonlight. Something in the faint phosphorus of the water made him think of Norway, of standing high above Trondheimfjord, the water like a slab of polished lapis lazuli beneath him; farther to the west, the wind-textured, blue-green expanse of the open sea, scattered with silver shavings by a setting sun. Norway. He had the wealth now, he had the dedicated nucleus of an army. Go home. And yet with that same thought he realized he could not. At the very least he had considerable doubt that the soul of his pledge-man, Asbjorn Ingvarson, had in fact been avenged. But now there were other souls crying out to him. Studion. The images of the wretches leapt at him like the fearless rats that would prey on their moribund flesh. He could not deal with those images. He could not leave them behind, either.

A bug rippled the water, and several fish thrashed to the surface in response. Destroy Joannes: Haraldr realized he could not help heal Rome or begin to assuage his own troubled soul without accomplishing that. And to destroy Joannes he would need to think with the Roman mind. To begin with, he would need Mar. Not a reluctant, grudging, boyish collaboration with Mar but a difficult, yet necessary, partnership with an ally he could not trust. Yes, he would embrace Mar; he would embrace the devil to slay the beast at Rome's dark heart. And when Joannes had been destroyed, perhaps he and Mar could part comrades, and perhaps they would have to ask Odin to choose between them. And should that turn out to be the case, the best way to learn how to defeat a man in single combat was to second him.

He could not sleep; his mind raced with the purpose before him. He took the route he and Mar had taken the night before and emerged onto the curious landscape beneath the Hippodrome. It was much like the previous night, the circus animals and the sad, tawdry performers, the booths of the palmists and the diviners. But tonight he was unaccompanied by the fearsome Hetairarch, and the people came out to meet him. "Saracen-Slayer!" "Manglavite!" Little boys rushed up to touch his cloak and scurry away. Two stooped old men scuttled along beside him, not daring to look up, satisfied with some silent conversation. A prostitute ran her fingers lightly over his sleeve, tilted her head, and cocked an eyebrow;

she was dark-haired and very pale and young enough still to be pretty, and for some reason he was moved by her. But he walked on, for a moment thinking he would actually go all the way to Studion and greet the people there.

The torso and head of a small boy rolled up to him in a little wooden cart. Haraldr looked into the brown eyes of this partially disembodied waif; they were frightening in their voracious, almost feral need, and yet their honesty affected Haraldr more than fawn-eyed supplication. He reached into his purse and gave the boy a silver nomismata; suddenly the boy's eyes had a heart-breaking innocence. As if by magic, a dozen boys appeared. Haraldr quickly distributed the rest of his coins, finally holding up his empty purse to show he had no more. The boys vanished, quarreling among themselves.

Haraldr remembered the way, the alley behind the row of wooden buildings. Why was he going here? he wondered briefly. But he knew. Maria had left his heart wounded and withdrawn, but she had left his body eager and questing. The sexuality of the Empress City was not hers alone; she had only initiated his seduction, not consummated it. And every woman he held in his arms from this moment on would be the answer to Maria's treachery, the denial of fate's caprice, reducing her at last to the anonymity of remembered flesh, and that alone. He exited the alley and saw the large, freshly plastered facade straight ahead. He went to the dark wooden door and knocked. The viewing grate slid aside. He had to wait for a while, and considered leaving. Then the locks rattled and Anatellon the charioteer virtually exploded in his face.

"Haraldr Nordbrikt! Esteemed Manglavite and Slayer of Saracens!" Anatellon took Haraldr's arms in his rock-hard fists. "You honor us, sir! Please, please come in!" As Anatellon ushered Haraldr inside, he giggled in his curious, genial fashion. "You don't even need to tell me, esteemed sir. You've come for my Alan girl."

† † †

"I don't care who was at fault here. This should have been brought to me. This is something the Manglavite and I should have settled among ourselves." Mar slapped his hands flat against his writing table. He looked at Centurion Thorvald Ostenson, and then addressed the uniformed Varangian standing next to Ostenson. "It's fortunate for you that no one was seriously hurt. But I need to impose some kind of penalty because I simply cannot afford to have the men of the Grand Hetairia quarreling with the men of the Middle Hetairia. I'm going to confine you for two weeks and fine you five silver nomismata. And you can tell your comrades that the penalties for future violations will be considerably more onerous. We are not here to settle personal grudges." Mar gestured at Ostenson to show the Varangian out.

When the Varangian had left, Ostenson closed the door again and studied Mar, frank, farm-boy astonishment on his ruddy face. "May I speak, Hetairarch?"

"I didn't appoint you Centurion because I thought you were a fool. Go ahead."

"Hetairarch, that was a very minor incident, and one that did not take place in the palace precincts. Some Varangians of both the Middle and Grand Hetairia were drinking at the same inn, and one of the Manglavite's men lured this man's whore away by flaunting the gold in his purse. And it wasn't just the whore they were fighting over. The men resent that the members of the Middle Hetairia are in most cases wealthier than them."

"I am aware of that, Centurion. That is why I want to make certain that whatever feelings of ill will that presently exist are not exacerbated."

Ostenson still looked astonished. "Hetairarch, I don't see how our interests are served by allowing the Middle Hetairia and the Manglavite to presume such importance."

"We are working with the Middle Hetairia toward a common objective. As soon as my plans are complete, I will explain them to you fully, and you will understand. In the meantime I need harmony among the two divisions of the Varangian Guard, and I am charging you with that responsibility. I myself will be working closely with the Manglavite Haraldr Nordbrikt."

"Hetairarch." Ostenson paused and then decided to test the limits of his relationship with his commander. "Hetairarch, when this common objective is achieved, won't it be dangerous to have so strengthened Haraldr Nordbrikt? He is already a hero in the city. You cannot drink anywhere without hearing his name. Saracen-Slayer. Saracen-Slayer. I think he has the potential to be a dangerous rival to you, and you are merely encouraging his rise."

It happened too fast for Ostenson's comprehension. He saw Mar leap to his feet and lunge toward him, and then felt the huge force of inertia as he flew into the wall behind him. When he came to, he was leaning against the wall, his feet outstretched, his head hammering. Mar was sponging the back of his neck.

Mar pulled Ostenson to his feet. "Never presume what I am or am not doing, Centurion," he said evenly.

he Bogomil twisted a lock of his long stringy hair and looked earnestly at Maria, with all sincerity trying to avoid so much as a glance at the jeweled icon of the Virgin hanging on the wall behind her; he regarded such images as manifestations placed upon this earth by Satanael, the eldest son of God, to confound those who truly believed in God and his two younger sons, Christ and the Holy Spirit. "The Antichrist," the Bogomil intoned in response to her question, "will be Satanael in his final form. When he is vanquished, the entire world will blaze with flame and a hurricane of wind and dust will scour the earth and raze the very mountains and obliterate the valleys, and all that will remain will be as flat and white as a sheet of parchment."

"How marvelous." Maria tried to envision that glazed, featureless, bone-white surface. Perhaps death was an all-consuming white light, she fancied to herself, not the darkness she had so often imagined. But of course these were the fables of heretics. She smiled at the gentle fanatic who sat on the carpet opposite her; before his conversion to the Bogomil sect the young man had been an idle Dhynatoi scion whose only passions were dice, polo horses, and betting on races in the Hippodrome; he had often kept company with Ignatius Attalietes. "So why do you Bogomils oppose the sacrament of marriage?" she asked, steering the impromptu sermon toward another of her favorite subjects.

"It is impure. The unchaste love of a man for a woman is an act of obeisance to Satanael, who created the physical world."

"But if God perfected Adam, who gave life to Eve, who was seduced by Satanael and gave birth to Cain and a daughter you Bogomils call Perfection . . . I am correctly stating your beliefs, am I not?"

The Bogomil nodded. His placid, dreamy eyes blinked once, then twice, suddenly wary.

"So if a perfect woman resulted from the illicit union of Satanael and Eve, was there not an element of purity in their congress?"

"But Satanael and Eve were not joined in the sacrament of marriage. Nor was there love between them."

"Exactly. So Eve and Satanael fornicated as beasts do, and yet their spawn was a perfect woman child."

"And accursed Cain."

"I am only suggesting that the woman fornicated and conceived a daughter who was without sin. I do not care what crimes your Satanael urges men to commit."

"Satanael is prompting you to say that."

Zoe appeared beneath the carved stone lintel of the door that connected Maria's antechamber to the Imperial apartments. She clapped her hands. "Little daughter! You have confounded the heretic!" The Empress walked over and rustled the Bogomil's hair; he shrunk away from her as if Satanael himself had reached forth his hand. "You would do better with the Euchitae, my darling," Zoe said to Maria. "They abhor the world of the flesh while permitting every kind of sexual excess." The Bogomil shot to his feet and scurried out of the room without another word. Zoe looked after him with mock despair. "Why is it that our invitations to Paradise are invariably extended by men with a peculiar, one would almost say, unnatural, horror of women?"

"Perhaps they remember that it was a woman's crimes for which they lost Eden." Her tone was suddenly wistful.

Zoe frowned slightly; even this casual distressing of her features seemed to age her dramatically. "Little daughter, you are not still reflecting upon the fruit you did not succeed in offering to your . . . companion, Haraldr Saracen-Slayer or whatever. I really believe that of all the melancholies you have nursed over the years, this is the most severe and worrisome. I can't imagine that you still dote on him. Perhaps he has not forgiven you your little betrayal of his earnest Tauro-Scythian passions, but he has certainly forgiven our sex. You do know that he has become a frantic devotee of Priapus in the months we have been confined here, do you not? Apparently he is intent on impaling a new woman each day; perhaps it is some Tauro-Scythian custom. He has taken a whore to live in his palace, and do you know Danielis, the wife of the Curator of the Magnara? She is one of his conquests as well. Can you imagine her? I always considered her to be so . . . conventional. When I heard of the two of them, I conjured the most remarkable image. And of course you have heard about our dear little Anna. I must say there is a point at which we must be just a bit . . . censorious of these affairs. She is just a girl."

"She is not a virgin," said Maria sullenly.

"Oh, dear. I seem to have missed that. When was it?"

Maria looked at Zoe as if reproaching her for her high spirits. Zoe frowned again and sat next to her; she stroked Maria's sable-soft black hair like an admiring suitor. "I am not mocking you out of spite or even boredom, my little darling. You know that in my heart you are my first-born, the dearest child of my soul, if not of my loins. This melancholy of yours, which has apparently driven you to interviews with Bogomils, has rended my own heart. So I have . . . negotiated in your behalf." Zoe kissed Maria on the cheek. "I have won your freedom to come and go as you please."

"Mother!" Maria threw her arms around Zoe. "So that is why you were teasing me!" She hesitated. "But I will not leave you here alone."

"You are not leaving me alone." Zoe's smile was enigmatic. Maria presumed that Zoe had taken a lover; she was often closeted in her sealed apartments late at night. "I think you should go out tonight," said Zoe. "Your friend Nicephorus Argyrus has initiated another clever enterprise. He has opened a hostel for the sumptuous lodging and extravagant entertainment of visiting merchants and embassies, this because he now has exclusive agreements with most of our major trading partners; I believe Genoa is the only substantial monopoly that has as yet eluded his grasp. His establishment has quickly become indecently fashionable; Symeon says that on any evening you could find enough Roman dignitaries there to convene the Senate, conduct the Palm Sunday procession, and conquer the caliphates. Argyrus has provided a dining room and boxes at the theater, suitable even for ladies of your class, and Symeon says the merchant invites scandal by encouraging the sexes to mix discreetly."

Maria said nothing, but her eyes glimmered with the ineffable confusion of her feelings: anticipation, dread, bitter longing, carnal heat. Would she see him?

Zoe cupped Maria's chin in her hand. "I know what you are thinking, little daughter. But you must be careful. If you encounter your Tauro-Scythian, you may be forced to decide if what you feel for him is love, or merely desire."

Maria looked quickly away. There was no answer to that dilemma that would not cause her pain.

† † †

"Uncle . . ." Michael Kalaphates turned to his Uncle Constantine and shrugged expressively. Constantine looked at his nephew with momentary exasperation and then reached into his cloak and pilfered his purse for a half dozen silver nomismata. Michael greedily accepted the donation and leaned back over the massive ivory gaming table. "I'll win it back double, Uncle," he said eagerly.

At least the boy needs me, thought Constantine bitterly, *even if only to fill his perpetually exhausted purse.* Constantine looked around at the jostling, garrulous patrons of Nicephorus Argyrus's new establishment; a Magister in a silk robe had just bumped into a Venetian merchant wearing an entire shipload of gold around his neck, the sotted Quaestor was somewhere—over there, taking bets on a pentathlon contest—and the puffed-up, pigeon-breasted Proconsular Patrician Digenes Ducas, whose voice so often stirred the Senate, whispered in the ear of the elegant whore on the arm of a young Topoteretes of the Imperial Excubitores. A sharp-nosed Patrician—what was his name? Evagrius?—with a precisely trimmed short gray beard nodded curtly at Constantine and turned away. Constantine imagined himself shaking the arrogant fop and shouting, "I am Constantine, to whom you virtually prostrated yourself in the Senate chambers last month! Constantine, the former Strategus of Antioch, Vanquisher of Seljuks, and Savior of your Mother, celebrated by the mob in the Hippodrome, and, not the least, brother of the Emperor Michael and the Orphanotrophus Joannes in the presence of whom even your silk-and-scent Magisters tremble!" Ah, but there, of course, was the thorn that so clearly kept Constantine from plucking the rose of Rome's adoration. Brother Joannes. A month ago such as these had indeed been ready to throw their faces to the floor before him. But a month ago Joannes had not yet made it entirely evident to the entire court that he regarded his brother Constantine as a temporary accoutrement, a discarded trumpet of his own power. Joannes had not sent for him once since the ceremony in the Hippodrome and the reception at the Senate, had not even inquired of him or their nephew. Such signals did not go unapprehended by the viciously acute eyes and ears of the Imperial Court. If Joannes had no further use for his brother, Constantine, then neither did these swaggering dignitaries.

Michael Kalaphates whooped at a successful toss of the dice. "Give me the trinity!" he crowed; three was his number. *At least the boy has use for me,* Constantine told himself again, his gloom deepening as he thought of the other Michael, his brother, too, his Father as well. Even Joannes had received them, appeared with them, if only briefly. Ah, well, Michael was so far away; it was as if the Imperial Scepter had finally severed the already tenuous blood ties as savagely as a Varangian's ax. They would go to their graves as strangers.

"Holy Trinity!" Michael Kalaphates leapt up from the table and embraced his uncle, showering him with silver. "Five times over, including what I had lost!" He danced around his uncle, his fashionable silk bonnet beginning to slide toward his right ear. "Let me keep it, Uncle. I have learned of a winning team of four that can be had for a pig's ear! We'll buy a trainer and a driver and rule the Hippodrome!"

Constantine smiled. "Keep it, of course. You are my family, you know." Constantine shook his head in amazement. The boy was as impetuous as a thundercloud, but half his schemes seemed to come to something. The others . . . well, they were best forgotten. Michael Kalaphates was his family now.

"Uncle, our friend the Manglavite has come in. With the Hetairarch."

Bile burned in Constantine's chest. The boy needed to choose his friends more carefully, that was certain. Thugs like that would buy him more trouble than even he could scheme his way out of. "Yes," said Constantine, his voice acerbic, "the Hetairarch and Manglavite are virtually without employment these days. It is difficult to go out at night without encountering one or the other, and sometimes the two together, arm in arm like Herod and Pilate."

"They are always courteous to us."

Constantine's brow furrowed. "They are both so . . . agile. When a beast learns its master's tricks too easily, the master should wonder if the beast doesn't intend to someday teach him a few tricks."

"Well, as we are not their masters, I intend to greet them." Michael held his arm up. "Manglavite!"

The two Norsemen worked through the crowd; some of the dignitaries greeted them eagerly, while others discreetly turned away as they passed.

"Manglavite. Hetairarch." Michael, joined perfunctorily by Constantine, bowed in greeting. "Now I know we have picked an auspicious destination for our evening's adventure. Do you intend to stay for the theater? They say this new drama is quite, one might say, transparent."

"So we have heard," said Mar, his manner genial. Then he grinned. "Look for us before you find your seats. And if your cup runs dry before then, tell your serving boy that the Manglavite is buying your drafts. You must relieve him of some of his gold before his vaults sink into the earth." Haraldr nodded his agreement. He had spent enough time working with

Mar to be comfortable with him, if still wary. And while Mar's Roman duplicity required a Norseman's caution, Haraldr had found Mar's Roman urbanity engaging, even beguiling. He had to admit he enjoyed going with him to a place like Argyrus's.

Haraldr and Mar bowed and went off into the crowd. "What does Nordbrikt do with all his money?" asked Constantine when they had left.

"Women," said Michael. "He has taken a whore, a girl from Alania who is said to rival fair Helen, and it is said that his mistresses include several ladies at court. Apparently there is also something to be made of his relationship with the daughter of the Grand Domestic. You have met her. Perhaps there is a match there."

"I thought he was quite set upon Maria, the Empress's dear companion. Don't I recall some mention of their liaison during our recent journey?"

"That ended some time ago. And were it to resume, I can assure that such a liaison would never be allowed to come to fruition."

Constantine laughed and squeezed Michael's arm playfully. "You have won a purse full of nomismata, so now you imagine yourself privy to the secrets of the Empress's apartments."

Michael smiled and put his arm across his uncle's shoulders. "I have certain . . . contacts, dearest Uncle."

† † †

"They interest me." Mar spoke in Norse as he and Haraldr walked away from Michael Kalaphates and Constantine.

"True, Joannes has shown them little favor," replied Haraldr. "But that is a far reach from saying that they might be inclined to conspire against him."

"You saw them in Antioch. What is your estimate of their abilities?"

"The uncle could not be expected to figure out how to dump shit from a chamber pot. Michael Kalaphates, however, I believe to be far more able than he is given credit for. A bit of the praise-tongue, but all in all a very worthy young man. Certainly very keen."

"And perhaps keen enough to realize that his uncle is not rewarding his talents in near the measure that his qualities deserve."

"Possibly. We should deliberate this matter before we proceed, though, and then proceed very cautiously."

Mar pursed his lips. "I am worried that we will not always have the luxury of caution. Joannes has made no move against us for weeks now.

You know how a camp is always the quietest when there is to be an attack in the morning."

"Hetairarch! Manglavite! Esteemed Dignitaries!" Nicephorus Argyrus's leathery face beamed with its usual effusion of genuine affection, moderate inebriation, and irrepressible self-interest. He swept the two Norsemen into the main dining hall, a miniature palace lined with sumptuously carved, emerald-shaded Carystos marble columns; the lofty, coffered ceiling had been painted a celestial blue.

"I insist that you join us!" boomed Argyrus. He guided the Norsemen to a large table set in the apse at the end of the room. The table was littered with goblets of fine glass, silver, and burnished stone, silver plates and utensils, and the savaged remains of a suckling pig.

"It appears you have finished eating," said Mar dryly.

"Gentlemen. Dignitaries. Esteemed colleagues!" The fourteen or fifteen guests at the table continued tearing at bits of pig, arguing, and shouting at the ceiling. Haraldr recognized a komes of the Imperial Fleet, who licked his fingers with a look of grave deliberation, two senators, and a Genoese admiral said to keep a Saracen mistress in a town house only two blocks from Haraldr's palace. A small man raised his oversize head from the wine-soaked white tablecloth and tilted it slowly as he appraised the new arrivals with glazed gray eyes. The Logothete of the Symponus, Haraldr observed, the official responsible for the financial administration of Constantinople. They are also drinking tonight in the Studion, thought Haraldr. Would the Logothete sleep as well, he wondered, if he could hear the oaths the cutthroats of Studion were growling into their cups?

Argyrus put his arm around Haraldr and addressed no one in particular. "I gave our worthy Manglavite his first employment when he came among us. You might say he learned his lessons at the foot of the master. My name means silver, but when I touch a man, he turns to gold!" Argyrus rapped Haraldr's massive shoulder as if he expected it to clink like a golden statue. "I'm proud of him; he took his advice from me and made himself a rival to Croesus. Of course I was generous when I dealt with him, and the only gratitude I asked was that he remember his mentor, Nicephorus Argyrus!"

Serving boys quickly cleared and set places before Mar and Haraldr could escape from Nicephorus Argyrus. They sat and looked about the room. With the current moratorium on Imperial banquets due to the Emperor's illness, Argyrus had drawn half the Imperial Court. Everyone seemed to enjoy the relative absence of decorum; the noise required

Haraldr and Mar to raise their voices in order to pursue ordinary conversation.

"Let us forego supper and ask the servants to bring us dessert." Mar smiled salaciously and looked around the room. "The Curator of the Magnara is here, so I imagine his wife has accompanied him to give the proper public display of their mutual infidelity." Haraldr noted this with interest, since he had slept with the Curator's wife, Danielis, a half dozen times. "And I do not see the Grand Domestic Bardas Dalassena—no doubt he is home wringing his hands over his dispatches—so we can assume that Anna has probably come."

Haraladr nodded and signaled the servant. He had at first been taken aback by the protocol of the Imperial Court, which was quite different from that practiced in the more liberal-minded private homes—like Argyrus's—or in a notoriously permissive environment like Antioch. Among dignitaries, it was considered scandalous for women to dine side by side with men; they instead dined in a separate chamber. But when dessert was served, the women were invited to join the men. At court, the suffocating protocol constrained this contact to elaborate formality. Here, however, the interaction frequently exceeded propriety—thus the popularity of Argyrus's venture.

The women had already begun to trickle into the dining hall, generally in groups of two or three. Here and there a man would stand and invite a lady to sit; she might accept, or she might pretend that she had not seen the gesture (even if the desperate gallant was flapping his arms in her face like a frantic bird) and hold out for a more desirable opportunity. Haraldr had come to enjoy the flirtatious ritual, the nods, the gestures, the raised eyebrows, the subtle communications and often quite complex strategies that the participants had evolved.

Haraldr sensed someone hovering at his shoulder. He turned and rose immediately. "Anna," he said, and bowed deeply.

Anna fixed her intense agate eyes on his and nodded. A servant brought her a chair. She and Mar greeted one another before she sat.

Each week she is more beautiful, thought Haraldr. Her coloring was still fresh, virginal, her cheeks and lips flushed brilliantly. But her eyes had become heavier, darker, more sensual, and full woman's breasts now swelled against her dark blue scaramangium. "You will make Eros weary of his errands tonight," he told her. "You are the most lovely woman here."

She put her hand lightly on his. "Tonight I only hope to dispatch Eros to one breast."

Mar coughed dramatically and jerked his head to the right. Haraldr wished he had a wizard's incantation that would turn him into a fly. But it was too late. She had seen him.

Danielis, wife of the Curator of the Magnara, walked among the tables, her long, swan-white neck erect, her arms relaxed, her fingers slightly poised as if she cradled some fragile, invisible object. Her husband, the dignitary responsible for not only overseeing but also financing all of the official diplomatic receptions at the Magnara Palace, was seated several tables away and had already deposited his decorum headfirst in the lap of an actress reputed to be the mistress of a famous polo player. That circumstance was hardly to Danielis's discredit—far more humiliating to have been invited to sit by her own husband. But with Haraldr, her widely acknowledged paramour, also occupied, she was in an awkward situation. As was he.

Mar stood, his face regal, his eyes waiting to make contact with Danielis's. She looked at him and the entire room seemed to hush for an instant. She then raised a sharp, dark eyebrow in a gesture that was at once almost imperceptibly delicate and wildly erotic. As Danielis moved to take her seat beside Mar, Haraldr nodded at him gratefully.

Haraldr had seen men's eyes in combat—even Berserks—more pacific than Anna's when she saw her rival seated only a place removed from hers. Danielis leaned forward and inclined her head slightly toward Haraldr. She had large, grayish-blue eyes that contrasted vividly with her dark hair, and a long, chiseled nose that seemed to pull her face down slightly, giving her beauty a hint of sadness that Haraldr found appealing. "Manglavite," she said in her demure, almost soothing voice. "Anna."

"Lady," said Anna as if she were an executioner addressing a client. She placed her hand on Haraldr's thigh. But Haraldr could not help thinking of Danielis. Unlike most women of fashion who now wore only the long, sheathlike scaramangium robe in imitation of their Empress, Danielis persisted in wearing both a dalmatic, a short, sleeveless tunic; and a pallium, a long, shawllike garment with an opening for the head—over her robe, a swathing of radiantly patterned silk that concealed her up to her chin. But once unwrapped, Danielis would insist that Haraldr perform as her "stallion"; he was never certain which role she enjoyed most for herself, the mare or the bareback rider.

Anna pressed her breast against Haraldr's arm. Anna, he reflected, for all her sparkling eyes and busy hands, was the opposite of Danielis. Anna had lost her maidenhood somewhere on the road to Antioch, apparently to some clumsy lecher who had made the experience painful. She was still wary, so Haraldr had not pressed her. They had twice been alone in his chambers and merely had stayed awake, conversing, occasionally caressing, almost until cockcrow, when he had ordered her guards and carriage to take her home. She had been very good for his Greek, and she made him happy.

"Anna, have you heard of the new drama?" asked Danielis as the servants brought out stuffed pastries, shaped like little churches, on silver plates.

"No. Oh, I see, I believe you have confused the genres. This is a mime, or rather a comedy in the form of mime."

"Yes. I think you are correct. How wise of you to know that." Danielis plunged her fork deep into her little pastry church. "The content is considered improper. I have been told that the actress will lay aside her cloak and bare her bosom in emulation of Aphrodite."

"No. She will remove her cloak and appear before us quite entirely naked, as the ancients have shown us in their statuary."

Danielis made a sharp, quick little inhalation, her public expression of shock. Hah, thought Haraldr, when Danielis is as naked as Aphrodite, she gasps like a post-horse. "Anna," Danielis asked, "do you think that viewing this spectacle will inflame the passions of the gentlemen present? How wicked it would be if this emulation of Aphrodite encouraged our gallants to an emulation of Hephaestus."

"But, Lady," said Anna, her pupils like needles, "Hephaestus was the lame husband of Aphrodite, cuckolded by the warlike and altogether more desirable Ares. Do we not see that emulation right here, even before our Aphrodite has yet appeared?"

Mar choked on his pastry. Danielis's nostrils flared and a vein stood out beneath her ear. "Indeed," said Danielis, her voice uninflected by the accusation and insult. "We have other emulations as well. I am certain that we also have an Athena among us."

Anna's nails clawed Haraldr's arm. Athena was a virgin goddess. "But where?" Anna's voice was faintly tremulous. "A maiden would hardly have the temerity to enter this company. Perhaps the error in your understanding is one of terminology. If I were, for example, to call a woman who squanders her . . . assets a spendthrift—and perhaps some would call her worse—I would not then be correct in considering a woman who merely prudently budgets her assets a miser."

Mar and Haraldr exchanged helpless looks. "And I would not consider a woman—" Danielis broke off, realizing that her voice was rising and the conversation around her had abruptly diminished. She looked straight ahead and lifted her chin. Anna breathed hotly against Haraldr's ear. "Tonight I want to emulate Aphrodite," she whispered with more anger than desire. Haraldr wondered why he could suddenly hear the clinking of silver and glass. A collective gasp drifted from the far end of the room. Anna turned her head and in spite of herself sighed the name. "Maria."

The cold knife ripped Haraldr from breast to belly. He could not turn his head. He could not be the only one who had not turned.

He did not recognize her at first. Her hair, loosely braided, glistening in the light of the candelabra, was arranged simply around her head in the fashion of the ancient statues and wreathed with a band of fresh flowers woven with almost tapestrylike intricacy. She wore no paint on her face, but her eyes were so deeply azure that they seemed, even from a distance, to have been colored in with some intensely concentrated pigment.

But it was her attire that had reduced them all to silence. Instead of a scaramangium, she wore a long, loose gown, again much like those depicted on the statues. Held by a small gold clasp at each shoulder, the shimmering white gown scarcely draped her breasts and seemed to leave half of her upper body exposed; the delicate yet proud sculpture of her bare throat and arms was as astonishing as any immortalized in marble. As she walked, the fabric teased her audience, clinging momentarily to the contour of her breast or thigh like another skin, then falling into complex folds to reveal glimpses of bare bosom. It was as if a goddess walked toward them, naked except for the iridescent cloud in which she had cloaked herself.

Every man who was free to choose her stood, more in homage than invitation. Homeric paens flew into the awed silence. "Helen, daughter of Zeus . . ." "She challenged Aphrodite the golden . . ." Serene, almost oblivious, Maria walked toward the apse at the end of the room.

Haraldr was numb. He had loved so many since her, had held so many tender breasts and opened so many white legs. Why had they all done nothing to make this moment easier? She could still choke the breath from his lungs. She was behind him, her presence so strong that it seemed to bind his limbs.

"Rome's goddess has returned! Welcome, precious light, we mortals beg even the merest moment of your grace!" Nicephorus Argyrus gestured to the chair that already waited for her. "You have no choice. I will close this establishment, dismantle it, sink the bricks and stone in the western sea if you take your seat beside any but your humble host!"

Maria laughed, the falling of liquid silver, and descended like snow. She was two seats down and across the table from Haraldr. He could see her face without looking at it, even taste her flesh. She nodded now, first at Anna, then at Danielis, at Mar, and finally her eyes passed like hot brands through his heart. They never paused, never reflected, only moved on like a great blue storm, unconscious of the destruction it left behind.

Anna put her hand gently on Haraldr's arm and whispered in his ear: "You still love her."

† † †

The great black horse struggled against the reins. Joannes shouted at the Komes of the Imperial Excubitores to grab the bit. The stallion jerked his head, jittered his flanks, and settled. Joannes quickly dismounted. The Topoteretes who had sent for him waited outside the abandoned warehouse, a blazing taper in each hand. "Orphanotrophus," he said as he bowed.

"How do we get down there?" asked Joannes brusquely. If this were anything less than reported, the Topoteretes's head would greet tomorrow's petitioners at the Chalke Gate.

"This way, Orphanotrophus." The Topoteretes held his torch up into the empty vault of the warehouse. Heavy, distorted shadows flickered over the brick ribbings. The floor had a thick layer of dirt. A small animal darted along next to the wall.

"The stairs were covered with freshly cut boards and a layer of earth for camouflage," said the Topoteretes. He plunged his taper into the dark hole in the floor. The ancient, crumbling steps had been cleaned and repaired with hastily set brick and mortar. Joannes followed the Topoteretes down, fifteen steps in all.

The floor below was hard earth, almost like fired clay. The Topoteretes thrust his torch up again. Joannes's jaw tightened, and his shoulders began to ache. It was an old cistern, probably one of the City's original water-storage facilities, long forgotten, drained, the residue of silt compacted and dried on the floor. The mortar had fallen away from many of the thin, slablike bricks used to build the vaults, leaving the masonry surface as jagged as old teeth. Beneath the vaults were stacked thousands of spears.

Joannes grabbed one of the spears and examined the shaft, threw it aside, and examined another. How could this be? How could this cancer exist in the body he knew as well as his own, and yet leave him unaware of the symptoms? No. He had known. And he had denied his own knowledge of this sickness, this plague.

"Who is responsible?" he asked the Topoteretes, his question more wondering than demanding.

"We are interrogating some individuals now, Orphanotrophus. I am certain we will have some names for you by tomorrow."

Names. Four, five, a dozen mutilated wretches yielding their final sobbing confessions. Pointless. This was the work of many. Well organized and, considering their means, well funded. There was substance here. Rage—channeled, directed, plotted into the uncertain future. And he was not ready for them.

"Thank you, Topoteretes." Joannes felt the weariness in his legs as he climbed back into the night. He had known, he had vacillated, he had postponed, he had hoped against hope. Soon it would be too late. What had to be done had to be done.

"Komes!" rumbled Joannes when he reached the street. "I want you to deliver a message for me. Tonight!"

† † †

"Altogether remarkable." Michael Kalaphates raised his cup to the stage just exited by the actress who had emulated Aphrodite. "Her subtlety was most affecting, was it not, Uncle?"

"Perhaps I am in a better position than you to appreciate her subtlety, or lack thereof," said Constantine.

"Ah . . . yes." Michael had, in his excitement, forgotten that his eunuch uncle had a rather different perspective on the female anatomy. He tipped his cup to Haraldr. "Well, for subtlety it would be hard to exceed the performance of our Manglavite, who this evening entertained three women with whom he is . . . well acquainted, all at the same table. A display of courage as well as subtlety."

"His courage has not been tested yet. He still has to go up there, if only to make his apologies." Mar pointed to the women's gallery on the mezzanine surrounding the theater; there was an open seating area at the rear, and rows of curtained booths along each side.

"Excruciating dilemma—" Michael broke off. "Is it possible that the divine emulation we have just witnessed has aroused the ire of responsible authorities? Look at the grim set on the face of that officer of the Excubitores. I believe he is coming our way."

"Komes," said Mar, identifying the man's title. "I hope he's not bringing news of another military debacle."

"I hope he tells me my officers have rioted and my men have invaded the Mangana Arsenal," mumbled Haraldr with genuine hope of some sort.

"Hetairarch, Manglavite." The komes bowed to his superiors and turned to Michael. "You are Michael Kalaphates?" Michael nodded, and the komes handed him a sealed paper, bowed, and shouldered back through the milling audience.

Michael identified the seal before he broke it. "My uncle. The Orphanotrophus Joannes," he said, suddenly seeming quite sober. He read the missive and rolled it up again before speaking. "He wants to see me as soon as the palace gates open in the morning."

Haraldr noticed the look that passed between uncle and nephew and realized that Mar had been right about them. Michael Kalaphates and his Uncle Constantine were indeed interesting.

"I believe you are receiving a signal," said Michael to Haraldr. He nodded at the mezzanine boxes, his carefree demeanor instantly restored, as if he regretted the lapse.

Haraldr looked up to a row of curtained booths separated by columns topped with madly foliate capitals; the drapes were tapestries woven to resemble animal skins, a detail that had aroused considerable favorable comment from the more fashionable patrons. The curtains of the fourth booth were slightly parted, and Anna peeked out. She beckoned him with a flip of her fingers.

Anna waited in the alcove that joined the booths. A little string of vial-like oil lamps along the wall cast a rich, almost silvery glow over her face. Anna took Haraldr's arms in her hands and folded her drowsy, thick, dark lashes. "Maria is my dearest friend." A tear left a silver track down Anna's cheek. She threw her arms around Haraldr and pressed her face to his chest. "I love you," she said. "But I love her more."

He stroked her soft neck. "I love you. I want to take you tonight . . ." He did not finish, realizing although that much was true, now it would only be to spite Maria.

"I am not ready," said Anna. "Perhaps later, when I have had more . . . experience." She looked up at him and smiled. "Danielis was right. I am not a woman yet."

Haraldr held her close. "You are a woman," he whispered to her.

Anna nuzzled him and then pushed him away gently. "Maria asked me to tell you something."

Haraldr shook his head. "I will not talk to her until she answers a question for me." He set his jaw. "She once mentioned a certain bird to me. I must know if this bird is entirely black, like a raven, or if its plumage is of a scarlet hue."

Anna raised her eyebrows discreetly, turned and opened the narrow door to the booth. She was gone only for a moment. Haraldr's heart pounded, his life again on a needle of fate, when she faced him again. Anna shrugged. "She says the bird in question is feathered like a raven."

Haraldr felt both relieved and saddened; now he could never truly hate her. Anna reached up, brought his head down, and kissed him, seeming both relieved and sad herself. For an instant Haraldr wondered, as he often had at greater length, if Anna had a secret dread of her fair-hair gallant, if he perhaps was a risk with which she taunted herself.

"She still loves you," said Anna, and then turned and ran down to the end of the alcove and danced down the stairs.

Maria's eyes were waiting for him when he entered the booth, the blue flames blazing. Her arms were folded beneath her breasts. Her bare skin was like white marble in white sunlight. Her sexuality seemed to change the very atmosphere of the room, flooding the chamber with a thick, drowning, honeylike liquor.

"I wanted to kill you once." Her voice had the strange detachment of a seeress. "In Hecate. The knife . . . it was not yours. I did not bring it for my protection."

Haraldr felt only a tinge of surprise. He had known that, really; at the time, drunk with her, he had not wanted to think what the knife had meant, and later it had not mattered.

"The second time I loved you, it was for her. So that you would kill for her. Not her husband. The Orphanotrophus Joannes. I am sorry I could not make the distinction more clear. We were desperate, and yet too cautious. We did not want to use his name until you had agreed. Our Mother is surrounded by spies."

Each word was a cold stone Haraldr had to disgorge. "If I had understood that a service to our Mother, and Rome, was at issue, and not a love that existed only in words lost to the night, then I could have made cause with you. I had something that in my folly I thought was real, and found that it was hollow. You had something real, your love for your Empress, and yet by making a mockery of me you fouled that love. My folly is a poison that corrodes only my own breast. Your folly is a poison that seeps into the world and corrupts everything."

Lyre music drifted up from the stage. The audience oohed at some revelation in a mime. Maria's breasts rose and fell in a slight, irregular rhythm. "Yes." Her eyes flinched from nothing, denied nothing. "Yes. I am the greater fool. I betrayed you, and I betrayed myself."

"Liar. You do not believe that."

"I have told you every truth now. . . ."

"I know nothing of you."

A vague blush spread over her breast. "I know nothing of you, land man from Rus." Her chin tilted up. "You have loved a dozen women since you held me. Do you sob to each of them that they have also abused your love?"

"And you have loved more than a dozen before me, no doubt. Did each of them earn your tearful remorse?"

Maria's left wrist, folded over her right elbow, began to twitch slightly. "I ask nothing of you tonight. Not even forgiveness."

"But you have asked me to hear your confession. Have you Romans not priests enough to attend to those needs?" Impulsively, Haraldr stepped toward her, unwrapped her arms, and seized her wrists. It was a mistake; he felt as if he taken hot irons in his hands and yet was compelled by some desire entirely his own to hold them until his flesh was incinerated. He had to grit his teeth in order to speak. "Perhaps you have other needs."

She resisted for a moment and then clutched at his robe, her lips savage and her teeth showing. "Yes, Manglavite," she spat out, "for those needs you are . . . superior. You are, of my dozens, by far the best. You alone drive me to madness." Her voice was monstrously mocking, and yet Haraldr glimpsed that she also mocked a certain truth that was too painful for her not to admit. "Make me your whore again, Manglavite!" she trilled angrily. "Make me your whore!"

Haraldr let her go. "I am sorry," he said.

For the first time she cast down her eyes. "No. I am the one who has made love a currency of exchange between us. Or perhaps I mean a stick with which to strike each other."

Haraldr's defenses sagged again. "Why would you wish to strike at me?" he asked sadly. "What did I do to invite your . . . contempt?"

The crowd below broke into raucous laughter. Maria sighed and folded her arms back under her breasts. She looked directly at Haraldr again. "You have not. You have only invited my . . . fear." The audience laughed even louder. Maria gestured with her hand toward the noise; the movement of her arm and the shimmer of her gown was almost magical. "This is not the proper place. I want to . . . explain. To understand for myself." She pursed her lips. "I have a villa in Asia, just above Chrysopolis. It is a short ferry. Will you go there with me? Not tonight. Tomorrow. In the light of day."

Haraldr nodded. Yes. Below him, the audience suddenly fell silent, and then a cymbal crashed like a tinny thunderclap.

his way, sir," said the Komes of the Excubitores. Michael Kalaphates had an almost overpowering urge to wet himself. The marble steps of the Magnara gleamed like ice on the cold sunny morning, but he had not been asked to ascend those steps to the waiting glory of Rome. Instead he was escorted down a side ramp that sloped gradually, then seemed to plunge straight to the bowels of the earth in a series of steep, poorly kept steps. The abrupt descent ended at a long, dark corridor lit at intervals with smudgy lamps.

Parchment. That was the smell. Musty, pungent, almost palpable. Chamber after chamber full of documents; halfway down the hall, a man worked inside one of the rooms, and his lamp illuminated the endless stacks, the layered shelves of rolled parchments. A compendium of Rome's centuries, each ancient decision, each long-forgotten act a parcel of the huge accumulation upon which each succeeding Lord of the Entire World would raise his golden throne. Men died, and yet here their deeds endured, a chorus of voices to render invincible, indisputable before man and God, the will of one man.

The long corridor ended at a plain wooden door. The komes knocked and was greeted by a small, aging eunuch who wordlessly pointed to another door at the end of the cramped antechamber; most of the floor space in the room was occupied by disordered stacks and tumbled piles of rolled documents. The komes knocked on the second door. A beast seemed to growl behind the sealed portal. The komes opened the door and waved Michael in.

Michael blinked. The windowless chamber was flooded with light from a stark, functional candelabrum fashioned from a single metal band. The room was all papers and parchment, and yet not a sheet was out of place, the stacks immaculate, the rolled documents set into plain wooden boxes. The smooth, whitewashed plaster walls were unmarked by any kind of decoration, not even a solitary icon. Joannes sat in a backless chair behind an unornamented wooden writing table; the varnished surface was eroded in places. His heavy iron sealing pliers were placed neatly next to a row of rolled and sealed missives; a pile of lead seal blanks glimmered dully in a little wooden casket, a common coin that would have the power of life and death once the jaws of the Orphanotrophus Joannes's seal-stamp had pressed his imprint into the metal.

"Nephew." Joannes held out his freakish, akimbo arms. "Please sit." His spade-tipped fingers seemed to fling the dense, smoky air toward the backless, canvas-upholstered chair behind Michael. "You are well." It was strange how Joannes never asked a question, only requested confirmation.

"Yes, Uncle. Sir."

Joannes brought the splayed ends of his fingers together just beneath his smooth, jutting chin. "Let us consider you, Nephew. I see before me a young man, robust, vital, well-formed indeed, of agile wit and intellectual acuity. A young man who, unlike his uncles before him, has not suffered the vicissitudes of the journey from Amastris to the Imperial Palace. A young man whose health, then, and mental equilibrium, are unmarred by the struggles that have bowed and cicatrized his illustrious forebears. Our father was disgraced before our eyes, a small man made smaller. Your father, in no little part due to the efforts of your Holy namesake and myself, is now a Droungarios of the Imperial Fleet." Michael's father, Stephan, a former ship tarrer, was married to Joannes's sister, Maria, and had proved his lack of military experience by taking a severe pasting from the Carthaginians in the waters off Sicily. "You share in your father's glory, and of course you bask in the reflected radiance of the Imperial Dignity; though the diadem does not rest on your head, it is close enough to accrue to you a station and consequence that most men would deem themselves the idols of fortune to enjoy, even after a lifetime of dedicated labor.

"Now let us consider what you have done, Nephew, with these gifts extended to you in such profusion that it burdens my tongue simply to enumerate them. Yes." Joannes nodded and placed his huge hands on the document over which he had been working. "Young Michael Kalaphates, after a fitful education in the Quadrivium in Nicaea, where he was more familiar with the actresses and prostitutes of the city than with his mentors in mathematics and rhetoric, proceeded on to Antioch, where under the aegis of his Uncle Constantine he embarked upon his military training. Yes, and dedicated he was to his new profession, assuming that one believes a besieged city might be relieved by a roll of the dice, or a fleeing army turned by the sight of a racing chariot and its team of four. For indeed Michael Kalaphates learned little of the arts of warfare but is widely considered the Levant's foremost expert on sporting contests and games of chance." Joannes's fingers drummed the table in a heavy, padding, ominous motion. "Well. Let us bring the brief tale of Michael Kalaphates to its conclusion." Joannes's eyes seemed completely shrouded in their deep, sunken sockets. "Michael Kalaphates, having been bludgeoned senseless in front of the Empress's carriage, is fortunate enough to hitch a ride upon the cart of a Tauro-Scythian bandit. He is invited to the Empress City to enjoy his undeserved celebrity, which he quickly squanders earning his own reputation as a tomcat, spendthrift, dilettante, petty speculator, and drunken idler."

Joannes suddenly stood, and Michael reflexively jerked his chair back toward the door. "You who were carried in a silken litter into the blazing light of the Imperial Diadem have already crawled off into your own shadow of iniquity!" Joannes's voice was like proximate thunder, and as his face darkened, the deep hollows of his brutish, distorted face seemed to become as black as his frock. His huge, spreading arms made him look like a great vulture about to enfold his hapless nephew. Michael's eyes were bright coals stoked by terror.

"Let me tell you now how I might deal with you." Joannes's tongue slid over his lips. "I could dispatch you to Neorion this very moment, you sniveling milksop! They would bring me your skin before the sun has set, and you would no longer be in it! Ah, but seeing that such summary judgment might leave you with little time for repentance, I could ask that you remain in a windowless cell in the Numera until you expire from utter desolation. Or, should I feel particularly benevolent, I might request that your talents be employed in distant Baku, loading petroleum into barrels so that our warships are assured a supply of liquid fire. Then again, the monastic life might suit you. The cenobium at Mount Athos—"

"Uncle, Uncle!" Michael Kalaphates fell to his knees. "No, Uncle!" Crawling on his knees, he maneuvered around the writing table like a large, eager dog, grasped Joannes's enormous black boots, and kissed them in supplication. The bluster about the Neorion and Numera and even Baku, Michael had identified as such. Mount Athos was quite another matter; his uncle would earn only the general approbation of court, church, and city for having dispatched a prodigal nephew to a grim cell in an isolated community where his only companionship would be stinking, burlap-shrouded, prayer-chanting eremites. Neorion would in fact be preferable.

Joannes allowed Michael to wipe his nose on his boots for a few moments, observing that his nephew had spent so much time consorting with actresses that he had acquired thespian abilities of his own. Still, the desired message had been delivered. Joannes viciously kicked his nephew's ribs. "Get away, scamp. Even your sniveling needs improvement."

Michael returned to his chair. He rubbed his throbbing sternum thoughtfully. What did his uncle want in exchange for sparing him even a few years of poverty, chastity, and, worst of all, obedience?

Joannes sat and appraised his nephew, wondering how many times he would have to whip this dog before it learned even a single trick. Still, Michael was energetic, clever, a natural dissimulator—all raw materials with which Joannes could work skillfully.

"I would like you to assume a position of some benefit to your family. Certainly you owe us that much."

"Yes, sir," said Michael sincerely. An office of some sort? Why, if it ensured his continued exposure to the . . . culture of this great city, why not? From what he had seen of men with official duties here at court, their interests were identical to his: horses, women, rich food, and strong drink.

Joannes leaned back in his chair. "You have heard, no doubt, that our Imperial Father, your uncle and my brother, is not well. He has borne the burdens of state for so long, and so diligently, that in the confidence of our familial sanctuary I confess to you that I fear for his life."

"Oh, no, Uncle. No!" So, thought Michael, the common gossip can no longer be denied. And a pity it is indeed. Without an Imperial relation, even one who pointedly disregarded him, life would be so much more difficult here. Perhaps he would no longer be welcome at Argyrus's.

"Our splendid Father is not in imminent danger, of course, but we must be concerned now to relieve some of the burden upon him; otherwise we may indeed have cause to mourn our lack of foresight. We who are closest to him must now circle around him, and, like the columns that thrust up the celestial dome of the Hagia Sophia, take a share of the weight that encumbers and threatens to bring our magnificent Father plunging to the dust."

"Yes, sir." Michael wished his uncle would get to the specifics. Something ceremonial, perhaps. That would be most desirable. A chance to sport about with the Hetairarch and the Manglavite; even the crumbs from their table, metaphorically speaking, would soon sate one to glorious excess.

"The position I have selected for you is that of Caesar."

"Caesar?" Michael knew that this was the title of the Emperor of ancient Rome, but with the endemic inflation of titles in the new Rome, a

Caesar might very well be the man who carted manure from the Emperor's stables. Caesar? Either the title was in fact that insignificant, or it had not been used for many, many years.

"I see you are not familiar with the dignity you are to be assigned," said Joannes, his shrouded eyes seeming to draw in light. "The Caesar is only designated when the Emperor, Basileus, and Autocrator has not sired a purple-born heir. In the event of the death of the Emperor, the Caesar would succeed him to the Imperial Throne."

†   †   †

"This is Her Majesty's galley," said Maria. The wind whipped at the black sable collar of her coat. Signal banners flapped in the rigging and the hull groaned slightly. "I am privileged to use it." Maria looked over at the group of a dozen servants, wrapped in heavy wool cloaks, standing by the railing amidship. "Please excuse me. I must instruct them on the cleaning and management of the villa. It has been closed for some months, and many of them will be new there."

Haraldr watched the Bucoleon Harbor recede with each powerful stroke of the bireme's eighty oars. The city was incandescent, the lead roofs and marble revetments glittering like jewels in the glancing light of late afternoon. Gulls screeched as they descended to accompany the ship across the Bosporus. Chrysopolis seemed to float by to the right, a city splendid enough to dazzle the world by itself, and then the urban clutter gave way to elegantly spaced villas surrounded by groomed cypresses, and gardens rendered by winter into brown-and-gray geometric sketches.

A large, canopied, richly enameled white skiff deposited Haraldr and Maria and six of the servants alongside the steps of a stone jetty; the skiff was quickly rowed back to the galley for the other servants and some supplies. The jetty crossed a narrow section of rocky beach and ended at an iron gate set in a stone wall; Maria's chamberlain unlocked the gate. Marble steps covered with dead leaves climbed through a series of terraces to the entrance arcade of a large three-story villa.

From the porch in front of the villa Haraldr could see gray, spiky orchards extending behind the house for some distance. They entered the house through a small, roofless atrium; a dead bird had fallen in among the leaves. A narrow hall led to a two-story peristyle surrounded by gold-veined marble columns. An ornamental basin at the near end of the peristyle was drained of water, and the tiles were dirtied with dried scum. "It will take some time for the heat to circulate after the furnaces are started," said Maria. "I think it is warmer outside." She put her hand on Haraldr's arm; it was the first time they had touched since the previous night. She guided him back out to the porch. They paused at a marble balustrade that overlooked the series of terraces. They were perhaps a hundred ells above the water. The sun had a rose tint as it flirted with the hills far to the west, and the vast cities across the water glowed softly in the final diffusion of daylight.

"My parents left me this villa." She ran her gloved hand over the smooth marble railing.

"You have never spoken of them."

She put her hand on his arm again. "There is too much of which we have never spoken."

"Who were your father and mother?"

Maria's eyes were a vivid reflection of the glistening sea. "I never knew them. They died . . . were killed, when I was an infant. They were involved in a . . . political matter. They were banished, their properties confiscated, their names expunged from record. Our Empress Zoe, then merely the niece of the Bulgar-Slayer, was my parents' friend. She was able to intercede and retrieve some of their estate, and their newborn daughter, in hope that there might one day be some sort of pardon. But the ship carrying my parents into exile was overtaken by a storm and they were drowned. The Empress has raised me as if I were her own child."

"So you consider her your family?"

"Her sister is also . . . my family."

"I did not know you were close to the Augusta Theodora." Strange, thought Haraldr; he remembered the interaction between the Empress and her sister in Euthymius's mime, a bitter rivalry generally acknowledged in palace circles.

"Yes. She is my other mother. I miss her." Maria bit her brilliant, wind-rouged lower lip. "Who is your family?"

"I am from Norway. It is a peninsula in the part of the world you call Thule. My father died when I was very young. He was an important man in Norway. A man of noble birth."

"And so you are of noble birth as well?"

"Yes."

"What dignity were you assigned in Norway?"

Haraldr regretted his partial honesty. "I was a member of the king's court. We do not have as many or various kinds of dignities in Norway as you do here in Rome."

"I cannot believe you ever bowed to anyone."

"I bow to our Father and our Mother, just as I bowed to Norway's king."

"Perhaps you will not always do so."

"I see. When I lead the fair-hairs to the despoliation of Rome?" Haraldr's tone was sarcastic.

Maria smiled. "It is appropriate that you should be annoyed with me. I was hoping that you would find my chronic melancholy seductive. A girlish conceit."

"I find you seductive."

"Yes." Her jaws clenched and her voice lowered. "I know that you are going to sleep in my bed tonight. I know what you are going to give me in my bed; I can see it in your eyes and feel it between my legs, feel it deep in my belly. Do you know that I am already wet?" Her eyes blazed back at the sun as it slid behind the horizon. "But how can I get you to give me back your love?"

"Perhaps love is not necessary."

She turned to him and he was astonished to see the tears. "It has to be," she said in a voice so small, so desperate, that he reached out to touch her burning face, then swept her into his arms.

† † †

"One of our treasures is sleeping," whispered Michael, Emperor, Autocrator, and Basileus of the Romans. He put his fingers to his lips to caution silence. Joannes glanced to the Imperial couch. Beneath the rich, gold-embroidered canopy that draped the enormous four-columned bed, beneath the breeze-soft claret sheets, lay the wizened, gnarled figure of a man who appeared to have just emerged from a half century of keeping company with snakes and scorpions in some cave, and indeed probably had. The latest of the Emperor's "treasures" snored in long, shallow rattles, and his unshorn, verminous hair spread out over the Imperial pillows like a halo of excrement.

The Emperor quickly guided his brother from the Imperial bedchamber, through a vast antechamber, to a smaller audience chamber, ringed with newly installed mosaics depicting the visions of Ezekiel. The monk Cosmas Tzintzuluces stood beside a small marble table and peered into what seemed to be a large gold reliquary shaped like a multidomed church; the miniature domes were tiled with red gemstones. Tzintzuluces greeted Joannes effusively.

Joannes grunted a polite greeting in reply. He tolerated Tzintzuluces, not the least because the intervention of this apparently sincere monk in the life of the Emperor was vastly preferable to abandoning His Majesty's spiritual care to the wiles of the despicable Patriarch Alexius. Praise the Pantocrator that He had created the monastaries, thought Joannes, for without the debilitating rivalry between the priesthood and the monks, secular government would soon be overthrown by ecclesiastical forces. Still, Tzintzuluces had to be watched. Like all truly religious men, he was a fanatic, and like all fanatics he had no plan, only an ultimate, largely abstract goal. And men without plans were dangerous.

"Come see this, Brother." The Emperor took Joannes's arm and urged him beside the table. He hefted the miniature church. "This is how Saints Cosmas and Damian will look. We are building around the existing foundations, with these additions and the construction of an upper story that will add a symmetry and magnificence that the previous architects neglected. We have already ordered the quarrying of the finest Lacedaemonian and Sangarian marbles, as well as Thessalian onyx. There is to be a fresco depiction of the martyrdom of the glorious saints, and our mosaics extolling the Pantocrator will emphasize the role of St. Luke. Of course, the edifices of the rest of the monastery will be adorned with the same degree of devotion and respect. And the surrounding neighborhood will also receive a renovation, as we have commanded the architects to consider new baths, fountains, a park . . ."

Joannes no longer heard his brother's raptures. He had already computed the cost of the Emperor's latest expiation within a few dozen solidi. A price that regrettably must be paid, he told himself. At least the Emperor's building projects were charitable, not self-indulgent; Saints Cosmas and Damian, after all, had been physicians who did not charge for their services, and this lavish reconsecration of their humble church would remind the vicious mob of the hospices, monastaries, and orphanages so recently endowed by their caring Father. And this activity would perhaps, in some way, serve as a rebuttal to the rumor mongers; a dying man would not rise from his deathbed to commission whole new monastic complexes that he would never live to see.

Joannes turned to Tzintzuluces. "Do you see how our Father spares nothing for the welfare of his children?" Joannes shook his head and attempted to smile wistfully at the monk. "He is so doting that I sometimes fear he will spoil them." Joannes approached Tzintzuluces more closely and whispered in his ear; the Emperor was still talking, almost to himself, going into further detail about where the various mosaic scenes would be placed in the chapel. "Blessed brother," said Joannes, "might

I borrow our Father for a time, even as I admonish myself for depriving him of even a moment of your salutary ministrations? What I hope to humbly offer him, will, I think, also ease his torment."

Just as effusively as he had greeted Joannes, Tzintzuluces bade him farewell and withdrew, content that even though he had momentarily released his sacred charge to the clutches of the world, it would be in the company of a man equally devoted to him, a man who, like Tzintzuluces himself, wore the black frock of worldly denial.

† † †

She placed her hand in his. The night was clear, cold, magical, the cities spread across the black water like carpets woven from the stars, the stars above them mirrors of the Great City's brilliance. She leaned back and looked overhead, her arching throat swanlike, erotic. "Do you think they ever collide?" she whispered. "They swirl about in the heavens, they are known to fall to earth, but do they ever collide?"

Haraldr looked up. "Perhaps they do, or have, in a time when there were no men to witness them, when only the gods saw. I know that like all things, each one of those fires will one day come to an end."

"Yes. Every fire must exhaust itself. But perhaps some burn longer than others. Do you know much of astrology?"

"I have met one of the astrologers attached to the Imperial retinue. I have also met others at court who consider the science to be pure chicanery. Is astrology an interest of yours?"

"An interest . . . but not a belief." Maria lowered her head and looked across the water. "I do not believe that the movement of heavenly bodies determines our fortunes here on earth. But I believe that like the stars, our fates move in certain patterns, and that we are bound to remain in those orbits no matter how strenuously we may hope and endeavor to escape them." Suddenly she turned and threw her arms around Haraldr. "What made you bring your ax down that day? How did you know that your stroke would not bring the sword down on my neck?"

"I did not know that." But he was not certain what he had known in the instant he had decided; later he had realized that if he hadn't killed the Seljuk leader at that moment, probably none of them, including Maria, would have left the kastron alive. Now he only hoped, in spite of himself, that his answer would hurt her. "I presented fate with an answer, and left fate to determine the question."

"Or perhaps fate had already told you the answer."

"You mean that what passes between you and I has already been determined?"

She let him go and walked a few steps away, her arms wrapped around her thick, fur-lined coat. The fine tip of her nose tilted to the stars again. "You and I are a moment when the stars collide. You came to me across all time, your path determined before the first stars were set in motion. We are bound together, your star and mine." She lowered her head and looked at him, and her eyes outshone all other lights. "I know this."

† † †

"We are alone," said the Emperor. "Please sit with me." Joannes awkwardly settled his enormous, distorted form on the gilded throne his brother used for the most informal, intimate audiences. Protocol insisted nevertheless that no one sit in the presence of the Emperor, much less on the throne beside him. But these were unusual circumstances.

Joannes studied his brother's swollen wrists, puffy cheeks, and shadowed, weary eyes. The deterioration was shocking; did the humors that afflicted his brain reside in the other parts of his body when they were not causing the mind storms? If so, they had begun to destroy the body which they had made their host. "It is sometimes wearying, is it not, to labor on behalf of so many?" said Joannes.

"And yet I must serve my children even with my last breath," replied the Emperor.

"They have never had a more just and devoted Father than yourself."

"Do not let modesty overlook your own contribution, dearest brother."

"I do not mind admitting that I have tried to serve you with every resource to my avail."

"Yes. You are my Peter, the rock upon which my throne has been erected."

Joannes paused, assessing the width of the portal that was opening before him. Finally he spoke. "I have given much thought as to how that foundation, which I hope I do in some small part provide, can be strengthened."

"Indeed? Tell me, brother." The Emperor's voice was earnest and somewhat solicitous, as if he could bestow a favor simply by listening.

"Just as the Son of God had both his Heavenly family and his earthly family, so does his Hand on Earth have two kinds of family, the spiritual and the corporeal. The spiritual family he has sought out and embraced, and the proceeds of that virtuous endeavor will accrue to his glory both in this world and the next. But he has not sought out his corporeal family with the same diligence."

The Emperor's expression changed from open curiosity to inscrutable deliberation; his dark eyes suddenly seemed flat, impenetrable, as if they would take in no more of this information. "If a man wishes to take his ship upon rough waters," the Emperor said at length, "then he builds his vessel with sturdy, well-planed boards. The rotten timbers he discards."

"I am sensitive to your . . . feelings concerning our brothers."

"Constantine's blundering in Antioch almost cost me my throne. Stephan will cost me Sicily."

Joannes trod warily. His brother was no man to be trifled with, even in this condition. If only God could have shown them another way to place the Imperial Diadem upon his head, he might have been the greatest of all Emperors. But guilt was eating away at him like a leprosy. "There is another threat to your throne."

"I am ill. I am not dying. With the Pantocrator's help and God's forgiveness, I will be cured of my affliction. In the meantime I am quite competent to govern my children."

"Neither do I think that your life is in jeopardy, nor that your abilities have been impaired. The danger here is not in what we know to be true but in what others perceive. Do not imagine that this disease that has temporarily afflicted you has gone unnoticed, and that it has not fueled the fires of rumor."

"I will soon appear before my children to assuage their anxiety and lay these rumors to rest."

"I think it will be some time before we can, with confidence, allow your children the privilege of seeing you. For your children to witness—may the Pantocrator forgive the boldness of my conjecture—one of your . . . attacks would turn these fires of rumor into a conflagration that would consume the entire Roman Empire."

"We will wait, then, until I have received absolution. St. Demetrius is working prodigiously on my behalf, I can assure you."

"If only the blessed St. Demetrius were able to proselytize in the inns and brothels of the Studion as effectively as he litigates before the Heavenly Tribunal, then we would have little to fear."

The Emperor seemed to jerk into a more erect posture, and for a moment Joannes feared that another fit was upon him. There had been two episodes the previous day; after the second his Majesty had remained unconscious for several hours. But the Emperor responded with the acuity that had been, in better days, taken for granted. "What reports do you have of insurrection?"

"I have myself seen an arsenal secreted by these rebels in an old warehouse just north of the Studite monastary. The quantity and quality of the weapons indicated that this group had resources we do not ordinarily associate with the unfortunate wretches who occupy that district. There is a danger that this . . . disease might be communicated to the classes of laborers and even the various professions and guild members."

The Emperor's broad shoulders and chest sagged with pain. "My children. Why would my children turn against me?"

Joannes wrapped his huge span around his brother's suddenly heaving shoulders. "It is not any lack of love for their Father, believe that. It is that few can now resist the rumors. There are many who claim you are already dead, and the majority are certain that you are dying. In their desperation and grief they wonder why their Father has not, like any good Father, provided for the future of his brood when he is gone. They think you are gone from them, and have left them no successor to your glorious and benevolent tenure. So quite naturally they are inclined, after enduring this lengthy period of distress, to think of placing their own successor on the throne. If you were to make a gesture toward them in naming a successor, I think this incipient insurrection would wither like a weed with its roots plucked from the earth."

"I will be unable to leave them an heir." The Emperor's eyes were profoundly sad.

"Of course you are unable to designate a Basileus and Augustus, as you could with a child of your own loins. But you could provide the children of your Imperium with a Caesar."

"Is this the help you would have me receive from our corporeal family? Then you must know I will not hear of it. Stephen would destroy everything that we have labored for!"

"I was not thinking of Stephan." Their brother-in-law, Stephan, was the closest male relative with the requisite reproductive organs.

"Who, then? Constantine, thankfully, is . . . disqualified."

Joannes observed to himself that this was not unlike the decisive moment in an interrogation in the Neorion, the moment when success and failure are both equally pregnant. "You have not met your nephew, Michael Kalaphates. I have taken it upon myself to become acquainted with him, and I am impressed with his qualities. He is intelligent, presentable, and is an experienced warrior. That he knows nothing of statecraft is of no consequence, because he need only offer the appearance of a princely character. We are not in need of a ruler to replace or even assist you, only a suitable image to present to your doubting children."

"I do not need this nephew beneath my feet like an unwanted pet."

"I assure you, Majesty, that will not be the case. I have already, discreetly and obliquely, approached him on this matter. I made it stridently patent to him that he would be your slave, a mere token of your God-granted authority. To this he agreed with touching humility and gratitude that even in the smallest fashion he might have an opportunity to earn your respect and affection. He is yours to command, to send through the city riding backward on an ass if you so wish."

"And what of Zoe? Without public expression of her approval to this . . . succession, any designation would be meaningless."

"She is in no position to oppose us. But even so, we would be less than fair if we did not approach her with a measure of compromise, even humility. The Christ forgave a harlot, and is it not our highest purpose in life to walk where He has walked? Let us suggest to her that with respect to her purple-born stature, we would not dream of offering this Caesar to her children without her blessing and sanctification. And in further acknowledgment of her Endowment by the very Hand of the Pantocrator, we would humbly beseech her to take this child, this Caesar, to her bosom, to metaphorically suckle him with the milk of her impeccable Macedonian lineage, and formally adopt him as her son."

The Emperor considered the matter for a remarkably brief interlude. His chin was set, his gaze decisive. "This is well conceived, my dearest brother and most faithful servant. I can only offer one caution as to this enterprise. If the Empress forms a personal enmity for our nephew, the plan will not work."

"Yes. I have dispatched him to her chambers this very evening, to dine with her and convince her of his merits, feeling that even if you did not signal your approval of this proposal, he might at least tell us something of her activities and intentions. He was quite quaking at the prospect, but I am certain that his boyish charms will arouse her maternal inclinations."

The Emperor stood. "How much lighter is my load than it was an hour ago," he said. "Come and embrace me, my Peter, my rock." The Emperor held out his arms and clutched the giant monk to his own thick chest. He was astonished when Joannes suddenly burst into tears.

† † †

She awoke to his kisses on her neck. She rolled over and took him in her arms and felt the length of his body against hers and pressed her breasts to his hard chest. Haraldr held her head and whispered in her ear. "You had a night vision," he said soothingly. "Why did you cry out?"

"I dreamed of you," said Maria in a voice like a hot breeze. They were so warm together, beneath silk and down, the heated floor baking the cold from the marble walls of her bedchamber. "I often dream of you."

"Are we lovers?"

"Often."

"Did I hurt you this time, to make you cry?"

"No . . ." She shuddered against him.

"Why were you frightened?"

She would not answer; she nuzzled his neck and gripped his shoulders tightly. "Make love to me again," she said gently, raspily.

"Tell me what you saw."

"It was . . . frivolous. A vision with no meaning."

"Then tell it."

She paused to bite him on the neck. "Very well." She relented, hoping that her acquiescence would indeed render the vision frivolous. She pushed away from him slightly. "I saw you sailing across a cold black sea with hundreds of ships in your wake. A man who was with you pointed to the heavens, and thousands of ravens tittered overhead, until they were like a cloud that blocked the sun."

"A portent of death. What happened?"

"I don't know. I cried out, and your kisses carried me away from the shores of sleep."

"Were you afraid that you would share my fate?"

"Perhaps I was afraid that I would not." She gathered him in her arms with a fierce passion. "Make love to me."

It began again, on a sea made of light, boundless, their frantic arms drawing each other into a single atom of being, this common soul expanding until it embraced all time, all creation. "I . . . love . . . you!" she screamed in her moment of paroxysm, and then she drifted slowly to his chest and wrapped her arms around him again.

Their kisses made him hard again before he had even left her. This time they clung to each other, flesh dissolving flesh, sleepwalkers meeting in a dream, lips to the other's ear, waiting for some enchanted revelation. "Love . . . love . . ." she said, her voice quavering. He waited, deciding he would not tell her of his love this night, might never tell her; but of course she already knew. She moaned softly and whispered again. "Tonight the world has changed forever."

"Yes," he admitted, controlling his voice. "I feel that."

"No, you do not know how I mean that. It is not just these two breasts, these two souls locked within. It is a thousand thousand souls for a thousand years."

He took her face in his hands and found her gaze with his. "I know," he told her, and in that moment he saw, like a distant image against an azure sea, the reflection of a raven as it tracked across the blue depths of her eyes.

† † †

"Look, Nephew, I have provided you with a final treat. Finish your pastry and you will see it." Zoe raised her hand at the hovering eunuch who had reached for her empty little silver dessert dish. "Away!" She looked at Michael Kalaphates and shrugged. "I do not know who is responsible for training the servants I am sent. Perhaps your uncle the Orphanotrophus Joannes. In any event, whenever Symeon finally instructs one in the proper decorum, he is snatched away and I am plagued with some new oaf. This one only arrived this very afternoon. Perhaps he will improve his performance."

Michael Kalaphates swallowed the last of his dessert and smiled effortlessly. He studied the images chased on his silver plate and laughed. "You remembered my fascination with pagan scenes. This is a satyr, I believe you once told me, and this lovely creature, though she is as pale as her aureate specter beside you, is a maenad."

"You remembered," said Zoe happily yet demurely. "We found we had much in common in Antioch, did we not? I am so pleased that your uncle has permitted you to renew our acquaintance." She cast her eyes at the servant.

"Although I am virtually terrified by the boldness of what I must remark, let me humbly beg you that our acquaintance be given the opportunity to ripen into friendship. I will beseech the Holy Virgin each night that before I have pined away each of my days, I might be invited to sup with you again. Until then I will mourn, deep-eyed Hera, that I am forever cast down from your Olympian immanence."

Zoe laughed huskily, perhaps erotically. "I have enjoyed this interview, Nephew. You may be certain that we will be more than strangers in the future. In the meantime I will propose to your uncle that you be offered a dignity more in keeping with your charm and intellect. Now I must regretfully ask you to take your leave."

Michael stood, bowed, and withdrew with his arms folded across his breast, his eyes seeming to plead what protocol, and the presence of

Joannes's spies, dictated that his tongue could not. Zoe nodded and the bronze doors slid shut on the shimmering vision of his Mother. Michael passed quickly through an antechamber dazzling with mosaics, and was escorted by a chamberlain down a series of hallways that turned twice before ending at another set of bronze doors. The Khazar guards at the gate to the Empress's apartments halted him; their komes carefully eyed Michael, then pulled a marker out of a little tally board before he finally opened the doors. "May I visit the Virgin of Kamilas to give thanks?" Michael asked the komes, referring to a palace chapel near the Gynaeceum. The komes reached for a document resting on the stone barricade and read it with dark, darting eyes. Finally he looked up and shrugged. "It is permitted."

The little church consisted of two apses stuck on the first story of a larger building used for wardrobe storage. Michael proceeded to the altar of the Holy Mother of Heaven, who floated serenely in the midst of a mosaic applied to the half dome of the apse. He stepped inside the silver chancel screen and placed a single silver nomismata on the gold altar table; metal against metal made a dull, mysterious ring in the absolutely still chapel.

Michael did not hear the priest until he materialized, seemingly as magically as the Holy Spirit, by his side. The priest picked the coin off the altar with slender, cadaverous fingers. He turned about, and Michael followed him into a little room full of sacramental candles. The priest pulled a battered, rusty knife out of his cloak and pried a slab of marble pavement from the floor. He lit one of the candles and handed it to Michael.

The first part of the passage was through raw earth; Michael cursed the gummy soil that quickly dirtied his best silk. After forty fathoms the dirt tunnel intersected what appeared to be the basement of a long-razed palace; a few bits of plaster still clung to the ancient brick vaults. Michael transited the unbearably dank basement to a crumbling perimeter wall, crawled through a small opening, and entered a stone-walled passage so narrow that he had to walk sideways. This ran for fifty fathoms before ending in stone stairs that climbed almost as steeply as a ladder. At the top of the stairs Michael perched himself precariously on a little ledge; a door that looked like it had been designed for a small child was just at his left. He removed the key from his boot, unlocked the door, and squeezed through into a treasury of little-used chalices, porcelain cups, glass basins, bronze lamps, and icons. The antechamber beyond was empty, and the lamps had been extinguished. He took a second key, quickly unlocked a small bronze door bordered with embossed eagles, and, at the end of a featureless but aromatic hallway, parted the dark silk drapes.

The bed beneath the great gilded dome reminded him of an altar: the gold-brocade canopy thrust up by twisting golden columns; the scarlet curtains threaded with thousands of tiny Chi-Rhos, the monogram of the Christ. He approached the bed with excruciating precision, then reached out, his hand steady, and flung the curtain aside.

"Wicked Nephew," said Zoe. She was naked except for her rings, her heavy breasts and sensuous belly thrust out, the jeweled fingers of her left hand beside the shaped, golden pelt between her legs. With her right hand she reached out and touched Michael's face. "Take that filthy thing off."

Michael stripped frantically and fell on Her Majesty, his face buried in her breasts. She laughed in great throaty peals. "Yes, little Nephew, I shall have you to dine again. That is, I shall have you dine upon me. You would have been a surpassing thespian, my little slave. I believe that your odious uncle is even now receiving a favorable report from his spy." She pushed him away and sat up, her hands cupping her own breasts. "Now tell your precious mother about this clever scenario in which you are to play the buffoon. Symeon has heard the most fantastic rumors."

Michael eyed the Empress's pubic triangle while he hurriedly spoke. "He wants to make me the Caesar."

"Yes."

"But you must adopt me first. I am to . . . charm you."

Zoe fell back with the force of her laughter. She writhed with mirth for a moment and then reached up and kneaded Michael's scrotum. "My little boy," she said, puckering her lips facetiously. "My precious little boy!" she shrieked. "Suck at my breast, my little cherub!" She let him go, arched her neck, and pressed her voluminous white bosom upward, a finger at the tip of each thick, erect, porphyry-colored nipple. "There, my child, my paps will give you life!"

Michael's attentions to her breasts calmed Zoe, reducing her boisterous laugh to gentle moans. She began to slide her pelvis over the silk sheets in snakelike motions. "Love slave," she said with a moan, "you must now play Sophocles's tragic hero and enter your mother's womb." She lifted his head. "Come to me, little Oedipus. I shall not even make you bawl for my favor. Give me your essence."

Michael eagerly lowered himself between the twitching Imperial legs. Zoe wrapped him with her gorgeous limbs. "Ah, my little slave"—she sighed—"my precious, tiny Caesar, my dear Nephew and soon adopted son." She gasped and fought for control as his buttocks pumped above her loins. "Listen to me, little one. Once you are named my husband's heir, you must reward the uncle who has enabled this delicious . . . incest. Do you hear me?"

"Yes . . . yes," he began to wail. "Reward . . . unnnh . . . Joannes . . ."

Zoe pulled her knees forward, reached back behind her buttocks, and wrapped her thumb and forefinger around Michael's thrusting member. She squeezed, first firmly, then so painfully that he stopped his motion and looked at her with watering eyes.

She pressed her lips toward him and whispered, her words hot on his heaving chest. "I want you to kill him."

thought it might be instructive for you to see this, Manglavite Haraldr." Joannes selected an instrument from the table and held it toward the light. "You might be called upon to spend more of your time here in the Neorion." He looked back over his shoulder, his eyes almost invisible inside his grotesque head. Then he walked over to his subject, his step heavy, his boots resounding in the sinister chamber. The naked man was chained between two bloodstained stone pillars, his legs spread slightly; a long wooden rail, supported by ropes that could be raised or lowered on pulleys, supported his arms. Two assistants waited dutifully beside the wretch. One was tall by all but Norse standards and had the charred blue skin and short, wiry black hair of Afrikka. The other was a small, noseless Armenian; Haraldr had been told that condemned prisoners might prolong their lives by assisting in the punishment of others.

"Interrogation, Manglavite Haraldr, is an art superior to that of the painter, the carver in stone, even the goldsmith who chases pure images of the Virgin with skill and delicacy." Joannes pointed to the helpless wretch who in his terror had already deposited feces and urine on the bare stone floor. "This inert clay, capable only of the most basic human responses, is the raw material from which I will fashion an object of both beauty and utility in the eyes of the Sacred State we both serve. Though some might perceive our creation as fearful, even repulsive, remember that the most hideous acts of cruelty are beautiful to the Pantocrator when they serve to create martyrs to our Glorious Faith, or when such acts serve to punish the condemned souls who have rejected His Sacraments. If the fiery lakes of Hell are beguiling to our Lord because they purify his Heavenly Empire, then we His servants must find pulchritude in the interrogator's designs, for by them do we purify the Earthly Empire."

Joannes turned quickly to face Haraldr, elbows whirling rigidly as if he were the enormous toy top of some evil Titan. "You, Manglavite Haraldr, are privileged to apprentice yourself to this art." He whirled back to face his raw material, a man of about twenty-five—or perhaps thirty-five?—

with short dark hair and a patchy black beard. It was impossible to tell who he might have been, what his character was, for Neorion had already taken the humanity away from him, as it did everyone, victim or victimizer, who entered its grim portals.

"Like any artist, the interrogator must carefully consider where to begin. The novice tends to strokes that are too delicate or, conversely, too broad. I rather prefer to"—Joannes nodded to the blue man, who seized the victim's head in his huge, dark fingers—"begin with an unexpected flourish, a conundrum to delight the eye of irony." Joannes took a short knife resembling the instrument of a surgeon and held it to the man's mouth; the dark eyes above the gleaming blade glared with a kind of noble defiance and Haraldr asked Odin to help this man die well, and quickly, for he deserved a good death.

"When a man undergoes interrogation, the object of greatest concern to him is his manhood. He is least fearful for his oral cavity and the organs therein, for he knows that he must be left his tongue if he is expected to provide us with the verse we have so arduously prompted him to compose." With a deft, instant motion, Joannes began to carve around the man's mouth, and in a mere moment he flung aside a small, bloody mass like a piece of rotten fruit. The Armenian scrambled after the discarded flesh and dropped it into a large wooden bucket.

Haraldr fought his swoon and surging gut. The poor victim jerked his head as much as he could, and his exposed, reddened teeth chattered while blood poured down his chin. He was in every other way intact, but he was already in countenance a cadaver, a fleshless skull.

"But a man still speaks credibly without lips," said Joannes. He stepped back and appraised his work. "The interrogator, like the artist, knows when his work is finished, for that is when the object he has created praises the Pantocrator in the voice he has intended for it." Joannes reached down and grabbed the man's penis. "This creation of mine can already praise the Pantocrator by informing us who is arming the rabble of the Studion." The man rolled his head with the great, gaping bloody smear where his mouth had been but said nothing. "If we take the testicles, as was my fate, we leave the means but not the desire. If we take the penis, we leave the desire but not the means." Joannes yanked on the penis and sliced it cleanly away. He turned and showed the bloody, limp member to Haraldr.

"Perhaps I should perform this alteration on you Tauro-Scythians." Joannes grinned, an obscene, heavy-lipped smile more terrible than his scowl. "I am concerned that yours, and those of your henchmen, will trouble you more than this is troubling our friend here." He tossed the penis into the Armenian's bucket, then wiped his hands on a towel offered by the blue man. "The slut Maria, with whom you are enjoying yourself, is a chronic malefactor, a delinquent whose immoral license flaunts every standard and expectation of a Christian community. She is anathema to all who worship the True Light of the World."

"She is not anathema to our purple-born Mother," said Haraldr. *When Mar and I destroy you,* Haraldr vowed silently, *her name will be one we shall invoke over your foul corpse.*

Joannes could scarcely conceal his astonishment. Haraldr Nordbrikt was challenging him. Haraldr Nordbrikt and the Hetairarch Mar Hunrodarson, fowl of the same feather. But to his face! Even the Hetairarch was not so carelessly impudent. But that was the difference between the two; the Hetairarch was much more clever, and more dangerous. And that was why Haraldr Nordbrikt's tongue would not earn him lodging in the Neorion that very evening. "Someday," growled Joannes, "you may be asked to assist me with the whore Maria in this place. I enjoy working with women. I often ask them which set of lips they are most loathe to part with. It becomes quite easy to distinguish between those who are vain and those who are lustful."

Ice clotted Haraldr's veins. She a hostage to him? He had not thought of that when he had so blithely taunted Joannes. Christ. Odin. The flame of rage collapsed into mocking embers.

Joannes turned back to his artwork, satisfied that he had made a useful point. Strange, he thought, how these huge Varangian brutes could be moved by tiny, chattering creatures like women. "Our talk has been most useful, Manglavite. It gives our creation an opportunity to reflect on his own reticence. Let him now praise the Pantocrator."

But the Pantocrator was only praised in the dignity of the wretch, a man who, Haraldr reflected, was probably innocent, and if not, then guilty only of righteous outrage. Haraldr was exhausted, brutalized, pained by his own agony in watching Joannes's methodical, deft dismemberment of this once human being; he could not imagine the courage and strength of the simple man who was mutely accepting this terrible attrition of his mortality. Finally, after the Armenian had filled his bucket, Joannes pronounced his creation a disappointment, if only because the clay was of too poor a grade to be molded into any object of value. He turned away from his failed creation for the last time. "Manglavite Haraldr Nordbrikt," he rumbled, "I have been musing, as I often do when I am at my ease in my workshop, and one of the subjects I have entertained while I have worked today is how to best employ your abilities. It comes to my mind that you are currently in complete disuse—in fact, one might claim, disutility—in your office of Manglavite. I have thought of a more useful vocation for you and your Varangian fellows until our Father resumes his customary protocol. Since our Christian community is increasingly plagued by this rabble in the Studion, an example of which we have before us, you and your men will be assigned to duty as cursores in that district until such time as I am convinced that these precautions are no longer necessary." Joannes walked to the forbidding steel double doors; he waited until his assistants had opened them and left the chamber with their bloody towels and bucket of viscera. Then he looked back at Haraldr with a grin like death. "I leave you today's legacy of my art, perhaps flawed, but one you might yet learn from." Joannes slammed the huge doors shut behind him.

The stench of filth and viscera was suddenly overwhelming. Haraldr was alone with . . . it. It was a demonic, crimson mask of bloody, pulpy, flayed facial tissue, without nose, ears, scalp, or lips, only glaring, lidless eyes and clenched, exposed, blood-smeared teeth. Its crotch was a bloody gash, its belly a gaping, reeking, empty cavity where the bowels had been ripped out. Its legs, truncated at the ankles, twitched frantically, the veins gently pumping blood into pools on the floor. Most horrible of all, its spurting, handless wrists jerked up and down with conscious articulation, as if trying to recapture with phantom digits the life that had been carved away from it, piece by bloody piece. And then the rolling, blood-washed irises made contact, and Haraldr realized that there was still a man inside it, just as there had been that terrible night in the Studion. He unsheathed his sword and prepared a quick end to this long, ugly, yet noble death. He came close, forcing himself to look in the eyes, and he realized that this death, and the one in that fetid ally, stained him with blood far more deeply than the many lives he had taken in battle. Now there were two; how many more wretches could he slay out of compassion before he had to question the quality of his mercy? He could never give this man what he was owed, but he could give him what he could. He drew back his blade.

"Wait . . ." The voice stood on the threshold of the spirit world. Haraldr held his blade at the beginning of its merciful arc. The man looked at Haraldr with a bitter yet kindred defiance. "The . . . Blue . . . Star," he croaked, barely audibly. Then with the last fiber of his strength he lifted his head. "Now," he pleaded.

Haraldr brought his blade screaming through the man's neck, his strength fueled not by Odin but by the desperate hope that somehow this stroke would sever the head of the Imperial Eagle.

✝   ✝   ✝

"What will you do?" asked the purple-born Augusta Theodora. Her pinched face and dull brown braids were unadorned; despite her gold-laced purple robe, she seemed as plain as a butcher's wife.

"I could refuse to crown this Caesar," answered Alexius, Patriarch of the One True Oecumenical, Orthodox, and Catholic Faith. His small black eyes stalked like agile panthers above the craggy hump of his nose. "Imperial protocol dictates that the Caesar be crowned by the Emperor, and so I could refuse to sanction the ceremony simply on that basis. But of course the paradox of our Caesar is that we must have him because the Emperor is not well enough to crown him."

"You would be . . . coerced if you refused to crown him."

Alexius smiled. "I fear no coercion. If my jurisdiction were merely the Empire of Rome, then I would offer this Caesar nothing about his head but penitential ashes, and glorify the Pantocrator with my own martyr-dom. But my Empire is that of all souls, and so my considerations are rather more complex." Alexius stroked the ornate rings on his left hand with the fingers of his right. "It is unfortunate that your sister Zoe has so warmly embraced her husband's heir. Were the Empress opposed even mildly, I could take her reluctance to the people of the City, and before the three days that it took our Lord to be scourged, martyred, and resurrected had passed, the people of this city would have hurled Joannes and his Dhynatoi accomplices into the abyss that spawned them. But now the fortunes of our secular Empire—and those of my beleaguered spir-itual Empire—will go from bad to worse. Your sister's husband has lis-tened to the Christ with one ear, and the demon Joannes with the other, and that is the source of the torment that is destroying his body if not his immortal soul. I believe and pray that when this Emperor supplicates the Heavenly Tribunal, he will find expiation. But when this Caesar inherits the Imperial Diadem, he will hear only Joannes, and his soul will endure the fiery lakes of eternal woe."

Theodora crossed herself. "Father, you cannot think that the Emperor is so close to his mortality. He will recover, certainly. He is an extremely . . . robust man."

Alexius stroked his silvery beard. "If he recovers, it will not be soon, and during his illness he will have yielded that much more of his authority, and perhaps his soul, to Joannes. My child, your love for your sister is an example to Christian charity, and I, too, pray for her soul each morning and evening. But Joannes has used the objects of your sister's lust to enslave her people. Whether we are to be ruled by Michael the present Emperor, or this new Michael, the Caesar, is of little consequence to the suffering folk of Rome, who know only that it is Joannes's boot on their neck. Yet as long as your sister continues to place her carnal aspirations above the obligations of her purple-born sanction, her people will obediently suffer that scourge. But God will not suffer this outrage with infinite patience. He has already risen up the Bishop of Old Rome and his blasphemous *filioque,* to warn us of our transgressions."

Alexius studied Theodora's troubled face; she wore her almost child-like expression of grief. Finally the Patriarch gestured at the barren walls of Theodora's apartment; his golden rings caught the light for an instant. "My child, your spiritual wealth has increased in this place of exile."

"Yes. I do not miss the palace. I prefer to dream of the Lord's mansions."

Alexius's thin, elegant lips parted with genuine warmth, but his dark eyes still paced menacingly. "I am certain you will be well received in those mansions. In your devotion to our Lord you are similar to your sister, Eudocia, may the Pantocrator keep her soul in His Eternal Light, though she came to her faith too late to save her mortal being from the consequences of her sin." Theodora seemed startled by this; her face retained the innocence of regret, but her eyes were alert, wary, the prey observing the stalking beast.

"Indeed," continued Alexius, "where the Christ's steps have gone, I see yours following. And yet there is another path that the Christ has also charged you to follow, a charge he gave you from the moment of your soul's conception, and now the Christ cautions us that you have strayed from this path." Alexius's eyes no longer paced; they crouched. "I need not tell you that Christ the Pantocrator, crowned in heaven, was also crowned here on earth."

Theodora's pale blue eyes shifted. "Yes. The crown Pilate gave him. A crown of thorns."

"Our Lord accepted the crown of thorns because beneath that excruciating diadem He would lead mankind to the resurrection and eternal life." Alexius smiled sympathetically. "All worldly crowns are crowns of thorns, my child. Mine own bleeds me even now. The Christ was offered all the Kingdoms of the world if only he would fall on his knees before

Satan. We who rule the world must turn away from like blandishments and take only the crown that earns us favor in the Kingdom of Heaven. And that crown is pain."

"I, too, have renounced the Kingdoms of the World. At last, Father, I have."

Alexius's eyes leapt forward. "No. You have renounced the crown that brings only blood and pain and death to your brow, and in so doing you have denied your people their hope of resurrection. You are the purple-born, child, chosen of God to do His will here in this valley of sorrows. What you have achieved here in your exile is a strengthening of your soul. But that soul must now assume the Holy Burden it is obligated to bear, or it will cease to quest for Eternal Glory. Soon our Lord will bid you rise up and bear your cross to Golgotha."

Theodora's features sharpened. "My Lord cannot mean that I should betray my purple-born sister."

Alexius inclined his head slightly, his thin lips almost musing. "No. I am not asking you to initiate anything against your sister. But the day will come, and soon, when the people of this City will appeal to their Christ to deliver them even from the tormented bosom of their purple-born Mother. And for that day you must be prepared. Your line, the great house of Macedon founded by your uncle, Basil the Bulgar-Slayer, is, through its unyielding defense of the One True Faith, the very artery that nourishes every soul born unto life. And that artery must never be severed, or we are all damned."

"And how would my barren loins perpetuate the dynasty of Macedon? If ever I was fertile, I am now too withered to bear fruit."

"You are not the last of the Bulgar-Slayer's line."

Theodora's eyes could not deny the shock of this jugular attack. "You . . . have known?"

"Yes. For many years. I know the circumstances. Your sister, Eudocia, gave birth to the child at the convent on the Isle of Prote. I do not know the child, or even its sex. But I know that it was not stillborn."

Theodora drew her tall, slender torso erect. Her pale eyes were steely and her tongue newly sharpened. "Then we will not discuss the child. I am in passing health, and when the Christ calls me to my Golgotha, I believe I can offer you ten good years of my life, years in which you can with all your resources wage your battle against the Bishop of Old Rome. Then if we are both still alive, we will discuss the child."

Alexius inclined his head slightly and smiled; the bargain was acceptable.

Theodora flushed, aware of how easily the Father had led her to this precipice of fate but now far less concerned for the consequences of that leap than she ever could have imagined she would be. The child. The child had to be protected. And so, ultimately, did her sister; they were her family. "Father, do you intend to employ the Hetairarch Mar Hunrodarson to hasten the moment when the people of the city cry out for their deliverance from my sister's lust? If so, I must have your assurance she will not be harmed."

"My child, I have not even met with Mar Hunrodarson. What would I have had to discuss with him, until I knew your wishes in this matter? Now that I understand your requirements, I will accede to Mar Hunrodarson's request for an audience and listen to what he has to offer. But first I must place a crown of thorns upon the head of our Caesar."

V

tandards, observed the Parakoimomenos—Lord Chamberlain—of the Imperial Palace. What is missing today are standards. Rome has been built on the rigorous observance of protocol and the unwavering preservation of dignities. Today this is all changed. Today would long be remembered as the nadir of the Imperial dignity. But what was one to do? Abandon the legacy of Rome entirely to the whims of these lowborn parvenues? No. One held one's head high and tried to preserve what one could.

The Parakoimomenos was a strikingly youthful-appearing man for his sixty years; castration had made him callow and plump for most of life, but his late maturity had finally brought out classic Thracian features. He had been born the same year the Bulgar-Slayer had ascended to the Imperial Dignity, had entered the Imperial household as a mere chamberlain-in-waiting when he was only sixteen years old, and his aptitude for the astonishing minutiae of Imperial protocol had advanced him inexorably through the various eunuch grades. Nine years ago he had realized his dream: Parakoimomenos, the highest of all eunuch offices, the official responsible for every aspect of public and private ceremony in the Imperial Palace, the man who presented the face of glorious Rome to an awestruck world. Then, three months after this apotheosis, Rome had fallen to the cruelest fate: the Pantocrator had asked the Bulgar-Slayer to set his throne beside those of the rulers of Heaven. At first the deterioration of standards had been gradual. The Bulgar-Slayer's brother, Constantine, had been a profligate, a petty tyrant, and a sloven, yet he had not simply discarded the prescribed Imperial protocols. His successor, Romanus, had been an even lesser man, but his efforts to transform his pygmylike stature into a giant reputation had at least provided the solidi to maintain some semblance of Imperial dignity and decorum. But the lot who had purloined the throne from Romanus! The Emperor was a good man, in spite of everything, but utterly devoid of culture, as one might expect of the station from which he had risen. Still, he desired, in his simple, uninformed fashion, to observe proprieties. But the Orphanotrophus Joannes! There was the source of this veritable river of ignominy that now polluted the memory of glorious Rome!

The Parakoimomenos looked out from the arcade of the church of St. Mary Chalkoprateia, confident that all was in order on the street. The facades of the buildings were cloaked with silk tapestries embroidered with the Imperial Eagles, and the enormous crowd, held at bay by the batons of the cursores, stood in their best wool-and-silk tunics, clutching armfuls of laurel, myrtle, and olive branches. Two hundred Tauro-Scythians of the Grand Hetairia, gold helms and breastplates explosions of light in the sun, waited at rigid attention. Arrayed behind them was the sublime vision of the Court of Imperial Rome, ranked as the Pantocrator Himself commanded. The first two rows were Magisters, in their white silk tunics spotted with gold medallions, and behind them the Proconsular Patricians, also in shimmering white silk but without medallions, arms cradling the porphyry tablets that proclaimed their rank. And then the Patricians, in light rose-colored robes, with their tablets of white ivory, and behind them the other fifteen ranks, each with its different color silk and particular insignia of dignity. Behind the court were the bands; already a few booms of the kettledrums and blaring notes on the trumpets rose above the anticipatory murmuring of the crowd.

The Parakoimomenos noted that the ranks were in good order, that no witless Patrician had, in a desire to see what was going on, wandered up with the Proconsular Patricians. He turned and faced the bronze doors of St. Mary Chalkoprateia. The Manglavite and Hetairarch flanked the portal of the ancient basilica. The Bulgar-Slayer would have been proud of the two Varangians, thought the Parakoimomenos, the Hetairarch with his ax motionless on his chest, red plumes rising from his gold helmet so that it seemed he would scrape the sky. The Manglavite was new, of course, but he learned quickly and had a noble bearing. Look how stately he holds the fasces, symbol of the centuries of Rome's uninterrupted hegemony; hopefully he will not fall to his knees like some unwashed pilgrim when he sees the interior of the Mother Church for the first time.

The Parakoimomenos reluctantly abandoned his reverie and stared at the bronze doors as if his imperious gaze could somehow keep what was inside forever incarcerated. Yes, in a few moments *they* would emerge and shatter this marvelous illusion of elegance and dominion.

As if to spite the Parakoimomenos, the doors flew open. The Caesar-to-be stepped into the shaded illumination of the arcade, wearing the long white silk tunic symbolic of Christ, crowned with a simple pearl tiara, and shod in purple boots. Behind this impromptu heir, this centurion in the ill-gotten cloak of the Christ, was the debaucher of every known canon of politesse in Holy Rome, the Orphanotrophus Joannes.

The chants began immediately; the political officers had rehearsed the crowd well. "Welcome, Caesar of the Romans! Welcome, strong arm of our Father! Welcome new luminary in the firmament of Imperial Rome!" The Manglavite stepped in front of the Caesar and led him across the church porch and into the street; the Hetairarch walked at his side. The Parakoimomenos watched with horror as the Orphanotrophus Joannes took his place *ahead of the Magisters.* He had known that the man intended to do it, had even forced his reeling mind to visualize it, but to actually see it!

The blaring, thumping band seemed to mock the Parakoimomenos as he took his place between the Manglavite and the Caesar. The Manglavite began to lead the multicolored army of splendor south to the avenue of the Mese, his long, powerful legs snapping in a ceremonial goose step that was impressive and intimidating. The glittering caravan wended slowly through the city, amid the huge, thunderously chanting, petal-throwing crowds, backed up for blocks on either side of the route. Eventually the procession transited the vast Augustaion square, passing beneath the towering equestrian statue of the Emperor Justinian, and exited into the garden in front of the Hagia Sophia. The Manglavite turned directly opposite the western entrance of the Mother Church and began the final leg of the journey. As the massive domes rose before him, the Parakoimomenos armored his spirit against what he would see within. Within? That in itself was an outrage that might indeed bring the great dome down on their heads this very morning. In all the centuries of Rome's greatness, had anyone other than the supreme authority on earth ever been crowned in the Hagia Sophia? Indeed not! Until today, when a ship tarrer's son would receive his crown directly from the hands of the Patriarch himself—not, as was prescribed by all that was holy, from the hands of the Emperor. Well, this entire scenario could have perhaps been even more devastating to civilized sensibilities; at least the Orphanotrophus Joannes hadn't insisted that the Imperial Diadem be placed directly on his own monstrous head! Standards. Today the word was meaningless.

† † †

The central dome of the great church rose like a mountain peak above the sheer massif of the Hagia Sophia's west facade. Haraldr concentrated on the relentless cadence of his steps and ignored the other rhythms, the chants of the crowd, the pounding of the kettledrums. The last hour had been perhaps the most powerful experience of his life, except for Stiklestad. Today, on the streets, he had understood the fundamental awe that overwhelmed this crowd, their sense that a god walked among them. It did not matter to them who this new diety was or where he had come from; the simple fact that he walked in the purple boots of Imperial Rome was enough to evoke an inexpressible, virtually paralyzing wonder. And beneath this wonder was another current of emotion that swept through the crowd, a current so powerful that Haraldr had felt it swirl treacherously about him on every step of the procession: fear.

The Patriarch Alexius waited on the porch of the Hagia Sophia, flanked by the hundreds of priests and deacons who attended the great church. Wrapped in layers of tunics, stoles, robes, and scarfs of embroidered, bejeweled, and enameled silk, the assembled clerics seemed like nothing less than a many-headed treasure trove. Unlike his priests, who were bareheaded, Alexius wore a towering crown of pearls, gems, and granulated gold; beneath this miniature cathedral dome his black, tiny eyes were so fierce that they actually seemed to disturb the air in front of his face, creating a vortex that no man could enter without trembling. Michael shuddered visibly as he bent to kiss the jeweled reliquary suspended from a gold-and-ruby chain around the Patriarch's neck.

Alexius led the entire procession into the Mother Church. *If I had been brought here my first day in the city,* Haraldr thought as he entered, *I would have lost my reason.* The structure, which seemed as solid as a great mountain from the outside, was constructed of pure light and diaphanous color on the inside. To either side of the nave were two levels of massive columns transfigured by light into floating bands of mossy green and rose and carnelian. Where the columns should have spread to receive the weight of the structures above them, they dissolved into a lacy embroidery of vines and leaves; the vaults that floated on this sculptured foam were glimmering mosaic halos. Above the two towering arcades were walls pierced so extensively with windows that they seemed like great sheets of sunlight, and above these walls, suspended so loftily that its presence could only be felt, not seen in its entirety, was a dome as vast as the sky, a pure golden canopy that seemed to float above the rest of the colossal interior. For a moment Haraldr had the vertiginous sense that he, along with the rest of the church and everyone within, was being lifted into the heavens by the dazzling light of Christ's being.

Alexius walked toward the eastern terminus of the nave, where an oval-shaped, colonnaded tower, a small cathedral in itself, rose beneath the great dome like a peak surmounted by a golden sky; from the vault within the tower, a white-robed boys' choir filled the great church with high, sonorous melodies. Alexius ascended the purple-tinted marble steps to the platform atop the tower; this lofty pulpit, called an ambo, was encircled with a balustrade of solid silver embossed with twining ivy and flowers set with sapphire stamens. In the middle of the platform was a golden table upon which had been placed several folded, gold-embroidered, scarlet silk garments. Alexius, his voluminous sleeves billowing like clouds of powdered gems, blessed the clothing in a deep, chanting polyphony. The Parakoimomenos escorted Michael to the golden table and assisted the Caesar-designate into the garments: first the eagle-medallioned robe, then a mantle, and finally a long scarflike pallium, stiff with jeweled and cloisonné plaques. During the ritual Michael recited the prescribed prayers in a noticeably quavering voice.

The choir lilted a final, soaring note that seemed to ascend directly to golden light above, then fell silent. There was a brief rustling as the ranks of assembled dignitaries composed themselves. Then the vast space became completely, supernaturally silent, as if all sound had been banished from the entire universe. The sound of eternity, Haraldr told himself.

Alexius moved as slowly as a dream, his swathing of silk and gold coruscating like liquid light as he moved. He lifted his own immense crown, revealing thin matted silver hair; placed the miniature jeweled dome on the altar table; and took up a diamond-and-pearl diadem. He stepped forward with the same unearthly deliberation and held the diadem high for all to see. He glared over the massed courtiers, almost as if he taunted them with his power over this symbol. "By the authority vested in me by Christ crowned in heaven," he chanted in extended, harmonic syllables, "I bestow this crown on earth." The ringing tones echoed and vanished in the light.

Michael stepped forward, his head bowed and his hands clasped in front of his breast. Alexius looked down upon Michael's bare, humbled head with a gaze so furious that Haraldr wondered if he was about to strike the young man. Alexius held the diadem high above over Michael's head, motionless, hovering, a cluster of light waiting to raise the head beneath it to heaven above or throw him down into the fiery depths. Michael's shoulders began to tremble, and the crowd's tension became audible, the cumulative sigh of hundreds of anxious inhalations.

The diadem plunged like an executioner's blade, almost miraculously halting a scant thumb's width above Michael's unsteady head. The Patriarch gently placed the jeweled cap over Michael's dark curls. Before Michael had even raised his head, organ music rolled through the vaults as if the dome of heaven had split open and unleashed the music of creation. The audience thundered in response. "Holy, Holy, Holy! Glory to God in the highest and on earth peace to all men! May the Caesar live long!"

Haraldr looked at Michael Kalaphates, remembering the young man he had jested with at Argyrus's. That man was dead, resurrected as Caesar of Imperial Rome. Already his face had been transfigured by the light perched above it; it was as if the bones had somehow been realigned to give his face a sharpness, a more powerful sense of structure. His neck erect, his entire body seeming to swell and rise with the deafening acclamations, Michael Kalaphates, Caesar of the Romans, made the sign of the cross over Rome's glittering elite, most of whom, only a month ago, had not even known his name.

Alexius allowed the acclamations to fade and die before commencing the final ritual. The silence was not so absolute as before, the tension eased, and somehow the Patriarch seemed reduced in stature and vehemence. Almost wearily, Alexius returned to the altar table and with tentative fingers picked up a small sack fashioned from plain white silk. He returned to Michael's side and displayed the insignificant parcel to the court. "The Lord marshals the armies of high heaven!" he chanted. "But all men are dust and ashes!" The silk sack was filled, as mandated by custom passed down through the centuries of Rome's greatness, with the ashes of a nameless pauper.

Michael accepted this token of his mortality with steady hands. He turned to descend and receive the homage of his court, and as Haraldr moved toward the new Caesar to lead him down the steps, their eyes met. For a moment too long, too piercing to be chance, the Caesar and the Manglavite remained locked in some ineffable communication that their terrified souls would not permit them to understand.

† † †

"It is a humiliation," said Mar angrily.

"The men are looking forward to it." Haraldr shrugged. "It gives them an opportunity to go out into the city and make contact with the people. I am certain they will have enough young, winsome customers to make the effort worth their while, even if they don't want the money."

"Look at them," said Mar, pointing to the Varangians who roamed the

Augustaion, collecting the sanctified boughs, branches, and twigs that had ornamented the Imperial coronation procession. They alone had the franchise to sell these remarkably valuable relics in the city, a custom established by the Bulgar-Slayer. "First they are janitors, then peddlers. In this worthy for warriors?"

"It is simply a custom the men enjoy. There are many ceremonial duties performed by the Varangian Guard that are not really warriors' work. I don't hear you object about those."

Mar's handsome mouth distorted and his nostrils flared. "Perhaps it is time we do object. When Rome wishes to flaunt its might, who marches ahead of all? We do. But when the Senators and Magisters and Sacrum Consistorum are dividing the proceeds of that power we in great part provide, where are we? We are picking up firewood like peasant women!"

Haraldr sighed inwardly, steeling himself for another argument. He and Mar had for weeks now disagreed, increasingly strenuously, about how to deal with Joannes. In Haraldr's opinion their alliance should be strictly defensive until the Emperor's true condition had been ascertained; even Mar hadn't seen the Emperor for more than a month. In spite of the rumors, or perhaps because of them, Haraldr was certain that the powerful-looking man he had met could best any illness, unless it was some sort of plague that would have long ago carried him off. Mar did not disagree with Haraldr's prognosis of the Emperor's health, but he wanted to confront the Emperor when the coup against Joannes had already been virtually completed. But of course they had no plans for this coup, because their accomplices so far consisted of only a few disgruntled minor officials. To strike at Joannes now would mean that a thousand Varangians would have to go to war with virtually the entire Roman Empire.

Haraldr looked around and lowered his voice. "I don't think it is wise to be discussing your discontent with the Dhynatoi and their accomplices in a public square. Why draw attention—"

Mar stuck his finger in Haraldr's chest. "I don't want you to think I am threatening you," he hissed, "but you are Haraldr Sigurdarson, rightful heir to Norway. You should be sitting on a throne instead of polishing someone else's. But now you seem only too happy to be Joannes's servant. You urge caution at every turn. 'Let us see if the Emperor recovers.' Now it is 'Let us see if this Caesar turns out to be as pliable as Joannes would hope.' You always have a reason to hold back."

"What alliances have you brought us? You yourself said this Caesar interests you."

"That was before Joannes bought him with a crown. And I am working on the most important alliance we could possibly have, and when I have enlisted this confederate, you are going to have to prove that your bluster is backed up by Hunland steel."

"Well, I certainly intend to wait and see what this miracle alliance is. I hope it is someone more important than that clerk in the Magnara, who is able to tell us when Joannes arrives in the morning and little else." Haraldr looked around again. "But I don't think this is the place to discuss this."

"And when will we discuss it, since you are always off plowing your woman? Your value as an ally has become virtually nil since you took up with Maria."

This was another theme Mar had begun to carp on, with constant jests and cryptic allusions about Haraldr's lover. Was he jealous? "Maria has encouraged me to pursue . . . our cause. If you will remember, that was once the source of a considerable misunderstanding between us."

"Well, now she is taking the opposite tack. A month ago you were cautious. Since you started fucking her, you are submissive. When she changes her mind again, will you rush over to the Magnara and try to assassinate Joannes and get us all killed? That woman is dangerous to you and to me." Mar poked his finger in Haraldr's chest again. "You argue with Joannes"—Mar lowered his voice—"over Maria, and he sends you to the Studion. You are fortunate he permitted you to leave Neorion. Now, with the entire Middle Hetairia stuck in the Studion, we have no chance of a joint defense if Joannes orders the Imperial Taghmata to move against us. And you are going to lose men in there trying to police those miserable swine. A lot more than you think. The Studion is going to swallow you up. And Joannes knows that."

"I think I can advance our purpose in the Studion." This was another area of disagreement; Haraldr was convinced that the city's wretched poor were valuable allies, and Mar completely discounted them.

Mar looked skyward for assistance. "Yes. Out among the people. That has become your special folly. That and Maria. You are a fool for that woman. And you are only beginning to dance the fool's ditty. She will break you. Do you think you are the first?"

Haraldr glared, but not with righteous denial. He had heard many of the stories, and she had never denied the substance of any of them. Nor had she apologized for them. "I know about her. Why bring that up?"

"Because the crow shit she drops on your head is going to get in my hair as well. I have known her much longer than you have. You are merely a lull in the tempest. Has she ever told you about us?"

"Yes." But he didn't know, really, and the thought sickened him far more than any of the others. "She said she has known you for some time. You were close once. I did not ask—"

"Don't worry, I didn't fuck her. To be truthful with you, I thought she was mad. She was even wilder then. She had such rage. Real rage, in a way that Odin would understand. She wanted me to punish her. Really. I do not mind admitting that I often enjoy punishing men. But not women. I have never struck a lover."

"You have never had a lover that I have seen," said Haraldr. Before he had time to regret the words, Mar's hand was on his throat. The force was so great and immediate that Haraldr thought his windpipe would instantly collapse. Almost as quickly, Mar took his hand away and looked around to see if anyone had been watching. His eyes were a murderous glacier blue.

"Don't overestimate your usefulness, Prince of Norway," he hissed, then turned and stomped off.

oannes stroked the neck of his snorting black stallion. "I hope it pleases you, Nephew," he shouted to Michael Kalaphates.

Michael craned his head to look up at the peristyle entrance of his new palace. "It is magnificent, Uncle. So . . . Hellenic. What do you think, Uncle?"

Constantine's horse clambered over the marble porch. "It is indeed magnificent, sir. It reminds me of Antioch. Out here you can open the entrance up with a freedom that is not afforded in the city. Well done, brother! It is a palace fit for a Caesar!"

Michael reined his gleaming white Arabian around and looked east toward the Golden Horn, the natural harbor that flanked Constantinople on the north. The great buildings of the surrounding cities were sparkling miniatures from this vantage, and the ships that crowded the narrow waterway seemed like expertly painted little toys. His new residence, which looked much like an ancient pagan temple with its two-story peristyle and clean, rectangular shape, was surrounded with beautiful cypress groves and a vast woodland park for hunting; the closest building, other than his own stables and servants' complex, was another ivory-white palace set on a gentle green promontory about twenty stades away. And although the Caesar did not know it, not considerably farther away was the country palace of the Augusta Theodora.

The three men dismounted. Joannes signaled to the retinue waiting on a paved road that ascended the hill in gradual loops. The hundreds of grooms, chamberlains, guards, cooks, wardrobe masters, huntsmen, and priests filed past in yet another procession to the glory of the new Caesar. Grooms arrived to take the horses, but Joannes waved off the boy assigned to his stallion and continued to hold the jittery horse's bit. "I must return to the palace, as you know how much of the burden now falls on my shoulders. I simply wanted to see you settled, and know that you will be happy here."

"Uncle, I am delirious," said Michael, doffing his scarlet bonnet in respect. "I only wish that your solicitude for my comfort had not inspired you to place me so far from the arduous toils and manifold concerns of the Imperial Palace. For to help you heft the burdens of our beloved Empire would in some small way relieve the enormous incumbency of gratitude your copious generosity has placed within my breast. As surpassingly splendid as these comforts are, it would equally gladden my heart to know that I could be immediately—yea, instantaneously—at my uncle's summon should he need even the merest assistance."

"This is where I need you, Nephew, resting, contemplating, building the reservoirs of strength and wisdom that you will need for the sake of all Rome should you ever be required to wear the Imperial buskins. Like the worthy stylite perched atop his column who praises the Lord with his utter immobility, your service is in your patience and sedentary devotion, as precious to the Pantocrator as the bustling about of all the Imperial Taghmata. Now, Nephew, brother, I must bid you farwell, and leave you to the pleasures your Father and I have long sought for you."

Michael and Constantine watched Joannes pound off on his powerful stallion, then walked through the bronze doors of the residence, admired the fountains in the inner courtyard, and found a small reception room that had only one door. Constantine looked about in the hall before he quietly shut the door behind him.

"Can you trust any of the servants?" asked Constantine in a low voice.

"Yes," said Michael. His scarlet boot distractedly nudged a ram-shaped bronze lamp set on the small marble hearth. "I brought my old cook, Ergodotes, and made him a vestitore. I am certain he is reliable."

"Good. You have someone who can get information in and out."

"Have I not you as well?" Michael seemed surprised.

Constantine cleared his throat. "I had rather hoped you might ask me to live here with you."

"Uncle!" Michael beamed and embraced his uncle. "Of course! I had not even dared to suggest you join my luxurious exile. You will make this elegant incarceration not only tolerable but also amusing!"

"And perhaps productive."

The shadow crossed Michael's face again. "Yes. What concerns me now is that our 'Father' might recover sufficiently, if only temporarily, to regret his acquiescence to Joannes's scheme. Then"—Michael looked at Constantine with vulnerable, pleading eyes—"this situation is more dangerous than I had expected. I am a decoration, so to speak, that could quickly become unfashionable." Michael erupted and viciously kicked the head off the bronze lamp. "Damn him! Damn him! We will be his hostages as long as he lives!" Michael's face was crimson, and his eyes had a curious opaque glaze. He exhaled sharply through his nostrils, twice in rapid sequence. "I have been considering a plan along with an . . . associate of mine. It is quite dangerous. I will understand if you wish to hear no more of it."

Constantine opened the door quietly and checked outside in the hall, then came back in the room. His forehead was perspiring, but there was grim purpose in the set of his jaw. "They took the manhood from between my legs," he said softly. "They did not take the manhood from here." He thumped his well-larded chest. "Tell me about this plan."

†　†　†

"Blood! Blood!" The girl stood as naked as Eve and shook her dirty burlap tunic in Ulfr's face. She spit, made a punching motion with her fist, then pointed at Askil Eldjarnson and rattled off a string of words that Ulfr guessed he wouldn't have known even if his Greek was as good as Haraldr's. He did recognize one of the words, however: "Rape."

Ulfr looked down at the shrieking, gesticulating girl; she had greasy brown hair and teeth like a glacier rift. Another word he could understand: "Virgin." She pounded on Askil's chest and spit in his face. "Look at her, Komes Ulfr," said Askil calmly but mournfully. "She has lice. And breasts like kneecaps." The gangly, thin-faced Icelander spread his hands in a gesture of incredulity. "If a man visits the butcher, why would he pay for the meat and steal the entrails?"

Ulfr nodded sympathetically. The girl was sixteen, if a day, and if there was a woman of sixteen summers in the Studion who was still a virgin, whether she wanted to be or not, she deserved to be appointed one of these Christian saints. Blood had been smeared on her tunic and around her pubic area in an improbable quantity; she was saying she had been raped, not sacrificed to Odin. Ulfr guessed she was a precociously shrewd whore with a clever new cheat; he would tell the men to watch out for yet another Studion snare.

"Varangian devils!" yelled another woman, a toothless, soot-faced hag of indeterminate age. "Devil sent you, Devil take you back!" Ulfr could not understand everything shouted by a burly man with a dirty rag over one eye, but the essence of it was that in addition to raping children, Varangians also fornicated with the Emperor. Ulfr looked around. More than a dozen people had congregated, most looking on silently with sullen, flickering eyes. Something was wrong. People in the Studion wouldn't assemble on a filthy street corner in the dead of night to involve themselves in an ordinary misery like the putative rape of a young woman.

And the young men—six, seven of them—were too well fed to be from the sounding blocks. They were professional trouble-rousers from down near the seawall, not the ragged beggars and petty thieves that afflicted this area.

"I'm going to pay her something for her virtue," said Ulfr to Askil in Norse. He had reached inside his wallet for a coin when a swaggering, swarthy young man of no more than twenty-five walked up and put his arm around the girl and said, "I am her father." Ulfr nodded at the word *father* and smiled sardonically. Very well. He produced a copper follis and held it out to the man; the girl swatted it away. "Silver!" shouted the father, who now caressed his alleged daughter's bare flank. Ulfr deliberated. His instinct was to offer Hunland steel as payment due this impudent little thug, or better still, break him with his bare hands. But he remembered what Haraldr said about how cheap trouble was in the Studion, and how dear the cost might be be to put an end to it if it ever got out of control. He produced a silver nomismata.

The girl snatched the coin and ran off, vanishing so quickly into the putrid shadows that it was as if she had never existed. Her "father" stood openmouthed for a moment and then scurried off in search of her. Ulfr looked at the crowd and told them in Greek to "be off." The burly man, the old hag, and two others went growling and mumbling into the night. Ulfr noticed that the band of toughs had swelled to a dozen. He was just about to tell Askil to unsheath his long sword.

A motion and a blur from the crowd. Askil grunted and fell to his knees and the stone plopped on the fetid pavement at his feet. Ulfr brought his long sword shrieking out of the sheath. He had no recourse. They had been attacked, and now they had to kill, or the life a Varangian would not be worth the dung on the streets of Studion.

Ulfr studied the flashing blades that now ringed him. Knives. No swords, no armor, no spears. He asked Odin to guide him to the most deserving victim and instantly whirred his blade halfway through the neck of one of the tallest toughs. The rest looked at the gushing, twitching body and reconsidered their boldness. Askil was on his feet, his long sword unsheathed. He charged and scattered a half dozen into the night. The rest backed away slowly from Ulfr, jabbing their knives futilely like performers in a mime. One of them yelled something about Varangians who slept with goats.

† † †

Ergodotes, former cook and newly appointed vestitore to the Imperial Caesar Michael Kalaphates, stabled his mule in the courtyard of the little inn on the outskirts of the Venetian quarter. His principal concern on this night was the unsavory proximity to foreigners; these Venetian sailors were scoundrels at the least, and most likely carried plagues that would make a healthy body rot like a melon left out in the sun. Well, they probably wouldn't be up this far unless they ran out of rats and dogs to eat down where they were.

As far as the other so-called danger was concerned, what to worry? He was now the trusted servant of a demigod, out on the Lord's good business for his holy master. Ergodotes flipped a copper coin at the stable boy, strolled behind the inn, and identified the entrance to which he had been directed.

The house behind the inn was a curious ruin, perhaps an old chapel of which only the basement remained; the plaster was completely peeled off, and only the bare bricks, set with thick courses of crumbling mortar, remained. The wooden roof stuck on top of this decaying foundation was of much more recent vintage than the brick walls but was not in considerably better condition. The door was solid and new, though, sturdy oak studded with iron braces and nails. Ergodotes knocked three times, waited, then knocked once.

Ergodotes thought he would collapse from the stench when the door was opened; he assumed the occupant must live atop a sewer or never discarded his own slops. And the shrieking and howling quite unnerved him.

"Come in before the demons snatch you!" The man inside chortled. He was short, fantastically obese, with a head as smooth and round as a marble sphere; this sphere pivoted back and forth on his neck as if run by some sort of clockwork mechanism. "Come in here!" The fat man chortled again, as if even his most mundane pronouncement were a source of great mirth. He waddled through the small dark vestibule of the dwelling, his stained tunic out before his stupendous belly like the sail of a Genoese merchantman.

The main room resembled the factory of a chemist or pharmacologist, a complex jumble of vials, jars, bowls, mortars and pestles, with all sorts of dried and fresh leaves, berries, chunks of rock, and dried mushrooms scattered among the utensils. Jars of reptiles stood in rows against one wall, and against the opposite wall were wicker cages full of howling monkeys.

"Well, you knew the street, you knew the knock, you knew this was me, because who else would be here!" The fat man chortled yet again. He needed to squat only about a palm's width in order to seat his amorphous rump upon a backless chair. "Let's hear who you are and what you want!"

Ergodotes explained his mission. When he had finished, the fat man whistled a tune for some time, his head swiveling periodically. "That's a big one," he finally said, for the first time looking crestfallen. "But I'd like to add him to my collection, you're certain I would!" He laughed wildly and the monkeys went into virtual hysterics in response. "When did you say you'd bring the money!"

Ergodotes finalized the details, getting a lengthy, chuckling discussion of how the poison would work and how his "specialist" would deliver it to the "acquisition."

"One thing," asked Ergodotes when he was satisfied that everything else had been taken care of. "How do we stop it if we must change our plans?"

"You can't do that!" said the fat man, howling as if it were the funniest thing he had said all night.

† † †

"Provocations," said Haraldr. "Four incidents last night, yours, and two others already tonight. He looked at Ulfr searchingly. "There is a plan here."

"Well, they're getting nowhere," said Ulfr. "Was anyone hurt tonight, other than the ache in Askil's head?"

"Hedin had his leg cut," said Haraldr. "That's what concerns me, that there is no apparent reason for these quarrels. Ulfr, the Studion is like no place we have ever known. The palace, for all its splendor and vastness, is like a court in the north, only more complex. The Studion is like a dense, almost impenetrable forest, with its own laws, its own warnings, its various hidden lives that can suddenly appear to challenge one's own." He pointed down the street at a vista of towering, brutely simple brick buildings, ramshackle balconies, reeking lanes, and wretches sleeping on the streets. "They are doing something out there, and we don't know what. But we are certainly part of it."

† † †

The Caesar looked out on his empire; a doe loped into a clearing and then darted back into the thick brush. On the Golden Horn, the sails were like bits of colored paper. Michael turned away from the window.

"When will he do it?"

"He says tomorrow night," replied Ergodotes. "He did not think it would be difficult to arrange, since I had given him most of the information he needed."

Michael recoiled from the sharp pain in his stomach. Was he moving too precipitously? Did he need more time to contemplate, to prepare? Then he remembered—no, felt, in his belly, almost as if a woman had grasped his manhood—that moment in the Hagia Sophia, the moment that had transfigured him, the moment that seemed like a thousand times the ecstasy of an ejaculation, a thousand thousand times more than the exhilaration of a wager won, a sensation that wrapped the soul like the arms and legs of Helen, who drove the strong-greaved Achaians across the water to Troy. That sensation would never release him: The beauty, the light, the chords of pure sound, the . . . godliness. God. Hadn't there been a moment, as the chants of Rome's dignitaries rose to beseech the Dome of Heaven, when the Pantocrator had answered? Yes. Yes. There truly had been. Only if a man had been there could he know this, even believe this, and how many men had ever stood where he had stood that day? The Pantocrator had answered, as if he had been right next to His Caesar and had whispered in his ear. He had even touched His Caesar. The Pantocrator already moved His Caesar's hand, was not that clear? Yes. The Caesar could not move fast enough now; had not God created all of this in scant days? And as God was present at His creation, so the Caesar would need to be there when his creation began. He was Caesar, heir to the lords of both the old and new Romes. He would look in the dying eyes of the man who denied him his indescribable passion, his eternity, his soul of pure light, and damn him to the tomb where the voices of the adoring multitude were forever silent.

"Ergodotes," said Michael, "tell the centurion of my guard that I am to be escorted into the city tomorrow."

"Yes, Majesty." Ergodotes withdrew with his hands crossed over his breast. He had reached the door before Michael remembered, with a jolt, the detail he had neglected.

"Ergodotes," he whispered, coming close, "where will it be?"

Ergodotes stepped back in the room, closed the door, and told his Caesar the secret.

he new moon floated over the Studion, her full, lustrous serenity a mockery of the squalid world below. The bonfire had been set at a crossroads, and the flames cast an orange glow on the surrounding facades and down the four arms of the streets, turning the intersection into a fiery crucifix. The young man had stripped off his tunic and stood in a dirty loincloth, his bare buttocks tensed. He let out a whoop and dashed toward the pyre of burning boards and branches. Just when it seemed he would plunge into the flames, he lifted, throwing his arms skyward and pulling his legs up. He hurtled through the raging tongues and rolled into a ball when he landed on the other side. After he had popped back to his feet he was given a drink of wine from a clay jar; his friends pounded his back and two young girls threw their arms around him and kissed him. The crowd cheered and another young man stripped off his tunic and prepared to take his leap.

"I don't like it," said Haraldr.

"I don't like anything in this Studion," said Ulfr, "but of all I have seen, this least offends the gods. At least there is some joy in this. They say it is an old pagan custom, to leap over the fires on the new moon."

Haraldr looked down the long blocks of misery. Another fire blazed at an intersection five blocks away. "Look at these," he said, pointing to two ponderous, listing, enclosed wooden balconies that met over the street and were saved from collapse only by their mutual buttressing. "This is why elsewhere in the city the Logothete enforces the separation of balconies by at least four fathoms. Here, one spark could turn the entire Studion into a pyre."

"Perhaps that is why the regulations are not enforced here," said Ulfr.

"I am certain that is the reason."

"Trouble." Ulfr pointed to the distant intersection where the second fire blazed. The crowd, perhaps sixty men, women, and children, seemed to have been sucked in around a single scuffling vortex. "Shall I call for a decurion?"

"No. We'll go down there." Haraldr had the notion that the worse the odds against the Varangians, the *less* likely these people would attack

417

them. Two Varangians against sixty or a hundred reinforced the notion that the fair-hairs had supernatural powers; a decurion and his squad of ten might make the Norsemen seem like mere mortals.

By the time Haraldr and Ulfr reached the crowd, the agitation had ceased and the group almost seemed to be waiting obediently for the Varangians. The desperate, dirty faces even backed away to form a little cordon. "This is one of them," said a rheumy-eyed man of about thirty; he shoved forward a scowling, curly blond-haired youth about a dozen years younger than himself. The boy had cuts on his lips and eye; blood spilled over his sparsely bearded chin.

The crowd erupted into a blizzard of accusations, arms raised, hands waving. Haraldr salvaged a few words from the hurricane of shrieking voices. Apparently a number of the youth's accomplices had thrown things at the crowd in order to distract them; the youth had then either purloined some clothing or fondled some women or both. Nonsense, thought Haraldr. These were not crimes in the Studion. What was really going on here? He nodded to Ulfr to be ready. The crowd continued to protest.

Finally the rheumy-eyed man grabbed Haraldr's arm and pointed skyward. The tenement rose eight, perhaps even nine, stories from the street, and the fire had been set on top of the highest balcony, just below the peaked wooden roof. Small figures gestured against the glow, and suddenly embers showered down; a large blazing coal plunged right into the middle of the crowd and everyone scattered, only adding to the chaos of oaths. Now Haraldr understood the alarm. As miserable as it was, Studion was home for these wretches'. And up above them in the night were the seeds of Studion's destruction.

"Ulfr! Grab some of the more able men!" Haraldr grasped the tunic of the rheumy-eyed man and pulled him along; the man understood and signaled to four of his friends. Another group of six or so young men followed Ulfr into the tenement. The dingy, smoke-stained building reeked of human waste. The stairs were narrow wooden slats with frequent gaps. At the third landing a little boy sat, deftly skinning a small rodent with a sharpened tile. The halls were grim and bare but surprisingly free of trash; apparently the tenants threw everything into the streets. In the hall extending off the ninth landing, two young men, their tunics pulled up, engaged in sex. Haraldr shoved the lovers aside and pushed the door at the end of the hall open. At least a dozen more young men sat on a bare wooden floor, passing wine jars and shouting at each other; a naked woman straddled one of them. They seemed curiously unawed by the giant fair-hair crashing in on them. "Stay! Stay! Stay!" shouted Haraldr, waving his short sword. "If you rise, your legs will be cut off!" He shouted at Ulfr to enforce the order and looked out at the balcony; the arch that opened onto the wooden structure had crumbled, so that the balcony seemed more like an extension of the room. The fire had just burned through the ceiling of the balcony and was now kindling on the floor. "Get their tunics," yelled Haraldr; he assumed that no water was to be found in the building and that the best recourse would be to smother the flames.

"Get them off!" Ulfr directed his helpers to collect the coarse burlap garments. A youth leapt up and lunged at one of the rhuemy-eyed man's friends. In an instant all was bloody chaos. Ulfr held back, not knowing who was friend or foe. Too late he discovered that their only allies had been the rheumy-eyed man and his four friends; the youths who had already been in the room and the six who had followed Ulfr quickly stabbed and bludgeoned them to the floor.

Haraldr did not hesitate; his sword cut down four of the youths before the rest squeezed out the door. The woman remained in the corner with a wine jar clutched to her breast. Haraldr hesitated, his instinct telling him to get out. But he looked at the twitching corpse of the rheumy-eyed man and his dead or dying friends—one moaned pitiably, flopping like a wounded seal in his blood-soaked tunic—and decided he owed the people of Studion this chance. "Let's get their cloaks," he shouted to Ulfr.

The balcony exploded and spit embers and searing drops of pitch, which had apparently been used to ignite it. A fiery curtain forced Haraldr back toward the door. Ulfr shouted and Haraldr turned. The hallway was a furnace, the floor awash with blazing pitch. Haraldr looked about at blank, windowless walls and knew that here, in this terrible place that offended the gods, he had finally lost Odin's favor.

† † †

"You are not the man I usually deal with."

"They told me to expect you," said the Cephalonian, so-called because he came from the Island of Cephalonia, off the west coast of Hellas not far from Athens. The Cephalonian had Hellenic coloring, the blond hair and light eyes, but he was no Apollo or Hermes. In fact, there was little about him that was memorable. In a crowd someone would walk past him and never remember that they had seen him.

"Indeed so." The eunuch who addressed the Cephalonian was young, still encumbered with a baby's fat, with puffy red cheeks and a sneering manner. "Just who did they tell you to expect?" He looked around at the candlelit vats and tubs of the small medicinal soap factory, wrinkling his nose at the astringent smell.

"They told me to expect the Orphanotrophus Joannes's Chamberlain." The Cephalonian looked at the eunuch as if sizing him up, then allowed his expression to indicate that he was impressed with what he saw. "That's what I was told. The Chamberlain himself. Which has to be you, sir, from the look and manner of your Eminence."

The eunuch, who was in fact a mere cubicularias—a glorified janitor—to the Orphanotrophus Joannes, tried not to look too pleased; indeed he attempted to harshen his demeanor. "Well, then, man, they must have told you what I have come for," he snapped.

"That too, Eminence." The Cephalonian wiped his hands on his tunic and went to a long, low shelf at the far end of the room. He came back with a little wooden box and displayed it to the eunuch. "Just manufactured this morning, special as he likes it. Be assured that the ingredient still has its pharmacological properties intact." The Cephalonian opened the box and let the eunuch inspect the foul-smelling piece of soap, laden with special unguents to treat an eczema that afflicted the Orphanotrophus Joannes. "I don't imagine I need to tell your Eminence not to let anyone else use this."

The eunuch appraised the Cephalonian as if he were some kind of lesser life-form. His lips curled contemptuously. "Surely you don't think we are operating a public bath, do you, man?"

† † †

The smoke would kill them before the flame. Then something, perhaps Odin, directed Haraldr's attention upward. The roof beams. "Ulfr," he shouted, his sword already poised. The two Norsemen hacked as they never had in battle. But the exertion was suffocating them, the smoke pouring into their lungs.

A muffled crack preceded a stunning cascade of timbers and tiles; not just the ceiling but the pitched roof of the entire building apparently had been supported by the beams. Air rushed in, briefly reprieved their lungs, and then fanned the blazing pitch. "Where . . ." mumbled Ulfr; his head was gashed and he seemed disoriented.

Haraldr glimpsed the moon through the rising smoke. The remains of the roof rose above him like a tiled cliff. "Ulfr! We have to climb!" He scrambled over the tiles with desperate agility and clung to the peak of the roof. Ulfr almost slid to the street but also attained the precarious perch. To the east the lights of the city ran beyond vision. Beneath them, extending south to the seawall and west to the land wall, the entire Studion had erupted into regularaly spaced conflagrations, not merely at the street corners but also in dozens of tenements like this.

"They're burning it," shouted Haraldr. The flames erupted through the tiles and collapsed another section of the roof. The choking smoke thickened and obscured the terrible lights of the Studion. Haraldr crept like a four-legged spider down the eastward pitch of the roof. He yelled up at Ulfr. "Balconies!"

Ulfr inched his way down and propped his feet on the cornice. The roof of the balcony below was on fire. "We'll probably fall through the burning timbers until we hit a floor or ceiling that isn't on fire," said Haraldr.

"Odin has told you this?" asked Ulfr. "What if they're all on fire?"

"Then we will not need a funeral pyre."

Ulfr nodded. "I have been ready to die with you more than once." He crouched on the cornice and prepared to jump. "I will see that a warm bench is waiting for you in the Valhol!" he shouted, and then he plunged feetfirst into the inferno.

Haraldr held his breath. He fell almost without impact through the roof of the balcony and felt only a slight scraping as he hurtled through the floor. Almost as soon as he knew that he had crashed through the next roof, his fall ended with a stunning impact and he felt a pain in his ankle. The flames were all around him. He smelled his hair singe. He rolled toward the adjoining room. The choking air seemed cool. He sat up and slapped at his smoldering cloak. Ulfr squatted on his haunches, looking at him.

Ulfr and Haraldr descended the stairs, shouting to warn the tenants as they passed each landing. The street was entirely deserted. No onlookers, no panicked residents scurrying out with their meager belongings. They saw someone running in the next block; behind the flailing figure a wooden hovel, several stories high, was almost entirely consumed by flames. The upper stories of the tenement they had just escaped were a blazing crown; the building resembled a giant torch thrust into the night. Embers showered down.

Ulfr shook his head. "What you said is right. The Studion is like no other place." Huge timbers fractured and plunged flaming to the street. Haraldr and Ulfr ran west through an intersection to escape the falling debris. They encountered no one. It was as if the devils had claimed all the souls of the Studion and were now razing it with fire. Ahead of them, the wooden building they had seen from a distance collapsed with an explosive *whoosh* and blocked the street. They went back, skirted the burning tenement they had just escaped, and proceeded north. No side streets intersected this thoroughfare for several blocks, and there were no fires up ahead.

The toughs came out of the shadows like silent, dark spirits. Maybe twenty, but no apparent spear shafts, Haraldr observed calmly; the spear was the only weapon that could reach him before his sword could reach the man who wielded it. Haraldr unsheathed his sword. "Too much killing this night," he said grimly. The sound of timbers cracking punctuated the enormous sibilation of the flames at their backs. The toughs formed a blockade. Haraldr held the Hunland steel high so that they could all see it. "We'll charge them," he told Ulfr.

The toughs scattered before Haraldr had gotten within a dozen ells of them; they jittered like anxious dogs for a moment before the shadows pulled them back into their lairs. Two blocks south, the entire crown of a tenement fell into the street with a tremendous roar and flash of light. Haraldr and Ulfr turned to watch for a moment, then continued north.

Haraldr rubbed his smoke-fouled eyes. He thought of bathing, he thought of the next time he would hold Maria and feel her silk next to his skin. He could no longer save the Studion. But Odin had given him another day. He was suddenly quite weary. Where was a side street? They needed to turn east.

The street ahead shimmered. The flames behind them soughed like a great wind, and embers floated past. The street was moving. Haraldr felt as if his legs had vanished. His bowels iced. Odin. Clever, tricky Odin. The prankster. The street ahead was alive with people. Not hundreds but thousands, backed up for blocks, a crowd like that on the Mese for the coronation of the Caesar. But this crowd was different, bristling, with shafts sticking up among it like the spikes of a sea urchin. Spears. Hundreds of spears.

† † †

"Nephew. I was told you waited on me."

How gracious of you to point that out, thought Michael Kalaphates, *since I have been waiting here in your antechamber since the third hour of the night. And it is now the eighth hour of the night.*

"It is quite late, Nephew," said Joannes. "Perhaps I was too strident in my previous criticism of your industry, or lack thereof. Since you have attained your lofty dignity, you have perhaps allowed the pendulum to pivot too far in the direction of application. It wearies me simply to observe the hours you obviously now devote to affairs of state."

"My profound apologies if I have momentarily deterred you from your verily unceasing pursuit of our Empire's concerns, Uncle, but I did have a matter of grave import to discuss."

"Indeed." Joannes's sluglike lower lip lapped over his thin upper one. "I had rather hoped to insulate you from grave matters, as your health is so precious to me."

"As yours is to me, Uncle." Michael paused. "I have heard rumors of a plot."

"It is not possible to walk beneath the Chalke Gate without hearing rumors of a plot, Nephew," said Joannes with deliberate weariness in his deep, growling voice.

"I believe it is, as much as it tortures my very soul even to contemplate the words, a plot against you, my dearest uncle."

Joannes's deeply socketed eyes rolled toward Michael like the swiveling spouts of an Imperial *dhromon*. "Let us not carry this amusement further, Nephew." A lightning bolt crashed inside Michael's skull. Joannes showed his awful teeth. "I know Constantine is your favorite uncle."

"You are both equally dear," Michael somehow replied. He was numb with relief. And fear, the fear of a possibility he had never considered. It had been a mistake to come here tonight, sheer hubris. No. It was not possible that Joannes could know.

"Well, Nephew, I am touched by your sincere concern for my welfare. But as I am most weary of, as you so graciously phrase it, my unceasing labors on behalf of the state, I would like to bathe first. I see no possibility of assassins lurking in my bath, however customary such venues have become for murders of all sorts, and even palace coups. I would like to think that my demise would require more imagination on the part of the miscreant." Joannes's Chamberlain opened the door to a hallway. As Joannes stepped beneath the lintel he whirled dramatically and faced Michael. "You have whetted my curiosity, Nephew. Why don't you join me in my baths and tell me of the imminence of this danger to my person."

† † †

Haraldr looked south. Flaming wreckage completely blocked the street. "It doesn't matter," he said to Ulfr as he turned back to face the mob. "They have seen us. We cannot let them know that we are afraid of them, or the lives of my pledge-men will be worth nothing on these streets."

Ulfr drew his sword. "An ax age, a sword age. The ravens will drink well tonight. And this mob will soon know with how many lives the corpse of a Varangian is purchased."

"No."

Ulfr looked at Haraldr incredulously.

"Not yet." Haraldr unbuckled his breastplate and sword belt, took off his helm and cloak, and handed all of his weapons to Ulfr. "Odin permitted me this once before," he said.

"My friend . . ." Ulfr trailed off. There was no use protesting; Haraldr had made too many mad ruses work in the past. But for a Varangian to perish unarmed, a prisoner, perhaps tortured, was a fate literally worse than death; his bench in the Valhol would wait, empty, until the last dragon flew.

"I won't deny you your place at the benches," said Haraldr. "If they come at you, take up your sword and summon the birds of death. But wait patiently for my return. I may be gone for some time."

Haraldr walked toward the mob. Stripped of the badges of the feared Varangians, he felt strangely free, and yet terribly frightened as well, almost like a man in the middle of some prodigious dive. He could hear no voices above the fire storms. He came within spear range and for a moment wondered what it would feel like to have steel thud into his unprotected sternum.

The faces had the frightening uniformity of misery. Pale, deep eyes, mournful lips, angry jaws. Men, many women as well. Burlap, cheap tattered linen, rags. Stringy, filthy hair. Scars, sores. A cleft palate, a man on bare stumps. They shifted as he approached, their silence as awesome as the stillness in the Mother Church. A middle-aged woman came forward and stood a step in front of the rest. Vividly Haraldr saw the Hound at Stiklestad, that step beyond the howling wall. And his brother's last steps.

"Why are you burning the Studion?" she demanded, her eyes flashing. She had a long, worn face, a face that never had had a chance at beauty and was now past the age for it.

Haraldr was stunned, and then he realized what she meant. Of course. Two birds with one arrow. Joannes had ordered the Studion burned and knew that the people would attack the Varangians as the agents of that calamity. "We Varangians did not set these fires."

The crowd erupted, as angry as a tempest. Fists shook and spears bobbed up and down. The woman screamed over her comrades. "See what they think of your lies!" The crowd seemed to lift her toward Haraldr. His pagan roots surfaced and he feared the spirit world he would enter without his sword. *Christ,* he wondered, *where are you? Will you receive me in your paradise if I am denied the Valhol?*

They were around him, the white heat of death. He was clawed and punched, and the woman was pushed into him. She glared up with gritted, decayed teeth. "Is there another reason why you should not die, Varangian?" she shrieked. He looked at her eyes, thinking she was not the face of the Valkyrja he had imagined, and spoke the words that needed no prompting from any god. "The Blue Star."

The woman's hate-filled eyes were suddenly as wondering as a child's. She thrust her arms into the air, screamed, and began to push the crowd back. The mob slowly quieted until the huge flames that were consuming their homes could be heard again. "What business do you have with the Blue Star?"

"I want to plead my case, to convince the Blue Star that we Varangians did not fire the Studion. I think I know who did order this."

The woman stepped back and studied Haraldr for a moment. Then she shrugged and led him through the crowd. Haraldr looked out across the expanse of faces, feeling another kind of Roman power, far different from the power he had felt at the coronation of the Caesar, but perhaps, in a strange way, greater. And he knew in that moment that the two powers of the Great City would someday come to a bloody reckoning.

As Haraldr had suspected, the Blue Star was among his flock, herding them from behind, his bulky form towering above the rest, his shelflike beard jutting out proudly. Haraldr looked at the silly, silken little henchmen beside their leader and wondered if he had done the right thing in so boldly confronting this very petty street prince.

"So you want to see the Blue Star," said the big man. He held up his hand so that the sapphire ring was visible.

Haraldr nodded; the man's manner convinced him he had made his final mistake in the middle realm.

The Blue Star looked at Haraldr for a moment and dipped his head. That was the last thing Haraldr saw, the Blue Star nodding at him.

† † †

Naked, Joannes gave credence to the Bogomilist heresy that man was created in the image of Satanael, not God. The smooth, hairless, white wax skin draped a demonically distorted form: the great, swelling knees and elbows; the breastbone that curved like the chest of an enormous, featherless bird; the penis a solitary, pathetic little pod dangling beneath an immense, shovellike pelvis. A torturous embroidery of scarlet eczema ran from his wrists to the shoulders of each arm.

"I do not like to stay long in the dry heat," said Joannes. He seemed curiously at ease. He slumped against the marble bench and languidly waved his grotesque hand through the mist of steam. "The wet heat does not deprive the skin of its oils."

Michael looked at the mosaic that circuited the walls of the steam room. Joannes's apartments were in one of the oldest buildings in the palace complex, constructed in a time when different fashions and canons of beauty had prevailed. Like this mosaic. A woman and a man walked before a graceful portico, the architecture convincing in its substance, the human forms swelling with the glories of the flesh, the green and gold leaves behind the buildings almost rustling with the breeze. It reminded Michael of Antioch, where ancient revelries of the flesh were still redolent in the hot nights. How different from today's Rome, the harsh, attenuated forms one saw in art, the airless ether that allowed only the spirit, not the flesh, to breathe. He looked at his uncle. Joannes's deep sockets were blank, lids folded over the deadly irises. What could he know of old Rome, him with his tiny, vestigial penis, his blind disregard for the beauty and splendor around him? Why did he then live amid the echoes of a pagan world he could never touch even in his imagination? That was obvious. During his residence in the cenobium Joannes had come to despise the church and even its symbols. And that was why the Pantocrator, His voice rising among the hosannas of the seraphim in the Hagia Sophia, had decreed that Joannes, a monk without faith, should die.

"Uncle, I am quite wilted. May I wait for you in the steam room?" Joannes nodded assent, his eyes still closed, his huge head lolling. Even the seven-headed beast has its moment of repose, thought Michael. He rose and entered the large vault that contained both the warm tub for washing and the cold pool for swimming. Lit by candelabra, the mosaics around the wall, all secular scenes, took on a sacredness, and Michael knew that even in this place the Pantocrator was still with him, guiding him. He saw the wooden box on the broad marble rim of the tub. How clever. The foolish conspirator would have brought the soap as an offering. But this was so subtle, so intricate. The Caesar was clever enough to rule Rome; this was proof. Even if Joannes did suspect him, he would never anticipate this. Strangulation, perhaps, or a knife concealed in a towel. Fool. When Joannes was dying, he would have that moment to know he had been a fool, to look into the laughing eyes that had cast him into the fiery lakes.

Michael entered the pool. Yes, stay at a distance, when the convulsions begin summon the servants. He will be seen to die untouched. The water was so vitalizing, made him feel so alert. He stroked and floated. Would they crown him again? Yes, they would have to. No longer merely the Caesar but Emperor, Basileus, Autocrator. His hand in that of the Pantocrator. Michael found himself growing erect. He fondled his stiffening penis and enjoyed the silky, surreptitious thrill. He remembered as he often did how his father had hit him for that, when had he found the Caesar—Michael had always been the Caesar, wasn't that clear, just as the Christ had always been the Lord?—touching himself at the public bath in Amastris, the filthy, cheap one they had to go to, carrying their own pails and greasy soap and dirty linen towels. Not simply beat him, his pitch-stinking fist crashing into the Caesar's face; his father had told the men at the shipyard, and they had held him over the nauseating vat of caulking pitch and told him they were going to burn it off, and then they had tarred it! His father and those men had tarred it so that he could not touch it! It had not burned off like his uncles', like they had said it would, but it had burned! And the Caesar had run home and told his mother (he and the Pantocrator so loved their mothers, they were so alike in that), and she had taken him to the baths and sponged him herself, as she had when he was smaller, and she had touched it again and again and cleansed it. And she had not let his father put his stinking hands on her after that. Never again. The Caesar stroked himself and realized that once he had destroyed Joannes, the Pantocrator wanted him to destroy his father.

"Nephew. I am ready to hear of this plot." Joannes settled himself into the long, rectangular marble tub. "This tub is not sufficiently deep," he said. "It was made for smaller men. You would find it comfortable."

Yes. But I will not have need of your apartments, Uncle, replied Michael in his own silent reverie. *I will sleep on the Imperial couch. With my mother.*

"Who is it that poses this threat to me?"

"The conspirators were not named, Uncle. But the attempt is known in some detail. The Vlach cheese you are so fond of is to have a poison introduced. Indeed this may be a mere charade, but would it not be prudent to avoid this cheese until more is known? Our Holy Empire can hardly afford the loss of its most devoted servant because of tainted cheese."

"Yes," rumbled Joannes. He splashed water over his torso and then opened the lid of his soap box. "I think we affront Providence if we take lightly such warnings, even if only founded on hearsay. You have shown prudence, Nephew, a quality I had not thought previously to ascribe to you. Perhaps we should discuss enabling you to attend to some duties of state." Joannes removed the soap from the box and studied it for a moment.

"The prospect lightens my heart," said Michael, his heart racing and his arms trembling beneath the water.

Joannes dipped the soap in the water and lathered the small, yellowish, tallowy brick in his hands. "This soap is my most sinful luxury. While I am certain that the Pantocrator has scourged my skin with this eczema to instruct me in Christlike humility, I am tempted beyond redemption by the soothing properties of the emollient ingredient. A chemist skilled in pharmacology prepares this especially for me each day. This was just delivered this very night. I quite forget all cares when it relieves the torment of my affliction."

Michael was so cold, he thought his teeth would chatter. Why does he go on so much, unless he knows? But why does he lather the soap if he knows it is a deadly poison? Joannes began salving the lather over the purple blotches on his left arm. Michael was astonished by the surge in his loins. In a moment he might ejaculate.

"Yes, Nephew, one can grow dangerously complacent at the word *poison,* as one is constantly besieged by such threats, and as so many clumsy hands, so to speak, have sought to emulate the poisoner's art."

Ice spread from the nape of Michael's neck down his back. Was it too late to stop it? What if the ingredient only made him ill? If he knew, how could he go on lathering? No. It would work. Caesar. Emperor. Basileus. Autocrator. Light of the World. His hand in that of the Pantocrator.

"Yes, the science of toxicity, which has an undeniable social utility, has few truly learned practitioners. There is one specialist, however, who has advised me on the use of certain paralytics that are useful in interrogation. I consider him the one true artist in his field, though you would not find him aesthetically pleasing in his own right. He is an immensely fat man."

There, in centuries-old baths where pagans gamboled in an ancient yellow glow, the Pantocrator spoke to Michael Kalaphates, as He had beneath the limitless golden dome of Hagia Sophia: "Save yourself. As I forgave from the excruciations upon My cross, so I shall ask the Father that you be forgiven."

"Uncle, Uncle, Uncle!" Michael shrieked like a dying beast and thrashed from the pool and fell to his knees beside the marble tub, his naked back as wet and trembling as a newborn foal. "Save yourself! Oh, Theotokos, save yourself, the soap is poisoned!" Michael seized the lathered lump from his uncle's hands, clutched at it desperately, and lost it to the floor. "Oh, Uncle, Uncle, Uncle, I would sooner die myself—I will die myself! Oh, Theotokos, oh, Uncle!" He wailed desperately, like a widow keening and, with his face to the opus-sectile pavement, shoved the soap into his mouth, his limbs mad, flailing, the tentacles of an octopus pulled from the depths to die on a rock. The scent of his urine mixed with the foul, fatal bitterness of the soap.

Joannes stood above him, terrible in his nakedness. He extended his distorted arms, a demon retrieving a soul from the very bosom of the Christ. He grasped his nephew's hair and jerked back. Michael's neck twisted and his terrified eyes rolled, to gaze into the face of death. Joannes snatched the soap from Michael's foaming jaws and threw it into the pool. "The soap is not poisoned, Nephew. I will not be dead as soon as you would hope, nor, unfortunately, will you. Your soul will be taken piece by piece, according to the schedule I set, in the Neorion." Joannes wedged his knee into Michael's back and pulled harder on his hair. "You might mercifully accelerate that schedule by telling me who is in this with you."

Michael Kalaphates, Caesar of Rome, stared ahead into the darkness and saw the fading golden arms of the Pantocrator begin to reach out to him again. "The slut!" he screamed. "The slut commanded me to do it!"

† † †

"Let him see me now," said the woman's voice. She was not the same woman he had spoken to in the crowd. This woman's voice was calm, grandmotherly, but with a timbre of great authority. Haraldr's hands ached but his head was clear. The blow had not concussed him, only blackened his vision for a few moments and brought him to his knees; the thugs had been able to tie his hands and feet and slip several cloth sacks over his head. Thrown into a cart of some sort, a blanket or carpet over him, he had jolted over the streets for a half hour. He had heard the faint whoosh of flames, some distant shouting, animal noises. The cart had turned many times.

The sacks were slipped off his head and Haraldr blinked into the torchlight. He was seated on the floor in a small, neatly kept room. The woman was standing. She was short, white-haired, with the inflated features of a woman whose beauty had aged into plumpness. She wore a threadbare, but clean, sleeveless linen tunic; her substantial bosom pressed against the fabric. Beside her, in a simple wooden chair with a curving back, sat a man, even older than she was. His eyes were milk-white with cataracts. Behind the the aged couple, looking down over their silvery heads, stood the Blue Star.

"I am the Blue Star," said the old woman.

Haraldr blinked. "You . . ."

The old woman reached back and snatched the ear of the big man and pulled him forward until his jutting beard seemed to perch on her shoulder. "This rascal is my son. He uses my name; it protects me. Confused you? Confusion is my livelihood now, you might say. I must be known, and yet not known. This devil helps me with that." She released the ear and batted her son's cheek. "That's all he's good for."

The Blue Star dropped her hand to the head of the old man and caressed his wispy white hair. "This is my husband. He doesn't hear, either." She turned back to her towering son. "I let the boy know what I am about." She looked at her son sharply. "So he won't blunder into something!" She came around and studied the bindings of Haraldr's hands. "Cut him loose," she ordered her son.

Haraldr rubbed his hands and ankles and looked up at her. "The Blue Star," she began, acknowledging his evident curiosity, "is a name that the people of the city once knew well. This . . ." The woman, with some difficulty due to the tight fit, pulled her tunic down almost to the nipple of her left breast. The birthmark on her ruddy, fleshy breast was not blue but a faded brown that might have been deep purple once, and not a perfect star but indeed had five somewhat irregular points. "The Blue Star. They saw it—believe me, they all did, from the Bulgar-Slayer down to the porters. In the Hippodrome. I could do things on a galloping horse you couldn't do on a gymnasium floor if you spent a lifetime trying. One foot, one hand, my leg up, leaps from one horse to the next. To start, to titillate them. Then swords and fire and what have you. I have seen two Emperors crowned. You have heard nothing like the way they acclaimed me in the Hippodrome." For a moment Haraldr saw the young athlete's eyes, and he imagined the beauty she must have been, the spectacle of her. And then he saw Maria, her beauty, still alive, still vivid, and he realized he could not see her old like this, could not see a time when she would not be fresh and in his arms.

The Blue Star was an old woman again. "One day, during a practice stunt I had done a thousand times, I fell. I could not get up. I walk now but with pain and difficulty." Her head bobbed slightly. "Everything gone, the silks, the town house, snatched away by God. I came back here, where I had started. This man taught me that I had lost nothing." She bent and kissed the old man's head.

"These are my people, Varangian. Devils, whores, thieves, vagrants. They were his people too. The Bulgar-Slayer. He raised many of them out of the dirt, gave them reason to walk in the Christ's path, proved that he would not let the Dhynatoi crush them if they even lifted their heads out of the offal in the streets. Then the Bulgar-Slayer was summoned by the King of Heaven and the Studion became a hell. But we survived." She fixed Haraldr with cold, brilliant eyes. "Now we are not to be permitted even to survive."

"Mistress—" began Haraldr.

"Don't call me mistress, boy. I am not one of the courtesans you fair-hairs fawn over."

"I swear to you by all the gods sacred to me and to Rome that Varangians did not light these fires tonight. We tried to prevent them. That I came to you like this should prove that I have no wish to punish those who have suffered enough."

"I know that now." The Blue Star barked at her son, and he ran out for a moment. When he returned, he handed his mother a plain clay bowl. She held it down for Haraldr to see inside. He looked back at her grimly. The bowl was full of noses and ears. Freshly cut. "This is the record of our conversation with the arsonists. We have not gone back as far as we can go, or will go, but the trail of noses, and worse, will lead us to the Orphanotrophus Joannes. We have known for some time that he is the architect of our misery."

Haraldr nodded. "You are correct. But you must understand that you are not alone against the Orphanotrophus. There are many working in this cause. I am certain that when the Emperor himself recovers—"

The Blue Star burst into a rich peal of laughter. "Boy, what use are you to me when you don't know the simple truths? This Emperor is not a bad man, we know that. But he is dying. He will not see the next full moon. And then his evil brother, Joannes, will put his newly anointed puppet upon the throne and bleed the people of Rome to feed his own ambitions and nurture his Dhynatoi accomplices. He will create a Rome that only the few will love, and robbed of the devotion of her people, Rome herself will perish."

"We believe we have time," said Haraldr. "Rome is not a corpse yet. Those of us who share your hatred of the Orphanotrophus have decided to wait and see if the Emperor recovers before we act. But we will act soon enough. Do not doubt that."

"And if the Emperor does not recover? Will you support this . . . Caesar?"

"I believe the Caesar has many good qualities, and I believe that he is not likely to blindly follow his Uncle Joannes's policies; in fact, he is inclined to the contrary. He should be allowed to prove his sincere concern for the people of Rome. I would think it would be to your benefit to take the same position. Why hold your nose and throw the fish out before you have even smelled it?"

"If he shows the respect due the purple-born and places his aegis over the smallest folk, then we will joyously acclaim this Caesar as our Emperor. If not, *we* will act. Do not doubt that. But I did not allow you here to speak of the future of Rome. It is the future of the Studion that I carry in my bosom. You say we are allied in a common cause, and the manner in which you have come among us tonight is a coin of good faith that I am too old and too clever not to accept. So answer me, boy, with the truth you have paid me so far. What will you Varangians do if the Orphanotrophus Joannes orders you to massacre the people of the Studion?"

Haraldr felt weak, cold, and sick in his gut. Would there be such an order? Likely there would. He rose from the floor and looked down at the Blue Star for a long moment. "If the Orphanotrophus Joannes gives that order, then I swear by all the oaths I have already pledged tonight that I will kill him myself."

hy have you come?" Maria's face was bloodless with fright. "What has happened? I know that Studion is burning. We went to the roof and saw the fires. He is not . . ." Maria lowered her head and her dark, loose hair tumbled over her shoulders. The candelabra in her bedchamber had been extinguished, and two oil lamps on long slender bronze stands sent strange shadows scurrying across the densely patterned pale blue Antioch carpet.

"He is safe," said Mar. "I sent some of my own men to find out. As I had feared, Joannes attempted to bury him there. I warned him."

Maria's breasts heaved beneath her sheer silk cloak. She was like a corpse returning to life, her lips suddenly flushed a brilliant red. "Yes. But you did not come here to bring me comfort."

Mar studied Maria warily. "No." He paused, wondering if his purposes were more clear to her than they were to himself. Why had he come? "Do you love him?"

"Yes."

"You are going to get him killed."

"Yes." Maria folded her arms under her breasts and looked at Mar with cold azure eyes.

Mar shook his head incredulously. "If you have contrived some insane plot of your own, I warn you that anything that now involves Haraldr concerns me as well. He is a Norseman, and my friend, and I will not lie to you, an ally whom I need above all others. Destroy another man with your foolish schemes and mad passions. Because if there is further danger to my ally, I will destroy you." In the silence that followed Mar realized that he had not conveyed conviction. Her eyes were too clever, too weary.

She looked down, her lips curling slightly as if concealing an amused disdain. "You aren't his friend. Perhaps you are his ally. Are we rivals?"

Mar stepped forward and slapped Maria perfunctorily, almost as if it were a ritual punishment. "That is a slander, bitch!"

Maria laughed and put her fingers to her bleeding lip. She dabbed and tasted the blood. "Yes. It was unfair of me to say that. I do not believe that you could not love me simply because you want to love men. I never knew why. Was I unattractive to you?"

Mar's face twitched slightly. He remembered the vision of her, naked, wanting him. Since then he had ached, thinking of what it would have been like to make love to her. Why hadn't he? She had not been the first woman he had turned away from (why? he had reasons he could not admit), but she had been the culmination, the one who had brought him closest and had therefore let him fall the farthest. Why hadn't he? He was not waiting for a woman who was pure; many who had offered themselves to him had been virgins.

The corners of Maria's mouth trembled and her nostrils flared. "Do you think of me, Mar? I want you to think of me. I want every man who has ever touched me to burn with the memory of me." She swished forward, her silk cloak like a cloud. "I think of what it would have been like with you. I thought of you once when I was with him."

"And this is how you love him? You are a bitch."

"I love him!" she screamed, her face brilliant. "I love him so much, I wake up in the night sick with dread that he will never love me again! I vomit! I heave my soul up for loving him!" Her hair fell around her cheeks and her shoulders jerked with strange, dry sobs.

Mar shook his head. "I pity you. You are addicted to your passions. You have taken everything as long as you have known life, and so you despise anything you cannot entirely consume, like a flame that hates water. You will never understand men like Haraldr and me. We are Norsemen. When we are twelve summers old, we go on the western sea in open boats and sail to lands you Romans have never heard of, where the ice floats in great islands and the absence of everything except his own will makes a man strong."

Maria cocked her head slightly, defiantly. "When I was twelve, I took my first lover."

"That man forced you, and later you killed him for it. I know the truth of that."

"I loved him. I liked it. It made a whore of me."

"So you pretend you are a whore with every man? As it was with me?"

"I make love but I do not love. As I had hoped it would be with you."

"But with Haraldr it is different?"

"Who is he!" she blurted with a desperate, bell-like voice. "When he is inside me, I feel his fate around my neck, and mine around his. We are strangling each other with this destiny, two vines sucking the life out of one another. You say I will get him killed. Yes, I have known it, I have prayed for it, I have tried to do it! And he gave me my life back, so I could try again." Her eyes were insane, incandescent. "Who is he!"

"He has not told you who he really is?" Mar sneered. "Perhaps your love is not returned, then. You would understand the fate around your neck if you knew."

"Tell me!" she shrieked, and fell on Mar, pounding his huge chest with her small white fists. He showed his gleaming teeth and she clawed his face. "Tell me!" He felt the blood on his cheek. She lunged at an object on the ivory-inlaid trunk opposite her bed. "Tell me or I'll kill you!" Mar looked at the knife and laughed. She swiped wildly, and he caught her wrist. She strained to reach him with the knife, and he deliberately wrenched her arm so that the blade touched his throat. "You want to kill me, little bitch. Look, it is only a thumb's width. Kill me." She grimaced and let the knife drop. Mar looked into her mesmerizing eyes: the rage, the danger, the invitation. He knew his purpose for coming here now. Why had he concealed it from himself? He brought his lips close to hers, and she did not recoil as he had thought (hoped?) she would. He grabbed her hair and pulled her to him and kissed her, and she pressed back, her lips angry yet soft, the kiss that had made him sleepless a hundred nights. Then she pushed him away. "Tell me!"

Mar ripped her cloak off, revealing a sheer silk tunic; her nipples were erect beneath the mistlike drape. She looked at him and pulled her hair slick against her head and held it, and for a moment she had the utterly wild aspect of a blue-eyed panther. She dropped her hands and placed them on the draped neckline of her tunic and pulled down and ripped the garment from her shoulders. The silk settled at her ankles like falling eiderdown. "Set me free," she said.

Mar stared at her, his desire a great engine in his throbbing chest. If Haraldr Sigurdarson wanted to fight over her, he would kill him. He was a hundred times a man in every way except that he had never been able to take a woman. And now he would. He studied her body again, reality exceeding even memory; she had had him so close then, now there was nothing about her he did not desire.

She helped him undress, silently looking in his eyes the entire time, her face inscrutable. She took him to her bed and he was hard. "My fair-hair," she said, pressing down on him, demanding what he had hoped to plunder. Her breathing was quick and harsh. "Destroy me," she said raspily. "Set me free." She clutched at Mar's hair. "Let him live."

Maria ground her pubis against him until he grimaced with pain. "I like it, my fair-hair, I like it. . . ." She clutched his head to her breasts. "Bite me! Harder!" She arched her spine and growled like a cat. "Harder! Make me bleed!"

Intoxicated beyond any sense he had ever known, Mar took the soft skin of her breast between his teeth and ripped and tasted the blood. And then his loins exploded.

They breathed in a furious contrapunto. Mar fell quickly from the precipice of passion, disgusted with himself, not because he had taken another man's woman but because he had fouled himself. What had been different this time, he wondered, to make him do it? Did he really hate Haraldr Sigurdarson that much? Or was death closer than he thought? His genitals felt cold and filthy with her wetness. She was a whore. He pushed Maria away and retreated from her bed.

Maria sat up and smeared the blood over her breast like a fascinated child. She watched Mar dress. "I liked it," she said in a voice that sounded as if it were coming from some great distance. "You were as inept as a thirteen-year-old boy. I have seduced boys with beardless chins and had to teach them. Now I have taught you. It is all for my pleasure. As you say, I am quite addicted to it."

Mar looked at her as if she were a leper. "You are mad and empty," he said, pulling his boots on and then standing to confront her. "You are like the western sea, with this great force, this great tempest, but like the sea you rage alone, in emptiness and in silence, without meaning, unless a man dares to challenge you. Every man who loves you is a fool. I was a fool to come here."

Maria watched Mar leave. There was a high-pitched sound in her ears. She felt as empty as the sea Mar had described. There had been no pleasure, only the gift of pain she had demanded. She had hated it, and herself, and it had not set her free.

lexius, Patriarch of the One True Oecumenical, Orthodox, and Catholic Faith, appeared in a burst of white silk
and gold embroidery. Behind the luminous Patriarch,
through the briefly opened bronze doors to his personal
apartments, Mar caught a glimpse of servants clearing
the silver and gold settings of the Patriarch's breakfast table. Mar fell to
his knees and lowered his forehead to a red carpet sprinkled with delicately woven gold chrysanthemums. A sweet incense filled his nostrils.

"Rise, Hetairarch." Alexius beckoned with his ring-laden fingers. "Rise
up." It was a strange, powerful face, the feminine lips contradicted by the
hawklike nose, the eyes still, guarded, but fearsome nonetheless.

"Father, you honor me—"

"Nonsense. It is my pleasure. Since His Majesty is no longer able to
join me for breakfast, I often feel that I am losing conversance with the
secular arms of our glorious Empire. I welcome this opportunity to conduct a private and, indeed, intimate interview."

Alexius showed Mar through a series of antechambers and Patriarchal
offices; the bustling secretaries with their armfuls of documents and the
hurrying dignitaries in silk and gold seemed little different from the
officials of a major Imperial Bureau. The difference, Mar noted, was that
here there was a powerful uniformity of purpose, a sense that these
officials served, with unstinting obedience, but one master.

"I thought we might converse in my church," said Alexius. "I am intent
on redeeming your soul for the Pantocrator, you know. So I will ask for
His intervention. It is hard to deny Him in the Mother Church." They
entered a short, vaulted hallway that opened onto the south arcade of the
Hagia Sophia. Alexius walked to a heavy marble balustrade and gestured
into the vast chamber of golden light that extended beyond, above, and
below them; everywhere Mar looked, scintillae of color accreted into
architectural forms and then dissolved into light again. This is Rome, Mar
told himself, a huge structure so disguised by the multiplicity and splendor of its parts that it is impossible to tell what is solid, real, and what
is illusion. But one must not be dazzled by the lights. There were real
walls, real columns here. And if a man had the intelligence to identify and

the temerity to remove the critical supporting structures, he could bring even this edifice down.

"It is quite fragile," said the Patriarch, almost as if he had opened a window into Mar's mind. "Look." He pointed to the massive pier at the end of the arcade, one of four that thrust up the soaring central dome. "If you focus through the light, you can see how it is inclined backward." Mar squinted; the pier indeed tilted noticeably, as if the weight of the presumably incorporeal gold dome were crushing down on it. "When I walk in here each morning," said Alexius, "I am in awe that God has permitted the dome to stand through another day." Alexius looked about the enormous golden shell with an unexpected warmth and familiarity, as if he were watching a small child he would someday have to send off to life, war, love, disappointment, death.

After a moment the Patriarch turned to Mar, the beasts in his dark eyes finally unleashed. "This is my fortress," he said, his voice even but now much deeper in resonance, almost supernaturally compelling. "It is the most powerful structure on earth. Its strength is not in the mass of its walls but in their fragility, the fashion in which they are transformed by the light of day into the pure light of God's Eternal Being. Someday men, perhaps with means we cannot dream of today, will defeat the walls of this city. But how can anything defeat the light in which the Pantocrator reveals himself to men?"

The dragon of Nidafell, thought Mar. The last dragon will consume even the light of the Pantocrator.

Alexius's eyes retreated. "I see I have failed to move you with talk of God. Let us then talk of Rome, and what we must render to, if not our Caesar then to the powers that have given us a Caesar."

Mar looked up into the golden carapace that seemed more an opening than an enclosure. Perhaps there was a power to this light. It enabled the Patriarch to speak with the direct tongue of a Norseman instead of the oily mendacity of the Roman courtier. *Do not disappoint him.* "We will not accept the continued intervention of the Orphanotrophus Joannes in the affairs of the Empire."

Alexius raised both wiry eyebrows. "And who are we, Hetairarch?"

"The Varangians of the Grand and Middle Hetairia."

Alexius nodded his head. "That is no small thing. One thousand warriors of proven, and more importantly, feared ability. And even more importantly, already quartered inside the palace gates, indeed surrounding the person of the Emperor. But do the Scholae, Excubitores, and Hyknatoi of the Imperial Taghmata"—these were all elite palace regiments—"share your resolution? If not, they would certainly deter the swiftness of your thrust. Perhaps with fatal consequences for all involved."

"Of course you are correct in your reservations," answered Mar. "If we had to defeat the Imperial Taghmata," he said, slightly smirking with the boast, "the endeavor might take us several days. By then the people would have become aroused and could possibly create a situation that would force us to accept any candidate they proposed. However earnest the intentions of the simple folk, we might be left with another unsuitable candidate. But if the Imperial Taghmata were convinced that both the people and other . . . powers were resolute in their wishes, they would acquiesce to our coup."

"An artful hypothesis, Hetairarch. But you fail to calculate the most significant of Rome's many powers, if only because in that power is the will of the Pantocrator manifest in human form. I mean the purple-born. And is not the purple-born currently an author of our predicament?"

"Indeed the older sister is. Fortunately she is not the last purple-born Macedonian." Mar paused for effect. "The Varangian Guards would defend your client Theodora to the last drop of our blood if she were to ascend to the Imperial Throne. We would, of course, hope to consult on the choice of her consort and Emperor."

Alexius clasped his hands beatifically. "Well said, Hetairarch! I applaud the economy of expression you Varangians are noted for." The eyes suddenly leapt at Mar, for a moment literally stifling his breath. "In matters according to God, I am undisputed on this earth. In matters that pertain to Caesar, my concerns are manifold. I govern a state within a state, with all the predictable difficulties of such administration. Fractious Metropolitans, incompetent bishops, rebellious priests in far-flung sees. Like a state, I have my enemies. Internally the growth of the monastic establishments independent of Patriarchal jurisdiction has become an epidemic that leeches the church of its vital resources. Externally I must contend with malignant impudence of the see of old Rome, which threatens every soul in my state. And let us not forget my mandatory allegiance to the Emperor, Basileus, and Autocrator of the Romans. I am crowned by him, and can in theory be deposed by him."

"This Emperor will depose no one."

Alexius made the sign of the cross, praying that the Emperor would be able to complete in Purgatory the penance he had begun here on earth. "Yes. It is the Caesar we must concern ourselves with."

"The Caesar is in Neorion." Mar caught the surprise, and new respect, in Alexius's cat-quick eyes. "Four days now. He is still alive. My presumption is that he was overly assertive and Joannes intends to knead him into a more pliable state. All the more reason that the succession to this Caesar be initiated."

Alexius looked again into the golden vault. "I had intended to convert you, and I see that instead you have begun to persuade me." Alexius turned away from the immense cavern of light. "God's patience is infinite. But as He endlessly cautions us to observe, our time here is short."

† † †

The centipede was as long as a man's hand, and when it crawled over Michael Kalaphates's thigh, it seemed to wrap his bare limb like a many-legged serpent. He began to scream hysterically and retreated to the corner of his cell, the slime wet and cold against his naked back. He could see nothing. He panted and tried to make his body pull in on itself, disappear, so that the beasts could not recognize him. But the screams reached in, sliding beneath the cracks in the door that even the light could not enter; he could see the screams, they were the only thing he could see, they were sharp, hot vines that curled around him and then grew huge red thorns that pierced right through his flesh.

On the fourth day the locusts came up from the shaft of the abyss, cloaked in armor and smoke. Their light was blinding. They flogged him with screams and led him into the abyss, driving him forward with thorns and brands. The fiery lakes burned on every side, and sulfur poisoned his lungs. The locusts would not let him retch the screams out of his intestines, where the thorns had planted their seed. And then they set him before the serpent, and the serpent spit thunder.

"Nephew."

The serpent touched him. It had the face of a man. The screams died and left only hard little pods that rattled in his bowels. Soon the warm liquid dissolved them.

"Nephew, do you know where you are?"

Yes. Yes. I would tell you but man can no longer hear me. I talk to demons in their own language. Yes.

"Neorion. Remember Neorion, Nephew."

Then there were dreams, and in them the armies of Gog and Magog marched upon the earth. The Pantocrator spoke to him, from a mountain far away. He spread out his hands and revealed the kingdoms of the world, all little cities seen from a great distance. And then Michael slept, alone; the demons could not discover him beneath a cloud.

"Nephew."

He awoke with a start, the recognition like the sun on a hot sea. Neorion. I have been in Neorion. How long?

"Do you know where you are, Nephew?"

Michael looked up and blinked. "Neorion."

"Yes. Five days. Your collapse was more complete than I had intended." Joannes held out a silver goblet; Michael could smell the wine. He took a deep, desperate draft. "I am quite confounded as to what to do with you," Joannes said. "I had hoped you might make the acquaintance of some of your fellow guests, perhaps attend them in their time of travail among us." He waved his hand around the dimly lit, forbidding chamber, and the wine surged back up Michael's gullet even though the racks and instruments Joannes indicated were not in use. "Now I feel that such a recourse would destroy your mind." Joannes picked up a pair of tongs and distractedly inspected them, clicking the jaws together. "You are so weak." He paused, as if this phrase were a matter of great philosophical interest to him. "You are so weak that I consider you too valuable to destroy. Yes. Consider it as I did. I am not unaware that the greatest prodigies of the sculptor are those in which the shape is first molded in some malleable substance such as wax or clay, and then fixed in eternal bronze by the foundry master's art. Because you can be shaped with such ease, you will be the substance in which I create works of astonishing complexity and endurance."

"I am certain you do not need my words to know how thorough my penitence is for my mad, utterly demonic, act against you."

"Yes. I observed your contrition." Joannes gestured to the goblet. "Drink, enjoy that. You have felt the lash. Now you have only to draw the cart."

"You know I will do whatever you bid, if only—"

"Do not go on, Nephew. What I saw in your eyes yesterday was worth a lifetime of supplications from your lips." Joannes set the tongs back on the table with the rest of his instruments. "You were quite voluble before your isolation. I was intrigued by the depth of your friendship with our Blessed Mother. Having forced you to endure such an ordeal here, I would not like to deprive you now of the opportunity to seek the comfort of your Mother's solicitous breast. I want you to go to her often, and seek her counsel about such matters as you have previously. I only ask that in exchange for your freedom you assiduously practice the mnemonic arts, and recite for me whatever Her Majesty has to say, however intimate or confidential. Should I discover that your recollection is less than complete, we will continue your instruction here in Neorion."

Michael Kalaphates looked up at Joannes, his eyes rapt with gratitude, and whispered his thanks: "Uncle, yours is truly the voice of the angelic host."

hoped you would not look for me." Maria stood on the porch of her villa, facing a murky, malachite-green sea. Dark, steaming clouds rolled over the city to the west, and a broad shaft of rain advanced along the Golden Horn. She waved her hand as if throwing something onto the terraced lawns beneath her, but nothing left her clutched fist.

"Why?" Women are a mystery, thought Haraldr, hoping that this vague boyhood platitude might explain her unfathomable behavior.

"I wanted to be . . . away."

"Away from me?"

"Yes."

"Then I will leave."

"Yes."

Haraldr stood transfixed for a moment, then realized that she would not stop him. His hands trembled as he turned to walk down the steps to the jetty.

"You are a liar." She did not look at him when she spoke.

Haraldr turned, grateful for any sort of reprieve.

"Who are you?" Her voice was so detached, it was almost as if she did not know she was asking a question. "You did not tell me the truth."

Haraldr clenched his fists and jaw with the excruciation of his silence. He had sworn that secret to his brother, and to Jarl Rognvald, and so far had nothing but proof that their long-buried cautions had been anything but essential to his survival. And what Jarl Rognvald had told him about condemning other men had even kept him from telling Halldor and Ulfr, whom he trusted with his life. Even for Maria to know would be a threat to her. But none of those reasons were conclusive, even the soul-binding oaths to dead men. Only one reason truly held his tongue: He could not trust Maria. What Mar had said, what many men had said about her still haunted him. He was one of many, a caprice, as evanescent as those loves who had parted her legs before him. Two great fates warred for him now, Norway and Maria, but only Norway would always be constant. To surrender that lifelong fate to hers, and then to see it discarded like a necklace she no longer admired, would kill his soul before it ended his life.

"Yes. I . . . withheld the truth. I will tell you what I told you the first time you asked that question, then. I cannot tell you."

"Mar knows."

The sensation of alarm seemed to lift Haraldr off his feet for a moment. He did not even know how to get at this. Mar would never risk their plans unless he had intended to betray them all along.

"He would not tell me, either."

Relief quickly spawned anger. "You endanger yourself, me, my five hundred pledge-men, and anyone you ask that question," Haraldr snapped. "We are not children playing some game."

"Yes. Your game is different." She whipped her head around and glared at him, her face distorted with anger and anguish. "You think that because people die in your games that they are somehow less trivial than a child's." She jerked her chin up violently. "I know how it is to kill a man, Haraldr Nordbrikt, Slayer of Saracens and Seljuks. I killed my first lover."

Haraldr was not surprised; he had known, almost for certain, when Mar had first suggested the possibility. It explained much. He would be patient with her. "I know," he told her softly, and he reached out for her.

Maria recoiled. "Get away. I asked you to leave, Manglavite. If there is a drop of civilized blood in your *barbaroi* veins, you will oblige me." Haraldr placed his hands on her shoulders. "Yes, Manglavite," she said in her high, mocking voice, then grimaced. "Answer my question with your savage manhood. Make love to me and I will forget your lies. Rut the little bitch until her glassy eyes no longer question your great and mysterious purpose." Haraldr ignored her; he had heard these words before. He swept her in his arms and carried her into her villa, past her gawking servants, and laid her on her bed. She did not resist.

She lay mute, her eyes flat, the fire receded deep within. He kissed her neck, swooning with the taste of her, the softness of her skin. He now suspected one of her caprices; when would she erupt with manic passion, surprising him with something he could not even imagine? She maddened him with desire; he felt himself harden and pulled at the ties of her scaramangium. He reached up her robe and touched her thigh. She shuddered and pushed him away.

"Stop." She sat up. "Do you care that I do not want to love you?" Haraldr kissed her neck, and she slapped him. The sound seemed like a thunderclap. "I don't want your touch. I don't want your stinking *barbaroi* hands on me." With trembling fingers he touched her face, gently, barely brushing against her burning cheek. "Since the last time I was with you, I have made love to another man."

Haraldr denied the knife in his gut. "You are lying."

Maria loosened the collar of her scaramangium and pulled the fabric down to reveal her left breast. The bite was a livid bruise, the teeth marks evident. Her eyes were furious. "I begged him to bite me. I asked him to do things you have never heard of. I was his slut."

Haraldr already had enough images of her with other men. "Who is your lover?"

She laughed wickedly, a laugh he had never heard before, not even in the passion of love. "Do you want to kill him?"

"You were not forced. You are not my wife. No." He made his decision and stood up. He watched her self-consciously stroke her bruised breast. "You love me. That is why you are driven to hurt me. You are as transparent as an image cut in glass. But I will not beg you for a love that causes you pain."

"You are a vain fool."

He turned and walked out. She went to the window and watched through the greenish-tinted glass as he descended the steps to the jetty. When he was well out to sea in the small skiff, she ran to the porch. She could still see him, the distant speck of his blue tunic. "I have undone what the stars commanded," she told him through the salty wind whipping off the Bosporus. "I have given you back your life." Then she prayed silently to the Virgin that once before he died—the death she blessedly could no longer bring him—he would understand that she had loved him.

ittle boy." Zoe stroked the curls from Michael Kala-phates's forehead. "You should have come to your mother more quickly. The weeks have been an agony for me."

"It has been . . . difficult for me, my beloved." Michael reclined on the sitting couch, his head propped forward by a damask cushion.

"Yes. That terrible place. It is appalling even to consider the things he must have shown you there." She looked at him with a wryly erotic, subtle puckering of her lips. "He performed no alterations on you, did he, precious little candle?" She placed her hand behind his neck and let her silk-restrained breasts touch his shoulder.

"I am still . . . frightened."

"Nonsense. Such plots are commonly initiated, almost as commonly forgiven. You will not spend the rest of your life dwelling under some cloud, little one. He will attribute your failed conspiracy to my antipathy, and soon overlook yours. You are too important to him now." Zoe looked away, lost in a reverie she would never dare to speak of. "In any event, I will involve you in no more plots. You are too dear to me. There are many brutes I can employ for assassinations. You alone can author my pleasure." She leaned forward and placed her dry, sweet lips just on his. He spasmed. Zoe observed his swelling crotch. "It seems I am the architect of your pleasure." She smirked regally. "I touch you and raise a column."

"I am so glad I am alive," he said almost deliriously.

Zoe stood and lifted his hand. "I have discovered an unguent that imparts an indescribable silkiness to my breasts and thighs. You must try to find words for it."

After the caresses, the sweating passions, the grateful reunion of their flesh, Zoe held Michael's head to her breast. "I will never let him hurt you again," she said. "I am now more determined than ever."

He lifted his head in alarm and looked at her with doelike eyes. "No. It is too dangerous."

She hushed him with kisses. "I know. That is why I have selected a man both fearless and . . . expendable."

"Who?" Michael whispered, his eyes wider still.

Zoe pressed Michael's head to her breasts again. "The Komes . . . I mean, Manglavite, the Tauro-Scythian, Haraldr whatever." She felt the sudden stirring against her thigh and laughed gently. "Why, Nephew, I seem to have raised another column."

† † †

"It was not necessary to bring that." Mar pointed to the ceremonial fasces that Haraldr carried in his arms. "There is to be no procession."

"Yes, I understand," said Haraldr. "But I thought that once on the grounds—"

"No." Mar was impatient and anxious. "In fact, you shouldn't even have that out where it might be seen." Mar slipped his cloak off and wrapped the thick-shafted ax in it. He looked around and then whispered to Haraldr. "They are bringing him in a covered litter. With maybe a dozen Hyknatoi to guard him. They want to get him here without anyone taking notice. That's why I am here, instead of with him."

"And they suspect something here? Is that why the Middle Hetairia has been summoned?"

Mar looked at his boots pensively. "I imagine so. You are the principal unit for dealing with riots." Mar leaned over and whispered even more softly. "I am not certain what is going on anymore. You know how long it has been since I have even seen the Emperor." It had now been several months. "It is possible his recovery has been complete, and the purpose of this visit is to establish that he can indeed appear fit and able before his subjects."

"So perhaps all my cautions don't seem so foolish now," Haraldr said goadingly. He was tremendously relieved to hear that the Emperor was mending, because otherwise he and Mar had gotten nowhere with their increasingly fitful conspiracy to rid Rome of Joannes. Even Mar had admitted he was making no progress on the miraculous alliance he had promised weeks ago; it was obvious it would come to nothing.

Mar shrugged placidly. "Well, we shall see what we shall see. Do you know what this is?" Mar pointed to the gleaming new building, set back from a quiet side street by a broad, tree-rimmed lawn. The two-story edifice looked much like a prosperous new monastery; a freshly plastered chapel with five tiled domes rose in the midst of a four-sided block of living quarters.

"They say it is a convent," said Haraldr.

"Yes. A peculiar convent. Come with me."

The entrance to the convent was beneath a large arch supported on polished columns of rare green porphyry from Sparta. The massive wooden door was carved with images of the life of Christ. A grate opened, and they were admitted by a young woman in the black frock worn by nuns and monks alike. A black cowl covered her hair, and she drew part of the cowl around to veil her face, but Haraldr glimpsed that she was strikingly attractive, so much so that he was ashamed of the thoughts he had about her. "He has come?" asked the nun anxiously.

"Soon," said Mar. "We are ordered to check the building. It is simply a ritual." The nun led them through a vaulted hallway into a large refectory lit by rows of circular bronze polycandelons. Beneath the lamps sat hundreds of nuns in uniform black; they tittered in a very undignified fashion when Haraldr and Mar entered, and many, if not most, forgot to veil their faces. Their meal seemed extremely lavish, the silver plates and glass ewers immediately apparent; servants scurried among the tables carrying gilt platters piled with roast meats. Most remarkably, many of the women were as young and attractive as the nun who had opened the door, although many others seemed careworn or had pocked faces.

"Do you see the way they are looking at us?" said Haraldr. "I thought nuns would have their eyes cast down in Christlike humility. These women are as brazen as—" He broke off in astonishment.

Mar nodded and tried to keep from staring. "You will probably recognize some of the faces. You may have passed them on the streets of the Studion."

"Odin. Theotokos. Whores."

"Every one of them."

The simple canvas litter was borne up the marble path a short while later; only a handful of armored Hyknatoi and a single sad-eyed eunuch, apparently the Emperor's personal chamberlain, were in attendance. Haraldr stood by, at a loss to determine the protocol involved in this strange circumstance, and then fell to his face as the curtains of the litter were drawn aside. When he stood again, he could not avoid the sight, though he damned his eyes for what they saw.

It was not the same man, of course, but an impostor, a decoy. No, it was the man; the essence, the profound eyes, and the decisive nose were still there. But the rest was a painful parody of the magnificent Lord of the Entire World who had awed Haraldr those long months ago. The Emperor had swollen grotesquely, his cheeks and limbs and torso as sickeningly bloated as those of a floating corpse; his fingers were like thick sausages. His skin was jaundiced, with red streaks. It clearly pained him even to set his feet on the ground. He looked around, as if searching for someone to comfort him. Haraldr could not bear it. He stepped forward and offered his arm. "Glorious Majesty, please let me help you."

The Emperor looked at him, his eyes struggling for recognition. "Hetairarch," he gasped, obviously mistaking Haraldr for Mar. "Thank you, Hetairarch. . . . I need . . . no assistance." And then he began to walk, an effort so pitiful to watch that it broke Haraldr's heart.

It seemed an eternity before the shuffling, hobbling Emperor could drag his stiff, dropsied legs across the inner courtyard to the chapel. The nuns already knelt before the glimmering silver chancel screen and the huge mosaic of the Virgin in the apse, and they bowed when the Emperor entered. Yet another lifetime passed before he reached the small rectangular ambo. Haraldr prayed that the Emperor would not attempt to climb the marble steps to the canopied platform, though it only rose to the height of a man's shoulders.

The sad-eyed eunuch tried to restrain the Emperor with a touch to his cloak. But the Emperor resolutely climbed, so slowly that he seemed a wooden figure poised at each step. He finally attained the platform, steadied himself on the rail, and turned about. A dreadfully long interval passed before he could compose himself enough to speak; his legs seemed to sway like fat bladders partially full of water. "My daughters," he finally said, raspily. "Our Lord the Christ implores us to judge not others lest you be judged yourself. As He cast the seven devils out of Mary of Magdala, so let His hand on earth cast out the devils that afflict these daughters. But I know, then, that my daughters would fear for the poverty of their mortal flesh if they abandoned all traffic in their beauty and, through this cruel extortion, might never know the face of the Pantocrator's forgiveness. But the Christ also told His disciples, whatever you pray for in faith you shall receive. So your Father instructs you, His daughters, that if you pray to remain free of your sin, and continue to abjure the flesh and renounce the profession of the harlot, you shall receive whatever bounty my offices can provide, and never labor again except to praise the Pantocrator."

Haraldr was stunned. The man was providing free and luxurious lodging for prostitutes while his Empire decayed like his own walking corpse. Better that he did die soon.

The Emperor finished his discourse and repeated his excruciating procession, the nuns kneeling throughout, no doubt profusely grateful to the Virgin for their extraordinary fortune. The Emperor reached the courtyard and looked up into the spring sky as if questing for some gesture of approval from the Heavenly Tribunal. His head twitched, then drooped slowly. He gagged and fell to the pavement before anyone could steady him. His limbs instantly stiffened and palsied. His head pounded like a coppersmith's hammer against the pavement even as Haraldr and the sad-eyed eunuch knelt to help him. Haraldr looked at the Emperor's face in astonishment. It was the color of blood, and his eyes were white, the demons having deprived him even of his vision. The Emperor's teeth gnashed like a beast's, and his limbs were utterly rigid beneath the spongy, morbid tissue that cloaked his entire form.

After many terrible minutes the fit passed and the Emperor's eyes returned to normal and he looked up apologetically. His head was bloodied from his exertions against the pavement. His breath rattled in his throat and he could scarcely lift his head, much less rise to his feet. Haraldr had a curious instinct that there were two maladies present, and that this one sapped his strength and left him vulnerable to the second, which swelled his limbs. But he was no learned physician. He only knew for certain that the rumors in the street, not the reassurances from the palace, were the truth. The Father he had admired and respected was already dead. And now even this bloated corpse would soon be mercifully interred.

✝   ✝   ✝

Haraldr stood in the Empress's antechamber, wondering if her invitation had anything to do with her husband's imminent mortality, and if he would see Maria. The eunuchs quickly ushered him into her dining chamber. The small table had only two elegant settings, chased silver dishes and goblets fashioned of engraved gold leaf pressed between glass. Haraldr's breast emptied of the last hope that bound his heart to Rome.

He performed the usual prostrations when Zoe entered, and she laughed as if the ritual were a jest, not an obeisance to her purple-born majesty. When he rose from the thick crimson carpet, Haraldr was not prepared for what he saw any more than he had been two days previously, when he had witnessed the sad spectacle of her husband. It was as if Zoe had taken youth from her consort's catastrophic deterioration, as if only here, in the palaces that were her native soil, could her true beauty be fully manifest.

Zoe wore the simple scaramangium that she had made fashionable, but this high-collared robe was completely beaded with pearls; her form appeared all light and silhouette, without apparent volume, much like a living mosaic. She wore her hair braided over her head, somewhat in the style that Maria had displayed to such effect at Argyrus's hostel, but with pearl- and diamond-studded ribbons laced through the stunningly gold tresses. Her blue eyes did not have the heat of Maria's, but tonight they were ineffably deep, almost like amethyst.

"*Keleusate.*" The eunuch helped Haraldr to his seat, after which Zoe sat, twinkling like a galaxy as she moved. A priest appeared and intoned the blessing, and servants brought in the miniature olives and caviar. The wine was poured and watered.

"I have missed you, Manglavite. Of course Maria speaks of you."

"I have missed you as well, Majesty," Haraldr said sincerely; he was bedazzled. "I must awkwardly and impudently confess that I had not realized the extent of my deprivation until I saw you a moment ago, and indeed shame myself with the fervent desire of my eyes at this moment."

"Your Greek is vastly improved, Manglavite." Zoe tilted her head slightly, and her deep red, almost amaranth lips gave a hint of amusement. Haraldr realized he had presumed too much; she was not only more beautiful here but also more regal. His forehead flamed.

Zoe devoured her little olives in silence for a while, occasionally looking up at Haraldr as if he were a servant in front of whom she could eat without any sort of self-consciousness. Haraldr was only slightly ashamed by the thoughts he had of her as he watched her sumptuous lips suck at the morsels. He had grown up at courts, and he knew that a dying king was a dead king, and that his widow would, if only by necessity, soon take another man into her bed. He remembered the way Zoe had looked at Michael Kalaphates in Antioch, and reflected that this Empress had no doubt already entertained her husband's successor; Maria had told him several times that she shared the same suspicion. Haraldr himself had had to consider a succession to the Emperor: The man he had fully expected to deal with Joannes and right the wrongs of the Studion was a grotesque, moribund impostor. Everything had changed. Mar had been right; they would have to take the intiative against Joannes. But how?

When the fish course had been served, Zoe peered from beneath her fine, paint-darkened lashes and blithely asked, "Are you in love with Maria?"

"Yes." If it is a single combat you wish, Purple-Born, then the King of Norway will oblige you.

"Are you aware that I have opposed her liaison with you?"

"No. But I am not surprised. She is a lady of the highest rank. I am merely a *barbaroi* Manglavite, a servant of Rome. I hope my service to her has brought her some satisfaction. I consider myself free to serve elsewhere."

"So you are angry with her."

"I am pained by her. But I am a Norseman. We do not curse the sun when it sets."

Zoe set her chin on her exquisite hands. "How candid you are. Your heart is great enough to confess the pain that it carries. I am sorry I have not importuned you about romantic matters before. Your outlook interests me."

Zoe ate her fish in silence, occasionally idly prodding the sauce-laden filet with a slender, two-pronged fork. When she had finished, she stared at Haraldr for a while, and he held her gaze, in equal parts defiant and mesmerized. "Do you think I love my husband?" she finally asked.

"I would not presume to know your heart, Majesty."

"I love him. I will never see him again. I will ask, but it will not be permitted."

Haraldr fell into the sadness of her amethyst eyes; he perceived that she did love her husband, even if she had taken a lover in his absence. *Perhaps much like me,* Haraldr thought, *with my Alan girl.* "You bear your pain with a grace that nourishes the soul, Your Majesty."

"Any moment we have with someone we love is time stolen from destiny. I had my interlude with the sun in my arms. Like you, I do not curse the sun when it embraces the night." Zoe paused while the meat course, a roast kid, was sliced by a eunuch. When the servant had moved away from the table, she leaned slightly toward him, her lips glistening in the candlelight. "I have heard that you keep, or have kept, several women. Have you gone back to them?"

"Only to the whore I purchased from Anatellon. It is a hollow joy."

"Yes. But most of our pleasures are small. And the great joys in life almost always turn on us and bring us pain."

Unwatered wine accompanied the dessert. Zoe talked gaily for a long while, regaling him with stories of the Bulgar-Slayer, ancient gods, and scandalous romances. When she called the priest to say the closing grace, Haraldr was greatly disappointed. He had hoped to hear her husky voice long into the night, and forget Maria for a few hours.

He stood as protocol dictated and crossed his hands over his breast. Her pale eyebrow twitched slightly. "It is the first night it has been warm enough to sit on my balcony. Come and talk with me."

Zoe's balcony was a large arcade opening off her apartments. The multicolored constellation of the palace complex sloped to the sea beneath them. Chrysopolis blazed across the water to the east. Haraldr remembered the other balcony across the water, and what he had felt as he stood by Maria and watched the Great City in the night. Now his soul faced a different meridian. *My return journey has begun,* Haraldr thought. *I leave behind not only Maria, but the other love that can no longer hold me, the Empress City. I have spent the night in these twin lovers' arms and have known their narcotic passions and their lethal madness. Now I want nothing more than to abandon them to their own tormented fates. I have a duty to perform for the people of Studion and the soul of Asbjorn Ingvarson to avenge. And then the vengeance that howls across the endless plains of Rus and shrieks in my breast like the ravens' song waits for me. Norway.*

Zoe stood close to him and put her hand on his neck, and the touch thrilled him as if a mosaic Virgin had reached out to him. She pulled his head down and whispered next to his ear. "Speak softly and the wind will carry our words away. It is said that you and the Hetairarch intend to strike at the Orphanotrophus."

Haraldr stiffened. But at least she had used her charm and not her sex; she had allowed him that much dignity. "We have intentions but no plans," he said honestly; he would not have told her if they did.

"You cannot wait," she said. My husband could die at any time now. . . ."

"If Your Majesty will forgive me, when that does happen, we must give the Caesar time to gather strength. If he could join us against Joannes, our chances of success would be immeasurably improved." Haraldr did not add that he and Mar disagreed on this point.

Zoe shook her head vehemently. "My nephew is a dear boy, but he is weak. He has been entirely subjugated by Joannes. When Alexius prepares to anoint him with the Imperial Diadem, I would not be surprised to see Joannes snatch the crown from the Patriarch's hands and set it upon his own grotesque head. He will certainly occupy the throne. My husband has restrained him. Under the next Michael, Joannes will unleash a terror on my people such as you have never even dreamed."

"You are suggesting that I personally swat down Joannes? Remember that you have asked me to butcher that particular bird once before. And you have heard my answer."

"You were an innocent then. You still are. But the next revelation may cost you your life."

Haraldr looked down on her intense, questing face. She was beautiful in this role as well. And yet there was truth to what she said. He had been taken totally unawares by the Emperor's condition; he could not afford many more revelations like that. Mar had become increasingly unreliable, if not treacherous; Haraldr had begun to suspect that Mar's goals extended well beyond the death of Joannes, and he had no idea how he and his men would then fit into Mar's plans. And now the Caesar could not even earn his lover's approbation. But what did this ally offer? "You did not summon me here to save my life, Mistress. What price do you offer me to save your own?"

Zoe smiled and tapped a perfect white tooth with a fingernail. "Indeed. Let me be candid. I must find a champion. In spite of our . . . estrangement, my husband would never let his brother harm me. If my husband were dead, and my people broken to Joannes's bit, I would be in great jeopardy." Her jaw set firmly, with true Hellenic nobility. "I am not afraid to die, Manglavite. I am afraid to let Joannes live."

"Yes. I saw the Studion burn." Haraldr once again felt fate gaming with him, forcing him to play. This wager would be huge. "Once I had severed the head of this black-frocked eagle, how could you insure that the Imperial Taghmata would not obey their Dhynatoi masters and massacre my men in reprisal? They would certainly not miss Joannes, but they would welcome the pretext to eliminate every Varangian in Rome."

"I would go to my people and ask them to rise up against the Taghmata. That would alter the equation in your favor, would it not?"

Haraldr ran through the myriad contingencies he and Mar had batted around for months. Yes. She was right; with the distraction of a civil uprising, the Taghmata could be defeated. Then he admonished himself to deal with Zoe, as one sovereign to another. He was no longer a mere servant of Rome. "Yes, I believe you can guarantee that my men would not be punished. But what would be my reward?"

"Rome."

What monstrous guile. Madness had seized Rome. The good were perishing and the rest lived in the vast structures of their lies. "Indeed, my Mother." Haraldr did not attempt to conceal the taunt in his voice. "You would adopt me, as you did the Caesar, and name me after some Emperor of ancient Rome, I presume. Or perhaps an invention more grand. King of Macedon, in honor of Alexander."

Zoe moved away from him and looked out over the pattern of brilliant lights and inky water. "I would anoint you myself. I would bestow on you the only real power that remains in Rome. The anointment in the Hagia

Sophia is an empty ritual without the coronation that can only take place between my legs."

Haraldr imagined himself captured by a whirlwind, swept up in the madness of Rome. To think of her naked, waiting, was intoxication enough; to think of the power that penetration would endow was to leave the middle realm and gambol among the gods. But it was fantasy. A boast on her part. She played the woman but in her loins was only power. And she would guard that power with empty promises. "Indeed," he said, his momentary madness now restored to wry reason, "and to celebrate our betrothal, I would pluck the girdle of Orion from the sky"—he pointed to the constellation wheeling above them—"and fasten it about your fair loins as a wedding belt. I have but to reach for it."

Zoe smiled as if restraining a laugh, like a child caught in some mischief. "My crown is not as inaccessible as your wedding gift. But in refusing it, you have given me the assurance I need, that your ambition has practical limits. Let me give you the assurance you need. If you wish, I will swear on a piece of the cross upon which our Savior died that I will keep the other promise I have made tonight."

Haraldr was aware of the importance of these relics among the Romans but he saw no reason to make her take an oath on them. "If I fail, I will be able to offer your complicity to barter for the lives of my men. That is the pledge you have given tonight."

Zoe resembled an ancient marble statue with amethysts for eyes. Then her lips twitched slightly. "You have become more . . . civilized than I had ever anticipated, Manglavite Haraldr. But you have not lost your . . . impetuosity, either. Since I find you so candid this evening, let me ask you this: When I offered you Rome, wasn't there a moment when you lusted for her, no matter the cost?" She paused, and pearls winked dully as her breast rose with an inhalation that was imperceptible on her face. "Wasn't there a moment when you desired me?"

Haraldr nodded. Zoe's gemstone eyes warmed and the stone became living flesh. She came toward him; he could feel the heat of her. Her face was beyond beauty. "So. If you fail, we will both die. That is a destiny that already weds us. If we are to be consummated in that death, then let us be lovers in this life." And then she slipped her silken arms around him and pressed her jeweled head to his chest.

She was everything he had wanted her to be: desperate, innocent, majestic, tender, her body and face a treasury of desire. He made love to her for an entire night. And as the dawn pinked the Bosporus, he wrapped his arm around her regal white bosom and realized two maddening truths: He could love this woman. And he could never stop loving Maria.

† † †

John Proteuon looked at his neighbor Stephan and threw his arms up helplessly. "Oxen stray," he said, not without sympathy, but trying not to be too encouraging. "Look," he explained as he wiped his hands on his coarse, rain-soaked tunic, "I have to help my brother with the plowing. Because I am a soldier doesn't mean I must go looking for stray animals. The next time some Emperor wants to attack them"—John pointed north to the Bulgarian border at the Danube River, a ride of two days—"I will go riding off and you will stay, and you will not be helping me fight the Bulgars any more than you are right now helping me to help my brother plow." John gestured out in the field where his brother trudged along behind an oxen yoked to the awkward, top-heavy, curved plowshare.

Stephan stood in the heavy mist, his brown hair beaded with moisture and his dull gray eyes swimming above gaunt cheekbones. He looked as if he hadn't been eating well, thought John, which he probably hadn't. With the increase in the window tax and the addition of the hearth tax and the constant work-levys taking men away from their farms to build these roads to nowhere, honest farmers like Stephan often looked like stray dogs. John began to feel guilty; as a military freeholder he was exempt from these additional taxes, and in truth he hadn't had to spend much time fighting. In fact, he had once been mobilized to go to Asia Minor, but that campaign had been called off or ended or something, and other than that, he just had to show his topoteretes that he still had a spear and helmet and a horse. And since he hadn't seen his topoteretes in two years, he hadn't worried much about that lately. And the rain would soften the soil so that it would go easier tomorrow, so what would be the harm in just looking for the animal for a while? After all, if Stephan had lost his ox, he would have to pull the plowshare himself, and it was clear he wouldn't last long at that.

John saddled his horse, decided his spear would be an annoyance, and helped Stephan up behind him. They rode away from the cluster of small brick-walled cottages and passed through the broad fan of tilled acreage that surrounded the village. The common pasture was just a rock-strewn expanse of green scrub bordered by a wood that grayed into the mist. It was empty. "Didn't Marosupous have his goats here?" asked John, refer-ring to another village neighbor. "They are gone too," said Stephan in his thick, slow, slightly Slavic accent; his mother had been a Bulgar who had been born here before the Bulgar-Slayer brought this area south of the Danube back into the Empire.

"They are gone too!" exclaimed John, leaning back so he could bat Stephan on top of his idiot skull. "Why didn't you say! Someone has stolen all the animals! It's clear!"

"I told you," said Stephan.

"You told me your ox had been stolen, ox-head, not your ox and Marosupous' goats!" John pondered the situation. He could go back for his spear, collect his brother, Marosupous, Gregory and his brother. But then he'd be leading that clumsy band all over creation with no idea where the animals had gone. "Stephan," he said, "run back to the village and tell everybody what has happened. I am riding over the ridge to see what I can see." Without a word Stephan slipped off the horse and ran, ankles flapping in battered knee boots.

John rode through the cold, wet woods and out onto a rocky slope that climbed to a little promontory marked by a pile of large, crumbling stones. A fine idea, he admonished himself sarcastically when he reached the lookout; he could only see about two stades into the mist, enough to make out a fragment of the narrow cart path that wound through the shallow hills before intersecting the big paved road to Nicopolis. John was about to pick through the scrub and take the path when he heard something strange out in the mist, coming from the direction of the Nicopolis road. He reined his horse still and listened for a while. How strange. A sound he had never heard before, gradually but steadily rising. A sound like some kind of heavy rain, perhaps, rain and hail, or a freak wind. But no, the sky wasn't right; in fact, a steady west wind was begin-ning to push the mist back from the Nicopolis road. Animals. Yes. But more than one ox and a few goats. A herd. That was it. These thieves had made off with every animal in Paristron theme, it sounded like, and were driving them down the road.

The first man to come up the cart path did not see John. He wore a steel breastplate and helm and was armed with a bow and quiver and small round shield. John didn't recognize the uniform, but he could well guess that the man was Imperial Taghmata—out here for what purpose, God only knew. John felt like riding up and telling this lout what he thought about the Taghmata stealing peasants' animals even during peacetime. But as he wasn't armed—and who knew what kind of renegade this man was or how many accomplices he had with him?—he'd wait. Maybe he would see a centurion or topoteretes he could complain to. John rode back up to the promontory and concealed himself behind the rough natural cairn on top. The wind continued to sweep the mist off toward the Nicopolis road, and five more men joined the first, all armored alike; one, however, had no bow. An officer; just the man to hear about this crime. John nudged his horse back down the cart path.

The men called to him in some vulgar tongue. John pulled back on the reins and looked down at them; they were still distant but he could see their flushed, smooth cheeks. Eunuch soldiers? Is that what they have serving in the Taghmata now? They called again and this time he recognized the dialect and realized that these men weren't eunuchs. He decided he had best return the way he had come and pretend he was just a frightened peasant. Which he was. He reached the rocks and looked back to see if they were following.

Below him, the mist had fled from a section of the Nicopolis road. Out of the opalescent fog marched grayish rows of spearmen in steel helms and hide jerkins flanked by horsemen armored like the six he had already encountered. How many? wondered John, his alarm building with every row that materialized out of the mist. He waited and counted. By the time he had reached one hundred ranks, he decided enough was enough and charged down the slope as fast as his horse could negotiate the rock outcrops. His horse was in full gallop and wheezing when he passed Stephan on the outskirts of his village. "Bulgars!" John shrieked so loud that the word burned his throat. "The whole Christ-forsaken Bulgar army!"

† † †

The woman had perhaps recently entered her fourth decade of life; she had a face that a passerby on this spring night would have found plain, certainly unalluring, but solid and well cared for. A face of the middle class, tending to lower, the wife of a guild tradesman more plodding than prosperous—perhaps her husband was a leather cutter or raw-silk processor who contracted work for more ambitious tradesmen who owned their own businesses. She wore a long wool tunic with a wool cloak over that, for there was a chill in the air, a crisp post-rain freshness, and she was returning from the public baths near her home in the Platea district next to the Golden Horn; she carried her pail and towel in her right hand. Fear was a dim reflection in her dull brown eyes, because although she was reasonably confident that the cursores were never far in her middle-class, tending to lower, neighborhood, there were some unsavory tenements in the area—one on her block—and there had been thefts and assaults. But this fear was a minor nuisance of life; what tormented her was the anxiety of what she was about this night.

He was waiting for her at the usual place, his black cloak a shadow that seemed to take life as it emerged from the darkness of the alley next to an arcaded fruit market. He quickly took her next door, into the graveyard of the small monastary at the end of the street. She placed her pail down on the grass next to the toothlike rows of grave markers, hating as always this business amid the screaming souls of the dead, and waited for him to begin.

"How many times did they meet this week?" asked Joannes, looking down on the women's plain, pained face.

"Three times," she said, her voice muffled by shame.

"So they are busy, are they." She did not answer the rhetorical question but looked at her sandaled feet; dainty and smooth, they were her most attractive feature. "What did your husband tell you they discussed?" asked Joannes.

Her eyes roamed as if she suspected the dead of eavesdropping. The monastery chapel, shrouded by trees, was a dark, forbidding presence behind the rows of gravestones. "H-he said they are against . . . y-you, Orphanotrophus. They are . . . planning something. He would not say what."

Joannes nodded. "Has he ever talked of any association between his group and certain malefactors in the Studion?"

"I heard him talk to a . . . friend . . ." She paused, aware that ambiguities annoyed the Orphanotrophus. "The . . . friend was the baker I already told you about." Joannes nodded that she could continue. "They said that this group in the Studion was . . . well organized and would be a . . . good ally. They said that the middle class and the poor would have to unite against y-you, Orphanotrophus."

Joannes bent over the woman as if he were about to grab her and shake the truth out of her, but he merely leered. "The name of this group in the Studion. Did they mention the name of this group?" The woman shook her head and stifled a sob. "But you will find out the name for me, will you not? I should think that when we meet next week, you will know."

The woman nodded affirmatively, her hands clutching at the borders of her cloak as if she were suddenly cold. She looked up with tears on her cheeks. "Have you brought a message from my boy? Is he well? Oh, please . . ." The desperation in her voice would have broken the heart of a statue.

"He is well," rumbled Joannes. "He is one of the Neorion's pets already. I will have a message from him for you next time, when you bring the name."

The woman looked up at Joannes with the curious gratitude that victims on the rack often displayed to their torturers. She sniffled and waited.

"Has your husband touched you this week?" asked Joannes.

She did not think to lie. "No," she said numbly. Joannes nodded. She mechanically pulled her cloak aside and then slowly pulled her tunic up to her armpits, leaving everything beneath that line of demarcation exposed. Joannes's eyes never left her flat, low breasts. Her veined nipples were puckered from the cold, certainly not desire. Her eyes were closed. Joannes's huge, deformed fingers reached out and spread over her breasts, and the spatulate tips pressed against her sallow flesh like the suction cups of a squid. There was no movement in his face, no expression in his shadowed sockets. After a brief moment he removed his hands and the woman slowly pulled her tunic down. She quickly picked up her pail and ran out of the graveyard and disappeared down the street. Joannes looked around the graveyard for a moment, as if he wished to frighten even the dead with his terrible visage. Then he, too, walked beneath the stone portal and disappeared.

The dead rose from behind a large, square-sided fountain in the middle of the haphazard rows of slabs. One was an enormous spirit, the other a small man who moved with the quick, furtive, utterly silent spurts of a creature used to going where it was not wanted. The two spirits huddled their heads for a moment and spoke to one another.

"You see. Once a week. This night, always the same time and the same thing." The little man smiled, showing crooked, partially rotted teeth. "The only thing that ever changes is, sometimes he feels her breasts and sometimes he doesn't."

Haraldr smiled grimly and placed five silver nomismata in the little man's hands. "My thanks to you, friend. And to our mutual friend, the Blue Star, my gratitude and greetings."

The little man scurried off behind the monastery, leaving Haraldr alone with the dead. He doubted that any of the souls buried in this hallowed ground were damned, but if any were, he had a message for them to take to the Prince of Hell: "At this time a week hence, I will deliver to you the soul of the Orphanotrophus Joannes."

† † †

There were tiny black clouds high in the otherwise perfect, porcelain-blue sky, and the sun was hot and his hair was golden with the heat. She could not touch him anymore, but somehow her mind was inside his and she could see through his eyes, though she knew she was so distant from him. For a long time she did not notice the little black clouds become ravens flocking ever lower, until she saw the glittering ice on top of the hill and felt the cold wind rip through his heart. But beyond the ice was a creek, gentle, a surface of many-faceted diamonds. She whispered to him, "The king is on the other side," and she knew when he reached the king beyond the creek, he would be safe. Then a single raven came from the zenith of the black sky, arrow-swift, its obsidian beak as sharp as death. She felt it hit his neck, and then she saw the blood pump out horribly, and she reached for him desperately. . . .

Maria awakened shivering, her tears like ice crystals·on her face. She sat up and listened to the stillness of the night and felt eternity around her like a black, weightless shroud. What does it mean? she asked herself, feeling as if her soul were a tiny flame fleeing ahead of her in the darkness. What does it mean?

ephew. You look so well this morning. Have you refreshed yourself with one of your sluts? Perhaps, being young and foolish, and this the season of renewal, you have dedicated your earnest heart to one in particular."

Joannes nodded to his secretary, who closed the door to his plain, immaculately cluttered office in the basement of the Magnara. Michael Kalaphates sat without greeting his uncle.

"So you have renewed your liaison with the queen of sluts. What morsels has the lovely woman given you to share with me?"

"Uncle, she has engineered another plot." Michael looked at Joannes as if this were one of the most painful utterances of his life. His dark lashes blinked furiously.

"Indeed. How is she to accomplish this assassination?"

"I do not know the details, Uncle."

Joannes picked up his pen, dipped it in an ugly little porcelain inkwell, and made a note on a document before him. He looked up at Michael once and wrote a few more words before placing his pen carefully in a small clay tray. Suddenly he rose like an eruption of black smoke, his huge arms flying, one deformed finger pointing to Michael's nose like the sword of the Archangel. "The slut has always had some plot against me, you sniveling moron!" he thundered. "I do not need warnings! I have the resources to deflect any of the blows that are directed at me!" Joannes lowered his voice abruptly. "I need to find a way of luring her into drinking her own poison. That is why I need details, you witless harlot-monger. Can you remember anything?"

"Yes." Michael's eyes were wide with terror. "Her confederate in this enterprise is the Manglavite Haraldr Nordbrikt."

"Thank you, Nephew. You may see yourself out." Joannes did not look up. "Next time we talk, I hope you will have a more persuasive and thorough argument against your return to Neorion."

When Michael had left, Joannes leaned back in his chair and rubbed the deep sockets of his eyes. So the Manglavite Haraldr Nordbrikt would come against him. Excellent. That made the decision so much easier. Yes, one of the two Tauro-Scythian swell-heads had to go; their connivance was too dangerous, particularly at this time, but then the preservation of one was just as certainly necessary. And since the Manglavite Haraldr Nordbrikt was clearly the more foolish of the two and would soon offer the same allegiance to the Orphanotrophus as had the pathetic Caesar, the choice simply had to be the Hetairarch Mar Hunrodarson. It was time for Mar Hunrodarson to conclude his lengthy stay among the Romans with a final, exquisite night in Neorion.

† † †

"I cannot tell you."

Mar slapped his powerful hands to his vast chest with a resounding thump, as if ascertaining for himself that he was indeed the person to whom Haraldr was speaking. "I do not believe what I just heard. I have spent months trying to goad you into taking some action, and now you have this insane plan that I can only assume has been inspired by your woman, and I am informed that you are going to strike directly at Joannes tomorrow evening, but you cannot tell me where this assault will take place, or who has convinced you that this scheme will not get every Varangian in the Roman Empire killed. Why do I see the hand of Maria in this?"

"Maria is not involved. I am withholding the details for your own protection. If I fail, the less you know the better. I simply want you to be prepared when it happens." Haraldr knew this wasn't entirely the truth; he didn't trust Mar enough to name the Empress. But the safety of his pledge-men depended on Mar knowing that the attempt would be made.

"Prepared? We are *not* prepared. If we move now without pledges from the Scholae, Excubitores, and Hyknatoi, everything will be lost. I don't think you are aware of the considerable effort I have made to convert several topoteretes to our cause. I am moving forward. You are about to rush off a precipice and you are going to take the rest of us with you."

"I have . . . pledges that assure much more than a few topoteretes of the Taghmata can offer us."

Mar walked over and kicked at a stack of canvas tents; he had agreed to meet Haraldr in the storeroom beneath the barracks of the Middle Hetairia. He looked about at the bags of field equipment, battle armor, and rows of ceremonial banners resting against the wall. For the first time he realized how dangerous the Prince of Norway really was. He turned back to Haraldr. "The lives of one thousand men are at stake. You had better name your confederates." Mar's face reddened ominously.

"Do you think I would take any action that would recklessly jeopardize the life of any Norseman? First of all, I am not going to have any trouble dealing with Joannes in the place where I am planning to do this. And when I succeed, I have guarantees that the Taghmata will be neutralized. I am virtually certain that when they see what they are up against, they will not even fight. If they do, we will crush them."

"And I am supposed to take your word for this?" Mar propped his hands on his hips. "Maybe you have forgotten the lesson I taught you the night we met."

Haraldr hadn't; he clearly remembered how easily Mar had overpowered him. "Do you intend to beat this information out of me?"

Mar walked toward him. "That depends on you, little Prince."

Haraldr had almost decided to reveal everything, reasoning that he had already trusted Mar with the lives of his pledge-men. But Mar's physical intimidation galled him. "Perhaps it does."

This time Haraldr was ready. He caught Mar's serpent-quick arm and threw him against a row of standards. Mar flailed at the clattering shafts and rebounded against the wall; in an instant he had lunged into Haraldr's knees and sent him sprawling. They grappled and rolled, pummeling limbs thudding violently into the stone floor. Haraldr could not believe how powerful Mar was; he remembered wrestling with Olaf when he was a little boy. And yet Mar was unable to pin him down.

They were on their feet. Mar glared; perhaps not the Rage but an inhuman fury. Haraldr put his shoulder down and bulled him into a pile of canvas bags. Mar was slapping him frantically at the ears. A bag slipped away beneath Haraldr and he pitched to the floor. Somehow Mar was at his back. Mar's arm was across his windpipe, shutting it off, and the knife was at his cheek.

"This is madness!" shouted Mar, breathing furiously. "This is doing nothing to stop Joannes." He let go of Haraldr's throat and put his knife away.

Haraldr angrily shoved the canvas gear bags aside and got up on his knees. It *was* madness. He told Mar where the assassination would take place, and how the Empress had guaranteed to exhort the City against the Taghmata.

When Haraldr had finished, Mar looked off to the side and rocked slightly on his heels for a pregnant interval. Finally he said, quietly, "I think it will work."

Haraldr rubbed his throat. *Yes, it will work,* he told himself. *And the next time we fight, Mar, if I am lucky and you are not, I might be able to kill you.*

† † †

Mar stormed through the halls of the Numera to the wing containing the private rooms of his centurions. He pounded on Thorvald Ostenson's door, and when it was opened a crack, he burst in. He ignored the young boy who cowered in Ostenson's bed and thrust his bronze oil lamp in his subordinate's face. "I want you to go into the city and arrange an interview for me tonight. Without fail. Immediately."

Ostenson gulped for words. "W-who is the concerned party, Hetairarch?"

"The Grand Domestic Bardas Dalassena."

Mar watched Ostenson dress, as if he were afraid his centurion might climb back into bed. When Ostenson had left, Mar slammed the door on the bewildered boy and walked quickly to his own third-floor apartments. He flung open doors and went out on his balcony, wishing he could vent his rage for the entire palace to hear. Incredible. Who did he hate most? Himself, Haraldr Sigurdarson, or the conniving, unbelievably clever slut? Sigurdarson! Incredible! Mar had spent months forging an alliance with Alexius and Theodora, and in one evening with the purple-born whore, the boy Prince had arrived at a plan that would probably leave the bitch Zoe in power for the rest of her life. Had she also promised to make Haraldr Sigurdarson *Hetairarch?* Or worse, would she allow him to return to Norway before he had even begun to be useful? This is what he had hated most about Sigurdarson all along, his extravagant good fortune, simply to be alive, and then his preposterous string of successes on top of that. Mar walked back inside his bedchamber, picked up the enormous armoire opposite his bed, and flung it into the wall. The massive piece of furniture shattered with a noise like a ship breaking up on the rocks.

Mar was placated enough by the explosion of wood and ivory to think clearly for a moment. Of course Haraldr Sigurdarson was no longer worth the trouble, of course he had to die; the decision he had made in haste once before had been right then, and it was the correct decision now. But, Mar now wondered, had he selected the proper instrument for Haraldr Sigurdarson's execution?

† † †

The enclosed atrium of the Grand Domestic Bardas Dalassena's hilltop palace featured a central fountain lined with gold tiles; a lion reared up from amid the water. Mar studied the reflection of the candlelight in the still pool; the fountain had been turned off. Five officers of the Imperial Taghmata stood guard a discreet distance across the vaulted marble chamber. Mar sneered inwardly. *He thinks that if I wanted to kill him, I would send my centurion to him in the middle of the night to ask for an interview? And does the fool imagine he is manifesting his strength by making me wait?*

The ninth hour of the night passed before a topoteretes assigned to the offices of the Grand Domestic descended the spiral staircase. "He will see you now," said the topoteretes. The Grand Domestic did not greet Mar when the Hetairarch stepped into his quiet office. Mar studied the massive polished bronze water clock beside the writing table. The whore flaunting her cheap jewelry, thought Mar with disgust.

Dalassena riffled through the dispatches on his writing table. A book on military strategy, opened to drawings of stockade configurations, rested on the lectern. He looked up as if momentarily distracted from issues of momentous gravity. The image of the military man, thought Mar; the thick chest and powerful forearms, the leathery, chiseled brow and clipped, wiry, dark beard. The image, like everything in Rome, merely an image. Dalassena finally nodded for his topotoretes to leave; conspicuously the aide did not close the door behind him and after a moment coughed in the hall so that Mar would know he was still there. Mar could scarcely keep the glee off his face. *Does Dalassena fear me this much?*

"I am busy, Hetairarch." Dalassena's voice had a rich, innate command.

Mar decided he had politely suffered enough of this display. He kicked the door shut and barred it with his back. "Turd worm! Do you think those six boys outside can prevent me from breaking your neck like a twig!" To Dalassena's credit, his dark eyes flared with his own anger and hatred; Mar surmised that the Grand Domestic would retreat from death as long as he could, but when he was finally trapped, he would turn and face the Valkyrja.

"Very well, Hetairarch." Dalassena shrugged; apparently he had decided he still had a few more avenues for retreat. "I have offered you an opportunity to deal once before. There is no reason why I should not offer conciliation simply because this time you are the supplicant. I have negotiated with the devil many times in my career."

Indeed you have, thought Mar, and fair enough warning. Mar moved away from the door; the topoteretes, backed by all five guards, lurched into the room and was quickly dismissed by Dalassena and told to close the door again. "Let me arrive directly at my point," said Mar briskly. "You were correct in your initial warnings about the danger of the Manglavite—then ordinary pirate—Haraldr Nordbrikt. He is a threat to all of us."

Dalassena's eyes were startlingly quick and alert. "And you, who can break necks like twigs—which I do not doubt—wish me to perform the execution. Why?"

"Because if I am the executioner, I will be unable to gain the loyalty of his men when he has left them bereft of his leadership."

Dalassena jutted his chin out. "But I do not wish you to gain the loyalty of his men. I consider them, and you, a scourge, and would hope to see them march leaderless back to the snows of Thule. Or perhaps the Middle Hetairia might fall upon the Grand Hetairia in a fratricidal orgy. How suited that would be to my ends."

"Just when I think an ass has learned to talk with his rear end, he turns around and brays at me," said Mar. Dalassena leapt to his feet, his face livid. With one hand Mar slammed him back down into his chair. "Listen to me, fool who has bartered away his wits to the devil. The deal you negotiated was with the Dhynatoi, not Joannes. Now Joannes is your master. We both know that. So far Joannes has confined his attentions to the details of civil administration and left military matters to the Emperor. When his brother dies, and we both know that is imminent, Joannes's malignant hands will seize the military establishment; surely you do not see the pathetic Caesar leading the armies of Rome? And many are likely to be strangled in that grip."

Dalassena's eyes said everything. He had already heard rumors of the campaigns planned by Joannes. Suicidal. And yet not to obey? Suicidal. Dalassena thrust his chest out and exhaled through his nostrils. "So. I bring you the head of Haraldr Nordbrikt, and you bring me the head of Joannes."

Mar nodded. There was a pounding at the door. Dalassena shouted for the topoteretes to go away, but the pounding continued. Dalassena stepped to the door, his face reddening. When the door was opened, Mar observed the face of the topoteretes. Something was wrong. "Sir, there is a state courier downstairs." The topoteretes's voice was dulled by shock. "You will want to hear his dispatch."

Dalassena followed the topoteretes downstairs. Mar studied a carved ivory plaque on Dalassena's wall; it depicted St. Demetrius, the "warrior saint," armored in the fashion of an officer of the Taghmata. Mar's heart pounded. Has it happened? If so, then his haste had been more than prudent. There would still be time; Joannes would be distracted by the massive obligations of a state funeral and the anointing of the Caesar as the new Emperor. And perhaps by genuine grief. Yes, there was still time. Mar thought his heart would leap from his breast when he heard Dalassena's boots click on the marble again.

Dalassena's face was not merely ashen but had a sickly, vaguely greenish cast. Mar wondered if the man would swoon; his eyes were stunned and impotent. Mar helped him to his chair. Dalassenna rolled his eyes to Mar like a dying man, his voice already from the crypt. "Bulgars," he said. "The Bulgars have already claimed Paristron and Macedonia and have blockaded Thessalonica. We have lost the Western Empire. And they are ten days' march from the walls of Constantinople."

Mar reached down, clutched Dalassena's collar, and jerked the Grand Domestic's deathly face up into the light. "That changes nothing we have settled tonight," Mar hissed. "We will throw the Bulgars back. And there are many perils that can befall a warrior as courageous as the Manglavite Haraldr Nordbrikt in the heat of battle." Mar let Dalassena sag back into his chair. "Don't you see it? The Emperor cannot lead his troops into battle. You will have supreme command of the armies of Imperial Rome. And you will have no more loyal colleague at your side than the Commander of the Imperial Grand Hetairia."

† † †

"It's madness!" Haraldr shouted over the din inside the Magnana Arsenal. The smoke from the torches of the Optimatoi—Imperial baggage handlers—fogged the light from the disc-shaped polycandelons blazing high above in the vaults. At the far end of the enormous warehouse, huge siege machines loomed through the haze like strange mechanical monsters. The quantity and variety of military equipment being carted out and loaded on the pack mules and wagons was staggering: strings of caltrops, siege ladders, bridge pontoons, tents, various sizes of portable liquid fire-throwers, as well as clay shells filled with liquid fire, tents, arrow containers, leather field baths; one Optimatoi rushed by with a stack of bound tactical treatises. "Why are they moving the siege engines out? They are simply going to slow us down!"

Mar shook his head quizzically. "They think that Thessalonica may fall!"

"It probably will," shouted Haraldr, "if we slow down to protect all this equipment!"

Mar nodded his agreement. "What are you looking for!"

"These!" Haraldr reached in the canvas bag he carried and pulled out a soft leather ankle boot from which dangled long leather straps. "You wrap the straps around and they can't come off even if you step in pitch. We're going to run into mud, and these"—he slapped his heavy leather knee boots—"are going to be trouble!"

"Is the middle Hetairia ready to march?" shouted Mar, just as an Optimatoi carrying a basketful of horseshoes ran into him.

"Yes!" The decision had been easy, Haraldr realized. First the body of Rome had to be saved; then he could deal with the head, and the body could be healed. Then he could go home. Haraldr hefted several of the bags of footwear and shouted at a dozen of his men to start carrying off the rest.

"Are you returning to your barracks?" screamed Mar. Metalworkers had started hammering on one of the siege engines.

"Yes! Then I'm going to my home in the city to get Gregory! My interpreter! I don't want any chance of misunderstanding a battle order!"

Mar looked around the huge, steaming, clamoring, sweat- and flame-smelling warehouse, his eyes jittering with excitement. He clenched his steel-hard fists and bellowed into the din: "I can already taste the raven's wine!"

† † †

Haraldr rode alone up the hill to his palace. Despite a steady rain, the city was alive with speculation, perhaps incipient hysteria. A huge crowd had gathered in the Forum of Constantine to listen to the simultaneous harangues of various speakers with widely divergent views; one long-haired youth, probably a Bogomil, attributed the attack to the sinfulness of the city, while a grizzled one-legged old man, probably a veteran of the Bulgar-Slayer's campaigns, recited a lurid litany of the atrocities the Bulgars were even now perpetrating on the people of Rome. Even in Haraldr's fashionable neighborhood, people clustered on the street corners in small, restive assemblies; their concern was an imminent invasion of the city. And it seemed as if every servant in the district was running to and fro on the street, arms laden with bags of grain and clay jars of wine and oil, as households stockpiled provisions for a siege. Some servants had even carted out large ivory triptychs or bronze sculptures to sell for ready cash.

Haraldr's own street was no different; the chambermaid from his neigh-

bor's house leaned over a balcony and asked him if he had seen the
Bulgar horde yet and was it true that they tortured women after they had
raped them? A cart groaned up the cobbled hill, two eunuchs lashing the
mule; the vehicle was loaded with three fat, snorting stoats, no doubt
illegally obtained from a pork wholesaler. A woman in an expensive fur
rain cape waited by the entrance portal of his palace. *No, I haven't seen the
Bulgars yet,* Haraldr rehearsed mentally. *They are ten days' march at least and
we will certainly throw them back before they ever see Rhegium, much less the walls
of the city. Go back to your husband and worry about the taxes that will be needed
to pay for this campaign.*

The woman walked over to Haraldr before he could dismount; her
drenched cape cowled her head. She put her hand on his boot and turned
her face up. Haraldr's head snapped erect with the jolt of her hot sapphire
eyes. Maria quickly took her hand away, as if she had touched a glowing
brazier. She stared at him for a moment before she spoke. "I have no
right. But I must talk to you before you leave. I must. I have been
waiting."

"I have no time for your particular game, Mistress," snapped Haraldr.
"I must play the game of war, which as you say is no less trivial than a
child's but one in which the wagers are paid in blood." Haraldr dismounted and stood over her. Her face was unpainted and her pale skin
was beaded by the rain. "Perhaps you can tell me how to kill a Bulgar if
he tries to make love to me."

"I did not come to mock you," she said softly, her voice like crystal
drops falling from the gray, ugly sky. "I know I have . . ." She inhaled
and stood erect. "I did not come to explain myself. I can offer no apology.
What is done is done. What can yet be undone, I wish to undo. What I
have to say concerns your life."

Haraldr shook his head wearily. "I should think I would be beyond your
intrigues where I am going."

"Please. You know I am not . . ." She paused, and her lips, tinted more
purple than usual, trembled. "You know the emptiness inside me. I know
you have tried to reach out to me. I am not happy in my being." Her face
had a desperate look he had never seen before. "I beg you to pity me."

Haraldr remembered something she had once said, and he wondered
which eccentric star now prompted him to indeed pity her. "Come inside."

Haraldr's servants were in a frenzy, rushing about with jars and granary
sacks and taking the silver plates to the basement for storage. His chamberlain, Nicetas Gabras, stood in the middle of the antechamber like a

general directing an invasion. Haraldr just glanced at Gabras in annoyance; he had kept Joannes's lackey on because it seemed that in Rome a confirmed spy was almost as valuable as a trusted friend. Every now and again, however, he had to resist the urge to stroll downstairs and literally tear Gabras in two in front of his entire staff of cringing eunuchs and maidservants. "Gregory," shouted Haraldr to the corners of the huge palace, "are you ready to go a-viking with your Norse comrades?" Gregory shouted back, a muffled response, and after a few moments the little eunuch appeared at the far end of the antechamber; he wore a linen cape and dragged a Norse-style hide gear bag. "In battle storm we fear no lee!" he exhorted with a self-deprecating flourish.

Haraldr grinned at Gregory's kenning. "You are the first Roman Norseman," he told Gregory affectionately. Haraldr looked at Gabras, who was still directing his own campaign, and had an inspiration. "Chamberlain," he barked, "leave this! You are going to war!" Gabras looked as if he had just had a knife plunged into his ribs. "Yes. You could be useful. My interpreter and brave comrade here, a veteran of much combat, needs a batman to carry his bag to the front. You are appointed to this position. Any delay in obeying this order will be punished by regulations governing the conduct of the Middle Hetairia." The astonished Gabras quickly capitulated to Haraldr's icy eyes and attached himself to Gregory's gear bag as if he had been born to the position.

Haraldr waved for Maria to follow him upstairs. He walked quickly ahead of her to his vaulted, candlelit bedchamber. His Alan girl stood in waiting, her sinuous body sheathed in white silk and her opal-gray eyes anxious. He kissed her marble-smooth white forehead and sent her out. She walked gracefully past Maria, looking at her keenly, almost like one stallion appraising another.

"She is like a white leopard I saw once," said Maria raptly, apparently unable to contain her admiration for an equally splendid female. "You must be beautiful together, your gold and her ivory."

"Yes," said Haraldr, "and tonight when she wraps her panther legs around me, she will truly regret that it may be the last time. Not because she loves me—she hardly knows me—but because I have kept her well. And I have grown to see the beauty in the simple truth of that."

Maria looked terribly pained; at exactly what he did not know, but he was pleased to see her anguish. She bowed her head so that he could no longer see. "I am a mean bitch. I did not want to speak of those things."

"No. Let us speak of love. Your lovers and my lovers. I have a new mistress now. When I am in her arms, I do not always think of you."

Maria looked up with a faint hope written on her face. "I always think of you."

"Even when you are tearing flesh with some new gallant?"

"There was a lover. That once. I did it to . . . I will not lie and say I did it for you. I did it to save myself. But there is no one now. I am empty."

"You have made your own bed, Mistress. If it is empty, then that is your own doing."

"Yes." She seemed to have made some decision, like a traveler who looks back on his home and knows in that instant he will never return. "I came to speak of a dream I had in that bed."

Haraldr felt fear like a brief, sudden gust in the room. Her dreams, if they were to be believed, had a curious prescience. It was quite likely, given her strange, sad soul, that she was one condemned to see ahead in time. A seeress, of sorts, though apparently she could not induce the trance. "Speak of it," he told her.

She described the dream, the ravens, the king beyond the creek, and the wound in his neck. When she had finished, she added, "I did not think it was important to tell you, because I thought it was really about me. That I missed you." She shook her head blindly, as if trying to toss some terrible thought out of it, and a tear streamed across her temple. "I wanted to kill you once. I thought you were the messenger of my death. You know that. But I don't want you to die." She looked up with brimming eyes, her lips contorting horribly. *For the first time in my experience,* Haraldr observed, amazed, *she looks ugly.* And in that moment his heart was touched. She was a woman, a human being, not a goddess after all. He had been no fool to seek her desperate, lost soul. "Please don't go to this war," she said, sobbing. "I will do anything you want. I will leave Rome forever, whatever. I will enter a convent." Her shoulders wrenched with sobs. "Please believe me. You are going to die out there. I saw it." She clenched her fists until her knuckles burned welt-red and then dropped her arms to her side as if drained of every feeling. Her voice fell; the whispered words seemed like a cry from an abyss: "I could not live knowing your soul was not somewhere in this world."

He reached for her, not so much from pity but from knowing that her fiery touch would perish this strange new incantation. But she was cold, almost lifeless, and when she fell against him sobbing, she was not an Aphrodite with searing, snake-stealthy arms, but a small girl in need of chaste comfort. And somehow he touched her lonely, flickering soul in a way he never had when he had felt himself deep inside her. He pushed her away and held her hands, afraid that at any moment the heat and light that obscured her real being might return. "I promise you I won't die out there," he told her.

"I am frightened."

"So am I," admitted Haraldr. "But nothing in life is certain. Even destiny must sometimes stray from its own path."

"Or perhaps destiny misleads us into thinking it has strayed." Maria wiped her nose inelegantly, and Haraldr could not keep himself from holding her again.

"You must go," he told her. "There is too much our hearts must say to each other to again place the barrier of our naked breasts between them. I will come back to you." She drew away from him with her own understanding of this new, virgin troth. She clutched his hands one last time, then dropped them and silently fled to the door. But beneath the ornate lintel she paused and turned awkwardly, as if her emotions had finally confused her limbs. She looked back at him, the blue eyes like a fjord on the last dying day of summer. "If I do not return," he told her, answering the question on her sad child's face, "then I want you to know that I died loving you."

† † †

The City of New Rome did not sleep. In the hours of the waning night it began to migrate from the street corners and anxious family enclaves to the Forum of Constantine. From the districts of Petrion and Xeropholios, from Phanarion and the Venetian Quarter, from Blachernae where the Great Land Wall meets the Golden Horn, from Sigma and Deuteron, even from the Studion they came, the guildsmen and laborers and merchants and vagrants and petty bureaucrats, gnarled old women who had not been outside their homes for years, babies at their mother's breasts, they all came to watch the invincible armies of Imperial Rome go forth against the Bulgar horde.

Dawn. Polished breastplates, scarlet tunics, golden standards, and banners emerged in the first diffusions of daylight. The Imperial Taghmata had already assembled in a great procession along the avenue of the Mese, extending down to the Chalke Gate and the Imperial Palace complex. Behind the mounted regiments the Imperial baggage train and the supply wagons of the Taghmata jammed the Augustaion and the precincts of the Magnana Arsenal; the mules were even wandering into the open atrium of Hagia Sophia. The head of the armored column waited beneath the statue of the Emperor Constantine in the Forum. The enormous bronze Emperor, his countenance patinated with the centuries, stood atop seven massive drums of porphyry. A crown of rays, like shafts of sunlight through a cloud, haloed his godlike features, and he stood with the trail of his simple tunic draped over his left arm, his right arm raised as if exhorting his people. He faced east, searching for the rising sun that would send the armies of Rome west to meet the enemies of his great city and the vast empire that he had founded.

The crowd that now ringed the Forum and surrounded every building, filled every street, yard, and park as far as one could see, issued no ringing acclamations. They were subdued, their anxiety a low, buzzing rumble like a distant windstorm. They waited to see if Rome would have a champion in this terrifying hour of need. And beneath the statue of the first great Christian Emperor of Rome, the aspiring champions contested that honor.

"The Caesar must lead!" Michael Kalaphates's face crimsoned like the flushed eastern horizon as he tried to restrain his voice. "I have been acclaimed by the people and crowned by the Patriarch. That is my claim to ride out first!"

Bardas Dalassena reined his Arabian, as equally white and gorgeous as the Caesar's mount, his muscular forearms corded with tension. "You yourself acknowledge that I have supreme command." The Grand Domestic grimaced. "When the Emperor is present, he leads the procession because of his stature as supreme commander, and that alone. None of his other offices pertain to this protocol."

"That is specious," replied Michael, his horse now circling Dalassena's as if the two stallions were preparing to settle the matter. "Nowhere in the protocols is it suggested that anyone precede the Caesar except the Emperor. Ever. Under any circumstance."

"This is a matter of military, not civil protocol!" shouted Dalassena.

"Understand that I defer to you in the matter of command, Grand Domestic," said Michael, perfectly content as he was to relinquish responsibility for this ill-starred campaign. "Permit me to allow my children the comfort of knowing that the Hand of the Pantocrator will be the first to smite their enemies."

Haraldr steered his dappled Arabian away from the circling combatants and looked over at Mar. "We need to do something," he said in Norse. Haraldr reined around to face the east. Thorvald Ostenson, at the head of the mounted ranks of the Grand and Middle Hetairia, held aloft the golden dragon standard of the Grand Hetairia; company banners demarcated the five vanda behind; the Varangians were uniformed in newly lacquered Roman steel byrnnies with brilliant scarlet plumes atop their helms. Behind the Varangians the units of the Taghmata, headed by the golden-armored Scholae beneath their gilded eagle standards, disappeared down the Mese, a metallic river of latent fury. It was not wise to dispatch an army of this size with any sort of doubts over their leadership. But weren't such doubts now unavoidable?

Haraldr wheeled and faced the crowd to his right. Most of these spectators were various dignitaries from the Palace precinct—he could see Anna Dalassena and her mother standing in front—a few were prosperous merchants from Haraldr's own neighborhood. Even these, with their sophisticated understanding of the predicament, had the look of peasants watching their village leader flaunt some ancient superstition. Haraldr could only imagine the speculation among the laborers and minor tradesmen whose dun-colored masses filled the western end of the Forum. If they did not get this column under way, this army's first action might be against the people of Constantine's great city.

Mar looked up at the green bronze face of the Emperor Constantine as if asking for advice. He shouted for the bandmaster, who commanded the two ranks of drummers, trumpeters, flutists, and cymbal players arrayed on either side of the Varangians, to count twenty and commence playing. Then he charged his Arabian between Michael and Dalassena. "The Manglavite will lead," Mar said, nostrils flaring but his voice even and dignified. "The Grand Domestic and the Caesar will ride side by side behind the Manglavite. The Hetairarch will follow the Caesar and Grand Domestic." Just then the band blared into the lightening sky, effectively cutting off debate. The Caesar and Grand Domestic, at a loss to do otherwise, lined up as Mar had ordered but edged forward as each tried to move a neck ahead of the other; Haraldr finally blocked them with the rump of his horse. Anna Dalassena ran out of the crowd and handed her father a spray of golden marigolds; he took them with a look of mixed surprise and anger. Then Anna came beside Haraldr's horse and handed him a single white lily. She held his hand as he took the flower. He could not hear her well but he could read her lips easily: "From Maria." Anna kissed his hand and ran back into the crowd. As if on her signal, the petals of spring flew into the air like snow.

The acclamation began at the Chalke Gate and swept forward with such force that it seemed like some great gust of wind. Even the band was palled to silence and the group of four horsemen at the front of the column turned in alarm; Haraldr wondered if the Excubitores back on the

Mese hadn't begun to riot among themselves. He looked at Mar help-lessly. The sound was a hurricane that seemed as if it would throw the statue of Constantine to the pavement. Petals flew into the air. What could possibly be going on?

The horseman rode alone alongside the ranks; in a huge rippling motion all the Taghmata cavalry dismounted and the infantrymen dropped to their knees. The oncoming horse was a white Arabian capari-soned with gold and purple, and the horseman, in the finest gold armor, wore purple boots with a purple cloak flowing behind. His head was bare save for a single jeweled band around his forehead. Is Joannes mad, thought Haraldr, engaging an impostor to play the Emperor?

The horseman was fifty ells away when Haraldr realized that what he saw was not an impostor but a vision, a miracle. The man in Imperial raiment was the Emperor Michael. Not the same man whom Haraldr had adored a lifetime ago, but not the same pathetic wretch who had writhed in dying agony at his convent for prostitutes. He was still noticeably swollen, but he rode erect in the saddle and handled his horse with power and ease. And when the Emperor was still a dozen ells distant, Haraldr could see that his eyes were more powerful, more resolute than ever, the eyes of a man who had seen the abyss and with the force of ultimate will had leapt over it.

"Grand Domestic! Caesar!" shouted the Emperor, his voice audible even over the storm of his fame. "You will ride together, preceding the Imperial Scholae." Michael Kalaphates and Dalassena made no attempt to compose their astonishment-slackened faces and spurred off, exchang-ing looks that might have been passed between the centurions of old Rome when they saw the door of the Christ's tomb rolled aside. The Emperor turned on Haraldr and Mar with a gaze of full recognition and furious purpose. "Hetairarch! Manglavite! You will ride behind me! I alone will ride at the head of the armies of Rome!" Mar and Haraldr bowed deeply and fell in behind. The Emperor made the sign of the cross three times. Then he spurred his horse slightly and the powerful beast took the first step west. Responding instantly to this signal, the ranks behind began their march toward the destiny of Rome. Above them, the first clear shaft of the morning light caught the bronze rays that wreathed the head of the Emperor Constantine and gilded that ancient metal with the brilliance of the sun.

nd so, I must reiterate my conclusion that the author of the *Taktika* cautions us against a frontal assault in this instance." The Grand Domestic Bardas Dalassena flourished his hand as if he intended to produce this long-dead military expert to personally support his views. The Emperor, seated stiffly on a purple-canopied portable throne raised on a dais covered with cloth of gold, studied the thick scarlet wool carpet spread out before him, seemingly more interested in the pattern of highly geometricized Imperial Eagles than his Grand Domestic's tactical discourse. Candelabra hanging from the lofty silk brocade vaults of the Emperor's campaign tent glittered the ornamental gold breastplates of the Varangians of the Grand Hetairia, who flanked the Emperor in perfect arcs. A priest set a gold-framed icon and ornate gold censer at the Emperor's feet.

"A persuasive and coherent summary of the advocacies of the esteemed Leo," said the Emperor noncommittally before he finally looked up. He directed his incisive eyes to the group of junior officers arrayed behind Dalassena; all of them, like the Grand Domestic, were attired in court robes rather than military uniform, even though reconnaissance units of the Bulgar army had already been engaged that very morning. "Domestic of the Excubitores," said the Emperor, "would you give us, in the spirit of free and open speculation, the views of the author of the *Strateghikon* in this matter, as I know that you are well read in his literature."

Haraldr peered over the heads of the officers ranked in front of him and tried to get a glimpse of Isaac Camytzes, the new Domestic of the Excubitores. Haraldr wished that his old friend Nicon Blymmedes could have been here to see this; unfortunately Blymmedes, former Domestic of the Excubitores, had been transferred to command of a garrison in Sicily, ostensibly for his failure to protect the Empress near Antioch—actually because he opposed Dalassena's chronically timid strategies. But Blymmedes had taught Camytzes well, and apparently the Emperor was giving a competent junior officer an opportunity to speak without exposing him to charges of insubordination by his senior officer.

477

Camytzes strode to a position equidistant between the Emperor and his fellow officers. He was probably only in his early thirties, of medium height, with the dark Armenian coloring that seemed to be characteristic of so many of Rome's best soldiers (although Dalassena himself also had the swarthy look of the Armenikoi.) "Nicephorus Phocus, the esteemed author of the *Strateghikon,* as many of you know advocates the use of cataphracti in phalanx formation in order to cleave a defensive formation—"

"Cataphracti!" Dalassena snorted with a discourtesy designed to humiliate his young subaltern. "Where are the cataphracti?" He looked about comically. "Rome has not employed heavy cavalry for almost a century, Domestic." Dalassena wagged his finger for emphasis. "Because they were too clumsy to be effective in battle." This time the Grand Domestic looked around with immense self-satisfaction.

Camytzes waited for Dalassena to step back among the other officers. "Majesty, I of course am aware that we no longer employ cataphracti. We do, however, employ a powerful force of heavily armored infantry accustomed to fighting in phalanx formation—"

Again Dalassena burst forward. "I must protest, Domestic. You are ill. I will summon your unit physician to attend you in the field hospital immediately. You imagine all sorts of mythical warriors have joined our campaign. Next you will call out for Achilleus himself to lead the strong-greaved Achaians in this attack of yours!" Dalassena guffawed boorishly at his own joke.

"Majesty," resumed the long-suffering Camyztes, "the force to which I am referring is the Varangians of the Grand and Middle Hetairia. I have heard reports of the effectiveness of the wedge formation employed by the Manglavite and his unit against the Seljuks in Asia Minor"—here Dalassena snorted again, since that battle had, in the balance, gone to the Seljuks—"and of course the effectiveness of the Grand Hetairia we have all seen with our own eyes." Camytzes stepped forward and struck his fist into his hand in a Blymmedes-like gesture. "We have a superior striking force here. We should use it to shatter the Hun front"—*Hun* was the derisive sobriquet for the Bulgars—"and split their strength. Then we would find that the altogether worthwhile light cavalry tactics suggested by the author of the *Taktika* could be used to surprise, pursue, and annihilate these remnants. But without a crushing frontal assault, the Hun will be like a fist we cannot open." Camytzes smacked his fist again. "With the fist open, we can easily hack the fingers off one by one."

The Emperor looked to Dalassena for a rebuttal. Dalassena paused, weighing his options. He decided that if there was a chance of success for this strategy, he would oppose it; if not, this could be a defeat that would firmly entrench his prudent strategies as well as destroy this absurd myth of Varangian invincibility. "The plan is crudely stated, Majesty, but not without merits in its primitive configuration, as it does combine elements of both the *Taktika* and *Strateghikon.* However, I would like to consult the meteorologist on this matter."

The Emperor signed for the meteorologist to step forward. An elderly man who walked with a stick carved like a serpent, the meteorologist spoke in a breathless, gasping fashion; he had been with the Bulgar-Slayer during his campaigns decades ago. "Rain tonight. Rain early. Rain midday. Rain late day. You will wonder that the forty days and nights have commenced," he concluded, gulping as if he were already submerged by the Biblical Deluge.

"Majesty," said Camyztes, "wet conditions will not favor an attack such as I have described. I believe in this case the author of the *Strateghikon* would caution us to postpone or revise our strategy."

"Majesty," said Dalassena, "we cannot postpone. The dispatches we have received by messenger pigeon from Thessalonica indicate preparations for an assault on the city. Once the Hun is invested in Thessalonica, our problems multiply a hundredfold. The Domestic has proposed an innovative and excellent strategy. He should learn to posit his theories with more conviction. And our dauntless Varangians, who cringe from nothing; surely we insult them with the suggestion that they would retreat before a foe as ephemeral as the rain."

"Hetairarch." The Emperor turned to Mar, who stood just to the side of his throne. "Can you execute this attack in the conditions described?"

Mar bowed. "Majesty, I have consulted with the minsoratores who have surveyed the terrain. I am convinced that the drainage is adequate to permit the Grand Hetairia to advance resolutely and without delay."

"Manglavite?" The Emperor's acute gaze identified Haraldr in the pack of junior officers. Haraldr was still puzzling over Mar's comments about the terrain. Haraldr had also talked to the minsoratores—the army's field surveyors—who had reported difficult footing in the event of rain. And Mar had discounted Haraldr's suggestion about footwear suited to muddy conditions. Still, Haraldr was convinced that his own men, properly shod, could deal with the footing. "Majesty," said Haraldr, "the Middle Hetairia is also prepared to execute this attack."

The Emperor placed his hands on his knees and leaned forward slightly. "Then after suitable preliminaries, our initial assault will be conducted by the Grand and Middle Hetairia." The Emperor paused and looked around the room, his eyes so intense that it seemed as if he were personally addressing each man. "I will take direct command of, and participate in, the Varangian assault."

† † †

Mar looked out over the lights of the Imperial encampment. It was as if a city had grown up in one evening on this empty plain north of Thessalonica. The fizzling, smoking torches and campfires outlined a broad cruciform shape, with the Emperor's brocade-domed tent, a virtual portable palace, at the nexus. Around this orderly city was a ring of pack animals and wagons, dimly visible in the rain, forming a substantial portable wall. Mar stamped his boot in a puddle. The Romans usually frightened off their enemies with this sheer display of material. The Bulgars knew better; they had been under the Roman yoke long enough to have borrowed Roman equipment and tactics. The truth was, a good bit of this display had nothing to do with fighting capacity, but with maintaining the Emperor's ceremonial magnificence out in the field; in many cases, particularly with commanders like Dalassena, the army seemed more intent on protecting the Imperial baggage train than on attacking the enemy. What fools. Two thousand Norsemen, their leader sleeping in his gear bag alongside his men, could best the entire Imperial Taghmata.

Mar looked for a tent on the northern wing of the temporary city's cruciform, in a section allocated to junior officers of the Imperial Hyknatoi. An incredible affront to the Caesar, thought Mar; he had not believed the Emperor capable of such petty animosity and jealousy. But it was just as well, he realized; it would make what he must do that much easier. A single akrites stood outside the tent; apparently the Caesar was not even allowed a mandator to relay orders to him from the senior command.

"Hetairarch!" blurted Michael Kalaphates. The Caesar was, Mar reflected, almost as genuinely surprised and happy as a man learning of his release from the Numera. Odin favors this, Mar told himself. Let the pieces fall as they may.

Michael offered Mar a camp stool and a goblet of poor local wine; they are even begrudging him Imperial-quality drink, thought Mar. "Highness," said Mar, "I know you as a man who understands risks, and who has also seen a good bit of warfare in the bargain. Since our Father for some reason neglected to solicit your opinion on tomorrow's enterprise,

I have taken the initiative—and I hope I am not overly bold in this—of seeking out your advice."

Michael didn't believe the flattery for a moment but realized that it was an auspicious signal. Mar wanted something. At least somebody still had use for him. "I would be happy to help as eminent a warrior as yourself in any way I could, Hetairarch, but I must confess I know vastly more of the risks of wagering on charioteers than I do of the risks of battle. Perhaps I could offer you some other assistance."

Good, thought Mar. *I didn't think Kalaphates was a fool.* "Well, Highness, I did come to discuss a wager of sorts. Perhaps—to use a term familiar in commerce—a speculation." Mar spread out his huge, elegant hands as if displaying the sincerity of what he was about to say, or perhaps his ability to impose whatever he intended to declare, sincere or not. "Let us say that it concerns the price of a certain piece of jewelry." Michael's eyes sparked with interest. "The bauble that I am interested in is presently worthless, because although there was a brief flurry of speculation in this particular piece of jewelry, the prospective buyer—let us call this hypothetical buyer 'uncle'—quite vanished when he discovered himself already in possession of a similar piece, which he had previously thought lost. This is a dreadful circumstance for the owner of this now worthless bauble, for it is virtually all he has of value, and without the income he had expected the sale to bring him, he might not be able to eat. He might even starve to death. So there he is, wandering the streets, alone, destitute, when a friend sees his plight and offers to do him a favor." Mar locked eyes with Kalaphates. "This friend offers to destroy the other piece of jewelry, immediately raising the value of the remaining item beyond reason." Mar continued his manic, glacial, almost mesmerizing stare. "This friend asks scant reward for this incredible benefaction."

"For what scant reward would this friend ask, Hetairarch?" Michael's dark eyes were almost as crazed as Mar's.

Mar stood up, his huge bulk seeming to fill the tent. His voice, in sinister contrast, was a whisper. "Your friend asks that once you receive payment from this 'uncle' for this piece of jewelry and are assured that you will want for nothing for the rest of your life, that you permit your friend to kill this 'uncle' and snatch the bauble back. You keep the money you have been paid for the bauble, and your friend now has the bauble."

Michael looked up at Mar, his voice like a falling feather. "The money, as I see it, is my life. I keep that."

Mar nodded. "The life of, let us envision, a Caesar of Rome, a well-respected, extremely well-protected Caesar, with his own personal treasury financed by a new land tax, an income he can enjoy free from the burden of attending to affairs of state."

Michael's eyes already savored the vision. "And the bauble you receive, Hetairarch, is . . ."

"The diadem, and the attendant office, of the Emperor, Autocrator, and Basileus of the Romans."

† † †

The dawn was unexpectedly luminous, the cloud vault high overhead like pewter, the clean, steady rain almost like a glass that captured and intensified the light. To a hawk soaring high above, the armies of Rome would have seemed a broad, rectangular belt of gold, silver, and scarlet spread out over a dull green plain.

The Emperor spurred his horse to the ranks of his senior aides, who were grouped in front of the standards of the Grand Hetairia and wore the gold-tinted mail shirts and plumed golden helms of the Imperial retinue. The Emperor, armored identically to his officers, differentiated only by his purple boots and cape, directed a command to his principal orderly. "Droungarios, the report of the Mandator General!"

The Mandator General rode forward and bowed; a stout, not particularly military-looking man who always wore a small enamel icon around his neck, he was responsible for the final summary of all intelligence gathered by the akrites whom he supervised, his spies in the enemy camp, and the local peasants. "Majesty, they are encamped roughly according to the Roman practice, though not without critical variation. In lieu of an earthwork perimeter and a cordon of caltrops, they have simply spread stakes. They may also have dug leg-breaking pits. They assume we will pursue a limited engagement today, striking at their flanks with light cavalry. As the ground is quite soggy at the Bulgar front, their deployment there will be light initially. However, the site is suitably graded to allow them to move reinforcements quickly."

The Emperor wheeled his horse and studied the Bulgar line, visible as a jumbled mass of wagons, horses, and mules. Behind this defense, the smoke from the morning campfires rose in thin dark tendrils that blurred, grayed, and merged into a huge foggy column, finally disappearing among the high clouds. It was a strange portent, as if the sky had hung a vast ashen shroud around the Bulgar camp. "Let the priests go among the men," said the Emperor softly. The hundreds of priests began to circulate, the wisps from their smoking censers marking their passage through the ranks, their sonorous chants like a dirge.

When the priests had worked all the way to the rear guard, the Emperor removed his simple gold-and-pearl diadem, handed it to an attendant eunuch; a second eunuch brought him his engraved gold helm on a silk pillow. The Emperor placed the conical helmet on his head. His chest worked in slow heaves. "Grand Domestic," he said evenly, "begin your diversion."

The band signaled the attack with the characteristic blaring of trumpets and pounding of drums and cymbals. "The cross has conquered!" bellowed the units of the Imperial Scholae—five ranks of mounted archers and lancers—as they lurched forward, picked up speed, and began their thundering charge on the Bulgar center. The Scholae quickly reached bowshot of the Bulgar lines and the first volley rose like a dense flock into the air, then abruptly alighted; here, there, a horse went down. The Scholae stampeded the Bulgars' outermost cordon of pack animals and wagons, then veered sharply toward the Bulgar flanks to divert the enemy's attention away from the center they had just left vulnerable. Soon the flanks were heavily engaged; Bulgar standards could be seen moving toward the left and right perimeters of their enormous encampment. After perhaps a quarter hour, hundreds of akrites rode from a small copse just beyond the Bulgar's left flank, directly through the remnants of the Bulgar's mule-and-wagon wall. Puffs of flame appeared as the akrites hurled clay shells filled with liquid fire into the wagons. The fire and smoke drove most of the remaining pack animals away. Visible behind the black pillars of smoke was the vast mass of the Bulgar army.

"Domestic of the Hyknatoi!" shouted the Emperor. The Imperial Hyknatoi charged off as the Scholae had before them. This time many horses and men went down as the charge hit the exposed center of the Bulgar formation. After several volleys of arrows and spears the Hyknatoi retreated to join the flank attacks; in the wake of their assault, wounded and dying horses could be seen kicking the air like toppled clockwork miniatures. A mandator came galloping back toward the Roman ranks, his horse steaming in the cold rain and his face bright red. "Majesty, the flanks are fully engaged."

"Domestic of the Numeri!" Haraldr felt fear, as if awakening to a knife in his ribs. The Numeri were the infantry division of the Taghmata; they would support the Varangian assault once—if the breakthrough was made. "Hetairarch! Manglavite!" Haraldr ordered his men to dismount;

batmen circulated among the ranks of the Middle Hetairia and led the horses to the rear. Haraldr walked to the horses of the Emperor and his aides. Mar, also dismounted, came to his side. His ice-hard eyes already glimmered with Odin's gift.

"Proceed in ranks, Hetairarch." Before Mar could turn and give the order, the Emperor astonished everyone within seeing by arduously dismounting from his towering white Arabian. If he felt pain upon standing, he did not display it; there was only a furious resolution on his powerful features.

"Majesty . . ." uttered the Droungarios helplessly.

"Send my horse for me when our attack has been successful, Droungarios," said the Emperor. "These men fight on foot, and as I am joining them, so will I."

Mar led the Grand Hetairia out in two relatively narrow ranks; the Middle Hetairia followed, also in two ranks of two hundred and fifty men abreast. The Emperor walked alongside Mar, beneath the dragon standard of the Grand Hetairia, his step heavy, purposeful. Fifty paces out of bowshot, Mar turned and shouted "Boar!" The ranks of the Grand Hetairia folded like wings against the Middle Hetairia, creating a layered flesh-and-metal pyramid, with Mar's men on the outside and Haraldr's men forming a compact, solid inner wedge. The Emperor took his place just ahead of Haraldr at the snout of the boar-within-a-boar. Mar stood alone at the apex of the outer boar, his face twitching with fury.

The guttural cries of the Bulgars stilled as the Varangian formation, a huge lethal arrow, pointed directly at their center. It was possible to hear a dying man wail "Theotokos" over and over. The rain fell in large, clear drops. Mar raised his gilded ax. In unison the Varangians slammed their ax blades flat against the hard oak planks of their shields; the sound was like the breathing of some colossal beast. Again, again, mesmerizing, terrifying. The boar advanced to this deadly cadence.

The Bulgar arrows descended in buzzing swarms but largely clattered harmlessly off byrnnies, helms, and shields. Shouts came back to watch for the rows of sharpened stakes, and the wedge rocked and surged as men maneuvered around the crude barriers. Two Varangians in the first rank tumbled into a shallow, concealed pit; one scrambled up but the other screamed as he was impaled on a stake. The Bulgars became individual faces, stubbled chins, red noses, bad teeth.

Mar's oath could be heard, curiously muted, above the almost deafening din. He pounded the canvas-clad infantrymen at the Bulgar front with huge, bludgeoning strokes, so relentlessly that it seemed his foes were ritualistically kneeling before him, except that these supplicants had been anointed with brilliant blood as Mar split their skulls and hacked off their arms. Mar stepped over his writhing, butchered victims, and before he had killed a half dozen men the Bulgars fell back without even offering him resistance, shoving and trampling their own in an effort to escape the Varangian scythe. The rest of the boar followed Mar into the frantic, scrambling Bulgar retreat, moving almost as steadily as it had when unopposed.

In the middle of the boar, Haraldr and his men had little more to do than protect themselves against arrows and step over the grotesque, akimbo corpses, most of them with gaping ax wounds. At first the bodies lay in only a few inches of dark, watery muck, but soon the dead and dying were virtually submerged in the clinging ooze. Both the Varangian advance and the Bulgar retreat slowed inexorably. The hail of arrows and spears became heavy and steady. Now Varangians fell into the mud. The boar stopped. Haraldr stood on a dead man's back and looked ahead. Mar was immobilized in muck up to his knees, crouched behind his shield as the archers and javelin throwers pelted him. Mar's men surged up to protect him, but many of them were forced back by spear-thrusting phalanxes of Bulgar infantry. Haraldr quickly ascertained that the men of the Grand Hetairia, hindered by their clumsy boots, could no longer advance. He relayed the commands back through Ulfr and Halldor: The Middle Hetairia will now move to the front. Haraldr shouted his plan to the Emperor, who fearlessly joined him in slogging to the mired snout.

"I'm taking the snout!" Haraldr yelled in Mar's ear. "When we have passed, your men will have time to take off their boots and can come in behind us." Mar nodded drunkenly. He is deep in the spirit world, Haraldr thought. "Did you hear me!" screamed Haraldr.

"Yes! We will fall in behind!"

Haraldr strapped his ax to his back and unsheathed his sword. The Rage seized him like an angry wolf. He leapt out at a short, stout Bulgar infantryman in a metal-studded leather jerkin and slashed him across his torso, severing an arm and crumpling his chest. The dead man's comrades fell back at the appearance of this new Norse titan, and Haraldr lifted his knees high to keep moving, to keep pressing them. His Varangians stayed tightly behind him. The Bulgars made a brief stand with long spears, but Haraldr and his men fended off the metal-tipped shafts with their shields, then with swords and axes made the Bulgars pay for their resistance.

Haraldr looked back across the corpse-strewn bog to make certain that

Mar's men were following. Alarm swept through him in a nauseating wave. Mar had not advanced a step and clearly had no intention to; he had drawn his men into a tight, circular shield fort. They were waiting for the Numeri to rescue them. In an instant Haraldr knew what had happened, though he probably would be unable to convince anyone who did not share Odin's gift: Mar was deliberately abandoning Haraldr and the men of the Middle Hetairia. *And if Odin gives me another day,* Haraldr vowed, *I will kill him for that betrayal.*

The Valkyrja hovered, preparing to snatch away that day. Bulgar infantry by the many hundreds, the vanguard of thousands, were now trudging into the muck that separated the two Varangian forces, intending to encircle them both. They were armed with long spears and good steel helms and metal-plated canvas byrnnies. Haraldr knew that if his men were stopped and forced to form a shield fort, the Numeri would never reach them. The Middle Hetairia would dwindle to a pile of twitching corpses over a long, desperate afternoon. There was only one escape: to continue relentlessly forward, to the very heart of the Bulgar army, and pierce it with Hunland steel.

Haraldr fought forward with a renewed frenzy and a solid front of Bulgars, spears set, panicked, and ran. Their retreat exposed a muddy little creek running perpendicular to Haraldr's advance. And behind the creek was a wall of wide-eyed, jittery horses, crowded flank to flank, their chests covered with quilted batting. The riders wore mail byrnnies and heavy steel greaves. This was the vaunted Bulgar heavy cavalry.

What had Maria said? The king beyond the creek. But the creek was not safety. In her dream he had died before he reached the creek. As he would here. But if he could cross that creek, could he defeat that fate? He screamed at Ulfr and Halldor. "Those men are not afraid, but their horses are! We must let them know the ax and push beyond the creek!" And for some reason he could not fathom, he added, "The Bulgar Khan is just beyond it!"

The little creek was muddied by the rain, not diamond-faceted as Maria had seen it in her dream, and the water was blood-russet. Haraldr waded in, prayed to Odin to accept these innocent animals as sacrifice, and buried his ax blade into a horse's quilted chest; the scream of the poor dumb beast sickened him. The horse toppled and Haraldr pushed forward to yet another slaughter; as he killed his second horse he realized that his feet were no longer in water. And the men behind him were now able to start coming across the creek.

Their masters brought the horses to what seemed unending slaughter; for a time the sky almost seemed to rain equine blood. Soon the shallow slope rising from the creek was littered with dead beasts and their riders. But Haraldr knew that the torturous ascent was rapidly draining his reserves; the ax was a weapon for short bursts, not this sustained butchery. Haraldr prayed to all the gods that this cavalry was the Khan's last line of defense.

The head-flinging frantic horses retreated. Haraldr looked back and saw most of his men advancing well up the slope. When he looked ahead, he saw the Khan's last defense and knew that he would never see the king beyond the creek. At the top of the rise waited another wall, not terrified animals but huge, fierce-eyed, red-faced men in long mail coats, armed with Hunland steel: the Khan's elite guard. And they were so many, they blocked the horizon.

Haraldr knew that there was nothing left but to take as many of these souls as possible with him to the Valhol. They came forward eagerly, grunting, thrusting spears, hammering at Emma's silky invulnerability; his ribs ached with the blows that had yet to break the links but were breaking him up inside. His men were dying all around him, and in some strange, reflexive requiem he silently tolled their names as they fell: Joli Stefnirson, Kolskeg Helgison; Thorvald Kodranson. A javelin glanced off his neck and he could feel the blood immediately. That was what her dream had promised him, that was the destiny he had seen in her eyes the first night she had drawn him into them.

He was isolated; it seemed that even the final desperate shield-fort had collapsed. His arm seared with every stroke, and yet the furiously cursing metal demons still could not overwhelm him. He had no idea where his men were—Ulfr, Halldor, the Emperor. Was he tolling their names because they, too, had fallen? A blow from behind almost knocked his helm off, and a light flashed before his eyes. He shook his head to clear it but the light still glared. The sun. The sun had burst through the clouds and driven a slender, brilliant shaft into the Bulgar horde just ahead of him. He knew that he must reach it. He hurled himself forward in one last, desperate assault before that light, like Odin's voice, faded beneath the black wings of the last dragon. He sent a jaw flying in a crimson spray. His sword crunched a byrnnie so hard, he could feel the bones shatter beneath the steel skin. He went forward on faith and courage, not knowing why he had to reach the light, and he realized that other men had joined him, the men he had thought lost: first the Emperor, and then Ulfr, and Halldor, and Joli's brother, Hord. He could look back now and see hundreds of his men still with him, still advancing, questing with him for the light. The push from behind was now the blood lust of the Middle Hetairia.

Something fractured in the great body of the Bulgar army. For a moment the Khan's guard hesitated, stunned at the resilience of the bloodied yet still furious beast that had penetrated to the living heart of their great horde, to the last human redoubt of their Khan. And then they gave in to some collective, primal fear. Many dropped their weapons and ran toward the encircling skeins of the Roman cavalry, preferring capture to a less certain fate on the tusks of the beast they could never kill. Some of those too close to the boar to think they could outrun it had simply dropped to their knees to beg for mercy. Among these terrified petitioners was the Bulgar Khan.

Haraldr looked around, wondering. He stood within the shaft of sunlight now, a light reflected off the helms and byrnnies of the Bulgars as they humbled themselves in sun-glazed mud. All around them was a litter of discarded weapons, as if a ghost army had vanished, leaving behind only artifacts borrowed from the living. Far to the left and right, the horsemen of the Scholae, Hyknatoi, and Excubitores could be seen, standards proudly aloft as they herded huge, ragged groups of Bulgar prisoners. Behind the bloody, horribly diminished ranks of the Middle Hetairia were nothing but corpses.

The Emperor stepped in among the kneeling Bulgars. "Alounsianus!" he commanded: the name of the Bulgar Khan. A desperate-looking, medium-sized man, whatever cleverness or courage he had employed to gain his throne utterly blanched from his face, rose up from the mud and clasped his trembling hands in supplication. The tossing clouds closed on the sun and the dimming light flickered over the defeated Khan. Then the clouds roiled aside, the sun exploded in its full radiance, and as he swooned from loss of blood, Haraldr was certain that he was floating up toward a golden dome.

he Prefect of the City and the Logothete of the Symponus waited for the Parakoimomenos of the Imperial Palace beneath the arch of the Golden Gate. The Great Land Wall loomed above them, the invincible ashlar expanse glazed with the morning sun. Attended by his retinue of Imperial cubiculari, gleaming like antimony in his white silk and crowned with his pure silver hair, the Parakoimomenos exchanged nods with the Prefect and the Logothete. "Exquisitely done," said the Parakoimomenos as he looked down the avenue before them. Freshly swept and watered, almost bone-white, the Mese extended east toward the distant Imperial Palace, and as far as one could see, the entire route was a multihued corridor of brilliant hanging carpets and tapestries. A human tide, held back by cursores and Khazars, crushed in on either side of the avenue.

The Parakoimomenos blinked into the ascending sun and gauged that it was time for the long day to begin. "Komes of the walls," he directed, "open the gates." The komes's ceremonially armored assistants cranked open the massive bronze gates and the dignitaries stood aside to let the procession enter the city.

The first rider was seated on a dull-eyed, decrepit donkey. He wore tattered rags, and garlands of pig intestines, swarming with flies, were draped over his shoulders. The rider could not see the spectacle before him because he was seated backward on his transport; he could not see behind, either, because his eyes, crusted with scabs and ooze, had been put out with hot irons. The sightless man raised his head in response to the fantastic gale of obscenities and jeers that greeted him, and the Empress City could now see the hideous, noseless face of the man who had dared assault her. Alounsianus, Khan of Bulgaria, had finally breeched the walls of Rome.

The Bulgar generals followed on foot, then their officers and men, an unending procession of haggard, confused, sullen faces and filthy brown tunics; as the Pantocrator is merciful, most had been spared their eyes and noses. The army of the vanquished, flanked by steel-trimmed Khazars, became a strange, dirt-colored serpent of misery slowly crawling through the brilliant polychrome of the triumphant city.

491

The Parakoimomenos again computed the time as the last of the Bulgars disappeared down the Mese. Incredible. He had had no expectation that so many *barbaroi* wretches had been taken prisoner. He signaled the Logothete of the Symponus, at whose order hundreds of street sweepers descended on the avenue. The newly swept streets were washed again, this time with rose water. Hundreds of laborers spread thick, richly patterned carpets over the perfumed pavement. Dozens more workers hung polycandelons and even ornate candelabra in the street-level arcades. Residents suspended oil lamps and pungently smoking censers from their balconies. Jeweled icons were placed on balustrades or cradled in the arms of their proud owners. The surging crowd of onlookers sprouted ceremonial branches and sprigs of laurel and olive. Then all the lamps were lit, completing the transformation of the entire city-long length of the Mese into a glittering cathedral nave.

Outside the walls, a band blared and the crowd answered with ringing cheers. The Parakoimomenos nodded to the designated cubicularius to bring forward the victory crowns—two simple yet precisely woven laurel wreaths—and the gold-and-pearl bracelet that would also be presented to the Emperor. Extraordinary, thought the Parakoimomenos. The Varangian Haraldr Nordbrikt would receive the second wreath of victory and walk directly behind the Emperor. Of course the Bulgar-Slayer would have approved, but nonetheless it was extraordinary. And the other changes! The Middle Hetairia would march directly behind their Emperor and Manglavite, and the Grand Hetairia would not march at all; they were apparently mopping up remnants of the Bulgar army near Nicopolis. And the rumors that the Grand Domestic would soon be "promoted" to Strategus of Cilicia, and the Domestic of the Excubitores named to replace him. Already the Imperial Chrysobulls appointing the heroes to their new dignities had become a virtual purple-ink deluge in the offices of the Parakoimomenos! Well, the Parakoimomenos reflected, such is the nature of war, to endlessly shuffle the offices and dignities of Imperial Rome.

The Parakoimomenos watched as the *voukaloi* took their positions by the gate; the ceremonial choralers wore black robes, velvet bonnets, and necklaces of fresh roses. He nodded to their leader to prepare himself. Then he walked through the Golden Gate into the shadows of the Great Land Wall and threw himself on his face in the street for the prescribed three prostrations. When he rose, he did not permit himself even to look upon the face of the Pantocrator's glorious Vice Regent on earth. With a trembling hand he gestured that the city awaited its god.

† † †

"Glory to God, who has magnified the light of the Emperor of the Romans!" choraled the *voukaloi*. "Glory to the Holy Trinity for returning our glorious master victorious!" The bell-clear chants echoed as the *voukaloi* repeated them again and again, interweaving the choruses into an intricate, continuous tapestry of sound. As he had been instructed, Haraldr made certain that he remained five paces behind the Emperor. He could already see the multicolored incandescence of the Mese through the shadowed arch of the Golden Gate, and the sight made his knees weak. He remained beneath the arch while the Emperor received the gold arm ring and then stooped slightly to allow the Prefect to place the laurel wreath upon his head. The acclamation of the crowd swept through the arch like a gale. Then the Emperor turned to Haraldr and beckoned him into the light. For a moment Haraldr had to shut his eyes against the glare, and with the thunderous clamor blocking all his other senses, he felt as if he no longer walked the earth but had been swept away by a rushing cyclone.

Haraldr bowed and the Emperor took the second laurel wreath and placed it gently on his head. His hands brought Haraldr erect; his weary eyes—the campaign and its final brutal assault had certainly taken their toll—glowed with profound gratitude. Then the Emperor stepped forward and led Haraldr into a whirlwind of glory such as only Rome could bestow.

The storm raged for hours, from the Forum of Arcadius to the Forum Bovis to the Forae of Taurus and Constantine, then the Augustaion, and into the Hagia Sophia for a reception by the Patriarch. Neither the tempest of acclaim nor the blizzard of strewn petals ever abated. Behind the Emperor and Haraldr, the Middle Hetairia and the Imperial Taghmata received the same joyous reception.

After leaving the Hagia Sophia the procession stopped in front of the Chalke Gate and the Emperor ascended to a golden throne that had been set up in the open square. The *voukaloi* were now accompanied by the pulsing notes of a golden organ; the ponderous sound machine rose like a small building beside the throne. When the music stopped, the crowd hushed magically leaving a ringing silence in the ears. The Emperor described the campaign in great detail and enumerated the spoils of victory. At prescribed intervals the crowd burst out in ritual acclamations. Then the Emperor turned to Haraldr and began to emphasize the valor of the Varangians of the Middle Hetairia and their Manglavite. "This man saved Rome," concluded the Emperor, eliciting a whooshing, wavelike oath from the crowd. Haraldr looked out at the glittering avenue filled with rapt faces and saw the funeral pyres of the one hundred and forty-three pledge-men of the Middle Hetairia who now wassailed at the benches in the Valhol. He prayed to Odin to give them this vision of the victory they had earned. And he promised them that when Mar returned to the Empress City, they would be avenged.

The final act of the extended drama was played in the Hippodrome. The Emperor was allowed to refresh himself in his apartments beforehand, and then he joined Haraldr and his retinue to climb the marble staircase to the Imperial Box. While the dignitaries prepared for his entrance the Emperor took Haraldr aside. It was not the first time they had talked privately; after the battle they had discussed the engagement as one warrior to another, and they had relived that fragile, immortal instant when the conjoined wills of just two men had somehow broken the collective will of the Bulgar army. In spite of, or perhaps because of, this day's apotheosis, the Emperor seemed even more human than he had in that earlier interview. "It is often said that it is less fatiguing to win victory on the field than it is to celebrate that victory in Constantinople," he told Haraldr softly, with a wistful little smile. Then two Patricians appeared, to escort him into the Imperial Box.

Haraldr followed and looked out on the scores of thousands of people who filled the stadium. The elongated oval race path was completely obscured by the Bulgar prisoners, who stood mute and motionless within a ring of Khazars. Amid this beaten mob emerged the ancient columns and obelisks and statues set upon the stadium's central *spina:* a great bronze bull; a beautiful woman said to be the Helen of the *Iliad;* a naked Aphrodite and an armored Ares; grotesque demons and a soaring bronze column formed of three twined serpents.

The Hippodrome was silent. The Emperor made the sign of the cross three times. He nodded at the request of the Parakoimomenos, and the *voukaloi* stood and chanted the Roman hymn of victory: "Let us sing to the Eternal God most high, for Pharaoh's chariots he hath cast in the sea ..." When the singing had been concluded, the stadium fell silent again. The Bulgar Khan Alounsianus was brought into the box and the swarthy Logothete of the Dromus threw the vanquished ruler down on the Imperial Dais and pressed his mutilated face against the gold-embroidered purple Imperial boots. The Emperor stood, his face to the crowd, and placed first one boot and then the gilded tip of a ceremonial spear against the Khan's neck. Down on the floor of the Hippodrome, the Khazars shoved the rest of the Bulgars into the sand, forcing them to emulate their Khan. The crowd reacted with manic, earsplitting glee. Haraldr saw in the sad eyes of the Emperor little taste for this ritual humiliation, demanded by ages-old protocol and the psychic needs of a frightened populace.

Haraldr thought again of how only a single step had separated these two men, the triumphant victor and the mutilated vanquished. He realized that if he had halted at that moment, when it had seemed that all that was left was to die well, then the Khan would be standing here now, displaying to the captive populace of Rome the head of their Emperor. What had pushed him on when even Odin had wearied of his fate? Perhaps Maria, and yet perhaps she had only been an agent of some greater fate, a destiny so profound that even Norway was only a part of it, a destiny that now encompassed all Rome, perhaps the entire world-orb. But even as saw the huge dimensions of that fate and felt himself drawn toward its whirling vortex, his soul was chilled with an equally profound foreboding.

Haraldr looked across the stadium, oblivious to the leaping, chorusing mob in the seats, and watched the setting sun spill over the roofs of the great city like a golden lacquer. The dust stirred by the groveling Bulgars rose in a faint fog to cast an eerie, apocalyptic dusk over the proceedings. Destiny whispered to him in that haunted twilight, an ineffable confusion of riddles and replies. *The gods commanded me to save Rome that day,* thought Haraldr. *Will they perhaps one day ask me to destroy Rome? Today I vow to serve this Emperor well. Yet why does my soul tell me that there will come a day when I will throw the sightless face of a Roman Emperor into the dust?*

† † †

Giorgios Maleinus considered himself quite gifted at his profession. A tall man who suffered from a rheumatism of the joints that was making him progressively shorter as he neared his sixth decade, he drank too much and had few illusions about his social standing in the city; he knew he'd never even be permitted to buy an exarch's diploma, and for that matter he didn't give a phony saint's splinter whether he ever got to stand in the same room as the Emperor or not. The fact that he was, at this moment, in a room face-to-face with the Emperor's brother proved how much all those cooked-up titles were worth. Yes, the swellheads at court came and went, but Giorgios Maleinus was always in business: the business of buying cheap and selling dear.

"Eminence," said Maleinus, his inflection deceptively rustic, "I would like to invite you as my guest to see the property. Make your own judgment of the facilities. When you compare what you see to the price I am asking, you will consider yourself Fortune's favorite."

Fortune's favorite, thought Constantine bitterly. The Emperor's miraculous recovery was Fortune's boot in the ass. His poor nephew the Caesar was in virtual exile, denied even the privilege of entering the palace. It wasn't fair, either; perhaps the Caesar hadn't been a hero in the Bulgarian campaign, but no one had given him the chance to be.

"Excuse me, Eminence," said Maleinus, rubbing at his swollen red nose with his stiff fingers, "but would you like to see the property?"

"Ah, quite. Tell me why this superlative establishment is offered at the price one might expect to pay for a rocky hillside and a wooden chapel?"

"Well, Eminence, you're not a man to toy with, that is certain, so I will give you the truth in the sight of the Pantocrator. The monastery on the Isle of Prote once enjoyed a generous typicon drafted under the Bulgar-Slayer, may the Pantocrator keep his soul, and it grew surpassingly wealthy, some say under the patronage of someone in the Bulgar-Slayer's family; they don't say who. Apparently the patron died and the typicon was not renewed. Now, just so you can't say Giorgios Maleinus concealed the entire truth from you, the reason the typicon wasn't renewed is because there was a bit of scandal out there."

"Really?" said Constantine, faintly interested. At least some outrageous rumor would enliven this dirt merchant's pedestrian presentation. Constantine looked out the window of the virtually nonfunctional office he had been so generously granted in the palace complex—the view was of the blank south wall of the Numera—and longed for Antioch.

"Yes, Eminence. It seems that the Chartophylax of this monastery, an ancient fellow, got it into his head that the Brother Abbot of the establishment was actually a demon. They say this old book-buzzard murdered the Brother Abbot and fled to Cappadocia. I think the sin of Sodom was about the place, and that was the cause of the trouble. But whatever, the Emperor wouldn't renew the typicon, and the establishment was out of business. But I'll tell you, Eminence, though the monks have been gone for four or five years, the establishment is a jewel in the diadem of the Pantocrator, so to speak. You'd just have to clear out the bird's nests and you would be back in business."

"So why hasn't someone already bought it for this 'immorally scant' price you have mentioned, arranged for a new typicon, and reaped the bounty of Prote? Surely anyone with even minor influence at court could obtain a new charter."

"That's the trouble, Eminence, and why I see yourself as a prospective purchaser of unusual qualities. It seems that your brother, the esteemed Orphanotrophus Joannes, has mandated that under no circumstances may a new typicon be drafted for the monastery at Prote. I thought that with you being cut from the same bolt, so to speak . . ."

"Indeed." Constantine hoped his flushed forehead would not bead so quickly as to betray his sudden fascination with the monastery at Prote. "Well, sir, you are a most persuasive orator. I can hardly see what harm could come from sailing out to view this establishment, particularly since we are enjoying fair weather."

he Emperor indicated to his chamberlain that he would speak informally with the visitor, and the white-robed eunuch backed away like a statue on wheels. Mar was invited to approach the immense, purple-canopied golden throne. The Emperor had resumed his daily audiences in the Chrysotriklinos, the main throne room for nondiplomatic receptions, and he presided beneath the exact epicenter of a huge golden cupola supported by eight regularly spaced apses; a ring of silver candelabra wreathed the dome with light. The day's business had run well into the night.

"Hetairarch." The Emperor's voice betrayed no weariness of his resumed duties. He assumed his usual perfectly erect posture, his hands resting flat on his thighs. His eyes were as hard as the gems of his diadem. "You are well?"

"Yes, Majesty." Mar wore no uniform or badges of his office, only a dark wool cape with a cowl he had been ordered to keep over his head. He had been brought from Paristron in a curtained carriage and had been escorted to the Chrysotriklinos as soon as he had arrived in the city.

"I have learned that you have completed your assignment in Paristron with industry and thoroughness. My children, particularly those of the Paristron theme who were displaced from their homes, are grateful to you, and in the name of the Pantocrator I thank you for them."

Mar bowed. "Majesty."

The Emperor flexed his fingers and propped his hands lightly on his thighs. "I have been considering your next assignment, Hetairarch. In your absence I have reflected upon the performance of the Grand Hetairia in the battle in which we were victorious over the Bulgars. I have concluded that your contribution, both personally and as commander of the Grand Hetairia, was short of the standards expected of a unit commended not only with the protection of Rome's Autocrator, but with the preservation of the glorious history and legacy of the Grand Hetairia." The Emperor leaned forward slightly and stared intensely at Mar, as if looking for something behind his glassy eyes. "There are those around me who suggest that the actions of the Grand Hetairia, and principally

498

the Hetairarch, were either treason or cowardice, or both. The man who led us to victory that day, your fellow Tauro-Scythian Haraldr Nordbrikt, is particularly suspicious. Having experienced that battle myself, and having seen the very real difficulty you and your men were in, I think Haraldr Nordbrikt's interpretation of your actions, while understandable, has been inflected by the loss of life of his men and the emotions of that day. But since I do understand the feelings of Haraldr Nordbrikt, and since I can hardly afford to have my Varangians fall on one another to settle this matter among themselves, I have made certain that you and Haraldr Nordbrikt have been separated so far, and I intend to continue that separation. Hence your assignment in Paristron, and the secrecy with which you have been brought here. Perhaps at a time when our borders are more secure, I will permit Haraldr Nordbrikt to discuss your actions with you personally. But for the moment I need you both in my service.''

The Emperor allowed his hands to settle slightly. ''Hetairarch, I know, as perhaps no other man does, that you are an officer who has served me well and faithfully through many campaigns, and who until this regrettable incident has had to apologize to no one for his courage or his loyalty. But you are also an officer who has let his performance erode to the point where comment has been occasioned. As I am certain you understand, such comment cannot be permitted of the Emperor's personal guard, for it invites active, indeed armed speculation that could be fatal not only to the Regent of Rome but also to the Empire itself. Accordingly, I have determined to relieve you of your office of Hetairarch, and to transfer you and your men to Italia. Henceforth your title will be Droungarios of the Catapanate of Italia. This new position, as you know, is a significant responsibility.'' In fact, the situation in Italia was critical, and the Emperor considered the dispatch of the suspect Mar a necessary gamble; right now the province was as good as lost to the Saracens, and any treachery of Mar's could hardly make the situation worse. And perhaps Mar would redeem himself. The Emperor regretted that Haraldr Nordbrikt would not have his vengeance as soon he had hoped, but the Emperor regretted many of the things this office had forced him to do. ''I intend that you interpret this appointment as an expression of my confidence that you will regain the discipline and effectiveness that have served your Emperor, and the Roman Empire, so well in the past.''

The Emperor made the sign of the cross, the indication that the audience had ended. Mar crossed his arms over his breast and retreated from the colossal throne. The deposed Hetairarch, concealed within a ring of Khazar guards, was escorted through the silver doors and ushered to the curtained carriage waiting beside the porch of the Chrysotriklinos. Before he was sealed inside, Mar took a final look at the black, light-rimmed Bosporus. The torches of his escort cast an orange reflection in his brooding irises, and for a moment it seemed that Mar was gazing out on a sea of fire.

† † †

"Hetairarch Haraldr, may I fill your goblet," said the wife of the Magister whose name Haraldr had not remembered. She fluttered lashes as thick as bowstrings and revealed her fleshy bosom as she filled her own gold cup from a stream of amber-tinted wine flowing from the lips of a bronze ram.

The tribute fame demands, thought Haraldr. He smiled politely and accepted. Above him, the gilded, intricately perforated cone of the Mystic Fountain of the Triconchus rose like a golden cypress; amber-hued wine gurgled from within the elaborate fountain and collected in the bronze pool at the base, then was spouted to the guests via the mouths of various bronze beasts. Plates full of nuts, pastries, and fruits surrounded the wine spouts, and marble steps descended to an open plaza crowded with the elite of the Imperial Court: Magisters, Patricians, Proconsular Patricians, Senators. The wives were deployed in force, for these open-air receptions readily encouraged the informal mixing of the sexes.

"Hetairach!" importuned the Logothete of the Dromus, his ragged rodent's teeth showing. "You must come to my offices and furnish me with the most current information on Bulgar infantry tactics. I need to know which of their weapons are most effective, from whence they are obtaining them, that sort of thing. Perhaps we can inhibit the trade in these materials." The Logothete peered into Haraldr's chased golden goblet. "Discard that common stuff, Hetairarch. Let me introduce you to a vintage from Italia." The Logothete pointed to a cubicularius standing near a larger-than-lifesize water-spouting bronze lion.

The eunuch tipped his silver ewer and poured Haraldr a goblet of ruby-colored wine. The Logothete looked up at the new Hetairarch with the dark eyes of Asia. "I believe there is some misunderstanding between you and the Orphanotrophus Joannes."

"No. The Orphanotrophus and I understand each other entirely." Haraldr silently reflected on that understanding. He had decided that he would wait and see if the Emperor was as courageous when seated on his throne as he was when slogging over Bulgar corpses, and if so, give him an opportunity to deal with his brother Joannes's crimes. But this delay did not concern him, because he realized he already had Joannes on the rack, just like one of Joannes's own victims in the Neorion. And until the Emperor—or, if necessary, Haraldr himself—meted Joannes the ultimate justice he deserved, Haraldr would force Joannes, in his own fashion, to praise the Pantocrator.

The Logothete licked his lips. "I would like to mediate your differences. As a servant of Rome, I am concerned with reducing fissures at the level of government you now occupy. And I believe that the Orphanotrophus currently finds himself in a posture that would encourage him to forge alliances on terms quite favorable to his newly won friends."

Haraldr drained his cup and handed it to the hovering eunuch. "Thank you, Logothete. The wine was excellent. At some time I should like you to advise me on how I can import this vintage. You may tell the Orphanotrophus that I have received his . . . invitation and am considering a reply."

Haraldr walked back past the Mystic Fountain; he was detained by the greetings of a half dozen dignitaries along the way. He looked enviously at a gull soaring in the lapis-lazuli sky and wished he could enjoy the beauty of this day and setting without the grasping company of the elite among Rome's elite, who merely seemed to increase in avarice, insincerity, and dissimilitude the higher they rose in their multihued hierarchy. Even the women seemed to have lost the joy of flirtation and approached their prospective liaisons with the grim intensity of grizzled field commanders. Of course, there was a battle to be won on that field as well, Haraldr reminded himself.

"Hetairarch." The wife of the Senator and Proconsular Patrician Romanus Scylitzes ambushed Haraldr in front of the gleaming silver door of the Triconchus, the domed palace that faced the Mystic Fountain on the east. She was blond, elegant, with small, perfect Grecian features and a beauty curiously enhanced by the evidence, found in small creases about her eyes and lips, that it had recently begun to fade. Her husband was the most notorious windbag at court, reviled by even the pompous Hellenes, with whom he affected intellectual kinship. "You will think me silly when I tell you my husband is watching us." Haraldr looked around and located the vigilant husband. The white-haired Senator and Proconsular Patrician, surrounded by his posturing cronies in the Attalietes Dhynatoi clique, was indeed conducting a clumsy clandestine surveillance; each time he sipped from his cup his eyes darted over the rim of the goblet and allowed him a glimpse of his wife. "Please do not think that I presume," she stammered, her cheeks flushed in vivid contrast to the high, pearl-studded white collar of her scaramangium. "He is watching to see if I do as I am told. He wants me to thank you profusely for stemming the tide of the Bulgar advance—I'm sorry that I cannot quite remember the phrase that compared your feats to those of Alexander— but I am to thank you because our own estates in Thessalonica theme were spared a great loss by your bravery."

"Tell him I accept his gratitude and am greatly pleased by the emissary he has sent to express it." Haraldr understood now; the Emperor had granted Haraldr one third of the tax revenues from Paristron, Macedonia, and Thessalonica for the next five years, and apparently the land magnate Scylitzes was hoping for some kind of reduction in the amounts his estates owed. "However, I cannot intervene in the matter of his taxes, which I understand have already been reduced by various connivances."

Scylitzes's wife almost purpled with shame, and Haraldr was sickened by the imminence of her tears. "I am sorry," he said. "You were only performing your filial duty. I should have been more gracious."

"No," she said, shaking her head and appearing to gain control of herself. "It is we who should be shamed. He would not approach you on this issue because he would never deign to speak personally to a—" She blushed again.

"*Barbaroi,*" offered Haraldr. He watched the insufferable Scylitzes spew forth his putative eloquence in accompaniment to the spouting of the fountain. "So with all those words at his avail, he must send his wife to speak for him. I appreciate your liberality in delivering his request."

"He . . . he says I should offer myself to you if necessary."

"Would you?"

"You would not accept."

"I would accept your offer. I simply would not agree to reduce his taxes, because I could not in fairness accept so much from him and give back so little in return."

The woman smiled at the flattering reprieve from both her husband's demands and the prospect of having this giant rip her in two, although she now wondered if the *barbaroi*'s tongue was capable of other subtleties. "You are a kind man, Hetairarch," she said, bowing slightly as she returned to her flatulent spouse.

For a *barbaroi*, Haraldr told himself, completing her thought. He was about to find some excuse to make to the Parakoimomenos when he noticed that even Scylitzes had been rendered momentarily speechless. He walked around to the fountain to see what marvel had occasioned this miracle. Maria. He watched her emerge from the ambulatory surrounding the Sigma. She did not wear her usual revealing costume but instead had donned a white scaramangium and pallium in spite of the heat. Still, there was the same sensual, graceful insouciance in her walk that arrested both men and women. Haraldr watched the eyes of the dignitaries as they studied her, and he realized that Maria was considered, much like him, an exotic, undeniably puissant force but also dangerous and unsavory. Because of her openness and candor, she had come to represent all the secret schemings and scandals locked in their own far less honest breasts.

She saw him and came directly for him, her face glowing and her fierce blue eyes wet. She held out her hands but did not embrace him. "I will not burden you with my questionable repute among these august personages," she said, smiling radiantly but with the tears now rolling off her lashes. Haraldr wanted to hold her but reasoned that she knew the manners of this court far better than he.

"I am sorry I have not been able to see you," Haraldr said. "This new office requires all my time. I am fortunate to be able to enjoy—if that is the word—even a quasi-official function such as this. But of course you are always with me. You were with me there."

She shook her head and the tears ran down her cheeks. "I am so glad you are alive. Just knowing that has made each day a joy."

"Do you know that you saved my life?"

"But I didn't," she said happily. "You went in spite of my warning, and yet you are alive." She looked up at him as if beholding the miracle of his resurrection. "My dreams are meaningless." She said this with such great happiness and relief that Haraldr decided not to tell her about the creek, and the king who had waited beyond it.

"You saved me because your soul helped me forward when there was nothing else," he improvised, a distortion that was less profound than the truth.

"You do not have to say that," she said. "What you told me before you left was enough." Suddenly her eyes doubted.

"That was true," he told her, "and still is. Why, in fact, I survived out there I do not yet know for certain. But you were indeed with me then."

"Yes. That has the resonance of truth," she said, drawing herself up and projecting her breast with wry self-confidence. She seemed very girlish and keen, perhaps more like Anna. "Since you have been gone, I have spent much of my time listening for the truth."

"And what have you heard?"

"A great deal."

"Will you tell me?"

Her eyes were utterly clear and guileless, like a completely still fjord. "I want to very much. You are the reason I have begun to hear these things, or if not hear them for the first time, at least begin to listen to them." She smiled at him and shaded her marble-hued forehead against the sun. "One thing I know is that I have always put the act of love—or perhaps in my case, act of hate—before the idea of love. What you said about flesh coming between our hearts is true. You know the love I have here"—she patted her abdomen with both hands—"but I want you to feel the love I have here." She touched her fingers to her breast. "And for all my . . . experience with the other love, I do not know much of this"—she pressed her fingers against her heart—"love."

Haraldr was so deeply touched, he doubted that his own sincerity was equal to hers. "Perhaps I am no specialist in this"—he touched his heart—"love, either."

"I believe it is a study that takes time. Its truths are not arrived at in a night of hot, wet embrace." She smiled deliciously but wistfully, as if remembering a pleasure she would not taste again. "Our passion was something grand and glorious, but it was a tower that rose too high on a foundation of air. Can we tear it down and begin again, and this time build something solid, even if less brilliant and overwhelming to the senses? Something we can live in?"

Haraldr still could not trust her—or himself—but she offered something that was far more rare than gold, or even Imperial diadems in Rome. Simple friendship, with the prospect of real love. And perhaps— he had wondered at her choice of phrase—they could build a roof beneath which they could live, perhaps together. "I want to try," he told her. "Not as your bedmate, or even as some silly, innocent gallant. You to me, like I am with Halldor and Ulfr. Besides, I am totally occupied with the responsibilities of Hetairarch."

"I know," she said, her face radiant. "When you are free for a moment, have a message delivered to me. I will meet you here, or in one of the gardens. We will be afforded only the time and privacy to talk."

"Agreed," said Haraldr, his golden face beaming at her. "Let us clasp arms in the manner of comrades." He clutched her lithe forearms in his huge grip and laughed. "I will consult with you at my earliest conceivable convenience, esteemed Eminence."

She bowed and smirked. "Verily, your Hetairarchship, it will be an overawing honor surpassed only by the appearance of the glorious Panto-crator Himself at my morning ablutions." They looked at each other and enjoyed their spoof of court flummery for a moment. Then Maria bowed and turned to leave. After a few steps she turned and said, "I am so glad you are alive," before waving farewell and skipping off among the gawking dignitaries.

† † †

"Uncle!" whined Michael Kalaphates. "How can you run off on this . . . this excursion at this time!" Michael swooped his dice off the ivory tabletop and bolted to his feet as if the Bulgars were at the door. "You are all that stands between me and a life of ascetic contemplation!" Michael swept his hand at the lavish trappings of his hall; the silk tapestries from Persia, the silver candelabra, the gilded chairs. "Pity me, Uncle! If I can scarcely endure the life of contemplation I lead in this palace, can you imagine me in a monk's cell? Uncle! You are all I have!"

Constantine threw his arms around the trembling Caesar. "Nephew, nephew, you know you are quite capable of fending for yourself."

"I am extremely anxious, Uncle," said Michael; he smoothed his silk robe as if in eliminating the wrinkles he was exerting control over himself. "Now I am not even admitted to the palace. I tried three times last week." Michael clutched the dice in his balled fist. "It is all so plain. Remove me from the public view, and when everyone has quite forgotten I exist, tie me up some night and carry me off to Mt. Athos. That is the plan, Uncle."

"I assure you that I won't permit that," said Constantine. "I may be of little consequence to our Emperor and the Orphanotrophus, but my blood flows in their veins and I can vouchsafe that I will remind them of that if they move you one stade from this house. I was Strategus of Antioch! They seem to forget that I am a man of ability!"

"I know you are a man of ability, Uncle, as well as my dearest relative and most cherished friend. That is why the thought of your leaving for even two days quite unravels me."

Constantine clasped Michael's shoulders. "We need to find a weapon to use against them. I have been sitting in that jail next to the Numera for two months to try to stumble over something. Nothing. Until this Maleinus individual appeared. I am not particularly given to the notion that the Pantocrator personally prepares our agenda for each day, but I must confess to the singular intimation that the Hand of Providence is guiding me—and you as well, Nephew—toward the Holy Establishment at Prote.

"Of course you are right, Uncle. I only wish I was not subjected to this confinement. Together we could have made a pleasant excursion of it. I'd wager this Maleinus is fond of dice and horses. When will you go?"

"The sooner the better, Nephew. I will be back in three days."

Michael nodded. "Bless you, Uncle. If I survive to tell this tale, I will reward you in any way I can."

Constantine and Michael embraced. The Caesar escorted his uncle to the door and watched him ride off, through the ring of Khazar guards and down the broad paved road, until he passed from sight behind a cypress grove. Michael turned and reentered his antechamber, then stopped to stare at the mosaic on the wall to his right, a lifelike depiction of an eagle devouring a snake. His face began to crimson deeply. Suddenly he threw his dice at the picture so savagely that the ivory cubes and ceramic tesserae exploded into shards and dust.

"Monastery!" Michael shrieked, his neck corded and every vein in his face seeming to stand out. He raised his head, his throat gurgling slightly, toward the gold-coffered ceiling. "This is not what you promised me, sir!" he shouted in vicious, spitting syllables. "This is not at all what you promised! Do you recall the conversation we had that day, sir? You stood beside me. Your hand was in mine. You made me tell you my secrets while all of them were watching. Do you remember I told you how I could see the music floating in the dome, and how I much I wanted to touch myself, and how my father wouldn't let me? And you told me that your father had never fouled his mother?" He screamed madly again. "You told me I could make them all pay for what they did to me! It was your idea, and now you have abandoned me to them! You are going to let them take me to a monastery!" Michael quieted, but his neck stiffened and his head jerked up as if he had been pulled by his ears. "What? What?" he said softly. He lowered his head slightly. "Very well," he said, seemingly half to himself, half to his unseen conversant. "But remember that I am not a patient man."

† † †

"Soon we will have the torpid heat." The Empress Zoe ran her finger along the surface of the silver wine cask, tracing the engraved outline of a dancing nymph in the finely beaded condensation. "Does the heat make you long for Thule, Hetairarch Haraldr?"

"I think of home often. The heat is not relative to the issue." Haraldr had dreaded this interview, and yet he would have requested an audience with her had she not requested to see him. The matter had to be settled.

"Yes," said Zoe. She leaned back against the cushions of her sitting couch. A gust of dry, warm wind swept through her arcaded balcony, and she blinked her gold-thread lashes. "I have often felt that there is a claim on you." She waved her hand, and her delicate fingers seemed to stroke the thick, fragrant air. "Not merely the kind of claim that one heart places on another but the claim a land makes on its people. Or perhaps the claim a land makes on the man who would rule over her."

Haraldr stiffened and drew his torso erect; he had been uncomfortable when she had asked him to take a couch opposite hers, and now he wished he had remained standing. She was certainly only guessing—this business of the prince who had come with the Rus fleet was still about, albeit now a vague, virtually forgotten rumor. But Haraldr had hoped he would never hear it again.

"Maria says you came from an important family in Thule," continued Zoe in a slow, deep timbre. "Do you aspire to rule over your home someday?"

Haraldr decided that she was not setting a trap, that in fact this was her way of pointing to the snare in which they were both caught. "Yes. I have thought of ruling someday. In Norway, my home. It is now my fancy. But then I once, for a moment of madness, fancied myself ruler of Rome. And in that intoxication I dreamed that I took Rome in my arms." Haraldr inhaled silently and held the breath.

Zoe's eyes blinked and closed. "I understand your vision. I saw it once too. It was a dream, exquisitely beautiful, as dreams often are." She paused and stroked her forehead lightly, as if brushing away a gnat. "My husband awakened me from this dream."

Haraldr's heart thudded. "Yes, I believe that I was awakened in a similar fashion and saw that I had dreamed."

Zoe's finger traced over the engraved silver nymph again. "The beauty of dreams is that life does not hold us accountable for them."

Haraldr eased backward, the relief surrounding him like an eddy of the warm breeze. "And life can never entirely destroy the beauty of a dream." In his gratitude he felt a residue of the passion that had joined them once.

"The beauty, no. The substance, yes. Life so often destroys the substance of dreams, and yet so often provides us with new dreams. New beauties." Zoe sat erect and propped herself up with a silk-sheathed elbow. Her blue eyes had a diamond-like glimmer. "I have already thanked you in the name of Rome and the purple-born Empress for the lives of my people and the safety of our Empire. But you also know me as a woman, Hetairarch." Zoe's full crimson lips curled with the merest hint of salacious irony. "And I have not thanked you as a woman for saving the life of my husband."

"He saved my life as much as I saved his, Majesty."

Zoe nodded. "Yes. Like Achilleus, he has taken up his sword again, clad in the armor of the gods." Zoe stared as raptly as if the Emperor stood before her in his golden breastplate. "He will come to me, Hetairarch Haraldr. I have beseeched the Virgin with my prayers. Now that he is well, he will come to me."

Haraldr sincerely hoped that Zoe would find this dream fulfilled. "Yes. He is a proud man, and justly so, and he did not want you to see him reduced by his illness. But I can assure you that his health grows more robust with each day. When he is the man you remember, then you will have him again."

"You are a gracious man, Hetairarch." Zoe eased back against the silk cushions. "You made love to me, and yet you do not begrudge me the resurrection of my love. So in kind I will not begrudge you the restoration of your love." Zoe leaned forward and looked at Haraldr earnestly. "Maria says that you two have conversed."

"Yes. We are starting to know each other."

"That will not be easy for you, Hetairarch. I have known Maria all her life, and yet she remains one of the great mysteries of my life. For all her beauty and . . . spontaneity, she has an ancient soul, profound and perhaps unfathomable. I do not know the depths of it." Zoe smiled warmly and the small wrinkles at the corners of her eyes became visible. "When she was a small child, my sister and I took her to summer at Botanci, on the sea. It seemed to us that she stared at the sea for weeks, nothing but that. And yet she seemed so happy to be alone, as if she had a secret child's friend, a nymph who came up from the water when we were not looking. Finally we asked her who was out there. I remember her words so clearly because they were too sad for any child to speak. 'Everyone,' she answered us. 'The world will end in fire. I want to remember the time when there was only water.' "

Haraldr tried to see Maria as a child and wondered if even then, as she sat before the sea that had watched her grow and would see her wither and turn to dust, if even then she was moving toward him, and he to her. "She has told me that you were her parents' friend. Were they worthy people?"

Zoe's eyes were distant, as if she now sat beside that little girl and also stared into eternity. "They were the best of people. There were none more . . . worthy. They loved her more than . . ." Zoe's lips quivered.

"How they loved her. Perhaps they would also have seen into her weary, tender breast and understood her. The rest of us can only love her."

"I want to love her and understand her."

"Yes." Zoe's eyes were flat again, unmoved. "Do you want to take her to this Norway when you return?"

"I don't know. It doesn't follow that what a man plants in a summer meadow he can reap beneath the winter ice."

Zoe laughed, a silvery chime that was pleasant despite its melancholy. "How apt, Hetairarch Haraldr. I am glad you have come to us from Norway. Well, we must enjoy this summer, for it may be the most beautiful we will ever remember." She pressed her hand flat against the cold silver cask and looked at him and smiled.

here you see it, Eminence!" Giorgios Maleinus shouted into the southerly bluster. The reefed sail of the small galley clattered the yardarm above him; sixteen crewmen, scruffy laborers who could scarcely row in unison, bent to and fro at the oars. "Prote! East to Eden, south to Prote, I say! Glorious, is it not, Eminence?"

Constantine thanked the Pantocrator that He had not brought him to the Isle of Prote to acquire a monastery. The island was small, rocky, graced only with a verdant, wooded spine like a green cap on a bald man's head. Even if the entire Imperial Palace had been placed somewhere behind those groves, the price Maleinus was asking would carry a loss. The island could not support any kind of profitable husbandry, not even a herd of goats or a single winepress, not to mention the vast acreage of arable land required to make a monastic establishment truly profitable. *If I actually had intent to buy,* mused Constantine, *I would at this juncture wring Maleinus's neck.*

The jetty on the northern end of the island was formed from large rocks, obviously stripped from the island's own craggy flanks and tumbled into the sea. The galley tied up at a wooden wharf, still in good repair. "My lady." Maleinus gestured gallantly to his "cousin," Irene, an ample-breasted woman with proportionately substantial hips and, observed Constantine, enough paint on her sagging face to decorate an Imperial galley. Constantine gratefully reflected that he was not one of those eunuchs troubled by such desires; Maleinus's inducement would perhaps be put to better use by promising her to this crew of cutthroats to ensure they didn't make off with the galley in their master's absence.

The stairs, neatly hewn in raw rock, led to a completely disused complex consisting of a small stone chapel and a row of uninhabitable—at least by any civilized standards—cells. "It appears that one would have to do more than shoo away the birds, Maleinus," said Constantine sourly; what could he possibly discover in this miserable wreck?

"No, no, Eminence," protested Maleinus, his face as red as his nose, his lips gulping like a fish as he gasped from the effort of propelling the considerable Irene up the steps. "This . . . this . . . is merely the convent!

It does not even figure in the price. Hasn't been used for two indictions, if that. No, Eminence, you have not seen the wonders of Prote."

Constantine walked over to one of the cells and kicked at the door. The decaying planks fractured, and one could hear the scratchy, alarmed rustle of small, unseen creatures. "It's a ghastly place," said Irene in the struggling chirp of a large bird with a small voice. "To think of the nuns, all closeted away in here." To think of you, Irene, thought Constantine, walking the streets of the Venetian Quarter.

"Well, as I understand, this was once the home to some relative of the Bulgar-Slayer."

"Indeed." Constantine felt the Pantocrator's hand lift his sagging spirits. "Which relative?"

"Well, most likely a woman, Eminence!" Maleinus laughed wetly at his own jest, ending in a hacking cough. "Other than that, well, Eminence, you know how rumor dodges our efforts to grasp her and get a good feel of her." He winked at Constantine and then at Irene.

The birds fled in noisy regiments as the intruders crossed the forested ridge atop the island. Constantine immediately noted the architectural detailing when the monastery complex revealed itself between neatly arranged rows of cypress trees: the multiple domes of the chapel set on elaborately patterned cornices; deeply recessed arched windows divided with slender marble columns; carved window panels even in the rows of monk's cells visible just above the thick defensive wall. Theotokos, exclaimed Constantine to himself. Someone with a great deal to atone for, and a great deal to atone with, had been the benefactor of Prote.

That conjecture was amply supported as Maleinus proudly displayed his merchandise: the chapel with its silver chancel screen and superbly executed mosaics; a storeroom full of golden censers and sacramental basins. The monk's cells had floors of the richest opus-sectile marble, and the gold-tiled fountain in the courtyard near the library would have been suitable for an Imperial residence. Theotokos! Constantine eyed Maleinus with new respect; the old bandit was still asking more than the salvage price of this booty, but not so much that he wouldn't find some fool at court to give him his price.

"You see what the word of Giorgios Maleinus is worth now, don't you, Eminence? Yes, you'll never see me with some fancy title, but those that have them are not loath to deal when Maleinus comes offering! Now, Eminence, let me lead you to the crowning glory of this Elysium."

"Theotokos." Constantine could no longer keep his tongue at the sight of the library. Theotokos! There was a profit to be made here simply in the sale of the gem-studded gold, silver, and ivory book covers, not to mention the value of the manuscripts. Maleinus must need the cash quickly, Constantine surmised.

"Indeed, indeed, Eminence." Maleinus brushed the dust off a gilded scriptorium; his red-rimmed eyes suddenly had the vigor—and greed—of a badger contemplating a field-mouse nest. "Perhaps not the most extensive library outside our Empress City or your Antioch, but certainly the richest. Yes, Eminence, even an illiterate would soon learn of the glories of Paradise were he to acquire these volumes!" Maleinus virtually collapsed from his rattling laugh and attendant cough.

"What is this?" said Constantine coolly, gesturing to the slightly open sliding door at the west end of the library; he had decided to consider this offering on its own merits. Of course there were details; the cost of shipping these items and the necessary agents in Constantinople had to be figured in.

"That . . ." Maleinus paused and shrugged, as if to say that the truth could not hurt him. "That, Eminence, is the source of the great mystery of Prote and, I might add, the reason these riches wait to be plucked for the price of a harlot's favors."

Constantine slid the door ajar with difficulty and squeezed through the opening. The room was lit by a solitary window that looked out over the exquisite gold fountain. Constantine stared in disbelief at the litter of scattered documents; it appeared as if someone had taken the entire contents of an Imperial bureau and simply had dumped them into this little room. A gilded lectern emerged above the pile of parchment like a lone tree poking above the pumice-buried slopes of a volcano.

"The Father Abbot was a prodigious correspondent, was he not?" Maleinus picked up one of the parchments and let it drop without reading it. "Letters. Probably would make interesting reading if one had the time or inclination. I saw one addressed to the Logothete of the Praetorium. As you can see, the Father Abbot had access not only to the Heavenly Tribunal but also to the Imperial Court."

"The one who was killed?" Constantine worried that his throbbing heart might burst; he was short of breath.

"No, the man who was killed was his successor. Father Katalakon. The name of the man who wrote all this was Father Abbot Giorgios. Strange, isn't it, him and me with the same name? Him having led a life of denial, and myself, well, my virtue would not heal the sick, Eminence. Yet here I am to dispose of his riches." Maleinus laughed and began to cough.

"The man who murdered this Father Katalakon, you say he has fled to Cappadocia?"

"The Chartophylax? Oh, the old book-buzzard's bound to be dead, no matter where he went. I don't believe much of the tale, anyway. An old man like that. No, you might say that rumor's breast was produced so that the truth would stop wailing, so to speak, Eminence. Like I say, the sin of Sodom was probably on the place. You know the vice is common among these cenobites, don't you, Eminence?" Maleinus winked at Constantine. Out in the library, Irene tittered.

Indeed, thought Constantine as he surveyed Father Abbot Giorgios's letters. *I do not believe the tale, either, and while this place reeks of sin, it is not that of Sodom.* But if there was a great secret among these papers, why wouldn't Joannes have burned the lot? Or was Joannes merely interested in concealing something else? Only one thing was certain: The arms of the Pantocrator verily embraced this opportunity.

Constantine closed the door completely and again looked around the dazzling library. Maleinus gave him a few moments to calculate before nudging him along. "Act quickly, Eminence. There are parties at court who are bidding to double my price on this. But I'd like to count the brother of our Holy Autocrator and blessed Orphanotrophus among the clients Giorgios Maleinus has enriched. . . ."

Constantine raised his hand to silence this astute prince of peddlers. "You will have your price—minus, I trust, a suitable discount for a single payment in gold—as soon as we return to the Empress City, good sir."

† † †

Haraldr set the canvas bag on the rough wooden table; the parcel was so heavy that the table creaked and canted a bit. The Blue Star folded her arms around her stout bosom and watched quizzically; she wore the same sleeveless linen tunic she had the first time they had met. Her white-eyed husband sat beside her. Haraldr opened the bag to show the Blue Star the hundreds of gold solidi. "I have a dozen of these bags for you," he said. "I reason that they are safer in my strongbox at my town palace. But they have been set aside for you and the people of the Studion. I'll bring them as you need them. I hope you will buy food with them."

For a mere instant the Blue Star's eyes seemed as innocent as a girl's, perhaps as she had looked when she had first dreamed of crowds cheering for her in the Hippodrome. She pulled Haraldr's head down from high above her and gave him a grandmotherly kiss on his cheek; Haraldr thought of his mother, Asta, and how long it had been since a woman had kissed him like that.

"The Theotokos just said a prayer for you, boy, right at the feet of God.

And if I get there, and that is no certain thing, I will say a prayer every day for you, until you join us." The tough look came over the Blue Star's face again. "But this isn't what the people of the Studion need, boy. Yes, this will feed them. For a while—not as long a while as you think, and not as many as you think. Do you know how many are out there?" Her question was rhetorical, but to himself Haraldr guessed as many as lived in all of Norway and Sweden combined. "When it gets bad enough, they'll tax the poor peasants in Hellas and Anatolia, take the food from their mouths, and give it to us, to take the bite out of our anger. So you might say that their tax collectors can bring us these bags of coins, too, boy, though not with the goodwill that is in your heart."

The Blue Star took Haraldr's hand in both of hers; he could still feel the gymnastic power in her fleshy grip. "What these people need is food for the soul. They need to believe that someone cares about them, and not just when they are so desperate with hunger that they might crawl out of the sewers and prey on the Dhynatoi. They need to believe that someone is looking over them, so that if they clear the lot next door and plant vegetables, the soldiers won't come and trample them. They need to feel that they can fix the holes in their roofs without being burned out when a cursore is murdered five blocks away. They need to believe that if their child gets a pox, someone up there on those hills cares whether that child lives or dies. The Bulgar-Slayer did that for the people of the Studion. He didn't do as much as you would think, boy, but he did enough to give these people hope. They did the rest. The Studion isn't dying because people have no food, boy. It is dying because people have no hope."

Haraldr tried to imagine what it would be like to awaken each morning in the hell of the Studion and look up at the great palaces on the hills. "Hope," he said at length. "Well, I will continue to bring you this gold, because I do not think a full belly will deprive anyone of hope. But I also believe I can send you the kind of hope you are talking about. The messenger of this hope will be an immense black bird."

The Blue Star looked at him as if he were mad.

† † †

"Hetairarch Haraldr Nordbrikt." Joannes stood in greeting and Haraldr reflected that nothing was more hideous than Joannes's smile; he looked like a horse baring its teeth. Joannes waved Haraldr to the simple canvas chair; Haraldr had to concede that the Orphanotrophus's office evidenced only industry, competence, and self-denial.

Joannes's face settled into its usual glower after the ordeal of the smile. "Hetairarch, I will not mince words with you. I have been wrong about you and have wronged you grievously; I will not pretend that an apology or a sniveling ingratiation would have meaning to a man who has overcome myriad obstacles, some of my own design, to rise more quickly than any . . . outsider before him. Now that the former Hetairarch, Hunrodarson, is out of the way, I have nothing to lose and everything to gain by making you my ally." Joannes placed his fingertips together and brought his huge face forward until his brutish, smooth chin hovered above the deformed digits. His voice, though restrained, seemed to pound the walls. "I want to deal with you. I want to make a gesture of good faith."

"And what would that be, Orphanotrophus? Would the serpent permit me to inspect its fangs as a gesture of its good faith? We Norsemen are naturally curious, but we are not by nature fools."

Joannes tilted his cathedral of fingers forward. "I want the gesture to be of your choosing."

"Then I shall arrange for a delegation from the Studion to visit with you, Orphanotrophus. Their request will be your gesture."

Joannes nodded soberly. "I am willing to address the grievances of the Studion." Joannes dipped his head for a moment, his eyes fading into deep shadows. "May I show you something, Hetairarch?"

"I have seen as much of Neorion as I care to see, sir."

Joannes sneered, apparently at himself. "I should have known a man of your intrepidness would not be persuaded by such displays. No, what I have in mind is a display that I feel will coerce your intellect, since your passions are clearly beyond my influence. Did you not say you Norsemen are curious? What I have to show you may explain the Roman Empire, and perhaps my own actions, more completely and convincingly than anything else you have seen in your time among us."

Joannes collected two resined tapers and a small bronze oil lamp in the antechamber of his office. He led Haraldr down the long hall of the Magnara basement; the Orphanotrophus walked in enormous lunging steps that flung his black frock out behind like the billowing sail of some death-ship. He turned left at a small corridor, unlocked a small, very dirty bronze door at the end of the little hall, and led Haraldr through the usual maze of the Imperial Palace's subterranean passageways. They emerged at a heavy, steel-banded door with two locks. Joannes lit the tapers from the oil lamp before they entered.

The light flickered up into a vault perhaps three stories high but no wider than a man's arm span. Without a word Joannes led Haraldr along what seemed a fairly steep decline. The vault curved noticeably as it descended, and soon Haraldr understood that this was some sort of enormous spiraling gallery, not unlike the chambers of a conch shell, that descended into the earth. On they went, to the accompaniment of dancing shadows and Joannes's scraping boots. For a moment Haraldr fancied that they would find the Bulgar-Slayer down at the end of this gallery, sending up Imperial Chrysobulls to his still devoted people. Or perhaps the embalmed corpse of Constantine the Great, attended by ancient eunuchs. Haraldr's imagination yielded to a sobering chill. What would he see? Was there a place more horrible than Neorion?

The ceiling lowered and the curves became tighter, until it seemed that the gallery could no long turn in its own width. Finally the descent stopped at a wall. A bare, flat stone wall beneath a ceiling that now almost grazed Haraldr's head. Joannes turned suddenly, his face a surface of deep, shadowed craters and smooth, jutting boulders. "This is the secret of Rome, Hetairarch." His voice echoed like a demonic oracle. "Tell me what you see."

Haraldr's flesh crawled. Surely Joannes had not arranged for his confederates to follow them down; the Orphanotrophus would be the shield behind which he would fight his way up. "I did not come here to play at riddles."

Joannes passed Haraldr silently and ascended until the roof of the spiral gallery became sufficiently elevated that he could thrust his taper up over his head. He turned again to Haraldr. "This is the treasury built by the Autocrator Basil, called the Bulgar-Slayer. There was a time when what you see here was a glittering warehouse of the wealth the Bulgar-Slayer's armies brought back from the ends of the earth. Chests stacked to the ceiling, full of gems, tableware, silken garments, Oriental carpets, heathen idols . . . Hetairarch, I do not have words to describe the wealth that was amassed here." Joannes shook his head. "Gone. Gone before my brother ever lowered his head beneath the Imperial Diadem. What the Bulgar-Slayer's brother Constantine did not gamble away, his successor Romanus squandered."

Haraldr could not contain his wonder. "But how? This . . ." He gestured at the huge expanse they had explored. "How, even in a century of spendthrift—"

"When an Emperor sends a fleet of *dhromons* to the pillars of Heracles because he desires a certain type of large fish to feast on, as Romanus did, when instead of exacting tribute from the Pechenegs, an Emperor pays them a ransom, when an Emperor supports whole establishments of monks in a fashion that a Magister of Rome would find profligate, then even a mountain of gold is not enough. You want to see where it went, Hetairarch? Look inside the churches and monasteries, look at the silver ciboria and gold icons reveted with gems, and the larders of the monks stuffed with pickled fish and black cavier from Rus; look inside the palaces of the Dhynatoi with their golden thrones and mosaic ceilings, look at the estates that the prostitutes of the Phanarion have purchased in Asia Minor because the powerful men of Rome are as generous with their favors as the harlot is with hers. But do not look here, Hetairarch; do not look about these empty vaults for the treasure of Rome. Because the people of Rome have stripped Rome bare."

"Your Dhynatoi accomplices and their attendant parasites have stripped her bare. I do not see the Bulgar-Slayer's missing gold on the streets of the Studion."

Joannes dropped his head wearily. "What would you have me do for the people of the Studion, Hetairarch? Do you think I can levy the Dhynatoi to provide a palace for every wretch in the Studion? You would be surprised how much of the Dhynatoi's wealth is owed to merchants like your friend Nicephorus Argyrus, and how much of the wealth of merchants like Argyrus is owed to the Venetians and the Genoese. Rome used to seek her wealth throughout the entire world, from the pillars of Heracles in the west to the gates of Dionysus in the east. Now the rest of the world comes to Rome to leech our wealth. Rome has forgotten that her destiny is at the ends of the earth." Joannes waved his winglike arms expansively, and the movement of the torch in his hand sent shadows racing through the empty galleries. "Hetairarch, do you think the walls of Constantinople can produce wealth, or can even protect that wealth without the attendant Empire? To conquer is to produce wealth. To rule is to produce wealth. To win the right to tax is to produce wealth. And that right, that power, is not won in the great houses along the Mese, or among the gardens of the Imperial Palace, or even beneath the golden dome of the Hagia Sophia. It is won at the ends of the world!"

Haraldr was taken aback by Joannes's passion. In spite of his overweening authority, his virtual omniscience, Joannes had always seemed fundamentally limited, a glorified, fantastically efficient servant. To see that he had a vision of Rome was disturbing, like learning that a huge beast was capable of human reason. "Yes," Haraldr admitted. "A Norseman would agree with you. Wealth and power are won at the ends of the earth. If we Norsemen did not believe that, I would probably be some ignorant farmer dreaming of the land beyond the next hill, praying that men do not come in fast ships to burn my crop and steal my wife. If we were not willing to go to the ends of the earth in our open ships, our lands would scarcely give us even that much. But a Norseman does not go a-viking and think nothing of the family and people he has left behind. It would shame a Norseman to win gold in some distant land and come home to a village where even one man lived as the tens of thousands do in the Studion."

Joannes studied Haraldr's pensive face. "I need you, Hetairarch Haraldr. I have already confessed that. I do not ask you to trust me; I ask you not to condemn me until you know more of my policies. Let me offer this as a gesture of good faith, to you and to those wretches, to whose plaints I am not entirely immune. There is nothing here for me to give them." Joannes fanned his torch through the empty vault. "However, I have resources of my own—acquired, I might add, by dint of unceasing labor compounded by unremitting frugality. From my own resources I will build a charity hospital in the Studion, the largest and finest the world has yet seen. I ask that you do nothing in return save wait for me to make this gesture, and to render judgment on me when you know more of Rome and my policies. If then we are still enemies, I will consider you a worthy adversary."

"And I would consider you worthy of destroying as well, Orphanotrophus. The next time we speak, I will expect to hear of your remarkable progress in the construction of this hospital."

Joannes nodded, the great hollows of his face suddenly seeming more like wells of weariness than pits of evil.

onastery! Uncle, you know that the word alone is anathema to me! Look, my hands are trembling!" Michael placed his palsied hands straight out and the beautiful dappled Arabian he had been examining whinnied as if verifying his master's claim. "Oh, damn me, I have disturbed Phaethon." Michael turned and stroked the horse's probing nose. "And I have shouted at you, my precious uncle!" Michael clasped Constantine's shoulders warmly. "I am certain your decision was judicious, Uncle. It is simply that with each week that passes, I feel my time in the world of . . . of pleasure running out. I hate to think I will never see a horse run again unless it is some mangy mule sent to fetch one of my eremite brothers."

"Nephew, trust in me. Remember, I have managed the second city of the world and the affairs of a vast and prosperous theme. I can certainly manage to make a profit on the sale of this monastery's property. In any event, I will not require a contribution from your purse. I have scraped together the requisite solidi and already settled with the former owner."

"Do you think your purchase will quite enrage Joannes?"

"It may discomfit him more than that, Nephew." Constantine went on to describe the letters of Father Abbot Giorgios. Michael listened so raptly that he even batted Phaethon's nose when the horse nudged him. When Constantine had finished, Michael embraced him. "Oh, Uncle, for the first time since our Emperor returned from the dead I have hope. When can we see the seraphim-sent correspondences of this Father Abbot Giorgios?"

"I have already dispatched a ship and porters to pack and deliver the items. I warn you that many tedious weeks of sifting through these documents await us."

"Uncle, you must remember that I am also not without certain qualities of industry when the rewards are sufficient. Until we find the treasure we are seeking amid this abbot's dross, I will display a dedication to the task that would make the stylite upon a column question the vehemence of his own commitment." Michael took Constantine's arm and escorted him away from Phaethon's stall without even a farewell to the neighing horse.

† † †

"This is the oldest part of this garden," said Maria. She stepped through a bed of metallic-orange marigolds and entered a dark sycamore bower. The evaporation from the trees sprayed the baked, late-afternoon air with a sweet, cooling mist. "We can sit there." She pointed to an almost sarcophaguslike bench; the thick marble base was decorated with marble carvings partially visible through clutching tendrils of ivy. A statue of a woman, her body stiff and geometric but with a soft graceful face and long braids gently falling over her shoulders, faced the bench from the middle of a small pool rimmed with crumbling granite bricks.

The cold touch of the stone bench was refreshing. "It is not Greek," said Haraldr, meeting the eternal gaze of the statue. "But it is not in the fashion of Egypt, either."

"I think it is Greek, at a time when the sculptors of Athens borrowed from the ancients of Egypt. Before they learned to surpass them. I am not certain. Anna would know."

"Is Anna well?"

"I think she will soon be betrothed. To an officer of the Scholae. He is a good man, both courageous and intelligent enough not to grovel before her father." Maria turned her head suddenly, as if just noticing something. "You are not sorry, are you?"

"No, I am happy that she has found someone worthy of her." Haraldr frowned at the stone face. "But I feel that she has taken a part of me."

"And you have taken a part of her."

"Yes. That seems to be the way of life, endless partings where something is always taken and something is always left behind. I wonder if at the end of that long road anything remains of ourselves."

"Perhaps the soul we began with is not the soul we are destined to end with. The destiny of the soul is immutable, but the soul itself is constantly transformed."

"Or perhaps the same soul is destined to wear many disguises. That is the way Odin more than once tricked fate."

"Then it is important to know when the soul has been transformed, or when it merely masquerades."

Haraldr fell silent and watched a mayfly skim over the surface of the pool. A shout floated distantly from the polo field. Had his soul merely deceived him, and her soul fooled her? That was the question that stood between them as they struggled to reach each other again.

At length Maria whispered into the rustling silence. "Perhaps that is the cruelty of fate, that until the end we do not know if our own soul was true, or merely lied to us from behind its mask."

"Might it not also be the cruelty of death that we will never know?"

Maria pulled her arms around her silken waist, as against a chill. "I pray to the Holy Mother that at death we will at least have the comfort of that revelation."

"I pray that when fate takes me, I will leave enough of my soul in another breast to know that I will live on until the day all souls are taken."

"You know that will be true. Look at the souls who already live in your breast."

"Yes. My father. My brother. Jarl Rognvald." He could not say the other name.

"You are fortunate. One of the souls who lives in my breast only stabs at my heart." Haraldr sensed that he would be a fool to presume that he was the cause of her pain. He waited. Maria moved her white silk slipper gently over the tops of the tall, slightly wilted grass. A sulfur-yellow butterfly drifted erratically through the bower and out into the bright sunlight. The small crowd at the nearby polo field acclaimed some feat of horsemanship with a muffled applause.

"Will you let me tell you about the first man who loved me?" Maria's question seemed directed to the statue. Haraldr touched her hand for a moment and let it go, then allowed her the silence to continue. "I was very young. Not even a woman. It was a time of great turmoil in the palace. The Emperor Constantine, who had been a very old man when he had inherited the Autocrator's diadem from Basil the Bulgar-Slayer, acutely sensed his mortality. If he was to perpetuate the Macedonian dynasty, he knew he had to find a son-in-law for one of his purple-born daughters. Romanus was Prefect of the City, apparently of some ability at that level of government, although he was utterly incompetent as an Emperor. But he had the majestic speech and stature expected of an Emperor, and for a man—may the Theotokos forgive me—for a man as shallow as Constantine, that was enough. He became fixed on this man as his successor, even though Romanus was already married to a decent lady. That was no matter; the wife was forced to retire into a convent, the divorce granted, and Romanus was offered up to Theodora. She had the courage to refuse her father and has been punished for her denial ever since. Zoe could never resist her father, and ever since has paid the wages of her acceptance. But that is another tale. The object of this prelude is to say that the two women I had always relied upon for love and guidance were suddenly undone by this fate, their lives swept away forever. And so I, who had always feared abandonment, was at last alone." Maria paused and worked at her lip with her pearl-white teeth. "A man came to me during this time, a man old enough to be my father, and at first he *was* my father. He was the father I had always dreamed of, a man of military accomplishments who had risen to high civil authority in the Senate, his hair still dark with youth, his hard blue eyes gleaming with knowledge."

Haraldr looked at Maria's elegant profile and realized that she still loved this man.

"He bought me books of romances with the most beautiful illuminations, talked to me of Iberia or Alexandria or anyplace I dreamed of going, told me wonderful secrets about the lofty dignitaries who surrounded me." Maria's lashes fluttered, as if she were viewing some beauty too dazzling for vision. "Shortly after Constantine died and circumstances made both Zoe and Theodora even more distant from me, I began to become a woman. My menses had begun to flow, my innocent breasts were now tender and swollen. Drunk with the wine of that first womanhood, I began to seek the love between men and women. And of course I fixed upon the most immediate object of desire. I embarrassed us both at first, and yet I almost immediately sensed a power I had of course never known I possessed, even though I had always been thought a beautiful child. It was gradual, as delicate as the rain that slowly wells out of a mist, but our relationship became no longer that of father and daughter but of . . ." Maria stroked her silk-sheathed knees. "We became like husband and wife."

Maria stood, her arms folded under her breasts, and studied the grass as she trampled it in short, somewhat pawing steps. "I honestly do not remember much of what that love was like. It seems so long ago. I only remember a kind of silver nimbus around it, an innocence that seems incredible to me now. But we held each other and made love like husband and wife, so I thought, and I believed that we had indeed pledged a troth. I begged him to marry me before this sin profaned my soul. He kept deferring, disclaiming about my age." The blue flames of Maria's irises began to glow. "Apparently I was old enough for his arms to wrap my naked loins but not old enough for a wedding belt to girdle my waist. But in my innocence I waited. And then one day I learned the reason for my waiting. I remember that like yesterday. A slut who hovered about the court, waiting for whatever dignity might fancy to dip into her, came skipping to my apartments where I was learning Homer, as a girl my age

is bound to do. She announced as gaily as her own betrothal the engagement of my lover to Anna Ducas, an arrogant Dhynatoi bitch who had
already inflamed my jealousy with little intrigues that had seemed great
at the time, and apparently were. I did not wait. I raced to confront him
at his apartments and caught him in a position with the bitch that even
the most skillful of lies could not extricate him from. She had the effrontery to seize a knife and threaten me with it. I kicked and punched the
sin out of her and sent her fleeing, and the knife clattered to the floor.
I saw it, and I saw him, too speechless with shame even to lie. I would
have accepted anything except his beaten-dog shame!" Maria's teeth
flashed between brilliant, grimacing lips. "It was as if the knife had been
set there by some greater hand than mine."

Even now Maria was rigid, coiled, as if responding to the grip of that
great hand. "I seized the knife and, in my fury, plunged it into his astonished breast. I still see his eyes. . . . And the feeling . . . the feeling of
entering him with that knife was as it had been when he had first entered
me and stabbed me with love." Her eyes glowed but her cadence faltered.
"Ever . . . ever since then . . . love and hate have been . . . inseparable
in my . . . soul."

Haraldr stared at the statue for a moment; its whimsical stone features
seemed for a moment sad, as if stone, like flesh, were also a prison. He
looked at Maria, still standing, her arms clutched as if her stomach ached,
her eyes feverish with pain. He reached out and extricated one of her
hands and pulled her down beside him. "I understand your pain," he told
her as he clutched her cold, stiff hand. "I tried to become a man too soon,
as I think you tried to become a woman too soon. I cannot be as honest
as you and tell you everything that happened. But there was a battle, and
everything I knew and loved was taken from me that day. Even my pride
and honor. It was as if fate stripped me and broke me and ground me into
the offal of my own fear. I remained screaming, unable to move, awake
in that nightmare for many years. Because of the love of an old man who
is dead now, and the help of the gods, I no longer live in that nightmare.
But my soul still sears with the shame and agony of that day. I am marked
by it forever."

Maria's grip was fierce, astonishingly powerful. "I am not ashamed of
what I did. But I am still angry. It is the anger that reduces me, because
I have let loose its misguided arrows all my life."

Haraldr could say nothing. She had bared her breast to him and indeed
had no reason for shame; there was nothing in her tale that did not make
him think more of her. He felt shame because the lie born at Stiklestad

was still with him, and the anger he should proclaim to the world was still hidden. But he could not answer her truth with one of his own. He thought again of the ambivalent fate that had whispered to him high above the Hippodrome, and heard again its caution. Was this new truth of hers merely another mask for her soul? Or was her soul merely a mask for some devious fate? He did not know. And so all he could do was hold her desperate hand and listen to the hot wind rise and rattle among the sycamore leaves.

† † †

"The Magister and Strategus of Armenikoi, Constantine Tztezes, paid a common prostitute to costume herself as the whore of Babylon, go about her business with a young man while he watched, and then . . ." Michael Kalaphates let the letter drop onto the stack, a look of profound disgust added to the weariness that creased his handsome young face. "You don't want to hear the rest, Uncle. Suffice to say that when the young man had finished with this ersatz Whore of Revelations, Tztezes proceeded to enact the rulers of biblical notoriety who had 'drunk deep of her fornication.' " Michael narrowed his eyes. "And this, Uncle, is the kind of narrow-minded prig who calls a sportsman like myself an apostate to Satan."

"It is remarkable that Father Abbot Giorgios did not despair of human nature," said Constantine wryly.

"Yes, the Father Abbot seems to have been remarkably magnanimous as long as human nature brought him marble revetments for his cenobite's cells and gold-and-ruby icons for his personal treasury. I tell you, Uncle, if I ever . . . I would make these pompous dignitaries think that the trumpet of judgment has sounded." Michael picked up the stack of documents and set it down on the table with a muted thud. "Well, enough of that. Let me review what we have."

Constantine straightened his pile of parchments and watched Michael attentively. It *was* extraordinary what the young man was capable of when he fixed himself upon some goal. Michael had first discerned Father Abbot Giorgios's filing system, then deciphered the Chartophylax's own rather cryptic system, cross-referenced all the documents, and within two weeks knew the identity and predicament of each of the Father Abbot's numerous highly placed correspondents. (The vast amount of purely scholarly and religious correspondence, of course, he had quickly identified and discarded.)

Michael placed his hands on two stacks. "These are living holders of Imperial dignities who would be subject to immense . . . embarrassment if the contents of these letters became known." Michael lifted the hand that rested on the other, taller stack. "These documents pertain to deceased individuals whose families still hold positions of responsibility." Michael strutted for a moment, enjoying his moment of latent power. "We will use this only as a last resort, or to protect ourselves if circumstances should prove to our benefit. I quite think extortion a rather limited sport. One always begins with an outcome, which becomes quite tedious to the true speculator."

Michael moved with new assurance to a small stack of perhaps a dozen letters and placed both hands upon it. "This, Uncle, has the all the indications of a superlative wager." Michael riffled the dry parchments. "The account is graphic, is it not? The purple-born Eudocia, the late sister of our present Empress Zoe and the Augusta Theodora, becomes enamored of a young courtier—by the way, Uncle, they say Eudocia was a fright, her face blemished by some pox. She becomes enamored of this young swain, lets him have his way with her, his seed bears fruit, she confesses to her father, and her young man mysteriously takes the tonsure of a monk and disappears to a lavra in Syria. She goes off to the convent at Prote and brings her bastard into the world, and the child's rather deeply blue blood—in fact, one could almost make the case for it being purple—is known only to Father Abbot Giorgios. Eudocia gives up the child and lives out the rest of her woefully brief years in an even more remote cloister, the Emperor Constantine dies, we even have the death of the child's father recorded. It is all here, the account of an artfully buried secret."

Michael sorted through the stack and picked up two letters. "Except for this. Here we have a letter in which Eudocia thanks the Father Abbot for seeing to the confidential delivery of her child and promises her confessor a new gold altar table." Michael waved the other letter. "Here we have the unfortunate woman's profuse gratitude for seeing to her own placement in another convent, and of course the promise of one hundred solidi to purchase bound manuscripts for the library. Both letters are marked in both the Father Abbot's and the Chartophylax's filing notations, and both sets of notations indicate that one letter is missing, the letter written between these two. The letter, I am willing to wager, Uncle, that describes the disposition of the child."

"Yes," said Constantine; he also rose and began to pace with excitement. "And the fact that the Chartophylax's notation indicates the missing letter proves that he was in possession of this rather propitious secret."

"Is it possible that the Chartophylax did kill this Father Katalakon in order to preserve the secret?"

"Possible. But remember that the scent—or perhaps one should say reek—of Joannes is on all of this."

"Yes, that is the key, Uncle." Michael pulled an ear thoughtfully. "Let us consider three possibilities. One, that Joannes found the letter and knows the secret. Two, that Joannes looked for the letter and did not find it. Three, that Joannes knows nothing of the letter and merely suspended the typicon for some other reason; you how meticulous his management is and how extensive his piques are." Constantine nodded agreement. "Two chances out of three, Uncle, is considered very attractive odds to an experienced sportsman. I say we should send someone to Cappadocia to locate this Chartophylax—or his remaindered effects in the event of his death, which seems likely—and bring us back that letter."

"There is no one we can trust with such a . . . treasure."

Michael's face collapsed into his usual boyish irresolution. "I had not thought of that. Poor Ergodotes, the only casualty of my plot against Joannes."

Constantine approached Michael and slapped his shoulders. "Of course there is someone we can both trust. By the goodness of the Pantocrator you have an uncle who knows the area passably well. The former Strategus of a neighboring theme."

Michael's lips were slack with shock. "Uncle, you cannot mean to . . . Uncle, the heat alone . . . No. Nothing is worth the prospect of having you away for those months, not to mention . . . I will not allow it."

"Nephew, you yourself have traversed most of the route. The caves of these eremites are only three days from Caesarea Mazaca. A most propitious destination, is it not, my Caesar? I should be able to join a caravan within the next two weeks, and be in Cappadocia by early September. I will be back before December."

Michael's eyes were wet with gratitude. "Uncle, bless you. I only hope that upon the occasion of your return I will still be here to welcome you."

aria awakened to the brilliant early September light streaming in her bedchamber. The drapes rustled with the already tepid morning breeze. Her arcade was a wall of gold. She had dreamed again, of thunderbolts fracturing a glassy sky, a flaming sea, her own death. *The dreams are what I fear, not what will be,* she told herself. *I have proof of that. What will be is today. I will see him, I will have hours to be with him. Enough time to break through this wall that still keeps us apart, as close as we have come these past months. Today he will share with me the secret that burdens his soul.*

Maria sat up at the knock on her door. Her chamberlain entered and ushered in Maria Diaconus, daughter of the Patrician and Senator Alexius Diaconus, and Maria's new lady-in-waiting; because of their shared name, Maria referred to her as Little Maria. Little Maria was fourteen, blond, as slender as a reed, and entirely too young to be gamboling about court, but clearly her parents were eager to auction her innocence in the interests of their ambitions. Maria had resolved to keep a keen eye on her.

"I couldn't sleep," said Little Maria in her flutelike girl's voice. "I have been up before the sun. I cannot believe this day is actually here." Little Maria walked to the open arcade and looked out over the domes of the palace and across the Bosporus. "They say there will be dancers and a drama in mime and an illusionist and acrobats and animals and that women will have their own hunt," she rattled off without pausing for breath. "Do you think we will be able to dance?"

"If the Empress decides we can dance, we will dance."

"With men?"

"Perhaps. If you are extremely good, you might be permitted to dance with men."

"So will you dance with the Hetairarch?" Little Maria smirked surreptitiously.

"How did you know he was coming?"

"I have been asking. Do you know who else is coming? That Saracen prince who wants to be Caliph of Egypt." Little Maria lowered her voice to a ridiculous hiss and steered her blue-green eyes about the room. "They say the Emperor may even appear."

I doubt that, Maria thought to herself, not wanting to spoil the girl's anticipation. It was enough that Zoe had been freed to entertain at her villa on the Bosporus, and that Her Majesty was conducting the event with the zeal of old. Maria only hoped that Zoe herself would not presume that the Emperor might attend her ball.

"Mistress, do you think I might be seduced this evening?" said Little Maria blithely.

Maria reached over and gave Little Maria's long blond braid a sharp pull. "Not tonight, little flower. When you are ready to be plucked, I will find someone appropriate to seduce you."

† † †

"Well, there it be, Worship. If you can find yourself this Charto-whatever out there, then you knows your way around better than me. And I've been running these ugly humped demons out here for two indictions. It's madness, Worship. I've seen it all happen, and it's madness. Kept me busy, though."

Constantine looked through the shimmering, late-summer heat that cloaked the Cappadocian valley. Incredible. Of course he had heard of it, but he had imagined a few dozen of these desert dwellers. Incredible. Spread out to the horizon was a land of dull almond and bronze colors, tortured by wind and rain into thousands and thousands of jagged, tooth-like spires, all of relatively uniform height, all crowded in dense, disor-dered row after row. The landscape in itself was something of a marvel, but what was truly remarkable was that this fantastic expanse of weath-ered stone was a city. Not a town or a village but a city of homes carved into these cone-shaped limestone spires; it was hard to distinguish a single spire that was not pocked with small square windows and rectangu-lar doors and even large recessed balconies. The rock city crawled with life; brown- and black-cloaked monks scrambled up and down the wooden ladders that led to their perches, and the roads that ran into and around this strange metropolis were crowded with these eremites and their donkeys, laden with sacks of provisions and clay jars of fresh water or wine. Thousands of cook fires further smudged the hazy atmosphere. Constantine could see a monk beating a rug on one of the balconies. The scene was not of this world.

Constantine tried to compose himself. The heat and dust were suf-focating. He would die before he could possibly find one old monk out there. But he could not allow himself that despair. He was a man of ability. And a man of ability would use his superior intellect to conquer this forbidding, holy otherworld. Constantine wiped his drenched face with his dust-soiled veil. The Chartophylax, coming here, would go to a world he knew. Books. Manuscripts. Eremites would not have these things, at least in any abundance. Only a church would. Constantine squinted over the spiky terrain. Certainly some of the larger, more complex porches indicated chapels, but there were bound to be scores, probably even hundreds. "My esteemed sir," he asked the camel driver, "where would one find the largest chapel in this district?"

The camel driver spit into the floury dust. "There, Worship." He pointed to a large conglomeration of blunted cones that seemed much like a ragged, natural version of the piled-up, multiple domes of an Orthodox cathedral. This rock chapel was a good eight stades distant.

"And where might one find a donkey and some water jugs?"

"You're in luck, Worship, as it is my cousin who sells mules to the eremites down there."

Constantine looked out over the sweltering, tortured city of denial and told himself that the Hand of the Pantocrator was indeed upon this enterprise.

† † †

"I am emphatically certain that his wife's father had an Armenian on his mother's side." Theophano Attalietes, wife of the Senator and Magister Nicon Attalietes, hefted, with a motion of her left elbow and entire vast bosom, the trail of her jeweled and gold-embroidered scarlet pallium as if the garment were some sort of volume bearing the genealogies of everyone present. She looked imperiously down her fat, painted nose at the almost as grotesquely splendid wife of another Senator. "By the Lord's Hand, woman, he allowed his daughter to marry a merchant. And he has had Venetians at his home!" As far as Theophano Attalietes was concerned, the matter was settled. She and her gaggle of bejeweled Dhynatoi cronies would not greet Andronicus Diogenes or his wife, despite the fact that Diogenes owned two dozen separate estates in Asia Minor and his father had been a distinguished general under the Bulgar-Slayer.

"I am faint," muttered Theophano, who appeared about as faint as a charging bull. She nudged her companion and nodded toward the gilded presence of Nicephorus Argyrus. Snapping her fingers quickly, she organized her eunuchs and ladies-in-waiting, all of them attired in white silk, into a gleaming mother-of-pearl wall before her, lest the preening merchant attempt to approach her. She could have strangled her husband, Nicci, for having had anything to do with that man, but at least that was over. At least her baby, Ignatius, had not been forced to marry one of the disgusting merchant's bastard daughters. "I am bleeding for our Empire!" Theophano erupted. "Do you see it, or have the demons been sent to test my incomparable piety!" She nodded her round, adipose head with frantic bobbing motions. "The brute! The Tauro-Scythian brute! He is in the costume of a stable boy, and with the Imperial Crest on his breast!"

"He . . . he is . . . rather well spoken," offered the wife of Senator Scylitzes timidly but nonetheless suicidally. "He . . . he did . . . save our Emperor." Theophano turned to Madame Scylitzes like an executioner. "Woman," she intoned in an acid voice, "the Emperor's horse also served him in battle. We do not invite the horse to walk among ladies of ancient and noble lineage, nor do we consider the beast 'well spoken' simply because it can stamp its hoof three times when its master utters the word *three.* I suggest that you endow an icon to the Mother Church, woman, and pray to the Holy Mother to be released from your untoward empathy for savages."

"I believe your costume has drawn the ire of Theophano Attalietes," said Nicephorus Argyrus to Haraldr; they were close enough to catch a few words of the woman's exclamations. Haraldr had worn the controversial new men's fashion to the Empress's ball, a thigh-length tunic worn with hose. "Or perhaps it is merely your fair complexion." Argyrus pointed to Theophano among the cluster of tongue-wagging Senatorial wives. "Do you realize I could arrange for you to own that fat sow before this evening was over?"

Haraldr laughed. "I would sign over to you my entire fortune for the privilege of not owning *that.*"

Argyrus gestured theatrically at the vast interior court of the Empress's villa; the colonnaded square was variously filled with set tables, a stage, fountains buried beneath trays of delicacies and silver ewers of wine, and a glittering crowd of hundreds of dignitaries in a display of silks and jewels beside which an Imperial coronation paled. Bonnets and pearl collars framed the beefy jowls of the magnates, and silk parasols held by uniformed eunuchs shielded the painted faces of their ladies from a sun that had already disappeared behind the court's soaring peristyle. "There are more prejudices here than gold earrings," Argyrus said. "The Dhynatoi of undilute blood—or so they think—look down on the Dhynatoi who have an Armenian or Persian in their history, but then any Dhynatoi from the Eastern themes looks down on the Dhynatoi from the western themes, and all the Dhynatoi look down on a merchant like myself, though I could buy any one of them. Needless to say, you *barbaroi* do not deserve consideration. Then there are the eunuchs, who think they are quite above everybody except another eunuch who holds a higher office. The priests, meanwhile, look down on the monks, whom they consider unwashed primitives, and the monks look at everyone else as sinful. The civil bureaucrat despises the military man, and of course the military man despises everyone except for the Seljuk warrior, whom he secretly admires. The Hellenes at court consider everyone else untutored louts, and everyone else considers them pompous, heathen windbags. It is a miracle that anyone in Rome talks to anyone else." Argyrus looked around and tipped his gold goblet toward the peristyle. "A friend of yours has arrived. Someone who really has risen above all this."

The level of noise was too high to hear the comments Maria inspired, but she clearly created a ripple of sensation in the crowd. Haraldr had wondered what new innovation would distinguish her attire, since her Greek-style costume had already inspired many imitations. This time she wore a dancer's uniform, except that her short, thigh-length tunic was cut from embroidered white silk and her long underskirt was of sheer chiffon and slit to the waist. The sight of her scarcely veiled legs gave Haraldr a queasy feeling in his stomach. The thought of wanting her that much frightened him.

"Hetairarch, have you ever considered making a wife of our Helen, our Maria?" Argyrus eyed Haraldr's frown warily. "I hope I have not presumed on our friendship."

"No. I have . . . thought of it."

Maria wended her way through the crowd, her teeth sparkling at the many compliments and greetings, her blue eyes blazing challenges at the disapproving Dhynatoi matrons. By the time she reached Haraldr, a troupe of young women and their ladies-in-waiting followed behind her, eager to watch the woman their parents so vehemently condemned. Maria greeted Haraldr and Argyrus with impeccable formality, nodding and then introducing her lady-in-waiting. But then she glanced over at Theophano Attalietes and the glaring Senatorial contingent and placed her hand on Haraldr's arm. "I must introduce you to the wife of our foremost Senator," she said. "And you as well, Nicephorus Argyrus."

Nothing, not even her fortress of attendants, could save Theophano; Maria's ceremonial title, Mistress of the Robes, was exceeded only by the dignity of purple-born Augusta, and of course that of Empress. Maria performed the introductions in front of the bosom-heaving, almost apoplectic woman. Theophano was forced by her own rigid sense of etiquette to croak "Hetairarch" and "Sir" at the two subhumans. Satisfied, Maria led Haraldr and Argyrus away. "She will suffer the torments of the damned when she sees that you are to be seated to the right of the Empress." Haraldr became almost rigid. "Of course," explained Maria, "I am always at the Empress's left, and you are across from me." Haraldr wondered at how small Rome had become.

✝ ✝ ✝

"I think the man you want never left Caesarea, my brother," said the monk, his eyes reddened and his brow furrowed from the effort of painting deep inside this rock . . . tomb. There was no other word for it, thought Constantine. Yet the raw fervor of this painter's vision had converted the rock chapel into a primitive paradise where brilliant polychrome apostles hovered in precisely carved niches and gold-haloed Pantocrators looked down from the smooth-surfaced, perfectly contoured apse and dome. The pungency of fresh pigment challenged the omnipresent smell of limestone dust.

Constantine thanked the monk, left him a copper follis from his dwindling supply of coins, and stooped beneath the arched doorway into the fast-approaching, still searing Cappadocian twilight. Despair had returned. He had already visited a half dozen of the largest chapels, and the suggestion that the Chartophylax had remained at the Bishopric in Caesarea was beginning to have credence, even though Constantine had already ascertained that there was no record of him in the Episcopal files. There was now only one large chapel left that might have any significant documentation. Constantine wearily mounted his wheezing mule.

The treacherous pathways between the cones were now crowded with monks scurrying to reach their sanctuaries before dark. This city of monks had attracted the usual urban vermin; Constantine had seen the secular "clergy" of this place lurking in the shadows or just blithely sleeping in the shade, waiting for the darkness to come so that they could perform their sacraments of assault and thievery. Constantine identified the final chapel, and when he reached the broad base of the spire, he could hear evidence of expansion going on within the cone. He laboriously ascended the wavering wooden ladder—his hands were already blistered—and pulled himself over the lip of the porch. The noise was thunderous and the dust a hot talc thrust up his nostrils. Constantine pulled his veil tight around his nose and mouth and entered the single doorway.

Inside, bare-chested monks were visible through the reddish pall; they pounded iron chisels with heavy mallets like wretches condemned to the inferno. A monk working with a file smoothed the surface of one of a whole row of columns that these men had hewn out of solid rock. The sound of the hammering caused actual physical pain to the ears, and Constantine's head ached. One of the brothers shouted at him through the din.

"How can I succor you, brother!" The monk was as powerful as a wrestler, and sweat yellowed with limestone dust beaded his entire face and beard. He signaled one of the brothers to bring Constantine a drink of water. The monk who brought the clay jug had dark, furious eyes; a strip of cloth was wrapped around the middle of his face, covering the slits where his nose had been. Constantine ignored the fearsome visage and greedily slurped from the noseless man's wooden ladle.

"The Lord's work is unceasing!" screamed the monk over the unremitting din. "I will not close my eyes in sleep, or my eyelids in slumber, until I find a sanctuary for the Lord, a dwelling for the mighty one of Jacob!" thundered the monk, quoting Psalms.

Constantine had no reason to be encouraged; even the least scholarly monk knew the Psalter by heart. He shouted back into the sweat-glistened ear of the monk. "I am looking for a Chartophylax, formerly of Prote! He would have come here five, perhaps six years ago."

There was a flash of recognition in the monk's eyes. He signaled his brethren to stop hammering. But his words were a disappointment. "A Chartophylax of Prote, you say?" The monk shook his head and wrung the silted sweat out of his beard. Still, Constantine noticed that the other monks seemed to betray some knowledge; the noseless monk's eyes shifted from Constantine's scrutinizing gaze. "Well, of course, we have archives that go back to the time of Gregory of Nyssa. You are welcome to inspect them." He signaled the noseless monk to show Constantine the way.

The noseless monk lit a taper and led Constantine through a narrow series of galleries, then up a carved staircase to a room fairly well il-luminated by two small square windows. Constantine sighed; the rock-walled scriptorium, with a single dust-covered writing table—apparently the monks here were more interested in works of stone than works on parchment—was lined with shelves full of dusty sheafs, many bound in ancient wood covers. He would be there late into the night, after an already exhausting day. But something told him that it was important he begin.

† † †

"If he slips," said Zoe, leaning forward in her golden throne and pointing to the oil-glazed acrobat performing atop a pole balanced in the middle of the table, "then Lady Manganes will have a virtually naked man in her plate."

"Yes," said Maria. "I wonder if she will ask for some garos sauce to be ladled over him."

Zoe laughed and lifted her fluted, scarlet-tinted wineglass. Haraldr felt both very sorry for her and very devoted to her. The pain of the continued separation from her husband showed in a kind of haunted darkness around her blue eyes; it was clear that she had hoped the Emperor might appear and surprise her. And yet in spite of how cruelly love had treated her, she obviously did not begrudge Maria and Haraldr their long, adoring looks. Instead she had played the gracious messenger of Aphrodite; she even had silenced the *voukaloi* and organs and made a toast to love, with an obvious inference to the couple sitting next to her.

"Well," said Zoe, her disappointment a thin edge on a voice determined to provide others joy, "I have tipped everyone, toasted everyone who deserves to be toasted, sent enough bared acrobats' breasts and buttocks among them to enact the forty martyrs of Sebaste"—the martyrs in question had been forced to strip and stand in the snows of Rus until they perished—"shown them the latest beasts from the Indus, provided them with unremitting chorales, and have successfully commissioned a mime of the liaison of Ariadne and Theseus so explicit that I believe Lady Attaliates split her scaramangium in a combination of ecstasy and outrage. I believe that I can only exceed myself by ordering our illusionist to begin."

Maria slid her arms across the table and leaned toward Haraldr. She was slightly taken by the wine but to charming effect. "You must tell me what you see," she said. "Some people will see nothing, some will see different things, many will see the same thing. It is interesting to compare."

Zoe touched Haraldr's arm. "Think of this as a waking dream. Do not be alarmed. The first time you see it, if you see it, you may think that angels—or demons—have taken hold of you, it is so wondrous." She smiled warmly and wistfully at him. Haraldr settled back, tense with anticipation despite the wine. He had considered much he had already seen in Rome magic. Now he would see what the Romans themselves considered magic.

The stage was a construction of gilded wood that had been erected at the east end of the courtyard, just behind the Empress's table. It was a virtually freestanding building, with a high, vaulted ceiling from which three elaborate candelabra hung, providing the platform below with an intense golden light. At Zoe's command the organs flourished and the tables full of diners hushed expectantly. An old, bowed workman of some sort shuffled out onto the platform. Inexplicably, the workman instantly vanished, and in his place was a much taller man, young and handsome, wearing a loose black scaramangium much like a monk's frock. "Who am I?" asked the man in a voice that carried like a herald's and yet at the same time seemed conversational, as if he were sitting across the table.

"Abelas!" yelled some of the young men and women who apparently had seen the man perform before. Abelas listened for his name and then whirled like a cyclone, and when he was still again, his face was as white as a corpse and streaked with brilliant tendrils of fresh blood that ran down from his thick black hair. "Who am I!" he shrieked, and whirled again. When he faced the audience this time, he was the old workman. He began to shuffle off the stage. Then a burst of light and a flock of white piegons fluttered above the stage and carried Abelas away, leaving only a mist where he had been. It was incredible; Haraldr could see the birds, a dozen of them at least, transport Abelas over the roof of the villa and off into the night.

Haraldr heard murmuring among the crowd and looked back to the stage. A dwarf in a black robe stood where Abelas had been. "Who am I?" asked the dwarf in a voice identical to Abelas's. "Abelas!" came the return chorus. The dwarf clapped his stubby hands as if applauding the audience for this feat of identification. "Who am I?" The dwarf flew up into the air, his black robe trailing like a column of smoke, and then the smoke cleared and a woman stood there, naked except for a single leaf over her pubic triangle. The crowd tittered. "Who am I?" asked the woman in Abelas's voice. "Abelas!" The woman bowed and skipped off the stage; two huge cranes rose up from where she had stood, flapped their wings, and flew off into the night. The crowd applauded wildly.

Haraldr took a deep draft of unmixed wine. Spectacular but explainable; he had recently been shown the complex hydraulic lifts that raised the Emperor's throne and had held in his hand one of the clockwork birds that had once bewitched him. Abelas was a wizard, but a wizard at mechanical stunts and sleight of hand. Haraldr drank again, relieved. He had feared that Abelas might have access to the spirit world. Fortunately that was not the case.

The organs flourished briefly and Abelas emerged again, a plain-looking man, perhaps late in his third decade, in a loose white scaramangium. He held up his hands for the crowd's acclaim and snakes coiled from his fingertips. He shook the snakes off and, in a prodigious, catlike leap, bounded to the Empress's table, almost weightlessly dodging the litter of plates and goblets with his dancing feet. He planted himself in front of Lady Manganes and leaned his torso far over her, seemingly in defiance of both anatomy and gravity. His hair seemed darker and his black eyes burned in the candlelight. "Who are you?" he asked her.

Lady Manganes, a fleshily attractive woman with a spark in her own eyes, smiled mischievously. "Anna Manganes," she said, a hint of invitation, and fear, in her voice. Abelas whirled his arms in front of her face and made a motion as if pulling her soul right out of her body. "Who are you?"

"Salome," said Lady Manganes in a voice quite unlike her own. She seemed to listen for distant music, and rose, swaying, tapping imaginary cymbals with her hands. Then she leapt onto the table and began to whirl, faster and faster, and yet her feet never disturbed a single utensil. Abelas let her go on for a moment and then touched her head lightly, at which she stopped and climbed down to her seat. Abelas leaned over her again. "Who are you?"

"Lady Manganes," she said, shrugging.

Abelas bounded across the table and stood in front of Haraldr, the fulfillment of a dread that everyone at the table had experienced. Haraldr glanced for a moment at Maria and saw her bite her lip; was it possible that she had engineered this trick? Haraldr vowed to resist whatever wizardry Abelas used to induce the trance; he had heard of old women from Biarmaland, seeresses who had similar powers to command other minds. "Who are you?" asked Abelas. Haraldr met the furious eyes, as black and deadly as hot pitch. "Hetairarch," said Haraldr. The hands whirled and Haraldr saw the rings flashing around him like dozens of brilliant moths. It is the hands, the lights that compel, thought Haraldr. He focused on Abelas's eyes and pulled his consciousness away from Abelas's darting fingers. "Who are you?" Haraldr's eyes flashed knowingly at Abelas. "Hektor," he said, so as not to spoil the wizard's show. He was trying to figure some stunt to perform when Abelas crouched over him and placed his hands on Haraldr's shoulders. They both shuddered from the jolt. Abelas's eyes retreated and then plunged like arrows into Haraldr's soul. *This man knows me,* Haraldr told himself with utter certainty. *This man knows who I am. Not simply that, but everything, things that I do not even know.* Abelas nodded drunkenly, as if in affirmation of a truth so terrible, it made even him swoon. For a long moment Haraldr and Abelas remained locked in the dance of fate. Then the illusionist dipped his head as if to kiss Haraldr on the cheek. "We are both merchants of destiny," he whispered to Haraldr in a harsh, frightened voice. He danced away and leapt to the stage. "The Hetairarch has suggested a fitting climax to my vision," he declared to the entire crowd.

The candelabra above the stage began to spin, slowly at first, then so fast that it was dizzying to follow the lights. Abelas was gone. His voice seemed to come from above the tables. Slowly, in a mesmerizing cadence, he began the story of the Creation. A nearly naked man and woman came on the stage, and it was obvious that they were merely actors. The light was distracting, whirling. Creatures and foliage appeared around Adam and Eve, somehow mechanically propelled onto the stage. Then a fish flew through the air, out over the audience, too brilliant to be a bird in some sort of guise, or even a lantern; many people pointed and watched. The characters on the stage vanished in an instant of flickering light, but some of the images lingered, like ghosts, a moment longer.

The lights of the spinning candelabra were joined by other lights, and all were in motion. "Go to the end," said Abelas. Haraldr did not notice that a Senator's wife had moaned and fainted only a few places down from him. Much of what followed was clearly a spectacular enactment of Revelations: the opening of the seven seals, the blowing of the seven trumpets, the horsemen of doom, the lamb and the beasts and the naked whore. Yet there were evanescent glimpses of less substantial things, great fires, and the star named Wormwood that glowed above the stage for what seemed a long while, perishing everything below.

Finally the stage cleared again and Abelas appeared alone. He reached up toward the spinning lights and began to describe the city of New Jerusalem. His arms and hands seemed to weave a tapestrylike image of the pearl gates and streets of translucent gold; the crowd gasped as if his hands were indeed building this marvelous city before their eyes. Haraldr saw only Abelas's flashing rings. Then Abelas intoned, "I am the Alpha and the Omega," and Haraldr could no longer blink away the fire in Abelas's cupped hands; the flame grew, expanding into a great, golden, shimmering globe that seemed to engulf the courtyard; the voices around him exclaimed in a chorus and Haraldr knew that they all shared this vision. The light within the globe became brilliant, almost blinding, and Haraldr remembered what Abelas had whispered to him, not the thing that he had heard but the thing that had been whispered when he was unaware he was hearing. "Look for the dragon," the voice had said. A point of darkness, like a black star against a golden sky, grew until its huge wings spread over the globe of light like an obsidian dome, and he felt the cold gust of doom, and the brilliant light vanished.

Haraldr shook his head. The vision faded into the reality of candlelit tables and silken dignitaries. Where had he been? Had Abelas entranced him from the moment their eyes met? The stage was completely dark, and Abelas was gone. The crowd was in a frenzy of speculation about, and recapitulation of, the wonders the illusionist had shown to them. Husbands attended women who had fainted, two men were almost to blows over something, and many simply sat in drunken, bemused awe. Then Haraldr realized that Maria was crying.

† † †

Constantine rubbed his eyes. The oil lamp cast spooky shadows over the rock walls of the scriptorium; were he the timid type, he probably should have begun to see demons crawling about the place. As it was, the demons were the doubts crawling about his mind. He closed the volume of archives he had just finished with; a poof of dust rose from between the wooden covers like a small djinn spiriting forth. He looked over the shelves, hoping against hope that he had missed something. No, he had been through all of them and found nothing. He wondered how late the hour was, and where he would go in the morning. This had seemed so promising: the looks in the monks' eyes this afternoon. That was what was wrong. They had certainly heard of the man, and yet there was no record here. No, this was the place. He could hire soldiers in Caesarea and return and demand the monks' cooperation. He could arrange a loan there, certainly, to pay the mercenaries. Suddenly the shadows did bother him. If the brothers had lied, it was not safe here. He remembered with a start that he had left his mule tethered to the ladder all this time.

Constantine picked his way nervously through the darkened galleries. At one point he reached a cul-de-sac and for a moment thought he would panic. Tombs. He hated being inside these rocks. He reached the chapel and was startled by the growl. No, snoring. The monks did slumber before the Lord's sanctuary was complete, but they slept beside their work. Constantine crept outside and set the lamp on the ledge and gingerly descended the ladder into what seemed a well of darkness. When he reached the base of the spire, he looked up at the light on the rock balcony above him and decided he should go back up and risk climbing down with it; otherwise he was blind in this strange and now pitch-dark otherworld. Then he glanced around the base of the ladder and realized that his mule was gone.

Constantine climbed arduously back up the ladder and retrieved his lamp. But as he set out on foot he quickly regretted having gone back for it. The shadows that danced around him, in and out among the spires, were more terrifying than any stumbling in the dark could possibly be. Where was he going? Surely there was an inn somewhere, or some cenobites who remained awake; he would pay them to lodge him. If only he could see a light.

Cold water seemed to drain through Constantine's bowels. Who was there? The same thieves who had stolen his mule? Constantine parried with the lamp as if it were a sword, thrusting it toward the craggy folds at the base of a cone. He saw red, feral eyes vanish into the night. Wild dogs, possibly more vicious even than thieves. He would have to get a loan in Caesarea now, simply to pay for his passage home, once he had reimbursed the mule's owner.

The scraping again. Constantine looked about the ground for some good stones to throw at the dogs; why hadn't he at least brought a staff? The black blur flashed from the shadows and punched the breath from him. His lamp spilled and burning oil washed over the rocks. Hands clutched at his cloak and probed for his purse. He rolled into the dust, gasping for air, the hands now pummeling his head. He forced himself to his knees and pounded back with his chubby fists, eliciting muffled groans from his assailant. The two men, entirely unknown and virtually unseen by each other, traded blows in the fading light of the spilled oil. Constantine's chest and arms seared with fatigue but he still flailed with unexpected force. The assailant fled, a clattering shadow disappearing into the night.

Constantine remained on his knees, gulping the dry, dusty air. His head ached and his temples thumped with raging blood. Even in his distress he could hear the footsteps behind him and he whipped his head around. The figure was over him and he looked at the face in the last flickering light of the spilled oil and screamed.

† † †

"He induces a trance, like a soothsayer," said Maria. "That is commonly done. His skill is that he can make hundreds of people see it at once. He has learned the ways of the mind, and how to make the mind see what it wants to see. He leads your mind to its own fantasies. But most of what you saw were tricks, to make you susceptible to the final illusion." Maria stretched her arms across the little dessert table and grasped Haraldr's hands. Zoe had set up the tables all across the porch of her villa, as well as on the terraces descending to the Bosporus. The entire hillside twinkled with candlelight like a miniature city; the stairs, marked with glowing silk lanterns, were brilliant boulevards. There was no moon and the sea was sable-black.

"Nevertheless, you cried at what you saw." Haraldr wondered if she had seen some new vision of his fate. Or perhaps her own.

"At what I let myself see. I saw the fire and the raven because I dreamed these things. Because I am afraid for you. Not because they will happen but because I care for you. Because I . . ." She trailed off, the missing words obvious. "You saw the dragon at the end, because that is your Norseman's myth. But you are the only one who saw it. We all saw the light of New Jerusalem because we have all been in the Mother Church, and Abelas persuaded our minds to see it again. Abelas is very gifted, some say dangerously so. Do you know that he was escorted to his ship by his own Allemanian guards and has already sailed off in the dark? He worries that people who saw terrible things will try to kill him. The church would like to see him out of the way because he casts doubt on the veracity of miracles. And he will probably be mad within a year. I would say his art will soon be lost, and even the chronologists will be too frightened to record all of what we have seen."

Haraldr clutched Maria's hands. What she had said about Abelas had, as she would say, "the resonance of truth." But if Abelas had the gifts of a soothsayer or seer, he could without question see into time. And he had known Haraldr, had seen him born, had seen him die, had seen the last dragon fly at the end of time. *And perhaps,* Haraldr thought, *Abelas saw my soul unmasked.*

"He knew you, didn't he?" said Maria. Haraldr's eyes registered the shock. Maria was also gifted, perhaps dangerously so. Haraldr wished that Zoe had not left them alone. He felt unsure of himself with her now; in the light of the candle she was not the same friend he had grown to love during the long summer afternoons. She was the lover he had known on those endless nights. He knew what she wanted, the unmasking of the secret that separated their questing souls, and he still could not give it to her. "No." Haraldr could not look at her. "He did not know me."

Maria looked down and her fine, dark lashes seemed to work at vanquishing tears. When she looked up again, there was a kind of tragic acceptance on her face. "Look," she said, "they are going to dance."

The dancers, a troupe of twenty beautiful young women dressed much like Maria, except in more colorful and less precious silk, formed a ring, their arms interlocking to form a continuous chain. To the music of flutes and cymbals they began to sway, first at the hips, sensually, then incorporating their entire bodies with fluid undulations of their locked arms and precise movements of their feet. Slowly they built to ever more elaborate, frenzied rhythms, movements added to movements until the ring swayed, twisted, and spun like a top with the power to change its shape endlessly.

Soon younger men and women, many quite drunk, began to form rings of their own, swaying and whirling with less grace but equal fervor. Maria impulsively grabbed Haraldr and led him to one of the rings on the terrace below him. They spun about with a large group for a while, and then the circles broke into fours, and finally couples were left to their own improvisations. The music whistled and chimed to an elaborate crescendo. The night was a blur of flashing silk and candlelight. Maria soon outpaced Haraldr and moved in with the professional troupe, her grace almost the equal of theirs and her undulant hips and bared legs even more erotic. On and on she went, her eyes and teeth shining fiercely.

Finally the music stopped to offer the exhausted dancers relief. Maria came to Haraldr, her breasts rising and falling rapidly and her forehead wet. She wrapped her arms around him and he could feel that her passion had only been momentarily diverted. She looked up at him, her eyes still on fire. "I would give my soul to make love to you tonight," she said. "Can you give me yours?"

He held her to him. "I know what I must say to you," he said. Tell her, he pleaded with himself. Every inhibition was gone at this moment—the oaths to Norway, the risk of exposure, the fear of her betrayal—and yet that truth had never seemed more deeply buried in his breast. If he told her, everything would change between them. And he loved her too much at this moment to want to change anything.

Maria's eyes teared as she waited. Finally she dropped her head. "Why? I will share anything with you. If you are a criminal, a traitor, a slave, if you have a wife, a queen, a whore, I don't care. I have to know who you are. Don't you see what it means that that is so important to me? I want to know how to place you within my life. I will do anything you want me to. But I have to know." She looked up at him again. At that instant Haraldr realized that they both stood on some great precipice, and they could either leap from it wrapped in one another's arms, or walk away from that brink separately, strangers forever. He could only answer that fate with silence.

"I have told you everything," she said, her voice the plaint of some small, doomed animal. She shuddered with a single sob, released him, and ran madly across the terraces, her legs pumping and her fists attacking the night air.

† † †

"You are an angel of the Lord," said Constantine as the noseless monk dabbed the cut over his eye with a wet cloth. "I apologize for regarding you as another cutthroat. Who knows how long I would have lasted out there."

"I followed you," said the monk. "They lied back there. The Chartophylax. Brother Symeon. He was once . . . of our lavra. He is in trouble. Men in Constantinople. We monks protect our own." The monk's voice had the curious resonance of the noseless; he spoke as if it took a great deal of time for his words to travel from his brain to his mouth.

"So why have you helped me?"

"Because he is a friend of mine. The Chartophylax. Brother Symeon."

Constantine decided not to pursue the matter; the noseless monk was a not too bright Good Samaritan, and perhaps he thought that Constantine was someone who could help his friend with his legal problems. And perhaps Constantine could. "Can you take me to see Brother Symeon?"

The noseless monk nodded and turned into the night, adeptly picking a path through the jagged bases of the spires. The darkness was overwhelming. It was as if the monk's single taper were a candle adrift in a vast dark sea. The monk moved swiftly and Constantine's heavily fleshed chest ached. Brother Symeon awaits, he told himself as he grimly pursued the black shape before him. The key to all Rome may be out there in this hideous night. They began to climb, scrambling over tortured, worn rocks. The air was suddenly cooler in pockets. To his left Constantine glimpsed a few glowing portals. He imagined the jagged presence of the cones around him without actually being able to see them.

"The ladder . . . needs repair," said the noseless monk. He thrust his taper toward a weathered wooden lattice that climbed into the blackness. "Watch that the steps don't break. You being . . . big." Constantine heard the old wood creak beneath him as he climbed. After what seemed an endless, purgatorial ascent the monk paused ahead of him and the timber beneath his foot groaned, cracked, and sagged. Constantine's foot flew out into the dead void and his shoulders seared with pain as he suspended his ponderous bulk from his burning hands. Where he found the will to pull himself to the next rung, he could not say. Perhaps the Hand of the Pantocrator.

The monk helped him over the ledge. Constantine guessed, from the condition of the ladder, that Brother Symeon was a true eremite who never ventured from his cone cell. He probably raised his food and water up with a rope.

"Brother Symeon," called the noseless monk as he stopped beneath the tiny hewn door. "Brother Symeon . . . I have brought . . . a man . . . to help you. A man from . . . Constantinople . . . Brother Symeon?" Constantine heard no answer. "Brother," called the monk to Constantine, "come. Brother Symeon . . . will see you." Constantine ducked beneath the entrance, scraping his head against the rough lintel. He could straighten up inside the cell. The noseless monk held his taper out so that Constantine could see Brother Symeon. Constantine moaned with shock and despair and his knees went out from under him, pitching him to the rough stone floor.

† † †

The fountain resembled an enormous pinecone; the surrounding cypresses echoed the intricately perforated marble shape. Water bubbled with a musical, faintly chiming sound. Maria was standing in the pool, her chiffon underskirt pulled up to her knees.

"Maria."

Maria turned. Her eyes seemed shrouded, swollen. "Why?" she said. "You asked me once why I wanted to cause you pain. Now I ask you. Why?" She thumped her breast with a tight fist and glared. "If there is some vengeance that you want now, my breast has no more armor. No need of armor. The knife is in it. Twist it if you want."

Haraldr waded in after her and she stood erect with her breast out, as if challenging him to a combat. He put his arms around her and pressed her warm cheek to his. Then he held her away and found her eyes.

"I told you once I was from an important family in Norway. That was no lie, but not all the truth. I am the rightful King of Norway, uncrowned only because I have not returned to claim what is mine."

Maria held him as if he were the last thing she would ever hold in her life. She kissed his face and neck with wet passion, her tears spilling onto his robe. "I knew you were no land man, no mere nobleman," she whispered. "I knew it the first time we talked. I knew you bowed to no one." Then Maria stiffened with shock. "Mother of God," she murmured as if greeting death. "When must you leave?" Just as suddenly, she smothered him again. "I will go to this Norway with you," she murmured hotly. "I will be anything. If you have a queen, I will be your concubine. . . ."

Haraldr held her to him and looked up at the brilliant mantle of stars. They were falling now, the two of them, falling from those heights, and while there was fear, there was also a joy he had never imagined. "I have no queen. And everything in my soul wants to make you my queen." He paused and stroked her hair lightly and listened to the sibilance of fate's warning as he plunged through the stars; could she hear it? "But there would be terrible dangers for you on the journey. And I see you here, in the light and sun and beauty of Rome, and it breaks my heart to see you there, in a night that lasts for months, with the rough men of my court, in the shrieking cold of our winter. I would die to see the light go out of your eyes."

She clutched his robe and looked at him with a new blue flame. "Would I have a life here without you? I have seen the beauty of Norway in your eyes, and there is no place on earth where winter is not followed by Persephone's return. There are rough men in our court, too, Hetairarch, even if their words are oiled." She pulled his mouth to hers and whispered before she let their lips touch. "And if the night is long, then we will kindle a fire inside it that will burn forever."

Maria pressed her breast tightly to Haraldr's, and he could already feel her naked body next to him, beneath thick down covers, in the Royal Hall of Norway at Nidaros.

† † †

"Brother Symeon . . . has not . . . been well."

Constantine gasped and clutched at his throbbing chest. Not well? Brother Symeon, who sat against the wall opposite the door, his legs crossed in front of him, was a pile of bones to which still clung not even a few desiccated shreds of flesh; apparently mice were agile enough to scale these heights even if dogs weren't. The scavengers had left some tattered fragments of the late Chartophylax's coarse wool habit. Constantine watched in astonishment as the noseless monk ladled water into the skull's gaping, intact jaws; apparently the demented monk had tied the bones together with leather cords as his skeletal companion had begun to fall apart, sinew by rotting sinew. Constantine recovered his wits quickly enough to decide on a course of action. "Do you think Brother Symeon is well enough to talk to me?" he asked the monk. "I wouldn't want to disturb him."

"He's . . . expecting you," said the monk somewhat irritably, as if this were a fact any fool should have known.

"Brother Symeon," said Constantine, "I believe that I can help you if I may presume to examine your correspondence." Constantine hoped that the monk would communicate Brother Symeon's assent. But after a moment the monk turned to him and stared, as if Constantine's reply were now expected. "I seem to be having difficulty hearing Brother Symeon," Constantine told the monk. "If you could perhaps help me by relaying his words . . ." The monk swiveled his head to Brother Symeon and shrugged. He waited a moment and turned back to Constantine. "He's talking as loud as he can!" shouted the monk to deafening effect in the bell-shaped cell. "Can't you hear him!"

Constantine reflexively put his hands over his brutalized ears and whispered, "Yes. Yes, I heard him. That was quite loud enough. Brother Symeon, thank you for your gracious invitation to examine your documents." He began to cast his eyes about the cell—whatever possessions the Chartophylax had left behind surely would be easy enough to locate—and hoped that he had not overestimated Brother Symeon's hospitality. Apparently he had not; the monk said nothing as Constantine walked over and picked up the simple wooden box that rested on the floor just to the right of Brother Symeon. Despite an unadorned exterior, the little casket was sealed with heavy, engraved bronze hinges and a sturdy bronze padlock. Constantine paused and considered his words very carefully. Finally he said, "Brother Symeon, if you please, would you ask your brother there to hand me the key to this lock?"

The monk swept dust from the floor, pried up a little stone slab, plucked the key out, and delivered it to Constantine. Praying fervently to the Pantocrator, Constantine inserted the key and turned the lock and was rewarded with the firm unlatching of the mechanism.

The box was lined with lead sheets and the papers were loose inside it. Constantine sat on the floor and held the taper so that he could read.

After a long while he shifted and said, "Interesting, Brother Symeon. I can see that you were quite blameless in that matter. And I can assure you that the responsible authorities in Constantinople will soon know of your innocence." Indeed they will, thought Constantine. In addition to the usual eremite meanderings about "the uncreated Light" and other such theological musings, Brother Symeon had chosen to preserve an account of his own fall from grace. Apparently he had discovered the evidence of the "bastard child" and communicated the secret to Father Katalakon, who had gone to Joannes with the information, apparently over the objections of Brother Symeon. Joannes had immediately incarcerated Father Katalakon in the Neorion and had dispatched some thugs to transport poor Brother Symeon to the same location. But Brother Symeon had been hidden by his brethren and then spirited off to the sanctuary where he had ended his days.

Constantine went back through the parchments, certain that the crucial letter had to be among these documents. But no. He peeled away the lead lining and found nothing. He went through the parchments again. Then he almost burst into a sob at the realization. Joannes had the letter. Still, all was not lost. It was conceivable that Father Katalakon still lived. No. But just the knowledge of the crime Joannes had committed, and the secret he suppressed, would be useful. No. Suddenly Constantine knew the utter despair of his position, sitting here in the hot Cappadocian night with an addle-brained, noseless monk trying to pull secrets from a pile of stinking bones, while his nephew might already be chanting the Psalter on some distant island. He wanted to let soothing, desperate tears flow, and yet he told himself that a man of ability does not succumb to such predicaments.

Constantine thrust his taper out into the cell; were there perhaps other caskets? No. Then something glimmered in Brother Symeon's tattered habit. There. Behind the empty rib cage. Yes, it was large enough. Yes. Indeed, yes! "Brother Symeon," began Constantine, his voice tremulous with excitement, "I am ready to return to Constantinople to plead your case. But in order to do so, I must take with me that letter you have sealed in lead sheets and sewn into the lining of your frock. Please excuse me while I remove it." Constantine crawled over beside the skeleton and reached warily; he prayed to the Pantocrator that he would not knock Brother Symeon's skull off its perch of strung-together vertebrae. The thin lead container came away easily, and with trembling hands Constantine peeled the pliable metal sheets apart. He saw immediately that the parchment was inscribed with the critical file numbers above the top margin. He rose to his feet as he read in the eerie torchlight. Incredible. It was all here. The name, the disposition of the child. Incredible. Had they ever told the child? Perhaps, but perhaps not. No wonder Joannes wanted this secret buried. It would change everything.

"Brother Symeon," said Constantine, bowing before the openmouthed skull, "these documents have convinced me that the entire Roman Empire will soon be indebted to your scrupulous regard for the truth."

† † †

"Each time will be better from now on," whispered Maria. "This was the beginning." Her wet body pressed against Haraldr's, and she kissed him on the neck. Their lovemaking had been different than before, with none of the sudden violence or exhausting ritual that had marked their passion in the past. Tonight had been tender and intimate in a casual, endearing way. They no longer clutched for each other in the huge vortex of fate but simply felt their closeness in the quiet room.

Maria propped herself up on her elbow. "I want to wait until we return to Norway to marry you," she said. "I want to become your wife in your land, by your custom. I want Norway to be my home."

"No, I want to marry you here as quickly as custom permits. I want you in my bed every night."

"That doesn't matter. I will live with you. As your mistress."

Haraldr leaned his head up and looked at her. "Are you telling me that your Orthodox Church would object to our marriage?"

"No, but they would submit you to excruciating rites of instruction in the One True Faith. May the Holy Mother forgive me, but I would rather have your heathen body next to me than have you off in the Hagia Sophia chanting with the priests. I will marry you in your church. It is Christ's church, is it not? I don't think I want this Odin to bless my marriage bed."

"Yes. My brother left a strong Christian church. I may have to rebuild it, but we will be wed as Christians."

"So that is settled."

"You will find churches in Norway very small. Palaces even smaller."

"This room is small, this bed smaller still." They began to kiss, simple kisses punctuated with whispered confidences, and slowly they made love again. And when they were done, they lay so close together that each seemed to be breathing for the other. But between them there were still secrets.

VII

etairarch." Joannes bowed and gestured for the Senators to remove Haraldr's drenched cloak. The cold December wind flung the rain at their faces like bits of scree. "I'm sorry that it is not a good day to be out, but then it is worse for them." Joannes nodded at the enormous crowd of miserable, soaked indigents who clustered outside the portal of the new Redemption of the World Charity Hospital. "You were correct, Hetairarch," said Joannes as he looked out over the sodden, dull-colored throng. "This was a shame that Rome could not long have suffered." Joannes took Haraldr by the arm and led him down the arcaded walkway to the street. "May I show you to them? You are a popular man here since you began distributing free food in the Studion."

And it will do you well to be seen with me, thought Haraldr. As he walked beside the giant monk, Haraldr glanced at the deformed face and thought of the vision Joannes had revealed deep in the Bulgar-Slayer's empty treasury. Could Joannes ever find in that vision a just Rome that served all its citizens? Unlikely, and that was why Haraldr would have to deal with him before he—and Maria—could in good conscience leave Rome. But the Emperor, despite a minor setback earlier in the fall (no doubt prompted by an overly hasty resumption of his duties after the Bulgarian campaign) grew stronger each day. He had exercised with the men of the Grand Hetairia two days ago, and it seemed likely that he would soon return to his wife's bed. Perhaps the Emperor could give Joannes's vision the depth it was missing. Perhaps Joannes would be forced by the sheer momentum of gestures like this to change his policies. A man could be ensnared by his good deeds as easily as he could by his sins. Haraldr entertained his own vision: being able to leave Rome without the blood-bath that would follow the final judgment of the Orphanotrophus Joannes.

"Your Hetairarch!" boomed Joannes. The crowd was mad with delight. "Hetairarch! Hetairarch! Hetairarch!" they chanted, waving their arms high. "I detest ceremony," said Joannes somewhat sourly as the acclaim finally ebbed, "or I would have arranged something. As it is, it seems that the appearance of the Hetairarch is quite enough ceremony for them."

He urged Haraldr back from the street. "You must see it. I readily confess to sinful pride over it. It is a marvel. No facet of the healing arts has been left unpolished, no comfort for the ailing neglected."

Joannes, the obligatory Senators trailing behind him like whipped dogs, was greeted at the entrance to the hospital by many of the staff of physicians, which included a half dozen women in long linen robes. Joannes gestured down the long, vaulted hallway to his left. "The dictates of modesty prevent us from visiting the women's wards. But I assure you that they are as well equipped and staffed as the men's facilities that we will see. Needless to say, our women physicians are a great comfort to the infirm of their own gender, for they allow our female patients to discuss freely symptoms peculiar to their sex, and submit to examination without exposing their female organs and their inherent delicacy to their opposite gender." Haraldr wanted to guffaw in open derision at Joannes's sudden concern for female delicacy—no such gender distinctions were made in Neorion—but it had long ago become clear to him that Rome was an empire built on saying one thing and doing another.

It is also an empire built on astonishing knowledge and achievement, thought Haraldr as the chief physician, a sagacious-looking man with a long silver beard and wide, worried eyes, led them through the wards. Row after row of beds—all occupied—with clean linen mattresses and pillows stuffed with wool, not straw, and with clean mats on the swept floors beneath them. Quilts covered most of the patients, and a hypocaust system just like those in the palace circulated hot air beneath the floor, providing a clean, dry heat; the chief physician explained that the different wards were kept at various temperatures depending on the nature of the ailment and which humors were contributing to the symptoms.

Joannes's entourage paused by the bed of a man with a face as yellow as Syrian silk. The chief physician pointed out the toilet that the man had been provided, the same as was furnished to all the patients: his own sponge, basin, towels, and soap for bathing, arranged neatly by the bed; and a chamber pot set at the end of the bed. An assistant brought the chief physician a copper basin full of steaming water, and the chief physician carefully soaped, rinsed, and dried his hands on a clean towel. The chief physician then pulled back the batted quilt, lifted the yellow-faced man's robe, and pressed his abdomen with long, searching fingers. He looked up at the group around him. "The rheumatics have yet to be evacuated," he said. "As there is danger that they may lodge in the body and be transported into the heart, I will ask the apothecary here"—he gestured to a younger, black-bearded physician—"to prescribe an herbal purgative." The chief physician stood and pointed to a pasty-looking wretch sleeping two beds down from the yellow-faced man; another physician held the man's elbow over a small copper bowl and collected blood from a slit just inside the crook of the arm. "If the purgatives do not induce the evacuation, then we will have recourse to a phlebotomy, as you see practiced there."

Six enormous wards of perhaps a hundred beds each occupied the main rooms of the hospital; subsidiary chambers housed a bakery, baths, a kitchen, and chemists' laboratories for the production of medicinal potions and salves. There was even a tool room where the dignitaries were shown a grindstone ingeniously attached to a whirling lathe for the purpose of meticulously sharpening surgical blades. Joannes watched the surgeon's assistant hone a small steel instrument. When the screeching of the grindstone stopped, Joannes turned and whispered to Haraldr, "I am beginning to understand your Northman's wisdom, Hetairarch. These blades"—he gestured at the shining rows of surgical instruments on the workman's bench—"will do far more to ensure the peace and stability of the Studion than the blades I have used in Neorion."

"I would like to believe that you have learned that lesson, Orphanotrophus," Haraldr whispered back. "You would save me the effort of putting a particularly keen edge on my own blade."

Joannes continued to study the immaculately honed scalpels. But he nodded his understanding.

† † †

"You must enjoy this while you can," said Maria. "It is not seemly for a man to bathe with his wife." She playfully splashed the cool but comfortable water in his face.

"Perhaps that is your custom. I will make the Queen of Norway sit in the sauna with me until she is as red as a lobster, and then take her outside and rub snow all over her myself."

"I do not wish to scandalize your people."

Haraldr pulled her almost weightless, floating body toward him and felt her hot, silky breast like a rare oil spread on his skin. "So a man troths you and suddenly you have become a woman of convention like Lady Attalietes."

Maria rose above him like a sea nymph, her wet breasts shimmering in the light. "Did you imagine that you made love to Theophano Attalietes last night? I am only concerned that my children do not have a mother of bad reputation."

Haraldr kissed her deeply and imagined the kings she would bear him—and Norway: fierce, powerful, with the passion to lead and the intelligence to mediate. Kings who would marry the strengths of Norway and Rome, and perhaps someday even rule over both.

Finally Maria pulled away and hung her arm around Haraldr's shoulder; her legs fluttered above the tiled bottom of the deep pool. "I am concerned about your reaction to Joannes's latest contribution to the welfare of his brother's subjects," she said; his enthusiasm had troubled her since he had returned home that evening with tales of quite ordinary healing arts. "He has built several of these hospitals already, usually coercing various dignitaries into financing them, and he always ends up appropriating most of the operating capital to his own coffers while the institution quickly declines into a putrid alms house. Or even a brothel."

"Yes, but that has always been in the middle-class precincts where the need for such care is not desperate. Believe me, little light, I have no illusions about the character of the Orphanotrophus. But now that he has extended his arms to the people of the Studion, the people are not likely to allow so easily those arms to be withdrawn. And the Emperor is, I believe, almost fit enough to impose his own stamp on the business of the Empire. Joannes will soon find himself wedged in on both top and bottom, and forced to make far more sweeping accommodations. If Joannes can be coerced into saving lives and offering hope, isn't that vastly preferable to the lives that would be lost if I were to attack him? Perhaps I am becoming too much like a Roman, but can't a better vengeance sometimes be achieved simply by the threat of vengeance?"

Maria let her body drift to face Haraldr and put her other arm around him. "I think it is dangerous for you to assume you have learned to think in the Roman fashion. There are layers of that mind which you do not understand. And I hope you never will. I will not share your optimism until the Emperor has acknowledged the wife who has given him and his brother their power."

"I can assure you that is imminent. Can you promise not to reveal this to her Majesty? I would not want her to know and then find that I am mistaken."

"Of course." She laughed. "You are my Majesty. She is just the Empress."

"I heard the Emperor discuss with one of his chamberlains the movement of some of his robes to rooms adjacent to Her Majesty's winter apartments."

"Oh, Theotokos, bless you," said Maria. "I am going to go to the church tomorrow and leave candles on the altar and pray that it is true."

"It means that you may soon have to leave her," said Haraldr soberly, looking at her directly. "Perhaps forever."

"I know," said Maria, her eyes already tearing. "But when she has her husband back, she will no longer need me so much. Besides, I heard a Venetian discuss a route through the Frankish lands that seems much safer than the one you took through Rus. I think we could return sometime on a pilgrimage."

Haraldr hoped they would be able to return. He would not want to leave, thinking he would never see the Empress City again. He pressed Maria's head against his. "I will bring you back."

Maria nuzzled his cheek. "Do you understand why I cannot leave Zoe until her husband returns to her?" she asked, even though they had already come to that agreement.

"Of course," said Haraldr. "I would not leave myself unless that matter was resolved. I have great devotion to our Empress as well."

Maria wrapped her smooth, strong legs tightly around Haraldr's waist and slid her arms around his neck. "Let me show you something," she growled sensually, "that would be quite beyond Lady Attalietes's comprehension."

ichael Kalaphates watched the servant ladle pungent garos sauce over his roast mutton. "Uncle, I hope you are pleased with the new cook. I imagine I haven't told you yet how his predecessor was afflicted. He maintains that a serving girl gave him the infection. So he has lodged himself in a room near St. Artemius, and goes there daily to coat the diseased member with wax melted from cakes bearing the saint's likeness. It sounds to me like a case of the cure being rather more excruciating than the disease. In any event, I should like this new cook to compensate for the deprivations you suffered on your surpassingly arduous and fateful journey. Although I must say that I have never seen such health and vigor on your face, my dear Uncle. You look quite like an Emperor with the luster of a successful campaign in the field about him. Uncle, forgive me if I do go on. You have no notion of how lonely it has been here without you. This is a miserable season here in the north. To think that Antioch is still simmering in fall's radiance.' "

Constantine smiled at his nephew across a tablecloth embroidered with gold peacocks. "I can assure you, Nephew, there were many evenings on the road between here and Cappadocia when I more than empathized with your loneliness. But I don't think you need to concern yourself with the fate of isolation any longer."

Michael squirmed in his seat like a small child anticipating his Easter treats. "You have no idea how madly I want to ride into the Forum of Constantine and proclaim the secret you have so assiduously uncovered. But I quite defer to your judgment in the matter. You have been unerring in your perceptions so far. I learned long ago that the time to bet with a man is when he seems to have won so many precarious wagers in a row that he cannot possibly win the next throw. When I hear about your ghastly adventures and think how close you came to not returning at all, I quite lose my appetite. I truly believe, Uncle, that it was the hand of the Pantocrator that brought you back to me." Michael paused and sopped up the thin, vinegary garos sauce with a piece of mutton. "Still, Uncle, I must remind you that all runs of luck inevitably come to an end. Even

Alexander of Macedon was felled, just when he seemed invincible. I have to confess to a certain disquietude despite our extraordinary good fortune."

Constantine wiped his mouth with a crisp linen napkin. "We must proceed very carefully, Nephew. I need to return to my putative office in the palace and begin deliberating on who shall be the first initiate into our exclusive little cabal. That is a very important selection. It is tantamount to naming your Chief Minister. Also remember this, because I consider this caution to be of utmost importance to your success in the office to which you will now unquestionably accede. Rome is like a horse, or let us say a team of four that has grown accustomed to a certain hand on the reins. If a new driver desires to race this team, he should first stand beside the old driver and observe his techniques in handling this team, his idiosyncracies and use of the whip, before attempting to take the reins, and whip, in his own hands."

"Believe me, Uncle, I am quite accommodated to the temporary usefulness of Joannes in our scheme. I sincerely think that there is a great deal to be learned in watching him. He certainly knows how to wield the whip effectively. He has erred, I think, in never allowing the beast a lick of salt or a soothing word and pat on the neck. Both are necessary to produce a swift team."

"Astutely put, Nephew. But I think Joannes may be realizing that. I have heard that the hospital he has endowed in the Studion is now accepting the wretches for treatment."

"Yes, it is reported to me that he had the mob assembled today despite the wretched weather. He even brought out the rabble's hero, our friend the Hetairarch—" Michael broke off as his chamberlain scurried into the room. He looked up quizzically at the slender eunuch's blanched face. "What is it, man?"

The komes of the Imperial Khazar Guard entered the room to the rattling of his armor and squeaking of his wet boots and leather fittings. He bowed. "I am sorry to disturb you, Majesty," he said to Michael, "but the Emperor has summoned you to the palace. He has provided you with escort for your immediate departure. Your uncle is to accompany you." The komes stepped forward to present the purple-tinted document. Michael rose and accepted the paper like a man walking in his own nightmare. His hands trembled and his face was the color of wet chalk. He stared at the purple text with wide black eyes. "God save us, Uncle," he whispered. "It appears our luck has already turned."

† † †

"What is that?" whispered Maria drowsily. Haraldr sat up and listened. A door closed downstairs and he heard someone clanking through the halls. "One of my men," said Haraldr. "Damn. I hope it is not something that will require my presence in the palace."

"I hope not too," said Maria, wrapping her warm arms around his waist. "It is sad enough to say farewell in the dawn light. At this hour of the night—"

The chamberlain knocked on the antechamber door and Haraldr called out to him to enter. The light from the oil lamp glowed through the archway that separated the two rooms. "What is it, John?" asked Haraldr.

"Haraldr." It was Ulfr's voice. "I am sorry, but the Emperor has requested that you attend him. He wants to be escorted to the Monastery of the Anargyroi."

"What?" whispered Maria to Haraldr. "I thought he was spending less time with his holy men. To go off at this hour, in this weather, will only make him ill again."

"I think this may be the day we have waited for," said Haraldr. "The Emperor is going to Anargyroi to ask the saints' forgiveness for once more entering his wife's bedchamber." Haraldr kissed Maria and got out of bed with a sudden eagerness to meet the cold, wet dawn.

† † †

"I don't want any more pastries, and I don't care for any more wine!" shouted Michael Kalaphates. "I am the Caesar, and I demand to know why I have been summoned here in the name of the Emperor and have traveled most of the wretched night only to be greeted by chamberlains offering me pastries and wine! I demand to know when I can expect his Majesty to receive me! My uncle and I have waited for what I count as three hours now. We did not come here to mince pastries and sip wine to the accompaniment of cockcrow!" Michael stood and glared at the trembling chamberlain, satisfied that his outburst had conveyed the importance of his abused Imperial dignity. The chamberlain bowed and retreated with his arms crossed over his breast.

Constantine looked around the sumptuously appointed antechamber; green Thessalian marble reveted the walls, and a silver candelabra illuminated the complex opus-sectile patterns on the floor. He plumped the scarlet silk pillow against which he was reclining, and fingered a gold tassel. "We are in the same building as the Imperial Apartments," he said. "As you know, I have never been invited there, but I have been privileged to familiarize myself with the location. Apparently our informal reception is in keeping with my Imperial brother's regard for our importance. When I think that he has not even had the courtesy born of blood to greet me in the time I have been here."

"Well, this is preferable to Neorion," said Michael with false bravado. "When that simpering chamberlain reappears, I think I will have more of that wine. It is quite a bit better than I am getting . . . ah!" Michael turned to the swishing of a silk robe but saw that it was not the chamberlain. The elegant, silver-headed Parakoimomenos entered the room and fell on his knees before the Caesar, as prescribed by protocol.

"Well, at last—someone who can tell us what is going on here," said Constantine.

The Parakoimomenos stood and bowed. "Majesty. Eminent sir. The Emperor has commanded that you be lodged here in the Imperial Apartments until such time as he asks for you. Please send for me personally if you feel that any courtesy has been withheld you. I will now direct the chamberlain to assist you to your bedchambers." The Parakoimomenos bowed and retreated as prescribed.

† † †

The renovation and expansion of the Monastery of the Anargyroi was still under way; a lattice of wooden scaffolding, visible in the first faint lightening of the sullen, wet sky, surrounded the unfinished west wing, and several broad areas of graded earth flanked the walls, awaiting the spring plantings. The reception portal in front had been finished, and the intricately foliate arches had a luster of newly cut stone that even the lingering night could not conceal. The Emperor's curtained litter was borne quickly through the south wing of the monastic complex and out into the newly landscaped courtyard in front of the church.

"Why the secrecy?" whispered Ulfr as the litter, carried by burly Khazars, halted beneath the open arcade in front of the church. "There is hardly anyone about in the city at this hour to see him. And I am certain he does not need to fear an assassin from among his people."

"I think," said Haraldr, "that he is overcome by a certain modesty, if I am correct as to what he is about. He has led a rather saintly life for many months, and now he is returning to more secular pursuits." Haraldr could not help but remember, with both acute guilt and pleasure, his night with the Empress. The Emperor would soon forget his saints and holy men.

The monk Cosmas Tzintzuluces looked inquiringly at the Hetairarch; Haraldr nodded for the monk to assist the Emperor from his litter. Haraldr liked Tzintzuluces, though he did not quite understand him; the monk truly loved the Emperor, and his ardent if extreme piety was, unlike that of most monks one encountered at court, unquestionably sincere. Haraldr also felt a certain sympathy for the frail, sad-eyed monk, who would soon have to watch his prize novitiate once again succumb to the perils of the flesh. With trembling fingers Tzintzuluces pulled back the curtain.

Haraldr and Ulfr prostrated themselves. When they rose, they clutched each other's arms in a desperate reflex. *No!* Haraldr's mind screamed. *By all the gods, no! I have seen this impostor before, and he is not my Emperor. By all the gods, no!*

Bloated beyond recognition, his purple robes and glittering Imperial Diadem the only indications of who he was, the Emperor, Autocrator, and Basileus of the Romans struggled to stand. Haraldr rushed forward to help him and was met with the appalling stench of a corpse. He was aware only of the tear-blurred aura of the brilliant lights and glowing altar as he virtually carried the limp, grotesquely pulpy body into the sanctuary. Tzintzuluces and two priests helped him lower the Emperor to his knees. Haraldr stood, his mind reeling, and backed away. Joannes was beside him. Tears fell from the recessed sockets of Joannes's eyes and glistened on the smooth slabs of his cheeks. "Holy Father," Joannes moaned in a weak, almost hysterical voice, a voice Haraldr had never heard before. "It was so sudden. The fit came on him two days ago. He suffered as never before. And then yesterday, I thought we had lost him. I thought . . ." Joannes's misshapen shoulders jerked spasmodically and he wailed. Tzintzuluces left the Emperor to the attentions of the priests and placed his spindly arms around the huge bulk of the fearsome Orphanotrophus. Joannes bawled like a child.

"We must allow him to make the sacrifice now," said Tzintzuluces gently. "We must."

Joannes fell to his knees and pounded his chest until it seemed the walls would shake. "Take me!" he pleaded to the altar. "Take me in his stead!"

Tzintzuluces continued to soothe Joannes. "Please. We must. He has so little time."

Joannes mastered himself with a great effort of will. "Yes," he whispered, his giant arms trembling with an animation of their own. "Yes. We must . . ." His voice trailed off to a strangled sigh and he slumped to the floor.

Tzintzuluces returned to the kneeling, quaking Emperor and whispered to him. The Emperor began to speak in rattling syllables punctuated by gurgling sounds; it was obvious that the same enormous courage and physical will he had shown against the Bulgars would be necessary simply to complete the ritual he now undertook. "Most Holy Lord . . . King of Kings," he pronounced torturously, "may you find me . . . a worthy sacrifice . . . accept me to Your unstained Bosom . . . receive me in pure grace . . . when I have achieved . . . my consecration." The Emperor lifted his bobbing, bloated head to the priests. "I am . . . your . . . willing . . . sacrifice."

The priests simultaneously signed him with the cross and began a long, mournful, slowly rising and falling chant. When they had repeated the invocations of the Lord's Sacrifice, they gently removed the Emperor's purple robe and placed over him a rough wool mantle. They removed the Imperial Diadem from his head and with scissors clipped away his hair and beard. Finally they signed the cross over him again and stood away. It was a miracle of sorts that the bloated corpse could continue to kneel without assistance. And yet as Haraldr watched the shorn face of the former Emperor, Autocrator, and Basileus of the Romans, now a simple monk about to humble himself before the Pantocrator to whom all men must bow, he realized that the newly initiated Brother Michael's eyes glowed with a happiness he had never before seen on the Emperor Michael's face. "I am . . . ready . . . to begin my . . . journey," Michael said raspily, tears of profound joy streaming down his waxy, stubbled, hideously swollen cheeks.

Halldor came to Haraldr's side; he alone seemed in command of his emotions. His cloak and armor were drenched from a renewed downpour. "You had better come," he whispered. Haraldr followed him outside into the courtyard.

The woman stood alone in the rain, her fur cape beaten down by the pelting cold drops. Haraldr did not recognize her tortured face until she spoke. "I must see him," said Zoe. "I must see him before—" The Empress collapsed to her knees and pounded the sodden earth. "I must—" Haraldr lifted Zoe to her feet and brought her beneath the shelter of the narthex arcade. He nodded at Halldor to take care of her while he went back inside the church.

Michael had been moved to a cot, and Haraldr was certain he had already completed his life's journey. But his head rolled and his gleaming dark eyes opened into the light. "Hetairarch," he gasped. "The Pantocrator . . . asked you . . . to give . . . me back . . . my life. Now he has accepted . . . that life. Bless you." Haraldr gripped Michael's monstrous dropsied fingers. "Your wife," Haraldr whispered to him. "Your wife wishes to see you."

The pain returned to Michael's eyes and he shut them as if the light pierced them with awls. "Lord God, help me, I cannot . . . oh, Lord." He opened his eyes again. "She must remember me . . . as I was. Tell her it is not her shame . . . but my own." Haraldr let go of Michael's hand and rose from his knees. Let him die in peace, he decided, let her have the beauty of her memories. He turned and walked outside.

Haraldr took Zoe in his arms and whispered in her ear. "He says it is not your shame but his own. Can you understand why he cannot—" Zoe slumped, her head fell back, and a terrible cry seemed to emerge from her distended neck rather than from her distorted mouth. Haraldr cupped her head and brought her face next to his. "Try to understand. Remember the man you loved." Zoe's neck went limp and she collapsed. Haraldr left her in Halldor's arms and rushed back into the church.

Joannes knelt at his brother's cot, his huge head on Michael's chest, his entire body heaving with sobs. Michael's head lay to the side, motionless. The monk Cosmas Tzintzuluces turned to Haraldr, his dark eyes transformed with an ineffable joy. "Brother Michael has been accepted into the arms of the Pantocrator," whispered the monk.

† † †

The rainbow colors of the assembled dignitaries of the Imperial Court had been replaced by robes of black sackcloth. Even the vast octagonal dome of the Hall of Nineteen Couches, wreathed in golden vines, was dulled by a mourning sky that pounded the clerestory windows with cold rain. Only one man was privileged to wear color at this ceremony. The Emperor, stretched out on a glided bier, was for the last time attired in the purple-and-gold robes of the Autocrator, the gold-and-pearl Imperial Diadem on his head. Michael had lain in state for three days, and in the chill of the hall his features had settled into a pale, claret effigy of the man who had once held hegemony over the entire World. The Orphanotrophus Joannes kneeled beside the bier, as he had without motion, without sustenance, for the entire three days.

The Patriarch Alexius signed over the body and nodded to the Parakoimomenos. The Parakoimomenos lifted his shrouded face slowly, as if the gravity of his task had turned his head into a ponderous granite effigy. The rain tapped faintly at the windows far above, and the great, still hall seemed suddenly colder. The Parakoimomenos's thundering voice rent the stillness with icy, knifing blows. "Arise, O King of the World, and obey the summons of the King of Kings!" The Parakoimomenos's words pealed through the huge dome and returned just as he began again. "Arise, O King of the World, and obey the summons of the King of Kings!" After the third repetition of the grim summons it seemed as if the dome would split from the shattering force of the resounding commands.

As the Emperor had wished, the procession to his final resting place in the Church of the Anargyroi was a simple one. Michael was borne from his bier as the Christ had been from Calvary, in the arms of those who loved him and had served him. Haraldr stood between the entranced Orphanotrophus and the steely-eyed Grand Domestic Isaac Camytzes; the body, drained of fluid, seemed so light that Haraldr was not conscious of a burden.

The people waited along the Mese, silent, wet, a colorless mosiac of tens of thousands of pale, stunned faces against the light-consuming backdrop of their coarse black robes and capes. Yet as he passed, Haraldr felt and heard an unmistakable undercurrent, a murmuring like a cascade of snow from a distant peak, and he realized how dangerous Joannes's immobilizing grief had become. Why had Joannes refused to allow the Caesar to appear in the procession? It was evident that the people who had come to bid their Emperor farewell were confused, even angry. And understandably so. Who would lead them? Did the Orphanotrophus now propose to have himself crowned against all laws of state, God, and nature?

Cosmas Tzintzuluces stood by the simple porphyry sarcophagus that waited to the left of the Church of the Anargyroi's golden altar. The blazing candelabra proclaimed the resurrection. The pallbearers lowered the body into the crypt. The Parakoimomenos stepped forward again and called out, "Enter, King of the World, the King of Kings, the Lord of Lords calls you!" He paused until the church was still again, and even the candles could be heard sputtering beside the altar. "Remove your crown."

The Patriarch Alexius stepped forward and removed the gold-and-pearl diadem from Michael's head. He placed the helmetlike crown on a silk pillow presented by a priest and accepted a simple purple silk band from another pillow. He slipped the purple band around Michael's brow and signed three times over the corpse's chalky forehead. Then he stepped back and the marble lid was lowered. As soon as the face of the Emperor, Autocrator, and Basileus of Rome had vanished forever from the world he had once ruled, Joannes turned and fixed his dark, barely discernible gaze on the Imperial Diadem.

etter stay back, boy. If they see us together, they'll want us to take them to the Chalke Gate tonight." The Blue Star tugged on Haraldr's heavy wool cloak, pulling him back into the narrow, refuse-glutted alley. Her towering, bearded son stood protectively behind her.

Haraldr moved back but stuck his head around the ragged brick corner of the tenement. At the street corner to his left a bonfire sputtered against the cold drizzle. A crowd of as many as several hundred, anonymous and virtually asexual in their tattered brown tunics, had gathered around the blaze, but not for warmth. The sound was a continuous murmur of discussion punctuated by periodic outbursts. They were asking themselves one question: Who would rule them? And they were offering themselves the answer that had brought them into the streets: Joannes. The name was a staccato epithet spit forth in harsh punctuation to the general anxiety. Occasionally wooden staffs jutted into the air.

"It's building, boy," said the Blue Star. "Joannes bought himself three days' grace with that hospital. But if another night goes by without the purple-born proclaiming her husband's successor, these people are going to know that Joannes intends to keep the Imperial Diadem for himself. When they realize that, one hospital isn't going to keep them from going up on those hills. And then it won't be just the Studion that will burn."

Haraldr drew his head back and turned to the Blue Star. He had seen at least two dozen street-corner gatherings like this on his way into the Studion; he wasn't certain these people would wait until tomorrow night. His own internal debate continued. Why not let loose this collective rage, use his Grand Hetairia to hold the Imperial Taghmata in check, and purge Rome of Joannes and his Dhynatoi accomplices? But there were several reasons why not. Foremost, with the traitor Mar and his men in exile and the terrible attrition of his own pledge-men in the Bulgarian campaign, he had one third the strength he had been able to count on the last time he had considered this equation. And the last time he had not had an opportunity to see his ally mustered for battle. He looked at the pathetic wretches with their staves and stones and realized how many of these innocents would be slaughtered.

"What will you do, boy?"

Haraldr gave fate a fool's reply, but to honor the only answer he could. "If Joannes crowns himself Emperor, the Grand Hetairia under my command will besiege him in the Hagia Sophia and demand that he relinquish the Imperial Diadem. I think we will be joined by many factions of the Imperial administration." And we will eventually be defeated and massacred by the Imperial Taghmata, he silently concluded. "It is possible," he offered with more hope than proof, "that Joannes's delay is due to genuine grief. I had never believed Joannes capable of any love except power, and yet I believe he truly loved his brother. In some strange way his brother seems to have been the repository of all the love and kindness that had otherwise been driven from Joannes's breast."

"That love is now buried," said the Blue Star, her irony ominous. She made a smacking sound with her lips. "But it is possible he will offer this Caesar up to conceal his own ambitions. Will you swear your loyalty to this Caesar?"

"Yes, presuming that the Empress will endorse him." That, too, was in doubt. Zoe herself had told Haraldr that she considered the Caesar to be too weak to challenge Joannes. "I think it is to the benefit of both Rome and the Studion to give this Caesar an opportunity to oppose his uncle, and to serve his purple-born Empress and her people. I have followed the Caesar's rise more closely than many, and I see a much more capable man than others credit him." Haraldr again was struck by the parallel between himself and Michael Kalaphates, how they had both been accused of lacking ambition, and how fate had given them both an opportunity to prove otherwise.

"Capable, perhaps. But capable of good or ill, boy?"

That was the question Haraldr had, with no little foreboding, just asked himself. What was it? That day on the ambo in the Hagia Sophia, when their eyes had met? "If he is capable of good, I will serve him until he can serve the people of the Studion. And then I will return to my people. If he is capable only of evil, I will consider him another account I must settle before I can leave Rome."

The Blue Star nodded approvingly. "If Joannes crowns the Casear, we will wait and see what he is prepared to render unto the Studion. But look for yourself, boy. Their patience is growing short." The Blue Star stuck her pudgy face around the corner. Her breathing fogged the cold, misty air. She turned back to Haraldr and looked up at him, her eyes gleaming with the power of the other Rome, the Rome that did not stroll silk-frocked through marble palaces. "These people have accounts to be settled, too, boy."

† † †

"This is not tolerable!" shouted Michael Kalaphates, Caesar of Rome. "I am led to understand that the burial has already taken place and that my uncle and I have not even been granted the courtesy of viewing the mortal container of our relative and sovereign! I don't think you understand the position you find yourself in, Chamberlain! You are inflaming the brow that will soon be illuminated by the Imperial Diadem!"

The chamberlain bowed smoothly. "I am to tell you that the Orphanotrophus Joannes will shortly join you. He is on his way." He crossed his hands over his breast and withdrew.

"The Orphanotrophus will now deign to join us, now that he has concluded the affairs of state!" Michael's face was brilliant red, his eyes like glass. "Who is the heir here, Uncle? Who will soon receive the crown that rules over humankind?"

Constantine grasped Michael's shoulders in his surprisingly powerful hands. "Nephew! Nephew! Master yourself!" Michael seemed jolted by his uncle's admonishment, and his eyes snapped back into focus as if he had just emerged from one of Abelas's trances. "I am sorry, Uncle. I quite forgot myself."

"Listen to me, Nephew," said Constantine with a firmness and authority that his voice had never had before; it was as if the Imperial Diadem had in fact been passed from the late Emperor's head to his. "We haven't much time. Remember this when Joannes arrives: *He* is the Emperor now. If you let that thought leave your head, you will find your head leaving your body."

"But what of our secret, Uncle? Isn't this the time—"

"Right now our secret is but an ingot awaiting the goldsmith's hammer. We have many laborious steps ahead of us before that lump of metal can be shaped to glorious effect. This is the first step in that process of transformation."

Michael looked at his uncle, his face as stricken with confusion as that of a schoolboy who understands nothing of what his master has told him but who also knows that the lash will be at his back if his does not commit it to memory. "Yes, Uncle, I trust you. You know that I will follow in your steps as obediently as if the Christ himself were walking before me." He embraced Constantine. "Thank you for saving me, Uncle. I will find some way to reward you."

The chamberlain arrived a moment later. "The Orphanotrophus," he announced. Joannes swept into the room, his distorted features inscrutable. Michael watched in rapt astonishment as Constantine dived to his knees before his brother and clutched his legs and smothered his thighs with kisses. He took the cue and himself fell to his knees and held out his hands to Joannes. The Orphanotrophus's eyes seemed to devour this adulation; it was as if fires were slowly kindling within the dark sockets.

"Brother. Nephew." Joannes gestured for them to rise. "Rome is now vested in our hands, and yet we cannot rule her without the generous endowment of our bereaved purple-born Empress." He turned to Michael. "Nephew, go to her, succor her in her grief. Remind her of the pledges she has made to her adoptive son, and pledge yourself to her again with your hand upon the Holy Relics. Beg her to sponsor you in your coronation as Emperor. And ask her to proclaim immediately her sponsorship to her people."

Constantine cleared his throat. "My esteemed brother, am I to understand that there is a threat of rebellion in the streets?"

Joannes glared at Constantine and did not answer. He turned to Michael. "Nephew, you must console our purple-born Mother before grief overcomes her. And the proclamation must be delivered before the people can gather tomorrow."

"Yes, my master," said Michael without even a hint of irony. He bowed and departed on his errand.

† † †

"*Keleusate.*" The eunuch, cloaked in black, bowed and withdrew as Michael rose to his feet. He hardly recognized Zoe. Her face was swathed in a black veil; only her eyes and the few rudely shorn strands of blond hair that fell onto her forehead were visible. And the eyes were those of an ancient woman. Michael had known that she was perhaps old enough to be his mother; now her eyes might be that of his grandmother. He had never been shocked at the notion of bedding his uncle's wife, but now he could not imagine how he had slept with this crone.

"My little boy," Zoe croaked in a voice as weary as her visible soul. Michael wanted to cringe as she came toward him. He watched her black-gloved hands reach out and for a fleeting instant wondered if the hands beneath them had become dry, cracked, spotted with age. And then he could only think, *Better these hands than those that would handle me in the Neorion.* To his enormous relief Zoe only maternally stroked the hair at his temples. "My little boy," she said again.

Zoe indicated for Michael to sit on the couch opposite hers; again he was flooded with relief. "I know what you have come for, my child." Now her eyes seemed powerful, alert, even slightly sensual. "Of course you will have my endorsement as our new Emperor. You are, after all, my son—if not of my loins, then of my heart."

Michael steeled himself for the proposal he knew he had to make. "I know it is monstrously audacious for me to presume, and an inexcusable transgression upon the sanctity of your grief, but my soul begs me to ask. Will you take me as your husband?"

Zoe's laugh, coming from behind her veil, was gentle and yet also slightly evil. "I would soon weary of the role of Jocasta to your Oedipus, my son." Zoe clasped her gloved hands and set them in her lap. "No, I do not want you as my husband. But I will endorse your Imperial pretensions, for a price that carries no carnal obligations. What I must have from you in exchange for my endorsement is a guarantee." Michael nodded, ready to offer anything in return for her somewhat unexpected and wholly welcome refusal of his offer. "You must promise to shield me from even the slightest hint of a threat from Joannes. Remember, you will not be protected by the status of husband to the purple-born. Remember that I have my own considerable resources in this court. If I even suspect an intrigue involving the Orphanotrophus, I will withdraw my acquiescence in your sovereignty and unleash the fury of my people upon you."

Michael was jolted by his sudden realization of what her refusal of his troth had cost him, even if only temporarily. Damn! She was still not one to challenge. But it was as Constantine had said. There were many steps to their goal. "You have my guarantee, and the devotion that even a son could not offer you, my Mistress, my Mother."

"Very well, my little boy. Now kiss your Mother's hand and leave her. The Empress must compose a proclamation to the people of her city."

† † †

"I grieve for her," said the purple-born Augusta Theodora. She seemed more thoughtful than mournful, her blue eyes focused on the ice-slick marble floor. Theodora wore a purple silk cape lined with sable; the single brazier in her apartment provided little heat. Except in extreme cold, she rarely fired the huge hypocaust furnaces that circulated warm air under the floor. "I cannot grieve for him. Not after the pain he caused her."

"He will be judged at the tribunal at which all souls are judged, my child." Alexius, Patriarch of the One True Oecumenical, Orthodox, and Catholic Faith, waved his beringed, lithely powerful fingers as if absolving the dead Emperor himself. He sat on a silk couch and was swaddled in a huge ermine cloak dotted with gold velour crucifixes. "I pray that in death the Pantocrator who has sat at his side will take him to His bosom. He was a good man, used to bad ends."

"To what ends will his successor be used, Father?"

Alexius smiled wryly. "I am pleased to see that your contemplation of the Lord's Mansions has not deterred you from occasionally giving thought to the Imperial Palace."

Theodora's eyes snapped up from the floor. For that moment they seemed every bit as quick and potentially lethal as the Patriarch's prowling irises. "From time to time I remember the cross we have discussed, Father. However, I do not think it is time for me to carry that burden to my Golgotha."

"Nor do I, child. It might surprise you to know that when I crown this Caesar for the second time tomorrow, I intend to do so with vastly more enthusiasm than I was able to summon on the previous occasion."

"That you are crowning him is no surprise, Father," said Theodora, a taunt in her inflection. She had become comfortable enough with Alexius, and had seen his own temporal needs clearly enough, that she no longer restrained the sharp tongue with which she dissected almost everyone else. "Your eagerness to do so does surprise me."

Alexius's thin lips compressed with a virtual smirk of self-satisfaction, as if he not only approved of Theodora's impudence but credited himself for it. His rich tenor also betrayed his good spirits. "It will be quite an unusual ceremony. I wish you could be there to see it, my child. But I believe it will hasten the day when you will see the same ceremony from the ambo of the Mother Church. Tomorrow Joannes will leash an Emperor in front of all Rome, but I do not believe that his creation will suffer that collar blithely. The master and his pet will soon be at each other's throats. The master will of course prevail, but his wounds may render him quite vulnerable to an attack from another quarter."

Theodora's eyes were as hard as sapphires. "And what then, Father? It occurs to me that the beast we had hoped to set upon Joannes is now sojourning in Italia, and it is not likely he will return to Rome for some time."

Alexius smiled amiably. "Mar Hunrodarson is gone from Rome, my child, but he has not left our heart. I still say a prayer each day for his heathen soul."

† † †

The transition of power was completed three days later in the Hagia Sophia. The day was so dark that the bronze lamps and rings of candelabra suspended from the dome had to be lit; the lights hovered in the vast space like clusters of stars. After Michael Kalaphates received the Imperial Diadem from the Patriarch Alexius and was acclaimed as Emperor, Autocrator, and Basileus of Rome, he was escorted from the silver-sheathed ambo to a throne set on a porphyry platform at the far end of the church. The new Emperor seemed numbed, distant, like a victim walking away from some great catastrophe. When he reached the throne, he motioned to the Parakoimomenos, who seemed to have aged ten years since the burial of the previous Emperor. The Parakoimomenos nodded at his own staff of eunuchs. The great church echoed with a murmur of astonishment as the eunuchs brought forth two portable thrones and set them on either side of the Emperor's broad, canopied throne. The Emperor gestured, and Zoe, dressed in her widow's veiled black, seated herself on the left-hand throne. "I am your servant," said Michael very clearly, and then he took his seat beside the purple-born Empress. One dignitary far back among the vestitores muttered aloud when Joannes, dressed in his monk's habit, then appeared and sat on the throne to the right of the Emperor, but the protest was lost amid the rising surge of more carefully whispered asides. "My master," said Michael in acknowledgment of Joannes, his homage spoken clearly enough to be heard over the speculation of his subjects.

After this curious beginning the ceremony of adoration proceeded in the prescribed fashion. One by one the dignitaries of the Roman Empire prostrated themselves before the new Lord of the Entire World and then crawled forward to embrace his knees. Haraldr's place in the adoration, as prescribed by protocol, was after the Disputers. *"Keleusate,"* intoned the Grand Eunuch after Haraldr had completed his prostrations. Haraldr embraced Michael's knees and felt nothing more than the cool, smooth texture of silk and gold thread; nothing to evoke the strange marriage of fates that had joined them in that moment during Michael's coronation as Caesar. "Autocrator, may you live long," said Haraldr, the same prescribed salutation Michael would receive from each dignitary present.

"May you be happy," replied Michael in a mechanical, insensate drone. Haraldr stood and withdrew with his hands over his breast, and the next dignitary fell on his face in front of the porphyry platform; the ceremony continued until late in the day.

And thus was the power and glory of Imperial Rome passed on, as it had been for more than a thousand years.

he Protostator completed his inspection, navigated the underground galleries that led from the Hippodrome stables to the spiral staircase, and ascended to the Emperor's box. He blinked away the bright spring sunlight and listened for a moment to the anticipatory fervor of the crowd. To his right and left, the Magisters and Proconsular Patricians, along with the ambassadorial delegation from Genoa, had already taken their seats in the loggias on either side of the Imperial Box. On the flat, rooflike terrace behind the Imperial Box, the Emperor waited, surrounded by Varangians of the Grand Hetairia. Michael Kalaphates wore the Imperial Diadem on his head; the train of his jeweled pallium was drawn up over his left arm, and he gripped the sapphire and ruby-studded scepter of his office in his right hand. The eagles embroidered on his pallium phosphoresced in the sunlight; it seemed as if the wings of gold thread were actually fluttering with motion.

The Protostator pressed his leathery face to the carpet upon which his sovereign stood. "Majesty," he said when he rose up, "we await Your light." With a slight motion of his hand Michael beckoned the Protostator to come close. The Protostator leaned forward until his lips almost touched the pearl-and-diamond lappets that covered the Emperor's ears and streamed down his cheeks like jeweled tears. "Epaphroditis has drawn the first race," whispered the Protostator. "He will start in the second position." Michael nodded and the Protostator backed away respectfully. Michael nodded again and the Grand Eunuch, the same sad-eyed man who had served the previous Michael, came forward and bowed.

"Approach the Genoese Ambassador," Michael told the Grand Eunuch. "Tell him that the Autocrator of Rome offers him a wager. I claim Epaphroditis, representing the blue colors, as winner in the first race. Offer him the team and driver of his choice, his choice to be made after fifteen circuits of the race are complete. I will put my galley full of Syrian silk, still under seals in the Bucoleon Harbor, against those six Genoese merchant craft that await unloading at the Neorion Harbor." The Grand Eunuch bowed and shuffled off and Michael winked at his Protostator.

"He will be quite unable to refuse the opportunity to select a winner after the race is three-quarters complete, when I have committed myself from the outset."

The Parakoimomenos nodded to the Emperor. Michael moved quickly into the arcaded box, his gold-armored Varangians fanning out beside him as he ascended the porphyry steps to his throne. The crowd hushed reverently. Michael made the sign of the cross to the crowd beneath and opposite him, then turned to his right and left and repeated the blessing. Organ music flourished and the crowd erupted into the prescribed chants of greeting. The Emperor seemed impatient with the adulation, and he shifted his weight from one purple boot to the other. Finally the chants were completed and the music stopped and the vast arena became entirely silent except for the crisp snapping of the ceremonial banners. Michael handed his scepter to a waiting eunuch and took the ceremonial mappa offered by the Parakoimomenos. He gravely lifted this swatch of white silk and watched it flutter against the glorious blue sky. Then he released it.

Four bronze gates clanked open at the north end of the stadium, initiating a rising fury from the crowd. In an explosion of gleaming horseflesh, gilded fittings, and multicolored caparisons, the four teams of four appeared, the anxious horses' hoofs chewing up the neatly raked sand of the track. The drivers, dressed in leather skirts with leather corsets strapped over tunics in the colors of their teams, leaned over the open backs of their light, two-wheeled chariots, the reins taut in their hands. They brought their head-flinging teams slowly forward to the triangular bronze start-and-finish pylon at the north end of the spina. As soon as all four teams were even with the finish line, the riders slackened their reins, brought their long-handled leather whips snapping over the necks of their horses, and the teams charged off, tossing clouds of sand behind them.

The crowd went into immediate hysterics; virtually every man seemed to rise from his seat and wave a towel with the colors of his team on it over his head; even the Emperor whirled his right arm above his head, as if this motion could somehow propel the teams more quickly around the track. On the spina, an elegantly robed attendant stood by a table on which twenty gilded ostrich eggs had been set in neat rows, and as the teams thundered past the finish pylon, he removed the first of the eggs.

As the race progressed, the spectators seemed to equal the fury of the foaming horses; here and there brief fistfights erupted in the stands. On the seventh circuit the red team clipped the south end of the spina and flipped out of control, and Michael grimaced and balled his fists as Epaphroditis and his blue team—which was actually three black horses and one dapple on the outside—swerved wildly to miss the careening red chariot. The red driver somehow survived the tumble and scrambled to the railing on the outside of the track. On the tenth circuit a brawl broke out among three dozen people seated high in the southern end of the stadium, and baton-wielding cursores scrambled through the seats to keep the peace.

By the fifteenth lap the green team led the white by a length, and the blue of Epaphroditis was almost the entire length of the spina behind. Michael looked down at the Geneose Ambassador seated in the loggia to his right. The Ambassador, a noble-looking man with a high forehead, bowed to the Emperor, then held up his arm and plucked at the loose sleeve of his ceremonial white robe. "White! White, you say!" shrieked Michael against both the noise of the crowd and the restraints of protocol. The Ambassador nodded.

On lap seventeen the white team overtook the green. The green fell back rapidly; the second horse seemed to have a troubled gait. The blues of Epaphroditis flew past into second position. Still, the white led by half the length of the spina.

On the eighteenth lap Epaphroditis made his move, bringing his whip savagely over the necks of his horses. A cyclone of dust trailed behind as the blues steadily gained on the whites. At the end of the eighteenth lap Epaphroditis came alongside the whites but could not pass before the turn. He dropped back slightly and then came alongside again on the next straightaway. But the whites held him off, and by the end of the nineteenth lap the blues had dropped off a length. One egg remained on the table, and the Genoese Ambassador looked up and waved at the Emperor. Michael glanced at him and again fixed his sharp, dark eyes on the track.

Epaphroditis's blues made another thundering advance on the penultimate straightaway. The whip struck again and again, and the white supporters in the crowd jeered; Epaphroditis was leaving everything on the next to last stretch. White would win easily. But with a look over his shoulder, the white driver saw the blue horses literally snorting at his back, and he went to the whip as he rounded the last turn. His sudden acceleration forced the white chariot wide, and the wheels slid sideways, losing traction. Epaphroditis's team hugged the spina, as if attached by rails, and suddenly squeezed through the opening provided by the centrifugal motion of the white team. Epaphroditis summoned the last resources from his team and lashed them on. The blues won by half a length.

"Six Genoese merchantmen!" shrieked Michael. He leapt from his throne and descended among the mere mortals to embrace his Uncle Constantine, who now exceeded all other dignitaries in the newly created rank of Nobilissimus. "Uncle! Epaphroditis has won me six Genoese merchantmen!" The Emperor gasped with excitement. "You would have to send out a fleet of *dhromons* for an entire summer to do as well as I have with a team of four in a single morning! Six Genoese merchantmen! Epaphroditis will receive one, and you two, Uncle!"

Epaphrodites received his laurel crown from the Prefect of the City; somehow the scarcely animate old Prefect had survived another winter. Then three races ensued in like fashion. After the fourth race the crowd quieted, expecting the usual intermission diversions—acrobats, trained animals, mock combats. Instead, Michael signed to the Grand Eunuch. The various starting and service gates clanked open, disgorging hundreds of eunuchs who carried enormous baskets of fruits, vegetables, and cooked meats. Soon the base of the spina was almost entirely concealed by the food-laden baskets. The crowd cheered wildly. At another signal from the Emperor the cursores stood away from the marble parapet that separated the audience from the track. The spectators clambered over the wall, traversed the dry moat, and poured out onto the track. The stands were soon half emptied, and the spina was swarmed by a well-ordered mob; this was a heavily middle-class crowd of tradesmen and lesser merchants, and even the laborers in the audience were far from desperate for a meal—most had brought their own lunch—but were simply enthusiastic over the Emperor's gesture. Their chant rose and quickly spread: "Michael! Michael!"

Michael nodded at the Grand Eunuch to signal the Hetairarch. Haraldr leaned over the Emperor's shoulder. "I want to go down there, Hetairarch!" yelled the Emperor. "I want only you and a centurion to accompany me!"

Haraldr looked over at Ulfr in silent desperation. Madness. Michael was overestimating his newly won popularity. It was hardly due to oversight that the Emperor who had long ago built this box had not provided any access between it and the crowd below; even the later underground passages were secret, circuitous, and well guarded. Out of the many, there were certain to be malcontents—the Bogomils, who had no reverence whatsoever for the Imperial offices, were sure to have some adherents in the crowd. With only two guards among that mob, even a lone assassin could get close enough. "Majesty—" began Haraldr.

"Nonsense, Hetairach. My children adore me. And I feel Fortune smiling upon me today." Perhaps so, thought Haraldr as he listened to the chants. He shrugged at Ulfr, and together they guided the Emperor down the staircase and through the passageways.

The marshaling area beneath the stands was antic with acrobats, jugglers, and buffoons waiting to begin the intermission entertainment. The Emperor paused to poke his hands into the cage of two performing bears while the astonished performers and stadium officials watched. He growled at the beasts for a moment, then darted over and swiped at a juggler's brightly painted wooden balls. He smiled down at an adolescent acrobat in a short tunic and chucked her under the chin.

"Follow me out, Hetairarch." The bronze door opened and the Emperor strode out into the mob. As soon as he was recognized, the men around him fell to their faces in the sand. Michael navigated the prostrate bodies to the spina, found a half-empty basket of fruit, and began throwing oranges and citrons to the people as they rose to their feet. The chant resumed: "Michael! Michael!" A starting gate opened, and Epaphroditis and his blue team wheeled out among the crowd as if by some prearrangement. Michael waved to the driver, and Epaphroditis guided his team to the Emperor's side. The Emperor removed his heavily jeweled Imperial Pallium and handed it to Haraldr. Then he pulled his scaramangium over his head, to reveal a chariot driver's tunic and leather skirt beneath his robes. He swung onto the back of Epaphroditis's chariot, took the reins, waved Haraldr and Ulfr away, and began a slow procession around the track. The Imperial Diadem was still on his head. The din of approval exceeded that moment when the Bulgar Khan had kissed the boots of that other, now thoroughly forgotten Michael.

"Has he gone mad?" asked Ulfr as he watched Michael steer the team around the spina.

Haraldr shook his head and shouted his reply in Ulfr's ear as the acclaim crescendoed to a numbing roar. "To this moment, he has obviously been anything but that! But what he is hearing now may indeed make him mad!"

✝   ✝   ✝

"Who is that man?" Joannes held the door to his office antechamber open and pointed down the hall to a portly eunuch swathed in the robe of a Secretikoi in the offices of the Sacellarius.

"Lebunes," said Joannes's own eunuch secretary. "You asked for his assignment. He is studying the thematic tax ledgers of the Emperor Leo."

"Just so I know who is here," growled Joannes. Why hadn't he remembered that?

"Orphanotrophus, the man you sent for is waiting for you." The secretary paused, waiting for a response that came only in the form of a dark, distracted nod. "The man from Amastris."

Joannes seemed almost jolted by his sudden recollection of the appointment. "Yes. Yes." He walked with heavy steps to his office, entered, and shut the door behind him.

The young man jerked to his feet when Joannes entered. He was about twenty, with a beard of sparsely woven fine, dark hairs, and wore the coarse wool robe of a provincial tradesman. His large, dark, innocent eyes registered alarm and then surprise when Joannes stepped forward and clapped his bony shoulders. His forehead had a curious bulbous projection, almost as if there were a fist inside of his skull pushing out. A vein in his temple wriggled with anxiety.

"Cousin," said Joannes in a rumbling effort at amiability, "please sit down." Joannes took his own simple chair behind his writing table and studied the entirely unprepossessing young man as if he were laying eyes on the incarnation of the Bulgar-Slayer. "So you are the grandson of my father's brother, Nicetas. I'm sorry we haven't been acquainted before. Do you know that the preoccupations of our Empire have prevented me from visiting Amastris since before you were born? It is a pity to loose touch with one's family. So you are a wool carder in Amastris. And a member in good standing of your local guild." Joannes paused to allow the young man an opportunity to speak.

"Yes, sir." The young man's voice was fluty and tremulous. Joannes was satisfied with the silence that followed; apparently, he observed, this rube scarcely had the wits or initiative for other than monosyllabic replies.

"Wool carding," said Joannes wondrously, as if he were describing some important office of state instead of the business of combing raw wool to prepare it for spinning, "an honest profession that affords a man a lifetime of steady earning and rewarding activity. Unless, of course, he runs afoul of his local Prefect." The young man's eyes popped open like a sheep's in the shearing pen. Joannes drummed the table for a moment, his crusty fingernails making a staccato sound like a marching tattoo. "I should like to free you from that anxiety," said Joannes at length. "That is why I asked that you undertake this long journey for me. I should like you to be my guest here in the Empress City. Forget the worries of your profession for a while. I will put my head to it and arrive at a more suitable employment for a young man of your abilities."

The young man stared at Joannes as if he had just witnessed the Archangel descend before his eyes, bearing a message from the Pantocrator Himself. "Yes, sir."

† † †

"Gregory!" Haraldr stood and gestured for the little eunuch to join him and Maria at the table.

"I cannot stay, Hetairarch, Mistress. The duties of the Grand Interpreter of the Varangians are manifold. I have come to you in my capacity as chief intelligence secretary in the offices of the Hetairarch." Gregory smiled and then composed himself. "This was sufficiently important to arrest your dining."

"At least sit while you tell us."

Gregory allowed the serving eunuch to seat him to Haraldr's right, and he looked for a moment at Maria, who sat opposite him. "I do not wish to jeopardize the Mistress with this," he said.

"Don't worry, my friend," said Haraldr. "I would have to tell her, anyway. I don't know half of what she does of this palace and its curious machinations." He looked at Gregory quizzically. "This doesn't sound like an ordinary intrigue."

"It may be nothing, Hetairarch, but as recent history has shown us, even the most insignificant seed can grow untended and eventually attack the great roots of an entire Empire." Gregory smoothed the embroidered tablecloth before him, almost as if he were going to write his information on it. "I have made the acquaintance of a Secretikoi in the office of the Sacellarius who has been assigned to the records bureau in the Magnara basement. I need not tell you of the importance of that location. This man has become friendly with the Orphanotrophus Joannes's secretary, and of course is well placed to monitor the comings and goings in the Orphanotrophus's office as it is. Yesterday he saw a young man—a young man whose only distinguishing characteristic seemed to be his utter mediocrity—visit the Orphanotrophus's offices for a private interview. He inquired of Joannes's secretary, and learned that the man was a young relative of Joannes's from his home in Paphlagonia theme. My acquaintance also learned that Joannes has provided this young man a comfortable lodging outside the city. Quite ironically, these lodgings are the same as those occupied by our Emperor during the time when he was merely our Caesar."

Haraldr looked at Maria and then back to Gregory. "An island going," he said in Norse.

"Island going?" asked Maria in her own increasingly fluent Norse. "I don't know that kenning."

"Single combat," said Haraldr in Greek. "It sounds as if Joannes has obtained the shield he needs, and from what I have seen, our Emperor is honing the sword he intends to wield to a fine edge. I think it is only a matter of time before they challenge each other."

Gregory stood and bowed. "That is my inference as well, Hetairarch. I will allow you to further digest this information while I return to my duties. And to the collection of more information on this matter."

After Gregory had departed, Haraldr and Maria stared at each other for a long moment. Finally Haraldr sighed. "I guess we are going to have another argument."

Maria's blue eyes ignited. "Of course we are."

"Well, you do agree with my interpretation of this information, don't you?"

Maria nodded. "Of course. It is obvious. Michael has not proved to be as malleable as Joannes had hoped, and now Joannes has begun to carve himself a new puppet." She signaled for the eunuch to remove her silver plate. "I don't know why he has even troubled himself with that formality. He already fancies himself an Emperor, with his private guard now, and the Senate always following behind him like a herd of sheep with golden fleece."

"I think that is good," countered Haraldr. "It makes Joannes's power evident to everyone. If he abuses the people, they will hold him accountable. He can no longer hide behind his monk's habit or the Orphanotrophus's office. And I think he knows that." Haraldr leaned forward earnestly. "He is making serious concessions now. Under Joannes's auspices the Imperial Treasury has financed the reconstruction of twenty square blocks of the Studion. Food distribution in the Studion is now a regular state program, vastly expanded beyond what I started. Joannes is even studying the thematic tax ledgers to find cheaters and absconders who are placing an unequal burden on their fellow villagers."

"And the Imperial Orphanotrophus can also reverse these reforms with several strokes of his pen."

"No. Once the people have received a lightening of their burden, they will be considerably more resistant to having that burden placed back on their shoulders. If Joannes wants to survive, he will have to continue his reforms.''

"I think Michael is every bit as capable of managing these reforms,'' countered Maria. "Look at the Imperial Court judges he has removed, and those he has appointed. And what about his demotion of both that idiot Strategus and his corrupt Chartalarius in Opsikion theme.''

Haraldr spread his hands with mock incredulity. "I have always respected Michael's abilities when he is motivated to employ them,'' he said. "You will recall that I was the first to bring those abilities to your attention, and at that time you argued that I was wrong about that.'' Maria stuck out her tongue. "Both men are capable of ruling Rome. The issue is, which one *will* rule Rome? I simply do not believe that Michael will be able to challenge Joannes sufficiently to rule on his own. That would require a courage that is clearly *not* one of his abilities. Having been almost killed in battle myself, I can see how his experience against the Seljuks might have stripped him of his courage. It took years for me to recover mine. But for whatever reason, Michael does not have the backbone required to win this sort of combat. At best he can rule over an Empire with disastrously divided allegiances.''

"So you are saying that because Michael cannot win, you are going to support Joannes in this combat? I cannot believe that!''

"No. I do not wish for there to be any combat. What I would like to do, in fact, is prevent this combat, and preserve Michael's lesser, but important, role in the government of Rome. Once Michael has been defeated, I will be unable to do that.''

"You forget the real issue of who rules Rome.'' Maria thumped her fist on the table. "Zoe is the government. The rest come and go. And of the two men who currently rule Rome, Joannes is a far more serious threat to Zoe. This is why I cannot countenance Joannes's participation in the Imperial Administration in any form.''

"I certainly have not forgotten Zoe's welfare and safety,'' protested Haraldr. "That is my entire point. The more visibly Joannes is identified with the rule of Rome, the more imperative it is for him to come to a public, binding, and lasting agreement with Zoe. I believe I can negotiate such an agreement myself.''

Maria put her hand on Haraldr's arm. "Be careful. You think you have become expert in the Roman arts of guile and cunning, but you are still merely a novice. I think you are too naïve and trusting to ever truly fathom the Roman mind. I suppose that is why I love you.''

"What if I can bring about this agreement?'' said Haraldr with a somewhat wounded edge to his voice. "A public pledge by Joannes, which it would be suicidal for him to deny later."

"I would say that in that case I would be satisfied that my Mother was well taken care of." Maria leaned forward and blasted Haraldr with her acute stare. "But consider this, esteemed Hetairarch. You say you hope to prevent this single combat from taking place. What if you cannot? Are you prepared to prevent Joannes from winning?"

"Yes. I have been talking with the new Grand Domestic Camyztes, and he is no Dhynatoi stooge like Dalassena. I believe he will defend his Emperor against Joannes."

Maria conceded the argument with a shrug. "I think that is the kind of persuasion Joannes would understand. Good. Now we can start worrying about your throne." She got up and put her arm around Haraldr's neck and kissed his forehead. "I think I am ready for that long northern night."

obilissimus!" Michael held out his hand to his Uncle Constantine and with the other gestured toward the outdoor polo field; one of his portable thrones had been erected along the east border of the broad green lawn, just in front of the salmon-tinted porticoes of the Imperial Apartments. "Look! Look! Look!" screamed Michael, rising to his feet, the pitch of his voice steadily ascending in accompaniment. "Glycas is driving!" A pack of horsemen in short riding tunics—either blue or red—thundered past in pursuit of a small red wooden ball; they came so close to the Imperial Throne that bits of earth showered the attending Senators. A bearded man in a red tunic, mounted on a nimble, fairly small Arabian, charged out ahead of the pack. He raised his mallet like a battle standard as he drew even with the slowing ball, whirled the slender wooden shaft, and with a cracking report sent a red blur flying between two marble pylons at the north end of the field. "Glycas has scored!" screamed Michael. He leapt onto the grass and applauded as Glycas galloped past in the other direction.

"Majesty," said Constantine with a certain urgency. As if his ceremonial title of Nobilissimus had actually imbued him with the qualities it suggested, Constantine seemed to have lost much of his pudginess, and his eyes were tougher and more incisive.

"Yes, Nobilissimus!" said Michael grandly, as if he were the Deity complimenting himself on one of His own creations, which in a sense he was. "Did I tell you, Uncle, that I am conducting a pentathlon on our Lord's Day this week? I would compete myself, but as you know, these affairs of state are inimicable to the preparation required for athletic performance. I intend to make a few tosses of the javelin, however." Michael reared his arm back and flung an imaginary spear.

Constantine drew Michael away from the body of Senators and eunuchs, who, with discretion inspired by the obvious relationship between Emperor and Nobilissimus, allowed the pair their privacy. Constantine pulled a rolled document out of his cloak, opened it, and displayed the purple-tinted paper to Michael. "This is your signature, is it not, Maj-

585

esty?" He pointed to the scarlet script, beneath which a coinlike gold seal dangled from a silk cord.

"Yes, my signature, my seal, Uncle," said Michael blithely. "That is the the Imperial Chrysobull to create a Magister that I signed two days ago. Magisters? Magpies, I say. Let them flock to my court. I have discovered the real power in Rome and am not concerned when these dignitaries protest that I have reduced the worth of their august titles by creating too many of like value. Yes, let the Magister-magpies flock. It is the offices of state, not the ceremonial titles that are important. And I can assure you, Uncle, that I take those appointments seriously."

"I am not criticizing your performance, Majesty," said Constantine, aware that his nephew was far more keen than anyone suspected. Perhaps too keen, as it was turning out. "I am directing your attention not to an error on your part but to a perfidy on the part of an officer of state."

Michael took the document and studied it carefully for a while. He shook his head. "I don't know this particular Constantine whatever," said Michael. "You are the only Constantine who concerns me."

Constantine looked grimly at Michael. "This particular Constantine, now Magister of Rome, is a distant cousin of yours. He is my uncle's grandson. A month ago he was a wool carder in Amastris. Your other uncle has him ensconced in the same villa in which you were housed as the Caesar."

Michael's face had grown progressively whiter; now it had the color of a linen sheet. His knees wobbled and Constantine had to steady him. "Nephew, Nephew," whispered Constantine, "this is not a defeat. It simply means that you have proven yourself too able, too popular with the people. It is Joannes who is frightened of you."

Michael controlled himself sufficiently to speak. "Uncle, w-we are not strong enough to act yet. I realize that my backing among the tradesmen and lesser merchants is . . . profound. But Joannes has the allegiance of the Senate, the Dhynatoi, and the great merchants, and lately he has mollified the rabble of the Studion to the extent that they would not rise against him. I am between Scylla and Charybdis, so to speak."

Constantine clasped Michael's shoulders. "No. You forget that the Empress is also your ally, and she could check any attempt by Joannes to rally the Studion against you. So we can presume that the rabble will remain neutral in this conflict. The great merchants have considerable resources and influence, but the small merchants and tradesmen have vastly greater numbers. So we are still even. The Dhynatoi in the Senate, of course, will go with Joannes. But the rest of the Senate may not. If we can maintain a small cadre of moderate Senators behind us in the beginning, I think we can achieve success."

Michael's eyes were glazed and his voice automatic, but the color had returned to his face. "Shall I begin persuading our Senators?"

"No, we haven't time for that. Tell the Empress what we are about. And then we must begin."

Michael looked at Constantine with the expression of a man peering over a very sheer precipice. "Uncle," he whispered, "can we do this?"

"We must," said Constantine.

† † †

"Hetairarch Haraldr!" Joannes swept through the empty entrance hall of his immense town palace. "You see that I am not quite settled in. He pointed to the high coffered ceiling. "I haven't even had the lights installed yet." He took Haraldr's arm and led him toward the marble staircase. "I spend so little time with these comforts, but I feel I must not neglect the property."

Neglect the property? thought Haraldr. *Is that why the craftsmen I saw out front were reinforcing your gate, and why I heard your private guard drilling in the yard? Apparently the Orphanotrophus intends to concede the palace to the Emperor and wage his siege from here.*

The second-story loggia was flooded with light streaming into the central court; the white Proconnesian marble pillars had a brilliant golden glow where the direct sunlight struck them. Joannes pointed to the courtyard below. Several hundred Thracian guardsmen thrust their swords at wicker dummies set in long, perfect rows. "You know what is about, Hetairarch, so I will not trouble you with ingratiating preludes. I am going to confront the Emperor with his crimes against the people and instruct to Senate to propose a successor to him."

Haraldr was in fact stunned by the directness of the appeal; he silently complimented Joannes on the skill and swiftness of the thrust. "In Rome the Emperor is the law," countered Haraldr. "How can you move legally against him?"

Joannes eyed Haraldr with respect. "You know that in Rome the law has many interpretations. I believe that the Senate and the common folk will find my interpretation satisfies their earnest desire for legal propriety. Of course, I will have to instruct the middle class in these new legal statutes."

"And you would like the Grand Hetairia to assist you in this instruction?"

Joannes's face contorted with his hideous grin. "You *are* a Roman, Hetairarch. Name your price."

"You may find it more onerous than you can bear, Orphanotrophus." Haraldr's voice was sufficiently grim to shadow Joannes's face. "First, I want you to understand that this instruction would consist of enforcing civil order, not punishing these small merchants and tradesmen for their support of Michael. Secondly, I would have a public pledge of your guarantee of the safety, happiness, and well being of the purple-born Empress Zoe. Finally, I want you to understand that I will protect the life, if not the office, of the Emperor Michael with my own life. I want a preservation of some honor for him, as well as a role for him, in the future administration of Rome. He has much to offer his people."

Joannes's eyes seemed to retreat to the black depths of his skull. "I believe you have just refused my offer, Hetairarch," he said with an ominous rumble. "I hope you will reconsider. I would hate to see a life of real account to Rome sacrificed for the sake of two who have merely plundered what others have built." Joannes signaled for the eunuch hovering near the entrance to the loggia to show Haraldr out. "Goodbye, Hetairarch Haraldr," said Joannes. "Remember this in parting: My course against the Emperor, the Emperor whom I myself have created, and whom I have the power to recast in whatever mold I choose, is irrevocable. But this failure to concur over a price seals nothing between you and myself. I will gladly offer you time and opportunity to renegotiate. Perhaps I can offer you some flexibility concerning the first and last matters you mentioned. As I said, you are a man of great account to the glory of Rome."

Haraldr bowed. "And I will consider at greater length the matter of price. But remember this, Orphanotrophus. Unlike our Emperor, I am not your creation."

† † †

"Black. It was as if the veil were a dark pane over my eyes, as if the blackness of my robes had fouled the entire world." Zoe laughed bitterly. "I actually thought that one day I would remove my black to enter my bath and find that my skin had taken the color. Like a Libyan." She pressed her hands to her cheeks as if her touch could ascertain that her skin was still its delicate porcelain white; her blond hair, shorn in mourning, had grown long enough to be braided and brought in little rows across her head. "I hated the color because it could never display my grief. It was a parasite, enjoying the moment of my tragedy without feeling anything in return. If I were to wear black again, it would make my skin crawl."

"There is nothing dark about the vision I see now, Mother." The Emperor Michael did not have to invent his flattery. Remarkable, he thought. Like a flower with the ability to shrivel and die and yet return even more brilliant and succulent the next spring. He looked at her flawless skin—perhaps there were a few more fine wrinkles about the eyes, but the spring-blue irises with their gorgeous amethyst flare were as beguiling as ever—and examined the voluptuous silhouette of her simple purple-and-gold scaramangium. The dried leaf was gone. The flower had bloomed again, and desire was the fragrance about it.

Zoe held out her shapely arms and beckoned Michael to sit on the couch beside her. She curled her knees up around him and stroked his hair. "Did you miss your mother's caresses?"

Michael burst into tears and cried for perhaps a quarter hour. Zoe held him and waited until his paroxysm had subsided to whimpering sniffles. She kissed his temple and said, "I am certain you didn't miss your mother that much, my little boy. What has that man done to you?"

Michael gave Zoe the particulars, punctuated with deep sobs, of Joannes's new protégé. "Uncle Constantine . . . the Nobilissimus, I mean, says we must challenge Joannes now. . . . I am utterly rigid with fright . . . Mother."

"What is the Nobilissimus's plan?" asked Zoe, her voice calm and her eyes as placid as a pond. She no longer feared death. She only feared black next to her skin.

"He intends to provoke him to treason. I . . . I think it is quite a dangerous game."

"Perhaps not," said Zoe. "Your uncle the Nobilissimus is a very shrewd man, and his tactic here is quite astute. He simply encourages Joannes to manifest the very intentions that Joannes is bent on to begin with. Clever."

"But . . . Mother, what if he is encouraged . . . too much? Joannes could have me struck down at any moment. He might . . . do it himself."

"He will not as long as the Hetairarch is attendant upon you."

Michael sniffled deeply. "Do you think the Hetairarch is that . . . loyal? He and Joannes have come to some sort of understanding, due to all the work Joannes has done in the Studion."

"He has no love for Joannes. Do not presume that his loyalty is limitless, but you can be absolutely certain that he will intercept any attack made on you in his presence. It is a Tauro-Scythian thing about honor. I should think you would already have enough evidence of his reckless devotion to the purple."

"You are right, of course. Securely placed between the Hetairarch and the Nobilissimus, I have nothing to fear."

"And your mother will always be here as well." Zoe pressed her thighs more tightly against Michael. "Now, can we imagine just for tonight that you are a big enough boy to be your mother's husband?" Zoe's hand slid across the lap of Michael's purple scaramangium, her slender white fingers marching across the gold-thread Imperial Eagles. When her fingers had completed their reconnaissance, Zoe put blood-red lips to Michael's neck. "Yes," she whispered hoarsely, "I can see that you have become quite a big boy."

† † †

The Monastery of Kauleas was one of the largest of scores of such establishments in Constantinople. The entire complex took up two city blocks. Four multistory wings contained monk's cells, storerooms, refectory, infirmary, kitchens, library, and bath; these enclosed a large central court, in the middle of which was a substantial pale red-brick church topped with several large domes. This palace of worldly denial had been built a century and half earlier, during a period of fervent religious construction, commissioned by a Dhynatoi family as their private spiritual retreat. The original owners had been forced to sell the monastery more than a century ago, shortly after a great famine (not because their finances had suffered due to the poor harvest but because they had soon thereafter proved incapable of managing the vastly expanded estates they had patched together by buying up, for next to nothing, the freeholds of starving peasant farmers). The purchasers were another Dhynatoi family, and they maintained the establishment in great splendor for decades. But a succession of increasingly dissolute scions had neglected and gradually plundered the establishment, selling off the marble revetments and ivory-bound books and gold fixtures, and allowing the population of monks, which had once numbered in the hundreds, to dwindle to less than a dozen. The family had finally given up the property three years ago; the typicon had been signed over in the Neorion as a penitential act. The current owner was the Orphanotrophus Joannes. In three years Joannes had neither visited the establishment nor allowed anyone else to enter its gates, except to have the remaining monks cleared out and new locks installed on all the doors.

But this evening the venerable Monastery of Kauleas once again teemed with activity. More than a hundred armored Thracian guardsmen bustled about in the weed-choked courtyard, assembling the new brotherhood in orderly rows just in front of an arcaded, three-story wing of monks' cells. The new brotherhood numbered in the hundreds. They wore the dyed linen or wool tunics of the city's small merchants and tradesmen, and indeed they were: grocers, butchers, shoemakers, fish sellers, silk weavers, soap makers, yogurt vendors, pepper grinders, silversmiths. All of them responsible guildsmen whose greatest indulgences were several glasses of wine one night a week in their local tavern, and attendance whenever possible at the races in the Hippodrome; they were family men who ordinarily would not be expected to abandon their wives and children for a life of contemplation.

But something was wrong with this group. Most of the brothers' tunics were spotted with blood, and some of them were torn. All of the brothers kept their feet precisely together and held their hands rigidly behind their backs, but often their knees swayed and their heads lolled, and they would not straighten up until the Thracian guardsmen prodded them with their spears. The brothers' faces seemed like hideous painted masks, with huge, bruised eyes. On closer inspection, none of them had noses. Only freshly carved slits crusted with dried black blood.

The rows were finally assembled. The one man present who wore actual monastic garb stood in front of these new brothers, his novitiates. Strangely enough, Joannes's deeply socketed eyes, glimmering with reflected torchlight, were the only distinct features of his huge, shadowed face. Joannes studied his unfortunate novitiates for some time before he addressed them.

"I grew up in Amastris, on the Black Sea. In circumstances, no doubt less auspicious than many of you enjoyed in your childhood; certainly no better. I was castrated at age six and educated by monks here in Constantinople." Joannes was speaking in a curious, conversational tone, as if these men were his intimates. "When I was thirteen, my tutors obligated me to become a monk like themselves, and I spent the next eight years in a monastery much like this, though not so grand. Not nearly so grand. When I left the monastery, I began work as a secretary in the office of the Sacellarius. By dint of unrelenting effort I have achieved the position of your Orphanotrophus. I like to think that my office in the Magnara basement, where I serve Rome, is much like the monk's cell where as a boy I served . . . God." Joannes paused and seemed to reflect. "I will share with you a most curious particular about myself. Since I left the monastery where I spent my boyhood, I have not set foot in a monastic establishment of any kind. Until this evening. Until you forced me to take this step."

Joannes shook his head sadly. His glimmering eyes fixed on the arcaded tiers of monks' cells that rose behind his audience. "It was in a cell like these you see here, though hardly as splendid, that I first learned that numbers were my friends." There was now something quite strange, quite irregular about Joannes's voice, even his choice of words; despite the low, mournful rumble, he seemed to be a small boy offering an exegesis. "I surrounded myself with these new friends, numbers that I chalked on my tablet and the floor of my cell, numbers that I conversed with in the refectory as I chewed my bread. Numbers filled me with delight. They explained to me that the burdens of each day, the unending sequence of fasts and prayers and sermons and chants, had meaning to them, and that they were pleased. And as I pleased my new friends I pleased myself. I knew a sinful joy, brothers, as my friends and I gratified one another."

A smile flickered horribly. "I took my friends with me to the Magnara when I went to serve Rome. And there they explained to me the meaning of Rome, as they had explained the meaning of my previous service. But Rome was not as my friends wanted it to be. Rome was like this place you see here, abandoned and neglected, as random and disorderly as a brothel. So my friends and I set to work to make Rome a thing of order and beauty. And the harder we worked, the more Rome became a place of delight to us. But there were those who envied the beauty of what we had constructed, and these delinquents began to deface the perfection of our edifice. This vandalism distracted from the symmetry and grace of our creation, so that others could not enjoy the beauty of what we had done. So that we ourselves were distracted by their depradations."

Joannes suddenly seemed twice as huge as his arms flew up, his great black shroud like the wings of a monstrous bird. "You are those vandals!" he shrieked. "You are those delinquents who have brought the serpent of your chaos into the garden of my Rome! And your serpent's name is Michael! Michael! Michael the gambler, Michael the speculator, Michael the idolator of unclean chance! Michael who has known the harlot who fouls all Rome!"

Joannes's arms were at his side again, and his voice fell to its original, curiously familiar rumble. "I have brought you here, brothers, so that you may understand what it is my friends and I are building here in Rome. So that you may know that beauty, and become part of its perfection."

Joannes signed to the Thracian guards, turned, and stalked swiftly toward the gate, his black frock billowing; it was as if he were the one desperate to escape the demon of this place.

onservat Deus imperium vestrum," chanted the five white-robed *voukaloi,* the language of the ancient Romans lifting with a clarion resonance into the golden dome of the Hall of Nineteen Couches. The *voukaloi* were eunuchs, and after the first few extended notes their smooth, pale cheeks puffed out and glowed like lanterns flickering on.

"*Bona tua semper,"* chanted the last *voukaloi* in the line, his solo voice ringing out to challenge the echoes of the chorus.

"*Victor sis semplar,"* rang out the next.

"*Multos annos vitae."*

"*Victor facia semper."*

"*Deus praestet."*

Michael, Emperor, Autocrator, and Basileus of the Romans, reclined on his couch at the head of the Imperial table. To the Emperor's left was the Orphanotrophus, his ungainly, extended form a sleeping black beast perched on the crimson silk-upholstered dining couch. To the Emperor's right reclined the Nobilissimus Constantine, resplendent in the purple pallium and scaramangium of his office. Next to the Orphanotrophus Joannes reclined the Hetairarch Haraldr Nordbrikt, placed there against the dictates of protocol at the request of the Emperor. Also at the request of the Emperor, the Hetairarch wore a dagger concealed within his scarlet scaramangium. The rest of the Emperor's long, narrow table, as well as the eponymous Nineteen Couches arrayed beneath the great dome and in the abutting apses, were filled with the dignitaries of the Imperial Court, all attired as prescribed by protocol. Gold plates lit by the candelabra glittered at every setting.

The Imperial Chamberlains moved among the guests, pouring the wine into goblets fashioned of gold leaf set between layers of glass. "*Bibite, Domini Imperatores, in multos annos, Deus Omnipotens praestet,"* chanted the *voukaloi* in unison. "May ye lead a happy life, my lords," chanted the second *voukaloi* in Greek. "Deus praestet," the first *voukaloi* chanted in counterpoint; he inhaled deeply, and then, as the chamberlains began to water the wine from silver ewers, began again. "*In gaudio prandete, Domini."*

"May ye be joyful while ye feast, master," concluded the second *vouka-loi.*" Michael rose and gave the ceremonial toasts, and then more chants accompanied the presentation of the delicacies. Michael's hand shook as he tried to spoon black caviar out of a silver dish; the eggs dribbled onto the gold-embroidered tablecloth in front of him. A eunuch whisked the little black pellets away, leaving an oily smear. The lesser dignitaries at the far end of the hall quickly grew raucous with the wine, but the Senators seated at the Emperor's and nearby tables limited their conversation to nervous whispers. At the head of the table, the Emperor, the Nobilissimus, and the Orphanotrophus made no attempt to converse with one another. After the serving of the fish course the Nobilissimus asked the Hetairarch if this particular type of flounder was found in Thule; Haraldr replied that he was not familiar with it, though it was hard to compare tastes when the fish was smothered in the omnipresent garos sauce. Three acrobats performed between the fish and meat courses—a burly man who balanced a long pole on his head and two boys who executed handstands and swings atop the pole, far up among the dazzling light clusters.

The Orphanotrophus seemed concerned only with ensuring that his goblet was filled as quickly as it was emptied, which was quickly indeed. Haraldr was soon certain, despite the fears Michael had professed to him earlier in the day, that Joannes was too drunk to be an effective assassin, and that his attack would take the more subtle form he had described at his town palace. Perhaps the dinner would pass without incident. Perhaps the differences between the Emperor and the Orphanotrophus could even be mediated at some point, in private. And Haraldr himself had not given up on coming to some agreement with the Orphanotrophus.

After dinner enormous gold bowls—large enough for a man to bathe in—filled with figs, apples, grapes, melons, and oranges, were brought into the hall on trolleys covered with purple cloth. One of the trolleys was halted at the center of the Imperial table; directly above it three gilded cables with thick gold rings on the ends descended from the ceiling like golden snakes gliding out of the night. Eunuchs attached the rings to hooks on the sides of the bowl; a mechanism in the ceiling lifted the bowl, swung it over the heads of the Senators, and lowered it into place in the center of the table. The rings were removed and the ropes slithered back into the dome.

The Nobilissimus Constantine appraised an apple thoughtfully, almost as if he could see his reflection in it. "I note," he said, his first words since he had spoken to Haraldr about the fish, "that the Pretender to the

Caliphate is enjoying the hospitality of Rome yet again." Constantine nodded at the Saracen prince seated at a nearby table, one of several such exiled leaders maintained at the Imperial Court, in sumptuous style, as potential instruments of diplomacy. "How long has this noble son of Hagar been a guest here in Rome?" Constantine looked directly at Joannes. "You would know, wouldn't you, Brother, since you have been the principal distributor of the largesse he enjoys."

Joannes's ponderous head lifted and seemed to yaw very slightly as he stared back at Constantine. He said nothing in reply.

"Consider the policy, Majesty," said Constantine, now addressing Michael. "The Orphanotrophus aspires to reclaim Tripoli from the Caliphate by the presence of a gilded camel driver at the court of Rome. He supports this rather oblique pursuit of our interests with the argument that the Imperial Taghmata is unavailable to offer more vigorous diplomacy, because the so recently humbled Bulgars are eternally restive." By the time he had completed these words, Constantine had an astonished audience of hushed Senators staring down the table at him; Senator Scylitzes, who had paused in his own discourses to sample a fig, set the half-eaten piece of fruit down as carefully as if it were a delicate piece of blown glass. "Majesty," Constantine continued, "I was rather more impressed by the policy *you* proposed concerning the governance of Bulgaria, one that would concurrently address the problem of the reduced strength and effectiveness of the Imperial Taghmata in other areas of strategic import."

"Indeed." Joannes's voice had the same effect that the sound of the dome splitting might have had. The hush spread backward through the room and within a few breaths the entire vast hall was silent. Even the eunuchs paused at their tasks, their glistening white forms rigid, as if they had suddenly turned to ice. "I am curious as to your musings on this subject, Nephew." Joannes's head extended forward from his supine body like the bobbing head of a serpent.

And the Emperor looks like a rat transfixed by the serpent, thought Haraldr. Michael would never have the courage to publicly challenge Joannes. That was the problem.

"Yes . . . yes . . ." Michael faltered, and glanced at Constantine, whose forehead had begun to bead with perspiration. "Yes." Michael cleared his throat and the entire assembly of dignitaries seemed to shift on their couches at once. "It . . . it is my thinking that the tax we now collect—or perhaps more often fail to collect—in Bulgaria is assessed in a manner that is injurious to our defense of that frontier and also deprives us of needed revenues." Michael seemed to have commanded his tongue, but his dark eyes were surrounded by gleaming whites, as if he were reading an order calling for his own execution. "It is customary among the Bulgar people to pay their taxes in kind with portions of their crops and herds, rather than to render payment directly in silver and gold, of which there is an acute shortage among the small farmers upon whom we rely for the preponderance of our revenues. The Bulgar-Slayer recognized this and allowed in-kind payments in lieu of coin, the result being a steady flow of revenue and relatively little discontent over tax exactions among the subjugated people. The recent policy has been to abolish in-kind payments and force collections in coin, which has actually decreased our revenues and inflamed sentiment against Rome, providing an opportunist like the Khan Alounsianus the necessary grievance to convince his people to rise against us. The net result, as I say, heaps predicament upon predicament. We lose the revenues needed to expand the Taghmatic regiments or employ suitable mercenary forces, while creating a situation that requires constant attention to our northern borders, at the added expense of our interests to the south."

Joannes ruminated for a moment, his head tilting gently, and then his voice slurred out. "Indeed—"

"Indeed," interrupted Constantine. "On the one hand we have our Emperor's astute policy, and on the other the belch of a drunken monk who should perhaps consider returning to the cloister, where he might find the frontiers of his cenobite's cell less demanding of his intellect than the far-flung polities that govern the fate of the Roman Empire."

A Magister knocked over his goblet with a dull thud. Joannes's head continued its sotted, marionette's bob. Finally he spoke, his words more distorted by drink than Haraldr had heard even on that first night at Nicephorus Argyrus's. "And what does our nephew think of this . . . suggestion."

Michael's eyes literally seemed to retreat from Joannes's droopy-lidded stare. "I—I—" he stammered, and stopped, his words fluttering from the dead air like birds struck with an arrow.

Constantine's flushed brow glistened. Then he erupted. "His Majesty does not concern himself with appointments on the level of Orphanotrophus. He is concerned with matters that attend to the eternal glory of the Roman Empire and maintenance of Roman hegemony in a Christian world. He is quite above the petty intrigues generated by his servants."

Joannes's entire body coursed with sudden, remarkably supple energy, and his huge python head snapped to confront Constantine. "Make your accusation, Brother!" he thundered, all trace of inebriation vanished from his voice.

Constantine's smooth face was as red as if he had raced fifteen circuits in the Hippodrome. His glaring eyes made him look more like Joannes than he ever had before. He gripped his apple with a whitened fist. "Your secreting of our young cousin to the Empress City!" The dome echoed with the shouts. "His elevation to Magisterial dignity without his presentation at court! This reeks of connivance, Brother!" Constantine's shoulders lifted as if he were straining to rise, but some fierce, contrary discipline kept him seated. "This reeks of treason."

Joannes's face flushed very slowly, like a corpse gradually revivifying. "Of course I have committed no treason, Brother." There was a remote edge of hysteria to his calm voice; not hysterical fear, but hysterical violence. "The Emperor himself signed the Chrysobull creating the dignity of Magister for his young cousin. I invite any of the esteemed dignitaries present to examine the document, which is now in the offices of the Parakoimomenos." And then he was on his feet. Goblets and platters clattered on the floor as Joannes's huge black span milled wildly; the Emperor dived for the floor and clutched madly at the tablecloth, trying to shield his body with the stiff brocade. Haraldr had risen in virtual concert with Joannes, his quickly produced knife still held close to his forearm in a last hope he would not need it. Constantine had reflexively cringed from his brother's sudden movement, but now he sat upright on his dining couch, his face so brilliant and glistening that one expected to see a cloud of steam around him. His jowls trembled slightly.

"Let us discuss treason, Brother." Joannes's even-toned menace held the entire hall transfixed; Haraldr stood almost at attention beside him, Constantine still sat, and the Emperor still cowered behind the tablecloth. "Let us discuss how you have already killed one emperor. Let us discuss how my Michael was destroyed by the burden he had to carry every day, the burden of his idiot brother-in-law and his pathetic, cringing nephew, and, most onerous of all, his corpulent, utterly incompetent brother, Constantine. Had he not carried all of you on his back each day, he would still be beside me. My Michael always despised you. He despised you for the way you sat on your fat ass in the cart that I pulled all the way from Amastris. But he never could hate you as I did. With every step I cursed every fiber of your bloated being. I prayed that you would no longer be useful to me, so that I could dump you in the gutter like so

much offal. I prayed that for so long that I finally stopped praying."
Joannes leaned forward; his boots creaked in the moment of silence.
Constantine's eyes were liquid with fright and pain; his lower lip pro-
truded and twitched. Joannes's next words were almost a whisper. "And
now that God no longer listens, I find that my prayers have been answered." Joannes leapt across the table, his motion mirrored in Constantine's recoiling eyes, but Haraldr gripped Joannes's huge shovel pelvis
and pulled him back. Joannes's arms flapped frantically, but Haraldr
easily pinned them. Haraldr embraced the struggling, deformed creature
until he felt the violence rush out like air from a deflated bladder.

Joannes turned to Haraldr. His eyes were incredible, repulsive; they
seemed to squirm within their dark pits, as if dozens of tiny, silvery
maggots worked in the skeletal sockets. "So you are one of them," he
hissed. He stepped away from Haraldr and surveyed the virtually motionless, utterly silent Senators for a long moment. Finally he turned as if to
leave. He did not look at Constantine, but he glanced down at the Emperor, who now sat staring distantly, seemingly without orientation, as if
he were a man who had suddenly found himself floating high in the air,
with no clue as to how he had gotten there. Then, in violation of all
prescribed protocol, Joannes walked away, unexcused, his arms at his
sides, from the Emperor's table. His boots rattled like drums on the
marble floor.

Constantine looked after Joannes's disappearing black back. He
blinked his eyes as if quickly and stoically settling with some great torment. When the sound of Joannes's boots had faded, Constantine raised
his apple to his mouth and took a bite that was audible throughout the
silent hall.

† † †

The main storeroom at the Kauleas Monastery was a long, vaulted
chamber; much of the plaster had peeled away to reveal the fine, almost
delicate brickwork that had created this massive, almost brutal architecture. The scored stone floor had been freshly swept. The storeroom
contained hundreds of large earthenware jars, as tall as a man's waist,
stacked in perfect rows against the long wall. The jars were all new, the
immaculate, lightly textured terra-cotta surfaces so vivid that they seemed
to be living tissue, like great ripe melons. Each was sealed with a lead
sheet, to preserve their contents for eons.

The Orphanotrophus Joannes had convened the Senate of Imperial

Rome in this storeroom. The location was not according to prescribed practice or protocol, nor was the manner in which many of the Senators had been summoned, pulled from their beds in the middle of the night by soldiers of the Imperial Taghmata. Now they stood, wrapped in their cloaks against the chill of the dank interior, and listened to the reason for this extraordinary convocation.

The light of the tapers threw Joannes's shadow across the rows of terra-cotta jars. "Brothers," he said, his tone as brusque as his greeting, "an extraordinary treason was revealed this evening. Evidence gathered by our Logothete of the Dromus"—Joannes gestured at the rodent-faced Logothete, who stood with the Dhynatoi Senators of the Attalietes clique—"has proven beyond doubt that our beloved Emperor Michael, the late and lamented Michael, may the Pantocrator keep his soul, was in fact poisoned by his own brother, the Nobilissimus Constantine. Having murdered our beloved emperor Michael, the felon Constantine has now corrupted the other Michael and promises to lure our new Emperor into errancies that threaten the foundations of Rome's thousand-year Imperium."

The Dhynatoi growled in an obedient chorus. "How can we stop them, Orphanotrophus? What will you do?"

Joannes nodded gravely at the clearly previously solicited questions. "It has occurred to me that the agent of our peril is this considerable ambiguity as to who rules Rome. In their confusion, many of the people have come to view as their savior this false Emperor, who is only leading them into perdition. I intend to make a gesture in which you are all invited to participate." The Dhynatoi Senators rumbled with grateful anticipation. "I intend to retire to my country home outside Galatea. In this way I will manifest my refusal to collaborate with the traitors. I am inviting all of the ranking dignitaries of our illustrious Imperial Administration to join me in that gesture of profound outrage. The people will quickly perceive the enormous consequence of allowing the treasonous Nobilissimus and his puppet Emperor to preside over our Imperium. The Emperor will be forced to supplicate our prompt return in order to preserve his own life amid the chaos of our untended city. And return we shall, on the condition that the Emperor acknowledges his criminally negligent congress with Rome's enemies and resigns his office."

The shouts of approval from the Dhynatoi chorus rang in the vaults. When the echoes had faded, a single voice emerged. "Where is this evidence of the Nobilissimus's treason?" The speaker was Theodore

Tziporoles, the leader of the moderate faction in the Senate. He was a small, balding man, with intense, perpetually questioning Asiatic features.

"The Quaestor will deliver the indictment to my home in the morning. You are welcome to study it there."

Tziporoles sniffed fearlessly and looked at the soldier standing next to him. "Has this evidence been presented to the command of the Imperial Taghmata? I think that the Grand Domestic Camytzes will want to read this indictment before he commits his forces to the usurpation of his Emperor."

"Camytzes no longer commands the Imperial Taghmata. He resigned his position as Grand Domestic a short time ago."

Tziporoles was visibly shaken, but he composed his fierce features. "You realize that you are inviting a bloodbath in the streets of the city? The small merchants and tradesmen will oppose even the Imperial Taghmata in defense of the Emperor who has brought them so much prosperity."

"I have spoken to the leaders of this faction," said Joannes. "They will not oppose the resignation of their benighted Emperor. I will let you speak to them." Joannes's eyes again had that curious, squirming animation. His voice was slightly distorted, as if he had a small bone lodged in his throat.

"This is madness," said Tziporoles. He was clearly more apprehensive about staying than making a motion to leave. "I regretfully decline your invitation, Orphanotrophus." As he turned to go, Joannes snapped at the soldiers and several of them blocked his exit. He turned frantically to face Joannes.

"Talk to them!" thundered Joannes. "Talk to them! They have been persuaded to join us! Soon they will all join us! We stand on the threshold of Rome's perfection, and only a handful of miscreants remain to deface that splendid creation. Talk to them!" As the Senators watched raptly, Joannes grabbed a spear from the hands of one of the soldiers. In a mighty motion he rammed the butt end into one of the terra-cotta jars. A thick, yellowish oil spouted from the rupture. Joannes continued to shatter the vessel, and in a moment something white slithered out. A human arm. As Joannes battered the jar to shards, additional limbs slid out like giant albino eels. The head tumbled onto the floor and came to rest near Tziporoles's feet. Tziporoles's face was paler than the noseless visage that looked up at him.

"If you cannot hear this man's petition to reason, Tziporoles, I can offer you a chorus." Joannes gestured at the rows of jars. Then he prodded the oil-soaked, disembodied head with his spear and looked directly at the stunned Senator. "His eloquence would shame the ancients, would it not?"

t was a dawn such as had inspired the Immortal Bard. This Aurora was not yellow-robed, however, but a cool pink flame that flickered above the domes of Chrysopolis, still tinted blue with night, and suffused her glow across the Bosporus to wrap the columns of the Imperial Palace in a mauve mist. Maria and Haraldr stood on the rooftop terrace of their town palace and watched the horizon flare in silence. The chill of early spring iced the thick clear air, and Maria slipped beneath Haraldr's cloak and wrapped her arms tightly around him. The movement of the wagons, horses, and litters on the streets below was strangely muffled, as if nature held sound in partial abeyance to celebrate the miracle of sunrise. The processions moved with the slowness of a dirge, the silken backs of uniformed retainers and the armor of the private guards still dulled by the dove-colored shadows in the streets of Constantinople.

Maria inhaled audibly, announcing that she was about to shatter the peace of the morning. "Do you think any have remained?"

"I doubt it," said Haraldr. He pointed to a large retinue of silk-clad eunuchs entering the intersection of the Mese and the Perama street two blocks to the south and west of Haraldr's town palace. "Look. That is the standard of Tziporoles. He is one of the most moderate men in the Senate. One of the last I would have expected to follow Joannes." But follow him he had, like all the other Senators and most of the dignitaries above Spathar rank who were marching—accompanied by their obligatory retinues—out of the City to join Joannes at his country palace north of Galatea. Some were headed out the gates for a long overland passage around the Golden Horn; most were wending their way through the streets to the Platea Harbor where the masts of their galleys had begun to blossom with signal flags.

"Is there hope for the Emperor? For us?" asked Maria.

"Yes. I have already sent Halldor to seek out the Grand Domestic Camytzes and discuss the situation with him. Camytzes is an honorable man. There is a good chance he will use force, if necessary, to defend his Emperor against Joannes."

"And if he does not?"

"There is still hope that Joannes will consider his display of strength sufficient warning and allow the Emperor to resign his office peacefully."

"And if the abdication is not peaceful?" There was dread in Maria's voice, and Haraldr remembered the look in Joannes's eyes. That was why Camytzes was so important.

"If the abdication is not peaceful, I will fight to protect the Emperor's life. I am sworn to it." Haraldr's voice was mechanical; he was describing a strategy already arrived at. "There is a good chance we can rescue the Emperor and escape with him. As reduced as our strength is, however, I cannot expect the Grand Hetairia to sit and trade blows with the Imperial Taghmata. Before the day is over, I will have arranged for you and the Empress to be escorted to the Bucoleon Harbor and taken to your villa. That is where we will meet you. And then we will sail north."

"The Empress will not give up her people to Joannes. And I cannot leave her to face Joannes alone. It is what I have sworn, not on my sword but in my heart."

Haraldr held Maria tightly. "We should wait until we hear from Halldor before we sing the Valkyrja song. This may all end well." They turned to watch the procession again. After a moment they were interrupted by Haraldr's Chamberlain, John.

The eunuch bowed. "I thought it important, sir. You have received a parcel from the Orphanotrophus Joannes."

Haraldr and Maria looked at each other in surprise. "If he is sending me gifts," said Haraldr, "he may be more amenable to negotiation today than he seemed to be last night." He held Maria's hand and followed the eunuch down the spiral staircase to the ground floor.

"Where is it, John?"

"In the antechamber—if you please, sir. It is quite a large clock."

Haraldr followed John across the big hall. The water clock stood on the floor of the colonnaded chamber, a substantial piece of architecture in its own right, with brass columns as tall as a man's waist and an intricate, templelike facade.

"It seems he does regret his impetuosity," said Haraldr. "Or perhaps this is merely his way of saying that time is running out for me to accept his offer." Haraldr sniffed curiously. "Smell that. Does it run on perfume or water?" The clock smelled like a garden.

"See if it has a message," said Maria. She pointed to the doors that seemed to open into the miniature temple. Haraldr stooped and pulled on the ornate little knobs. The doors opened.

"Get the Mistress out of here!" Haraldr shouted to John. "What is it?" said Maria, her voice high and anxious. "Just leave!" screamed Haraldr. Her face flushed; Maria allowed John to escort her out of the chamber.

Haraldr reached inside the little temple and removed the perfume-drenched contents. The features were intact. As he had feared, the head had once belonged to the Grand Domestic Isaac Camytzes.

† † †

"Excellency!" The Emperor's voice echoed through the heavy gilded coffers of the Senate Chamber. "Sit still and listen to what others tell you, to those who are better men than you, you skulker and coward and thing of no account whatever in battle or counsel. Surely not all of us Achaians can be as kings here! Lordship for many is no good thing. Let there be one ruler, one king, to whom the son of devious-devising Kronos gives the scepter and right of judgment, to watch over his people!"

Michael looked around at the empty Senatorial benches. He wore the robes of his office as well as the Imperial Diadem. "A rather denotative selection from the Bard, is it not, you skulkers and cowards! Or should I say, my precious children." He stepped down from the Imperial Dais and strolled alongside the benches as if he were still haranguing his imaginary audience. "Yes, good sirs, in a few hours you will assemble here to learn of the new destiny I have modeled for our Empire! You will hear how the Orphanotrophus Joannes, who has mocked and reviled the architect of that destiny, and has afforded that noble Emperor the unprecedented affront of stalking unbidden from his Imperial dinner table, is no longer permitted to share the rewards of that destiny. Scurry now from your palaces, sirs, because the whirlwind of history and the sweet lyres of immortality await you!" Michael's face was as red as the blood-colored streaks in the columns of Iasian marbel that surrounded him. "Come forth, Rome, and greet your Father and worship your Deity!"

Michael breathed heavily and surged his loins so that his growing erection might be stroked by the heavy weight of his Imperial robes. His head snapped around when he heard footsteps at the end of the chamber. "Nobilissimus!" he exclaimed. "I have extracted a passage from the Bard that shall place this day in both the annals of the chronologists and the rhetoricians!" Michael set himself in a stance with one leg forward, pallium over his left arm, right arm gesturing heroically forth, much like the great statue of Constantine in the Forum. The stance collapsed when he observed his uncle's grim, ash-gray countenance. "What . . . is it, Uncle?"

"They are gone," said Constantine flatly. "All of them. The entire Senate, as well as the Logothete of the Dromus, the Quaestor, and of course the Sacellarius, have followed my brother into his self-imposed exile. They have taken many of their bureaux with them. The government has been eviscerated."

Michael dropped slowly to his knees and then collapsed almost gracefully onto his side. When he revived a few moments later, he looked up at his uncle with glazed eyes for a long while. Finally he spoke in a scarcely audible whisper. "Uncle . . . what . . . do . . . we . . . do?"

"Our response is quite basic," said Constantine, his face set like stone. "We draft a letter to the Orphanotrophus, begging him to return and rule Rome on our behalf."

Michael fell back into his faint, and this time the Imperial Diadem clinked against the marble floor and almost slipped off his head.

† † †

"You are certain the Empress could not be persuaded?"

Maria stood with her arms folded, her face pale and her eyes red but her posture resolute. She had just returned from an urgent interview with the Empress Zoe. "You of all people should understand why she cannot abandon her people to Joannes. Even at the cost of her life."

Haraldr nodded. "My brother died to preserve the honor of Norway's kings. I do not think his death was meaningless." He took Maria in his arms again. "I will remain and fight to protect you and the Empress. I will release my men from their pledges in that case, but their honor will almost certainly compel them to stay with me. We will give meat to the eagles in the east. And this, then, is where our bones will stay."

Maria clutched so hard that Haraldr's breath was constricted. "If you fall, I will not let them take me. I will put the dagger in my own breast. You know I am strong enough."

"Don't make me think of that," said Haraldr. He caressed her hair and nuzzled her forehead.

"I simply want you to know that I will not die in Neorion. I have promised myself, and I promise you." Maria's hands were like powerful claws. "This is so abrupt," she said, suddenly relaxing, her voice breaking slightly. "But then, that is how dreams end."

"Our dreams have not ended. A dream is not truly ended until the dreamer dies. And who is to say we do not dream in the Valhol or in Paradise? Only the dragon of Nidafell can swallow all dreams."

Maria blinked away her tears. "When this dragon flies, I will be content to surrender the memory of us. Until then, wherever my soul is—" Maria broke down for a moment and pressed her wet face to his chest. "You must know what that memory is to me." She threw her arms around his neck and whispered in his ear, her cheek blazing against his. "These last months with you have been my life. All of it. To hold you in the dark, to see the light of morning in your eyes, this closeness we have shared . . . it has given life to a dead soul. Do you remember the Empress's tale of Daphne, how she traded that moment in Apollo's withering arms for an eternity of virginal repose? I would not trade our moment, however short it may be, for any kind of eternity."

Haraldr held her as desperately as life and let his own tears answer the eloquence of her love. And in his heart he prayed to all the gods to deal with him as they would but to mercifully leave him not a single breath in a world without Maria.

† † †

"What divine efflatus has been brought forth unto your coruscating resplendence by the offices of swift-footed Hermes, hence to your Olympios of fair-girded columns, Oh Zeus!" The Senator and Proconsular Patrician Romanus Scylitzes flourished his arm at the black-frocked Orphanotrophus. Joannes was too pleased with the enormous outpouring of—if it was not love, then what was it? Yes, love that his constituents had displayed to him, to bother swatting away the otherwise unbearable Scylitzes.

Joannes had set up his court in the great hall of his country residence, a dwelling similar in Hellenic majesty to the palace he had so graciously loaned the former Caesar (soon to be former Emperor, he reminded himself). His throne was a massive ivory-and-gold dining chair; the concentric rings of dignitaries surrounding the throne were the same who yesterday had attended the Emperor. However, one of the dignitaries who might ordinarily have attended him was missing; having learned from his woeful experience with the Caesar, Joannes had banished the new Magister Constantine to a position of responsibility in the stables. Once this Constantine's docility had been irrefutably established, he would be permitted to kick the horse dung from his boots and don the Imperial buskins.

The Orphanotrophus contemptuously ripped the gold seal from the purple-tinted document. "Our Emperor's hand seems unsteady," said

Joannes to the Logothete of the Dromus as he began to read the crimson script. "Touching sentiments indeed," said Joannes when he had finished his quick scan. "The boy has begged for his life." Joannes mused for a moment; the heavy reptilian lids of his eyes slipped shut. Scylitzes stood by anxiously; the attendant arcs of dignitaries were utterly silent. "The Nobilissimus Constantine, of course, will never achieve perfection. We will strive mightily on his behalf, we will labor over him unceasingly, and yet he will never become an object of our pleasure. We shall be forced to discard him. But the boy might be the culmination of my arts, the vehicle through which fair Calliope will articulate the concentric harmonies of the Roman universe. The boy will stand before the Heavenly Tribunal and proclaim in a voice that shall silence the cherubim that the thousand years of mankind's perfection are at hand, and their name is Rome. And then our boy Emperor shall gratefully offer his soul to that millennium." Joannes's eyes had been closed throughout this vision. He opened them and looked over at the Logothete and showed his repulsive teeth. "The boy Emperor is sending a galley to transport me back to my palace. The thousand years begin."

"O Son of Kronos," spouted Scylitzes, "O Olympian who has with the unparagoned industry of an arm both cogent and omnipotent hurled forth the lightning of his imperium, unto the egregious usurper—"

"Shut up, Scylitzes," growled the Logothete of the Dromus, his feral eyes sparking. "Orphanotrophus." Joannes nodded for the Logothete to speak. "Permit me to caution you. This galley the Emperor has so humbly dispatched may have a Ulysses at the tiller. I would suggest you order him to send a vessel under the command of an officer trusted by you. We have already requested the Droungarios of the Imperial Fleet to remain in Neorion Harbor should we have need of him. Since we clearly do not need to be concerned about a military challenge, I think a more immediate utility of the Droungarios would be to command this craft, along with a crew of his choosing. It would be a gesture of appropriate significance. The Imperial Galley under the command of your officers. And we would have no treachery to fear."

"Well noted, Logothete," said Joannes, his thoughts already on the Empress City. The black-frocked monk rose and turned his back on his glittering, aristocratic supplicants. "Please arrange the details with my secretary, to be forwarded with my acceptance of our Emperor's gracious gesture. And now I must prepare myself to return to the inevitable and unrelenting duties of state." The assembled dignitaries erupted into spontaneous applause.

† † †

"Accept the condition." Constantine stared up at the soaring dome of the Chrysotriklinos.

"But, Uncle, this was our last opportunity. We had three well-trained men among the crew, any one of whom—"

"Accept it. You are a sportsman, are you not?" Michael nodded numbly. "Accept that the wager has been increased. Now, I have ordered the gates closed early this evening. There is no point in maintaining the charade of government. Compose your acceptance to the Orphanotrophus's gracious conditions and then dismiss your secretaries and go to your baths. You must try to find some comfort and rest this evening. I am going to try to raise our own stake in this matter."

"Uncle . . ."

"Continue to trust me, Nephew." Constantine patted Michael's arm and stepped quickly away from the throne.

† † †

Rumor stalked the streets of the great city on a cool, windless night. Haraldr could hear the low, murmuring anxiety that drifted in the still air, and he awakened often to its fevered, wordless voices. For a long while he listened to Maria's troubled, fitful breathing and wondered if she dreamed tonight, and what fate she knew. Toward dawn he was awakened by a rattling at the window. It was too insistent to be a bird. He kissed Maria's shoulders and got up and opened the shutters. For a moment the face at the glass startled him. He peered into the gloom and recognized the white streak in the black hair: an "associate" of the Blue Star's son. With hand signals he directed the little man to come around to the front gate. He threw on a silk cloak and silently padded downstairs.

The little man scurried through the big oaken doors, glancing up at them anxiously, as if he had never entered a house in this fashion. He wore a black hooded cloak like a monk's. "Haraldr Nordbrikt," he whispered quickly, "the Blue Star is aware that you might be experiencing some difficulties. She says she intends to help you, but she is having difficulty convincing the people of the Studion that Joannes is their enemy. Or at least that it is worth dying to oppose him. But she offers you what resources she can muster. She says she owes you this much." The little man nodded vigorously as if to second that judgment.

Haraldr had already considered the issue. "Even united, her people would not be able to tip the balance against the Imperial Taghmata. My Varangians are far too reduced in strength. I see no purpose in sending innocents to the sacrifice in a lost cause when the only result would be to focus the wrath of Joannes on the Studion. And he may decide that with his other enemies in the city, it is prudent to continue his programs there. But tell my comrade the Blue Star that her offer alone is worth a thousand men at my side. And tell her that should I soon find myself at the feet of the Pantocrator, I will say a prayer for her each day."

The messenger nodded grimly and offered Haraldr his hands. As he gripped the little man's forearms, Haraldr was struck that he felt far more sincerity and honesty in the parting clasp of this petty thief than he had in the lavish greetings of the men who ruled Rome.

✝   ✝   ✝

One hundred marines of the Imperial Fleet stood at attention along the flat stone surface of the jetty. Armored from head to toe in steel mail-coats, helms, and embossed greaves, they were a wall of silver in the morning sun. Behind them, the brilliantly enameled scarlet-and-white superstructure of the Imperial Trireme rose above the massive black hull. The Droungarios of the Imperial Fleet, attired in gold ceremonial armor and attended by four komes of the Imperial Fleet, waited to welcome the Orphanotrophus. Joannes descended the marble steps to the jetty, his enormous black form a curious magnet for the sparkling dignitaries who trailed behind him like rapt children. The officers fell to their knees and the marines bristled a line of spears in acclamation. "Orphanotrophus!" The shouts rolled across the Bosporus, a warning to the city that now awaited its conqueror. "Orphanotrophus! Come forth, champion of Christ! Come forth, victorious Lord of Rome!"

Joannes's misshapen fingers urged the supplicant Droungarios to his feet. "Well executed, Droungarios," rumbled Joannes as he surveyed the fearsome marines. "Are you confident that the Imperial Taghmata understands my instructions?"

"They await your personal signal, Orphanotrophus."

"Very well. Let us embark and reclaim our City from the usurper and his *barbaroi* accomplices.

✝   ✝   ✝

"Hetairarch." Halldor stepped forward, his mail byrnnie chinging as he walked. "The barricades are set." Halldor pointed with the polished steel blade of his broadax, noting in turn each of four entrances to the main hall of the Imperial Gynaeceum; the tall bronze doors, visible behind the columns of dark red Carian marble that supported the building's main dome, were bolstered with heavy ceremonial dining couches. Twenty Varangians clustered at each door, talking quietly and adjusting their armor or inspecting their weapons. The sound of axes being fine-honed shrilled through the hall. The Valkyrja song, thought Haraldr. But there was a beauty to that music when he thought how unhesitatingly his pledge-men had vowed to remain at his side in spite of the Emperor's craven capitulation to Joannes. They were fighting for him now, and for their own honor. They would not be known as the Varangians who had been driven from Miklagardr like whipped dogs.

The Decurion Stefnir Hrafnrson ran over from the north end of the hall, where the bronze gate was still slightly ajar. "Hetairarch!" he snapped as he handed Haraldr a rolled document.

"The new Grand Domestic," Haraldr told Halldor as he broke the lead seal. Haraldr read the text quickly and looked at Halldor. "Ducas is the new Grand Domestic. You remember him, of course. A Dhynatoi stooge in the tradition of Dalassena. His men will not fight well for him, but being good soldiers, they will fight. Ducas writes well. He calls upon the men of the Grand Hetairia to surrender and end this day before it begins." Haraldr's pause was punctuated by the shriek of a whetstone across Hunland steel. "Decurion," he told Hrafnrson, "have a reply drafted. Tell the Grand Domestic to prepare himself for the longest day of his life."

Haraldr dismissed his officers, strode to the west end of the hall, and climbed two sets of marble staircases to the roof of the Gynaeceum. Ulfr stood on the terrace that ringed a large, colonnaded cupola used by the Empress and her ladies to view the races in the Hippodrome; the enormous, empty, bleached bulk of the stadium extended beneath them to the north. The sun was three hours above the horizon, and the surrounding domes of the palace complex seemed coated with quicksilver. No sails or painted hulls marred the sky-blue Bosporus; the docks had been rife with rumors of some sort of naval engagement between supporters of the Emperor and the Imperial Fleet, elements of which were visible as neat rows of miniature *dhromons* in the distant Neorion Harbor. The single dark shaft of Neorion Tower stood against the brilliant red and white of the ships like the sole remaining column of a temple raised in some distant time by an evil god. Haraldr thanked the Pantocrator for allowing him to love a woman whose courage would not allow her to enter the black steel doors of Neorion. May the Christ forgive him, but he would plunge the dagger in that beloved breast himself before he abandoned her to that place.

Ulfr scanned the northern horizon. "I expect Joannes soon," he told Haraldr without looking away from the sea. "If there is to be fighting, he will want it to start promptly. I'm certain he wants to make his triumphal entry before dark."

Haraldr laughed derisively. "The Orphanotrophus will wait in Bucoleon Harbor for many days before he makes that entry. And he will have to climb over the corpses of his Imperial Taghmata when he does. The defenses you and Halldor have prepared are excellent."

Ulfr looked around as someone emerged from the staircase.

"Gregory!" said Haraldr. He had tried to think of some excuse for getting the brave little interpreter to some place of safety but had decided that Gregory would perceive any such effort as an insult. "You have come to soar with the Norse Eagles!"

"I am afraid you will want to see if I actually can fly from this perch when you hear what I have to say, Hetairarch," said Gregory with none of his customary levity. "First, I have discovered the signal that Joannes will give the Taghmata to begin their attack. The Imperial Trireme will hoist a black flag to the center mast before it docks in Bucoleon Harbor."

"The color is apt," said Haraldr. "That is important intelligence, Grand Interpreter. Why did you think I would—"

"That was merely the flower on the dung heap, Hetairarch. The piece of intelligence that you will find most foul is this: The Nobilissimus has not been seen this morning. He was last seen during the night last, in the inns near the Pisan Quarter. Looking for a ship."

"Damn!" Haraldr smashed his ax against his shield, and the thunder boomed off into the sky. "I knew from the moment I laid eyes on that . . . that . . . I knew he was a craven, praise-tongued, charcoal-chewing . . . damn!" Haraldr stood fuming at the sea for a moment, as if he hoped he could spot the fleeing Nobilissimus and cut him down with a prodigious toss of his ax. "Does the Emperor know this?"

Gregory shook his head. "Since we are discussing cowards," said Ulfr, "where is our Emperor?"

"He is in the Empress's chambers," said Haraldr. "The purple-born and Maria are trying to steady him." Haraldr again pounded his shield with his ax and glared at Ulfr. "Get our Emperor up here, Centurion, if you must carry him over your back. I'll tell him myself about his uncle's defection. And then I am going to make him stay here and watch his fate sail toward him."

The Emperor followed Ulfr up the stairs a quarter of an hour later. Michael wore a purple scaramangium but no other insignia of his office. His face was flushed but his dark eyes were blank, as if his soul had fled, leaving only its shell to confront fate. "Majesty," said Haraldr, trying to conceal the disgust he felt, "I am concerned about the Nobilissimus."

Michael's eyes darted from side to side. "He is—working on something," said the Emperor, his words coming in rapid bursts. "He—has a plan." Suddenly Michael fell to his knees. "Hetairarch!" he shrieked, his hands clasped before his hysterical face, "he has left me!" Michael clutched Haraldr's legs. "I am lost, Hetairarch. Hetairarch, swear to me you will not let me die. Swear to me . . ." He rubbed his nose against Haraldr's boots. "If there is mercy in you, swear it to me."

Haraldr could only feel pity. He remembered how Jarl Rognvald had both literally and spiritually lifted him up after Stiklestad. "Majesty, Majesty," said Haraldr as he lifted the sobbing Emperor to his feet. "You had courage once. I saw the proof of that courage pounded into your armor that day near Antioch. Today you will find that courage again."

Michael made a worthy effort to draw himself together. "You are right, of course, Hetairarch." He looked out to sea resolutely. "I hope this—outburst will not—prejudice your loyalty. You and your men are all I have."

"Majesty," said Haraldr, "I swear by all that is sacred to me that as long as I remain in Rome, I will defend your life with my own."

"Thank you, Hetairarch." Michael's eyes teared, and he looked down at his purple boots. Ulfr motioned to get Haraldr's attention and pointed to the neck of the Bosporus, to the north. Haraldr left the Emperor and walked around the cupola to get a better look.

The masts were clearly visible on the horizon. "Joannes and his Senators," whispered Ulfr. "I think I can make out the Imperial Trireme—" Ulfr stopped as both he and Haraldr saw the activity along the portico-lined avenue that ran between the Hall of Nineteen Couches and the Sigma, the principal north-south axis of the palace complex. Preceded by gold-armored officers mounted on white horses, the units of the Imperial Taghmata were moving into position.

The next hour was excruciating. The Taghmatic units surrounded the Gynaeceum while Joannes's flotilla moved steadily south. The Senators' galleys steered into the Golden Horn to make their anchorage at Platea

Harbor, while the Imperial Trireme bearing Joannes sailed conspicuously alone around the tip of Byzantium, heading well past the city so that
the populace would have time to watch as the imposing, seagoing fortress
turned back to the north and came head in to the Bucoleon Harbor.
Somehow Michael was able to watch it all without another breakdown,
and Haraldr was touched by his composure. It was no easy thing for a man
to march with his head up into battle after he had already soiled his
breeches in front of his comrades.

The Imperial Trireme trailed white wake and the three rows of oars
dipped and rose inexorably; from a distance the armored marines looked
like granulated silver spilled on the deck. Haraldr watched as the swift-
moving craft plunged like an elaborate spearhead directly toward the
Bucoleon quays just below them to the south. Then something at the
periphery of his vision distracted him. Another wake streaked the finely
silvered water; a ship had emerged from the Harbor of Contoscali, a very
small U-shaped bay about five bowshots west of the Bucoleon.

"What is it?" asked Ulfr.

"A *khelandia* of the *pamphyloi* class. Imperial Fleet," said Haraldr. The
pamphyloi were half the size of *dhromons* but still lethally armed and faster
and more maneuverable. The single tier of oars fluttered in rapid cadence
and the narrow-beamed vessel moved quickly on an intercept course with
the Imperial Trireme; as Haraldr judged it, the two craft would make
contact just a bowshot beyond the Bucoleon breakwater.

"A curious rendezvous for an escort vessel," said Ulfr, pointing to
where the wakes would converge. Haraldr looked at Ulfr and shook his
head. It was obviously a desperate rendezvous for a Nobilissimus intent
on begging for his life.

Michael pointed at the racing *khelandia* with a limp finger and quaking
arm. "Uncle is on that ship, isn't he?" he said in a voice so low that had
there been wind, his words would have been lost.

† † †

"Signal him to return to his anchorage!" shouted the Droungarios of
the Imperial Fleet. He stood at the stern of the Imperial Trireme, high
above the hissing sea, atop a cottage-size stern-castle that resembled a
small palace in its ornate gold fittings. The Droungarios was a slight man;
no doubt he had been tough and wiry in his youth, but now that he was
well past seventy, shriveled and stooped, his authority was in his rough,
wine-pickled voice and insignia of rank rather than his physical presence.

His command soon produced a sequence of flags along the yardarm of the trireme's central mast.

"He's not responding!" shouted one of the Droungarios's attendant komes, shortly after the flags had been raised.

The Orphanotrophus Joannes appeared at the Droungarios's side and leaned against the gilded railing. "Let him come on," Joannes said, his face struggling with a grin. The Droungarios looked at him in surprise. "See that man," he said, pointing to a purple-clad figure at the bow of the *khelandia*, now only two stades distant. "Those are the robes of the Nobilissimus. My brother has come to negotiate the terms of his nephew's abdication."

The ships slowed as they reached hailing distance, and the komes at the bow of the *khelandia* asked permission to come alongside. "Ship port oars!" commanded the Droungarios. The two craft swung around, and crews threw rope bumpers over the sides. The *khelandia* thudded along-side the trireme and crewmen on the deck scrambled to secure mooring ropes. The Droungarios looked down at the komes in command of the *khelandia;* the komes was a short man with a chest so massively powerful that his silver breastplate looked like an enormous kettle. He had a short dark beard, a sun-blackened face, and flint-hard gray eyes. "What is that man's name?" the Droungarios whispered to his aide. The Droungarios had more than two hundred komes, each in command of anywhere from one to four vessels, beneath him; he vaguely recalled having given this man a reward for some role he had played in a battle off Italia.

"Moschus, Droungarios. John Moschus. The hero of Taranto."

"Find out what he is about." The Droungarios shook his head. Hero . . . Taranto . . .

Moschus walked to the stern of his vessel and shouted up at the Droun-garios. "I would like to come aboard, sir, and negotiate for the safe transfer of the Nobilissimus to your flagship. I believe it is in the interest of the Imperial Navy . . ."

"You presume what is in the interest of the Imperial Navy, Komes!" shouted the Droungarios angrily. This so-called hero would soon be pulling an oar on an *ousiai.*

"Let us play this out," countermanded Joannes. It amused him to think that Constantine was already concerned about his immediate safety. In Neorion he would wish that he had met with a quick death out here.

The Droungarios, followed by his aides, scuttled down the stairs to the deck to avoid having to deal with a potentially insubordinate officer in front of the all-conquering Orphanotrophus Joannes. It wouldn't do to have a man like that perceive weakness in his commanders. "Komes Moschus!" the Droungarios shouted, his face livid, "come aboard and explain your treason!"

Moschus scrambled up the rope ladder and climbed over the heavy, gilt-and-red railing of the Imperial Trireme's main deck. He strode right up to the Droungarios and in a lightning-quick movement was behind him; one powerful arm pinned the old man's neck, and the other pressed a knife to his nose. "One movement and this blade will be in his brain!" shouted Moschus to the four stunned aides. "Order your marines to hold their places!" At the same time two dozen marines clambered out of hatches on the deck of the *khelandia;* some of them brandished liquid-fire grenades.

"What did he offer you?" the bulging-eyed Droungarios asked raspily.

"I am to be the Droungarios of the Imperial Fleet," said Moschus.

"I will give you my estates near Ancyra. Fifty villages," croaked the Droungarios.

"I am a sailor," growled Moschus; suddenly he seemed truly enraged. "You might remember that. I saved your fleet and your command at Taranto. You gave me five pieces of gold. I am still waiting for the command of *dhromons* you promised me that day." Moschus jerked the old man off his feet. "We are finished negotiating. My men will burn this ship if you do not deliver the Orphanotrophus to me."

Joannes's voice exploded from the lofty stern-castle. "Droungarios, order your marines to kill him!"

The Droungarios's throat gurgled as he quickly decided that the Orphanotrophus was not a man he was willing to die for; he had enlisted in this cause to aggrandize his land holdings, not sacrifice himself to some transient tyrant. "Will the Nobilissimus grant me a pardon?" he said raspily, rolling his ancient eyes back at Moschus.

"Nobilissimus!" shouted Moschus. "Will you pardon the Droungarios if he yields up his passenger?"

"Yes!" shouted Constantine from the deck of the *khelandia.* He was surrounded by Moschus's marines.

"Order your marines!" screamed Joannes. He came down the ladder with his arms akimbo, like a huge vulture descending to earth. His face was so dark with anger that it seemed like something viewed in the shadows at night. He waved his black wings at the marines. "I order you!"

"The Droungarios of the Imperial Fleet commands these men, not the Orphanotrophus!" shouted Moschus. The marines remained motionless.

"I will destroy every man on this deck." Joannes stood near the main mast, and his voice carried without any apparent effort at projection, as if it were a pocket of cold, foul air that slowly seeped over the deck. The mysterious power of the black-frocked Orphanotrophus to bring fear among men brought silence like a sudden night. The hulls thumped together twice. Constantine's chest burned and his breath strangled in his throat. "Kill him or you will all die in Neorion." The signal flags lifted in a faint breeze, and the ranks of the marines seemed to waver, their armor shimmering like a mirage. The gulls wheeled and cawed overhead.

"Neorion." Constantine's voice was a steady, calm tenor. "The Orphanotrophus will kill us all in the Neorion." With remarkable agility Constantine scrambled up the rope ladder to the deck of the Imperial Trireme. His voice rang out from the higher platform. "The Orphanotrophus says he has the power to kill us all!" Constantine walked over to Joannes and set himself a fathom away from his brother. They were the same man viewed in a strange, distorting mirror: the one eunuch black-frocked, his face carved by some demon into grotesque hollows, his immense limbs and swollen joints projecting at angles like the legs of a monstrous insect; the other purple-robed, his beardless features haggard from a night of desperate solicitations and arrangements, his still fleshy chin set hard with purpose, his heavy chest heaving gently.

Joannes's eyes fired from deep within their recessed sockets. "You are prolonging your death, Brother."

"He will kill us all in the Neorion!" repeated Constantine. "So then, mighty Orphanotrophus, kill me now!" Constantine's robes swished, and he stepped forward with his right foot and raised his thick, fleshy hands in a pugilist's stance. "Take me now, all-powerful Orphanotrophus! I have no weapon, Brother!" Constantine's face burned with anger and he gritted his teeth against the pain in his chest.

Joannes seemed to rise up off his feet, his entire form swelling like a preening bird of prey. He lurched forward and Constantine cringed reflexively. And almost in the same instant, Constantine's arm shot out. His balled fist smacked into Joannes's brutish nose with a crack and a deep thud.

Joannes slowly brought a huge paw to his gushing nose and dabbed incredulously. He studied the rich, red slick on his spatulate fingertips. The man who had drained the blood of thousands in Neorion seemed astonished to find that the same mortal stuff flowed in his veins. He leaned over and numbly watched the spurting blood dribble onto the white enamel deck. Then he crouched, slowly, almost as if he were trying to capture a butterfly. He knelt, dipped a forefinger in his spattered blood, and began to draw perfect concentric circles on the deck, pausing only to dip his finger again and again, as if it were the quill of a pen.

The wind came up and gusted. Joannes's black frock flapped around his jutting limbs; it was as if only a wooden armature remained, where moments before there had been a man's body. He continued to make perfect circles with his own blood. "None of them could ever see how long it would have lasted." His voice was a rasping, strangled whisper. "Except Michael. Michael would have made me complete. They took him. Now they are going to take me, my friends, and you will have no one left." Joannes smeared his circles with an angry motion of his vast, square palm and turned to Constantine. His sockets were alive with that strange silvery movement, the dance of thousands of tiny wraiths. He crawled on his knees and put his arms around Constantine's legs and embraced them like a desperate child. He nuzzled his monstrous head against Constantine's thigh. "I am so tired. Someone help me. I am so tired."

Constantine reached into his cloak. "I have here an Imperial Chrysobull charging this man with treason," he said quietly, as if afraid to wake the child at his feet. "Arrest the Orphanotrophus." He held up the gold-sealed purple document, and marines moved forward to execute his command. Joannes did not resist when the marines peeled his arms from his brother's legs and shackled him. His eyes were completely alive now, seemingly separate organisms.

Constantine turned to Moschus. "Droungarios Moschus, in the name of Michael, Emperor, Autocrator, and Basileus of Rome, I order you to transport your prisoner to his place of permanent exile at the Monastery of Monobate."

Moschus nodded. "You are certain?" he asked matter-of-factly. "We could with no difficulty drop him overboard on the way."

Constantine's eyes were dark, wicked, as if the evil that had fled Joannes's defeated soul had found this new home. "No. This is the one punishment he fears more than death. He went mad in the monastery when he was a boy. They had to send him home for a time. He was only fourteen years old."

† † †

The entire drama had been clearly visible from the roof of the Gynaeceum. Michael had said nothing and registered no emotion, even when it had appeared that Constantine had clearly defected to Joannes. Now, as the two ships moved apart and dipped their oars back into the water,

Michael only breathed steadily and shallowly, almost like a man in a brief doze. His dark eyes watched as Moschus's *khelandia* moved away quickly to the south. The still, black figure of Joannes stood like a charred statue at the stern.

The purple robes of the Nobilissimus coruscated in the sun as he stood in the bow of the Imperial Trireme. The huge ship almost immediately veered left and prepared to dock. Constantine looked up at the palace and waved, though it wasn't certain he knew where his nephew actually was. Michael waved back. Then the Emperor lifted his head to the sun and quickly brought his hand up to shield his dazzled eyes.

IX

ou are impressed with this?" The Droungarios of the Capatanate of Italia Mar Hunrodarson gestured in passing at the mosaics. He governed the province from a Basilica in Bari, an ancient structure from the time of the Emperor Justinian, with heavy arches and a flat, coffered roof. Mar signed his eunuchs to bring his guest wine and seated him on a couch at the east end of the hall, where a large blue carpet had been spread over the marble floor. "The wealth you see here in Italia," said Mar as he sat in his chair, "is the shit of the Imperial Eagle. You will see well enough the truth of that when you get to Grikia."

Mar beckoned to the prostitute and she came forward in a rustling of rose-colored silk. Her tough blue eyes registered shock when she saw the face of the man she had been paid to entertain. But she quickly sat next to him and placed her slender arm on his huge, sloping shoulder. The guest placed his brutish hand around her waist; the sun-baked skin was crisscrossed with dozens of scars, and most of his forefinger was missing. "The reason I summoned you is this," continued Mar. "The Great King of Grikia has died, and I have just learned that the brother who was his marshal has been defeated." Mar used terms he knew his guest would understand. "The Great King who has been named the successor once promised the high seat to me. I am certain that when I remind him of his promise, he will gladly yield to me. If he will not, the Chief Kristr Wizard of the Griks will help me evict him."

"Then why do you need me and mine?" The voice from the bearish chest was incongruously gentle.

"I told you that I knew where you could find the prince who did not die at Stiklestad."

"Yes. Haraldr Sigurdarson. That is why I have come. He is in Grikia?"

"Yes. He is an accomplice of this Great King who has cheated me. I expected him to be my ally in my worthy cause. But he is also a serpent-tongue and I am certain now that he will oppose me."

"How many men will you need?"

"A great many. I believe the army of Grikia will oppose me. They do not want to be ruled by a fair-hair. However, I also know that a son of the Great Prince of Rus now has a grudge against the Griks. One of his comrades was slain in a brawl in the Great City. This Rus prince is ambitious as it is, and this gives him an excuse to attack. But of course you know the Rus. Without Norsemen to lead them, they are women."

"King Sven will allow me ten times three hundred men. Will that be enough to lead these Rus?"

Mar thought for a moment. "Men like you?"

"You know there are not many like us. But these are well-tested men. Many fought for Sven's father Knut at Stiklestad."

"Yes. That will be enough. I am going to send my marshal Thorvald with you. He will arrange your counsel with the Rus prince. I will instruct Thorvald as to the time for you to strike. You must be very careful to follow what he says, so that you will arrive at a time when the patrols cannot detect you until you are on the threshold of Miklagardr. And then everything you see here in Italia you shall have for yourself a thousand times."

"If I can kill Haraldr Sigurdarson, I will already have more than this. King Sven has added to King Knut's bounty. Will I be allowed to kill Haraldr Sigurdarson?"

Mar looked into the fiery, dark, insane eyes of his guest. "Yes. You have already killed the King of Norway once, have you not? You will not find his little brother nearly as formidable a warrior. But then I forget. You already know that."

† † †

The yacht's deck swayed in a scarcely perceptible motion. The lights of the city blazed off the starboard railing. A eunuch walked forward from the stern-castle, his white silk like some phosphorescent sea creature. "You will miss it," said Haraldr.

Maria's hands gripped the railing tightly. "Of course I will. It will probably make me melancholy. You will find me unendurable."

"I will find you seductive," said Haraldr, recalling an earlier conversation.

Maria put her hand to his face, but her melancholy seemed genuine. She turned to him suddenly. "No. I could not leave quickly enough. I am serious, my darling. I have a foreboding."

"You have not dreamed again?"

"No. This is . . . I do not like the Emperor."

"I don't understand. He has proven himself just and capable beyond

my imagining. Consider. He has not executed a single man for the treason against him and has imprisoned but a few. His reforms have so
encouraged the people that he cannot enter the city on even a secret visit
without them spontaneously flocking to throw flowers and carpets on the
streets before him. Believe me, I have seen this, and it is not a case of the
cursores rousting people out of their homes. He is truly loved. And most
importantly, he is deeply devoted to the Empress. Anyone can see his love
for her." Haraldr shrugged. "I believe he is somewhat deficient in the
area of military preparation, but his first challenge will bring out the
warrior in him. You, yourself, saw him fight once."

"Yes. But I also saw him cringe once. That morning when Joannes
sailed into the harbor. Ever since then he has looked at me as if he fears
I will reveal his secret shame."

"I know that he harbors guilt about that day. I see it in his eyes as well.
But I have also in my life suffered from that guilt, and I understand how
it can rend a man's soul. He will outgrow it."

"I don't trust him."

Haraldr realized he had pursued his argument to outpace some of the
same doubts. But then there were few men in Rome one could not doubt
in some fashion. "Most of the men I have talked to at court feel that
Michael may be the most able Emperor since the Bulgar-Slayer. He is
clearly dedicated to the Empire above all else; he dismissed his own
father, the Droungarios Stephan Kalaphates, as commander in Sicily, and
the man he appointed in his father's stead, Maniakes, has dramatically
improved the situation. He is Zoe's lover again, I am almost certain, so
he obviously has her interests at heart. And while Rome enjoys this good
fortune, Norway now suffers under the boot of King Knut's son, Sven. It
is Norway, not Rome, that I am now concerned about."

"I am aware of that."

Haraldr looked south to open water, as if the city that was clearly his
rival offended his sight. He had forgotten that a woman could love her
too. "This is your fashion of refusing me, is it not? I understand if you
are frightened of the journey north. I am frightened myself, and certainly
I fear for you. But you must refuse me in your own words, from your own
breast."

"You are an enormous pig, Prince-King Haraldr!" Maria pounded the
railing with her fists. "I said I wanted to leave as quickly as it can be
arranged!"

"And leave your mother with this man you cannot trust."

"She is not my mother, pig head!" Tears glimmered on Maria's lashes.

Leave her to her anger, thought Haraldr. The scar from a deep wound takes many years to heal. Haraldr stepped away, having learned that intimacies only fanned the flames at these times. "Very well, Maria. I am going to ask to see the Empress tomorrow. I am going to discuss with her in terms of greatest candor her dealings with Michael, suggest the possibility that he may pose some threat to her, and discuss any fears or even intimations she may have. But if she assures me that she has no reservations concerning the Emperor—and I believe she is in a far better position to divine his intentions than you or I—then I am going to the Emperor and make arrangements for my leave-taking. It is not necessary for me to say that my heart cannot leave without you. But it is necessary for me to tell you that I am going to leave, and I will leave with my heart torn from my breast if that is how it must be."

Maria did not answer, and her blue eyes blazed back at the City.

ou are certain I cannot interest you in breakfast?" Alexius, Patriarch of the One True Oecumenical, Orthodox, and Catholic Faith, gestured toward the silver double doors of his private dining chamber.

"No, Father," replied the Emperor Michael. "I am more in need of spiritual nourishment. Might we walk together in the Mother Church?"

Alexius's dark eyes sparkled. "Indeed we might, Majesty. I completed the morning Mass only a hour ago, and yet I already long for her. And unlike physical nourishment, which when consumed in excess can encumber the flesh with corpulence and corruption, each spiritual repast lightens our burden and cleanses our souls."

Alexius escorted Michael through the various antechambers and sitting rooms of his personal apartments, through the Patriarchal offices, across the carpeted causeway to the second-floor gallery of the Hagia Sophia, and then down the stairs at the southeast corner of the enormous cathedral. They walked out into the nave. In the morning light the central dome shimmered as if it would break loose and float into the heavens. Polyphonies drifted gently through the light-filled ether; the white robes of the chanting priests could be glimpsed behind the two-story latticed screens of green Thessalian marble that shielded the altar. The two most powerful men in the world were a strange and marvelous sight as they strolled side by side, both of them swathed from chin to ankle in layers of metallic silk; the Patriarch predominantly in white, with embroideries of gold crosses; the Emperor in vivid claret purple sprinkled with golden eagles. In the golden light of the Mother Church they seemed more akin to the glittering mosaic deities floating high above them than to human figures.

Alexius took Michael's arm. "Our Lord transformed His Word into the light of the world, yet here in our Mother Church, I often feel that the primordial light is transmuted back into the Word. Does that sound strange to Your Majesty?"

Michael's face twitched curiously, first the lips and then the eyebrows. "That fascinates me, Father. Do you refer to the hosannas and holy sacraments with which our church is even now redolent?"

"That, certainly, Majesty. But also the Word of Our Lord without the intervening medium of human voices. When I am here, I often have private, intimate conversation with the Pantocrator."

Michael skipped forward a step, as if seized by some irrepressible impulse. "Father, is . . . is it possible that the Pantocrator would speak to me in that fashion?"

"But most certainly. You are his Vice Regent on Earth. I would be disturbed to know that Our Lord had not communicated His wishes to you."

"He has communicated His wishes, Father. He spoke to me for the first time on the ambo when you crowned me Caesar. Now we converse frequently. Even in my own chambers."

Alexius squeezed Michael's arm in a gesture of encouragement. "And what are the Pantocrator's wishes, Majesty?"

Michael's eyebrows twitched quite noticeably. "He has asked me to go forth and multiply."

Alexius's eyes paced rapidly. "Indeed. Is it our Empress He has asked you to wed so that you may bring forth this fruit?"

Michael tilted his face slightly upward, as if basking in the light from the dome. "No. That lovely blossom has not borne fruit all these years, and it most certainly will not now."

"You are correct in that assumption, Majesty. While our Empress has preserved the exquisite bloom of her youth, she has passed the age of fertility. However, Majesty, you must know that while you are the adopted son of the Empress, you are in the eyes of her people her consort. You might compromise that relationship if you were to take a bride."

"But if my bride were also purple-born?"

It was as if Alexius could scarcely restrain his eyes from leaping out of his head. "I am afraid the Augusta Theodora is no more likely to bear fruit than is her sister, Majesty."

"I have heard an interesting rumor, Father. That the purple-born Eudocia gave birth to a daughter in a convent somewhere. It is presumed that the child died. But what if the child had been adopted and lived somewhere, unaware of her noble Macedonian lineage? She would be of childbearing age now."

Alexius hoped his pounding breast would not give him away. "I have heard these rumors, too, and think there is some truth to them, at least where the birth is concerned. But we cannot presume that the child was born alive, or, if it was, is still alive. And if that Imperial progeny were alive, how can we presume that it is of the female gender?"

"But if Eudocia's child could be found, and if it were a woman in good health, would you object to this marriage, Father?"

Alexius commanded his arm not to tremble. "The lineage of the child would be suspect, Majesty. She would not have been born in the porphyry chamber of the Imperial Palace, so she would not be a true purple-born. And of course the child was born outside the sacrament of marriage."

"But if the Patriarch of the One True Faith, knowing of the legitimacy of the Macedonian blood in those veins regardless of the circumstances of birth, were to assure his people that the necessary conditions for purple-born status had been met, the lineage would no longer be suspect."

Alexius's shoulders ached from the burden of self-control. "But I could not give my people those assurances of my own volition. I would have to wait and receive the Pantocrator's instructions on such a vital matter. But of course this is all speculation, and most likely will remain so."

Michael seemed to listen to someone else for a moment. "Yes. Quite. Father, let me ask you to speculate on another subject. Let us presume that when the Christ lived on earth as a man—"

"You mean when the Holy Spirit took on the form of the Christ. You must not become careless and lapse into the Latin error by denying the procession of the Holy Spirit from the Father through the Son. If you do so, you deny Christ the Pantocrator His divinity. And you know what a scourge that heresy has become."

Michael nodded impatiently. "When the Holy Spirit occupied the body of the Christ, He had an earthly father: Joseph. Now this Joseph was a virtuous man. But let us assume for the purpose of speculation that Joseph was in fact an evil man. Let us assume that he mocked the Christ as did Caiaphas, that he scourged Him as did the soldiers of Pilate. Let us assume that he brought shame to the Holy Family. Let us assume that he fouled the Mother of God with his lust and corrupted Her virtue."

Alexius raised both wiry eyebrows. "Do not let speculation lead you into blasphemy, Majesty. You must remember that the Fallen Archangel can often speak to us in the guise of the Pantocrator, and convince the unwary that Satan's beguilements are the words of the Christ."

Michael's entire body went rigid, and his eyes darted for a moment. Then he almost convulsively relaxed; Alexius could feel the tremor. "But let us assume that these crimes did take place. Who would be the agent of retribution in this case? Would it be the Holy Spirit in the form of the Father, or of the Son?"

"Christ the Pantocrator would offer this corrupt Joseph the opportunity to repent and earn forgiveness. And then this corrupt Joseph would be judged at the Heavenly Tribunal alongside all souls, and held accountable for any sins of which he had not been cleansed. And at that Tribunal the Father and the Son and the Holy Spirit will all three preside."

Michael pondered this information for a moment. "I must return to the duties with which Christ the Pantocrator has charged me, Father. But I feel a remarkable spiritual satiation after your wise and loving counsel. Indeed, I felt that even as you spoke, the Christ was whispering in my ear."

† † †

The Patriarch Alexius greeted the Augusta Theodora by signing the cross on her forehead. She had been gotten out of bed and now wore a plain purple robe; her lusterless brown hair was set in a single braid.

"It is time, my child," said Alexius.

Theodora calmly showed Alexius to a couch and signaled her eunuch to offer him wine. "What has happened, Father?"

"I had an extraordinary conversation with our Emperor this morning. I am certain that madness is the will of Divine Providence, and is given us either to scourge us or to allow us to enter into a state where we can more closely know God. Yet I also think madness is sometimes passed in the blood, from generation to generation of the same family. The Emperor's uncles were both mad, though in one case it was a demonic possession, while the other was a fury of true repentance. But this Emperor is quite the maddest of all. And the most adept at concealing his madness behind the masks of reason, intellect, and dissimulation. Quite extraordinary. He has embraced the most profound heresies. Even the Bishop of Rome would consider our Emperor a heretic. The Emperor insisted in the Mother Church that Joseph might have attempted carnal congress with the Mother of God."

"But you did not awaken me in the middle of the night to tell me of this heresy, did you, Father?"

"No, child. Today our Emperor revealed to me that the child born to your sister Eudocia on Porte was a daughter."

Theodora leaned forward so abruptly that it seemed she was going to leap at Alexius. "He knows?"

Alexius smiled thinly. "I think he does. He pretended to know only the

the rumors of the birth. But he posited that the child was a daughter, and now you have confirmed it."

Theodora flushed with anger and embarrassment; Alexius was maddeningly clever. "Perhaps he was only playing the same guessing game that you are, Father."

"Perhaps. We had better hope that he is. It is clear that he intends to marry the last Macedonian and bring forth his own dynasty, something his equally mad relatives were unable to do." Theodora was so pale, her face seemed tinted with blue. "Yes, my child, I think that you will soon have to shoulder your cross. And while I do not think it is time for your climb to Golgotha to begin, I think it is time that we prepare for your entry into Jerusalem."

he *dhromon* of the Thematic Fleet of Sicily approached the harbor boom in the moonless night. The captain ordered the oars shipped, and the huge vessel drifted sideways and thudded against the log bumpers. The prisoner, chained and gagged, a black sack over his head, was loaded into a skiff along with an escort of six thematic marines. The small boat was lowered on the other side of the boom. With four of the marines at the oars, the skiff moved away toward Neorion Harbor. It came alongside a small dock just inside the boom; the *dhromons* of the Imperial Fleet were dark silhouettes off to the right of the little-used stone jetty. Four Khazar guards waiting on the quay communicated the correct password and hoisted the passive body up onto the dock. The prisoner, still attired in the now-fouled silk tunic of his rank, resisted briefly when the Khazar guards slipped a large leather bag over his entire body and carried him off on their shoulders.

The four Khazars carried their package quickly through the streets that angled among the military warehouses of the Neorion district. Twice the escort was confronted, then passed along by sentries. The Khazars came around the back of Neorion Tower and halted before the black steel gates. Their pass was accepted and they moved their prisoner up the dank, reeking stairs to the interrogation rooms on the tenth level. The prisoner was tied faceup on a wheellike wooden rack, and the Khazar guards left the prisoner with the interrogators, two smooth-faced Pechenegs who worked silently over their instruments at an adjacent table, honing blades and setting out leather straps.

The Emperor Michael arrived a quarter of an hour later. He wore the scaramangium, pallium, and diadem of his rank. When the Pecheneg interrogators had finished their prostrations, the Emperor signaled for them to leave. The huge steel doors slid and clanked. The prisoner breathed in even, shallow wheezes. Michael walked around the wheel for a moment; as he did, he placed his hands in front of his chest and touched the tips of his fingers together again and again in light, rapid movements. He closed his eyes and became very still and his entire head and torso inclined forward very slowly, as if he were a wax sculptor's model gradually slumping in a fierce heat. Then his eyes popped open and his dark irises struck out at the bloodstained floor, as if the shafts of pure malevolence they projected were all that prevented his collapse. He stared for a long moment, and then his hand shot out and jerked the sack from the prisoner's head. The prisoner's eyes blinked in the lamplight. "Father," whispered the Emperor. "It is time for you to repent."

Stephan Kalaphates, recently recalled Droungarios of the theme of Sicily, was a small, paunchy man; his belly, distended over the rack, quivered like an aspic. He was tightly gagged, but his dark eyes, writhing head, and gurgling throat conveyed the terror, outrage, and astonishment of his strangled words.

Michael prodded his father's bound hand with trembling fingers. "Look, Father, your hands are still dirty." Stephan stopped writhing and merely glared at his son in mute fury. "I remember how you used to take me down to the shipyards, as if to see you smear pitch on the sides of boats was some great marvel, like watching the Emperor in procession. I hated the pitch. I could not get the stink of it off no matter how I washed. Those men and you stank of it. Those men and you showed me the stinking vat of hot pitch and said I would burn in it because I touched myself. And then you tarred it! You tarred it!" Michael's face was livid, and he grabbed his crotch violently. "Because I did that! For doing that! I do it all the time, Father, and God has not punished me. I touch it all the time, Father! I touch it in God's presence. I place the Pantocrator's hand on it!" Michael leered over his father like a drunken man, and Stephen's head jerked up and down, cracking against the hard wooden wheel. "Mother touched it too. Mother cleansed me. Mother still touches it. And I still touch her."

Michael ran his hands down his stiff, jewel-studded pallium, his fingertips grazing the raised gems as if they were women's nipples. "I am a splendid Emperor, am I not, Father? My people love me. They do not call me, as they do you, 'the pygmy playing Heracles' or 'the ass costumed as a Droungarios.' They call me their father. Their beloved father. The light of their world." Michael stared into the oil lamps on the grim stone wall behind the rack. He cocked his head once to each side. "The Pantocrator and I are together inside a light. Do you know that we have talked about our fathers, not the Holy Spirit who begat us, but our worldly fathers. His father was a tradesman, a good carpenter who loved his son and never fouled His mother. I told Him how you had scourged and mocked me and what you had done to my mother, and He told me what I should do so that you might repent and be cleansed. So that you will no longer stink of pitch."

The Emperor exhaled deeply and closed his eyes. Stephan's head resumed its grotesque protest, pounding the wheel with sickening thuds and hideous, thwarted cries. "Shut up, Father!" Michael blinked his eyes in furious concentration. He turned away from the struggling figure on the rack. "I know he isn't the only unclean father," he said to someone else. "I know that the other father tried to trick me. He tried to get me to tell him our secret. He thought he was so clever. He doesn't want me to have my new mother." Michael leaned his head back and issued a strange, barking laugh. "He tried to tell me that you lied to me! He tried to tell me that you are Satan!" The strange laugh again. "He is Satan! They are *all* Satan! They don't want me to have my new mother! They are all going to have to be cleansed!"

Michael smiled as he listened to the echoes in the chamber of death. When he could no longer hear them, he tapped on the door to signal the interrogators. The steel doors opened and the two Pechenegs entered. Michael nodded at them and they removed the appropriate instruments from the table, walked to the rack, and ripped Stephan's robe from the hem to the chest, leaving his spasming legs and pulsing, flaccid abdomen fully exposed. "I am going to see mother," Michael said. "I am going to tell her that you will never foul her again." Michael turned and left the interrogation chamber before the Pecheneg eunuchs began the incision around his father's scrotum.

† † †

"Keleusate." Haraldr rose and faced the throne beneath the golden vault of the Chrysotriklinos. The Grand Eunuch indicated that he could approach the Emperor and speak. The Nobilissimus Constantine sat impassively in a simple chair just to the right of the dais. Also in attendance were the usual white-robed secretaries, interpreters, and the Emperor's new astrologers.

"Majesty."

"Hetairarch."

"Majesty, may I preface my request by remarking that Rome now enjoys a stability and unity that I have not seen before in my time here. I say without resort to flattery that no sovereign in my experience has ever enjoyed the love of his people to the extent that you do. I say with all honesty, as one who has been privileged to know you in times of both adverse and beneficent fortune, that I feel that the entire city has supplanted me in my office as Hetairarch, in that as I walk the streets behind you I know that any one of Rome's citizens would lay down his life to protect your own as readily as could myself. Seeing that there is so little danger to your person, and that no foreign powers currently menace us, I believe that the time is now appropriate for me to take my leave of Rome. It is not without regret that I ask for leave, but I am bound by loyalties to my own family and people in Thule, and now I believe that they are in greater need of me than is Your Majesty. I humbly beg your permission to resign my office, and those offices held by the men of the Grand Hetairia, and be granted my leave as a devoted friend of the Roman Empire."

Michael's eyes were red-rimmed, no doubt from his always lengthy sessions in the Chrysotriklinos, and Haraldr worried that his speech had been too long. But he had learned that the Emperor was quite susceptible to well-intended cajolery and had reasoned that a show of respect would hasten him along.

Michael's chest sagged somewhat, and Haraldr was now certain that the Emperor would implore him with desperate words to counter some new threat. "Well, Hetairarch, no sovereign, no matter how well loved, can afford to lose a servant and comrade in arms as dedicated as yourself. But then, no sovereign worthy of that love could deny one who has dedicated so much to him. You have my leave, my blessing, my gratitude. Rome will mourn your departure, of course. If I do not presume, can you tell me if you plan to take our beloved Empress's Mistress of the Robes with you?"

"Yes. Maria will become my wife in Thule."

A strange flicker crossed Michael's face, a brief, passing shadow. He does not like her, thought Haraldr. Or perhaps he is secretly smitten with her. "Does our Empress know this, Hetairarch?"

"Majesty, I beg you to allow the Lady Maria and myself to plead our case to her directly. We do not intend to leave without her permission, either."

"Very well," said Michael. "My only reservations concerned her Majesty's wishes in this matter. When that is settled between you, I will do everything I can to facilitate a prompt and safe return to your people." Michael was about to make the sign of the cross when he remembered something. "Counsel with me for a moment longer, Hetairarch. Indeed, as you say, I can confidently bask in the light of my people's love, but who knows what external agents might wish to send clouds my way? I will need to replace your Varangians, and I am loath to summon your predecessor, Mar Hunrodarson, back from Italia. He is doing a far better job there than he did in protecting my late uncle, may the Pantocrator keep his soul. I have, however, recently purchased a contingent of Pecheneg eunuchs already educated in the Greek language, trained at arms, and even now performing well at various odd tasks for me. What is your estimate of their value as a temporary guard until I can obtain the services of loyal Varangians?"

"Majesty, I believe that your perceptions of Mar Hunrodarson are characteristically acute." Haraldr did not add that he would be returning to Norway via Italia, and that Mar Hunrodarson would soon be unavailable for any sort to service. "As for the worth of Pechenegs, I have fought against them and have always felt that were they instructed in bathing, reading, and military discipline, they would be the scourge of the earth. They are certainly fearless of death. These men should serve you well."

Michael nodded and made the sign of the cross. As Haraldr departed with his hands over his breast, Michael and Constantine immediately found each other's eyes.

† † †

"Call me husband."

Zoe laughed and rubbed the slick, sweet-smelling emollient over her bare white leg. Her scarlet silk robe was slit to the waist; she had spread the fabric out behind her like a peacock's tail, and thus sat bare-bottomed on her silk sheets. "That is not the game I want to play tonight, precious one." She leaned forward and hissed through her gleaming white teeth. "I want to play bitch and hound."

Michael blinked earnestly. "I really mean you must call me husband."

"Husband!" Zoe leaned her head back and snorted regally. "My first husband was impotent, my second could only make love to me when we were adulterers upon my first, and you wish me to call you that." Zoe puffed her lips into a crimson pout. "I want you to stay my little boy."

Michael thrust his hand between Zoe's bare, succulent thighs. "It is quite important that you call me husband." His eyes glimmered brightly in the oil light.

Zoe removed his hand. "You have not asked me for that, precious."

"A husband does not ask."

"The wife of a fishmonger does not expect to be asked. I am the purple-born and you are my child. You will ask me."

"I am the Emperor and the beloved of my city."

"And you are my darling as well. But you must ask before you can open your mother's pink-fleshed reliquary."

"My people would bid me have you whenever I wish."

"Your people give you only what your mother is willing to give you. You must not delude yourself that your people love you simply for yourself. You are loved because I have made you my child."

Michael could not speak for some time, and there was a moment when his face hardened, until it seemed as if his skin was a porcelain that might shatter from the force of his grinding jawbones. "I am not asking for your troth again, as I did after your husband's death," he finally said in a curious, quavering tone that caused Zoe's blue eyes to widen. "I simply want you to pretend that I am your husband from now on. In your bed." He thrust his hand between her thighs again and moved it to her crotch. "In here."

Zoe gripped his hand but he would not move it. "You are becoming quite your mother's little man," she said slowly.

"I am not a little man!" Michael screamed, his face almost instantly livid. He stared at Zoe with murder in his eyes before he collapsed into sobs. She held him for a long while and let him smear his running nose over her silk-sheathed breasts.

"Husband," said Zoe at length, her voice firm and inviting. "I am sorry that I did not recognize your dominion. I want you to rip my robe away and savage me with your manhood." She spread her bare legs wide, and Michael lifted his head to show her his burning eyes.

† † †

The people danced, twisting and swaying and whirling in mad circles. Inside their frantic ring, the two kings casts the lots of fate. One was tall and golden, the other black-bearded and cringing. The people began to chant as they danced, and the song they sang was Death. Over and over and over they called down Death until their faces darkened with the wings overhead, and then they became the birds, fat, obsidian bellies glistening as they whirred in a cawing cyclone around the two kings. The raven appeared in the hand of the golden king, and the black king looked up at it, his eyes filled with unspeakable terror. The eyes of the raven glowed orange like burning embers, and the golden king brought the raven down into the face of the black king.

"Haraldr!" Maria bolted upright, her breasts heaving and her eyes burning into the dawn.

"What did you dream?" His arms were already around her. "I was awake. I watched your eyes."

Maria shook her head numbly. "I dreamed . . ." She paused and recalled the vision to herself. "I dreamed . . . that you killed the Emperor."

"I have no intention of doing that." He kissed her forehead. Maria described the entire vision, however, and he listened intently. When she had finished, he said, "I know that many of the details of your dreams are accurate, but the prophecies of life and death are not. My experience against the Bulgars proved that. Your dreams are warnings, not the decisions of fate. It seems more likely that they have the power to reverse fates."

"Perhaps. But perhaps the Emperor means to provoke you somehow into striking him. As they did with Joannes. I don't want you to dine with him this evening."

Haraldr's gut knotted for a moment. He considered the matter. "I don't think the circumstances will be as they were in your dream. You say there were many people present? An enormous crowd? But this will not be an official banquet. It is only the Emperor, the Nobilissimus, and myself in the Imperial Apartments." Haraldr squeezed Maria tightly. "If the eunuchs start dancing in circles, I will leave."

Maria did not see the humor. "No, this was outside . . . a procession. You must not—"

"I will no longer follow him in procession. I have resigned my office. My men are already lodged in St. Mama's Quarter, preparing our ships. The new Pecheneg guard led him through the city yesterday. There is no chance of that." Maria exhaled futilely, her fears exhausted. "You are apprehensive and I understand. And I think you and Zoe are going to miss each other more than you have imagined." Haraldr paused. "Has she said something to you since she gave us her permission to leave?"

Maria stared raptly ahead. "No," she said in an entranced voice. "She is happier than ever with Michael. She has hinted that she can think of him as a husband."

"And you wish to wait for their wedding?"

"No. I believe she is only amusing herself." Maria dipped her head as if letting the vision go. "I don't know," she said. "It is as if, as you say in your tongue, I can hear the Valkyrja singing."

† † †

The Church of St. Mary Chalkoprateia was located just outside the walls of the Imperial Palace complex, north of the huge bronze Chalke Gate and virtually within bowshot of the Hagia Sophia. It was one of the oldest churches in Constantinople, an austere Roman-style basilica with a flat, coffered roof and a single large apse. It might have looked like a large warehouse save for the brilliant frescoes and mosaics covering the interior walls, the result of an extensive restoration more than a hundred and fifty years previously. The visitors, six in all, seemed to have dressed in concert with the architecture; their rough wool cloaks concealed the rich silk and gold vestments beneath. They entered the vaulted narthex at the front of the church, were greeted by four of the resident priests (who wore their vestments openly), and were quickly escorted to a door at the north end of the narthex. A colonnaded walkway led to the priests' apartments, a cluster of brick buildings of much later construction. Shafts of sun lanced through the columns and illuminated the visitors' jeweled silk slippers, just visible beneath the hems of their brown cloaks. The visitors entered a square, marble-framed portal and were shown down a short hallway. The room at the end of the hall was large and set into a curving apse at the end of the building. The walls were buff-tinted plaster, set with tall arched windows. The shutters remained closed. Two gold-framed icons glimmered on a small cupboard. The bed was covered in blue silk. The resident priests and four of the six visitors made the sign of the cross and left the room. The carved wooden door closed behind them.

The Augusta Theodora lowered her woolen hood and looked around the room. "I am certain that Pilate did not lodge Our Lord so well on the eve of His excruciation," she said; her blue eyes were girlish, mischievous.

"You may be kept waiting longer than was our Lord," said the Patriarch Alexius; he continued to wear his hood. His beard looked like spun silver against the the coarse wool. "But when I need you, it will be important for you to be close to the Mother Church. Though, of course, it would far too dangerous for you to spend that length of time within the palace precincts. Someone would talk."

"How will you proceed, Father?"

"I believe that if necessary, I can bring down our Emperor with the patent evidence of his heresies. But I believe that his madness will soon provide his own undoing. We will wait. At least until Mar Hunrodarson arrives." Theodora betrayed her surprise. "Oh, yes, my child, I informed him that my need for him was imminent shortly after our Orphanotrophus Joannes enrolled in one of the monastic establishments he had so energetically advanced against the interests of the One True Faith. If Mar Hunrodarson has kept to my schedule, he will have entered the Sea of Marmora already. He will wait for instructions off Arcadiopolis. And then, if necessary, he and the Tauro-Scythians will extirpate the unwanted growth from the Imperial Palace."

"You may find Mar Hunrodarson an even more luxuriant and far more resilient growth, Father."

"He is ambitious but not a fool. He knows that he cannot rule without your sanction. Let him be the man at your side. You will need neither to crown him nor to bed him. I believe his robust thinking will strengthen the secular arms of our empire while I carry forth the standards of spiritual Rome." Alexius tipped his head in a wry gesture. "And we could turn the people against him whenever we wished."

"It is a pity you cannot lead the secular arms of our Empire, Father. In your own fashion you are a very robust thinker."

Alexius responded to the sarcasm with a fond smile. "You know, my child, my thinking on this matter could be considerably more vigorous if I knew the identity of your sister Eudocia's child."

No trace of amusement remained on Theodora's face. "No. Father, I am willing to become your sacrifice, but I do not want that for . . . the child. That is one matter on which my sister and I agree. Perhaps when she is older. But she is—" Theodora broke off, unwilling to give up any more information.

"Very well, my child. I was only considering the girl's own safety. Assuming the Emperor knows."

"I do not think he does."

Alexius nodded cryptically. "I must go, then. If matters develop as I expect, I must prepare the Mother Church to withstand a siege."

† † †

"Hetairarch Haraldr, this is where I find myself unable to accommodate myself to the risk of war." The Emperor nodded that he wished his goblet refilled, and the chamberlain inclined over him for a moment. "I can race a team in the Hippodrome and wager on them according to their fitness, the experience of their driver, the condition of the track. If I lose, I can train the team more vigorously, hire a better driver, or perhaps sell two of the horses and replace them with others. But in war, if my team loses, I have lost the capital I need to continue in the sport, so to speak. I can hire new generals, of course, but I cannot sell dead soldiers for live soldiers. And my people suffer the loss, not only those who die but also those who grieve for them. So I consider the odds in war to be generally unacceptable."

"But you have moved boldly in appointing Maniakes to command in Italia," said Haraldr. He was enjoying the wine, the unexpected informality of the dinner, and the chance to deal with the Emperor's only critical shortcoming: his reluctance to assume field command of the Imperial Taghmata. "Maniakes's successes in Sicily have already rewarded your wager."

"Ah, Hetairarch," said Michael, raising his finger in the manner of a rhetorician, "in Sicily I bet the man. I knew that Maniakes could win for me and for my people. But had I been there to decide on each day's movements of our forces, I would have been quite beside myself. Let me bet on my generals, yes. But do not ask me to wager on the actual battle." Michael took a deep drink and the red wine spilled onto his dark beard. "Now you, Hetairarch Haraldr, are also a man upon whom I would wager to bring me victory in the field. How do you do it?"

Haraldr paused and also took a deep draft. He looked over at Constantine, who was so drunk, it appeared he might collapse into his roast pig. "I allow only the best men at my back, and then make certain that I am always at the front to lead them. I do not command my men to do anything I am not prepared to do myself. I am certain that my men are drilled in every tactic that I might wish to employ, and I remember that in battle the memory grows weak, so I make certain that my tactics are simple and direct to begin with. But at the moment when fate hinges, I am not unlike yourself, Majesty. I trust in luck."

"Indeed!" Michael spilled his goblet as he lurched forward in excitement. "Tell me what you mean. I had always considered you a kindred sportsman of sorts, but I thought you entirely grim in battle. What do you mean?" Michael nodded for the chamberlain to refill Haraldr's cup. "This is a different wine, Hetairarch," he offered as the eunuch poured from the silver ewer. "From Dyracchium. If you do not like it, pour it out."

Haraldr drank deeply; he didn't like the taste of the Dyracchium vintage, but he was enjoying himself too much to complain. "Majesty," he said, conscious of a slight slurring of his words, "we Norsemen believe in a god called Odin. But you do not have to consider him a god if it offends your Christian piety. You could consider him a talisman, like a splinter of the True Cross, or even a personification, like Fortune. But we believe that Odin sends his favor to certain men in battle and witholds that favor from others. If he sends his Valkyrja, these being his angels of death, to pluck a man from the battle, then nothing that man can do can arrest his fate. We have a saying: 'No man lives to evening whom the fates condemn at morning.' "

"Does this Odin enjoy any sports besides war?" asked Michael ebulliently.

Haraldr jerked his head up. What had the Emperor asked him? Had he been asleep? His head snapped up again and a surge of alarm brought his wits back for a moment. How could he be this drunk? He had not consumed enough wine to have already summoned the herons of forgetfulness. He felt the drowsiness in his arms and legs, and his terrified heart pounded life back into his limbs. He lurched to his feet and his spastic arms sent his cups and dishes clattering; his spilled wine spread a broadening red stain over the white-and-gold tablecloth. His feet seemed stuck in mud, but he staggered toward Michael and reached with arms that felt like huge logs. "You . . . have . . . poisoned—" He gasped, suffocating. Then the room whirled and he fell forward onto the table with a tremendous crash.

Michael and Constantine stood up. They looked over Haraldr's twitching torso like hunters examining a slaughtered beast. A long golden lock of Haraldr's hair rested in the garos sauce on the Emperor's plate. Michael lifted the sodden strand of hair from the golden dish with the tips of his fingers and looked over at his suddenly alert uncle. "It appears," he said, "that when this Odin decided to bring our friend here to a timely end, he also divined to ruin my roast pig."

† † †

"Do you smell it?" Halldor stood on the St. Mama's Quarter wharf and stared toward the Great City. The setting sun flared off the soaring round towers of the main land wall.

"I am gagging from the stench." Ulfr looked back at the three light galleys tied up on the wharf. Varangians poured over the ships, attaching rigging, finishing out the oar ports, checking caulk, and loading kegs of provisions. "Even if he was with Maria, he would have come out here to check on this. No Norseman takes the sea that lightly."

"I don't like the whole business," said Halldor. "The way those Pechenegs were waiting to move into the Numera before our mattresses were cold. It was as if the Emperor were only too eager to have us out of the palace."

"Where did Haraldr go last night? Did you ask Maria?"

"I sent a man to Haraldr's house. Erling. I told him not to come back until he found her. He hasn't come back." Halldor shifted on his feet. "We need to arrive at a plan."

"Unfortunately we don't know what to plan for or against."

"Let's consider the two possibilities. If Haraldr is in trouble, we need to find him, rescue him, and prepare to depart immediately. The other possibility is that Haraldr has met with some treachery that has placed him beyond our help." Halldor looked at Ulfr and astonished his friend with his tearing eyes. "In that case I intend to join him in the Valhol. But before the Valkyrja wrap their cold limbs around me, I will reduce the palaces of Rome to a pile of cinders."

"I will join you if it comes to that. So will they." Ulfr pointed to the Varangians. "But if he still needs our help, we must find him. . . . Look."

Gregory, mounted on a horse vastly oversize for him, galloped along the wharf. The hoofbeats pounded against the shouting of the workers. "Comrades!" he yelled. He swung off the horse expertly. "I have information." He took a moment to catch his breath. "Haraldr went to the Emperor's apartments last night. None of my informants saw him leave."

Halldor and Ulfr exchanged ominous looks. "Was there anything else?"

"Yes," said Gregory. "The Emperor has been consulting with his astrologers all day. I have become acquainted with the chamberlain who attends one of these scientists, and he overheard this gentleman working on his astronomical calculations with his assistants. The Emperor has asked them if the stars will be auspicious for a man who takes a very great risk."

"For what day are they calculating, Gregory?" asked Ulfr.

"Tomorrow."

"As I said, that whole city reeks right now," said Halldor. "I suggest we march in there and demand that the Emperor tell us where we can find

Haraldr. And then we should march right out again and leave Rome before the Emperor takes this great risk of his."

"What if the Emperor does want us out of the city, and Haraldr out of the way, as it would look right now?" asked Ulfr. He pointed to the massive towers of the land wall. "Those walls aren't going to tumble down because all three hundred and sixty of us demand to see the Emperor. And even if we do get in, we can hardly hope to attack the entire Imperial Taghmata, particularly when they are the ones who will be fortified behind the palace walls."

Halldor nodded impassively. "Of course." He seemed almost embarrassed by his impulsiveness. He looked out over the harbor for a while. "This is what we do. We begin to go into the city in small groups. Not all of us will make it through before they close the gates at sunset. The rest can come through during the morning."

"And how do we deal with the Taghmata?" said Ulfr.

"Allies," said Halldor. He looked grimly at the towers of the Great Wall; only the crenellated tips were still glowing. "Our Varangians will rendezvous in the streets around the Devil's Walking Stick Inn during the morning. And by then I expect to have asked for and received the help of a lady.

"A lady?" asked Gregory.

Halldor nodded. "A very formidable lady."

† † †

"I don't wish to be exhausted by your preliminaries concerning the ruling planets and the relative position of the planets in the zodiacal signs and aspects and limits." Michael leaned forward in his throne and glared at the trio of astrologers. "I simply want the answer to the question I put to you this morning."

Cyril, the spokesman for the group, was an elderly man with a gray beard and a black-and-silver widow's peak. He wore a white pallium with his white silk scaramangium and carried the trail of the pallium very elegantly, as if he were posing for a statue. "Majesty," he intoned with the rolling speech of an educated Hellene, "I must warn you that the positions of the stars for the period of time you have mandated to us portend only blood and sorrow. Might I recommend that you put away the idea of this venture, or at least postpone your enterprise until the planetary aspects are more favorable?"

Michael tilted his head back and issued a loud, hacking laugh that clattered around the dome high above him. He turned to Constantine. "These frauds could not portend the falling of a stone to earth once it has been dropped." He reappraised the apprehensive-looking astrologers and shrieked, "Science! Your only science is mendacity! I will show you science! Get out!" The astrologers quickly scuttled back from the throne, hands over breasts. "Your exquisite knowledge is a child's babbling to the eloquence of my daring venture!" he shouted after them. "Damn your science to Hell!" He looked at Constantine and stood up. "I am going to attend to that matter this very moment, Uncle." He gestured at the Grand Eunuch to assemble his Pecheneg guard. Another eunuch responded to Michael's nod by bringing him a small sheaf of documents.

Surrounded by his guard, the Emperor left his apartments and climbed the terraces to the Hippodrome. The Imperial entourage skirted the pale, satiny flank of the enormous structure, paused at the entrance to the Gynaeceum, and were quickly admitted. Michael ascended the stairs with a small escort. At the door to the Empress's antechambers he told the new captain of his Pecheneg guard, a Roman officer, to wait outside. He shooed away the eunuchs with fluttering, whisking motions and walked in unannounced.

Zoe was working over her perfumes and unguents when she looked up and saw Michael. She signed at her two ladies-in-waiting, who were grinding with mortars at a long table jammed with glass, clay, and silver containers; the women bowed and hurried out. "You are early," she said, smoothing her unornamented blond hair back. Her nipples were vague, dark spots beneath her thin silk scaramangium. "But then you have been very eager lately."

Michael looked at the paraphernalia on the tables. "Are you working on your poisons, bitch?"

Zoe's hands froze on the stone container she was sealing. She did not look up. "I have quite forgotten that art, my child," she said softly. Then she slowly lifted her head and hard blue eyes. "It is vulgar of you to mention it," she snapped. "What I started with Romanus I have been punished for. What I tried to help you do to Joannes, you have now been rewarded for. If you are going to be vulgar, leave me, child."

"So you admit that you poisoned an Emperor, and my uncle the Orphanotrophus!" shrieked Michael. He swiped his arm across the nearest table and the vials and beakers and ewers went flying with a tremendous crash. "I have the proof here!" He waved the documents. "I have proof you tried to poison my uncle the Nobilissimus! You poisoned my uncle the Emperor!" Michael's screams rasped painfully and his face was gorged with blood. "You have tried to poison me, bitch!"

"You are not well, child." Zoe's calm betrayed a hint of fear. "Perhaps I have gone too far in indulging your newfound . . . virility."

"You have been charged with treason! Answer the charges, bitch!"

"You are mad. If you do not leave and return to apologize to me tomorrow, I may ask my people to consider a new consort for me. A mature man who might serve as my husband and Emperor."

Michael flipped the long table onto its side and screamed incoherently above the racket of breaking vessels. He walked forward and seized Zoe's arms and shook her furiously. "You treasonous bitch, you cannot take my people away from me! They love me! They no longer love you! I am their only love! The only one!"

"You are about to discover how easily that love is lost when I am not beside you to permit it."

Michael let go of Zoe and walked around the wreckage of the perfume factory, kicking at metal bowls and crunching broken glass. When he spoke, he was more composed. "We are going to find out if they love you or if they love me." His voice became very mild, as if he were afraid of offending someone in the room. "I am sending you away. You are going to become a nun at the convent on Principio."

Zoe emitted a mocking, chiming laugh. "And you will play the naughty priest and visit me in my cell."

Michael's voice was chillingly earnest. "I am through with our games. I am sending you away."

Zoe laughed again. "Do you think I will simply order my yacht to transport me to Principio?"

"I have a ship waiting for you."

"I will decline your hospitality."

"You will accept. Or I will kill your sister's child." Zoe's eyes widened and she wavered, as if his words were a hammer that had struck her on the forehead. Michael nodded, his eyes black and cold. "She is my prisoner."

"Her betrothed will not allow you to—"

"He is dead."

Zoe crossed herself and her skin seemed utterly bloodless; even her lips became a pale lilac. "Swear to me you will not harm her," she whispered.

Michael nodded. "Does she know?"

"No." Zoe's answer was scarcely audible.

"Good. That will make it easier."

"What do you intend to do to her?" asked Zoe desperately.

"I promised you I would not harm her." Michael smiled. "Now it is time for you to repent your treason, Mother. Your ship is waiting."

† † †

"Of course I remember you, boy. Halldor the Varangian. The ladies on our streets still speak of you." The Blue Star had received Halldor in her neatly swept two-room cottage. Her ancient husband sat beside her and his sightless, milky eyes seemed to search for Halldor's presence. Halldor proceeded to tell the silver-haired woman about his suspicions concerning Haraldr's disappearance.

The Blue Star's massive bosom surged as she pondered the matter for a moment. "I never liked that boy Emperor, no matter what our friend Haraldr thought of him. He turned the heads of the tradesmen and their ilk, but we in the Studion have learned to distrust promises made in the Hippodrome. He's a clever schemer to have bested the Orphanotrophus. Capable of anything, I think that one is." The Blue Star stroked her husband's parchmentlike forehead. "When will all your men be in the city?"

"Tomorrow morning," answered Halldor.

"That's good enough. We'll need to move carefully. Without the tradesmen behind us, we can't expect to stand up right in front of the Imperial Taghmata and announce ourselves. The tradesmen have most of the weapons."

Halldor didn't like the sound of this. "I fear we are running out of time."

"We in the Studion love your Haraldr as much as you do, boy. But he's either alive or dead now, and your fears or mine won't change that. I can have an answer for you by tomorrow's meridian. That's as soon as you could do anything. And by then I will have a hostage against his life."

"A hostage?"

"Yes. His uncle the Nobilissimus has a palace in the city."

Halldor shook his head wearily. "And a considerable private guard, and the Imperial Taghmata only a quarter hour away from his summons. Even my Varangians could not storm the place in that time. The very confrontation we both agree would be suicidal would ensue."

The Blue Star girded her imposing breadth with her arms; her meaty hands and forearms still had the firmness of the athlete she once was. "The Taghmata will be powerless against the army I am sending against them. Now you get some rest, boy."

† † †

"You do not prostrate yourself before your Emperor?" Michael had removed the Imperial Diadem but otherwise wore the full robes of his office. His eyes swept around the ornate antechamber as if looking for witnesses to this affront.

"You do not have the graciousness of an Emperor." Maria's eyes hurled fire at Michael. "Why should I show you respect in return? I presume it is you who have confined me here these hours. I have asked about my betrothed and about my Mother Zoe and have received only the snarling contempt of these castrated nomads you now employ."

Michael looked at Maria with a lightly cocked head and the bemused expression of a man contemplating a great vision. "You are the most beautiful woman in the world. I lie awake on my Imperial Couch and think what it would be like to see your white breasts and legs and hips in front of me. I touch myself and think of your touch. I think of you and that golden brute of yours and I imagine how . . . graceful you must be to absorb his . . . thrusts. There are also other men who say they have slept with you. They say your skin is like molten silver, so hot and smooth. You quite burn them up. They say you make a torch of the heart."

Maria listened entirely impassively. "I am pleased to think I amuse Your Majesty during the moments he is unattended."

Michael's face reddened. "You will attend me." His lips moved wordlessly for a moment. Then he screamed: "You will attend me, bitch! You will take me inside and marry your raging fire to my golden light and call me husband! Husband! Husband! Husband!"

Maria smiled. "There is only one man I will ever call husband. And he is not the little King of Rome."

Michael bounded forward and stood a step away from Maria. He looked at her with demonic, dark eyes and a hideous grimace that bared his teeth and left his purple lips and livid cheeks trembling. "Then you call a corpse husband, bitch!" He screamed so loud that it seemed he would vomit his throat up. "I have killed him! I have poisoned him!" Michael's grimace became gleeful and he danced in little circles in front of Maria, his legs and arms jerking up like a marionette's.

Maria fought against the horrible stillness, the huge, cold hand of fate that grasped her heart and brutally crushed it. No. He is not dead. I would know. I would know anywhere in the world. And yet her heart felt the real pain, the icy grip. No. She mastered her voice. "You are a liar."

Michael let his hands drop. "Indeed. You, yourself, have expressed concern about him. And your mother."

"Yes. Where is your mother? I wish to ask her—"

Michael clapped his hands. "That is my gift to you, my little bride. I have sent her away. You are my . . . m-mother now." He lifted her hands gently. "You will sleep with me every night and call me husband." He dropped her hands and erupted into his dance. "You will be my whore! My unrepentant Magdalen!" He stopped and looked breathlessly at Maria. "Do you know that He knew the Magdalen? It's not written in the Holy Scriptures but He did. He has told me about her. Her hot skin, a whore like you."

Maria stared at Michael for a moment. "I want to feel your lance now, Husband," she whispered. "Unlace me." Michael's jaw dropped. "Unlace me. Did they not tell you that in the heat of lust I abandon all reason?" She turned her back to expose the ties of her scaramangium. "How can I burn your heart out unless you can press it to my naked, flaming breast?"

Michael reached out with trembling fingers and began to fumble at the fine silk loops. "Kiss my neck," whispered Maria. Michael hesitated for a long moment, as if he actually believed her skin were on fire. Finally he leaned closer. Maria reached inside her loose sleeve. Then she whirled and kneed Michael in the crotch and threw her entire weight against him and brought them both down. She came to rest on top of Michael and thrust the point of her dagger into his neck. He howled with pain and his blood trickled onto the opus-sectile floor. "He isn't dead!" she screamed in Michael's face. "He isn't dead! Where is he? Tell me where he is!" The guards battered the door and she could see the motion of their entry, and she thrust the dagger more deeply into Michael's rigid, corded neck.

"He is in Neorion!" screamed Michael. At the same moment the Pecheneg guards tackled Maria and sent her sprawling. "Don't kill her!" bellowed the Emperor. He staggered to his feet, his hand on his wounded neck. Blood ran out from beneath his palm and trickled off the golden eagles on his shoulders. "You must never kill my wife, my queen," he told the guards numbly. "She is our mother." He took a step back from Maria. She knelt, her braids uncoiled, glaring at Michael and his four guards. "I did not lie to you, my love," said Michael. "The fair-hair brute who tried to abduct you from my arms is now in Neorion. But he will never be able to see you, touch you, speak to you, or force his filthy manhood upon you again."

Maria collapsed to the floor, and her quenched eyes rolled into her head. Only a sliver of blue iris remained visible.

he enormous statue of Constantine the Great stood over the Forum, vainly awaiting the first rays on its bronze head; the day would likely remain cloudy, threatening rain. Good, thought the new Prefect of the City, Stephanus Anastasius, as he entered the vast column-ringed oval. He noticed with satisfaction that the crowd was sparse, in anticipation of the weather. The pharmacological vendors, their wooden boxes full of vials and jars, already had lines, as people who had become ill during the night were wont to come here early. The shopkeepers in the arcades had begun to arrange their displays; bright piece goods flashed here and there behind the columns. The indigent scholars sat beside their books, waiting for pupils or, more likely, a good argument with which to while away their day. Fortunately none of the usual rabble-rousers were about; they would generally begin their harangues later in the morning. Two Venetian sailors in short tunics walked around the great column, staring up and gawking.

The Prefect spurred his white horse to a quick canter across the paved Forum. He reined to a halt beneath the statue; his horse was dwarfed by the massive pyramidal stone base. The seven porphyry drums lifted the colossal bronze figure of the long-dead Emperor far overhead. The Prefect dismounted and quickly unrolled his purple-tinted text. A group of laborers heading for the docks pointed and hurried over. Two meat vendors in stained tunics left an apothecary's line and walked across the plaza. The Prefect looked around at the timeless audience, the statues that stood atop the arcade roof all around the forum. They were always listening, he thought. He decided he must begin.

"Children of Rome, your Emperor, Autocrator, and Basileus greets you. He asks that you acknowledge a new triumph which the Pantocrator has enabled him to achieve. A treacherous endeavor to deny the authority of the Pantocrator and usurp His Vice-Regent, indeed cleave from His Eternal Body His hand on Earth, has been crushed by the diligence of your Father and his beloved children. The two traitors have been identified, yet with Christlike forbearance they have been spared a punishment in kind for the crimes they intended to visit upon your Father. Instead they have been mercifully relieved of their offices and invited to repent at the Lord's bosom. The names of the two traitors are Alexius, Patriarch of Constantinople, and the Empress and Augusta Zoe."

The four laborers looked at one another in disbelief. One of the meat vendors flushed deeply. The Prefect quickly mounted, thanked the Heavenly Father for having created the swift-footed horse, and galloped out of the Forum, heading east toward the palace gates.

† † †

Michael sat on his throne in the Senate chamber. His purple boots jittered slightly on the gold-embroidered stool; his fingers tapped against the gilded armrests. Did Scylitzes ever close his mouth? The Emperor realized with immense satisfaction, however, that he could no longer hear Scylitzes's words, only see his lips move. Michael continued his private conversation with the Pantocrator.

The Senators sat in tiers on either side of their Majesty, Magisters in their white-and-gold tunics, Proconsular Patricians with the purple porphyry diptychs of their dignity propped in their laps, Patricians displaying their inscribed ivory tablets. The white heads of the Dhynatoi nodded in senescent delight as Scylitzes's intricate encomiums climaxed a morning of slavish approbation for their master's bold stroke. They had lived to see the last legacy of the Bulgar-Slayer trodden into the dust. Both purple-born whores cast out in one daring venture: Zoe in exile; and the Patriarch Alexius, the only man who could bring Theodora back into the Imperial Palace, now besieged in the Mother Church, would soon be forced to give up his office, his church, and his ambitions for his client. "Who could deny," concluded Scylitzes with pallium-pumping grandiloquence, "that this paragon of infinite virtue, this treasury of unsurpassed merit, this avatar of boundless magnanimity, now leaves the chronologies of the great Emperors, the Constantines and Justinians, to emblazon the earth far below his soaring majesty, and now ensconces the manifestations of his ever-endeavoring imperium in the exalted vaults of the firmament, to set his splendid throne among the deities!"

Michael nodded, indicating that he had received the Senate's blessing with pleasure, and that the Senators should now come forward to kiss his knees. As the procession of supplicants went on to the shuffling of slippers and the rustling of silk, Michael and the Pantocrator discussed their mothers. *You came to Your Mother, Your Maria, in the form of Holy Spirit,* remarked the Emperor. *And so it was that you begat yourself by Your own*

Mother. I will visit my mother, my Maria, with my holy essence and beget myself again and again, through the centuries that Rome will rule the earth, until we call down the Final Judgment, and then together You and I will sit side by side again, in our golden throne in New Jerusalem. And I shall know Your Mother, and You shall know mine, and together we shall beget eternity from their loins.

Michael noticed that the Senators were leaving en masse, their hands crossed over their breasts. He nodded them out the vast doors at the end of the chamber. When he was finally alone with his eunuchs, his seraphim and cherubim, he rose from his throne, descended from the dais, and danced in little circles on the floor.

† † †

Mar Hunrodarson was awakened two hours after sunrise by his second in command Gris Knutson, who had replaced Thorvald Ostenson while Ostenson conducted crucial business in Rus. Mar arose and slipped the ceremonial tunic of Droungarios over his head. Bianca Maria, the twelve-year-old virgin with whom Mar had chastely spent many of the nights of his exile in Italia, stirred in the bed and looked up at him with wondering dark eyes. The trip from Italia had held many astonishments for her. And yesterday afternoon she had stood atop this villa just off the Via Ignatium and seen the distant but clearly distinguishable wall of the great city.

"Droungarios," said Knutson, extending a rolled and sealed document. "I thought you should read this right away. It bears the seal of the Patriarch Alexius." Knutson bowed and turned to leave. "No, Turmarch," commanded Mar. "You need to hear this. Soon you will have many more responsibilities than simply dealing with queries from a priest of Rome." Mar opened the seal and read quickly. He looked up at Knutson. "This is most interesting, Turmarch. The Patriarch Alexius has been deposed and the Empress Zoe has been banished. The Patriarch is besieged in the Hagia Sophia. He says his client Theodora is secured somewhere in the city. The wily old fox does not say where. He begs us to relieve him, and then he will lead us to the new Empress."

"Isn't that entirely to our purpose?" asked Knutson, his gray Danish eyes thoughtful. "With the Empress Zoe banished, Theodora would have no rivals."

"Except the Emperor."

Knutson blinked away his confusion. "I thought the Emperor was ... well, you know all the nights we have joked about what we would do with an Emperor in the interrogation chambers of the Numera."

"Yes, Turmarch, but that was before little Michael had displayed this unusual ability to rid us of our problems. Consider that under the patronage of Theodora we will always be subject to the coercion of her purple-born status. But with Michael as our patron, we will have only to overcome the legacy of a parvenue. We might even be hailed as liberators when we usurp him."

Mar crushed Alexius's missive in his huge fist. "Turmarch, convey a message to his Imperial Majesty. Tell him I have returned from Italia on a mission of necessary secrecy and utmost urgency. I will be arriving at Bucoleon Harbor this evening to discuss matters of vital importance to the future of Rome."

Knutson snapped out of the room. Bianca Maria sat up; a silken white night robe draped her bony shoulders and barely pubescent breasts. "Will I see the city tonight?" she asked in a high, clear voice like the ringing of the finest glass.

Mar gently touched the straight dark hair that cloaked her slender neck. "Yes, little candle," he said softly, "tonight you will see the Great Palace of the Roman Emperor."

† † †

Constantine slammed the wooden shutter and pressed his hands to his ears. "Even their noise is an assault!" he shouted to Demetrius Metanoites, the young Roman commander of his Pecheneg guard. Metanoites opened the shutter again to see for himself, and the intensity of the shrieking drone rose perceptibly. He shook his head in amazement. Two stories below him, the street was awash with women and children, all of them wailing as if the Last Trumpet had blown; their brilliant, beardless faces, flushed with rage, were like a field of rose blossoms amid the dull colors of their tunics. The wooden shafts of various tools rose above them here and there, but the principal weapons of this army, other than noise, were stones. With every heartbeat another missile pelted the front of Constantine's town palace; not a single pane of glass remained intact. And now the raging, wailing maenads had begun pounding away at the walls with large rocks.

"We are going to have to summon the Taghmata!" shouted Metanoites.

"They won't slaughter these innocents!"

"Then we must break out! My Pechenegs have no such reservations about killing the women and children of Rome."

"We still could not get through. You have seen how many they are!"

Metanoites pulled his wiry black beard for a moment. "We will send the Pechenegs out the front gate, and we will leave through the rear entrance. We will need to change into simple tunics!"

A quarter hour later Constantine unbolted the front gate and sent two dozen Pechenegs, swords unsheathed, into the street. The screams rose to a hideous din; Constantine saw a flash of enamel-brilliant crimson before he turned away. He and Metanoites raced through the main hall and kitchens and slammed against the rear door. They surprised several women who were setting refuse afire in the alley. The smoke provided good cover, and after a short dash to the street they were able to merge unnoticed with the crowd.

It took a half hour to work through the mob and reach the Mese. The broad avenue was frantic with merchants and tradesmen and even some barebacked porters up from the docks; most were running toward the palace, and many carried bows and spears. A portly man in a plain wool tunic puffed along with a rusty sword in his ruddy fist. Women were also about on the Mese; one dashed past, clutching a linen veil to her face. "Where is our Mother, our beauty, our noble Empress?" she moaned.

The arcades of the shops along the lower Mese were shuttered. A crowd blocked the entire Milion Square near the end of the Mese. Spear shafts rising above the milling wool-and-linen-cloaked figures were now common. "Where is our Mother?" every rage-rouged face seemed to be screaming. Metanoites stumbled over a middle-aged woman dressed in widow's black who had slumped to her knees; she beat her breast with her withered fists. "Oh, Theotokos! Oh, Theotokos! Deliver our Mother!" she wailed.

"The Mother of Rome!" boomed a male voice. "The Bulgar-Slayer's niece, and him from nowhere!"

Metanoites led Constantine through the mob, shoving bodies aside with fierce determination. Constantine could only thank the Pantocrator that his rough servant's tunic had spared him the deadly recognition of the mob. At the entrance to the Augustaion, Constantine looked to his left. The enormous bronze equestrian figure of Justinian charged above a lake of wailing faces that filled the entire square and spilled over to the porches of the Hagia Sophia. "Heavenly Father!" he shouted to Metanoites. "The entire city has come out!"

The giant Imperial Eagles embossed on the Chalke Gate loomed ahead. Constantine and Metanoites struggled with terrified urgency through clusters of well-armed tradesmen arguing about how to assault the palace. Close to the gate, the crush was so oppressive that Constantine was lifted off his feet from time to time. His chest ached and at one point it seemed that the pressure of the crowd would suffocate him. Somehow Metanoites got him close enough that he could have spit on the huge bronze doors. But that was as close as they could get. Metanoites was also blocked by the surging mass, and he looked back at Constantine desperately.

"I know one of the guards!" shouted Constantine to a beefy-faced man next to him. "Let me up there and I will get him to open the gate!" The beefy-faced man shouted to someone next to him, and soon a group of five or six pushed Constantine toward the small, man-sized door set within the colossal gates. The security grate, set at eye level, had been battered away. Constantine removed his seal ring and dropped it through the opening. A face flickered at the grate. "Let me in!" screamed Constantine.

"Let us in!" bellowed the tradesmen who had pushed Constantine forward. "Let us at the swine who have taken our Mother!" Suddenly the small door cracked open and arms thrust out and yanked Constantine inside. Metanoites tried to follow, but he was not recognized by the Khazars. Their swords ripped open his belly. The beefy-faced man also charged. His neck was hacked to the bone, and he slumped, blood gushing. The door slammed shut.

Constantine's chest burned like the fires of Hell and his head whirled. He was alive. He wished he had gold to give the Khazars; he promised them gifts as they returned his ring. He requested an escort to the Chrysotriklinos. As he headed past the Hall of Nineteen Couches, Constantine was shocked to observe business as usual in the palace precinct. The silk-clad eunuchs and bureaucrats glided along the colonnaded avenue; only once did Constantine see two officials—lower-level secretaries to the Sacellarius—stop and discuss the furious din beyond the walls, a sound as clearly audible as an approaching cyclone.

Michael sat on his throne beneath the gold dome of the Chrysotriklinos, listening to a report on the virtually defunct tax-collection apparatus in Theodosiopolis theme. His eyebrows shot up when he saw Constantine approach in his soiled servant's tunic. Michael nodded at his eunuchs, and the vast chamber was quickly cleared except for the Grand Eunuch and the Pecheneg guards in their gilded breastplates and plumed helmets. "Whatever are you doing, Uncle?" asked Michael, as if he were merely concerned about some prank. "I am so disappointed that you

could not attend my presentation to the Senate. They were quite taken
with it."

"Majesty, I have scarcely escaped with my life from my own house. The
captain of my guard is dead. The entire city is up in arms."

Michael fanned his hand languidly. "Then I shall announce an event
in the Hippodrome and put an end to it."

Constantine approached the throne. "Nephew," he whispered, "would
you please walk outside with me?"

Michael's face contorted with boyish displeasure, but he nodded for his
guard to surround him and followed Constantine out to the porch of the
Chrysotriklinos. The vast dirge from the city came like a gale from the
west; it was perceptibly louder than when Constantine had gone inside
only moments before. Michael listened for a moment, then studied his
purple boots for a long while, apparently carrying on some inner conversation. He looked up and smiled. "How incredible," he said effusively, his
dark eyes glowing. "The Pantocrator has already sent the means of our
deliverance from this rabble." Constantine looked at his nephew with
concern. "Yes, Uncle. It is true. The former Hetairarch Mar Hunrodarson has returned to save us."

† † †

The interior of the Hippodrome was already in twilight. Halldor was
the first into the vast, empty stadium and his boots crunched in the neatly
graded sand. He and Ulfr walked to the spina and stood beneath the
bronze pylons at the south end of the stadium. Behind him followed the
Blue Star, a short, plump figure firmly mounted on a donkey. The Varangians came next and clustered about the south end of the spina. And then
the army of the city began to enter. Rank after rank after rank marched
through the gates. They wore coarse wool and burlap tunics; some were
in beggar's rags, some in fine Greek wool. The men with spears entered
first, then men with swords, hoes, rakes, scythes, hatchets, bows,
butcher's knives. And the women came in their own contingents, armed
with stones and clubs. The track was quickly covered with these unlikely
soldiers, and then even the seats began to fill up.

Halldor pointed to the Imperial Box, high up on the east side of the
stadium. It was an enormous oblong structure that projected vertigi-
nously over the tiers of seats below, its weight supported by thick marble
columns. The Emperor's seating pavilion resembled the portico of an

ancient Greek temple, and this was flanked on both sides by balustraded balconies where dignitaries were usually seated; directly behind the Imperial seating pavilion was a long, flat terrace that bridged over to the adjoining Triclinium in the palace complex; the entire ponderous marble platform allowed no direct access from the seats below, unless one could shimmy up the marble pilings. And even if one could, armored units of the Imperial Hyknatoi already waited on the balconies.

"Those balconies are where the battle will be won or lost," he explained to the Blue Star. "They are an excellent platform for the defenders, but if we can take them, they will be the platform for our attack on the entire Palace. This is clearly our best opportunity to breach the palace defenses. Elsewhere the walls are sheer, but here the seats give us a natural incline. It is never wise to attack up a hill if it can be avoided, but attacking up a hill is better than attacking straight up the sheer face of a mountain."

The Blue Star nodded. "This is very different than what we expected last night, isn't it, boy?"

Halldor looked around at the still-filling stadium. "Very different. But that is the nature of conflict. It always presents us with the unexpected."

† † †

"It is as if God sprinkled the earth with stars," said Bianca Maria. She stood at the railing as Mar's *dhromon* glided past the city to the south. "What are the fires for?"

Mar looked at the conflagrations along the city's affluent spine. From the vantage of the Marmora coast, the huge tongues of flames seemed painted in eerie, brightly enameled miniature against the darkness. The palaces of the Dhynatoi were coming down. "There is some trouble in the city tonight, precious," said Mar. "But it will be over tomorrow, and then you will be able to see everything."

The massive galley turned larboard to head into the Bucoleon Harbor. The lights of the palace burned with their usual brilliance. "That is where the Emperor lives," said Bianca Maria with rapt self-confidence.

"Yes. Remember what I told you about the proper way to greet him."

Khazar guards waited at the jetty when the *dhromon* docked. Only Mar, Gris Knutson, and Bianca Maria disembarked. They were escorted up the statue-lined terraces, around the soaring apses of the Imperial Baths, and then into the Chrysotriklinos. The trio performed the prescribed prostrations and then stood before the Emperor Michael.

"What a lovely child," said Michael. "What is your name?" He leaned toward Mar's adolescent companion.

"Bianca Maria, Majesty."

"Well, Hetairarch, if I may reinstate you with your former title," said Michael quickly, "your return is so provident that I quite believe you are moved by the Holy Spirit."

"I am moved by a desire to preserve the office of Emperor, Autocrator, and Basileus of the Romans," said Mar.

Michael shifted uneasily in his throne. Mar had said *office*, not *person*. "Well, Hetairarch, I am grateful to hear that your former respect for the Imperial dignity has not been compromised by your tenure in the provinces. However, much has happened to alter the value of the Imperial Diadem since you and I last speculated on its worth. My uncle, the Nobilissimus Constantine, and I placed a considerable investment at risk, and have been duly rewarded. But you would not know of that, because due to your misbegotten fortunes in the Bulgarian campaign, you have been away from the vital center of our Empire."

"You have done well in aggrandizing your investment, Majesty. But I fear that the value of your commodity has once again plummeted. It seems to me that the vital center of Rome is now the Hippodrome, where the Varangians who so recently served as your guard are preparing to lead an assault by the wretches of the Studion and their new allies, the tradesmen and merchants. Only the Dhynatoi and the Taghmata stand with you now, and I question how vigorously the men of the Taghmata will enlist in the slaughter of the women of Rome, who have risen against you as vehemently as their husbands, fathers, and sons."

Michael seemed to regard the threat as a minor negotiating point. He smiled at Bianca Maria. "I have developed a special relationship with the Pantocrator, Hunrodarson. He will not permit me to surrender the troth that links us." Michael bowed his head for a while. "What? What?" he whispered. Then his voice seemed to buzz, very low, like an insistent insect. "So it would be the three-in-one, as it was in your mind in the beginning, because in the light all souls will hear the word . . ." The buzz trailed off. Michael lifted his head and clapped his hands three times. "He has no objection to a trinity! Here is how we will have it. You shall be Basileus, Lord of the Entire World. I shall be Autocrator, Lord of the Universe! And He shall rule for us in Heaven until we come to share His throne! Indeed! Kiss my hand, come forward and kiss my hand, Basileus, Lord of the World!"

Mar's pale eyebrows twitched as he came forward, ascended the golden dais, and knelt at the purple boots of the new Lord of the Universe.

"Are you ready to lead our seraphim against the thrice-damned rabble, Basileus?" whispered Michael.

"I will send for my men and be in position to slaughter every living soul in the Hippodrome by first dawn, Autocrator." Mar rose warily, afraid that the slightest tremor on his part might bring the fantastic, wondrous edifice of Michael's madness tumbling down. He backed away with his arms crossed, took Bianca Maria's warm little hand, and prepared to take his leave.

"Basileus! I forgot to mention that your friend, Nordbrikt, will be unavailable to oppose you. You can visit him this evening if you have time. In the Neorion. I'm quite afraid you will not find him with his usual vigor, however. He is . . . changed."

Mar's spirit ebbed slightly; he had so often dreamed of being the architect of Haraldr Sigurdarson's demise, perhaps even himself cleaving Norway's skull and seeing the last instant of terror in his eyes. He bowed to Michael. "Perhaps I will console Nordbrikt later, Autocrator. I have told Bianca Maria that the Emperor of Rome has a golden lion that roars, and she wants very much to see it tonight."

† † †

"Get out, you gelded swine!" Maria plucked the dish from the hands of the appalled chamberlain and hurled it at the Pecheneg guard who had escorted him into her antechamber. As the guard cowered from the hurtling silver disk spraying garos sauce, she bounced a goblet off his breastplate. "Get out!" she screamed at the chamberlain; she kicked him in the seat of his white robe and shoved him out the door, on the heels of his retreating Pecheneg escort.

Maria returned to her bedchamber, leaned against the ponderous sleeping couch, and grunted as she slid it across the smooth marble floor. She hiked up her scaramangium and knelt beside the knife that had been concealed beneath the bed. Still on her knees, she ran the point of the knife along the fine seam between two sections of marble flooring. She popped up the slab of purple Docimian marble—it was no thicker than an ivory bookcover—and slid it aside. She lifted several more of these thin revetments before she finally exposed the underlying, fathom-wide masonry flooring tile she had been working on all day. She knocked out the few remaining chinks of mortar and arduously pried up the limestone slab, which was as thick as a bound Psalter. Once she had a handhold, she was able to slide the slab out of the way. She reached into the hypocaust heating duct and felt the oak slats of the ceiling below. She took a deep breath and slid into the duct.

She could not lift her head enough to see even in front of her. She wriggled along in the dark, choking on the fine layer of dust. She wondered vaguely what it would be like to become stuck and die like this.

Finally her outstretched hands grasped dead air. The heating closet, she thought with relief. She squirmed along until most of her torso projected into the dark cubicle. She could feel the opposite wall almost against her nose, and she panicked. No matter how she contorted herself, she would not have enough room to maneuver her legs out of the duct. She reached down and felt the round bronze lid of the furnace just below her. She prayed that it was not sealed. She pulled with desperate fingers and got the lid loose, then slid it off; it clattered to the floor of the closet. She realized she might have alerted the guards, and she put her arms out and dropped headfirst into the bronze belly of the furnace. There was not even a layer of ashes at the bottom. She thanked the Theotokos that this terrible day was at least not a cold one, and that the Empress's servants were made to keep the furnaces clean.

She was still stuck like a circus buffoon headfirst in a barrel. She lowered herself onto her elbows and pushed at the furnace's fire door. It opened with a metallic scraping sound. She extended her arm and felt the wooden door of the surrounding closet. She prayed that it would not be locked. She pushed. It was. How long would it take to cut out the lock? She would have to right herself and somehow get the furnace out of the way. Was that possible? She thumped the door in frustration.

The door flew open, and light burst like flame through the fire door. A face loomed, a demon waiting at the gates of Hell. A ghost, a specter of the damned. Symeon.

"Mistress," whispered the ancient eunuch. "Let me help you." He gave her his fragile yet surprisingly powerful hands and pulled. Like a serpent in dirty red silk, Maria slid headfirst into the storage room adjacent to the heating closet.

"Symeon. You are truly the angel of my deliverance. Is it true about our Mother?"

"Yes." Symeon seemed concerned but not desperate. "They have shorn her and sent her away. But I expect her return shortly. The city has risen to defend her." Now Symeon was troubled. "Mistress, your Tauro-Scythian has been taken to Neorion. I am afraid his execution has already taken place."

"That cannot be. It cannot be. It simply . . ." No, she told herself. His light has not gone out. No. Maria looked around the storeroom. Zoe had stockpiled hundreds of jars of her skin emollients and beauty unguents and face paints. "Symeon," whispered Maria, "I have to make myself presentable. And I am going to need your help."

Symeon nodded with timeless grace.

† † †

Haraldr moved his fingers. The pain shot through his arms. He moved his toes. It was a start. The poison had left his entire body without feeling. He had no idea how long he had been unconscious. When he had first awakened, he had not been able to see or hear. He still could not see. But he could hear now, though he wished he could not, and so he knew where he was. Neorion. His eyes felt as if daggers were piercing them, but he could not move his arms to touch his bloody sockets. He could not feel his arms, actually, but his fingers had moved. He still had a tongue, though, but so dry and swollen that he could hardly breathe. *Let me live, Odin, let me live to destroy Rome. Like blind Samson, I will pull down the pillars.* Maria had warned him. God the Father, if only he could touch her, he would live on the memories of her vision and her living touch.

It was as if the halls were trumpets that amplified every noise, every scream. The Neorion was a vast conch, and the scream that started at the top would wind its way down and enter the ears and shatter inside the head so that the screamer died in one's brain, clawing for life in a stranger's skull. Things crawled out of the sludge and onto his legs and chest, and he could not pick them off. They bit him often; were they also chewing his shoulders? He prayed they would kill that man.

The fire exploded in his face, and when they jerked him to his feet, he thought they had ripped his arms off. He tried to see them and butt with his head, but they kept the flame in his face and he could smell his hair burn. Demons! This was the Hell of Satan! Demons ripping his arms off! He slammed into the wall, trying to crush the creature beside him. They screamed in their demon tongue. Pechenegs! Haraldr slammed again and again against the wall and they beat him about the head, and the flames seared his face and dozens of arms grappled around him. He knew now that he was not blind. He could see them screaming. Then a flash and he could see nothing.

When he awoke, he wondered if knives had been stuck in his neck and shoulders. He could see the interrogation chamber clearly, as if pain were a glass that distorted his thoughts but placed his vision in sharp focus. Four smooth-faced Pecheneg guards stood by while the two Pecheneg interrogators prepared their instruments. He cursed the gods who had lured him to this ignoble death and did not ask for their help. Then he remembered the wretch from the Studion he had seen butchered in this very room, and he felt the man's soul still lingering, offering him courage.

The shorter of the two Pechenegs, a man with brown chancre scars on his face and wide-set black eyes, picked up a steel brazier full of glowing coals and held it beneath Haraldr's face. The heat seared his nostrils and baked his forehead. Haraldr tried to swat the fire away, and he realized that he was hanging off the ground, suspended by his bound hands; his arms were pulled up behind his back in an excruciating posture. He jerked his feet up, but they were held fast by chains and his ankles burned. He glared futilely at the instruments of darkness. Two irons the width of a woman's little finger rested in the coals; the brands were white-orange at the sharpened tips. The second, taller Pecheneg put on thick leather smith's gloves and rotated one of the irons. Embers flew up into Haraldr's face. In some corner of his mind he observed the senseless humor of that; the last thing a man who is about to be blinded sees is flying sparks. No visions of golden cities, no final sunset.

The door slid open and the Pechenegs turned. A fifth guard brought in a fowl on a spit and a basket of fruit. The two interrogators set the brazier at Haraldr's feet and descended on the food with the rest; they placed the plucked bird on their table and sliced the nearly raw meat with the blades of their trade. One of them turned and made some joke about Haraldr in his guttural tongue. The rest began to eat noisily.

† † †

"That is not enough." The commander of the Neorion's Pecheneg garrison was a tall, ugly Asian, probably of mixed Saracen blood; his broad nostrils were in grotesque opposition to the sinister verticality of his long, hooked nose and dour, drooping chin. He pointed to the three gold solidi the elderly priest had placed on the table. "This prisoner is . . . *was* an important man. Wealthy. Wealthy friends. You can pay more for the privilege of providing him spiritual succor. And I have to collect for both of you. A double toll, so to speak." He grinned, exposing rotten front teeth, and pointed to the black-swaddled and veiled nun, a stooped crone with some kind of skin disease; her wrinkled eyes were almost crusted shut.

The priest, who wore the gold-embroidered shawl of a deacon of the Mother Church, emptied his purse with frail, trembling hands. Three more solidi spilled onto the table. The garrison commander grinned again. "Very well. But you don't have much time. They have already gone to work on him." The priest and nun crossed themselves quickly.

A single Pecheneg led the priest and nun up the dismal, mysteriously cold, endless flights. The wolf-shaped oil lamps seemed to struggle against the damp and darkness, the flames pitiful and stunted. At the tenth landing the Pecheneg knocked on the steel door, the security grate slid, and finally the door screeched open and offered up the reek of death. The priest and the nun were admitted to an antechamber a short distance down the icy hall. The black steel double doors of the interrogation chamber faced them. The five Pecheneg guards played a game on the floor with knucklebones. The priest gave each Pecheneg a copper nomismata. Two of them got up and slid the immense double doors open.

The two interrogators were sharpening their blades again, having dulled them on their dinner. Haraldr lolled his head toward the new arrivals. A priest. His eyes teared with gratitude. The Pantocrator would also be with him in the end. Haraldr thought he had never seen anything more beautiful than the golden crosses embroidered on the priest's shawl. The priest moved excruciatingly slowly. He gave coins to each of the interrogators and brandished his jeweled cross at them. They bowed and retreated; as part of their indoctrination they had been shown the Hagia Sophia, and subsequently they had no wish to offend any of the wizards who could bring the sun inside at night and bridge the sky with molten gold.

The old crone nun came forward, too, her veiled, crusted, hideous face lowered to spare her the sight of Haraldr's bloodied head and filthy, almost naked body. The priest chanted and knelt at Haraldr's feet. Haraldr could not understand why the priest was tugging on one of the thick hide ankle collars, looped through chains, that restrained his legs. He looked absently to his feet. The priest, now furiously chanting, clutched a dagger in his withered, corpselike hands. He was sawing away at the collars. Haraldr looked up in horror at the two Pechenegs. They busied themselves shining their new coins, then held them up to the oil lamps and played with the reflections. Who was this unlikely savior? If he could just get his legs loose before the Pechenegs lost interest in their new-found wealth! The old crone was looking at him; she had forced her crusted eyes open. . . .

Holy Father. Just to see them again, even if he died now. They were two sapphires with fires behind them. He mouthed her name in spite of his swollen tongue. Maria's shoulders heaved and her eyes teared, but she steadied herself. She looked over at the Pechenegs and came around Haraldr's back. The priest had cut one of the collars loose. Haraldr's wrists were bound but not chained, and Maria hacked at the ropes. One of the Pechenegs was distracted from his coin, focused his black eyes for a moment, and barked at his companion. They stepped forward, not yet alarmed, and peered curiously at the priest. Haraldr whipped his free leg up and cracked the short Pecheneg on the side of the head with his foot; the man fell like a drunk. The second interrogator ran for the steel doors, and Maria dashed after him and plunged her knife in his back; the Pecheneg's arms shot out sideways and he turned and looked at her in amazement. He shouted as he fell. Haraldr pulled desperately and the bonds at his wrist loosened as the doors slid open. One of the guards looked in. Maria stabbed at him but her knife clattered off his breastplate. Haraldr pitched forward on his face as his wrist came loose; the priest, who had been working all the time on the second ankle collar, crumpled beneath him. The muscles in Haraldr's shoulders seemed to rip as he pulled his arms free, but he had the strength of Odin now. He rolled to his feet and whacked the guard with his still-numb arm and sent him sprawling. The priest struggled to his feet and Haraldr realized he was Zoe's eunuch, Symeon. Haraldr's head roared with the howling winds of the spirit world. Another guard peered into the interrogation chamber and Haraldr slammed the steel doors shut on his head; the Pecheneg's face seemed to blow up with blood, and his nose and eyes spurted. Haraldr let the limp body slump inside, removed the sword from the belt, threw the doors open, and faced the remaining four men; the guard in the hall had joined the three Pechenegs. Haraldr was not even conscious of how he killed them, but the strange sword sang to him in the same melody as his own.

Haraldr came back into the interrogation chamber and methodically slit the throats of the men he had left unconscious. He looked at Maria, who had retrieved her bloody knife, and with some removed consciousness contemplated the terrible spectacle of their reunion. Then he embraced her. "Father, I am glad I did not die before this moment," he told her.

"Oh, Mother of God!" she gasped cathartically. She broke down at last and tried to rub the blood off his face.

Haraldr turned gratefully to the determined-looking eunuch Symeon and wondered how courage had ever come to be associated with a man's testicles. "Symeon, you and Maria must go down now, before someone discovers this."

Maria looked up at him and sobbed. "How will you . . . escape?"

"I cannot go down with you," said Haraldr. "There will be too many guards. They still think you are a priest and a nun. They know I am not supposed to be leaving." He looked around the room, studying the ropes and various paraphernalia of torture. "I have to go up." He let go of Maria and began gathering supplies. As he worked, Maria and Symeon told him of the incredible events that had ensued in his absence: the banishment of Zoe and the charges against the Patriarch; the rising of the city; the encampment of his Varangians and a citizen army in the Hippodrome.

When Haraldr had assembled his gear, he bagged it in one of the Pecheneg's tunics. Then he led Maria and Symeon back into the stairwell. "Go now," he whispered. Maria hesitated. She threw her arms around him and clung fiercely. "We are taunting destiny with these farewells," she whispered harshly. "Fate will not always give you back to me; it cannot be that generous." Haraldr took her arms from him and looked into her blazing eyes. "The gods serve those who obey their summons. You have proved that by giving me back my life." His voice rose in the dismal shaft. "Go. Go." She turned, looked back at him again, and then Symeon gently urged her down the stairs. She was gone before the gods whispered that he might never see her again.

Haraldr ascended the last flight. As he had expected, the stairwell ended at a steel trapdoor. He crushed the padlock with the steel mallet he had found in the interrogation chamber. He climbed out onto the roof. The wind whistled and he immediately saw the conflagrations along the spine of the city. He paused for a moment, rapt with the spectacle. The palaces of the Dhynatoi were crumbling into gutted hulks. To the south, thousands of torchlights moved in and around the Hippodrome.

Haraldr looked over the low parapet that ringed the roof. The pavement was twelve stories below; the intervening walls of Neorion were sheer gray rock articulated with only a single band of small windows on the lowest level. Haraldr used the mallet to drive a steel spike—one of the brands intended for his eyes—into the stone. He looped a length of rope over the spike and fastened the other end under his arms. He slung his gear over his back and crawled over the wall. Odin, Christ, he prayed. He let go of the parapet and allowed the rope to take all his weight. Iron and stone screeched faintly, like an insect dying.

Driving spikes as needed and reusing his short lengths of rope, Haraldr rappeled to within a dozen ells of the pavement before his spikes ran out. He jumped the rest of the way, landing hard. He heard shouts from the road to his west: Khazars, about a dozen. He did not wait to satisfy their curiosity. To his left was a small wooded area that ran south toward the Church of St. Irene. The cool fragrance of the trees engulfed him. He heard shouts and realized that the Khazars had followed. He thrashed through several rows of shrubs and saw the huge, brightly lit apse windows at the eastern end of St. Irene. He crossed the lawn that bordered the church; off to his left, the windows of the neighboring Hagia Sophia glowed like golden studs set into the night. Shouts came from the walled courtyard on the south side of the church. He looked back; Khazars had followed him across the lawn. He heard more of them coming around the apse from the north. They seemed to be everywhere.

Haraldr leapt to the ledge beneath the towering apse windows. He kicked out glass panes and wooden lattice and jumped. He landed in the midst of a group of exclaiming, fervently praying priests; they had been seated, as was customary, in tiers just behind the altar. Haraldr clutched the robe of the first priest he could get his hands on. "Where is your underground!" he bellowed at the dazed cleric; the entire palace complex was linked by a network of subterranean passageways.

"If it is sanctuary—" began a white-haired old priest.

"Show me the passage!" shouted Haraldr. A young priest rushed forward and pulled him to a small door set into the wall behind the altar. They ducked into the dark storeroom as the Khazars climbed through the shattered window. The priest threw open a wooden hatch set into the floor. "Bless you, Father!" shouted Haraldr as he descended the steps into the darkness.

Haraldr navigated the abrupt turns of the damp-smelling passageway; he had to duck his head to keep from hitting it on the low ceiling. After a while he could see the slight illumination of his pursuers' torches. The passage forked. Which way? He was uncertain now if he was pointed south or east. Or west? One fork led to the Hagia Sophia, he reasoned; the priests there, no doubt still led by their besieged Patriarch, would surely conceal him and show him a way out into the city. Fate instructed him and he took the left fork.

The passageway lowered and he had to crouch. He could hear the Khazars shout to one another. He scuttled along desperately through the claustrophobic tunnel. And on and on. He realized that the Mother Church was not this far from St. Irene, but he was beyond turning back. He remembered the cul-de-sac in the Bulgar-Slayer's galleries and wondered when he would encounter a similar dead end and have to turn and face the Khazars.

The floor became slick and he could smell the water. Not just seepage, but oppressive, cold, dank, a wetness that thickened the air like a wind off an icy lake. The passageway ended beneath an arcade. Flares a good bowshot away rippled in golden rivulets across an onyx-black underground lake, illuminating the hundreds of columns and brick vaults of the Cisterna Basilica. Haraldr gasped with involuntary wonder; he had heard of the great "sunken palace" but had never before seen it. He could not appreciate the beauty of the intricately carved floral capitals that thrust up the honeycomb of groined vaults; the cistern seemed only like a vast stone forest rising from a Stygian swamp.

Haraldr sheathed his blade in his burlap loincloth and lowered himself into the icy water. The submersion of his chest left him gasping for breath. He stroked furiously. A third of the way across, he heard the shouts roll through the vaults and looked back to see the Khazar torches in the arcade from which he had embarked. As he approached the far end of the cistern he paused and treaded water while he studied the guards on the small landing ahead of him. Khazars. Four of them; they were obviously standing guard over an entry point from the city. A rowboat was tied up at one end of the wooden landing; Haraldr hoped that the Khazars would be foolish enough to paddle out after him. But the Khazars simply unsheathed their swords and waited for the inevitable finish of his swim.

Haraldr paddled to within fifty ells of the landing. He continued to tread water and taunted the Khazars in Greek. They responded with curses in their own language. One of them sheathed his sword, swung his bow off his back, pulled an arrow from his quiver, and took aim. Haraldr ducked under the water and swam forward. When he came up for air, he was only twenty ells away. Another Khazar aimed at him and he took two quick breaths and ducked under again.

The two other Khazars quickly sheathed their swords, strung their bows, and joined in the sport; all four of them crowded toward the edge of the landing and began wagering on who would hit the "big white fish" first. They studied the surface intently, arrows drawn. Nothing. Then the water splashed right in front of them, and one of the guards pitched forward into the inky void, immediately disappeared, and a moment later bobbed up, his neck tilted unnaturally. The astonished bowmen shouted and fired aimlessly into the dark water. More thrashing at the end of the landing. They turned.

Haraldr was already on the dock. He decapitated the nearest Khazar and with a single swat sent another sprawling into the water. The third Khazar dropped his bow and went to his knees on his own accord. "You know who I am?" Haraldr said in Greek. The trembling Khazar nodded. "I let you live." He pointed to the boat. "Go back to your unit and tell them that Haraldr Nordbrikt and his Varangians will come against them soon, and there will be no mercy for those who oppose us. But there will be amnesty for all who refuse to take arms against us and the Empress of Rome." The Khazar dipped his head to the wooden slats. Then, still crouched and looking back at Haraldr like a frightened cur, he crawled to the boat, tumbled in, and paddled back toward the palace.

† † †

"I am . . . inspired, Uncle," said Michael, flourishing his gem-encrusted pallium. His dark eyes flashed beneath the blazing candelabra of the Chrysotriklinos. "I am not a fool. The employment of Hunrodarson is merely expedient. I have no more intention of making him Basileus than I do of placing a dead fish on our glorious throne. Do you think the Pantocrator would continue to sanction me if I were that foolish? No, Mar Hunrodarson will serve his purpose and then join his former accomplice, Haraldr Nordbrikt, in the Neorion." Michael's lips quivered and his teeth flashed momentarily. "I rather fancy that little girl he has abducted. She is so . . . pristine. I quite see her as my mistress. My virgin Magdalen. 'White Mary' is what her name means."

Constantine's forehead prickled and his stomach roiled. How had his nephew fooled him for so long? Or, perhaps, why had he for so long dismissed his nephew's obvious symptoms as mere impetuosity or youthful caprice? But he should have known, he should have been alarmed, he should have slowed things down. But Michael could be so brilliant, so able. Was it a family curse, or was it in the nature of the Imperial Office to drive men mad? Perhaps the man supplied the madness, but the office supplied the form of that madness. The endless enactment of the Pantocrator's life in the ritual at court, with each journey through the city a restaging of Christ's triumphal entry into Jerusalem, with each state banquet a repetition of the symbolism of the Last Supper; the implication, by the very breadth of the Imperial Throne, that the Pantocrator himself sat next to the Emperor. Little wonder that Michael had come to believe he knew the Pantocrator intimately; it was perhaps a tribute to Michael's qualities that he did not yet believe he *was* the Pantocrator. Perhaps it was

Christian Rome itself that suffered from the delusion, and Michael was only afflicted with the contagion of that hubris. Or perhaps it was true that Satan himself did dispense the keys to the kingdoms of the world.

"Majesty," said Constantine delicately, "I fear that the Pantocrator is . . . testing us with yet another travail in this enterprise of ours. I am informed that both the Tauro-Scythian Haraldr Nordbrikt and the woman Maria have escaped from their respective confinements."

Michael's eyes widened for a moment. He tilted his head slightly, listening. "My mistake was in choosing a Magdalen who was both sullied and unrepentant. That is why my White Mary has now been sent to me." His gaze was distant, as if he looked off toward the vast, shimmering golden domes of new Jerusalem. "My mother must be a virgin. I know that now."

"Nephew!" snapped Constantine in desperation. "If Haraldr Nordbrikt has escaped to lead the citizen rabble, the consequences could be grave. You, yourself, have said never to bet against a man who has won so many times that it seems he cannot possibly win again. Haraldr Nordbrikt has cheated destiny so often, I am most reluctant to wager against him now."

"Mar Hunrodarson is also a man favored by fortune. I rather think that the good fortunes of both brutes will quite cancel each other."

Constantine nodded, grateful that the Pantocrator's companion still enjoyed moments of lucidity. "Still, Nephew, even if the Tauro-Scythians neutralize each other, we are confronted with the unabated wrath of the rabble." Constantine steeled himself and offered the only counsel that a man of reason and ability could in a situation like this. "Majesty, I think we should call the Empress back from the convent at Principio. We merely need have her read a proclamation to the citizen rabble, and then maintain her under house arrest, as your predecessor did. I am certain she will be amenable. They say she was entirely undone with the prospect of leaving her city when she was taken aboard ship."

Michael paused and waved his hand airily. "Oh, that, Uncle. Yes, quite. I have already dispatched four of my fastest galleys of the *ousiai* class toward Principio, with extra complements of rowers and relays waiting for the return voyage. The Empress will be here shortly before cockcrow. And after the Tauro-Scythians have successfully eliminated each other in the morning's combat, I will produce her to quiet the rabble."

Constantine bowed. "Majesty," he whispered with relief, "I believe you are indeed inspired."

† † †

"So I will place my linen weavers and bakers and grocers here," said John, a thick-armed, short-haired leather cutter who had emerged as the leader of the guildsmen. He knelt and pointed at the rough map Halldor had sketched in the sand of the Hippodrome track.

Halldor forced himself to concentrate, as he had all evening. He was certain now that Haraldr was dead, and his implacable shell was beginning to crack. But he had to hold himself together until tomorrow. Until the day of vengeance. He prodded the indicated place in the sand with the point of his sword. "Yes. Tell them that the diversionary attack at the Chalke Gate is of crucial importance. And if they can force the gate, all the better. Our success here depends on the vigor of their assault there." Halldor turned to the Blue Star's son, who leaned over the scrawls in the sand and studied them so intently that it seemed his jutting beard would erase the plan. "Nicetas," said Halldor, "your . . . associates will be the first to strike. Just before dawn, at the Bucoleon gates. That is the last quarter from which they expect an attack. You will probably achieve initial success and then meet strong resistance. Remember that holding your ground is just as important to us as an advance." Halldor looked at the Blue Star, who stood with her arms folded and a keen, steely look in her eyes, as if she heard the echoes of her earlier triumphs on this track. "Your attack is the most important, Madame. Especially since we know that Mar Hunrodarson's Varangians are coming against us tomorrow. I am certain that they will defend the Imperial Box. It is imperative that the Imperial Taghmata is not permitted to come down into the stadium and encircle my Varangians while we assault the Imperial Box."

"Tomorrow the high and mighty will reap the whirlwind of the Studion," said the Blue Star. "There are accounts to be settled."

Halldor dismissed his curious assortment of officers and looked up to the Imperial Box. "Mar will have the advantage of high ground and numbers," he told Ulfr. "When Odin sends me a Valkyrja, I hope she is tight and wicked."

"The web of man is now being woven," said Ulfr somberly. "The Valkyrja will cross it with their blood-red weft." He looked at the stars, only faintly visible throught the pall from the fires and torches. "We have an account to settle as well. I hope Odin will spare me long enough for that."

"Yes," said Halldor, his voice breaking for the first time in Ulfr's memory. "We will never see our comrade again in the middle realm. But tomorrow we will see him in the Valhol. If there is joy in this, it is that I will drain Odin's mead trenches with Haraldr tomorrow." Halldor's voice firmed again. "And bring him a thousand souls as a gesture of my love and respect."

Ulfr manfully grimaced to stop his tears and pointed down the track where a contingent of guildsmen were practicing their spear assault. "We will bring many souls with us. Your idea of forming units according to profession was a good one. These guildsmen are already becoming an adequate army. And what the folk of the Studion lack in tactics they will make up for in ferocity and courage."

"And I have never seen Varangians so thirsty for the eagle's brew. It is as if every man has Odin's Rage." Halldor nodded to the groups of Varangians, many already in full armor—they would sleep tonight with their helmets as pillows—as they worked over their blades or assembled siege ladders. Halldor turned and observed a Varangian in a ridiculously undersize rough wool tunic stagger through the ranks of the drilling guildsmen. "All eager except this sot," said Halldor with mild derision. "He must have found the only inn open in the city. Tomorrow he will think that someone is pounding his helm with a broadax before he even sees Mar's men." Halldor squinted into the flickering light provided by hundreds of torches. "Who is that? Erlend?"

Ulfr lurched forward as if drawn by a stunning vision. He stopped after a few steps and an incoherent sound came from his throat. Then he dashed toward the stumblebum Varangian and almost knocked him down with a frantic embrace. He sobbed like a woman. The drunken Varangian pulled Ulfr to his feet and virtually carried him over to Halldor.

Halldor grinned broadly in spite of his effort not to. "Haraldr," he said, his impassive voice betrayed by the tears in his eyes, "I thought that was you. You look like something a gull has dropped. No wonder the black-bitch Valkyrja sent you back to us."

he quiet seemed supernatural, a thick, soundless ether that lay over the great city, disturbed only by an occasional haunting animal sound, a distant cockcrow, or dog's bark quickly muted by the gray predawn haze. It was as if the human inhabitants of the city obeyed a single collective fear, that in speaking or moving they would set in motion the terrible day that lay ahead.

In the Imperial Gynaeceum, Michael, Emperor, Autocrator, and Basileus of Rome, clutched the hands of the Empress Zoe, a communion as silent as the city. He could not confront her haggard, black-rimmed eyes and shorn hair, and so his bare head slumped in apology. The darkness of Zoe's bedchamber hid his tear-coursed face. Finally Zoe separated her fingers from his. She reached out and stroked his dark curls. "I forgive you, my little boy," she whispered. And with those words the huge engines of destiny began the new day.

† † †

Mar Hunrodarson stood on the catwalk atop the roof of the Imperial Box, a living titan among the immortal statues that ringed the highest level of the Hippodrome. Mar's Varangians were a dull gray shield wall surrounding the Imperial Box. Archers and javelin throwers of the Imperial Taghmata, also a wall of faint pewter in their steel breastplates and helmets, had crept over the highest tiers on the north side of the Imperial Box and waited for the slaughter that would fill the scores of rows of empty seats below. On the track directly beneath them, the ragtag army of the Studion had assembled; they wore almost uniform brown tunics and were armed with wicker shields and an assortment of clubs, tools, spears, and knives. The women among them could be identified by the coarse linen veils that concealed their hair. Haraldr's Varangians stood in full armored formation in front of the stadium's central *spina;* wooden siege ladders threaded their ranks.

Haraldr knew that the question between himself and Mar would be settled before this day was ended, and yet the imminence of death did not

673

concern him. Where was Maria? Had she and Symeon been caught, and was she even now undergoing the tortures she had spared him? That excruciating doubt made him consider the certain death of reentering the palace alone, and yet what if she was safe now, only unable to come to him? How would his death then reward her courage? Destiny commanded the day, he realized. Whoever would leave the middle realm before this day was over, the fates had already condemned.

The clearly audible chorus of shouts from the vicinity of the Bucoleon ripped the batting of silence off the vast stadium. A chant rose from the ranks of the Studion army. "Michael, Michael, upside down! We'll hang you from a column and crown your ass!" High above, Mar's Varangians answered with the chilling pounding of axes on shields. Haraldr strode through the ranks of his men and stepped up onto the stadium seats to face them. "Varangians! What you hear is the breast-beating of the men who cowered in their own slime while our comrades died in the fight against the Bulgars. For our comrades who now wassail in the Valhol, let us bring them those"—he thrust his hand upward toward the Imperial Box—"to bow before their courage tonight!" The Varangians erupted into shouts of "Haraldr, Haraldr!" and began a drumbeat on their own shields.

An arrow clattered on the stone at Haraldr's feet. He turned and defied the archers, waiting for the signal that the diversion at the Chalke Gate had begun. Another arrow clattered. Haraldr watched the backdrop of brightening sky behind the archers at the top of the stadium. A moment later the dragon-shaped red kite wriggled up into the lightly pinked sky. Even before Haraldr turned to give the command to his own forces, he could see that archers of the Imperial Taghmata were being taken off the stadium wall to counter what seemed to be the much more imminent threat of the well-armed guildsmen at the Chalke Gate. Haraldr signaled the Blue Star to begin her assault. Then he pointed his sword upward. "Vengeance!"

Ducked beneath his shield, his men grunting at his back, Haraldr quickly climbed the tiers of seats; the ends of the siege ladders jutted out ahead of him. "Set the ladders!" he shouted as he neared the top of the stadium. Javelins thudded against shields and sparked against the stone benches; Mar's men hurled down obscenities along with their spears. Haraldr looked at the red, bawling faces on the balcony above and marked the men who would precede him to the Valhol.

The five heavy wooden ladders rose almost in unison and then tilted toward the marble balustrade of the Imperial Box. As soon as the ends of the ladders made contact, Haraldr's men leapt on the lower rungs, their weight resisting attempts to throw the ladders off. The boldest began the climb. Mar's men waited, swords poised, red-rimmed eyes glaring, teeth bared; some of them beckoned with bearish, pawing motions. They had every reason to expect a slaughter; Haraldr's men advanced in curious echelons, each climbing file led by a man with a spear followed by an archer—both virtually useless in the close combat in which they would engage at the top. The spears prodded forward and Mar's men swiped at them playfully; one of them actually captured a shaft, jerked it violently, and sent the man who had wielded it plunging to the steps. Almost as if by that signal, Haraldr's archers rose and fired. Mar's men had been too distracted by their game to guard their faces with their shields. Virtually every shot struck home, and the entire rank at the balustrade toppled or flailed wildly at the feathered shafts sprouting from jaws and eyes.

The momentary advantage was quickly seized. Haraldr and his men spilled over the marble balustrade and hammered back the surprisingly thin second line of defense. As he clambered over the corpses Haraldr wondered with profound apprehension why Mar had posted so few men at the most critical point of defense. He pushed Mar's token resistance back toward the terrace behind the Imperial seating pavilion. He wheeled to his right, looked down the long, narrow terrace, and saw what Mar had held in reserve. Mar's men barred the narrow platform, five men wide, almost a hundred men deep, a plug of seemingly solid steel. The infrangible steel seal to the Imperial Palace.

For a moment the two Varangian forces hesitated and the metal music stilled. Haraldr looked into the fierce blue eyes of Mar's men and for a moment wished he could offer them something less bitter than the ferric draft of blood and steel. But the Bulgar war had settled that. He studied the man with a thin blond mustache opposite him; he had seen him in the palace but did not know his name. With a lightning-quick motion he raised his sword and brought it down; the man's clavicle collapsed, his mouth contorted, and he pitched to his knees.

Time ended. The sun rose and iced steel byrnnies and helms and blades, but no man could register the length of its silvery ascent. The fighting was unrelenting in its brutality, a confrontation of seasoned warriors who had determined to abandon all the artifices of their trade and exchange blows of pure, desperate hate. There were no battle cries, no false courage, only the endless, harsh choral of steel on steel, and the regular, sickening thuds of swords and axes into flesh. The only thing that separated their motions from the deft, mechanistic slaughter of a butcher was their voiceless rage.

At first Haraldr, Halldor, Ulfr, and Hord Stefnirson took the snout of a slender boar, exchanging places at the front every few moments, a relay passing on the terrible hammer of Thor. Gradually they expanded their front to the entire width of the terrace. Haraldr's arms still ached from his ordeal in Neorion, and he noticed that Halldor and Hord—fired by vengeance for his brother, Joli—were his champions now, pushing forward where even he could not go. And over the course of what might have been an hour, what for many was eternity, Halldor and Hord prevailed; it seemed as if Mar was now losing four men for every one of Haraldr's.

Soon the resistance perceptibly sagged, and the bloody stalemate quickened to a steady shuffling advance. Haraldr glanced off to his left and could see the ringed silver domes of the Chrysotriklinos glitter in the morning sun, and he realized that if he could live another few hours, he could settle with the man enthroned beneath those domes. But first he had to settle with the man who waited ahead. And the gods were telling him that even they feared that moment.

Mar's men fell back suddenly and the din of conflict abruptly subsided. A voice barked from behind the bloodied, disastrously thinned ranks of Mar's Varangians. "Haraldr Sigurdarson! We must deal!"

Halldor simply charged forward to finish the fight, and Haraldr had to pull him back. "I am Haraldr Sigurdarson," said Haraldr. Halldor's jaw slackened and he stared in shock. The Varangian ranks on both sides became absolutely silent. The vague shouting from the fighting in the stadium only added to the sense that they all stood in an eerie, soundless vortex. Haraldr walked forward to confront Mar Hunrodarson.

"There is no reason for our men to continue to settle the quarrel between us, Prince of Norway." Mar's byrnnie glistened with fresh, unmarred lacquer. His eyes were like diamonds and his nostrils flared. "You knew this time would come," he said with a sneer. "I have always despised you. You are weak and stupid."

Haraldr now understood Mar's strategy. He had sacrificed his best men, and his honor, to exhaust Haraldr and save himself for their reckoning.

Halldor shouldered past Haraldr and pounded Mar in the chest with his flat hand. "I will settle with you, Hunrodarson! I am not afraid of your vaunted arm! Coward!"

Mar simply grinned at the provocation. "It seems that your Prince Haraldr is the coward."

"He has been poisoned and bound and beaten in Neorion!" shouted Halldor, so that everyone would hear. "And he has fought this morning, slime crawler! There is no shame in my appearing as his champion!" Halldor shoved Mar again. "I do not need Odin's favor to meet you, Hunrodarson."

Mar shook his head and laughed. "He will want to fight me when he learns that I fucked his woman." Haraldr's head snapped and the blood drained from his face. "You don't believe me?" said Mar. "Let me describe the bite I took from her soft breast. She begged me, little Prince. Ask her how she begged me." Mar pointed to Haraldr and snorted derisively. "He wants to make his woman Queen of Norway. But she is just my whore."

Haraldr refused to lower his eyes. If he could see Maria again, he would forgive her a thousand men. But he could not forgive himself if he yielded to Mar's challenge. Were he only Haraldr Nordbrikt, yes. But Haraldr Sigurdarson, King of Norway, could not turn away from this any more than Olaf could have walked away from Stiklestad. And for the first time in all his years of dreaming and yearning, he knew what it was to be a king: always to be in front; always to be the first to accept the consequence of decision, especially when he blundered, even when the men who served him blundered. A king had to be the one man in the world who could say to his people: "I hold myself accountable, for my honor and for yours. Always. Not merely when it is easy to do so."

"You are a small man, Mar," said Haraldr softly. "The weapons I choose are one sword, one shield, no replacements."

Halldor turned to Haraldr. "No! We don't need to do this. You have already won. Let us begin again until we have slaughtered them to a man."

Haraldr shook his head. "I must do this. I fear running again more than any death. I owe the men who have been brave enough to follow Haraldr Nordbrikt at least this much." Ulfr stepped forward and nodded at Halldor. Halldor would not yield. Haraldr seized Halldor's shoulders and looked between him and Ulfr. "The last time you seconded me I fought for the right to lead five hundred men. Today I must fight for the right to lead Norway."

Halldor finally stepped away, his eyes wet. Then he turned and addressed all the Varangians with a flat, implacable statement. "The tale that Haraldr Sigurdarson was a coward is a lie."

Mar unsheathed his magnificent engraved blade and examined it in the sun. Then he slammed his sword against his shield and Haraldr turned to meet him. Haraldr knew he would be able to make but one savage assault with all his remaining strength. He closed with no preliminaries and pounded Mar's shield to kindling amid a gale of cheers. Mar countered deftly, and moments later Haraldr tossed aside the useless, rattling frame of his own shield. The energy-sapping, screeching quarrel of blade on blade quickly drained his exhausted shoulders, and yet Mar still could not overpower him. Haraldr had expected no reprieve from Odin, but he thanked the one-eyed god for today withholding his favor from the craven Mar.

Haraldr allowed Mar to drive him in a continuous, circling retreat; he hoped to tire him. Finally Haraldr broke and turned and leapt to the ell-wide wooden catwalk that ran along the ridge of the peaked roof of the Imperial seating pavilion. He walked steadily backward, to the very end of the precarious walkway. The tiled roof sloped away to the stone seats fifty ells below. Mar looked down and hesitated. Then he advanced carefully. Haraldr swayed and looked over his shoulder at the drop. He was certain he was losing his balance and he deliberately lunged forward so that he would not topple backward to his death. His chest slapped to the catwalk and he clutched for his life. He realized he had lost both his nerve and his sword.

Haraldr's sword distantly rang against the steps. Mar walked steadily forward, to the accompaniment of a gentle, evil laugh. He came close enough to sever the neck so neatly presented on this lofty scaffold. "Norway," said Mar, "this is a fitting end to you. Nose to the ground." He lifted his sword. "Odin spits on you, little coward. . . ."

Haraldr's arm swiped out and caught Mar's boot, and Mar's blade whirred past his face. Mar lifted a leg and milled his arms in a desperate effort to adjust his balance. He pitched sideways and Haraldr was able to raise himself to a crouch. He had time to nod knowingly to the astonished blue eyes before Mar fell on his back, onto the tiles, and began sliding to the cornice of the roof. Now Mar's sword chinged against the stone below. His legs were already over the cornice before he was able to turn onto his stomach. His momentum continued to pull him down. His icy eyes glimmered as his head disappeared. His huge hands clutched for the cornice. His hands did not disappear. Mar clung to the lip of the cornice like a strange human banner, arms outstretched, his entire body suspended in the void.

Haraldr knelt on the catwalk and waited. He glanced to the north and saw that the Blue Star's army had captured the highest tiers of the stadium; the seats beneath held an audience of corpses. Down on the track the guildsmen, in neat ranks, spear shafts held high, began entering to reinforce the push into the palace. They shouted their improvised oaths for a while and then grew silent as they turned their attention to the curious drama high above them. Haraldr could hear his own steady exhalations. Eventually every head in the stadium was directed to the roof of the Imperial seating pavilion. And still Mar's hands did not move from the cornice.

The sound was like no human sound: the last dragon, its black entrails ripped out so that the corpses it had devoured could bellow their dying rage. Mar's hands flexed and his knuckles surged. Haraldr watched as the head, no longer Mar's but the wolf's, the dragon's, his complexion as dark as a dead man's blood, rose slowly above the cornice. Mar's mighty arms propelled his entire torso above the roofline. He swung his leg over the cornice. The demon had climbed back from the abyss, and the favor of Odin was on his face.

Haraldr was beyond terror. Mar's eyes had turned red, as if washed in blood. Haraldr was drawn to them with dreadful fascination, lured as he had been by Abelas. Mar was a destiny that could not be killed.

"Jump!" growled Mar in the spitting voice of the beast. "Jump before I tear out your throat with my teeth. Jump." Mar crawled slowly up the perilous tiled incline, as if now even gravity was subject to his Rage. He was almost able to reach out and grab the catwalk when he began to slip back again.

"No! No!" bellowed Halldor. He watched in horror as Haraldr extended his hand to Mar. Fighting broke out as Mar's men blocked Halldor and Ulfr from reaching the catwalk.

Mar's grip was like a thunderbolt, and Haraldr knew that Odin had sent Mar back to settle the question he could not live, or die, without answering. He pulled Mar up to the catwalk. They both rose from their crouch. Mar stood an ell away and his breath was as foul as the slime of a carrion eater. His entire face twitched, as if hundreds of strings had been attached to his skin by some demonic puppet master. His trembling hands reached for Haraldr's neck.

At the coldest, infinite core of his being, Haraldr acknowledged the bargain he had long ago made with fate. He lunged for Mar, clutched his arms around his byrnnied girth, and lifted him off his feet. Mar's hands clamped Haraldr's throat and his windpipe collapsed, and he knew that he would not breathe again in the middle realm until he and Mar had settled what lay between them deep in the spirit world.

For an immeasurable heartbeat there was a profound stillness as the

two Berserks' flesh met on a plane where flesh did not exist. Haraldr was
in the darkness entirely; he could not even see the black flame blasting
him to numbness. He only knew that he at last held the dragon in his
arms, could feel the huge, scaled beast throttling the last surge of life
from his desperate, pumping neck. *Embrace that death,* the voice whispered.

The Varangians watched in awe as the two giant Berserks danced
death, their faces purple, their eyes blooded with Odin's insane favor.
Mar's head arched back with the mad force of his grip, and Haraldr's
knees sagged. And then a crack, a hideous, muffled, mortal crack, the
sound of will and bone breaking in concert. Mar's face instantly blanched
and his hands fell from Haraldr's neck. His head lolled and he went limp.
His back had been snapped like a twig.

Haraldr felt the dragon burst into pure light. He held that light for a
moment, as if embracing a dead comrade, and then flung Mar out into
the void. He watched the body fall away like some fading vision in a
dream. Mar hit the stone seats far below with a wet, melon-splitting
sound.

Haraldr walked off the catwalk. The faces of Halldor and Ulfr were as
chalky and wondering as Mar's dying visage. "Who is in command now?"
shouted Haraldr to Mar's men. Gris Knutson came forward, his eyes
frightened, vacant. Haraldr jerked Knutson up by the collar of his byrnnie; Knutson's feet barely grazed the pavement, and his legs fluttered like
a hanged man's. "This is over," growled Haraldr, his voice still from the
spirit world. "Disarm your survivors and take them north on the next tide.
And tell the Northlands that the King of Norway is coming home, and that
he will sate the ravens with his vengeance."

Haraldr parted the silent, reverent ranks of his Varangians and descended the siege ladders to the stadium. Mar's body lay on the steps
beneath the Imperial Box. His fingers twitched and blood gushed from
his mouth and pooled behind his head. His eyes were almost ice-white,
a uniform color to the delicate pale blue of his skin. He still lived. Haraldr
bent and whispered, "You did not die a coward. In the Valhol tonight,
tell the Kings of Norway the name of the champion who sent you as a
sacrifice to them." Haraldr touched Mar's forehead gently, almost as if
consoling a child. "It was you who had my pledge-man Asbjorn Ingvarson
killed, wasn't it?"

Mar's gory head tilted slightly forward. "Yes."

Haraldr took his hand away. "Then we have settled between us."

The blood gurgled in Mar's throat, almost as if he were laughing. His

words were whispered through pale red froth. "I left . . . you . . . a legacy
. . . King . . . Haraldr." His purpled lips moved without speaking, and his
feet twitched. Haraldr stood, descended to the track, and left Mar Hunrodarson to die alone, his last words, if any, heard only by ears of immortal
stone.

ather!" The Augusta Theodora rushed forward and kissed the Patriarch Alexius's jeweled hands. "Father." She stood speechless, blood visibly pumping into her pale cheeks, unable to ask all of the desperate questions that had been running through her mind.

Alexius made the sign of the cross at her forehead and then, uncharacteristically, gently stroked her braided brown hair. He had never looked more defeated. In his rough woolen cloak, his face virtually the color of penitential ashes, his pacing eyes now exhausted, wounded gravely, he looked like the survivor of a shipwreck. "My child," he said quietly, "we may never see another day like this."

"Father, I was not even certain you were still . . . that you were safe. After what we heard yesterday . . ."

Alexius stared at the beige plaster walls of Theodora's temporary refuge in the Church of St. Mary Chalkoprateia. "The Mother Church has withstood the assault of the mad heretic Michael. The siege of the Hagia Sophia was lifted a half hour ago when the forces that had imprisoned me were called away to counter a greater threat." Alexius shook his head wearily. "I confess that the effluence of love and support for your sister has been a revelation to me. She has raised all Rome against the demon."

Theodora wrapped her arms tightly around her torso, as if she were on the verge of doubling over with pain. "Father, is she . . ."

Alexius smiled as thinly as a dying man mocking himself. "Your sister is safe. I have been told that the mad heretic brought her back to the palace this morning. No doubt to save his own skin from the wrath of her people."

Theodora seemed to breathe in the news of her sister's deliverance; her torso straightened and her small, pained face became fierce and punitive. "Father, you must know now that I cannot do it. I have suffered the agonies of the damned just knowing that my sister might be . . . Father, last night . . . Father, I do not know if my sister still loves me. But nothing in my heart can make me betray her now. If Our Lord had wanted me to make that sacrifice, He would not have put so much love for her in the hearts of her people. Or in my heart."

Alexius was too weak to resist. His black eyes lay still. "Of course, my child. I am returning you to your home immediately. I, too, believe Our Lord has asked us to consider another means of defending our spiritual empire." Alexius paused and touched his fine silver beard, as if to ascertain that he still possessed corporeal form. "Mar Hunrodarson betrayed us. That does not surprise me. I had reasoned that in such an event we could still deal with him. But he turned against his fellow Varangians. Now I am told that he has been defeated in a great battle that took place in the Hippodrome this morning. He broke his sword, and ours, in the defense of a usurper who never could have been legitimized. I can only assume that Hunrodarson believed that he could place his own *barbaroi* feet in the Imperial buskins. I knew that the Emperor was mad. I had no idea that Hunrodarson shared his affliction." Alexius again stroked Theodora's hair. "My secular sword no longer exists. And your sister's sword, the love of her people, is a vastly more formidable blade than I had ever imagined. You have made your sacrifice for myself and for Our Lord, my child. Now you may return to the mansion your Lord intended for you."

Theodora nodded. "If I may, Father, I would like to stay here until all this is resolved. My sister . . ."

Again the weak, moribund smile. "Certainly, child—" Alexius broke off but did not turn to the insistent pounding on the door. Finally Theodora crossed the room and cracked open the heavy wooden door.

The priest burst into the room, his wool hood flung back, glimmering slices of his white silk vestments visible under his dull brown cloak. His face was brilliant with exertion. "Father, this could not wait." He handed Alexius a small parchment.

Alexius received the missive with indifference. His long, elegant fingers fumbled with the parchment. His eyes were so dull as he read that it seemed he was only staring at some design. And then, almost miraculously, he returned to life; but not even Lazarus had returned so quickly or vehemently. His face, a moment earlier as gray and coarse as weathered stone, became flesh again. His eyes flickered, awakening rested, eager. He clutched the parchment in a powerful fist. "Perhaps our Lord has merely divined to test our faith."

"Father . . ." Theodora was clearly frightened by the Patriarch's resurrection.

The eyes offered no mercy. "My child, the situation has changed. You must now prepare yourself for your climb to Golgotha."

Theodora flinched but did not retreat. "Father, I will not. The crown of thorns I must wear is my love for my sister. And I will never remove that crown, no matter how painful it has become." Theodora's lips set grimly and her eyes were like bits of lapis lazuli. "Father, I will not do it. I will *not* do it." She squared her broad shoulders as if preparing for a physical confrontation. "Do you think you can chain me and drag me screaming to the ambo and place the Imperial Diadem upon my writhing head?"

Alexius was stunned into silent acquiesence. Perhaps his ordeal had left him irreparably weakened; perhaps he had always known that his protégé would someday challenge his strength. He looked away from Theodora and walked slowly to the simple oaken cupboard. A pair of gold-framed icons had been set on the top shelf. Both depicted the Virgin; one was an intricate cloissoné, a surface of vivid colors and fine gold striations, the other a faded encaustic, many centuries old. Alexius looked between the two images for a long while, his palms pressed together and fingers touching the tip of his powerful humped nose. Finally he turned.

"My child, would you be agreeable to sharing your sister's Holy burden? If you will not, I fear that both your sister and the Roman Empire will soon be lost."

"What has happened, Father?"

"I am not yet certain. That is why I must know what you are prepared for me to offer in your name."

"Yes. I will share the throne with her. If it is necessary to save her and to save Rome."

Alexius made the sign of the cross three times and without another word strode urgently from the room.

† † †

The future of Rome had been drawn in the sands of the Hippodrome. Haraldr stood over the hastily sketched campaign map; at his side were the co-commanders of the citizen army of Rome, John the leather cutter and the Blue Star. John had a bloody gash over his forehead, but his eyes blazed with triumph; his guildsmen had taken the Chalke Gate, with the help of some Khazar defectors. John pointed to the small square that indicated the Numera, where Michael's Pecheneg guard was quartered. "I have left my bakers and grocers to harass the Pechenegs. When should I give them the signal for the afternoon attack?"

Haraldr looked around the stadium. Ulfr and Halldor and the rest of his Varangians now stood where Mar's men had that morning, on the commanding vantage of the Imperial Box, ready for the final massive assault on the Imperial Palace. The Blue Star had removed her wounded from the stadium steps and the ranks of the guildsmen and the army of the Studion had reassembled on the track; they were already going over the chants they would sing when they had the usurper Michael before them in chains. He realized that there was no reason to wait. And in an awful way he wanted to wait, because he knew in his soul that when he entered the palace, he would find the answer to the question that now pierced his being. And if fate had answered him with Maria's death, her life for his? Then fate would have killed them both.

"Haraldr!" Ulfr's voice boomed down from the Imperial Box. He waved. Behind Ulfr were the luminous white robes of the palace chamberlains. The eunuchs rapidly filled the Imperial Box and stood at attention as they might on a race day. The army on the track below looked up and erupted with speculation. Had the Emperor Michael come to capitulate?

A few moments later the solitary black-shrouded figure appeared against the wall of white-robed eunuchs in the Imperial Box. Her head was veiled in a black nun's hood, her eyes black holes, her face aged decades in days. Only the voice proved that this ancient woman was Zoe the purple-born, Empress and Augusta of the Romans.

"My children!" proclaimed Zoe. Her words brought an absolute silence to the huge throng beneath her. "I am well. I have not been harmed. My son, your Emperor and Father, and I have quarreled between us, as a mother and her son are wont to do. He has taken actions in his anger that he has now repented of. I am satisfied of his sincere contrition. He has promised that he will respect the dignity of your purple-born Mother as long as he wears the Imperial Diadem. He has sworn to do penance to the people of the city with distributions of food, entertainments, remission of certain taxes, and a lifting of the Prefect's profit ceiling for the guilds. I have taken your father Michael to my bosom and forgiven him. Now I beseech my children to show him their forgiveness, for love of me." Zoe stepped back and made the sign of the cross over her people.

The first reaction was applause from some of the guildsmen, particularly the small merchants who would most benefit from the lifting of the profit ceiling. Someone in the Studion ranks shouted, "That is not our Mother. She is an impostor!"

"That is no impostor," said the Blue Star, her eyes stricken. "She has been coerced. There are knives at her back."

"A more dangerous coercion, I fear," said Haraldr. "A coercion of the heart."

"I think she wants to avoid further bloodshed," said John. "If she is willing to guarantee these reforms, we have no further quarrel with the Emperor. He was good to us before all this, and now that he has brought our mother back . . ." John shrugged.

"You would abandon her to them while you go back to your salted fish and Vlach cheese!" snapped the Blue Star. She whipped her powerful arm and pointed at the terrible litter on the seats behind her; at least a thousand lay dead. "We did not die here so that the tyrant could imprison our Mother in his palace and appease the guildsmen with more races in the Hippodrome where so many have now died!"

"You have not seen the dead at the Chalke Gate, woman!" John's swarthy face darkened. "If this bloodshed is no longer necessary, it must end. If your cutthroats desire more blood, let them prey on their own cutpurses and whores!"

The two factions slowly gathered around their leaders and began their own chorus to this argument. "We were not whores when we slew men!" shouted a woman standing behind the Blue Star. "Rabble!" cursed the guildsmen. "Sluts and thieves!"

Haraldr watched the two sides converge from the ends of the track; it was as if they were two roiling cloud masses about to collide as a thunderous storm. "Ulfr! Halldor!" he shouted to the Stadium roof. "Bring the men down!" He turned to mediate but could not make himself heard. The factions shrieked at one another and scuffling broke out. Haraldr broke up one fight only to have another, and then another, flare up around him. He prayed his men could get down here before the first death. A combined assault on the palace was impossible now, but a civil war in the city was not unlikely. Fists cracked into faces. Haraldr saw bright blood again, and it sickened him more than all the day's carnage. He fought desperately to keep men apart. A guildsman fell, howling, clutching his stomach.

And then the shrieks of conflict subsided slowly, and men and women paused, still clutching their adversaries' cloaks. The fallen guildsman moaned. Haraldr looked over the heads of the crowd, toward the bronze starting gates at the north end of the stadium. The army of the Studion was parting, to allow the army of yet another Roman Empire pass among it. Mounted on his donkey in emulation of Christ, flanked by scores of his priests in white-and-gold vestments, himself a jeweled icon in the billowing robes of his office, the Patriarch Alexius rode among his flock.

The donkey blinked, his gentle gaze a pointed contrast to the equally dark and feral but far more deadly eyes of his master. Alexius was assisted from the saddle by his deacons. He studied Haraldr, John, and the Blue Star silently for a moment. He spoke first to Haraldr. "Is it true that Mar Hunrodarson is dead?" Haraldr nodded. Alexius turned away and faced his flock. "Your Mother has borne the cares of her people for many years now!" His voice thundered and echoed through the stadium. "Now she is weary of her travails; she is too exhausted to revoke the sanction she has granted to her treacherous son." The ranks of the Studion murmured assent. "And yet she is not the only purple-born daughter who can offer"—Alexius paused meaningfully and his voice roared—"or revoke that sanction! The purple-born Augusta Theodora, daughter of the Autocrator Constantine and niece of the Autocrator Basil, called the Bulgar-Slayer, also carries the blood of Macedon in her veins. She is willing to sacrifice the life she cherishes, that of contemplation, to share with her sister the burden of caring for her children! Would you deny yourselves a love this generous?"

The folk of Studion erupted into spontaneous acclaim. "Theodora! Theodora! Purple-born Mother!" John and his guildsman lieutenants considered the matter at greater length. Their informal caucus reflected on the succession of men Zoe had brought to the throne of Imperial Rome; they decided that a prosperity hostage to Zoe's whims was a false security. Theodora would stabilize the throne. John brought his arms up and began to lead the guildsmen in a chant. "Theodora! Theodora!"

Haraldr shouted to the Patriarch. "Father, what of Michael?"

Alexius looked at Haraldr with his glaring panther eyes, then pulled Haraldr's shoulders down so that he could speak in his ear. "By the sanction of the purple-born Zoe, my hand placed the Imperial Diadem on his head. Under command of the purple-born Theodora, that Diadem will now be plucked from his skull!"

Haraldr nodded and listened to the chants. For the tyrant Michael it was finished. And yet for him it had only begun. Where was Maria?

† † †

"That porcine sot." Michael crumpled the message and glared at his Uncle. "This is gratitude!" His voice was high-pitched and whiny. "I have provided these luxury-loving monks with *typica* so generous that they are all but a license to plunder, and not one of them will come to my assistance during a period of transient difficulty. I tell you, Uncle, when my throne is again secure, there shall be a wholesale redrafting of these *typica*. And I can assure you that many of these fatted monks will be as lean as desert goats when I am through with them." Michael fanned away a silk-robed chamberlain with an impatient hand. "Reject the offer. We will remain here and weather this outburst."

Constantine mopped his brow with a delicate linen handkerchief. "Majesty, I do not think it wise for us to remain in the palace. Mar Hunrodarson is dead, Haraldr Nordbrikt is even now negotiating the surrender of the Scholae and Excubitores of the Imperial Taghmata, and the Augusta Theodora is already in the Hagia Sophia."

Michael stared sourly at his purple boots. "That dried-up old thing. Uncle, you cannot think she will depose me. Zoe will have her out of the palace before the day is over. There is no love between those sisters."

"The Patriarch Alexius seems bent on preserving his client's privileges this time."

Michael leered over at his uncle. "The Patriarch Alexius is a Satanic apostate, you know that, don't you? The Pantocrator will never receive him. He is adamantly opposed to it." The Emperor straightened. "I still have the the loyalty of the Numeri and Hyknatoi units of the Imperial Taghmata. I will have them throw the unclean Alexius out of our Holy Mansion. He quite disgraces it. And the bitch with him!"

"Majesty . . ." Constantine paused and accepted the dispatch from a chamberlain. He read it quickly, his face drawing taut with shock. "Nephew," he finally whispered, "the Varangian Haraldr Nordbrikt has received the surrender of all units of the Imperial Taghmata."

Michael shot up from his throne and kicked away the gilded stool at his feet. "Nordbrikt! Nordbrikt! It was his whore who tempted me to begin with! Nordbrikt!" Michael stood, glaring; his chest surged wildly. "Tell my Pechenegs to destroy Haraldr Nordbrikt!" he screamed with neck-cording rage.

"Nephew," said Constantine, "Haraldr Nordbrikt also requested the surrender of your Pecheneg guard. When they refused, his Varangians slaughtered them to the last man." Constantine walked forward and clasped Michael's arms. "We must accept the offer of sanctuary."

Michael was suddenly calm, again introspective, hearing other voices. "Yes. Quite. We must save our lives and await the collapse of this absurd coalition against us. Whom did you say had the charity to receive us?"

"The blessed Brothers of the Holy Studite Monastery, Majesty."

† † †

The lowering sun bored through the windows high above and projected great tunnels of light directly across the vast, darkening interior of the Hagia Sophia. The subdeacons and doorkeepers moved about on the arcades and soaring ambulatories, beginning the lengthy ritual of lighting the bronze and silver candelabra, lamps, and polycandelons. The Augusta Theodora, clad in the purple robes of state, was seated on a throne beneath the semidome at the west end of the nave; the bejeweled diadem of the Imperial Augusta seemed like a piece of ornate architecture perched atop her small head. The improvised court that knelt one by one in obeisance before her was unlike any Rome had seen before. The dignitaries were present in their robes of state and emblems of rank, but the new Empress was also attended by the people of the city—guild members, merchants, the humble poor of the Studion. And women had been admitted to the floor of the great church, as only befit an Empire that was now ruled by two sisters.

Haraldr was one of the first presented to the new Empress, as Alexius had wisely proscribed formal protocol during this acutely delicate time of transition. After the ritual prostrations he knelt at Theodora's feet and was offered her hand to kiss. "I know of you," she told him in a flat, faintly wry voice. Unlike her sister, who had a face for pure pleasure set off by pain-ravaged eyes, Theodora had melancholy features countered with flashing, almost girlish eyes. "You want to take my Maria away from me." Haraldr was weary, hungry, and he hoped that his plunging spirit did not register on his face. Where was Maria? All day he had sent runners out to comb the palace, and each had returned with the same report: No one had seen her, even heard of her whereabouts. And even if she was safe somewhere, would he now need this Empress's permission to take her to Norway?

Theodora laughed. "I will let her go," she said, but Haraldr was not certain if she was sincere or merely placating him to another end. Theodora became serious again, and Haraldr identified the fear communicated by her small, pinched mouth. "This seat is not the most comfortable," she told him. "It is broad enough but not stable. One expects to fall off at any moment." Haraldr nodded. "I need a man to steady it for me. A strong and loyal man. I know you have the first-mentioned quality. Maria says you are also the second." She looked at him gently. "I am not asking you to stay by me for long. My sister will marry again. Soon, I hope, to a man who can govern justly. And then I will return to a more modest yet more secure perch."

Haraldr was taken by her directness and apparent guilelessness, though who could tell with these Romans? "Majesty," he said, "I am more than willing to discuss a temporary service to your person and office. But my strength is twined with another, as you know. And I do not even know her fate now. Can you help me?"

Theodora's wincing eyes convinced Haraldr that his concern was shared. "I am looking for her as well. But I am also looking for my sister. I believe there may be the same solution to both riddles. Those two know places in this palace that have been forgotten for centuries." Theodora looked about uneasily at the representatives of her unlikely coalition. "I think Maria is trying to mediate for me. I pray she is, because the success of this enterprise is still in grave doubt."

Haraldr bowed, overcome with mere hope. But the idea of Maria having gone to Zoe, if Michael still held Zoe under his sway, was chilling as well. Fate had made this day too long. He looked up at his new Mother. "Majesty, I will serve you until such time as you feel this enterprise is no longer in doubt."

Haraldr withdrew and was immediately accosted by a member of Alexius's staff. "The Father wishes to see you," said the priest, an aggressive-looking young man who might have been a military officer except for his red-and-white vestments. He led Haraldr to the second-story gallery and then across the sumptuously carpeted walkway to the Patriarchal offices. In spite of his oppressive melancholy, Haraldr could not help but marvel at the richness of the arcades beneath which even ordinary officials worked—and today they seemed to be working extraordinarily feverishly. The walls sparkled with jeweled, gilded, and enameled icons. Writing tables were surfaced in ivory veneer. Mosaics covered the spandrels of the arches.

After passing through a series of antechambers and sitting rooms as splendid as any in the Emperor's apartments, Haraldr was admitted to the most elegant dining chamber in New Rome. The vaulted room was octagonal, with a gold dome three stories above the floor. The walls were carved with elaborate arched niches filled with white marble reliefs representing various saints. Alexius sat alone at the end of a table covered with a red-and-gold cloth. He had removed his towering diadem but wore his usual encrustation of jewels and gold thread.

The Patriarch gestured for Haraldr to sit in a gilded, backless chair opposite his own. "I know you like fish," he said. Haraldr had no idea how Alexius presumed to know this. "May I offer you some?" Haraldr was famished and he nodded, though Alexius made him sufficiently uneasy to curb his appetite under ordinary circumstances. Almost immediately a servant set a silver plate embossed with a large Chi-Rho, the monogram of the Christ. A second servant served the fish from a large golden platter, and yet a third ladled the garos sauce from a silver pitcher. Haraldr had to restrain himself from shoving the entire fish into his mouth and swallowing it like a bear.

"You are a Christian?" asked Alexius. Haraldr nodded. "And what is your church like in this Norway?"

Haraldr's accelerating pulse registered the warning. He needed to sharpen his wits for this exchange. "It is a Christian church, Father."

"But its bishops hew to the authority of the see of Old Rome and practice the Latin creed, do they not?"

"Father, you must understand that the Christian faith is only a few decades old in my country, and that I left home when I was too young to know that the Christian faith had several factions."

Alexius's wiry eyebrows lowered. "There are no factions, my son. There is only the church, the One True Oecumenical, Orthodox, and Catholic Faith. And the schismatics who would deny the divinity of the Christ." Alexius took a bite of fish and chewed it carefully, then patted his elegant lips with his embroidered napkin. "An interesting rumor has emerged from the tumult of this day. It is said that you are in fact the King of this land of Norway."

Haraldr dropped his fork in his plate. "Father . . . I have pledged my loyalty to the Augusta, as I have to all who have worn the Imperial Diadem, at least all who have proved themselves worthy of that office."

Alexius raised his hand. "My son, I do not accuse you of treason. You could have taken Rome this morning had you that ambition. Yes, there is always a great deal of concern about an invasion from the north, and there are the prophecies as well. I am sure you are quite weary of hearing them. Those are not my concerns. I am only troubled by fair-haired Christians who might embrace the Latin creed and be led to eternal perdition by the pontiff of Old Rome."

Alexius ruminated on another bite of fish before continuing. "I would like to propose this to you. The truth of your lineage is certain to become common knowledge, indeed has already circulated fairly widely. I will pledge to you that I will make certain that no consequence of any sort arises from these revelations. You in turn must promise to me that when you return to rule your Norway, you will permit my priests to bring the One True Faith among your people."

Haraldr fought his numbness, trying to tell himself that fate had offered another boon. For the mere price of passage for a few priests, he now had an immensely powerful ally who actually had an interest in seeing to his prompt return to Norway. But was this another mocking mask that destiny wore? What would he return to without Maria? "Father," he forced himself to reply, "I do not see how my people could but benefit from this instruction."

"Excellent," said the Patriarch. He pushed his plate away and a servant immediately removed it. "We have girded ourselves for the eternal struggle. Now let us consider a conflict of a more immediate and temporal nature." Apprehension churned Haraldr's hasty meal. He realized that this man, like fate, made no easy bargains. "Our position is currently very tenuous. Our factions are held together by the hope that the purple-born sisters will rule jointly. Unfortunately Zoe has not appeared before her people with an endorsement of her sister. I fear that she may even have fled with Michael and will attempt to rally her people to his cause."

"I have the same fear, Father."

"I now know where the tyrant has fled, although I do not as yet know if Zoe is with him or whether she has assisted his escape. The Emperor and his uncle are petitioning the monks of the Holy Studite Monastery to accept them into their keeping. I need not tell you that our Emperor's sudden piety will last only until he can arrive at some new scheme for seducing Zoe to his purpose."

Haraldr saw the awful dimensions of this bargain taking shape. He remembered his strange covenant with Michael on the ambo at the Hagia Sophia. He forced himself to challenge Alexius's pacing eyes. "So. If the tyrant is to be killed, better that the deed be done by a man who has the support of the people, yet represents no particular faction. A Varangian."

Alexius did not humor Haraldr with a smile. "I want you to perform an execution. Not of death, however. We are a Christian nation. Blinding should be sufficient to render Michael's . . . vision harmless."

"Yes," said Haraldr, "I should like him to enjoy the fate he intended for me. But have you considered that I might also have reason to kill him?"

"The matter of your . . . betrothed? I think he has been too busy with other worries to have harmed her."

"And if he has?"

"As I say, it would be better for our Christian nation not to be tainted with the blood of the Pantocrator's Vice Regent on Earth. And of course the boy's death might unduly prejudice Zoe against our cause, though the Empress has displayed a remarkable capacity to embrace life again after the deaths of her previous lovers." Alexius paused and then uncaged his menacing black eyes. "Let me offer you this, King Haraldr, if I may call you that. It is not unknown for the sentence of blinding to wound a man so severely that he dies shortly afterward, sometimes within the very hour. But in that case the sentence of death would have been pronounced and executed by the Heavenly Tribunal, and not by this corrupt flesh here below."

† † †

The first shadows of twilight painted the Mese a melancholy purple tint. Clouds in neat, cobbled formations crept across the sky from the north. Cold gusts stinging with dust ripped along the filthy side streets and swirled to meet the horsemen head on as they turned southeast toward the Golden Gate. Haraldr had taken only Halldor and Ulfr on this ugly journey. Whether one believed that kings were descended from gods or were simply endowed on earth with the sanction of God, the killing of a king was a challenge to the gods.

The horsemen passed four men and a woman running south; their coarse tunics were whipped by the wind. The citizens cheered the Varangians as they galloped past. "Michael! Michael! Upside down . . ." they shouted, their words fading behind the flying horses.

"At least you offer him mercy!" Halldor shouted into the wind. "The citizens want to chain him upside down to a column and take him apart piece by piece!"

"Let us hope they have not already!" shouted Haraldr. "We confront the gods in this. Let us not profane them as well!" The avenue quarter-turned to the east, and the three Varangians rode between aging but clean tenements. People stood on the balconies and cheered as they passed; it was almost as if they were waiting for the Emperor in procession. And perhaps they were.

The groups on the street increased in size as the Varangians approached the Sigma, a marginal district on the borders of the festering Studion. Well-kept tenements rose next to gutted wooden shells. Some of the shuttered shops and inns had signs with bright new paint, while other arcades gaped dark and empty and drew packs of dogs. Vegetable gardens grew in the cleared lots. The rushing crowds had new verses to their ditty, recounting their successful assault of the palace. One group still carried their spears and hollered, "Haraldr! Haraldr! Emperor slayer . . ."

Near the west end of the Sigma, the Mese ran directly through a broad, poorly kept park. Noxious grit howling up from the Studion filled the air with a dull, sandy haze and obscured the spring verdancy of the vast lawn. Haraldr called for Halldor and Ulfr to slow; he lowered his head to blink away the scouring grit. When he had cleared his eyes, he squinted obliquely into the wind. An enormous crowd was spilling into the park from the west end. The vanguard of this throng, their individual features blurred by the haze, danced in rough circles and chanted raucous ditties.

The crowd surged forward and soon surrounded the three Varangians. They cheered the Norsemen furiously and sang a fractured verse about Haraldr sending the hated Mar off as a messenger pigeon to his Emperor, but that this bird had failed to take wing. The prostitutes who had fought in the morning had painted their faces again and came forward and kissed the Varangians' legs and offered them a lifetime of gratis pleasures. The cutpurses and petty thieves had exchanged their spears for wine bags and sang and hopped about with flushed faces and wine-stained teeth and chins. A chorus of preening thugs battled forward for an impromptu performance. "Michael stuck it in Zoe, he stuck it in us, now we'll stick it in his mouth!" they shouted with appropriately obscene gestures. Haraldr wished the Blue Star was not back at the Hagia Sophia. Her people had become a mob now, as intoxicated with their power as Michael had been with his.

Haraldr pushed on toward the vortex of the celebration. He was relieved to find that the center of this storm was relatively calm; more responsible men, wearing the threadbare but clean linen tunics of the laborers who worked honestly to rise above the squalor of the Studion, moved along with controlled malice in their eyes. They paused when they saw Haraldr, as if awaiting his authority in whatever matter they were about, and stood respectfully away from his horse. A young man in an official silk robe got through and anxiously confronted the Varangians. Haraldr recognized him: Michael Psellus, a young Hellenistic scholar and Imperial secretary who had not had a hand in Michael's crimes. "Sir," called up Psellus, "the mob has driven them from the Holy Studite Monastery! They mean to rip their very limbs apart!" Psellus, unlike such presumptuous Hellenes as Senator Scylitzes, was a man of true learning, but panic had clearly overcome his usually carefully considered Attic eloquence.

The Varangians dismounted. "Where is the Emperor, Psellus?" asked Haraldr. The laborers stepped aside as Psellus preceded the Varangians into their midst. Masses of men, women, and children continued to flood into the park, and already the crowd was so enormous that the distant outer perimeter was masked in choking ocher dust.

Haraldr was rendered dumb by the apparitions at the very epicenter of the whirlwind. He recognized Constantine, though the Nobilissimus had exchanged his purple robes for the sackcloth of a monk. Constantine looked defiantly at Haraldr, his care-hollowed countenance so much like his brother Joannes's that Haraldr was momentarily startled into thinking that some monstrous transmutation had taken place.

There was nothing left of the Emperor, Autocrator, and Basileus of the Romans. The boy who stood next to Constantine was beardless, his dark curls shorn like a novitiate's. Michael's head bowed, his shoulders trembled, and he whimpered like a wounded dog. His entire body seemed drawn in, as if fear had eaten away his internal organs.

"They have petitioned to take the vows," said Psellus. "Can you appeal to the crowd to spare them and allow them to return to their sanctuary?"

Haraldr looked at the young scholar and realized that for all his classical erudition, there were things that Psellus could learn from even the sotted derelicts of the Studion. "And how long would Michael and Constantine wait to discard these monastic robes and take up their former purple when this danger has passed?"

Psellus collected himself and nodded. "Of course. It is simply that to see the power of our glorious Empire degraded in this way moves me to compassion. And such spectacles can only inflame a lust for rebellion among the people. What are your orders?" Haraldr showed Psellus the order, signed by Theodora, commanding him to blind both Michael and Constantine. "I think that sentence will assuage their lust," said Psellus. "I also think you had better show that order to them." Psellus gestured to the crowding laborers.

Haraldr nodded, his estimate of Psellus's wisdom rapidly rising. He passed the order among the laborers. As the purple-tinted document circulated, they began to voice agreement. "Yes, that is just. Theodora is right in this."

Michael's head lifted. "I will carry my cross." Haraldr looked into the eyes he had been sent to destroy. "He suffered these scourges as well. He wants me to carry my cross as he did. What? What?" Michael's words were barely distinguishable above the clamor of the mob.

He is completely mad, thought Haraldr. Will he even remember Maria? "Majesty," said Haraldr evenly, afraid that a stern tone might precipitate a hysteria from which no answers would be forthcoming, "where is Maria?"

Michael stared into the void only he occupied. "With my Marys." He cocked his head. "They don't like her. Even the Magdalen repented. No, I have rather decided that White Mary will be my mother."

Haraldr was chilled almost beyond hope. The nature of the sentence Theodora had pronounced sizzled through the crowd like liquid fire. Evidently few in the outer circles approved of the new Empress's leniency. "Michael, Michael, upside down!" came the thundering chants. "Death to the tyrant!" "Skin him!" "Crown his ass!"

Michael clutched Haraldr with clawlike hands. "Nordbrikt! What can the bitches offer you that I cannot?" His eyes were suddenly brilliant and aware. "Together we will conquer the earth from the Pillars of Heracles to the Gates of Dionysus. They will call you the Macedonian, after Alexander. You will have a hundred tributary kingdoms and a thousand Marys. You have proven yourself worthy. I have tested you, Nordbrikt, and you alone are the man who can bring these victories to Rome. Rule with me, Nordbrikt. You the Autocrator, I the Caesar. My Father in Heaven sanctions it."

Haraldr clutched Michael's shoulders, and the Emperor recoiled with pain and fear. "Where is Maria?"

Michael collapsed to his knees. "Oh, Father!" he wailed. "Oh, Father!" He pounded the earth. "Father, you have forsaken me. Oh, Holy Spirit, smite my foes!" Michael tore at the sparse clumps of grass and tossed handfuls of dust and chaff in the air. "My Father, why have you forsaken me!" He wailed hysterically, his shorn boy's face livid with distress, his eyes luminous with tears that left dusty tracks on his face. He sobbed and then shrieked, "I cannot forgive them and neither could you! Don't lie to me! Don't lie to me! You always lied, didn't you? You are Satan. You are Satan! You tricked me!"

The crowd surged inward and the vortex compressed. Constantine was pushed into Haraldr. "Oh, Lord, have mercy on us sinners," Constantine sobbed. The crowd hurled oaths wildly. "Skin them!" "Cut their throats!" "Death to the tyrant! Death! Death!" Haraldr remembered Maria's description of her dream in every chilling detail. She had the gift, and yet fate did not always obey her. "Death to the tyrant!" shouted the mob again and again. The sun had set and there was a final coppery tint in the thickening, swirling dust.

"You must act!" shouted Psellus. "In a moment the mob will have its way. That lust must never be consummated or all Rome will perish in its heat." Halldor held up the sharpened spikes and looked grimly at Haraldr. "Psellus is right. You must act now if you wish to spare them."

Constantine clutched Haraldr's arm, his grip firm and his face now resolute. "You!" he commanded Haraldr. "Please order these people to stand back. I will show you how a man of ability bears his calamity!" Haraldr pushed the laborers away and cleared a space for Constantine to lie down. Constantine sat on the scoured, dusty turf. Haraldr signaled to Halldor and Ulfr to lay him down flat and hold his arms and legs securely; if he moved about, he might be wounded even more severely. Constantine looked up at Haraldr, his eyes spitting their final rage. "Look, you! If you see me so much as budge, then you may *nail* me down!" Haraldr motioned Halldor and Ulfr away, and Constantine reclined with trembling determination. Haraldr begged the forgiveness of the gods as he straddled him, kneeling. Constantine convulsed, then became still. He made no appeal for mercy. The Emperor beside him bellowed incoherently like a sacrificial calf, pounded his fists together, and then began to strike himself in the face.

Haraldr worked quickly. He pressed the right eyeball to one side of the socket, jabbed it firmly with the sharpened spike, and the sight flowed out in a glutinous serum. He took the left eye and stood up. Constantine rose with him and Psellus helped hold the blind man up. "I do not fear the darkness," said Constantine to that darkness.

"Please spare me, Nordbrikt! Satan lied to me! He said he was the Pantocrator! I let them live! He wanted me to kill them but I let them live!" Michael spat as he screamed. "Satan has fouled me! The true Pantocrator will have to cleanse me!" Michael threw his arms around Haraldr's knees and clung to him, trembling with spastic fury. "Father! The Pantocrator must cleanse me. I must live to be cleansed. My mothers must cleanse me. Mother, oh Mother, oh Mother, oh Holy Father! Let me live so that I may be cleansed."

Michael's pleas only inflamed the surging lust of the crowd, and Haraldr forced him to the ground in the tiny space cleared by Halldor and Ulfr. He pressed heavily on Michael's chest, compressing his lungs so that he could no longer cry out. Michael's legs and arms continued to twitch madly. Haraldr lowered his face to the already unseeing eyes. "I will let you live," he said, "if you will tell me where Maria is."

Reason flew over Michael's face like the shadow of a passing bird. "Oh, Holy Father, let me live," he said raspily. "I do not need my sight to repent in the pure light of Your Being." He blinked again, and his dark eyes saw for the last time. "I did not harm her. She is with Zoe." Michael strained forward and focused on Haraldr. "This was arranged for us, was it not? In the Mother Church that day."

Haraldr nodded. "Yes. I, too, felt . . . it."

Michael's head fell back and he awaited fate. "Someday a king will show you mercy," he whispered. Haraldr brought the spike down twice, swiftly but carefully, to destroy the raven's reflection in the dying sight of Michael Kalaphates.

Haraldr helped Michael to his feet and Constantine reached out for his nephew. The former rulers of Rome were guided to each other's arms and they embraced in a darkness they alone could share. The noise of the crowd receded outward from the vortex, fading like the denouement of some vast orchestration. The wind was audible again, a harsh, scouring sound, as it buried the twilight in a shroud of dust. Silently the great crush of people fell away, recoiling more with fear than satiation from the evidence of destiny's implacable hand; they retreated through the shadowed borders of the park and left Michael and Constantine to the soughing empty night. Yet no sooner had the crowd vanished than a new chant began a haunting ascent from the surrounding city, rising to confront the swirling wind. "Theodora! Theodora!"

† † †

"Children! Children!" pleaded Alexius. "The weight of all of you will collapse your Mother Church! As many of your brothers and sisters as this sacred roof can shelter have been admitted! Let them be your eyes! And the purple-born daughters of the Pantocrator will appear to you soon to bless you for your forbearance!"

The crowd let loose a thunderous acclamation and halted its menacing surge against the west facade of the Hagia Sophia. Haraldr looked out from beneath the arches of the narthex; he stood just behind the Patriarch. The area encompassing the porch, portico, and garden in front of the church was a black-and-gold tapestry of flaming tapers; the gradually diminishing pinpoints of light filled the Augustaion and ascended the Mese toward the Forum of Constantine. The entire city had come to welcome its Mothers.

Alexius turned to Haraldr and asked him to precede him through the mob that had squeezed into the narthex. The faces that blocked the way were a cross section of the great city: dirty-haired laborers; a puffy-faced, silk-garbed merchant; scented bureaucrats; even a beggar crawling with lice. These heads lowered deferentially and the bodies tried to move respectfully back, but the crowd was so dense that they could scarcely move, and Haraldr had to bull through with the Patriarch tucked in behind him.

The immense circular candelabra floated with galactic splendor beneath the light-wreathed dome. Glowing stringcourses of candles and oil lamps ran along every cornice and ledge. The floor was a solid mass of people, and the towering second-level arcades were filled with entire populations. The carved balustrades of the narrow walkways above the arcades seemed on the verge of giving way beneath the weight of the people squeezed behind them; the slender stone ledges in front of the railings were perches for hundreds who clung precariously to the intricate grills. The people had even found their way to the catwalk that encircled the base of the hemispherical central dome, and hung in even more perilous positions more than a dozen stories above the heads of their fellow citizens. It was only a matter of time before someone plunged into the crowd.

Theodora, flanked by her chamberlains, stood on the silver roof of the ambo, directly beneath the central dome. She was attired in the same purple-and-gold robes and ponderous diadem she had worn throughout the afternoon. Haraldr pushed through the crowd and after an arduous journey delivered Alexius to the marble staircase of the ambo. Alexius motioned for Haraldr to come up the steps behind him.

Theodora's lips puckered with fatigue and fear. She looked gratefully at Alexius and then Haraldr as they stepped onto the roof beside her. Alexius stood next to her and motioned to Haraldr to stand directly behind the Empress, so close that he could have embraced her. The glittering pearl-and-diamond lappets that coursed over Theodora's ears trembled slightly, reflecting the agitation of their wearer.

"I must acclaim you," said Alexius. "They are growing impatient."

"No," said Theodora," her voice slightly tremulous. "Wait another half hour. I know she will come."

Alexius looked out at the sea of expectant faces. "I will delay for a half hour," he said. "Then I must, and pray that our Holy Father's sanction can overcome your sister's enmity." He stepped back from Theodora and pulled Haraldr aside. "You have been through the city and dealt with the factions. What is your assessment?"

"The poor folk will accept Theodora alone. The guild and trade factions expect to acclaim both Empresses," said Haraldr grimly. "If they are not both presented here tonight, the factions will turn on one another. The guildsmen are already rumbling their threats." Haraldr pointed to the Varangians who ringed the base of the ambo. "I am certain my men can escort the Empress safely to your apartments, but we will have to stain our swords with the blood of this morning's comrades and profane the floors of this holy place. And by tomorrow morning there will be a full-scale civil war in the streets of the city. Even my men and the Taghmata will not be able to quell the violence. Rome will be destroyed."

Alexius blanched slightly, but his eyes did not flinch from Haraldr's forecast. "Yes"—he nodded gravely—"you are quite astute. You will be an able king." His eyes slowly swept the huge church. "I will wait as long as I can. Then I must acclaim her. Better that we please half of these than no one at all."

The half hour passed beneath the blazing lights. "Where is Zoe?" shouted a guildsman near the ambo. The cry was taken up briefly. "Zoe! Zoe!" The poor folk countered with "Theodora! Theodora! Give us our Empress!" A fight broke out just beneath the ambo, and Halldor's shoulders cleaved the crowd as he waded in to separate the combatants. At the back of the church another scuffle erupted and began to spread. Soon there was a twenty-person brawl just in front of the narthex. The shouting became general, and many of the people on the catwalks and arcades leaned over and shook their fists.

"We are losing the moment God has given us," said Alexius. He stepped forward. "Children of God!" the Patriarch's voice rang through the domes. He made the sign of the cross and the crowd quieted. "Where is Zoe!" shouted someone defiantly. The shoving near the narthex resumed.

A roar came from within the narthex. Haraldr realized that the violence was probably much more ferocious outside the church; now the mob outside was forcing its way in. He sickened at the thought of killing these people. The pressure of the crowd outside surged against those inside, and they began to fall to the marble floor in successive waves. Haraldr shouted to Halldor to ready a boar to carry Theodora to safety. The roaring from outside continued. "Forget the acclamation! We only have time to save her!" shouted Haraldr to Alexius. Haraldr took Theodora's bony elbow and urged her toward the steps.

"No!" Theodora shook her arm loose and stood stiffly, her head erect. "They will have to carry me from this place." Haraldr looked desperately at Alexius. The cost of the Empress's safety was rising with every oath the crowd uttered. Alexius shook his head helplessly.

Haraldr turned toward the narthex. The crowd had quieted, and those who had fallen remained prone without struggling to rise. The Imperial Diadem and purple-and-gold robes glittered beneath the massive pediment of the church's main door. The Empress and Augusta Zoe stepped through the prostrate forms of her subjects with the grace of a dancer. Behind Zoe walked the Mistress of the Robes in a celestial white-and-gold scaramangium. Maria's blue eyes were visible even across half the vast nave. Her pearl-wreathed head never dipped to observe her feet despite the awkward path. She always looked directly at the ambo. Theodora's slender shoulders heaved once, and she gasped with relief and joy. Alexius made the sign of the cross and his terrible eyes enjoyed an instant of triumph before they focused on the unseen foe he was now girded to meet.

Zoe ascended the stairs of the ambo in a silence so absolute that Haraldr could hear the click of her pearled hem against the marble steps. Her face was heavily masked with paint and powder, but her reddened, shrouded eyes betrayed both the terror of the last few days and the emotion of the moment. Her gaze swept quickly past her sister and Alexius as she mounted the ambo and turned to her people. Maria looked steadily at Haraldr as she came to the top of the steps, and there was as much passion in her glistening eyes and faintly twitching lips as he had ever known when he had held her naked in his arms. Then she turned, bowed to Theodora and the Patriarch, and stood between the two sisters.

Zoe looked down on her still-prostrate subjects. "Augusta Theodora," she said without looking at her sister, "I offer you the equal share of my office and my throne."

"Not equal, Augusta Zoe," said Theodora, her face brilliant with emotion. "You have precedence. I acknowledge that. And you are free to marry if you wish, and place an Emperor above us both. I owe you that much."

Zoe's breast surged and she blinked rapidly. Her sensual lips trembled, naked with emotion. "I have missed you," she whispered.

Theodora turned to Zoe with abrupt, artless sincerity; for a moment it seemed her precarious crown would topple. Tears moistened her dry, red cheeks. "Sister," she whispered. Zoe turned. "Sister," she said, her eyes welling. They confronted each other for a moment, and then stepped forward and embraced.

Maria came to Haraldr's side. The last time he had seen her she had been disguised as a hideous crone; now he had never seen her more beautiful, her eyes more supernaturally radiant. She grazed his sleeve with her finger; he thought his knees would buckle with the intoxication of that mere contact. "I love you," she whispered as the sisters continued to exchange caresses and their own intimacies. "I could not send word to you. Symeon and I hid all night. We were able to get Zoe away from Michael and have spent the rest of the day persuading her. We knew that everything depended on it."

"It did," whispered Haraldr. "It seems that today you and I, with considerable help, have given Rome a new fate."

"Yes. I wonder if that is the destiny we have so often felt in each other's arms."

"Perhaps. The only destiny I am concerned with now is the one that places you in my arms tonight."

Tears beaded Maria's fine dark lashes, and she touched Haraldr's sleeve again.

"Rise up, Rome!" Alexius's voice resounded through the domes and the crowd seemed to stand as one. "Rise up and welcome the Light of the World! Rise up and welcome the purple-born Majesties the Empress and Augusta Zoe and the Empress and Augusta Theodora!"

"Long life to Zoe and Theodora!" thundered the crowd over and over, an acclamation of such pounding resonance that Haraldr actually looked up to make certain that the groaning walls still supported the immense domes. Alexius made the sign of the cross and held his hands over the heads of the Empresses to symbolize that they had both received the crown from the Hands of the Pantocrator. The chants continued for some time. After a while Theodora beckoned Maria, embraced her, and bid her stay at her side. The three women looked from one to the other, their faces jubilant.

Haraldr studied the three faces with his own joy. There seemed to be a magic about them; not just the beauty of two of the women, or the spectacle of the Imperial raiment, but something much more familiar: the charmed way their pearllike teeth flashed as they smiled and whispered close to each other's ears, the sense that something more profound than even fate had brought them together. He remembered how Maria had said that Zoe and Theodora were both her mothers. That thought prompted a strange shift in his vision, almost as if he had removed a distorting glass from his eyes; suddenly he could see something he had not noticed before because he had never thought to notice it. He had long since forgotten how much alike Maria and Zoe had appeared to him the first time he had seen them together, and yet now with Zoe's very different sister present, he was struck by the subtle similarities between all three of them, a certain line to the mouth, the structure of the bones around the eyes. They were as much alike as a daughter and . . . Haraldr felt a cold finger trace up his back and he realized that destiny had not yet finished its game with him. Maria's parents, he was now certain, had not merely been friends of Zoe and Theodora. One of them, most likely Maria's mother, had shared the same purple blood.

X

uck!" Halldor gestured to the Imperial Chamberlain. "The Varangians are eating the duck," he explained to the desperate-looking eunuch. He pointed to the other end of the long table. "The Senators are dining on pork." The harried chamberlain hissed a flurry of new directions to the servants. The suckling pig that the servants had tried to serve Halldor was hurriedly transported directly in front of the ever-regenerate Senator and Proconsular Patrician Romanus Scylitzes. Large grilled ducks were placed on silver platters in front of Halldor, Ulfr, and Hord Stefnirson. Halldor politely told the hovering eunuch that the Varangians would carve their own meat. The tablecloth fluttered in the strong, dry September wind; the weight of the Imperial Eagles embroidered in gold thread kept the fabric from being whipped away in the occasional gusts. The sun was brilliant and the sky as clear as blue porcelain.

"Where is Haraldr?" asked Ulfr, nodding to the empty place setting next to Halldor.

"He is working on another petition," said Halldor.

Ulfr rolled his eyes. "I hope this one works. In another month it will be too late to start out. We will have to wait until next spring. And by then we may be too fat to move."

Senator Scylitzes stood and began a celebration of the "demi-deified Achillean virtues" of the new Emperor Constantine Monomachus, whom Zoe had taken as her husband only two months after the deposition of Michael Kalaphates. (According to court gossip, Constantine Monomachus had been one of Zoe's lovers during her first marriage, to the Emperor Romanus.) The Monomach, as he was known, was virtually everything the Imperial Court valued in an Emperor; he was handsome, graceful in his movements, charming and adept in his speech, and an able military commander. But the august Imperial dignitaries had quickly discovered one particularly egregious flaw in their new Emperor. The Monomach prefered coarse companions: innkeepers, merchants, and professional loungers, many of whom he had promoted to Senatorial rank immediately after receiving the diadem and scepter of his office. And many of whom were now seated at the end of table, utterly ignoring Scylitzes's endless discourse as they played with their food, knives, and a wooden court ball that they casually lobbed across the table in curious concert to the rhythm of Scylitzes's sentences.

"Does that man ever shut up?" asked Hord in disbelief.

"Senator Scylitzes has received a suitable reward for his remarkable adaptability," said Halldor. "He succeeded in rescuing his fortune from the mob, in which he was more fortunate than many of his Dhynatoi comrades. But Scylitzes, who once would not have deigned to walk on the same side of the street as an honest merchant, must now acknowledge as his colleagues some of the foremost rascals of the lower Mese. Notice how they appreciate the Senator's attic eloquence."

A group of masons walked by, pallets of thin clay bricks loaded on their backs. "Does the Emperor usually go to these lengths to inspect a building project?" asked Hord.

Halldor laughed. The table at which they sat had been set up in a large open yard behind a fairly modest town house just northeast of the Forum of Constantine. The busy masons were laying a foundation for a considerable annex to the house, an expansion twice as big as the original structure. "For this particular building he does," said Halldor. "The Emperor is particularly interested in inspecting some equipment in the existing house."

Hord understood. "Who is she?"

"Her name is Sclerena. She is the niece of the Emperor's first wife. They have a touchingly intimate relationship."

Hord shook his head. "So he goes to all this trouble, telling us that he is inspecting this highly important construction project, and sets this table and serves us whatever we wish so we won't grumble while he plows his niece. And he has only been married for three months."

The chamberlain appeared at the head of the table and cleared his throat. "Sirs, Mistress Sclerena sends you a small token of her esteem for her Emperor's guardsmen and Senators." A dozen young women in diaphanous white tunics pranced into the yard and began a sensuous, whirling dance. "This Sclerena is apparently a very clumsy builder," said Halldor. "I am beginning to think that this construction here will require frequent inspection and supervision."

Hord and Ulfr laughed and joined the newly minted Senators in pounding a rhythm on the table. Some of the dancers had already begun to leap onto the table when Haraldr appeared and stood at his place setting. He was dressed in the robe of the Hetairarch, the office he had agreed to assume temporarily for Zoe's new husband. Beside Haraldr, resting on the tabletop at the level of his hip, was a pudgy, apparently disembodied head. The head made a few ridiculous faces and then sprang onto the table, propelled by the suddenly revealed, squat body of a dwarf. The dwarf sprinted the length of the table, pausing along the way to swat the rumps of two dancers. He halted dramatically in front of Scylitzes and made motions, as if drawing out his own tongue. He turned his rear end to the Senator and made loud farting sounds, then sped off, as if propelled by his feigned flatulence. He lay beneath the legs of one of the dancers and stuck his tongue out obscenely. Finally the dwarf leapt off the table and ran into Sclerena's house.

"Who was that?" asked a stunned Ulfr.

"That is Theodocranus the Dwarf," said Haraldr. "He was a famous buffoon in Adrianopolis and promises to succeed here as well."

Halldor looked down at the Senators, who were still in hysterics over the diminutive clown and were already emulating a few of his more vulgar gestures with the dancers. "I believe he already has," said Halldor wryly. "This Theodocranus the Dwarf is likely to be our next Senator. How do you know him? He doesn't seem like one of Maria's friends."

"He is my petitioner." Haraldr folded his arms and smiled smugly.

"What?" Ulfr groaned. "Now we will be forced to stay here, but in the Numera Prison instead of the Numera barracks."

"So you think," said Haraldr confidently. "I believe the Emperor will find Theodocranus a man of exceptional eloquence." This statement was greeted with incredulous head shaking, and Haraldr sat down to share his insight. "I have observed that the Emperor hates dealing with anyone who reveals any kind of serious intent. If a minister comes to him with a well-conceived plan to drive the Seljuks out of Taron theme, the Monomach will scowl and throw that minister out before he can finish the introduction to his discourse. But send a one-legged comic in there to stutter the latest banter from the marketplace, and the Monomach is all ears. I believe Theodocranus will get the Monomach's attention in a way that I never could."

Haraldr watched the dancers for a while, hoping that Theodocranus was having a successful interview. After a quarter hour of waiting, the Imperial Chamberlain approached. "Hetairarch, His Majesty would like to see you."

Haraldr was escorted into the modest hall of the house, then to a dressing chamber where the Monomach stood in his purple scaramangium and smoothed his luxuriant silver hair. Theodocranus stood on a chair placed directly in front of the Emperor and held up a bronze mirror for his sovereign. He had just begun a ribald jest about the Emperor's notorious sexual appetite. "The Emperor visited the Imperial stables," prattled Theodocranus in his warbling voice. "He saw that one of his prize stallions couldn't hump the mare he had been penned to stud. The Emperor asked the stallion what was wrong and the stallion said, 'I am afraid of losing it in there.' The Emperor pulled his out to show the stallion and said, 'I've put this in many a mare of my own, and look, it is still here.' The stallion's eyes grew wide when he saw how the Pantocrator had endowed the Monomach, and he said to the Emperor, 'Well, if mine was that big, I certainly wouldn't be worried about losing it, either!'" Theodocranus clapped his stubby hands and Haraldr winced. The Monomach clutched his stomach in a paroxysm of mirth, finally tumbling to the floor in comic rapture.

Haraldr waited until His Majesty had recovered his breath; however, the Emperor seemed in no hurry to get to his feet again. Finally Haraldr said, "Majesty, has Theodocranus mentioned to you the matter—"

The Monomach held up a powerful, squarish hand. "Yes, yes, Hetairarch, my dear little friend here has presented the matter with a delicacy and subtlety you would do well to emulate. And therefore I have agreed to consider the matter." Haraldr waited while the Emperor wiped the tears from his eyes; His Majesty remained on his haunches. "Oh, well, quite," said the Monomach, suddenly remembering what he had just said. "I am amenable to the matter if your Mother Zoe is. You know how devoted I am to her happiness. Yes, I fear you are becoming too sober-minded here, Hetairarch. Perhaps you do need a winter in Thule to help you appreciate the delights of the Imperial Court." The Emperor held out his arms to Theodocranus, who bounded into the Imperial embrace like a small, cuddly child. The Monomach covered the dwarf's squat face with friendly kisses. "Now, my little friend!" The Emperor chortled with renewed enthusiasm. "Tell what I did when a dozen naked whores awakened me in the middle of the night!"

† † †

Maria's hand felt like a dry, warm cloud in his. She led him up the gently rolling slope toward the back porch of her villa. Along the narrow path, grapevines grew in neat, perpendicular rows, and she paused and stooped to examine a cluster of dark, heavy grapes polished like agates by the bright late-afternoon sun. Maria plucked one and popped it in her mouth. "I will drink from this vine again," she said. "I know I will." She clutched Haraldr and gave him a kiss, wet and sweet with the juice of the grape. "When we visit from Norway."

Haraldr held her and stroked her thick, silky black braids. He had not even brought her Argyrus's uncharacteristic offer of a good price for her villa; he knew that she would need this place as a symbol and a hope when she was so far from home. "We have not been given leave yet," he told her. "We may yet drink this harvest. This winter."

She tilted her chin up against his chest. Her eyes were more perfectly azure than the sky. "I am not melancholy about leaving," she said defensively. "You do not need to lift my spirits with such doubts. Zoe has already given her permission once. And I am ready to sail. I would like to give you a child before I am an old woman."

Haraldr kissed her forehead and shared that vision. They held each other tightly and rocked in the breeze. After a while Maria turned her chin up again. "I can hear your troubles pounding away in your chest, King Haraldr. Are you thinking about the lifetime of cares I will bring you?"

"I am worrying about beginning that lifetime. I am . . ." He squinted into the sun. "I am worried about the length of that lifetime."

Maria pulled loose and took his hand again and led him to the steps on the sunny southern porch, which afforded them a panorama of the glitter-sprinkled cities to the southwest and the vineyards and cypress groves to the east. She sat beside him and looped her arm in his. "Tell me what concerns you," she said. "Leave nothing out."

Haraldr watched a *dhromon* slide past on the Bosporus, banks of oars dipping leisurely, the red-and-black hull and deadly golden spouts vivid. His sigh was his preface. "Zoe is not the same Zoe. So much has happened to her."

"I know things are different with her. And I have not been able to . . . I don't know. I have forgiven you for sleeping with her, which is the least I can offer, since you have forgiven me . . . Mar. But I cannot . . . I knew she was opposed to you, and I thought I understood. But for her to then take you to her bed, when she knew that I still loved you. And she knew that you still loved me. I cannot forgive . . . I know it is wrong, and I know I will one day understand. But it is hard for me now." Maria found his hand and twined her fingers in his. "It is of no consequence. You will obtain her leave, and if you do not, I will. I persuaded her to embrace her sister, and they are still as thick as thieves, particularly now that the insatiable Monomach has found a new amusement. I can certainly persuade her to release me." Maria kissed Haraldr's temple. "So I am confident that we will soon begin our lifetime. Why do you worry that our time together we will brief?" She asked the question matter-of-factly, almost gaily.

Haraldr hung his head and looked at his boots. "I have made the east-journey. I grant you that our return will not be as dangerous as our coming, since the Pecheneg horde will not expect us, and our ships will be light and few enough that we can more easily avoid the cataracts. But it is still an enormously dangerous journey."

Maria jabbed Haraldr in the ribs. "I am worried about encountering your little love, the Princess Elisevett, when we arrive safely in Kiev. She is probably not so little anymore. She might try to poison me. And you might be smitten by her again."

"That was a boy's love."

"Well, her's was not a girl's trick. You still don't believe that she was really a virgin? When I was fifteen, I could play the false virgin very well myself."

"I don't think she was playing."

"I can see you are still smitten with her. So that is what I am worried about. What else?"

The grin fled from Haraldr's face. The sun seemed strangely cold, as if the white fire had turned to ice. "My enemies in Norway are very powerful. I have to overcome them before our lifetime can begin."

"Look what you have overcome here in Rome," said Maria with high-pitched incredulity. "You are a legend here. Here? Throughout the world. These men will flee when they hear your name. And don't tell me that these foes won't be daunted, simply because they are Norsemen. Mar and his men were Norsemen, the most feared in the world." Maria threw her hands up in exasperation.

"That is here. Norway is where I lost . . . I lost my strength. I am afraid I will lose it again. Even Olaf could not defeat these men."

Maria nodded slowly, knowingly. "Olaf," she said softly. She paused for a moment, considering her words. "Haraldr, have you ever considered that perhaps you might be a greater man than Olaf? That perhaps Olaf, however brave and heroic he was, might have had neither your wits nor your strength. That perhaps Olaf blundered at Stiklestad and lost everything, and that you had no part in it except to be a brave boy trying to be a man. You did not lose that battle or your throne. Your brother Olaf did!"

"Perhaps that is what troubles me. That I will be a greater king than

Olaf, and yet someday will also blunder more gravely, and cost many people everything. Perhaps cost your sons their lives."

"At least you admit that we will probably survive long enough to have sons."

Haraldr smiled ruefully. "I have never told you this. That night at Zoe's, when Abelas performed, he called me a 'merchant of destiny.' I feel the power of my fate to command the collective fate, and it has begun to frighten me."

"I felt your fate the first time I looked into your eyes. Do you remember? At Nicephorus Argyrus's palace. That look we exchanged at the table. It chilled me and excited me at once. That was when I decided I had to make love to you." For a moment Maria sounded like the old Maria, wild and spooky. "I thought you would bring me a new, all-engulfing darkness, a more excruciating prison in which I could conceal my soul. Instead your destiny brought me to the light. Your star is a bright and joyful one. That is what your destiny brings."

Haraldr stood up, still unsatisfied, unable to resist her persuasion while he sat next to her. He could not face her eyes. "What if I were killed trying to reclaim my throne? You would be alone, in a strange and distant place. I cannot bear to think of it."

"I would marry Halldor!" Maria laughed out loud.

Haraldr turned, a look of relief on his face. "I would want you to," he said eagerly. "I am serious. To think of you alone . . . I would come back from the dead to prevent that."

"If I were to die at the hands of your Pechenegs or to be flung into the Dnieper, who would you marry? Elisevett?"

Haraldr's face immediately furrowed with pain. "I would marry no one! I would mourn you for the rest of my life. I would wither and die. I would suffer every time I looked at a woman."

"So I would be condemned to an eternity of looking down from Paradise and knowing the unhappiness in your breast?" Maria's lips twitched with amusement.

Haraldr shook his head, as if that terrible fate were virtually imminent. "How could I ever replace you?" he asked plaintively. "It would profane your memory. I would never let someone else displace you from my soul."

Maria shot to her feet, her eyes on fire. She grabbed Haraldr's arm and turned him to face her. "Do you think anyone could ever remove you from my soul?" she shouted angrily. "Even after a lifetime? Even after a thousand men had had me?" She shook her fist at him. "How can you imply that one woman could take me from your breast? I will always be inside you. Even if I never touch you again, I will touch everyone you touch for the rest of your life."

Tears ran down Haraldr's cheeks. "I did not mean that. I only mean that it would be unbearably painful to live a lifetime with someone else, when I would always remember that our time was so short."

Maria brushed at his tears with her lithe white fingers and put her arms around him. "Time?" she murmured. "There is no time. There are only the moments when we are together. That is all the time there ever was, and ever will be. How can you measure that much time?"

† † †

That night Maria dreamed it all: the ravens and the fire and the king beyond the creek and the beardless king vanquishing the bearded king. When she awoke, however, she remembered only the last. It was still dark, and she slid next to Haraldr and pressed her naked flesh so tightly to his that he finally roused from his own dreams. "Darling," she whispered, still partially entranced by drowsiness, "I remembered the name of the beardless king. It is William." She kissed him on his shoulders and neck. "But it will happen after we are both dead. And we will be together then, in the purest golden light."

Haraldr was fully awake. He smelled her hair and whispered in her soft, warm ear. "I know," he said. "I dreamed that we were always together, and that the light you have lit in my soul was never quenched." Their lips almost touched, and they paused and felt each other's warm, moist breath. "I have never loved you more than I love you at this instant," said Haraldr.

† † †

Symeon raised a hoary eyebrow. "Hetairarch," he said in his imperturbably decorous voice, "if you do not have a handkerchief, might I offer you one? Or several." Haraldr looked at Symeon with curiosity, decided that the old chamberlain was anything but senile, and accepted three of the soft, embroidered linen handkerchiefs from Symeon's translucent hands. Without further preliminaries Symeon nodded at the doorkeepers, and they slid open the bronze doors to Zoe's apartments.

Haraldr immediately understood Symeon's strange consideration. The antechamber was like a dry sauna; there was even a mist of intensely pungent smoke in the air, as if every form of incense known to the Orient were being burned. The large adjoining reception chamber was the obvious generator of this atmosphere. A half dozen servants worked at three large tables, tending rows of smoking braziers, heating flasks, grinding herbs, and sealing bottles. The heat from the braziers would have brought a camel to its knees. Zoe was once again in the business of perfume and unguent manufacture, which according to Maria was her habit when she was neglected in love.

Haraldr had already had to mop his drenched face twice before Zoe appeared. She was as miraculous as ever, her skin like smooth marble, moist but not wet from the heat. She wore a red scaramangium cut from silk so sheer that no contour of her body was left to the imagination. And the contours were as beguiling as ever. But the eyes were different, more opaque, set at an angle slightly oblique to him as she addressed him. "Hetairarch . . . No, I don't like that for you. King Haraldr is much more suited. Such a secret to conceal from your mother. Had you told me during our dalliance, who knows what madness might have possessed me." She led him into her bedchamber. The arcade facing the sea was shuttered despite the beautiful late-summer day.

Haraldr was glad to have the heat as an excuse to mop his brow again. She had not spoken of their affair since that single conversation after his return from the Bulgar War. Then he realized he should be relieved; Zoe never leapt at what she really wanted. Like a true Roman tactician, she always leapt at something less important first. He decided to humor her diversion. "Yes, Majesty, many opportunities were probably lost that night."

Zoe laughed. "My queen to your king. We should have been very wicked together. Could you have loved me?"

"Yes. I believe I have expressed my love for you in different ways since then."

"Could you make love to me again?"

"Majesty, I am in love with Maria. . . ."

"You will never marry Maria." Zoe's eyes were glacial.

"Majesty . . ."

"Do you know what my skin feels like in this heat?" With magical grace Zoe slipped her scaramangium over her head and stood as naked as Eve. Her vast white bosom, set off by erect lilac nipples, was as astonishing as ever. Her pubic triangle was flossed with gold. She cupped her breasts in her hands and approached Haraldr. "Think what these would feel like hot and wet on your thighs." She pinched her nipples and ran the tip of her tongue over her crimson lips. "Perhaps you could kill my husband and add Emperor to your titles."

Haraldr stepped back and looked up. "Majesty, I have come humbly and respectfully to beg your leave. I have served you and your Empire with as much loyalty and devotion . . ."

Zoe sat on the end of her sleeping couch and spread her legs so that the pink lips between them were visible in every detail. "You will make love to me before you leave Rome," she growled. "It is the duty you pay on exiting Rome."

Haraldr laughed. "Majesty, I can think of scarcely anything more appealing at this moment. I would have my pleasure, tell Maria what I did and why, and she would forgive me. But my enjoyment would damage what she holds in her heart for you, and I would never subject her to that hurt. So I will exit without paying you your customs exaction."

Zoe's legs lolled obscenely. "You won't exit without my permission."

"These walls can keep an invader out. But I don't believe they could keep a simple beggar in. I will leave with or without your blessing."

"Then you will leave without Maria."

"I will let Maria decide that."

Zoe leaned forward and leered with a blade-sharp gaze. "You had better think before you challenge me on this, King Haraldr. The last king to challenge me to a contest of love lost dearly."

"Maria loves you, I grant that. But I would stake my life on her love for me."

Zoe laughed wildly, setting her great breasts in frantic motion. "You think you hold her with your love?" she shrieked. "I hold her with a love so powerful, she will never deny it."

Haraldr allowed Zoe's fierce laughter to subside. "I know she is of your blood."

Zoe's head snapped and her eyes were like adders. "You don't know what you know, King Haraldr," she said with teeth-gritting malice. "You have my permission to leave Rome. Maria does not."

Haraldr made his decision. "Majesty," he said as he crossed his arms over his breast, "might I humbly suggest that you open your shutters? I believe that the cool sea air would have a most salutary effect on your demeanor."

† † †

Halldor stuck his fingernail into the pitch. "It's still pliable," he said, slapping the hard wooden strakes of the *ousiai*-class galley. "They build these hulls so stiff that they hardly need to caulk them. Of course they wouldn't last a week in the western sea. A hull needs flexibility to handle the big waves." Halldor straightened up and looked out over the other two *ousiai* tied up at the St. Mama's Quarter docks. "No, a summer in the water hasn't hurt these hulls. But they'll need to be retarred in the spring. Of course, that won't be our worry."

"I wish we weren't leaving like fugitives in the night," said Ulfr. "After all we have done for Rome, we should have a fleet of *dhromons* leading us out of the harbor instead of having to worry about them chasing us through the Bosporus." Ulfr turned to Haraldr. "I hope your plan for getting over the harbor boom works."

"These stiff hulls will make it work," said Haraldr. "Just make certain that no one straps any gear down. Particularly the chests of gold. Anyway, I will be down here tomorrow night to rehearse the drill with the men. We won't have time for mistakes."

"If we are drilling at night," said Halldor, "how are we going to provision the ships during the day without arousing suspicion?"

"I made a deal with Argyrus when I sold him my estates and tax privileges," said Haraldr. "His men are going to load the ships and tell any of the Prefect's meddlers that the vessels are being outfitted for one of Argyrus's ventures. We even had papers forged."

"So Argyrus has turned out to be a true comrade, after all," said Ulfr.

"I would trust him with my back," said Haraldr. "Of course, I would keep my purse attached to my belt in front. We won't be out of the Bosporus before he has doubled his money on the resale of my properties. But I am certain he will keep his mouth shut until we are away."

The three Norsemen looked toward the sprawling ring of lights around the Golden Horn and the great massed clusters of Galatea and Constantinople. "I wonder if we will ever see this heaven bound to earth again," said Ulfr softly.

"Nidaros will seem like a sleeping closet," said Haraldr.

"But it will be your land and your people," said Halldor.

"It will be your people as well. You and Ulfr will no longer be guardsmen to a king. You will be Marshal and Counselor to the King of Norway."

"I look forward to fighting for Norway," said Halldor. "I also look forward to a tall, silk-thatched, northern woman. The hair on her thighs so pale that it is almost transparent. Legs like a colt. The kind that likes to drain a mead horn at your side and keep you up all night."

Ulfr gazed off at the lights of the city and Haraldr pulled Halldor aside. He kicked at the wooden planks of the wharf for a moment. "Halldor," he said secretively, "are you attracted to Maria?"

For once Halldor seemed startled. "I have no intention of cuckolding you, if that's what you mean. But . . . I would worship that woman." Halldor sounded rapt. "She would chain me with desire. My career would be finished. But as I say—"

"No, no. That is excellent. Now, I want you to make me a promise." Halldor nodded unconditionally. "I do not believe that anything can stop us from wresting the throne of Norway from King Sven. With my money and our pledge-men, ultimately nothing will prevent that conquest. Not even my death. If I were by some chance killed trying to regain my throne, I want you and Ulfr to carry on and rule in my stead. Rule jointly, or one take the north and one the south, as was done in my father's time . . . whatever. That is between you two."

"Of course," said Halldor, "but I don't think—"

Haraldr jabbed his finger in Halldor's chest. "Here is the important pledge. I want you to promise that if I die, you will marry Maria and love her for me."

"I will promise, but I don't really . . ."

"Just make your pledge."

Halldor shrugged. "I hope circumstances will never compel me to keep this pledge, but if they do, I will not find it difficult. I pledge it on my honor as a Norseman."

Haraldr surprised Halldor with an embrace. "Thank you, my friend. Now I have been freed to go north."

had no idea I actually possessed so little," said Maria. "Growing up in the palace, I simply assumed that all of those things were mine. Now I see that all I have are these two chests full of robes and jewelry." She watched somewhat anxiously as Argyrus's porters hefted the two large wooden caskets and carried them out into the courtyard.

Haraldr locked his arms around her waist. "In six months you will own Norway. In eighteen months you will hold a Prince of Norway to your breast."

Maria turned and placed her hands flat on his chest. "Are you certain you will still desire me when you once again behold the fair-haired maidens of Thule? When my breasts and stomach sag with childbirth?"

"Certainly. Who else will love me when I grow fat from the labors of the ale halls? The King of Norway is expected to drain the mead trench with his court men almost every night. Olaf looked like a pregnant cow. They even called him Olaf the Fat. That is what you will have to sleep with."

Maria slipped her hands into Haraldr's belt and bit at his chest, pulling up the silk robe in her teeth. "Each night after you have labored with your subjects, you will labor so hard in my bed that you will look like a starving crane."

"I have survived so far without significant diminution of my stature. Though I have noticed that my byrnnie is not as tight as it once was."

The bronze water clock in the corner of the room rang the hour. Maria pushed Haraldr away and her forehead puckered. "I have to do it," she said. "You understand."

"Why do you imagine that I wouldn't? I am tremendously relieved. This will solve every problem. I am certain that because of our past relationship, and her present predicament, I incited Zoe. With you it will be entirely different. She and Theodora will probably even want to sail with us as far as her villa. We will have a joyous farewell, with every expectation of an equally joyous return. I just want to make certain that if she refuses, you will still be willing to join in our dramatic escape. Which I don't think will be dramatic at all. Gregory says that the patrols on the Bosporus have been reduced to almost nil, while many of the ships are being refitted. I've seen them hoisted to the docks in Neorion Harbor myself."

Maria smiled slyly. "I was a wild girl when you met me. Have you forgotten some of my escapades? Love has not made me altogether docile. And as you say, this will probably be the least dangerous portion of our journey." She smoothed her robe and pursed her lips. "I just want to make her understand. I want her to see that in her own erratic way she has helped me find the happiness that I now have in my life, and to ask her to share my joy."

"I don't want you to be tortured by guilt if you must leave against her wishes."

"I will feel guilt, but I will not let it torture me. She did not feel guilt when she abandoned me for the love of her men. I see that now. She has always been selfish in love, which is why the sum of her loves is so paltry. Just as the sum of my loves was so meager before you came to me."

Haraldr looked at Maria's marvelous blue eyes for a moment. "My darling, have you ever considered that there is a blood relation between you and their Imperial Majesties? I believe that there is, and that Zoe may try to use this bond to hold you here."

Maria's gull-wing eyebrows lifted. "I can't believe you don't know that!" she said with girlish astonishment. "Did I never tell you? My mother was their cousin. A very distant cousin. The relationship is never acknowledged because the scandal that engulfed my parents might impeach the Imperial Dignity. That tenuous blood tie is nothing next to the bonds of the heart." She rushed up and clutched him tightly. "Feel my heart and yours," she said breathlessly as her chest fluttered away against his. "They are the same."

† † †

"Little daughter!" said Zoe. "He told me you would come. Now I must share him with you." The little ivory statue of the Christ was almost entirely concealed by Zoe's delicate hands, but the tiny white head, ringed with a golden halo, peeked above her thumbs. Zoe looked at Maria like a child about to share a secret. "This little image is extraordinary, Daughter. You will understand when it speaks to us."

Maria followed Zoe into her sweltering bedchamber, hoping that the little Christ would turn out to be another harmless caprice. The brilliant candelabra added to the infernal atmosphere in the shuttered room. Zoe motioned for Maria to crawl up on the bed beside her. She hiked up the hem of her tight scaramangium and sat cross-legged, the ivory figure still cradled in her hands. "This is extraordinary, Daughter. Now, be very quiet." Zoe bent over and brought the little head to her blood-red lips. "My pale beauty," she whispered, "my precious eternal being, creature of light. My darling, my love, my sweetest embrace. Talk to us." Zoe paused and kissed the tiny head. "My little daughter is about to embark on a journey. My blessed beauty, tell us if this future is a propitious one for her."

Zoe rocked back and forth slightly, still cupping the figure and intermittently kissing its golden halo. After a long while she opened her hands carefully and studied the figure, now revealed in its entire miniature exactitude. Only the change on her own face was extraordinary. Her eyes seemed to retreat into her sockets and her cheeks appeared to contract. It was as if she were very slowly becoming a corpse. She wrapped the figure in her tremulous hands and then pounded it to her chest. "Oh, Holy Beauty!" she screamed. "Oh, divine spirit. Oh, first and Purest Light! I will save her from that fate if I must chain her here in this room. Oh, why, my beauty, have you revealed this terrible vision if not to permit her rescue! Blessed are you, blessed are you . . ." Zoe turned to Maria, tears bright on her pale cheeks.

Maria put her arms around Zoe and clasped her head to her shoulder. "Oh, Mother, I will miss you desperately too. If I thought that some prophecy could ease our pain at this parting, I would have procured every soothsayer and palmist from the shadows of the Hippodrome and brought them here. I already take with me my own forebodings. Please allow me to challenge my fears with your blessing on my journey."

Zoe struggled free from Maria's embrace. "The statue is extraordinary," she said, as if explaining to an intractable child. "I did not mean that he would literally speak. If this journey of yours had Divine Sanction, he would have glowed with the fiery radiance of the candles of the Heavenly Seraphim. I cannot believe you question this. You, whom I have seen more than once discard an otherwise blameless lover because of some presentiment offered you by a withered palmist."

"I still believe in fate, Mother, but not the selfish fate I once worshiped. I have embraced the fate that is my life and will not let him go."

"Even if it means your death?" Zoe's voice had the timbre of grim reason again. "My child, those men are savages. I know they are as charming as chained and perfumed leopards when they are paraded before us, but in their own frozen habitats they revert to their animal state. You will end up caged with a menagerie of their doxies. You will perish from the brutal life. I say this because I love you."

"I know you do, Mother. But I do not see how you could have known these men as you have and think that . . ." Maria paused and her eyes flared. "Mother, I know that you and Haraldr were lovers. And that he never lied to you, but that you lied to him!"

Zoe turned with a nervous, feline motion. "I loved him and lied to him because it was in the interest of my state and my people to lie to him. To use the brute for the purpose for which he was intended. To further the power and glory of Rome." Zoe leapt up from the sleeping couch and began to pace. "Holy Mother, child! This man of yours is the Pretender to the throne of some iceberg that is likely to sail off the ends of the earth. We have almost as many would-be caliphs and cast-out princes of his ilk at our court as we have senescent Magisters in the Senate. Some of them are little more than clowns!"

"This clown saved your life and mine more than once! He saved your Empire and your people from the pathetic madman you took into your bed! Haraldr is the only one of your lovers who was not a danger to your people!"

Zoe stopped and her grimacing lips relented. "I admit my . . . errors. But it is easy for you to criticize my conduct when you have enjoyed the luxuries of my court and none of the responsibilities. Luxuries, I might add, that you will be fortunate to enjoy as memories in Christ-forsaken Thule."

"Yes. Luxuries such as having a man three times my age cajole himself into my bed and then break my heart. Such luxuries as my mad . . . passions that you found so gay and charming. Such luxuries as a dark, frozen heart that every glowing candelabra and gilded mosaic in this palace could not pierce with a splinter of light. My heart will be a thousand thousand times as brilliant on the bleakest, coldest winter night in Norway as it ever was in the splendor of this palace."

Zoe crept back onto the bed beside Maria and put her arm around her shoulders. Maria's breasts heaved with sobs, and tears flooded her eyes. "Little Daughter," Zoe whispered, "I wish I had told you the truth when I first held your little head to my breast. We are not meant to be happy here. Only to serve our people. If I could offer you any caution derived from my bitter experience, it is that when we follow our hearts instead of our true destiny, we end up punishing both ourselves and those we must serve."

"You, yes," said Maria, wiping at her tears. "Perhaps that has been your lot. But I have my life to live. I have a separate destiny now. It is to be with him."

"It is not to be with him. Don't you understand? He is not your destiny."

Maria pressed her eyes with her palms and straightened her back. "Mother, I will leave with him whether or not you bless and permit it. This is our farewell. Please let my heart go without the weight of your censure."

Zoe let go of Maria's shoulder. "This is a farewell only to the innocence I have so long sought for you." Her voice was hollow and haunted. "I realize now I have spared you nothing by not telling you." Maria turned to Zoe and could not stifle her shocked gasp. It was as if in the few moments of Maria's tears Zoe had become an old woman, her face more sunken and drained of life than when she had imagined the prophecy of her statue.

† † †

"It was as simple as the seduction of a whore," said Halldor. "Here's how it worked. Theodocranus went along with the rest to Sclerena's house. As you know, Theodocranus is permitted to enter the Emperor's presence at any time he wishes now, without prostrations or even 'Good afternoon, Majesty.' So instead of waiting the requisite five courses while the Monomach sated his own appetites, Theodocranus left the banquet table and bounded into the Emperor's presence while his Majesty was presenting himself—all of it—to Sclerena; apparently the Monomach's virtuous niece is as skilled as some of the sword swallowers we find in the Forum. Which is what Theodocranus told the Emperor, who proceeded to laugh like a goat without interrupting Sclerena, whom I presume was also tickled, though perhaps not by mirth. In the midst of this good cheer Theodrocranus blurted out, 'Majesty, the Grand Hetairia is required to inspect the outer perimeter of the Great Land Wall this evening. May I order the Komes of the Walls to permit their exit later this afternoon?' The Emperor, who at this point seemed on the verge of plucking delicate Sclerena's hair out by the roots, shouted his assent in a voice so commanding that the state messengers were already conveying his order to the Komes of the Walls before Theodrocranus had even left the room."

Ulfr shook his head. "Incredible. But it did indeed work. Is everyone checked off?" Ulfr nodded toward the hundreds of Varangians milling on the dock and climbing through the open-decked hulls of the three light galleys. They moved in darkness; Haraldr had ordered that no torches be lit on the docks.

"Every last man," said Halldor, "except the four from Hedeby who are staying to command a private guard. Haraldr released them from their pledges. Most of the rest are eager. A few are nursing aching breasts. I am still burning for the wife . . . well, that is all behind me. Norway. There probably isn't a woman there who has even heard of me."

Ulfr laughed. "Have you forgotten that in the north, adultery is not so casually regarded as it is here? You don't want to become known as a husband killer."

"I know. I will probably have to wed some precious, silky little virgin and make discreet calls on widows."

"I am certain you will find a bride lovely enough to keep you in your own hall for at least a month." Ulfr stamped his feet on the dock, as if expecting an icy north wind. "Haraldr should be here soon to tell us one way or another."

"Yes," said Halldor. "But I don't think we will have to steal out of here in the night. Haraldr is confident that Maria will obtain the Empress's leave. We will be able to sail leisurely out of the harbor in the morning. With a suitable escort as well."

Ulfr walked over to the nearest galley and kicked the hull with a resounding thump. "Good. Because I don't agree with the two of you on your plan for getting past the harbor boom. These hulls aren't as sturdy as you think."

† † †

Maria's eyes were engorged with tears. She fell into Theodora's arms and cried for a long while. Finally Theodora placed her long, slender fingers beneath Maria's chin and gently tilted her head up. "She told you."

Maria nodded and sobbed. "Is it true?"

"It is true," whispered Theodora.

Maria lifted her head up to the light and her eyes seemed to be glazed with ice. "Why did you wait? And why did you tell me now?"

"We loved you. We wanted it to be different for you. Both of us. You must believe that. And now . . . we truly thought your Haraldr was just another plaything. We thought we were indulging another of your wild romances. I think until this very evening we did not believe that you really intended to marry him and leave Rome. That was our folly. But would it have been fair to you, or to him, to let you leave without knowing?"

"Yes! You knew how much I loved him."

"There is a greater love we are bidden to. It is far less comforting and far more painful than the love of a man. But it is a greater love."

"No. I will not live your lives!"

"Maria, we are not like other people. Our lives are given us by the Pantocrator. They are His to dispose of."

"My soul is mine to dispose of. And it is going to Norway!"

Theodora cupped Maria's chin. "Wait. Decide nothing for now. You have not had time to consider what all this means. If after reflection, in the light of what you now know, you still love this man in the way you think you do now, we will think of something. Customs can be changed. You might . . . I don't know. He could certainly stay as your lover."

Maria put her hands to her ears and screamed. "No! His dreams are in Norway. To keep him here would destroy the light that is my life! No! I am going with him! I am going *now*! He is my destiny!"

Zoe appeared in the doorway of Theodora's chamber, her face weary, the faded mother of the beautiful woman who had greeted Maria an hour earlier. "Maria," she snapped, "it is impossible. Your legacy is too great. Go to your Haraldr and tell him that he has my leave to depart our City and Empire tomorrow morning, with all the gold he and his band can carry. But you will never leave Rome."

Maria ran from the room, her face distorted and lantern-red. "I am going with him!" she said, sobbing.

Zoe turned and called after her, "Maria! I will not permit you to leave! And if he tries to assist in your flight, I will have him destroyed!"

† † †

Haraldr listened to the water clock ring the third hour of the night; he was grateful that Norway did not have such sophisticated mechanical devices. The relentless timekeepers were the clarions of anxiety. Why had she not returned? He never should have let her go. Zoe, like every person condemned to that diabolic purple cloth, had gone mad. Haraldr paced a moment and then decided to make one last sweep through the house to ensure that he had left nothing of value. Value? Everything that could possibly matter would soon be on three ships. The future of Norway. And nothing Zoe could do could stop it.

To the flickering light of his taper, Haraldr descended the marble staircase for the last time. If he felt any nostalgia on leaving this oversize, empty shell, it was only because of the nights he and Maria had held each other there. He stopped in the large entrance hall and thought of the first time he would make love to Maria as his wife and queen. Odin, your skalds will spend the next ten centuries singing of her beauty— He was startled by the noise. You are welcome to the water clock, he wanted to tell the thief. He poked the taper in the direction of the rustling.

"Darling!" he cried out, his joy visceral. "I thought you were some . . ." His voice fell off as the light revealed her agony. He rushed to her and held her. She sobbed for a painfully long while. The unforgiving clock racheted in accompaniment. "I am so sorry," he finally told her. "Oh, I did not want this. Darling, darling," he said, trying to lift her stubborn, leaden chin, "I will have my men return to the Numera and we will wait for another day. We will both go talk to her. I won't let you leave your home like this."

Maria looked up. The color of her eyes was a shimmering blue fjord in the darkness of a shadowed gorge. "I have made my farewells," she said fiercely. "I want nothing more in this life than to sail with you to Norway tonight."

† † †

"Who is at the Blachernae Gate?" asked Halldor.

"Erling," said Ulfr.

"I think I will ride up there and wait for another hour. Then I'm afraid our 'inspection' of the walls will have to be concluded. I'll ride into the city after that and find out what happened to Haraldr. Hopefully he has been detained because he and Maria are celebrating a successful petition to the Empress. I'm worried about leaving too late in the evening. Even the Monomach is going to be suspicious if he finds that his entire guard has been gone half the night."

Halldor had saddled his horse when he heard horseshoes clatter on the pavement near the dock. He reached for his purse; he intended to pay off the cursore. Then he noticed that the horse was transport for both a man and a woman. "Ulfr!" he shouted. "Haraldr!"

Haraldr dismounted, swept Maria into his arms, and carried her onto the dock. She was pale and hollow-eyed. Halldor looked at her with concern. "It appears that Zoe did not give her consent," he said to Haraldr. He looked off toward the distant mouth of the Golden Horn, a vague aperture between the hills of light. "Haraldr," he said firmly, "I propose that we return to our barracks. I am certain that suspicion has already been aroused by our absence. And now Maria looks ill. Let us wait. We can go tomorrow. Or in a week."

"Put me down," said Maria to Haraldr, as annoyed as if she had been abducted. "I am not sick. I am . . ." She breathed deeply and arranged her robe nervously, then looked searchingly at the three men, her head held high. "There is something I must tell all of you before you take me on your ship." She turned to Haraldr and put her hand on his arm. "I was going to wait to tell you until we had seen the last lights of the city disappear. But on the ride through the city I thought about what I, myself, have said about selfish love, and now I realize that I am guilty of that." She looked again between Halldor and Ulfr and her lips quivered. "You are all in grave danger if you take me with you tonight." Maria clutched Haraldr's arm tightly. She faltered and blinked away new tears. "I have just learned that my . . . mother . . . was the purple-born Eudocia, daughter of the Emperor Constantine, niece of Basil the Bulgar-Slayer, and sister of their Majesties Zoe and Theodora. I . . . I am the last Macedonian heir to the throne of Imperial Rome."

The night was infinite in its vast hush. The whispered conversations of the Varangians on the docks created a cathedrallike murmur. A hull groaned slightly. Finally Haraldr very slowly took Maria's face in his hands. "Oh, my love." The pain in his voice was for both of them. "Oh, my love," he repeated numbly. He stared at the city for a long moment and then returned to her with tears in his eyes. "I . . . I will understand if you must . . . remain with your people. I . . . of all here I should understand what you feel now. Your obligation. But if you still . . . If your fate and mine can still be joined . . ." He trailed off hopelessly and shook his head in shock and bewilderment, a man confronted by a catastrophe for which he had no solution. Finally he could only take her in his arms. "I . . . it doesn't matter. I cannot ask these men to take that risk. I will stay here with you."

"No, that is not what I want," she said, her voice soft and high and her eyes like starlight. "I want to go with you more than ever. To forge a new fate with your people. We could never have a life here now. An Augusta could never marry a"—she looked down at her feet and then into the eyes of the Norsemen—"*barbaroi.*" She inhaled deeply. "Zoe will do everything she can to keep me here. She has returned in her emptiness to her oldest passion, the House of Macedon. She has already warned me that she will kill you to preserve that legacy. It is as if her dead uncle the

Bulgar-Slayer has ruled her heart all these years, and she only now realizes the terrible implications of that overweening love." Maria sobbed quickly and regained control. "All of you may be destroyed because of me."

"That is a risk I am willing to undertake," said Halldor.

"For once I have no words to add to Halldor's." Ulfr nodded.

"May I put the question before your pledge-men?" Halldor asked.

Haraldr looked at Maria before nodding assent. Halldor hurried down to the end of the dock and stopped at each ship in turn. He left the crew of the first ship to a low, fevered buzz of activity. The second and third vessels followed Halldor's hurried inquiries with their own murmured choruses. Men leapt into motion, pulling oars up from the hold and scrambling to loosen mooring lines. Halldor came running back. He looked directly at Maria. "They are all willing to risk whatever Norway's queen is willing to risk." Tears streamed down Maria's cheeks. Halldor turned to Haraldr. "But we must leave immediately."

The ships were pushed slowly past the dock, and then oars dipped and turned the prows east. The first full surge of all sixty oars buckled Haraldr's knees momentarily, then seemed to free the enormous weight on his chest. He could not conceivably assimilate the full import of what Maria had told him, but his heart thrummed with the stunning testament of her love. He paced the catwalk between the rowing benches, making certain that the chests and gear bags were arranged as he had intended. The first of many obstacles lay directly ahead in the night. But now there was only a single destination in his mind and in his heart.

The wind rustled in his ears as the brilliant city floated past in the night. He looked at Maria, seated at the stern, wrapped in her fur cape, gazing at the brilliant lights of Blachernae, the ancillary palace at the northwest corner of the city, where the Great Land Wall and seawall met. He would never miss these lights as long as he had her blue fires to dazzle him. He had given much to Rome, but now Rome had given him her greatest treasure.

The wharves blazed with the tapers of the porters, who customarily worked long into the night. Haraldr took the tiller from Ulfr and talked to Maria; together they recited the names of the towering, broad gates in the seawall as they glided past: Basilica, Phanarii, Petrion, St. Theodosia, Ispigas, and Platea, with its huge complex of wharves, warehouses, and endless rows of merchant and pleasure craft. The high, round hulls of Venetian merchantmen were dark silhouettes at Droungariou Viglae

Gate. On the north shore of the Golden Horn, the city of Galatea glimmered with a brilliance that would have made it the wonder of the world, were it not for the great city little more than two bowshots across the water.

The splendid spine of the city was strung with necklaces of light; already the great palaces of the Dhynatoi had been rebuilt and filled with new riches. The lights of the Imperial Palace and the ring of glowing golden windows around the dome of Hagia Sophia winked into view from the hills to southeast. At the Perama Gate, Haraldr gave the tiller back to Ulfr and told him to steer to left center of the channel. Haraldr joined Halldor in the prow of the galley.

"Not good at all!" shouted Halldor. He pointed at Neorion Harbor, a lattice of lights cradled in the slightly hooked end of the peninsula. Most of the small patrol craft were still on lifts, but Haraldr could distinctly see the hundreds of tapers milling around the *dhromons* like luminous ants. "Our passage has been reported! I presume they know what they are after!"

"They haven't left anchorage yet!" shouted Haraldr. "We'll outrun them easily!"

"If we make it over the boom." Halldor looked out on the black water. The Bosporus, glazed by the luminous backdrop of Chrysopolis on the Asian shore, opened up ahead. They were almost directly opposite the Neorion docks. One of the *dhromons* blew its air horn; the frightening bellow almost certainly signaled the departure of the huge fire-ship. "There!" shouted Halldor. He pointed to the northeast, near the point where the Galatea coastline veered north. "I can see it already!" The boom was an ebony sketch on the water. Haraldr called out to Ulfr to come larboard a quarter to meet the angled chain head-on. The other ships made the same turn and came abreast.

The massive log floats of the harbor boom became distinct three-dimensional forms. Each float was several ells high and thirty ells long; the sections were joined by iron links as thick as a man's arm. Haraldr walked back to the stern and took the tiller from Ulfr. The log barrier was three bowshots away. He picked his spot. On the periphery of his vision he could see the lights of a *dhromon* as it left the docks. Another horn bellowed across the water. "Begin the drill!" he shouted. The rowing cadence immediately increased and the ship lunged forward. Varangians deep in the hold began sliding the heaviest chests toward the stern, along greased planks set especially for the purpose. The bow began to plane up, and the railing at the stern dipped toward the waves. As they closed on the boom, the cadence went higher, more chests were moved, and the angle of the bow increased.

The log barrier suddenly looked like a wall. "Fifty ells!" shouted Haraldr. The rowers took fast, deep strokes and the men in the hold braced themselves. Haraldr and Ulfr steadied the tiller with both arms. Maria ducked her head. Water whooshed along the hull.

Wood screeched against wood. The planing bow slid over the log float as if cresting a wave, then decelerated with a tremendous shudder. The stern began to settle, and the entire hull teetered on the fulcrum of the log float, the bow ten ells clear of the water. Men leapt onto the floats and began to secure heavy ropes between the mast and the boom. Oarsmen joined the frantic bailing at the stern. Haraldr was already up to his calves in water. He realized they were losing their first battle of the long journey back. He shouted for the men in the hold to go ahead with the drill. The chests were now pushed frantically forward along the greased planks. As the weight of the cargo was shifted, the hull protested with a deep, almost animate keen. The stern began to lift.

The ship slowly leveled, until for an instant it was perfectly balanced on top of the log fulcrum. Timbers screeched and the ropes that kept the hull from yawing over hummed with the strain as the ship tilted first to one side and then the other. And then the descent began; after a moment the bow slapped reassuringly into the water on the other side of the boom. The bow oars dipped and wood shrieked as the ship began to slip off the boom. They were free in the Bosporus.

"You are luckier than Odin!" crowed Ulfr. "We . . ." Ulfr's joy vanished in the thunderclap that came from the left. Every head turned. Only fifty ells away, the second ship was poised at the critical balance point atop the log. Within a heartbeat the ship fractured in two, as if it had been dropped against the log barrier from some great height.

"Cut the lines and make ready to pick them up!" shouted Haraldr. His ship scraped free from the boom, and he looked to his right to see how the third galley had fared. It, too, had dipped its bow and was sliding off the boom. Still farther to the right, the lights of the *dhromons* moved on the water.

The rescue was orderly; Haraldr praised the gods that Norsemen did not panic when plunged into a dark sea. Most of the Varangians had evacuated their gear bags and clung calmly to the shattered hull of their galley. The surviving galleys divided the crew of the wreck; the extra men were quickly distributed on the benches. *The next time there will be fire on the water,* thought Haraldr. *And none of us will be so calm.*

Haraldr looked south. Apparently the harbor boom had been partially towed away at the Constantinople end, and the *dhromons* were coming through along the coastline. He turned to Ulfr. "This was my fault. I should have known that at least one of the keels would fail and fitted an extra ship. Now our two *ousiai* are so heavily loaded that we no longer have the advantage of speed." He paused and counted the *dhromons* as they passed the boom and began to turn to the north. Eight. "Before we lost that galley, this pursuit was not a contest for us. But we are in a race now."

t is strange how an entire life must suddenly become a memory." Maria looked off the stern and wrapped her fur cape up to her chin. A night wind had come up from the north and the galley pitched rhythmically through the rising seas. The lights of the city were now a golden haze on the southern horizon. The lanterns on the masts of the *dhromons* were distinct stars against this luminous band, gently lifting and falling with the motion of the waves.

Haraldr snugged Maria's cape around her shoulders and held her; he was unable to entirely banish the great city to his own memories. "If I had known the choice I was forcing on you . . . it is still hard to believe." He paused for a long while. "I will go back with you. I would not be some helpless consort. Perhaps I could never be crowned, but then Joannes did not need a crown. I would rule."

"You would rule a dying empire, and in your own fashion you would become a Joannes. You did not grow up next to the heart of Rome. I did. And I know that Rome is dying. And everyone close to that heart is corrupted and dies in emptiness and darkness, no matter how long their span and how glorious the honors heaped upon them by the sycophants at court. Their souls are stolen when they ascend that golden throne, and at that moment they die, alone and empty."

"But you would have the love of your people."

"These people I would somehow reach out to from the prison of the Imperial Palace? These people who would perish in a civil war if my true identity were even known? Those who want to restore the Macedonian line would fight to seat me on the throne so that my young loins could bring forth the next Macedonian, and those factions whose interests lay elsewhere would raise their swords on protests of my illegitimacy." Maria turned to Haraldr. "It is so strange. Zoe and Theodora knew what I am telling you now, and yet in their secret hearts I guess they always dreamed that I could follow them. The shadow of their uncle the Bulgar-Slayer is still over Rome. And because Rome cannot escape a dead man's legacy, Rome will soon join him in death."

Haraldr wrapped his arms more tightly around Maria and nuzzled her ear. "As King of Norway I will find no better counsel than in my own marriage bed. I, too, have smelled that fetor of death. In the Studion. Among the corpses of a thematic army ill prepared and even more poorly led. And most strongly within that glittering circle at court, that splendid, scented illusion that masks a power that has decayed at its very core. The foundations of Rome are crumbling, but its caretakers have chosen to regild the exterior rather than shore up the columns that actually support the edifice." Haraldr looked out at the wavering constellation of the pursuing *dhromons;* the lights were now strung out in single file. "The great beast is dying from within. But its teeth are still deadly."

"Will we outpace them?"

"We have pulled away slightly. This north wind holds them back more than it does us because their hulls are higher. But the *dhromons* can slip in behind one another, and the crews in back can save their energy until it is their turn to challenge the wind. See, that is how they have formed up. As I said, the teeth are still sharp. And I must take my spell at the oars." He kissed her and let her go.

"I wish I could row," said Maria.

Haraldr looked up at the sky. The stars were fading beneath a rapidly thickening haze, and the scent of an approaching storm was on the wind. He pointed to a bucket. "Well, you have already proven yourself a good bailer," he said. "I think you will have an opportunity to practice your skill again before the night is over."

† † †

"*Khelandia,* " said Halldor flatly. "And there are ten *dhromons* instead of eight."

"I can't see them," said Ulfr. "I can't see—" Ulfr stopped and squinted at the line of lights trailing behind them. Except for an occasional light or two on the shoreline, the rest of the horizon was black and featureless. The Great City was a memory. Even the stars had vanished entirely. "I can . . . *Skita!* Where did they come from?"

"They have been hanging back and running without lanterns. Very clever. Put bells on the oxen and let us exhaust ourselves racing against them, then silently bring up the horses." Halldor turned and studied the bowing backs of the Varangians and shook his head. "They are at their limit right now." He looked back at Maria, still vigilant at the stern, her fur cape bound tightly around her. "Have Haraldr spelled," he told Ulfr. "We are going to have to decide what to do when they catch us."

Haraldr came to the stern, sweat beaded on his forehead. He listened to Halldor, squinted past the *dhromons,* and his ruddy complexion faded as he verified the observation. He looked quickly at Maria and she smiled at him. He beckoned her with his hand. "She will want to know," he said softly.

Maria looked up at the three Norsemen, her eyes the only bright surface on the entire galley. Haraldr pointed to the south. "They have sent out more ships than we thought. *Khelandia.* The fastest fire-ships. I think they are waiting for some sign of our weakening before they unleash them." Haraldr looked quickly over his shoulder at the swaying oarsmen. "And that will be soon."

Maria lips parted silently, and she inhaled quickly before she spoke. "This race is ended, then." Her voice was resolute. She looked at Haraldr. "You have a dinghy. Set me in it and give me a lantern. I am the prize, not your lives. When they have collected me, they will turn back." Haraldr immediately shook his head and Maria grabbed his arms. "Listen to me!" she commanded. "This is not the end. I will find some way to come to you. Rome will never hold me again. But what prison would I escape from if you were not free to welcome me? This is the only way now. For *your* people. For us." Haraldr stared into her steady blue eyes, her unimpeachable logic ripping at his heart. He shook his head again. "What other way is there?" protested Maria.

"Very well," said Haraldr. "We will lower the dinghy. But I will be the captain of that vessel."

"No! Zoe might . . . who knows what she might . . . She has gone mad."

"I am not afraid of Zoe," said Haraldr. "And I do not intend to see Zoe. I intend to bribe the Droungarios in command of those *dhromons.*"

"You should know by now that even all your chests of gold cannot purchase the fate of a purple-born."

"It suddenly occurs to me that the Droungarios almost unquestionably does not know why his Empress so desperately demands your return. You, yourself, spoke of the threat to Zoe's own status if a more fecund Macedonian were to become available. I don't think Zoe is yet as mad as you think."

Maria looked at Haraldr with sparkling astonishment. Then her white teeth flashed and she reached up and touched his face. "Why do I sometimes forget, my darling, that you are a very wise man?" She threw her arms around him. "You won't even have to offer him a chestful of gold. A Mistress of the Robes, particularly a discredited wanton like myself, is probably only worth a bag of silver."

† † †

The hulls of the Varangian galleys vanished behind the dark waves. Spray whistled along with the wind and soon drenched the passengers in the wildly pitching dinghy. Maria's teeth chattered and Haraldr used one oar to steady the dinghy and the other to hold her. "Darling, I must tell you something. This wager may be lost. There is a chance that I am wrong about Zoe."

Maria spoke firmly in spite of her quaking body. "Feel this." She guided his hand to the lining of her cape. The hard blade of a knife lay beneath the soft fur. "If they threaten to take you, I will use this. You know I will."

"No. I will get in the water somehow. Halldor and Ulfr will come back to look for me. I will live and you must not die." A wave picked the dinghy up and dropped it with bowel-numbing suddenness. "What I must say is what I did not have a chance to say the other times we have taken such risks. There is so much that can happen now if this does not work. We could . . . it could be a long time before we hold each other again. Years. I could die in the north before . . ." He shook his drenched head as if in flinging away the drops of seawater he could cast off that destiny. "Fate is suspended, that is all I know. And I may not have this reprieve again." He turned to her with blue lightning in his eyes. "Wherever you are, I will find you again. I will hold back the last dragon for all eternity if I must to hold you again. I promise that. I will keep that promise beyond my own grave. I will find you and hold you again. This will not be our last embrace."

They held each other, unspeaking, until the lights of the *dhromons* came over them like terrible stars in a dark universe.

† † †

The Droungarios John Moschus stuck his powerful hands into the ivory casket and pulled up fistfuls of gold. The solidi fell back into the pile, the sound a dull clink in the shrieking wind. He fixed his cold gray eyes on Haraldr. "It's a hundred times more than I could expect to leave this office with," he said. "But my life is ships. It would be death for me to live on some estate in Armenikoi after I am relieved of my command."

"You could buy your own ships. Pursue Saracen brigands. Sail when you please and fight when you please, instead of waiting on the docks until your Emperor decides to frighten some naked children on the beaches of Kherson." The *dhromon* lifted in the mounting sea. "Look at this. Is this an effective sortie for thirty fire-ships? To bring back Her Majesty's Mistress of the Robes? Next you will be asked to send twenty *dhromons* to Libya to capture a black man to fan the Empress's face. Besides, she doesn't make the ultimate decisions. The Monomach knows you are an able commander." Haraldr reached in his cloak, produced a large leather purse full of gold coins, and set it on top of the gleaming contents of the casket. "Here. Give this to a dwarf named Theodocranus. Tell him that you want the Emperor to preserve your command."

Moschus rubbed his scratchy black beard. "I've heard of this dwarf," he said as he shook his head. "I don't know." He shook his head again.

"Look," said Haraldr, "my men will come back for me. A lot of your men and my men will die. For what? For a glorified serving girl. If I did not love her so much with the head that doesn't think, I probably would just give her back to you and shrug it off. But I burn every time I think of her. Why don't you keep the money and let me keep the Mistress?"

Moschus looked at Maria and then at Haraldr. "I think you might misunderstand. I have orders to let you go. Maybe you should try to forget her."

"Look at her," said Haraldr. "Could you forget her? She's not a woman, she's a demon. She possesses the soul. You know what they say about her."

Moschus laughed. Maria's eyes never flinched. "I've heard about her as well." He cocked his head at Haraldr. "You're certain that it isn't the Emperor who really wants her back? I mean . . ." He lifted his wiry eyebrows suggestively and threw his hands up.

"She's faithful to me. I keep her locked up."

Moschus dug his hands into the gold again and then stood up. He stamped the deck. "Damn! Women! That's the beauty and the curse of the sea. No women. Damn!" He looked at Haraldr. "I need to think about this."

† † †

"Halldor, your eyes are intoxicated with their earlier success." Ulfr winced into the screaming north wind and flying spray. Hord Stefnirson leaned over his shoulder. They silently studied the sea for a long while.

"Odin!" Hord jerked erect as if he had been struck by an arrow. "Odin! No! Who?"

Ulfr looked at Hord and shook his head as if to say, "Don't tell me you are as mad as Halldor is." Halldor shook his head back at Ulfr. "You're not talking about that squall line?" said Ulfr, still peering at the sea. "That . . ." Ulfr went rigid. "Holy Mother of Christ. Holy, Holy Mother of Christ. That is no squall line. That is . . ." He turned and looked at Halldor. "That is a fleet."

"Yes. I think about three hundred ships," said Halldor, not at all enjoying his triumph. "Now let us see," he said grimly. "Who can be the first to discover whether they are merchantmen or warships?"

✝   ✝   ✝

Maria pressed her chin to Haraldr's chest. "If he does not accept, I will threaten to kill myself. I will. His mission could hardly be considered successful then."

"He will accept," whispered Haraldr. "The fact that a man like Moschus says he must think about it convinces me that he has already accepted. He knows that he could do exactly as ordered and still be dismissed because of some Imperial caprice. Rome does not reward loyalty sufficiently well to be accorded loyalty. The only thing I am worried about now is this storm that is coming."

"A mere hurricane," said Maria with a wry smile. The call from the lookout high above blasted through the wind. Haraldr turned to the mast and saw Moschus pulling himself up the rope ladder. Moschus hung about halfway up the enormous mast and looked into the night. His body yawed as the wind whipped at the ropes; then he jerked abruptly with alarm or astonishment or both. He shouted down the deck. Haraldr heard part of the command but it was too late. The Imperial Marines, spears lowered, were already encircling Maria and him. Haraldr thought of leaping the railing at his back but instantly knew he was defeated. He could not leave Maria to an unknown fate.

Moschus came back down the rope ladder like a huge, thick-bodied spider clambering through its web. His face was livid. He shouldered through the arc of his marines. "If you think you can coerce me, think again, Varangian!" he shouted, clenching his powerful fists. "I don't understand your game, but while I have been hesitant to quarrel with you over this woman, I will be more than eager to accept a challenge from your fleet! You cannot see them yet, but I ordered another three dozen *dhromons* and support vessels to follow behind this group, simply as an exercise. I will crush you!"

Haraldr looked at Moschus in astonishment. "Droungarios, my fleet, as you put it, was reduced by a third when one ship foundered on the boom. And why would I ask that fleet to challenge you now? You were about to accept my offer, were you not?"

"I was," snapped Moschus, "until I discovered this treachery. By my count it would take a hundred wrecks to reduce your fleet by a third. Do you plan an invasion? Perhaps the Empress had good purpose in putting my fleet in your pursuit, and I better Fortune by ordering my strength to sea."

Haraldr looked to the north. His two galleys had approached to within less than a bowshot of the *dhromon,* which surprised him, but not as much as the fact that that was all he saw. "I left with two ships," he said in bewilderment. "I don't know why they are coming up, but I can assure they do not intend to attack without my signal."

Moschus stepped forward and seized Haraldr's arm. "Very well! You climb up there, and if you can still maintain there are only two ships, I will turn over my baton to you!"

Haraldr was only a third of the way up the swaying rope ladder when he looked out and gasped. The dark hulls virtually spanned the width of the Bosporus and disappeared back into a lowering mist. Haraldr hoped that what he saw was only a small wrinkle in the fabric of fate. He shouted down to Moschus. "Those are Rus ships!"

Haraldr studied the ships for a few more moments before he climbed back to the deck. The Imperial Marines surrounded him again. He faced Moschus. "I swear to you I have no collusion in this. But those are the hulls of Rus merchantmen."

"Which can also be used as warships!" growled Moschus. "It's late in the year for a trade flotilla, don't you think?"

"Perhaps they have been delayed by the Pechenegs," said Haraldr. "I am certain their business is peaceful."

"Droungarios!" Haraldr's galley had come within fifty ells of the larboard, and Halldor hailed from the stern. "Droungarios! Permission to come alongside!"

Moschus barked orders and the lion-shaped bronze spout at the stern of the *dhromon* swiveled to address the Varangian galley. Then he gave Halldor his permission. The ships drifted to within ten ells and pitched alongside each other in the heavy chop. "Haraldr," shouted Halldor, "the fleet is Rus, commanded by Vladimir, Prince of Kiev." Haraldr sighed with relief; Elisevett's brother, Vladimir, had been a puny idler the last time Haraldr had seen him. He couldn't attack a nest of mice. "Droungarios!" shouted Halldor. "The leader of the Rus fleet wants to negotiate with the commander of the Imperial Fleet."

"I know this Vladimir," said Haraldr. "Believe me, he is without hostile capability."

Moschus shook his head. "This is all too neatly contrived." He scratched his beard. "Here is what I will offer you in good faith. You go and bring this Vladimir to me as my hostage, and I will not attack his fleet pending inquiries to the Prefect and the Logothete of the Dromus. In the meanwhile I will keep the Mistress of the Robes in my custody."

Haraldr looked at Maria. It was clear she liked this compromise less than he did, and he wondered if she was at last losing her courage; he would not blame her. How many times could they dance on the needle of fate? He nodded to her that they must play this out.

Maria rushed to him and clutched him with stunning power. "No," she gasped. "You cannot go out there!" She shuddered violently. "Hold me," she pleaded, "hold me. I am so cold. I am so cold." Her teeth chattered and she grimaced so that she could speak. "You must not go out there. I will never see you again." She began to cry and her entire body trembled.

Haraldr could not fathom her premonition. It was only Vladimir. This would be settled in an hour. He rocked her and stroked her hair. "I must," he said. "The sooner I begin, the sooner I will be back for you." He forced her chin up. "Darling, remember my promise. If Satan himself is out there, I will still come back for you."

† † †

Haraldr's galleys pulled north through the pitching rows of Rus ships. According to the slit-eyed little Rus functionary Halldor had taken aboard, Prince Vladimir was tucked safely in the middle of his enormous fleet. Haraldr wondered how the hapless scamp had even gotten this far, with so many ships still intact.

The functionary pointed to a fat river ship identical to the dozens around it. Haraldr told Ulfr to stay aboard and take command if anything happened, though he was confident nothing untoward was about. He strapped on his sword and laughed. "I would tell you to wear your byrnnie, Halldor, but when you see this Prince of Rus, you will be so frightened that you will leap into the sea, and I don't want you to sink."

Haraldr rowed the Rus functionary and Halldor across in the functionary's dinghy. He helped the other two over the railing of the fat merchant-man and then swung himself over. For some strange reason the ship smelled like Rus, though he couldn't say exactly what scent produced that effect. He looked up. Raindrops hurtled out of the darkness.

Vladimir waited by the mast. He wore a bronze breastplate and was surrounded by several wispy-bearded, heavily armored Rus Boyer whelps no more impressive than himself. Vladimir, observed Haraldr, had his father's unimpressive height and extensive girth, his mother's fair skin, and his sister's delicate hands; his blotchy, adolescent face had at last been overgrown by thin blond whiskers. In addition to his armored retainers, Vladimir also employed several hulking Norse bodyguards who lounged in the darkness at the stern of the vessel.

"So," said Vladimir with a smirk and a nonchalant flip of his head. "Haraldr Nordbrikt Sigurdarson. The coward of Stiklestad. Running errands for the Greeks, I see."

"How is your Mother, Vladimir?" asked Haraldr genially. He had nothing to prove to this pathetic lot.

"She misses your cock-hound brother."

Haraldr struggled for control. "And is Elisevett well?"

"She is still sitting on her little twat and waiting for you to come back and marry her, even when she heard that you are the famous coward. You must have fucked the wits out of her."

Haraldr stepped forward and jammed his fingers under the lower lip of Vladimir's breastplate and lifted him off the ground with one hand. "Your sister was very dear to me. If you speak about her again in such a fashion, I will make you swim back to Kiev to apologize to her. Now, I can help you gain entry to Byzantium if you promise to watch your manners." He set Vladimir down slowly. "The Droungarios of the Imperial Fleet—"

"I didn't come to beg my way in," interrupted Vladimir, apparently undeterred by his humiliation. "I came to ask the city to surrender." Halldor burst into laughter.

Haraldr was less amused. "You little fool. Have some of your Norse bodyguards blown you up with dreams of conquest, or is this a self-invented folly? Whatever the source, I suggest you reconsider. There are enough fire-ships waiting for you out there in the night to turn the Bosporus into a river of flame."

Another voice responded from the darkness. "And there are enough Norsemen here to bring down the walls of the Great City." The shrouded Norseman came forward along the catwalk and drew back the hood that concealed his steel helm. Haraldr immediately recognized him.

"Thorvald Ostenson," said Haraldr, greeting the former Centurion of the Grand Hetairia. "I should have known that the hand of Mar Hunrodarson was in this." Haraldr recalled Mar's cryptic words upon dying.

Ostenson bowed. "We have three thousand Norsemen and five thousand Rus. This morning Mar will attack the walls from within the city and open the gates for us. Apparently he has spared you to flee from our triumph. So go. And leave the pillage of Rome to true warriors."

Halldor looked at Haraldr with a rare expression of uncontainable mirth. He laughed again and looked at Ostenson. "The last time I saw your Mar Hunrodarson, he was trying to imitate a pigeon taking wing. Unsuccessfully."

Ostenson drew his sword. "You crow-shit eater! I'll take you back to Mar and let you share your jest with him."

Halldor stepped forward and sent Ostenson plunging into the hold with a single shove. "I'll wait to jest with your Mar when the Valkyrja take me to him, boy-lover," Halldor called down to Ostenson. "Your Mar is drinking with Odin tonight."

"Liar!" shouted Ostenson. He struggled to his feet and his head emerged above the catwalk. "No man could have vanquished Odin's champion!"

Halldor pointed at Haraldr. "This man did. He hugged him to death. Broke his back with one squeeze."

This time the laughter, a soft, quiet chuckle, came from the vicinity of the cowed young Rus nobles. Haraldr wondered which one of these hapless whelps could possibly find their situation amusing. Then he saw the second Norseman. The bearlike giant wore a hide cape. He came around in front of Vladimir and his retainers. Haraldr knew the face at once and felt the sudden lightness and liquid knees of terror. The hacked-away eyebrows, the white-streaked beard, the horrible, truncated nose and huge, sucking nostrils. "I am Thorir, called the Hound," said the Berserk in his curious, quiet voice. "The Haraldr Sigurdarson I remember soiled his breeches when I killed his brother. He was then a coward, he is now a coward. And a liar. Mar Hunrodarson is one of us."

Haraldr and Halldor stood transfixed by the fearsome Hound. Ostenson seized the opportunity and pulled Halldor's legs out from under him, pitching him into the hold; he cracked Halldor on the head with a loaded bucket and stunned him and drew his knife to finish him off. Haraldr jumped down into the hold and grabbed Ostenson's arm with both hands and snapped it; the crack was like an old, dry tree trunk snapping. He dragged the astonished Ostenson to the catwalk and clamped his hands on either side of his face and picked him up. "Ostenson!" he demanded, "were you privy to Mar's plan to abandon the Middle Hetairia to the Bulgars? If you were not, I give you this chance to beg for your life!" Ostenson's face reddened and he glared with defiance. Haraldr roared from the blackest pit of the spirit world and snapped Ostenson's neck instantly. He seized the suddenly limp body and, almost unseeing from inside some red-hued haze, flung the huge, fresh corpse into the mast; the vehemence of the throw was so great that the sturdy wooden trunk fractured with yet another crack and began to tilt toward starboard. The mast cracked again, came down with a huge boom, and fell over the starboard side of the boat. Ostenson's mangled body lay beneath a web of toppled rigging.

The utterly dumbfounded Rus nobles leapt for the sanctuary of the hold. Haraldr turned to the Hound with a blood-red glow in his eyes. He whipped his sword out of his scabbard with a terrifying screech and stepped forward, within reach of the Hound's own murderous blade. "I am one of you as well," he said in a fierce, rapt voice. "But I am not a cowardly Berserk who needed two of his comrades to kill Norway's king. I am Haraldr Sigurdarson, King of Norway." He remembered as clearly as yesterday the Hound's own words at Stiklestad. "When we begin, I will kill you."

The Hound's brutal jaw was as slack as an old dotard's. His huge sloping shoulders sagged. His eyes were burned-out coals. He slumped to his knees like a figure of melting wax. Haraldr looked down on him with pitiless eyes. "You have told the world for years how you slew a king in single combat and then fouled a prince's breeches. Half of that is true. I was a coward then. But you were a coward then, and you are a coward now. And you will die a coward." Haraldr brought his blade screaming down on the thick, brutish neck. The head jerked and then slumped to the chest, held by a flap of flesh. The neck gushed bright blood, and the body of Thorir the Hound pitched into the hold. Prince Vladimir screeched in terror.

Haraldr yanked the Rus Prince back up on the catwalk. "You need to agree to the Droungarios's conditions immediately. The fire-ships will not wait forever on your answer." Vladimir stood mute, his lips beginning to twitch. He burst into tears.

"It is too late!" shrieked the Rus Prince, tears streaming down his cheeks. "This negotiation was only to deceive the Greeks! The attack has already begun!"

Haraldr ran to the bow. The front echelons of the Rus fleet were advancing through the whitecapped sea, a wall of thick hulls descending on the *dhromons*. The wind hurled scudding black clouds after them, and sheets of rain ripped by at a sharp angle. Haraldr could only stare in rigid agony. The advance echelon was already within range.

The night turned to fire.

† † †

"It is impossible!" shouted Halldor. "We cannot sail through it! As soon as the fire touches the pitch on our hull, we will become a floating torch!" Halldor and Ulfr and Hord wrestled Haraldr until he stopped resisting. The burning sea lit their faces an eerie orange and brought sweat to their foreheads. The scene before them was unimaginable, the fiery lakes of damnation raised to the surface of the earth. The entire Bosporus, as far as one could see, was a sheet of flame, and upon this floating pyre scores of ships had become towering, wind-whipped flares. Here and there the flares exploded in immense orange fireballs that illuminated the glowering, low clouds; it was as if enormous, black-shrouded lanterns had been suspended over the sea. The rain, descending in sheets, did nothing to quench these flames.

"Get the dinghy from the other ship," Haraldr said. "Its hull is not caulked."

"I'm going with you," said Ulfr.

"And I," said Halldor.

"No. I want you two to stay and lead my men and rule Norway. This I alone must do. Bring the boat up."

"Haraldr," pleaded Halldor, "Maria was on the Droungarios's *dhromon.* She will be safe. Wait at least until the fire burns away." A ship exploded and the light and sound flashed over the water.

"No one is safe out there." Haraldr nodded numbly at the fire storm. "We now see the limitation of liquid fire in a general engagement. When the entire sea is set on fire, it burns indiscriminately. The ship that just exploded was a *dhromon.*"

Halldor and Ulfr could offer no rebuttal as the dinghy was quickly ferried over from the second galley. They knew that they would honor Haraldr Sigurdarson more by living to conquer Norway in his name than by leaping into his funeral pyre with him. Haraldr stripped off his cloak and wrapped a hide cape around his short wool tunic. He unstrapped his sword and inserted his dagger in his belt. He turned to Halldor and Ulfr.

"I promised her I would come back for her. I wish I could make you the same promise." He paused, thinking of an old verse. "This is how the skalds said Ragnarok would be. 'The sun grows dark, earth sinks beneath the sea. The stars fall from the skies. Flames rage and fire leaps until heaven itself is seared to ashes.' " He looked steadily at his two friends. "I know I could live for three score more years and never have better men for my comrades. In the Valhol I will tell them to await the two best men who ever lived. Rule well."

Ulfr rushed forward, sobbing, and embraced Haraldr. He had no words for this. Finally Haraldr had to prise him away. Halldor, grim and implacable, wrapped his huge arms around Haraldr. "We . . ." His voice choked. "We love you, comrade."

Haraldr leapt over the railing and into the dinghy.

† † †

The heat at Haraldr's back was so intense, he thought even his wet hide cape would burst into flame. But there were passages through the blazing waves, twisting, treacherous, evanescent currents of orange-tinted water. And he could see Moschus's *dhromon*, ringed by fiery patches but still intact, the bow spout still spitting flame.

Haraldr rowed furiously between crests crowned with fire. He turned to adjust his course, an orange burst greeted him, and he smelled his singed hair. Burning globs rolled off his hide cape and sizzled on the hull of the dinghy. He passed a blackened, floating corpse; the man's arms were seized up, as if he were trying to claw his way out of Hell. Finally Haraldr reached a large, clear path and closed to within a hundred ells of Moschus's *dhromon;* he could see marines operating the missile throwers on the deck and repulsing Rus boarders at the stern. A blackened hand swiped in front of him and he had a terrible glimpse of desperate white eyes against a greasy wave. He put his back to the oars. A fire-peaked wave rose up before him and then fell away to reveal a giant beast from Hell. Another *dhromon*, its pitch-smeared hull completely engulfed in flames, came hurtling out of the enraged sea. It was a wall of fire descending on him.

Haraldr threw aside his cape and leapt. He swam under water for perhaps fifty ells. He saw no flames above him. He surfaced to an immense crash and felt the shock even in the water. The burning *dhromon* had collided with Moschus's flagship, bow to bow. A blinding explosion flung shattered, glowing timbers into the air. Haraldr went under again.

When he surfaced, embers still drifted to the sea around him. Both bows were now rapidly descending beneath the waves.

Moschus's ship listed to the larboard and fire spread along the hull. The stern was still free of flames and Haraldr stroked wildly for it. Fire began to leap along the pitch-slathered strakes but the tacky surface gave Haraldr's slippery feet purchase. He scrambled across the slope of the vast, tilting hull. He reached the railing and saw marines trying to walk upright on the steeply inclined deck. The bow was an inferno; dead marines lay on the deck in blackened armor. The ornate cabin at the stern was still intact, and Haraldr scrambled for it, ascending the increasingly sloping deck. The gilded door had been flung open and he ducked into the chart-strewn office of the Droungarios. "Maria!" he screamed. An officer in a gold breastplate appeared, a small lacquer casket under his arm. "Where is the woman!" bellowed Haraldr; he grabbed the officer's arms and shook him. The casket tumbled to the deck and gold coins scattered. The officer shook his head numbly, and Haraldr released him and stepped back through the door. The slender but powerful arms seized him from behind.

"God, you are alive!" gasped Maria as Haraldr turned to wrap her in his arms. "Holy Mother, you are alive!"

"I promised I would hold you again, even in the shadow of the dragon." He held her as if this embrace would last them for eternity. And because his eyes were closed, he could only feel, not see, the line of flame bursting through the deck of the *dhromon* in the instant before the ship exploded.

alldor rolled over the floating, blackened corpse and studied the charred lump that had once been a head. Unable to identify it, he pushed the corpse away with a staff fitted with an improvised grapple on the end; the body was quickly rejoined by dozens of nipping fish. "Who can tell?" he said wearily to Ulfr. "You cannot even tell a woman from a man, much less a Rus from a Roman." He straightened and looked out over a calmed sea littered with countless fragments of flickering wreckage and a few still-blazing hulks.

"Should we wait until dawn?" asked Ulfr. "It is only an hour."

Halldor shook his head. "We probably would have no better chance of finding them in the light of day. And who could sleep?"

Halldor hooked another floating corpse, a legless form with curled, fetal arms; the hands were merely crusted bones. He pushed it away after the most cursory examination. "This is no way for men to die," said Halldor bitterly. "To a flame that has no courage or loyalty, that kills friend and foe alike, that does not even allow a man the dignity of seeing the face that has sent his soul on. If this flame were set loose upon the earth, it would mean the end of all that is noble in the world. And it would shame the very gods at the moment of their death. When the gods destroy Rome, I pray that they will also bring about the end of this fire of doom."

"There will always be another Rome," said Ulfr sadly. "Good men, not the gods, must banish this fire from the world." Ulfr looked out over the strange, flame-flecked calmness of the sea. The wind had pushed the clouds to the south, and stars were becoming visible on the northern horizon. His head snapped forward and he pointed. "There is one who lives!" Halldor ordered the ship to maneuver for the rescue. "There are two of them!" shouted Ulfr.

"One living, one dead," said Halldor. "That is devotion to a comrade."

"A Norseman!" shouted Ulfr as the forms drifted closer.

"One of the fools who started this. He's still got his boy lover under his arm—" Halldor froze with a sickening collision of recognition, exultation, and horror. Not a boy but a dead woman. A woman with her hair singed to a matted cap. But the man lived. "Get this boat over there, you mindless swine!" Halldor screamed to the crew in general. He pounded Ulfr on the chest. "Haraldr! Haraldr! Haraldr is alive!"

Haraldr cradled Maria's body with his left arm, her head to a sky bluing with the first hints of dawn. He stroked weakly with his right arm, so slowly that he only succeeded in remaining afloat. His cheeks were bleeding, and much of his hair had been singed away. Ulfr and Halldor leaned over the top frame to receive him. Haraldr spat water, and his white teeth grimaced like a demon's. "Help Maria," he said.

Halldor gently lifted the body. Only tatters of clothing around her torso had not been burned away, and parts of her legs and arms were covered with blackened flesh that stuck to Halldor's hands. He gritted his teeth and prayed for the gods to curse any man who took this fire in his hands ever again. He laid her gently on the decking by the tiller and found a linen rain cape to cover her. He could not bear to pull the shroud over her head; even as seared as her face was, there was still the beauty of her features, an exquisite marble darkened with soot.

Haraldr's wool tunic was intact, and his head and hands seemed to have suffered the worst burns; the skin was raw but not badly charred. Ulfr lifted him over the top frame and he found his feet on the deck. He slumped with his hands on his knees and looked up with white, stunned eyes as Ulfr steadied him. "I lost her," he said, sobbing. "If only I could have held her tighter. She was ripped out of my arms and I lost her." He fell to his knees beside Maria's body. "Oh, God, save her! Give her back to me!" He turned to Halldor and Ulfr. "She is alive," he said frantically. "She talked to me in the water. She forgave me! Oh, merciful God . . . All-Father!"

Ulfr knelt beside Haraldr. "Haraldr, no one survives such wounds. Let Maria have her death."

Haraldr calmed himself. "She is alive." He reached over and grasped her hand, oblivious to the sticky serum that coated the skin. "Darling, don't go." Reason struck him like a thunderbolt and he remembered how she had stilled in his arms at least an hour ago. She was . . . He turned to Ulfr and whispered, "She is gone. I know that. If I could only talk to her again. Just once. If only I could say one thing . . . it . . . it would be my eternity."

"She is watching you from Paradise." said Halldor. "She knows. I swear to you she knows your heart at this moment." Almost perfunctorily, Halldor bent over and felt the pulse at Maria's neck. He knelt, his finger still to the artery. He looked up, expressionless. "There is life. But the thread that holds it is gossamer."

Maria was wrapped in blankets, and Eilif, a Varangian who had learned some Roman and Saracen healing arts, put a greasy salve on the worst burns and gently prodded Maria's abdomen. She stirred and groaned slightly. Eilif looked at Haraldr, still clutching Maria's hand, and then at Halldor and shook his head sadly. He whispered to Halldor, "She's broken inside as well. She will be gone soon. There's nothing more I can do." Halldor motioned everyone away.

Haraldr maintained his desperate vigil, trying to will her back. His soul was cold to the core, and yet somewhere a light flickered. He struggled for that light, as he had when it had meant his own life.

The tips of her fingers twitched slightly. And then the life came back, slowly; her hand no longer simply rested in his but knew his touch. She pressed his fingers as weakly as an infant. Her head rocked and her eyes fluttered beneath her scorched lids, and then the miracle, the thing he had willed and prayed for, a glimmering like sapphires hidden among ashes. He squeezed her hand gently and leaned over her.

"My darling, my lifetime."

"Don't . . . look . . . at me," she whispered hoarsely. "I am . . . a cinder."

Haraldr struggled to control himself. His entire life was here in these blessed few moments, to be lived with dignity or squandered in futile tears. "You were never more beautiful to me than when you played the old crone in Neorion," he whispered, fighting his tears with all his force. "Until now. Now I see the soul without any artifice, and it is more dazzling than any sight I have ever seen."

Maria's body shuddered and her breath came in short, uneven gasps. Her eyes closed but she fought her way back. "Darling," she whispered, "you must . . . know this. That day . . . we wondered if death could tell us . . . if our souls had been true to us . . . or had only worn masks." She fought again for breath. "I know . . . now . . . that my soul has never lied to me . . . or to you . . ." Her throat rattled and her head rolled from side to side, but her eyes became lucid again.

Cold tears burned Haraldr's raw face. "I believe more than anything in the truth of your soul. To you and to me. Your soul will always be in my soul. You will touch whomever I touch for the rest of my life—" The gates of resolve shattered and he broke down. "Oh, my love, I would give anything if God would exchange our fates. Oh, God, I did not mean to kill you."

"Stop this," she hissed, tilting her head up with an enormous will. "You were my miracle . . . my resurrection. Listen to me. I have seen what follows the fiery end of the world. It is not the darkness I lived in before you came inside me. Death is not dark. There is the light . . . There is only light. You promised me, darling . . . now I promise you. I will come to you and hold you again. Even after the last black dragon flies. I promise you I will hold you in the light. There is only light . . . And only . . . love . . ."

Maria's head fell back from the great effort of speech. Haraldr felt the strength ebb from her hand, but he would not let her go in the darkness. He spent the long hour to the dawn in a lifetime of memories, smelling her dark hair and feeling her white skin and hearing her crystal laugh.

Just as the sun brought pink life over the death-fouled Bosporus, Maria's head turned to him. She did not open her eyes but her lips moved several times. Somehow she formed the words. "The king . . . beyond the creek . . ." Her head rolled back. A short while later she whispered, "Love," and a smile flickered over her face.

The sun rose above the green banks of Asia and glittered the water. A brilliant shaft slanted over the railing and struck Maria's crusted face. Her eyes opened and Haraldr clutched her hand tightly and leaned over her. The color of her irises was like some rare and impossibly lovely blue gold. Then Maria simply closed her eyes, and Haraldr felt her soul leave her body and enter his.

EPILOGUE

NORTHUMBRIA, ENGLAND 25 SEPTEMBER 1066

he trumpets sounded and the ducks flocked skyward from the calm surface of the River Ouse. As if by this command, the egg-blue mists began to lift. The Norsemen began to leap over the sides of their dragon-ships and assemble on the damp, grassy flats beside the river; there were enough of them to populate an entire city. The clearing air had the dry fragrance of a lingering summer that would not yield to fall. The day would be hot.

The King of Norway waited on the bank, his diamond-sharp blue eyes sweeping over the long rows of lean, swooping-prowed Norse dragons. The most powerful invasion force the world had yet seen awaited his bidding. His army gathered in a vast cordon, his court men crowding next to him, eager for the honor, their banners, limp in the quiescent air, proudly set. The warriors fanned out in a vast cordon that blanketed the tree-dotted slopes to the north. The King waited for their jubilant banter to fall to a reverent hush.

"Comrades!" bellowed the King. "Northmen! Men of Ireland! Men of Scotland! Men of Flanders! Men of England!" He waited for the answer.

"*Alvardr* Haraldr! *Hradskyndir* Haraldr! *Hrodaudiger* Haraldr! Haraldr Hardraada! Haraldr Hardraada!" The gale of Norse acclaim was mixed with the oaths of the other tongues. Ducks raced overhead, their startled protests unheard. A golden sliver of sun shimmered on the horizon.

"Brave comrades!" The King's seamed face blazed with the force of his words. "Five days ago we showed England the iron fist of our allied might! The corpses of the fyrd of Northumbria built a bridge for you across the River Humber!" The army exploded in another chorus of triumph, and King Haraldr waited until the echoes vanished. "Today we go to Stamford Bridge to accept the victory we won at Fulford Gate! We come to accept all of England north of the Ouse." Again the chorus of triumph. "But today we must show England the open hand of our just intentions! We have come to rule, not to pillage! We have come to govern, not to slaughter!" The army cheered with lessened enthusiasm. Haraldr looked around at the sea of blood-eager faces that could have inundated him in an instant if they did not at this moment worship him.

He caught the sparking blue eyes of Eystein Orre, the ferocious, already legendary "orcock," his fiercest commander, the man who had annihilated the English rear and center in the overwhelming victory at Fulford Gate. The man who reminded Haraldr of the untroubled glories of his own youth. The man who would be husband to the King's firstborn, his most beloved, his daughter Maria. Eystein dipped his shaggy blond head in understanding. If necessary, he would second his King in this.

Haraldr turned to the other young man, whose martial spirit he did not have to rely on but without whose understanding he could not endure. His son and heir, Olaf, did not need to nod his approval; this had been the precociously wise Prince's counsel the previous night. Haraldr sought the love in his son's lucid blue eyes and considered the legacy Norway's King was now forging for his people. A mighty northern Empire, at last on the verge of unification. Eystein Orre with the sword to preserve it, quiet Olaf with the wisdom to govern it. And, of course, Maria. Eystein and Olaf would be their own men, and that was all Norway would need. But in his daughter Maria, the King himself would live on.

Haraldr waited for the halfhearted cheers to erode into the inevitable murmur of relatively polite grumbling. Then he signaled for his stewards to unlace the leather thongs that tightly cinched his byrnnie. The stewards lifted his byrnnie away from him like foundry workers removing a plaster cast from a statue. The King emerged in a glass-smooth blue silk tunic, and his army buzzed with astonishment. "Warriors! I do not need armor to accept hostages and appoint governors. So I leave behind my Emma, the woman who has been truest to me in battle. Besides, the day will be hot. And this lady's tight embrace would boil me like a fat goose in a kettle!" The King stroked his thickening middle to illustrate the reason for the tight fit. The army followed with a vast exhalation of laughter. Eystein Orre stepped out of his byrnnie and the fashion of the day was established.

As the Norsemen stripped off their body armor—they retained their helms, spears, and swords, as they would on a journey to a market or church—the English Pretender Earl Tostig sought Haraldr's ear. "My Lord," he said, his ruddy forehead scowling, "I do not advise this. I have ruled over Northumbria myself, and if the English are the most untrustworthy of folk, the Northumbrians are the most untrustworthy of Englishmen."

Haraldr studied Tostig's perpetually tormented face. He often wondered what fate had encouraged him to care for this difficult man, whom he had disliked so much at first. Tostig's offer to sponsor a conquest of

England, against Tostig's own brother King Harold Godwinnson, had seemed preposterous as well as treacherous at first. And yet as Tostig's case had unfolded, as Haraldr had learned how he had been favored for the succession by old King Edward, only to be undone by his rivals at court, Haraldr had pitied him. And when he saw the man's remarkable, unwavering love for his wife, Judith, the sister of the Duke of Flanders, he had begun to like him. (If only Haraldr's love for his Queen Elisevett had been as constant.) And finally it had been Ulfr who had convinced King Haraldr that Tostig was a man who would be true to him. Ulfr. God in Heaven, if only Ulfr could be here! What fate had taken dear Ulfr on the eve of the triumph he had so long labored for, even during the times when his King had lost hope?

"It is a risk I must take," Haraldr told his English ally. "I learned that bitter lesson in Denmark. To rule without the affection of a people is to wage endless war. Crush the army, yes. But the people are won with fairness and mercy. However, I do not entirely discount the risk you remind me of." Haraldr recalled the portents that had pursued his great fleet like screeching gulls throughout the long voyage from Norway. Someone had dreamed of ravens perched on the stern of each ship; another man had seen a wolf precede the English armies, a Norseman in his bloody jaws. Haraldr himself had spoken to his dead brother Olaf in a dream and had received a foreboding of danger; but then perhaps that was merely his own fear of conquering where Olaf had never dared. All great ventures spawned great anxieties; so far the ravens had fed only on English corpses. Still, when fate cautioned, only a fool laughed. How ancient were the scars of that truth on his weary heart.

Haraldr beckoned to Olaf and Eystein Orre. "My eaglets!" he said in greeting to their unlined, ready faces. "I go to accept a surrender, which is a duty appropriate to a man who has been bowed by five decades. I want to leave behind my strength, however. I will take most of the allies and half our Norsemen with me; that should be sufficient to impress the English. But I want my best Norse fighters to remain here and guard the ships, without which we are all lost. Eystein, you will command them in my absence. And, of course, Olaf, you must also stay. I go to grasp the future. But without my brave and able eaglets to nurture it, that future will be as good as stillborn."

Eystein and Olaf gave their assent, and Haraldr Sigurdarson, King of Norway, the greatest warrior of his age, made the announcement to his army. Overhead in the warming azure sky, a line of ducks soared south in a sharp, dark vee.

† † †

The last butterflies of the season still frolicked over the verdant banks of the River Derwent. Stamford Bridge, the crossroads leading to the city of York, was less than a rowing-spell away across the gentle green land. Haraldr walked with his new Marshal Styrkar and the Earl Tostig. The unarmored army behind them was almost ten thousand men, a loose, lazy formation that frequently lost many of its constituents to the beckoning meadows and cooling river.

"You know this William the Bastard, do you not?" Haraldr asked Tostig.

"Yes. Duke William of Normandy is married to my wife's niece."

"Do you believe that his invasion fleet has already sailed?"

"They have been gathered at the mouth of the Dive for some time. The weather delays. Or perhaps William's caution. But should they land, the Normans and their allies will only be a factor after we defeat my brother. My brother is no fool. He will turn to meet the greater threat with his strength undiminished. Duke William is an able huntsman. You are Haraldr Hardraada. My brother Harold will face you first."

"But will your brother come north to confront us, or wait in defense of London? If he is as skilled as his reputation suggests, he will wait and allow us to extend ourselves."

"He is unpredictable and moves rapidly. But if he comes north, we will have at least a week to prepare for him."

Haraldr nodded. "Whether he comes north or not, I must rely on the goodwill of the people of Northumbria to guard my back. That is why no armor can help us win the battle I am waging today."

The King suddenly increased his stride and walked out ahead of Tostig. The Royal Marshal Styrkar held Tostig back. "The King wishes to take his own counsel," whispered Styrkar.

"I understand him," said Tostig. "I entertain my own demons. When my wife is with me, they are kept at bay. I presume his daughter does the same for him. The pretty daughter. The changeable one. Maria."

Styrkar laughed. "We say that our King and his daughter Maria are so close that there is but one life between the two of them. You can see the way their eyes go to each other at the table. They know what the other is thinking. He will begin a sentence, she will finish it. They will both laugh when no one else does. It is shame that he cannot be as close to her mother. Queen Elisevett is a fine woman."

Tostig's scowl seemed to deepen. "Why did he take a second wife?"

Styrkar shrugged. "To bear him sons. After Elisevett bore him the two princesses, she could no longer conceive. Haraldr said that he had known two women condemned to offer their love on the altar of state, and he would not permit that for his daughters. So he got the bishop to accede— he has great influence over the church, as you have seen—and wed the eventual mother of his sons without a divorce from Elisevett."

"Yes, I have met her. Tora. A noble woman."

"Elisevett still has precedence. You saw how he allowed her, and of course Maria, to sail with us as far as the Orkneys, while Tora had to bid him farewell in Nidaros. He loves Elisevett the best of his wives." Styrkar grinned. "And she loves him the best of her husbands! But it would take an Irish scribe to trace the jealousies that separate them."

"They say he has always loved a Greek woman."

"That was before I knew him. It may be one of those tales invented by the skalds."

† † †

The King walked ahead for a long while, alone, as if drawn to Stamford Bridge by the sun-colored butterflies darting before him rather than the imperative of the impatient armies at his back. The day was his vindication, his . . . resurrection. There had been so many times through these long years when he had wondered why fate had taken Maria and spared him. The constant quarrels with fractious Jarls; the long, bitter, inconclusive war in Denmark; the guilt he felt about Elisevett—circumstances that never would have come about if he were only a man and not a king. So many times he had thought of Halldor and his friend's strange renunciation, and he wondered if Halldor had been perhaps the wisest of them all. It was Halldor who had never really recovered from that night so long ago, who had always been haunted by the burned and broken body of the one woman he had never made love to. Halldor had helped Haraldr regain his throne, and then he had gone back to Iceland, to live quietly on a farm. Haraldr wondered if Halldor had received the news of Ulfr's death yet. The road of life, so many turns.

And yet now that road had leveled into a glorious autumn. Today would at last consummate what he had so long ago dreamed of with her. For her. This would have been Maria's Empire, she who had left behind her own Imperial legacy to join him in what had then been only a promise, what for her had meant only death. He wondered if she approved of him now; he knew there had been many times over these years when she had not. That, too, was one of life's strange paths, the route her spirit had taken through his life. Sometimes he could reach out and touch her; at other times he could not even remember her voice. He could never see her in her entirety, but often he could recall distinctly the parts of her, the incandescent irises, the gull-wing eyebrows, the soft white inside of her thigh. He thought of the Maria who had taken her place in his life; she was as distinct as his hand before him, not only the young woman she was now, but the infant, the child, the adolescent, every phase of her life. Even the first Maria never could have been that close, to have been created by him, to become a woman as he watched in wonder. And yet his daughter Maria could never share with him the supreme intimacy that the other Maria had shared with him. Perhaps, he often thought, the two Marias, the daughter and the lover, were different aspects of the same soul, that through him his first Maria had so deeply touched her namesake that she lived again, to restore that joy to his breast. There were times when the two Marias were that much alike, or so he remembered, and yet times when they did not seem alike at all. There were even moments, albeit fleeting, when he thought of Elisevett as the first and greatest love of his life. In the world as it was, not as it had seemed to be so long ago beside the Bosporus, what more could a man ask from a wife, except to know that from time to time he loved her above all else? And Tora, who had given him sons and love, how could she be denied her claim to his heart? Perhaps they were all aspects of the same soul, of the great love that only youth can know, just as an old man's shattered dreams are all fragments of the single, pure, incandescent purpose he had imagined as a young man. The dream seemed pure and whole again today, but he would give it away to the young men who could truly believe in it. But the love was not the same as the dream. The dream had faded and crumbled, and had now been restored. But the love had never faded. It was only in many different places now. She had been the source of the light, and as best he could, he had shared it with many.

† † †

"Let them raid the cattle," Haraldr said to Styrkar, his voice edged with annoyance. "I will pay for whatever they plunder. But if they begin to molest the peasants, I will send my house-karls down after them." Haraldr watched the Norse warriors wade the reed-choked shallows of the languid Derwent, then scatter over the broad, very gradually sloping meadows on the west side of the river. Several bowshots to the north, where the little river narrowed and the banks steepened, stood Stamford Bridge, a simple structure of wooden trestles and rotting planking. The King and his retinue stood on a grassy flat about thirty ells above the dull silver water. The sun was at its zenith, the heat oppressive. Haraldr wished the wind would come up and evaporate the sweat from his soggy silk tunic.

"What is that?" asked Styrkar. He pointed to a thick haze visible at the western horizon, just above a ridge line about eight or nine bowshots distant.

Haraldr shaded his eyes with his palm. "I imagine it is the people of the countryside come out to see us," he said. "They will find we are no different from them." Haraldr turned and watched his house-karls wager on spear tosses. He remembered that he had played the same game with Olaf's house-karls on the magic, innocent day before Stiklestad had sent his destiny gyring. *I will never have more courage than I did the day before Stiklestad,* thought Haraldr. *No man who has seen battle can ever be as brave as one who has not. And yet I can be proud that in every one of my fights, while I was always afraid, I never turned my back. Of course I have never met the ultimate test of courage, either, as so many of my foes have. As Maria and Ulfr and Olaf and Jarl Rognvald and so many of my comrades have. Each of them showed the valor I have yet to prove. And the woman had been the bravest.*

"I hope the next battle is my last," he told Styrkar, his voice musing, distracted. His marshal lifted his fine golden eyebrows in surprise. "When we go south to meet King Harold Godwinnson," clarified Haraldr. "When he is defeated, that will be the end of my wars of conquest. You and Eystein Orre can settle with my remaining enemies. I wish to govern. I have fought my entire life and I have seen too many terrible battles. I will soon have grandchildren."

"You showed no reluctance to fight five days ago," said Styrkar. "The fashion in which you drew the English vanguard on, holding back your strength, and then crushed them at the center and rear. I learned a lesson that day."

"I learned that lesson from a Greek. His name was . . . It is impossible I could have forgotten. I can see his face before me. I will remember it before the day is over. He was a friend of mine." Haraldr frowned. "Nicon Blymmedes. Domestic of the Imperial Excubitores. He was transferred to Italia. I should have liked to have known what happened to him."

"If he lives, he has heard of you," said Styrkar, intending no flattery. Styrkar looked west again. "Are those our men that far off?" he asked.

Haraldr looked toward the ridge and saw, through a rising haze of dust, the glint of sun off steel. "Those are not our men," he said. "Bring Tostig to me."

A few moments later Tostig came to Haraldr's side. A broad front of armored men had begun to spill down from the ridge, a descending wall of ice-of-battle. Tostig stared out and then turned to Haraldr, his eyes sharp with frustration and rage. "English," he said. "You have perhaps risked too much today."

Haraldr studied the rapidly moving vanguard. Fast cavalry, thousands of them. That was why there was so much dust. "The fyrd of Northumbria could not have that many horses left," he observed to Tostig, his own logic chilling him.

Tostig and Haraldr watched in silence for a long while as the horsemen, followed by a solid mass of infantry, came spilling down the ridge in glittering rows. The banners in the vanguard were like gold lanterns flickering in the dusty pall. Across the river, the cattle raiders abandoned their few trophies and began to form for a valiant defense of the river. Haraldr did not order them called back. He would need the time their lives would buy.

The wind at last blew, almost as if the huge vault of Heaven had been stirred by the massive movement across the River Derwent. Haraldr felt the chill against his back. The gold-embroidered English banners lifted. Styrkar pointed to the tiny figures in the distance, two gold-threaded scintillae rising above the steel-silvered English vanguard. "There," said Tostig softly, incredulity reducing his voice almost to a whisper. "The Dragon of Wessex. And the Fighting Man of Harold Godwinnson. The banners of the King of England. Somehow my brother has attached wings to his army and flown it north."

"The wings of the dragon," said Haraldr as he watched the huge army come down to the river like a silver avalanche.

"We must withdraw to the ships," said Tostig. "Our armor and our reinforcements—"

"No," said Haraldr. "Their horse would overtake us easily and cut down our backs. I will dispatch couriers to the ships to summon Eystein. And then we will stand and fight."

✝ ✝ ✝

The reed-stubbled shallows were coppery with blood. The Norse cattle raiders had fought valiantly, but the English van had forded the river and now waited just out of bowshot on the banks below the flats on the east side of the river. Their ranks were disciplined and murmuring quiet, a sound far more frightening than the pointless bravado of a rabble. The English ambassadors, a group of about twenty richly armored officers, rode forward on their horses; at their head was a medium-sized, red-bearded man who wore a golden helm and carried a red-enameled shield embossed with a gilded hawk. The man announced himself as a representative of the English King. Haraldr ordered his spear-bristled shield-wall to open and admit them.

Haraldr dispatched Tostig as his ambassador. He watched from thirty ells away as Tostig conversed with the King's representative, who remained sitting proudly in his saddle. It was obvious that the dialogue was as stiff and formal as the emissary's posture. After a curt exchange the horsemen bowed and rode back through the shield-wall. Tostig returned to Haraldr.

"He offers me a third of his kingdom if I will abandon you," said Tostig.

"Indeed. And what is offered Norway's King?"

"He offers you seven feet of English earth."

Haraldr laughed. "Well spoken. Do you wish to accept his parlay?"

"Too little and too late. I will take what is offered the King of Norway."

Haraldr nodded; Ulfr had not been wrong. "Who was the man you spoke with? He was a fine sight, so tall in his stirrups for a little man."

Tostig dropped his dark gray eyes. "That was the King Harold God-winnson."

Haraldr's rage flared momentarily; had he known, he might have sacrificed his honor to save his men. But kinship was the strangest of all bonds; he had seen that time and again in his life. "I understand why you would not give him up," said Haraldr after his anger had subsided. "I am grateful you did not give me up." Haraldr laughed again. "Seven feet of English earth. A man once told me that a king would one day show me mercy. But then that particular man was a craven liar." Haraldr turned to Styrkar. "We have not accepted terms. Tell the men their king has composed some verse for them."

Haraldr was announced, and for a moment he stood silently at the center of the immense, square shield-fort. He wondered if Odin had merely fooled him with the verses that had seemed so fully formed minutes ago. He had become too much a Christian. Odin had been the boy's god. And then the wind rustled from the spirit world and he found the words. The ring of spear points around him seemed ineffably beautiful, like a garden of silver blossoms.

> *In battle-storm*
> *No refuge we seek*
> *Behind our hollowed shields.*
> *As once I was bade*
> *By the highborn maiden*
> *High to hold my head*
> *When the Valkyrja flock*
> *To the clash of swords and skulls.*

When he was finished with the words, he could hear only the wind whistling in his ears.

† † †

"Hold them back, Styrkar!" The grotesque carpet of fallen Englishmen sprawled over the slope beneath the Norse shield-wall; the shadows of the dead had lengthened in the descending sun and begun to take on eerie life, as if they were dark little demons fleeing the flesh. The English cavalry had not sortied against the invincible Norse defenses for a quarter hour now, a quarter hour in which the frenzy of the Norsemen had built with the violent suddenness of a summer storm. And now came the thunder of axes on shields, the footsteps of an army of Titans, unbidden by the Norse commanders, the spontaneous rage of men who had fought well all afternoon as defenders and now lusted for their own attack.

"Hold them back!" Haraldr shouted again, but he was already too late. The shield-wall bulged into a broad snout, and then the bright cloaks and gleaming steel blades and helms swept down the rise.

Nothing could be done to stop the mass suicide. The wall that the overwhelming English force had been unable to dent had now been broken by the very will that had kept it intact all afternoon. The din below was deafening as English cavalry and infantry rallied along their broad front on the river. Even Styrkar and Tostig had disappeared into the raging fray. As the Norse charged to the river, the entire English formation seemed to contract, an enormous organism preparing to engulf and ingest the Norse salient. Quickly the massed Norse attack was isolated into desperate pockets of survival. Haraldr had fostered the cult of bravery among his men, and now their deaths were their terrible homage to him. Haraldr stood on the plateau above the trickling, coppery Derwent and realized that there was only one way to save Norway's legacy. Follow the doomed attack with an assault of such devastating force that the shield-wall could re-form.

Haraldr turned and faced the weapon-bristled ring of his house-karls, four score strong, the bravest men in the north. No words were necessary. Their proud eyes glowed with the fury of their calling. He wondered for a moment if he was still equal to such youthful passion. And then he mastered his fear with the reflex of a lifetime. Too many had gone before him, were waiting for him, for death to daunt his breast now.

†   †   †

The Norse boar plunged down the embankment, at its deadly snout the King of Norway, the gold-threaded banner called Landravager snapping in the breeze above him. And as the Norse house-karls ripped aside the English ranks, the golden dragon above the head of the King of Norway moved inexorably toward the golden Dragon of Wessex flying above England's King. But Haraldr Sigurdarson was only vaguely conscious of this collision of destinies. He knew only the cold black wind of the spirit world. He did not know how long he remained in the underworld, only that his quest in the darkness was much longer than ever before. And he emerged to a silent world viewed through a strange glass that scattered images of banners and bright cloaks and thrusting diamond-tipped spears like the tesserae of a shattered mosaic, yet presented the tiniest details in the sharpest focus: the white halo on the edge of a swinging sword, the sparks leaping like tiny fireflies as a javelin pierced a steel byrnnie.

Finally Haraldr saw the golden Dragon of Wessex, just beyond the cobbled ford a hundred ells south of Stamford Bridge; he could almost distinguish the separate threads of the embroidery. The King beyond the creek . . . and destiny's conundrum. Would he die this time, to serve the fate he had cheated once, or had he always been fated to conquer this way? The King beyond the creek. Odin chose for him. With a scream that literally brought the rank of English infantry before him to their knees, the Norse King charged forward, leaving even the precarious sanctuary at the snout of the boar behind.

The mounted guard of the English King fell back from the single scything ax of Haraldr Sigurdarson, transfixed by the inevitability of his blade. Haraldr charged them, mindless of the corpses he stepped over, and felt the water cold in his boots. For an instant he met the eyes of Harold Godwinnson, before the English King was crowded back by his retreating guard. Destiny's merchant began to ford the shallow Derwent to victory.

After three steps Haraldr focused on another fragmented epiphany across the river. The thick, rough fingers whitened against the bowstring, and Haraldr glanced up at the English archer's eyes and saw the red-black gleam of the raven. The arrow was still for a moment, and he could see the trueness of the shaft and the black steel barb at its head. Then the arrow blurred and flew across the river. Haraldr heard the instant, thrumming skirl just before the barb struck him in the neck. The contact felt like nothing more than a hard blow from the hand in a wrestling match. Haraldr braced himself, awaiting the adversaries who even now would not come against him. His house-karls closed behind him. Then he felt the warmth over his collarbone and was surprised to find that he had fallen to his knees. His guard swept past him, and now every sound of the battle came to him: the music of steel, the shattering of wood and the cracking of bones, the curses and grunts of men, and the high-pitched terror of horses.

He could no longer stay on his knees and fell back, but something caught his head and held him up. He did not recognize the face looming above him until the skald Thjodolf spoke; he could not make sense of the words but somehow knew the voice over the shouts of his house-karls. He was conscious; he knew that Thjodolf and some of his house-karls had pulled him to the east bank of the narrow river. He thought he would live until he tried to breathe and felt the blood in his windpipe.

Tostig was beside him. "Accept . . . your brother's . . . terms," gasped Haraldr, "as . . . I have. Save yourself . . . and my men."

"They will not accept that, nor will I. I will drink with you tonight, Haraldr Hardraada." Haraldr could not answer, and he closed his eyes and accepted the beauty of his death, in the arms of a skald and a brave man, his house-karls still fierce around him. The gods loved him still. He saw the beautiful, vivid images of the life that lingered in death's shadow: eight years old, in a dark cool forest, his fingers against the grainy surface of a rune stone. Olaf bringing him a toy ship. Elisevett as a girl, her downy cheek. Maria, her eyes like blue lanterns in the night. Daughter Maria, making a face at him as he sat in counsel on his high seat. Even his father, Sygurd Syr, more clearly than he had ever seen him. So much beauty, the deaths forgotten, only life. And then the cold hands closed around his neck and the shadows deepened and the rustle of the huge wings announced the darkening sky. Fear ran cold through his dying limbs. He girded his will to face the final test of being, to meet the last dragon. He could not even draw a final, desperate breath as he fell away from life into the dark well of oblivion.

There was no dragon, he realized at the end, nor had there ever been one. In reality, the last dragon had no shape or form but was merely a blackness so complete and devasted that to give it any shape, however terrifying, was to endow it with a mercy that did not exist in the last endless night of the world. Here at last was the cold, dark core of being and creation, and here at last was true fear, the fear that only the dead could know. From this horrifying vastness Haraldr cried out in unspeakable, craven agony, unheard in the emptiness, crying out for himself and those he had loved, for all mankind who would someday know this terrible loneliness. Had he known death as the living never can, he would have cursed the day he was born to serve fate. Darkness would always win the final victoy.

In the unforgiving pall a light flickered, a pinpoint in the limitless void. He watched in wonder as the single star grew suddenly, expanding like a golden dome beneath an obsidian sky. The dome came over him and she came toward him out of the light, a creature of light, and he knew at once the liquid gold of her walk and the blue gold of her eyes. For a moment he was surprised that she was his other Maria as well, but then he understood. She reached out and took him in her weightless arms of pure light, as she had promised so long ago on the Bosporus. And in the last moment before his reason became infinite, Haraldr knew the truth of all she had told him. In the end, beyond the dragon, there is only light, and only love.

AFTERWORD

he English King Harold Godwinnson did extend Haraldr Sigurdarson a certain posthumous mercy; he permitted Haraldr's son Olaf to bring his father's body back to Norway. King Haraldr was laid to rest in the royal cathedral that he had built in Nidaros, the Maria Kirke. But the King's beloved daughter Maria was not waiting among the mourners; history has recorded that she died, suddenly and inexplicably, on the exact day and hour of her father's death. King Olaf Haraldrson ruled Norway for several decades of such unprecedented peace and stability that the son of the world's greatest warrior became known as Olaf the Quiet. So it was that Stamford Bridge marked the end of the era of Norse conquest in Europe. The Viking Age was over.

But even in death, Haraldr Sigurdarson served as destiny's instrument. Immediately following the dearly purchased victory over the unarmored Norsemen, King Harold Godwinnson of England was forced to march his severely mauled army south to meet the Norman invasion force under Duke William the Bastard. On October 14, 1066, near the town of Hastings, the two forces met to determine the fate of England. Despite their reduced strength, the English were on the verge of victory when a premature pursuit of the beaten foe brought them the same fate the Norsemen had suffered at Stamford Bridge. Duke William, by far the least of the three men who contested for England in the fall of 1066, became, almost by default, William the Conqueror. The Normans were able to exploit the wealth of England to dominate Europe for the next century and a half, as well as lead the Crusades to the Holy Land; by the time this "Norman century" had ended, the shape of the modern world had begun to evolve. If Haraldr Sigurdarson had not removed his mail coat on the morning of September 25, 1066, the politics and culture of that world, even the language we speak, would most likely be very different today.

Fate reckoned with the Byzantine Empire just five years after the death of Haraldr Sigurdarson. On August 26, 1071, at Manzikert in eastern Asia Minor, the poorly maintained armies of Imperial Rome were routed by the Seljuk Turks, and the Emperor Romanus IV was taken prisoner. The loss of the Empire's breadbasket was a mortal blow followed by an ex-

767

tended, agonizing death. The city of Constantinople fell to Venetian treachery in 1204, but a pathetic vestige of the Empire was restored in 1261. Finally, in 1453, with the city virtually depopulated and most of its glories fallen into ruin, the Ottoman Turks succeeded in breaching the walls and deposing the last Roman Emperor. Today the towering walls have crumbled and there are but scattered fragments of the Imperial Palace. Only the fragile magnificence of the Hagia Sophia, stripped of the symbols of the Pantocrator who once anointed the Rulers of the Entire World beneath its golden dome, remains as testament to the enduring glory and invincible might of Byzantium.